The
Collected Papers
of
Sherlock
Holmes
Volume V – Chronicles
(20 Holmes Adventures)

New Sherlock Holmes

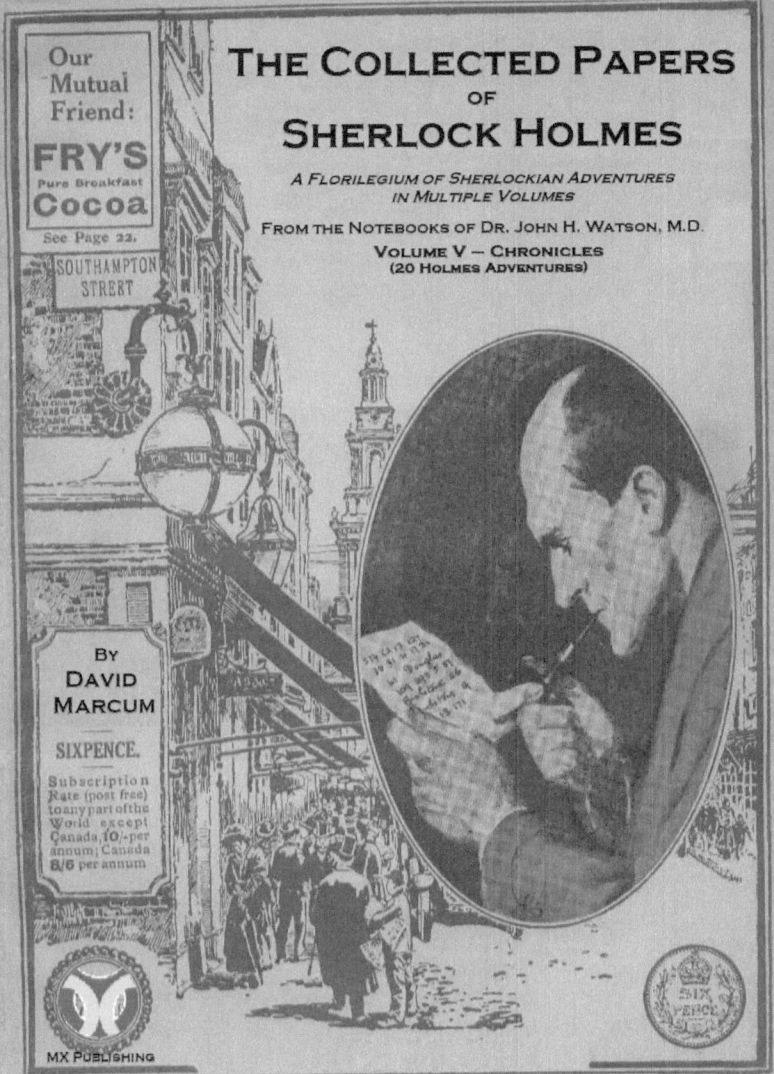

THE COLLECTED PAPERS
OF
SHERLOCK HOLMES

*A FLORILEGIUM OF SHERLOCKIAN ADVENTURES
IN MULTIPLE VOLUMES*

FROM THE NOTEBOOKS OF DR. JOHN H. WATSON, M.D.

VOLUME V — CHRONICLES
(20 HOLMES ADVENTURES)

BY
DAVID
MARCUM

MX PUBLISHING

Published by MX PUBLISHING, 335 PRINCESS PARK MANOR, London, England.

"Watson's Descendants" ©2021 by Nicholas Meyer. All Rights Reserved. First publication, original to this collection. Printed by permission of the author.

ISBN Hardback 978-1-78705-915-3
ISBN Paperback 978-1-78705-916-0
AUK ePub ISBN 978-1-78705-917-7
AUK PDF ISBN 978-1-78705-918-4

Published by
MX Publishing
335 Princess Park Manor, Royal Drive,
London, N11 3GX
www.mxpublishing.com

David Marcum can be reached at:
thepapersofsherlockholmes@gmail.com

Cover design by Brian Belanger
www.belangerbooks.com and *www.redbubble.com/people/zhahadun*

Internal illustrations by Sidney Paget

CONTENTS

Forewords

Chronicles

Sources

"The Stolen Relic" **The MX Book of New Sherlock Holmes Stories – Part V** *MX Publishing, 2016*

"The Helverton Inheritance" **The MX Book of New Sherlock Holmes Stories – Part IX** *MX Publishing, 2018*

"The Carroun Document" **The MX Book of New Sherlock Holmes Stories – Part XIV** *MX Publishing, 2019*

"The Reappearance of Mr. James Phillimore" **The MX Book of New Sherlock Holmes Stories – Part XVII** *MX Publishing, 2019*

"The Keadby Cross" **The MX Book of New Sherlock Holmes Stories – Part XX** *MX Publishing, 2020*

"The Rhayader Affair" **The MX Book of New Sherlock Holmes Stories – Part XXIII** *MX Publishing, 2020*

"The Cliddesden Questions" **The MX Book of New Sherlock Holmes Stories – Part XXVI** *MX Publishing, 2021*

"The Affair of the Mother's Return" **Tales from the Stranger's Room – Volume III** *MX Publishing*

"The Painting in the Parlour" **Sherlock Holmes: Before Baker Street** *Belanger Books, 2017*

"The Two Bullets" **Sherlock Holmes and Doctor Watson: The Early Adventures – Volume I** *Belanger Books, 2019*

"The Coombs Contrivance" **The Irregular Adventures of Sherlock Holmes – Volume I** *Belanger Books, 2019*

"The True Account of the Bushell Street Killing" **Beyond the Adventures of Sherlock Holmes – Volume II** *Belanger Books, 2020*

"The Polmayne Puzzles" **Dear Holmes** *Subscription Serialized Letter Delivery Service, 2020*

"The Curious Cardboard Boxes" **The Strand Magazine** *Issue LIX, 2019*

"The Bizarre Affair of the Octagon House" **The Meeting of the Minds: The Cases of Sherlock Holmes and Solar Pons – Part I** *Belanger Books, 2021*

"The Peculiar Persecution of Mr. Druitt" – *Previously Unpublished*

"The Service for the American Colonel" **Sherlock Holmes: Stranger than Fiction** *Belanger Books, 2021*

"The Rescue at Ypres" **After the East Wind – Part I: The East Wind Blows (1914-1918)** *Belanger Books, 2021*

"The Problem of the Hindhead Minister" **The Strand Magazine** *Issue LV, 2018*

"The Edinburgh Bankers" **The Strand Magazine** *Issue LXII, 2020*

These additional adventures are contained in
Volume I – Tales
(9 Short Stories and a Novel)
The Papers of Sherlock Holmes (9 Short Stories)
The Adventure of the Least Winning Woman
The Adventure of the Treacherous Tea
The Singular Affair at Sissinghurst Castle
The Adventure of the Second Chance
The Haunting of Sutton House
The Adventure of the Missing Missing Link
The Affair of The Brother's Request
The Adventure of the Madman's Ceremony
The Adventure of the Other Brother
and
Sherlock Holmes and A Quantity of Debt (A Novel)

Volume II – Records
(5 Short Stories and a Novel)
Sherlock Holmes – Tangled Skeins
The Mystery at Kerrett's Rood
The Curious Incident of the Goat-Cart Man
The Matter of Boz's Last Letter
The Tangled Skein at Birling Gap
The Gower Street Murder
and
Sherlock Holmes and The Eye of Heka (A Novel)

Volume III – Accounts
(22 Holmes Adventures)
The Adventure of the Pawnbroker's Daughter
The Problem of the Holy Oil
The Trusted Advisor
An Actor and a Rare One
The Unnerved Estate Agent
The Cat's Meat Lady of Cavendish Square
The Hammerford Will Business
The Farraway Street Lodger
November, 1888

(Continued on the next page . . . .)

As always, this is for Rebecca and Dan, with all my love

"It's all one case."
by David Marcum

It's all about playing The Game.

That's the bottom-line reason behind these stories. And what is The Game? For those who don't know, it's reading the Sherlock Holmes stories with the firm belief that he and Watson were real historical figures. That Dr. Watson wrote the stories, and Sir Arthur Conan Doyle was his Literary Agent. That Our Heroes actually lived in Baker Street (for a couple of decades, off and on, and not forever) and solved real cases for real people, even if names and places and dates were changed and obfuscated to protect the innocent, or maybe because Watson's handwriting was bad, or because of some hidden agenda that the Literary Agent needed to fulfill.

By acknowledging that Holmes and Watson were real, living, breathing, functioning people, then it's a given that were born, lived, and died. (No magic immortal detectives need apply!) And if they were born and lived and died, then these lives occurred across a fixed period. These men aren't Time Lords who can be picked up and dropped into other eras, or supernaturally gifted monster hunters in a world where such things exist, and they cannot be remade into a plethora of completely different people to fit whatever agenda some current reader needs to project upon them.

No, the stories in these books are about the same Sherlock Holmes and Dr. Watson that one finds in the original Canon – those pitifully few sixty stories that were published from 1887 to 1927.

I've enjoyed the notion that Mr. Sherlock Holmes was real from nearly the same time that I discovered him – as a boy of ten in 1975. Before I'd even read many of the Canonical adventures, I found two other books that reinforced this idea: William S. Baring-Gould's biography *Sherlock Holmes of Baker Street* (1962), with its chronology of the events in Holmes's long and amazing life (1854-1957), and also Nicholas Meyer's *The Seven-Per-Cent Solution* (1974), in which Holmes meets historical figures such as Sigmund Freud. How could one read those books, especially at that age, and not be convinced that Holmes was real?

In the decades that have passed since then, my interest in Mr. Holmes has only grown. While I read and collect a great many volumes about my other "book friends", as my son called them when he was small – and there

1

are a great lot of them besides Holmes – I've always had a special interest in the consulting detective in Baker Street and his Boswell. Since obtaining my first Holmes book in 1975, I've managed to collect and read (and create a massively dense chronology for) literally thousands of traditional Canonical adventures. I've worn a deerstalker as my only hat, all year long and everywhere since age nineteen. I've been able to make three extensive Holmes Pilgrimages to England and Scotland (so far), wherein I pretty much visited only Holmes-related sites. So it was probably inevitable that, in 2008, I started writing Holmes adventures.

I'd always wanted to write, all the way back to when I was eight years old and intensely reading about The Three Investigators and The Hardy Boys. Not satisfied with just the official publications, I wanted more new stories too. I spent quite a few Saturdays of my young boyhood tapping away on my dad's typewriter to create new "books".

As I grew, I dabbled with writing little short pieces, mostly humorous, just intended to make family members laugh, because I loved to write, and it always came easily to me. By the late 1980's, I was a U.S. Federal Investigator employed by an obscure government agency, often sent away from home for long periods, conducting investigations that lasted anywhere from five weeks to three months. Once, when I was sent to Albuquerque for several months to conduct extensive field investigations, I impulsively stopped at a local Walmart and bought a hundred-dollar typewriter and a big pack of paper with some of my *per diem* money. (This was the early 1990's – a long time before personal computers or laptops.)

It was there that I sat down for my first real effort at being a writer – and before I departed I'd finished most of a 600-plus page Ludlumesque novel. (One can get a lot of writing done night after night in a bleak hotel room.) The book was coincidentally about a heroic federal investigator – not unlike myself – who stumbled into a vast Russian-led conspiracy in the American southeast where I'm from. I still have that book – *Civil Servants* – stored in my old federal investigator briefcase, pushed underneath my bed. Its plot is mired in the early 1990's when it was written, locked to the aftermath of the Cold War, but it isn't half bad, and it taught me the valuable lesson that other writers also know: *The secret to writing is to put your butt in the chair and do it.*

After that particular trip, I went back home, finished up what was left of my epic adventure novel, and then settled back into writing the occasional short piece for our private amusement – but it was inevitable that at some point I would write a Holmes adventure.

In the mid-1990's, the federal agency where I'd been employed was abruptly eliminated, a victim of the end of the Cold War and a move to reduce the size of government. (After all, the higher-up wise men thought, who needs security now? We won!) Over the next few years, I went back to school and obtained a second degree in Civil Engineering. Then, in 2008 at the start of the Great Recession, I was unexpectedly laid off from my engineering job. With time on my hands, and a desire to try my hand at Sherlockian pastichery, I began writing each morning after the daily job searching was finished.

I ended up with nine of Holmes pastiches, written over several weeks, and then . . . I did nothing with them. That's right. Simply satisfied that I'd written them and that they existed, I put them in a binder labeled *The Papers of Sherlock Holmes* and shelved them with the rest of my Holmes Collection, happy with my secret collector's item.

But eventually I began to wish for other Sherlockians to see them. I shared one with a Sherlockian friend here and another one there, and the response was very positive. Finally I became bolder and wanted more people to see them, asking myself: *Why not put them in a real book of my own?*

I communicated about it with a Sherlockian publisher from whom I'd bought books in the past. He immediately offered to publish *The Papers*, and after a great deal of back-and-forth, my first book eventually appeared. For those who have had that experience – Opening the newly delivered carton to see *your book!* – there is nothing like it. It's a satisfaction that cannot easily be described.

That was in 2011. Over the next couple of years, I became aware of MX Publishing. I saw that an acquaintance of mine who'd also had his first book published with the same original publisher as mine had switched to MX, and I reached out to him. He informed me that he was happy to have switched to MX. With that in mind, I sent an email to Steve Emecz, Sherlockian Publisher Extraordinaire – and that was truly life-changing and improving decision.

In 2013, Steve republished my first book, *The Papers of Sherlock Holmes*, and he made the whole experience so painless that I set about writing a Holmes novel, *Sherlock Holmes and A Quantity of Debt*. That same fall, I was making my long-planned first Holmes Pilgrimage to London, and Steve arranged for me to have a book-signing in The Sherlock Holmes Hotel in Baker Street, where I was staying (when not traveling about to Dartmoor, the Sussex Coast, Edinburgh, and other locations). I was able to meet Steve for the first time on that trip, and found him to be one of the nicest, most supportive, and most thoughtful people around – and that hasn't changed a bit.

Jump ahead a little bit: In early 2015, I woke up early from a dream in which I'd edited a Holmes anthology. Instead of rolling over and forgetting the idea, I arose and started thinking about authors whom I admired and that I might want to invite to write stories. I ran the idea by Steve, and he was willing to publish it, so I began sending invitations. I hoped that I might get a dozen stories (at best) for a modest paperback volume. Fearing a lack of response, I kept sending invitations to everyone that I could think of – and then, amazingly, people started signing up. New Sherlock Holmes stories started to arrive in my email in-box – which quickly becomes addictive. More and more authors heard about it – some that I didn't even know about yet – and before we knew it, the little idea had grown into a three-volume hardcover behemoth of over 60 new Holmes stories – *Parts I, II,* and *III* of *The MX Book of New Sherlock Holmes Stories*, the largest collection of its kind ever produced to that point.

Early on, Steve and I had decided that the royalties from the project would go to support the Stepping Stones School for special needs children, located at Undershaw, one of Sir Arthur Conan Doyle's former homes. The books were a smashing success and received a lot of attention, and I was able to go to London in the fall of 2015 for the release party – what turned out to be Holmes Pilgrimage No. 2. There I was able to meet a number of the contributing authors in person – and to my everlasting regret, I was so thrilled that I barely remembered to take any photos!

After I returned home, I began to receive more emails, now asking when the next book was planned – *Good grief! A next book?!?* – and also stating that many authors (both returning and new) wanted to contribute.

I'd had no plans to do any more books, thinking that the first three were lightning in a bottle that couldn't be recaptured . . . but then I realized that the heavy-lifting in terms of decision-making and set-up and formatting and process-building had already occurred, so Steve and I decided to keep going. (I think I said to him "Let's do one more . . . .")

Part IV came out in the spring of 2016 – and after that, more people kept sending stories for *the next books* and wanting to join the party. We came up with the plan to have yearly books. But we received so many stories that it grew to twice a year. We now have an un-themed spring collection – the yearly *Annual* – and also a fall collection with a specific theme, such as Christmas adventures, seemingly impossible crimes, Untold Cases, etc. As more and more stories kept rolling in, it became necessary for each season's particular set to grow to multiple simultaneously published volumes. That's how, in just a few short years, we're now up to *Parts XXVIII, XXIX,* and *XXX* (to be published in Fall 2021), and as I write this, I'm already receiving stories for the *Spring 2022 Annual, Part XXXI* (and *XXXII* and *XXXIII* too . . . ?)

4

So far the books have raised over $85,000 for the school, and it's my hope and expectation that they'll go over $100,000 within the next few months of writing this foreword.

As part of editing these books, I couldn't let them pass by without adding my own stories – editor's prerogative. Thus, that helped to motivate me to sit my butt in the chair and write more about Mr. Holmes. By way of these books, I've met some really incredible people, including the incomparable Belanger Brothers, Derrick and Brian. Derrick initially contributed short stories, while Brian – a truly gifted artist – became the MX cover artist after the original artist passed away.

At one point, the two Belangers wrote a series of Holmes books for children. Eventually they formed Belanger Books – another amazing Sherlockian publishing venture. Between MX and Belanger Books – both of which cooperate beautifully with one another – the Sherlockian publishing field is amazingly well covered, providing an opportunity for so many people to be Sherlockian pasticheurs when they would otherwise be excluded by those who happily and aggressively seek to squash that aspect of the Sherlockian experience.

In 2016, the Belangers asked me to assemble and edit a Holmes story collection for them. I did, and as it also consisted of traditional and Canonical adventures, and had many of the same authors as in the MX anthologies, I formatted it the same way. After that, I edited another one for them, and another, and those also grew to simultaneously published multiple volumes. This extra editing also served to motivate me to write more Holmes stories for each of those collections as well – because I didn't want those trains leaving without me being on them.

From there, I began to receive invitations to write still more stories for other editors' anthologies and magazines. Along the way I published a couple more of my own books – *Sherlock Holmes – Tangled Skeins* (2015) and *Sherlock Holmes and The Eye of Heka* (2021) – but most of my stories that I wrote over those years remained uncollected within the various anthologies and magazines in which they had originally appeared. All along, I stayed too busy with real life and family and my dream job (as a civil engineer working for my home town's public works department), along with writing more stories and editing various books, to take the time to properly collect them all into my own books.

But within the last few months, I looked up and saw that (as of right now) I've now written 86 Holmes pastiches, (along with 20 pastiches about Solar Pons, "The Sherlock Holmes of Baker Street" – but that's another story and another hero.) Thus, the idea of this collection was born.

These initial five books of *The Complete Papers* contain 77 of those 86 stories. The others are still in the pipeline to be published elsewhere. Right now (as of mid-September 2021), I also have five more Holmes stories promised to be written for various editors before the end of the year, and all of these, plus whatever I'm able to write in 2022 – with a plan to reach Pastiche No. 100 – will be published in Volume VI of this set in later 2022 . . . *Fingers crossed!*

Many people have sports figures or musicians or actors or (curiously) politicians as heroes. My heroes have always been my book friends and authors – all the way back to when I was eight or nine and wondering about why I couldn't track down satisfying biographical information concerning the brilliant and prolific and mysterious author Franklin W. Dixon. I've always admired writers for what they accomplish and create while spending great chunks of their lives self-imposed isolation – something which I now understand. And at least if I had to set aside all that time to put my butt in the chair, I've been very fortunate that all of these stories almost told themselves. I almost never outline or plan. Instead, when I write – when I find that it's time for another story – I simply open a blank Word document on the computer and then wait for Watson to begin whispering to me. It's scary, but I trust the process now, and when it works – and it always has so far – there's no feeling quite like it.

Through these stories, I've achieved two important personal goals: In my own small way, I've become a writer, and I've also added to *The Great Holmes Tapestry*, a phrase I coined several years ago to describe the massive collection of narratives about the true Holmes and Watson – novels, short stories, radio and television episodes, movies and scripts, comics and fan-fiction, and unpublished manuscripts – that tell the complete and entire course of their lives from beginning to end. The Canon serves as the supporting structure – the wire core of the rope, the heavy steel girders of the skyscraper – but the thousands of traditional post-Canonical pastiches provide essential depth and color, filling in all the spaces around The Canon, and adding important information about The Whole Lives of Our Heroes.

I've long described myself as a missionary for The Church of the Traditional Canonical Holmes, preaching that the bigger picture of both Canon and the traditional pastiches should be seen and supported. This means giving respect and value to additional Holmes adventures, and not just those original sixty because they were the ones that came across the first Literary Agent's desk.

Ross MacDonald – (Real Name: Kenneth Millar, another of my authorial heroes because of his incredible private eye, Lew Archer) – said

"It's all one case." In other words, a *Great Tapestry*. He meant that even though he'd written eighteen Archer novels and a number of short stories from the 1940's to the 1970's, they were never meant to stand alone. They were all part of one overall arching story – Lew Archer's story – spanning across multiple narratives.

It's the same with the Holmes adventures – *all* of them, Canon and traditional pastiche, mine and everyone else's. They fit together to tell the *entire* story of Sherlock Holmes, and with the stories in this collection, I'm incredibly proud to have added my own contribution.

* * * * *

"Of course, I could only stammer out my thanks."
– *The unhappy John Hector McFarlane, "The Norwood Builder"*

At some point during the foreword-writing for the various MX anthologies, I began to use the quote shown above from Mr. McFarlane in regard to Thank You's. It's fitting – I can only stammer out thanks, and never adequately express how grateful I am for all the help and encouragement I've received over the years in all aspects of my life – not just the writing and editing of Sherlock Holmes stories.

First and foremost, I am always overwhelmed at how incredibly fortunate I am to have my wife and son in my life. In all aspects, my wife – of 33 years as I write this – is the kindest and wisest and most beautiful person inside and out I know, and she has been there throughout with complete support and encouragement when we went through such things as some terrible jobs and the grind of my returning to school. We have pushed through together, and anything that I can ever accomplish I owe to her. And equally amazing is our son, so incredibly funny and smart, and truly an amazing person in every way. I enjoy every minute spent with him, and it only gets better. I love you both, and you are everything to me!

Then there are my parents and sister, who put up with me during those first couple of decades – I probably don't even realize how bad that was for them. My parents did everything to encourage me – music lessons leading to a piano scholarship in college, all the books that I could read, and generally anything to help me grow as a person, so that it never occurred to me that I couldn't do whatever I wanted. And my sister was my best friend then, patiently listening as I rambled about whatever interested me. Even then, she probably heard more about Sherlock Holmes than she'd ever bargained for!

There is a group that exchanges emails with me when we have the time – and time is a valuable commodity for all of us these days! As the years have gone by, we've gotten busier and busier, and I don't get to write as often as I'd like, but I really enjoy catching up whenever we get the chance. These people are all wonderful writers, and I recommend them highly as both friends and authors: Mark Mower, Denis Smith, Tom Turley, Dan Victor, and Marcia Wilson.

Next, I wish to send several huge Thank You's to the following:

- *Steve Emecz* – When I first emailed Steve from out of the blue back in 2013 – *Only eight years? So much in eight years!* – I was interested in MX re-publishing my first book. Even then, as a guy who works to accumulate *all* traditional Sherlockian pastiches, I could see that MX (under Steve's leadership) was *the* fast-rising superstar of the Sherlockian publishing world.

  The re-publication of my first book with MX was an amazing life-changing event for me, leading to writing many more stories and then editing books, along with unexpected Holmes Pilgrimages to England. By way of that first email with Steve, I've had the chance to make some incredible Sherlockian friends and play in the Holmesian Sandbox in ways that I'd never before dreamed possible.

  Through all of it, Steve has been one of the most positive and supportive people that I've ever known. He works far more than a full-time week at his day job, and he still finds time to take care of all aspects of MX Publishing, with the help of his wife Sharon Emecz, and cousin, Timi Emecz. (That's right – MX is just the three of them who get all of this done!)

  Many who just buy books and have a vague idea of how the publishing industry works now might not realize that MX, a non-profit which supports several important charities, consists of simply these three people. Between them, they take care of running the entire business, including the production, marketing, and shipping – all in their precious spare time, in and around their real lives.

  With incredible hard work, they have made MX into a world-wide Sherlockian publishing phenomenon, providing opportunities for authors who would never have them otherwise. There are some like me who return more than once to Watson's Tin Dispatch Box, and there are others who only find one or two stories there – but they get the chance to publish their books, and then they can point with pride at this accomplishment, and how they too have added to The Great Holmes Tapestry.

From the beginning, Steve has let me explore various Sherlockian projects and open up my own personal possibilities in ways that otherwise would have never happened. Thank you, Steve, for every opportunity!

- *Derrick Belanger* and *Brian Belanger* – I first "met" Derrick Belanger when he graciously reviewed one of my early books, and we quickly became friends. Then he interviewed me several times for his online blog, and when I had the idea for the first MX Holmes anthology in 2015, he quickly joined the party and contributed a fine pastiche. From there he's written a number of others, and then he formed Belanger Books with his brother, Brian. It's turned into a Sherlockian powerhouse, working in tandem with MX Publishing, supporting each other to produce more and more wonderful Holmes adventures. I've very grateful to have had this additional opportunity to further contribute to The Great Holmes Tapestry by editing and writing stories for their different anthologies. Derrick continues to write, but he also stays quite busy as a noted aware-winning teacher, husband, and father, as well as running Belanger Books with Brian.

Over the last few years, my amazement at Brian Belanger's ever-increasing talent has only grown. I initially became acquainted with him when he took over the duties of creating the covers for MX Books following the untimely death of their previous graphic artist. I found Brian to be a great collaborator, very easy-going and stress-free in his approach and willingness to work with authors, and wonderfully creative too. His skills became most apparent to me when he created the cover for my 2017 book, *The Papers of Solar Pons*, which was one of the most striking covers that I've ever seen. Later, when the Belangers and I began reissuing the original Pons books in new editions, and then new Pons anthologies, Brian's similarly themed covers continued to astound me. He truly deserves an award for these.

In the meantime, he has become busier and busier, continuing to provide covers for MX Books, and now for Belanger Books as well, along with editing and occasionally writing.

I finally met both Brian and Derrick in person in early (pre-pandemic) 2020 at the annual Sherlock Holmes Birthday Celebration in New York City, and they're just as great in person as they were by way of email. I immediately felt like I'd known them both forever. I cannot express to either one of you just how grateful I am.

- *Roger Johnson* – I had known of Roger for quite a while, having seen his name connected with the "District Messenger" newsletter of *The Sherlock Holmes Society of London Journal.* I could tell, even then, that he represented the finest kind of Sherlockian. When I wrote my first Holmes book, I sent him a copy – out of the blue, as he had no idea who I was – as a thank you, and with the timid and dim spark of a hope that he would review it, because having him do so would mean (to me) that what I had written was legitimized. He did write a wonderful review, and we began to correspond. When I was able to get to England for my first Holmes Pilgrimage in 2013, I made arrangements to meet with Roger and his wonderful wife, Jean Upton, in person, and I discovered that what I'd already known by email was true: They are both the very best people!

Later, in 2015 on Holmes Pilgrimage No. 2, they invited me to stay with them for several days in their home, and that was one of the best parts of all the trips. They gave me tours, they showed me their incredible collection, they let me see life in a real British household and not just from a hotel room, and we had some wonderful conversations along the way. I was able to see them again in 2016, Holmes Pilgrimage No. 3, when we attended the Grand Opening of the Stepping Stones School at Undershaw.

I'm more grateful than I can say that I know Roger. His Sherlockian knowledge is exceptional, as is the work that he does to further the cause of The Master. But even more than that, both Roger and his wonderful wife, Jean, are simply the finest and best, and I'm very lucky to know both of them – even though I don't get to see them nearly as often as I'd like, and especially in these crazy days! In so many ways, Roger, I can't thank you enough, and I can't imagine these books without you.

- *Nicholas Meyer* – I started reading Nick Meyer's Holmes books before I'd even read all of The Canon, and for that I'm eternally grateful. It was through his first two books, *The Seven-Per-Cent Solution* and *The West End Horror* (the latter of which is still one of my favorite pastiches to this very day) that I firmly understood that The Canon wasn't the be-all end-all of Sherlockian story-telling. I obtained Nick's first book as part of a free book give-away at school, and I found the second not long after when my mother took my sister and me to buy school clothes and I spotted it in the mall bookstore. (I sat cross-legged along an out-of-the-way wall in a Sears while my mother and sister shopped and started reading *The West End Horror* straight out of the bag.)

    After those first two books, Nick went on to have a very successful career in film. (More about that in a minute.) But he has continued to dip in an out of Sherlockian pastichery with *The Canary Trainer* (1993), *The Adventure of the Peculiar Protocols* (2019), and *The Return of the Pharaoh* (2021). He is a Sherlockian legend, and it's an indisputable fact that the publication in 1974 of *The Seven-Per-Cent Solution* – a pastiche, mind you! – was the beginning of the Sherlockian Golden Age when has grown and grown, and has never stopped, all the way to today.

    If it was just that, Sherlockians – and especially pasticheurs – would owe him an unpayable debt. But then there's *Star Trek*, which he also saved. As mentioned above, I have lots of interests besides Mr. Holmes, although he does demand more and more attention as my years pass. But I've been a Trekkie (or Trekker, or whatever the correct term is) since I was a wee lad in the late 1960's, when my babysitter happened to watch one of the original prime-time episodes. After that, I grew up seeing the original series in re-reruns, and then I was among those who saw the first Star Trek film in 1979 (and truthfully felt mightily disappointed. I do like it better now.) But it was Nick Meyer's *Star Trek:*

The Wrath of Khan (1982) which electrified the Trek Universe, jump-starting it into motion in a way that – like the Holmes Golden Age – has only grown. And how it's grown! Hundreds and hundreds of Star Trek novels and comic books, multiple films and television shows, with more in planning and production all the time, and fan interest around the world at an all-time high. As a nearly life-long Star Trek fan, who loves it nearly as much as The World of Sherlock Holmes, I credit the origin of this original escalation entirely to Nick Meyer.

I generally despise social media, but it's a very useful way for Sherlockians to connect. Imagine my thrill when I began to see occasional online posts from Nick Meyer – and when I dared to respond, sometimes he would respond back! I've learned that if you don't ask, you'll never know, so I connected with him a bit more often, and eventually I boldly asked him to write a foreword to one of the MX anthologies that I edit, and he most-generously agreed. After that, we've stayed in touch off-and-on, and that still never ceases to amaze me.

I met him in person at the 2011 *From Gillette to Brett* conference in Bloominton, Indiana, where he was the featured guest. I took my Holmes book, asked him to autograph them, and asked – like everyone does – when he'd write his next Holmes book. He certainly doesn't remember that, but he was the main reason I chose to attend that event.

One of my greatest regrets is that, while attending the 2020 Sherlock Holmes Birthday Celebration in New York, I was almost able to meet him in person again – and this time he'd know who I was – but I didn't get to speak with him, and it was my own fault. We had emailed ahead of time, planning to meet, and that day I entered the famed dealer's room and saw him seated at a table near the door, surrounded by many fans. I wandered away, intending to return in a just a very few minutes and dive into the crowd, hoping that it might have thinned a bit. But when I got back over there, he'd already left! Hopefully I'll get another chance, sooner rather than later, where I can thank him in person for so many things
. . .

. . . including generously writing a foreword for these volumes. When I was considering who could write a foreword, I couldn't think of anyone more fitting. Through Nicholas Meyer I found pastiches, which have been so important to me over the years. Nick, thanks from the bottom of my heart for taking the time to be part of these books!

And finally, last but certainly *not* least, thanks to **Sir Arthur Conan Doyle**: Author, doctor, adventurer, and the Founder of the Sherlockian Feast. Honored, and present in spirit.

As I always note when putting together an anthology of Holmes stories, the effort has been a labor of love. This time the labor and love have been mine. These adventures are more tiny threads woven into the ongoing *Great Holmes Tapestry*, continuing to grow and grow, for there can *never* be enough stories about the man whom Watson described as *"the best and wisest . . . whom I have ever known."*

David Marcum
September 8th, 2021
A most important day,
for all kinds of reasons

Questions, comments, or story submissions
may be addressed to David Marcum at

thepapersofsherlockholmes@gmail.com

A Note on the
Modern Publishing Paradigm

For the longest time, publishing something was mostly impossible for most people. The Great Publishing Houses – which sounds like something from *Dune* – are giant machines, with carefully calculated formulas to know just how many books they need to sell to make a profit. It's no different than selling cereal: Many of the boxes of cereal on grocery store shelves won't be sold, and they were never meant to be sold, and the manufacturers are okay with that, because they've calculated the amount that they do need to actually sell in order to stay profitable while figuring in just how much can be discarded.

It used to be the same with books. Publishers would create a print run of a certain number of copies, sending out so many of them to bookstores across the country. Some would be sold – enough, hopefully, to cover costs – while many copies would just sit there, unsold, forever. Then, after a certain amount of time, they would be removed – either destroyed, or "remaindered", to be sold at rock-bottom prices in bargain bins.

It's an investment by the publishers to go to the trouble and expense to create all of those physical books, hoping to make their money back on enough of them to justify the waste of the others. That's why they're so restrictive about what they publish: They must meet the razor-thin edge of profit. But that makes the path to being published a very narrow needle's eye.

Several years ago, the paradigm began to shift. Online sales began to disrupt the physical bookstore model. And as people ordered online, some publishers figured out that they didn't have to have back rooms and warehouses jammed full of physical books sitting around waiting for a physical customer to enter a store or a dealer's room, examine it, and possibly buy it. Instead, when an online order arrived, the manufacturing of the book could commence right then, only as needed, and not months or years earlier.

This print-on-demand idea had been around for a while. (When I was going back to school for my second degree in civil engineering, the campus print shop did the same thing for certain locally produced textbooks, printing them as they were purchased on fancy copying machines.) Publishers and authors began to take advantage of technological advances to produce their own books – straight from author to reader, happily eliminating the giant publishing middlemen.

Steve Emecz of MX Publishing brilliantly took advantage of this, building his business and allowing authors who would have never had a chance otherwise – like me – to create and connect.

But there are certain legitimate complaints.

In the olden days, the giant publishers slow-walked books through the process, so that it sometimes took literally years for a book to actually be published. Authors could actually die before ever seeing their work excreted at the far end of the giant publisher's process. The print-on-demand process, by comparison, is nearly immediate. As part of the large publishers' slow walk, there were battalions of editors who went through books forwards, backwards, and upside down. With the new technology, where a file can be loaded with the book manufacturer with very little effort and time spent, there is clearly less editing . . . and mistakes slip through.

Some readers continue to expect flawless and perfect works, as if legions of editors were behind the curtain as in days of old, still involved in the process. For this type of reader/consumer, the new format of publishing will always be pain they just can't ease. That's why, with this set of my stories, I want to apologize up front to those who will find typos – *because in spite of every effort, there will be some typos.*

In my own case, I love to write and edit, and I spend a sizeable amount of time doing both, but I also have a very busy and rich life doing other things. I spend time with my family, and I work more-than-full time as a civil engineer, fitting in these Sherlockian writing and editing projects during lunch hours, evenings, and weekends. It's a high wire act with no safety net. I'm the writer and sole editor of the stories in this collection. My wife, with a Bachelor's Degree in Journalism and two Master's Degrees in English Literature and Library Science, and with a first job as a copy editor, used to go through my stories and catch what I missed – because you never *ever* see your own mistakes – but she works way more than full time at her own job, and she just doesn't have any extra time to spare for playing uncredited editor on these projects. So they're all on me.

It's the same with the anthologies that I edit – any mistake that slips through in the end is my fault, because there are no other editors. When assembling a Holmes anthology, I receive the stories, format them to the "house style", print them on 8½ x 11-inch paper, edit and revise, go back and forth with emails to the author – sometimes a lot of emails – and then plug them into a giant Word document for more editing and revision. But from the time I get the story until I send the final file to the publisher, there isn't anyone else to edit, and no time to work one into the process. It's the new publishing paradigm.

As a print-on-demand publisher, MX does not have squadrons of editors. The business consists of three part-time people who also have busy lives elsewhere – so the editing effort largely falls on the contributors. Some readers and consumers out there in the world absolutely despise this – apparently forgetting about all those self-produced Holmes stories and volumes from decades ago with awkward self-published formatting and loads of errors that are now prized as collector's items.

These critics should recall that every one of these new volumes by various authors – even those that have typographic and formatting errors – are the very best efforts that can be produced by very sincere people who don't have professional full-time editors to help, and who would never ever have had the opportunity to publish otherwise, and because of these authors, there is thankfully more Sherlockian content in the world.

I'm personally mortified when errors slip through – ironically, there will probably be errors in this essay – and I apologize now, but without a regiment of editors looking over my shoulder, this is as good as it gets. Real life is more important than writing and editing, and only so much time can be spent preparing these books before they are released into the wild. I hope that you can look past any errors, small or huge, and simply enjoy these stories, and appreciate the effort involved, and the sincere desire to add to The Great Holmes Tapestry.

And in spite of any errors here, there are more Sherlock Holmes stories than there were before, and that's a good thing.

David Marcum

Watson's Descendants
by Nicholas Meyer

It is generally felt that the short story was Sherlock Holmes's best venue. The novellas, by contrast, are judged to be . . . lesser. Even the fabled *The Hound of the Baskervilles* suffers from the detective's absence for many pages. Though *A Study in Scarlet*, *The Sign of the Four*, and *The Valley of Fear* remain deliciously absorbing, it is in the short stories that Holmes and Watson truly flourish.

As Michael Chabon has observed, all fiction is fan fiction. Almost from the beginning, Sherlock Holmes has prompted imitators of his creator's creation. Arthur Conan Doyle wrote sixty Holmes cases in all – fifty-six short stories and four novellas. When they ended, boys and girls, men and women of all ages mourned Watson's silence and the series' cessation. But it wasn't long before others took up – or attempted to take up – Sir Arthur's pen.

Writing a full-length Holmes novel has always posed a challenge, even for Doyle himself, to say nothing of generations of later writers and filmmakers. Short stories, on the other hand, pose problems of their own. A good short story must compress action and character. It must – obviously – be short. The gift of writing compelling short fiction remains in a class by itself. Poe, Doyle of course, Twain, Saki, and Hawthorne are among the masters of the form from the Victorian and Edwardian eras, but over the years, the short story has produced many masters.

I alas am not among them. Even as a kid in art class, my paintings were so huge the murals I attempted had to be unfurled in the hall, not the studio. And so it comes as no surprise that writing a short Holmes story does not come easily to me. In fact, it does not come at all.

I retain nothing but admiration for those writers who *can* create short fiction, and a special respect for those who can bring off simulacra of Doyle's charming and distinctive Holmes tales. There many practitioners, including some whose efforts, unfortunately, resemble nothing so much as taxidermy. But among the best I must number David Marcum, who, by this point has written more Holmes stories than Doyle himself. Characterized by unflagging imagination and ceaseless ingenuity, along with felicitous prose, these tales continue to provide what we all crave: More Sherlock.

All Sherlock Holmes stories, (except Doyle's), are of course forgeries. And it's the rare forger who can resist signing his own work. See if you can spot David Marcum's fine Italian hand.

Enjoy.

Nicholas Meyer
Los Angeles, 2021

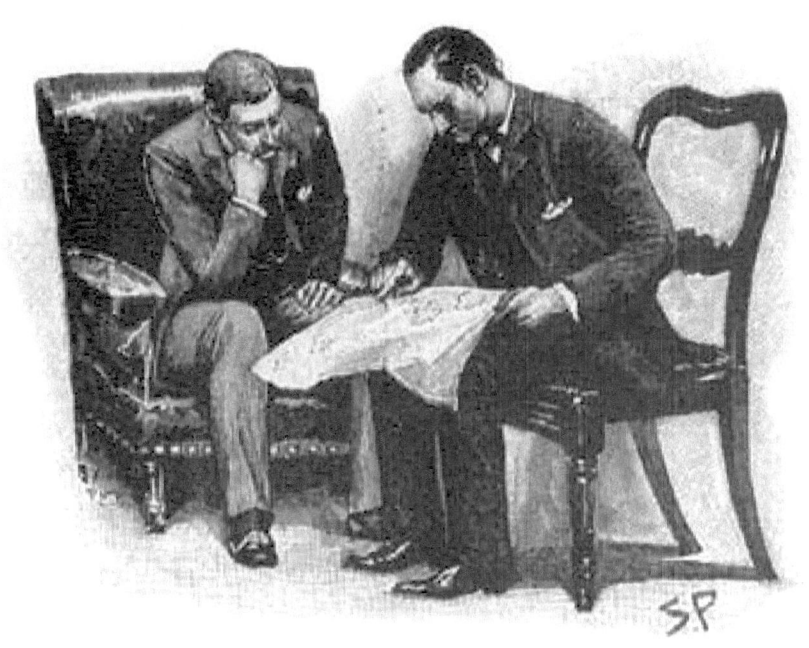

Sherlock Holmes (1854-1957) was born in Yorkshire, England, on 6 January, 1854. In the mid-1870's, he moved to 24 Montague Street, London, where he established himself as the world's first Consulting Detective. After meeting Dr. John H. Watson in early 1881, he and Watson moved to rooms at 221b Baker Street, where his reputation as the world's greatest detective grew for several decades. He was presumed to have died battling noted criminal Professor James Moriarty on 4 May, 1891, but he returned to London on 5 April, 1894, resuming his consulting practice in Baker Street. Retiring to the Sussex coast near Beachy Head in October 1903, he continued to be associated in various private and government investigations while giving the impression of being a reclusive apiarist. He was very involved in the events encompassing World War I, and to a lesser degree those of World War II. He passed away peacefully upon the cliffs above his Sussex home on his 103rd birthday, 6 January, 1957.

Dr. John Hamish Watson (1852-1929) was born in Stranraer, Scotland on 7 August, 1852. In 1878, he took his Doctor of Medicine Degree from the University of London, and later joined the army as a surgeon. Wounded at the Battle of Maiwand in Afghanistan (27 July, 1880), he returned to London late that same year. On New Year's Day, 1881, he was introduced to Sherlock Holmes in the chemical laboratory at Barts. Agreeing to share rooms with Holmes in Baker Street, Watson became invaluable to Holmes's consulting detective practice. Watson was married and widowed three times, and from the late 1880's onward, in addition to his participation in Holmes's investigations and his medical practice, he chronicled Holmes's adventures, with the assistance of his literary agent, Sir Arthur Conan Doyle, in a series of popular narratives, most of which were first published in *The Strand* magazine. Watson's later years were spent preparing a vast number of his notes of Holmes's cases for future publication. Following a final important investigation with Holmes, Watson contracted pneumonia and passed away on 24 July, 1929.

Photos of Sherlock Holmes and Dr. John H. Watson courtesy of Roger Johnson

The
Collected Papers
of
Sherlock
Holmes
Volume V – Chronicles
(20 Holmes Adventures)

The Stolen Relic

I paused in the doorway of 221 Baker Street, anxious to make my way inside and out of the bitter wind, but held in place by the sound of the approaching carolers. They were singing "The Moon Shines Bright", a song I remembered from my youth, and the lilting refrain brought bittersweet memories to mind, despite the cheery major key. It recalled times long gone when, as a child, our family had traveled south to visit my mother's people during the Christmas season. It was only then that I was able to see a traditional English celebration, and with it all that I missed during those other years while being raised in Scotland, where Christmas is not celebrated as such.

As the carollers came closer, I heard the words more clearly: *The moon shines bright and the stars give a light, little before it is day; Our Lord our God he called on us, and bids us awake and pray.*

I took another step into the building, but caught myself as they began the next verse, which I also recalled and which seemed to reflect my thoughts from this seemingly grim December: *The life of a man it is but a span, it's like a mourning flower; We're here today, to-morrow we are gone, we are dead all in one hour.* Shaking my head at this decidedly dark sentiment, and trying to imagine how it could possibly fit into a Dickensian holiday, I went inside and shut the door.

I had not intended to return home so early that Christmas Eve, having meant to spend the morning at Barts, followed perhaps by a rare afternoon at some theatrical entertainment, and then possibly a meal. I was feeling distinctly antisocial, and sought solitude. However, I was not needed at the hospital, and I found that I wasn't in the mood for the rest of my plans. With nowhere left to go, I glumly returned home.

While hanging my coat, I could see light shining at the top of the stairs, indicating that the sitting room door was open. But even as I watched, the stairwell darkened when the door closed with a solid thud, followed immediately by Mrs. Hudson's determined descent. I had only known our landlady for slightly less than a year, but I recognized this as the tread she made when irritated.

Seeing me standing there, she said, "Doctor Watson, I am *so* sorry. I've tried to do what I could to make your sitting room more festive, but *he* will have none of it." And with that, she cast an angry look back over her shoulder.

"It's quite all right," I said. "As you know yourself from being raised in the north, all of this Christmas merriment is, even now, still occasionally somewhat foreign to me."

"I felt that way as well, when I was younger," Mrs. Hudson replied. "But I've grown to love it. The decorations and the songs. The food and the tree. It's certainly better than how we did it when I was growing up in Scotland, where Christmas was just another day."

"I suppose," I agreed halfheartedly and, with a nod to her, started up the stairs. The truth was that I had enjoyed the British version of the holiday at times in the past. But this year, I was finding it more difficult to embrace any celebratory feelings whatsoever.

When I was a child, my parents' marriage had never set well with my maternal English grandfather, and in spite of his widely read experience and knowledge, he simply could not understand why Christmas wasn't observed in Scotland. My father would attempt to explain how the Church of Scotland, strictly Presbyterian as it was, had no use for Christmas, or *Christ's Mass*. Long before, it had been decided to be a Catholic affair, and thus anything remotely "Popish" was abolished in Scotland in the 16th century. And so it has remained.

But my mother was English through and through, and she had made sure that in our home, at least, some sort of Christmas was acknowledged. It was nothing like that which we saw on those few occasions celebrated at Grandfather's, and her efforts did little to otherwise alleviate the dour northern winter that held the rest of our town in its grip every December.

After I came to London to study medicine, I truly found myself in the midst of the seasonal excitement. In my student days, while living in Bloomsbury, there was no happier celebrant than myself, though perhaps for all the wrong reasons. I was in the thick of every party, and it was said by many that no one kept Christmas better than John Watson. But then came the army, and Afghanistan.

Now, in that late December of 1881, I found myself at the end of a difficult year. In July of '80, I was wounded at Maiwand, and then sent back to England, my health irretrievably shattered. I was set ashore on the Portsmouth jetty during a wet snow, with neither kith nor kin left in England. After that rather miserable Christmas had passed, I was acknowledging Hogmanay with a drink at the Criterion, and sourly contemplating the need to find cheaper lodgings to reflect my limited half-pay, when I was hailed by an old acquaintance, Stamford. What followed was an introduction to Sherlock Holmes, and the amazing series of events that had come over the past year.

Amazing they had been, but some had also been disappointing. Just months earlier, following a great portion of the year spent enduring a painful recovery, I had been notified that the army officially had no further need for my services. Each day that had passed since then reminded me in some way that I was marking time, and not going forward with my life. I had made myself useful, filling in as a *locum*, or assisting at Barts and a few of the other hospitals. But I knew that I should be devoting myself to something more permanent. The thought would not leave me.

And now, standing in the doorway of the sitting room, I felt the same thing. I was too happy to return here, when I should be looking for a more effective and prosperous alternative.

I only paused in the doorway for an instant before propelling myself forward. My friend was there, lounging in his chair by the fire and puffing on his cherry-wood pipe, and scowling at a veritable mound of holly and ivy lying across the mantelpiece.

"Ah, Watson. Come warm yourself by the fire. You'll see that Mrs. Hudson just brought tea, along with this pestiferous sampling of *Ilex Aquifoliaceae* and *Hedera Araliaceae*, detritus from some forest that has been killed before its time to rot above our fireplace."

"*We're here today, to-morrow we are gone, we are dead all in one hour,*" I muttered to myself.

"What was that?"

"Nothing," I replied. "Nothing at all."

"My dear fellow," said Holmes, rising suddenly. "You're freezing. Sit down, while I pour you some tea." And he moved to the table, showing that hidden compassion of his that appeared in the most unexpected moments.

Soon I was thawing out, and my mood increased exponentially. I was even able to look with appreciation at the difference made by having the decoration draped in front of Holmes's criminal relics that still rested, now hidden, upon the mantel.

We sat in companionable silence for a while, both looking into the fire with our own thoughts. Therefore, it was with some surprise when the bell rang. Holmes glanced at me. "Rather late in the day for the usual clients who help me earn my bread and cheese."

"Perhaps it is a crony of Mrs. Hudson's, here to wish her the compliments of the Season."

"True enough. We shall soon see."

It quickly became apparent that the caller was not there to visit our landlady, as we heard steady footsteps ascending the stairs. In a moment there was a knock, and Holmes called for the visitor to enter.

As we stood, the door opened, revealing a man in his mid-thirties, dressed in the habiliments of a plain priest's cassock. He wore no coat, paying no deference to the British cold, and he was clearly a stranger to our shores.

"Mr. Holmes?" he said, looking from one to the other of us, and speaking in an accent that betrayed his Italian origins. Holmes nodded, and gestured the man towards the basket chair facing the fire.

"May we offer you some refreshment?" I asked.

"Nothing, thank you."

"This is my friend, Dr. Watson. You may speak freely before him."

The man greeted me with a friendly and open countenance. I revised my opinion of his age. Upon closer inspection before the light from the fire, I could see that he was in his early forties.

"My name," said the priest, "is Father Abele. I am of the order located at the *Basilica di San Nicola*, in Bari."

Holmes nodded and stood. "One moment if you please, Father." As he walked over to the shelf where he kept his indexes, the Father smiled patiently, glancing my way in a friendly manner before turning his eyes to the fire. As he warmed, I could see him visibly relax.

Returning to his chair, Holmes sat and began to leaf through the volume. "Hmm. Interesting indeed," he murmured. Then, looking back at the priest, he said, "And how can we help you?"

"You were recommended to me, Mr. Holmes, by a man to whom you provided a previous service, Father Gregor, of the Orthodox Church, regarding the recovery of some stolen icons."

Holmes nodded. "I remember the case." Glancing my way, he said, "Quite before your time, Watson."

Father Abele continued. "I hold a unique position within the *basilica*. It is my duty there to be something of a roving agent, tasked to deal with those issues which might have cause to require a more substantial . . . interaction with the outside world." He looked from one to the other of us. "In short, I am here because a relic from the church has been stolen."

Holmes's eyes brightened, and he tapped his finger on the index. "Indeed. Might I ask – ? But no, let me not anticipate your story. Please tell it in order, from the beginning."

The priest nodded. "As I said, I represent the church of *San Nicola*, or as you would call him, Saint Nicholas."

My eyes widened. "Saint Nicholas. *The* Saint Nicholas? As in Father Christmas?"

Father Abele smiled. "There is that connection, of course," he said. "Even as the Americans have corrupted his name into the garbled appellation of *Santa Claus*."

"The Americans are not completely to blame," added Holmes. "The Dutch called him *Sinterklaas*, and carried that name with them when they immigrated to the United States."

The priest nodded. "As you can imagine, we are quite aware of the different iterations and adaptations of our patron's name throughout the world. But you are correct, Dr. Watson. I am referring to the *true* Saint Nicholas, of historical fact, and so canonized by the Church.

"Quite odd," I said, "the way a man who lived and breathed can, over time, come to be perceived as a make-believe character."

"Indeed," the man continued. "If I may, I would share a bit of history with you. I assure you that it is relevant, and I will not waste too much of your time." With a nod from Holmes, Father Abele continued.

"In case you were not previously aware, Saint Nicholas was born in the year 270 A.D. in Myra, an Asian part of what is now Turkey, and in what was then the Roman Empire. From an early age, he was quite religious, and entered the church while still a boy. Throughout his life, his kindness for both children and sailors was highly recognized, and it was through stories spread across the known world at that time by these very sailors that his fame grew.

"Throughout his life, he performed a number of miracles, including resurrecting the dead, feeding the hungry from food stores that did not decrease as they were used, no matter how much was used, and performing acts of great kindness and then directing the gratitude to God. An example of this was when he provided the dowries for a man's three daughters when the man could not provide it himself. The story goes that the Saint did so," continued the priest, looking at us significantly, "by dropping gold coins down the man's chimney and so into the daughters' stockings, hanging there to dry – hence, the variant form of receiving gifts now credited to Santa Claus.

"When the Saint was in his mid-fifties, he was quite respected within the church, and was invited by Emperor Constantine himself to attend the first Council of Nicaea, where he was one of the signers of the Nicene Creed. He died in 343, and within a few hundred years from his death, he was recognized as one of the Saints of the Church.

"At the time of his death, his body was entombed in Myra, where – for over six-hundred years – his grave was a destination of pilgrims and worshipers from all over the world.

"But in 1087, following several decades of unrest, sailors from Italy, fearing that access to Nicholas's tomb would become unreachable for pilgrims, seized a number of the bones from his tomb in Myra and brought them back to Bari, where the *Basilica di San Nicola* was constructed, and where pilgrims have journeyed ever since."

"A number of the bones, you say," interrupted Holmes. "But not all of them, I believe."

"That is correct. The others, initially left behind in Myra, were later seized by Crusaders and taken to Venice, where they are also kept in a church dedicated to the Saint."

Holmes nodded. "And you mentioned that a relic from the church has been stolen. Are we to assume then that one or more of the bones of St. Nicholas has been taken?"

"One bone," replied our visitor.

"And you need our assistance to locate it."

"That," said Father Abele, "is somewhat accurate. I know who took the relic. But I have not yet located where he is in London, and as a stranger in your country, I do not have the authority to retrieve it from him."

"I'm afraid that you're mistaken, sir, if you believe that I have any such authority."

The priest nodded. "That is understood, Mr. Holmes. But your involvement in helping me to locate him will go a long way toward clearing the matter up, and will prevent me from blundering in and making a bad situation worse by my ignorance of your customs."

"So," I interrupted, "you simply wish to retrieve the relic, then? And by not involving the police, as you clearly do not wish to do, you do not intend to prosecute?"

Father Abele nodded. "My only interest is in retrieving the object. The thief's punishment is beyond my influence."

"And you are certain the thief is in London?"

"Yes. I believe that you will be able to help me determine his location."

"And this relic?" said Holmes. "You said it is a single bone?"

"Yes. A *distal phalange*, as I think you would call it, from the Saint's left hand."

"The tip of a finger, then," I said.

The priest inclined his head. "More specifically, that of his left thumb. It was stolen more than a week ago. We must retrieve it as soon as possible, before any of the *manna* is lost."

I raised my eyebrows, but Holmes's lips tightened. "My index mentions this phenomenon. I will be happy to help you reacquire the object, but I'm afraid that I cannot give any credence to this supposed miracle."

"Miracle?" I asked. "*Manna?*"

Holmes gestured toward the priest, indicating that he should elaborate upon the matter. "Following the Saint's death, his tomb in Myra was always said to have a sweet smell resembling roses. And it has excreted a liquid, known as *manna* or *myrrh*, which has healing powers."

"I'm afraid that – " interrupted Holmes, but the priest continued.

"I understand your disbelief, Mr. Holmes. It is difficult sometimes to have faith in the manifestation of God's miracles. But I have often seen this for myself. After the bones were brought to the *basilica* in Bari, the smell of roses from the tomb has continued, as well as the appearance of the liquid, to the present day. And I have watched how it has been used to perform many miracles."

"And the tomb with the other bones in Venice? Does it also produce this *manna*?"

"I have not been there myself, but it is my understanding that they also have vials of the liquid."

"But surely," said Holmes, "there is another explanation. Seepage of groundwater into the tomb, perhaps? Or condensation?"

The priest shook his head, a tolerant smile dancing upon his lips. "No, Mr. Holmes. The tomb has been verified to be watertight, and no water is entering through the stones. The bones themselves ooze the liquid, much more than could be accounted for by simple condensation. Enough, as a matter of fact, that it is bottled in vials for use, along with Holy Water, in the performance of miracles."

Holmes frowned, as if looking for another argument. Finally, he shook his head. "That is all neither here nor there," he said, "in terms of recovering the bone. As you say, it is important to you to do so sooner, rather than later, but the idea of this *manna's* existence in and of itself has no impact on the actual recovery. What were the circumstances of the theft?"

The priest nodded, as if some sort of accord had been reached, and there was now enough to be going on with. "A little over a week ago, a British ship was docked in Bari. St. Nicholas always had a special relationship with sailors, so it is not unusual for them to visit the *basilica* in order to honor the tomb. Many are simply curious, but a few are genuine pilgrims who wish to worship.

"On the day in question, a group of sailors were there, including one who was recognized as having been there before on several occasions. On previous visits, he was always reverent and respectful, and had asked a number of intelligent questions. This time, however, he did something unusual.

"One of the novitiates noticed that this sailor, a Russian who had previously introduced himself on an earlier visit as Grigori Golov, had stayed behind when his compatriots departed. No other visitors in the *basilica* were present at the time. The novitiate thought nothing of it until, a few minutes later, he returned from an errand to discover that the stone cover of the tomb had been shifted. He called for help, and a number of priests, including myself, quickly determined that the thumb bone had been removed. It was obvious that only Golov could had taken it. There was no damage to the tomb itself, and no other relics were moved.

"As I indicated, it is my position within the church to act in matters relating to the outside world. I quickly made my way to the docks, only to determine that the ship upon which Golov served, *The Good Catherine*, had just left port for England. Obviously, Golov had planned his theft to the minute, allowing for a successful escape.

"Not wanting to involve the police, I decided to follow Golov on my own to retrieve the relic. There were no ships leaving immediately, and I did not want to take the time to follow in so leisurely a manner in any case. Therefore, upon returning to the *basilica*, I arranged to travel by rail, setting foot here three days ago.

"I had just missed the arrival of *The Good Catherine*, but I was able to determine that Golov had disembarked from the ship. It is scheduled to sail again in two days. I have been unable to locate him, although I suspect that he lives in the East End of London. The officials at the shipping office became decidedly uncommunicative when I pressed my questions, and rather than wait for him to reappear at his ship, I decided to see if someone else could help me locate him sooner. I had been given your name, Mr. Holmes, and here we are."

Holmes patted his hand twice upon his index, and then stood abruptly, as he was wont to do upon making a decision. "I believe that I can assist you." He walked around the two of us, replacing the scrapbook. "If you will come back in three hours, I should have the information that you need."

If the priest was surprised at this sudden burst of activity or the promise of a quick solution, he did not show it. He rose from his chair, and I did so as well. With a nod and a small bow, the priest agreed to return, and walked from the room.

Holmes moved into his room, removing his dressing gown as he did so. "Watson, I shall be back in time to meet our client. Do continue to warm yourself in front of the fire." And then, reappearing and wearing clothing suitable for the cold, he departed.

Rather than reseating myself, I stepped over to the shelf holding Holmes's scrapbooks, pulling out the one that he had recently replaced. I found the entry on the Saint, but it gave no more additional information than that which had been recently provided by Father Abele. Unsatisfied, I returned to my seat.

Growing up, I had been exposed to the stories of St. Andrew, that Galilean fisherman who accompanied Christ during his lifetime, and who later carried on the work of the church. I knew about the story of the miracle associated with his name, in which King Angus had seen a vision of St. Andrew's Saltire Cross in the rising sun, and it had inspired him and his men to win a decisive victory over the opposing Saxons, thus leading to the adoption of that Cross as the Scottish symbol. But, in spite of this tale, stories of miracles like the healing fluid produced from the bones of St. Nicholas were not regularly part of the strict Church of Scotland Presbyterian fabric of my boyhood.

I was still brooding upon these questions nearly three hours later when Holmes reappeared, followed almost immediately by the priest. "I have found your sailor," said Holmes as we stepped outside.

"I had no doubts," said Father Abele.

Soon, we were in a four-wheeler, making our way to the south and east. Looking at the priest, sitting across from me in the bitter cold, and without a coat but seemingly indifferent to the fact, I began. "This *manna* . . . ."

The man nodded. "I understand, Doctor. You are curious about the healing properties. You perhaps believe that there is not a true power within the liquid, but rather that the ills are cured by the power of suggestion, and the patient's own desperate desire to be well once again."

"Such things are not unknown," I said. "I could tell you stories of men on the battlefield, during times when we had completely exhausted our supplies. They were given water and told that it was, in fact, morphine. Their belief was enough to convince them that their pain, sometimes from horrible wounds, had been reduced or even eliminated."

Father Abele nodded, and with a kind smile stated, "God has blessed us with minds that have great powers indeed. After all, these minds are created in His own image. One does not realize what the mind is capable of, whether in terms of great reasoning, or the expression of beautiful art or music, or even in terms of healing. But," he added, his face now quite serious, "none of that negates in any way the actual power of a true miracle, which is a separate and distinct thing from that which is conceived of within the mind. A miracle is a gift, granted to us by the Grace of God." And he settled back with finality.

Holmes had a slightly troubled look upon his face, and he was silent throughout this conversation, remaining so throughout the journey. I wondered what he was thinking, although I could imagine. The priest and I also sat quietly, and soon we were at our destination.

We stepped down from our cab, and Holmes led us to a dark arch, from which we signaled for our cabbie to wait. We passed through a tunnel-like passage into a tiny court, and inside were several doors. Holmes stopped in front of the second on the left. It was part of a mean cluster of dark brick buildings, yet surprisingly well kept, considering the neighborhood in which it had been built. "Golov lives on the third floor," said Holmes as we entered the building and climbed the stairs.

Inside, the air was somewhat warmer, although not much, and there was the stale smell of cooked cabbage that is so often found in buildings in that part of London. The stairwell was quite dark, but the treads appeared to be solidly placed, and there was an absence of the refuse that clutters buildings of this sort.

Stopping at the door indicated by Holmes, we caught our breath. From beyond it, we heard quiet conversation. Then the priest knocked solidly, and the voices stopped immediately. After a very short wait, there were heavy footsteps, and the door opened.

We were faced by a tall man, wrapped in a pea coat to ward off the chill. Behind him, we could see a woman with a sad face, standing beside a table where she had apparently been sitting. The man, undoubtedly the sailor Grigori Golov, looked from one to the other of us before settling on Father Abele. A look of sadness crossed his face as he identified the priest's cassock, and he said, with only a trace of accent, "So. You have come, then."

"Was there ever a doubt?" asked the priest, not unkindly. "You did nothing to hide your tracks, my son. We knew your name from when you visited the *basilica* on previous occasions. You waited until no one was there before you opened the tomb, so that it was unavoidably certain that you would be the one identified as the taker of the relic. You made no effort to hide your return to the ship, and your action was apparently planned so as to be able to leave with the vessel at its planned departure time."

Golov nodded. "As you say. But you must understand. I had no choice."

"May we come in?" asked Holmes. "Then, you can explain your reasons."

Golov stepped back, gesturing for us to pass by him. Shutting the door, he said, "This is my wife, Maria."

We nodded at the woman, who simply looked at us, a fearful expression upon her face, pinched with a kind of dread and terror.

"Are these policemen, then?" asked Golov of the priest, looking from Holmes to me. "Are you here to arrest me?"

"No, my son. These men are from here in London. I requested them to help me find you, as I do not know this city very well." He looked around. "Do you still have it? The relic?"

Golov nodded. "I do. And you must believe me that, after I had used it, I intended to return it. I would not have taken it for anything. But, you see, I had no choice."

Holmes nodded. "Is it your child?"

Golov nodded, while the priest looked to his side at my friend. "Child? What do you mean, Mr. Holmes?"

Pointing to several items that I had also spotted on the table in the center of the room, Holmes stated, "Surely it is obvious, from the medical accoutrements placed here and there, that there is illness in the home. There is indication of a child's presence from some of the objects in the room, but he or she – yes, a girl, I believe – is not present. Based upon the various icons placed on the walls, this is a family of deep faith. No doubt Mr. Golov intended to use the power of the relic to heal someone who is ill. Neither Mr. nor Mrs. Golov appears to be sick, so the relic was taken to aid someone else, most likely the child."

Father Abele looked back at the sailor. "Is that so?"

Golov nodded, and his wife began to cry softly.

"And did it help?" asked the priest. "Has your child been healed?"

"No," said Golov sadly. "She has been too ill to even be aware that the Saint's bone is now here."

"Surely," said Father Abele, "she does not need to know it is here for its healing power to make itself manifest."

"That may be," said the big sailor. "And yet, from the time that I returned with it, she has been asleep, suffering from a fever, and unaware that I brought it, as she had asked. I believed that she would know of its power if she recognized that it was here."

"Your daughter requested for you to bring the relic?"

"She did. Many has been the time that I've told her of my visits to the tomb of the Saint, when I've had the opportunity to travel to Bari. When she was scratched several weeks ago, the wound quickly became much worse than one would expect. The doctor came and speculated that the scratch might have simply brought to light some other illness that might prove to be incurable. When it did not seem to get any better, and it appeared as if the doctor could be proven right, our daughter mentioned that perhaps one of the bones of the Saint could be used to heal what the doctor could not.

"I do not know if she really meant for me to bring it, but I resolved that I would do so. Thus, on my last journey, I made my way to the tomb, and as you know, removed the bone." He swallowed, and continued. "I swear, Father, that I was as respectful and as careful as I could be. I would not have desecrated the tomb under any other circumstance, but . . . but . .

. ." He broke off with a sob and hung his head. His wife took a step closer and pulled him to her.

"We are afraid," she said, speaking for the first time, "that she will die."

"I am a doctor," I said, stepping forward. "May I see her?"

At the same time, the priest also said, "The relic? Is it with your daughter?"

Golov looked up, from one to the other of us, and nodded. "In here."

He led us into the other room of the tiny flat, a dark chamber with most of the space taken by a small bed. Lying in the middle of it was a wee girl, probably about seven or eight, but appearing more insignificant due to a likely lack of nutrition during the early years of her life. She was huddled under several blankets, her breathing raspy and labored while she shifted from side to side, moaning lightly with each exhalation. Asking "May I?" and receiving a nod from both her parents, I leaned down and felt of her forehead. She was burning.

While I began to examine the girl, I heard the others talking softly behind me. "The relic?" asked the priest. "Where is it?"

"Here," said Golov, reaching for a small tin on a shabby table beside the bed. "I have not opened it since taking it," he said. "I wanted to keep it safe in transit, as you will understand, and there was no need to see it once I arrived, as Alina was too ill to take note of it."

"Then surely there may be enough . . ." said the priest softly to himself.

I glanced over my shoulder to see the Russian handing the tin to the priest. Father Abele took it and carefully raised the lid. Then he turned it slightly from side to side, in order to catch the faint light from the single-paned window. He stopped turning it when he found the angle he wished, and then he simply looked at it for a long moment. I continued to watch him, curious as to the apparent mesmerization that the object seemed to hold over him.

Finally, he looked up at Holmes, and then toward me. "Gentlemen? Would you like to see?"

He held it out, and I rose, even as Holmes took a step forward. Leaning in, we both saw inside the tin. It contained a small whitish nub, undoubtedly the bone from the tip of a thumb. It rested in the corner of the tin, nearly covered by an oily looking liquid. Even as I realized it, the scent of roses seemed to fill the room.

The priest smiled. "Mr. Golov," he said. "Did you also take any of the liquid that was in the tomb when you removed the relic?"

The sailor shook his head emphatically. "No, Father. I was careful to reach in and retrieve only the bone. I was praying as I did so, in order to be as respectful as possible. Some of the liquid lying around the bones in the bottom of the tomb got on my fingers as I picked out the bone, but I shook it off before I put it in the container. It was damp, but that was all." Suddenly, with a realization crossing his face, he asked, "Why?"

Turning slightly, the priest showed the girl's parents what Holmes and I had just seen, the fragment of St. Nicholas, nearly covered with a fluid that it had apparently excreted between the time it was taken in Bari and now. If one believed that sort of thing.

"But surely, Mr. Golov," said Holmes, stubbornly trying to make sense of what he had seen, "you added the liquid at some point. Or your wife."

"We did not!" cried the Russian, while his wife shook her head emphatically.

"Then someone on the ship from Bari," said Holmes. "Some other sailor who knew what you carried, and got at it at some point."

"No one knew that I had it. I did not tell anyone. I did not want to take the chance that it might be taken from me before I could return with it to Alina."

"A miracle, Mr. Holmes," said the priest simply. "A miracle."

Turning away from the frowning expression on my friend's face, I returned to my examination of the girl. She had a long scratch on her leg, quite infected, and suppurating. Around it, her leg was swollen, with streaks stretching above and below. I had seen this before, and knew that there was more going on beneath the skin than was easily seen.

"She fell," said her mother. "Outside. She said that as she did so, her leg dragged itself across a broken board."

I nodded. "No doubt there are splinters buried in the wound, adding to the injury. This and the fever are the body's way of fighting back. How long has she been like this?"

"She became ill about two weeks ago, not long after the injury. The doctor gave us this." She reached behind to a cabinet affixed to the wall and turned back with a brown bottle. I examined it with disgust, seeing that it was among the worst of the patent medicines available to the ignorant, prescribed by charlatans.

"Which doctor gave you this?"

"Doctor Anglesey," replied the girl's mother.

I snorted. I was aware of the man. In the year that I had been back in London, while volunteering my services at Barts, I had more than once come across the victims of this mountebank's practice.

"This concoction will not help her," I said, shaking the bottle and then handing it back. "She is in danger." I saw no reason to keep them from knowing the truth. "The treatment she received from your Doctor

41

Anglesey did not help. In fact, letting her go for so long without true medical attention has only made the problem worse. She has blood poisoning, and . . . and there is a danger that she might lose her leg."

Golov's eyes widened, while his wife gave forth a sob. "Will she die?" asked the women quietly.

I shook my head. "It is not too late. She can be treated, but we must get her to hospital immediately."

I leaned down and began to wrap her tightly in the thin blankets. But as I was doing so, Father Abele spoke. "Doctor? If I may?"

I turned to see him holding the tin, a questioning look in his eyes. I knew what he was asking.

"Father, I simply cannot. We do not know what is in that liquid."

"We do not know what is in it, but we do not need to. We know from whence it comes."

"It may do more harm than good," I answered with exasperation. "It has been in contact with a bone, for goodness' sake."

"Exactly," said the priest. "For goodness' sake."

I hesitated, uncertain as to whether to allow it. I noticed the girl's father staring intently at me. He nodded. "Let him, Doctor," he said. "Please."

I straightened and glanced at Holmes. His eyes were in a frown, but, sensing my uncertainty, he nodded. With a sigh, I stepped back, allowing the priest access.

He sat himself on the edge of the bed and, laying a hand across the girl's brow, began to pray in low, even tones. Mr. and Mrs. Golov bowed their heads, silently mouthing the words to the prayer as well. Meanwhile, Holmes watched intently.

Father Abele took his open palm from the girl and brought it to the tin, held in his other hand. Placing a finger carefully inside, he brought it back out, now damp from the liquid *manna* within. Moving carefully, so that none of it would drop off, he extended his hand back to Alina's forehead, where he traced the figure of a cross, lengthwise and then side to side, still praying as he did so. Suddenly, almost the instant that he had finished and lifted away his fingertip, the girl gave a gasp and flickered her eyes, but then settled back into the same condition in which she had been when we found her.

Pulling aside the blankets, he then repeated his actions, carefully tracing the length of the girl's wound with the oily substance from the tin. This time, the girl gave no reaction, and the liquid simply shone in the dim light from the window before gradually losing its sheen as it dried.

With a solemn "Amen," the priest arose and made room for me. Not wanting to disturb the fluid, still faintly outlined on the girl's forehead, I placed a hand against her cheek. Was her fever already lessened? Surely not. And yet, I could not be sure in that cold room, and I did not want to take time to find out otherwise. Bundling her up, I rose and carried her out of the bedroom, and so on until we reached the street, where our four-wheeler was waiting.

Talking to our cabbie was another driver, apparently a friend of his, who had tarried for a while during the time that we were inside. The two were talking and smoking, while the second driver's hansom was parked nearby. "*How fortunate to find a second cab in this neighborhood,*" I thought to myself as I climbed with the girl into the four-wheeler. "*Almost a miracle,*" my mind added as I settled back on the seat, carefully holding my patient. I was joined by the girl's parents, while Holmes engaged the hansom for him and the priest to follow.

"The Royal London Hospital, Whitechapel Road," I called to our driver. "And hurry!"

"Right away," the man answered, gigging his horse. Within minutes we were in transit, and not long after, I was carrying the girl inside, explaining the situation, and being directed to a room in order to begin treatment.

Even as we had traveled, the girl had inexplicably and impossibly begun to show signs of recovery. I would like to believe that it was due to the uncomfortable shock of being taken from the womb-like atmosphere of the bedroom and out into the cold December day. How could she not react in some way? But a part of my mind could not help but wonder if the priest's ministrations had not had something to do with it.

Within an hour of our arrival at the hospital, the girl's wound had been debrided and treatment was being given for the fever. Careful probing had revealed a long nasty splinter, black and slick, invisible from the surface and resisting to the end as it was pulled from the girl's wound. The streaks of blood poisoning had already unexplainably commenced to recede back toward the puncture. And, in all honesty, the fever had already started to abate well before the efforts at the hospital began. Within a short while, it was with a great feeling of satisfaction that I was able to call in the sailor and his wife, who joyfully reunited with the now conscious and smiling girl at her bedside.

Some time later, in the hallway outside, Holmes and I stood with the priest.

"She will be fine," I said. "They will be able to take her home within a few hours."

"And now, Doctor? Mr. Holmes?" asked Father Abele. "Now do you see the power of the miracle?"

I wanted to answer, but my response was torn. As a doctor, I could credit the effect of the mind in letting the body cure itself. As a man of science, I wanted to reject the moonshine associated with a miracle. In the end, I said nothing, looking toward my friend.

With a tight smile, Holmes simply said, "There are all sorts of miracles, Father."

Seeing that this was the best that he was going to get, the priest nodded. "Your fee, Mr. Holmes?" He reached within his cassock, pulling out a worn leather purse that jingled with heavy coins. Holmes waved his hand.

"Not necessary, Father. My assistance was minimal."

"Nevertheless," said Father Abele. "I insist."

"If you must," said my friend, "then use it to assist the poor. Perhaps the Golov's could benefit from it. Anonymously, of course."

"Of course. And Doctor? May I compensate you for your troubles?"

"Not at all," I said. "Add my portion to Holmes's. For the Golov family."

"Very good," he replied. He replaced the purse and patted his chest, where the container holding the relic of the Saint now rested. "Then I must get this back to where it belongs. May you both go with God."

"And you, Father," I replied, while Holmes simply nodded.

Later, as we were leaving Whitechapel behind, I turned to Holmes, sitting beside me in the hansom. "Father Abele," I said with a false heartiness, as I attempted to place these events in some sort of container in which they could be examined and understood, "certainly believes in the power of this supposed miracle."

"Indeed. He has dedicated his life to such an idea."

I was silent for a moment, before I felt the need to say, "I must confess, Holmes, that the girl's response following the touch of the liquid, and the subsequent and unexpectedly immediate improvement in her condition, is unheard of. It seems to give some validity to the Father's argument."

"There are all sorts of miracles," said my friend, repeating his comment of a few minutes earlier.

I smiled. "I'm surprised, Holmes. You are the ultimate defender of the scientific and rational explanation over that of superstition. What credence do you give to miracles?"

Holmes was silent for so long that I thought he had chosen not to answer. The sound of the horse's steady tread went on for quite a while before he spoke. And then, finally, "Ah, Watson, how can I explain it? I seek rational explanations to questions, because if I cannot define a mystery within the known rules and laws by which we exist on a daily basis, what hope do I have? No ghosts need apply. If the possibility for a supernatural explanation *does* exist, then when do we choose to carry on and find the truth if a human agency is responsible, and when do we abandon our efforts and throw up our hands, declaring that the problem has no solution, for it is the fault of a spirit or god beyond our understanding, and therefore the solution cannot be perceived by our mere mortal minds?

"If I am to function within my chosen field, I have to believe that there is a rational and worldly explanation for every action. There have to be some defined parameters within which I can work. If a person believes himself to be haunted, I must determine who is doing whatever is being done to make him *think* that, and then relieve him of the problem. I cannot simply assume that the possibilities are endless. You, as a doctor, must do the same thing. You must seek the cause of a disease, and treat it with the best defined methods in order to achieve real results, rather than stepping back and simply counting on the effort of a prayer, hoping that some magical culmination to the situation will be achieved."

I started to reply, but Holmes added, "But, as I said, Watson, there are all sorts of miracles."

"That," I said, "is contradictory, and does not seem to fit with your previous statement."

"But it does. I cannot refuse to make an effort to find a solution, simply on the surrendering assumption that it is beyond my powers. Nevertheless, as a scientist, I must also be aware of the smallness of man in the great scheme of the Universe, and how little we truly know. We have so much more understanding of the physical world than we did even a hundred years ago, but it would be foolish to think that we now understand all of it, and that all the mysteries of existence are now solved. There are so many things that we think we know with certainty that we probably have wrong, and so much more that we do not even *know* that we do not know. Our understanding of the actual world is like that of an ant's knowledge of the workings of a steam engine."

"You astound me, Holmes. I was certain that you would have had a much different point of view."

"I'm happy that, even after a year, Watson, I can still surprise you. Would it also astonish you to learn that I believe in the human soul?"

"Frankly, yes it would."

"And yet, given my statement that we really know nothing about the Universe around us, how could I not? For what is it that gives us a self-awareness? What is it that takes all of the various separate substances that make up our bodies, each a miniscule dead piece of matter that has never been alive and will never be alive as we understand it, and brings it all together into a unit that functions together for a while as a cohesive unit, with thought and action and purpose, before separating again into dead pieces, each one going its own way. And for that matter, what is it that allows us to change the world around us, with or without a plan, in violation of all the natural laws of the Universe?"

I found myself fascinated as this conversation spiraled from the discussion of a sick girl to the laws of the Universe. "What do you mean by that?"

"Simply that the Universe works by following a defined set, as we understand them, of natural entropic laws. Heat disperses into coolness. Higher energy decreases into levels of lower energy. The force of gravity pulls a smaller object towards a heavier one, but with a mutual attraction always existing between both of them. Any random particle in the Universe will follow these natural laws governing its motion and behavior.

"But this," he said, raising a hand in front of us, "this simple action of raising my hand and holding it there because I *choose* to do so, defies all the laws of the Universe. The Law of Gravity states that I should not be able to voluntarily and decisively raise my hand, going against the pull of the entire planet. Everything in the Universe says no. And yet . . . I choose to do so, and then I so accomplish it.

"What is it that makes me decide to do this, to take this random collection of dead substances held together for a while as *me*, and place them in opposition to the will of the Universe? As a scientist, I see this action accomplished. It has happened, and happens everywhere, every day, whether raising a hand or a pyramid. It must be achieved by something. For lack of anything else better to call it, it must be a *soul*."

"But animals choose to move independently," I countered. "Plants grow in opposition to gravity. Are you saying that they have souls as well?"

He shrugged. "Who is to say? Perhaps we all have a fragment or spark of the Divine within each of us, to a greater or lesser degree. I know as little about it as an ant knows of a steam engine.

"But let me give you another example: If I choose to roll a boulder up to the top of a hill, something that would never happen naturally in this entropic universe, gravity immediately wants to pull it back down to the bottom. Suppose then that I brace it, where it cannot roll away. My action has thus defied one of the basic natural laws of the Universe. Wind and weather – both caused, by the way, by convection currents and other phenomena related to natural laws – will wear at the boulder and the earth beneath it for countless ages. They may do so for so long that the hillside itself erodes away, thus allowing the boulder to be freed again from its support, whereupon it will follow the natural laws and again roll back to

46

the bottom. But in the meantime, during all those years, the boulder has been sitting where *my* own will and *my* energy and *my* choice placed it, where it never would have been located before, according to every natural law in the Universe. The same is true for a statue or a building made up of bricks and alloys and other materials that never would have been combined or formed together in that particular way or shape if someone had not intentionally done so, defying the laws and will and intent of the Universe.

"Knowing all of that, and additionally realizing how small we are in the great scheme of things, how can I doubt that there must be different sorts of miracles?"

I was quiet for a moment, contemplating the vast scope of his statement. Finally, I said, not knowing how else to reply, "I never knew that you felt this way."

"It has never come up. But how can we ignore it? When trying to determine that which is greater than us, there is nothing so necessary as deduction. And if we believe that existence is essentially good, as I do – in spite of much that I have seen – then the greatest assurance of that goodness seems to rest in the extras that we are given, such as flowers, for instance. Their beauty is an extra, an embellishment of life, and not a condition, and one that I am thankful for.

"But, even if I am thankful for this extra, I must conduct my work with a degree of separation from it, so that I do not end up counting on miracles. Yet, I do believe them, and the events of today convince me of that even more."

"How so? In what way?"

"We may or may not believe in the power of the *manna* from the St. Nicholas relic, although '*there are more things in heaven and earth, Watson, than are dreamt of in your philosophy*', to paraphrase the Bard. The relic's liquid could have contributed to the girl Alina's recovery, or not. But I do believe that your unexpected return today, allowing you to be present in order to participate in our trip to Stepney, was part of a bigger plan. For you, a doctor, were with us when we visited this girl who needed medical attention. You had, I believe, intended to spend the day at Barts, and then at other pursuits. What if you hadn't been at home when Father Abele arrived? I would have found the Golovs, but would we have known to seek immediate additional treatment for the girl? Would we have recognized the seriousness of her illness? Or that her wound was much graver than it appeared from the surface? Perhaps the anointment of the *manna* would have healed the girl, but I have to believe that she needed the immediate attention of a physician as well – and you were there."

47

"The second cab," I said softly. Holmes raised his eyebrows. "I thought at the time that it was unusually fortunate that a second cab was waiting in that neighborhood when we carried the girl outside."

He nodded. "Another minor miracle, perhaps?" Then, lowering his voice, he continued. "And then there is the other occurrence, which might also be something of a miracle."

A silence fell as he ruminated for a moment, until I prodded him to continue. "I didn't tell you about how I located the Golovs," he said.

"I had assumed it was a straightforward investigation."

"I should have been. I was able to speak to my various contacts near the docks, and I was quickly given the man's address. But then . . . then I *couldn't find it.* Watson, you know that I have an encyclopedic knowledge of London, but in this case, it failed me. And everyone that I asked was uncertain as well as to the location of the little court where the sailor and his family lived.

"Time was passing, and soon I would need to return to Baker Street to meet the priest. Just when I was feeling most frustrated, I heard a soft voice behind me. Turning, I discovered a tall old man, with a white beard and a high forehead, smiling at me with a most warming expression. He spoke with an unusual accent that I couldn't quite place, clearly foreign, and with something of the Mediterranean about it. 'The house you seek is there, my son.' And he raised his arm, pointing toward that same dark passage, previously unnoticed by me up to that moment, where I later returned with you and Father Abele. Then he lowered his hand, his smile becoming possibly even more filled with pure joy than before. I wanted to speak, to ask a question, to thank him, but I found that I could not. And as he turned and walked away into the gloom, I was aware of his eyes, Watson. They were perhaps the kindest eyes that I have ever seen . . . ."

His voice faded, and I knew the unspoken thought between us. Who could the man have been who knew just where to direct Holmes in his moment of desperation? Someone from that neighborhood, perhaps, who had heard Holmes's attempts to locate the address, and had simply offered assistance. *Or could it have been . . . ?* But no − for that would be impossible. Still, one somehow knows that at Christmas, above all other times of the year, the possibility of miracles might somehow truly exist.

I raised my eyes to find Holmes smiling at me, obviously reading my thoughts. "So there are different sorts of miracles, Watson, and I think that today's events count. Most fittingly, they were Christmas miracles."

And as we rode in silence, I found, with further examination, that I agreed with him. I recalled my feelings of just a few hours before, as I had looked about me with a sore lack of appreciation for the season. In fact, considering the circumstances in which I might have found myself at this point in my life, had I not met my friend when I did, I was very fortunate indeed. If, in fact, there is an overall plan, as Holmes espoused, one that is greater than our understanding, I could only be thankful that I could dimly recognize and appreciate my place in it, and thus count my many blessings.

"Merry Christmas, Holmes," I was moved to say.

"Indeed, my friend. Indeed it is."

The Helverton Inheritance

On that particular Saturday in October 1883, I nearly reached a crisis. Looking around those rooms that I had shared with Sherlock Holmes for over two-and-three-quarters of a year, I was hard-pressed to find either a single object of my own that wasn't covered or crowded or obscured by some criminal relic, and there wasn't a single empty space upon which to lay an additional item of my own, should I have desired to do so.

Perhaps my frustration was not wholly due to the overwhelming state of the sitting room that I had just entered upon that brassy afternoon. I had recently concluded one of several tedious consecutive days as a *locum* for a doctor on holiday from his practice near St. Pancras Station, and I was facing another bleak week of the same until his return. Every physician's office cultivates a certain *ambiance*, as the French so aptly put it, and the professional abode of Dr. Weaver was singularly constructed to weary a man's soul, consisting of plain and rather dark rooms without windows, frequent train-related rumblings – some obvious and others almost below one's awareness, except for an unsettled feeling in one's bones from arrivals and departures at the nearby station – and most of all a set of patients who were decidedly unfriendly toward this poor doctor who had agreed to treat them while their regular physician was pursuing his own likely prurient interests along the French coast.

It was with a day of this experience as my foundational basis that I returned to Baker Street in the mid-afternoon, with only the desire to put my feet up at the fire, sip a generous restorative, and lose myself in a novel of high adventure set upon the sea. Instead, I opened the door to find the sitting room especially avalanched, if that may be used as a word, under mounds of paper, stacked hither and yon across the path to my chair, which itself held a stack of books so high and skewed that I feared its imminent collapse into the fire.

Oblivious to what he had caused, for it could only have been caused by him, was my friend Sherlock Holmes, curled into his own chair opposite my own, some sort of document held close before his face, catching the last of the afternoon light from the west-facing window behind him. He looked far younger at that moment than his twenty-nine years and I, only about a year-and-a-half older then he, suddenly felt like a middle-aged parent who had returned home to find that a sheepish little Johnny or Mary had spent the afternoon making mud pies upon the carpets.

Even as I planted my feet, afraid to try and cross that battlefield of papers before me and preparing to roar at my flatmate, he looked up with that enthusiasm of old, while waving the document this way and that.

"Morgan's palimpsest!" he cried. "I've cracked it! We only need to journey out to Hornchurch, and then a little pick-and-shovel work should set the matter right as quick as the greyhound's mouth, to borrow a bit from the Bard."

I had been prepared to list grievances, and they were still on my tongue, but they turned to ashes and, with a sigh, I let them run away. Instead, I counted to three and then stated, "That's good news for Morgan, then. Have you let him know?"

"Not yet. I only just now understood the puzzle in the moments before you arrived. I have spent the afternoon . . . ." He trailed off, looking around the room at the dunes and drifts of paper. Having been there upon previous occasions when he discovered a trail and set off where it would take him, I knew how such a mess of stacked books and scattered documents could occur. When Holmes perceived a connection, he would search and shift and sort while following the elusive fact until he found the way to the next, and so on. Only after the prey had been run to earth, so to speak, would the fever slowly dissipate, and he would peer around, as he was doing now, realizing just what his quest had wrought.

He smiled ruefully, set the palimpsest aside on his little octagonal table, uncurled from the chair, and leapt to his feet. "My dear fellow," he said, taking a few steps to my chair and effortlessly lifting a nearly three-foot stack of volumes before pivoting with them toward our dining table. "I do apologize." Setting the books down upon the table top, he ran his hands from bottom to top to align them, and then made his way to the sideboard. "A brandy, perhaps? Or no. I should think a whisky will do." He began to pour while I was left to navigate through the papers on the floor.

So after only a minor delay, I was finally ensconced in my chair, a fine old friend that I had bought from a used furniture dealer in nearby Dorset Street within a day of first moving to Baker Street. I tried not to sigh audibly with satisfaction, a reaction made more tempting as I received my curative beverage. In the meantime, Holmes turned his attention to the herding of his papers, gradually combining and collapsing the stacks until they were replaced from whence they had come, even as he explained the process that had led to his understanding of the message on the document that Morgan had brought 'round only that morning – a solution that would mean rescue from penury to the gruff old man and his two worthy granddaughters.

I only half-listened, wondering how I would get out of a planned day at Doctor Weaver's practice in order to accompany Holmes to Hornchurch, to participate in what could only be described as a treasure hunt. It was a bit awkward, asking someone else to serve as a *locum* for me, while I was already acting as *locum*, but I'd done it before. It crossed my mind, as it sometimes did, that someday, when my health was finally as good as it was going to get and I found a full-time practice of my own, I would have to discover a way to force myself to stay there every day, facing the same progression of tedious illnesses that would shuffle in and wander out of my premises with the monotonous regularity of a ticking clock. I took a sip of good whisky to chase away the thought, and that is when the doorbell rang.

Holmes glanced up from the midst of his task, a familiar gleam in his eye. We heard the sound of conversation below as Mrs. Hudson answered the door, and then steady footsteps climbing the stairs. Holmes just had time to put the substantial stack of papers in his hand upon a desk – my desk – and straighten his dressing gown. Then, following a knock at the sitting room door and, with Holmes's bid to enter, we were faced by a stranger, a young man in his mid-twenties, not much younger than Holmes or me.

I stood while Holmes spoke a greeting, directing the distraught-looking fellow to the basket chair directly facing the fire. I questioned whether he would join us in a whisky, perhaps, or something else. He declined and, with all of us seated, he began to speak.

"Thank you for the gracious welcome, gentlemen." He looked from one of us to the other. "I apologize for arriving without an appointment. I was returning to town, following the events of last night, and I fear that I allowed myself to become indiscreet upon the train, as I felt the need to discuss what happened with someone. Fortunately, I found myself sharing a compartment with a policeman returning to London from some business of his own, and he suggested that you might be able to shed a bit of light upon my dilemma."

"And this policeman was . . . ?" asked Holmes.

"I believe he said that his name was Youghal, if I'm recalling it correctly."

Holmes nodded. "Indeed. He is an inspector, and quite competent, in his own way." Turning to me, Holmes said, "He must be returning from that business in Exbourne. No doubt we'll receive a report shortly."

Holmes then gave our visitor an appraising glance, and I knew that he was seeing quite a bit that I'd likely miss. However, as I'd studied my friend's methods for a while now, I could recognize some of the more obvious things, including the fact that the man in our basket chair was a left-handed bachelor with a *penchant* for lime hair cream, someone with an office job requiring that he do a great deal of writing, perhaps in a law office, and with a nervous disposition.

Holmes said, "Watson, in addition to what you will have just observed, you might avoid making the leap to identifying his professional position as that of a law clerk, based upon the legal-looking paper peeking from his pocket. In fact, I can see that he actually works in the book publishing trade – although in the dreary business side – and that those documents you see instead relate to the matter at hand. Additionally, his nervousness is not typical, for his nails are newly chewed to the quick, and not those of someone who has an ongoing need to pursue that habit. Finally, he has had a rough night. The stains on not only your shoes, sir, but your suit from shoulders to feet indicate that you have spent some time, probably unplanned, in the woods."

The young man appeared surprised for just a moment, and then smiled. "The inspector said to expect as much," he said. He glanced at his fingertips. "You are correct about being outside and in the trees. And I am not normally nervous. But the events of last night were certainly enough to knock me off my regular perch."

"Pray, enlighten us then, Mr. . . . ?"

"Hayden. Jerrold Hayden."

Holmes nodded, and the man began his tale. "I've only just returned on the train from Exeter. I should have been back sooner, but there was a track fire along the way. I walked straight from Paddington to speak with you, Mr. Holmes, and I – "

Holmes held up a hand. "You were returning specifically from Exeter, Mr. Hayden, or one of the surrounding areas?"

"Ah. I'm sorry. From Exeter, and before that just west of Chudleigh, in Devonshire. Near the River Teign."

"Yes, I know the place," replied Holmes. "I was able to be of some service to the family at Hams Barton, back in '78. As I recall, that area you mention is just a mile or three northeast of where I visited."

"As you say, Mr. Holmes. Before I went down, I did a bit of research on the countryside, and I recall reading of that place."

"And why were you in that location?"

"I had been notified that I am the heir to a house and some land there."

"Indeed. Was this expected? I perceive that it may have been a surprise."

"Oh, I was very much surprised. I received a confidential letter on Tuesday, informing me that I had been located by a firm of West Country solicitors, seeking individuals that had been named in the will of one Clark Helverton, in order to dispose of his estate."

"Sent to your place of employment."

"That's right. How did you know?"

"From the address on the legal papers protruding from your pocket, care of the publishing firm where you are employed. You say that you had no previous knowledge of this man, Helverton?"

"You are correct. I'd never heard of him before. According to the letter, he had married my great-aunt, late in her life, and as he had no close relatives of his own, he had willed the house and land to his wife's heirs. It turns out that she also had no other remaining family but myself. I should mention that I have no personal memory of this great-aunt, as she had drifted beyond the sphere of my own family long before I was born."

"And you have no brothers, sisters, or cousins who might have also benefited from this unexpected windfall?"

"I do not. My father, who was apparently my great-aunt's only other relation, died when I was but a small child, and my late mother never remarried. I am an only child, and apparently my great-aunt – as far as I ever knew – had never married before Mr. Helverton. Thus, she had no children, and therefore my father had no cousins on that side of the family. Therefore, I am the end of that particular branch. And this was confirmed by the solicitor's representative."

Holmes leaned back. "Perhaps you need to tell me more about the circumstances."

"But don't you need to know what happened at the house last night? I can – "

Holmes smiled and shook his head. "All in good time, Mr. Hayden. Lay the proper groundwork. Surely your own experiences in the book publishing profession have taught you the importance of assembling of each element in the proper order."

Hayden nodded, took a deep breath. I again offered a tot of whisky, but he thanked me and declined.

"As I said, I received a letter early this week from the firm of Stoddard and Stoddard, of Exeter, informing me that I was the heir to the property."

"May I see the letter?"

"Certainly." Hayden retrieved the previously mentioned letter from his pocket and handed it to Holmes. "After the events of last night, I was reading it on the train, and I had also showed it to the police inspector. As you can see, it rather specifically describes the nature of the inheritance, the research showing I am the only remaining heir, how I was located, and also the suggested arrangements for journeying to the West Country this weekend."

Holmes turned the sheet this way and that before reading it. "Curious," said he after a moment. "The paper and letterhead appear to be rather aged, based upon the spotting. I see that the writer, one Ethan Stoddard, had already determined that you are unmarried, and he suggested that you keep the matter secret, even from your employers."

"That is true. As he wrote, the story of the discovery of a long-lost heir might be of interest to the press, and would bring undue attention upon the matter."

"And did you keep it secret?"

"I did. I obtained leave from my employers on Friday, yesterday that is, without telling them why, and traveled down to Exeter by the late morning train, whereupon I made my way to the law offices, as suggested in the letter."

"And what of the Stoddards? I confess that, while my knowledge is not extensive upon the subject, I did have reason a few years ago to learn a bit about the legal firms of that part of the world, and I don't recall them."

"I gathered from my visit to their offices that they are a rather small concern, dealing with just a few old and established clients. I must say that I found them to be quite humble indeed. There was no clerk, and the offices are on a side street beside a haberdasher's shop. They had a feeling of neglect – an excess of dust about the place and so on, if you follow me."

"I do, indeed, Mr. Hayden. Did you have the sense that the firm had been in that location for a while, or had moved there quite recently?"

"Oh, quite a while, Mr. Holmes. I see what you are getting at, but it is a real firm, and not a quickly rented room with the intent to fool me. The sign on the wall by the front door was ancient looking and well established, and there were various certificates and photographs on the walls that testified to the long-standing presence of Stoddard and Stoddard in that area. In fact, one of the framed documents near the entryway had become crooked upon the wall, perhaps from someone brushing against it or from the vibrations of the nearby closing door, and a less-faded patch matching that object was revealed, running alongside the frame. Clearly, it had hung there for a long time. The document itself was quite faded as well."

Holmes clapped his hands. "An observant man after our own hearts, Watson!" he cried. "Clearly then, that evidence, coupled with the age of the paper, establishes their legitimacy. Do go on, Mr. Hayden. What about this Ethan Stoddard, who summoned you to Exeter?"

"He is a young fellow, about our age I would think. He apologized for the condition of the office, explaining that the original Stoddard and Stoddard had been his two uncles. One died years ago, and the other only recently became incapacitated due to apoplexy. His prognosis is not good, and Ethan, himself a lawyer, moved down from London just a few weeks earlier to take over the practice.

"We made conversation for a bit, about living in Exeter versus London and so forth, before turning to specifics, and that was when he told me that the firm had been established long ago to manage the affairs of just a few well-placed clients with interests in and around Exeter – including this Clark Helverton. A week or so ago, just after Mr. Ethan Stoddard came down to assume his new duties, he received a letter informing him of Mr. Helverton's death in New York.

"Although the old man had left England years before, he'd maintained ownership of the house near Chudleigh, out along the river, and it was this that he'd willed to any relatives of my great-aunt. In fact, in this particular case, managing the care of the old house – maintenance, taxes, and so on – was really the only thing that Stoddard and Stoddard ever did for Mr. Helverton, as the rest of his affairs were handled in America. Ethan Stoddard informed me that for a long time, the house had been rented, but sadly it has stood empty for a number of years, partly due to the decline of the elder Stoddard who ran the firm – he had been lax in finding a new tenant. As I mentioned, Ethan Stoddard's researches had revealed that I was the only heir to this particular bequest, and thus he had summoned me down to get a look at my inheritance.

"He gave me a look at both the letter from America, and the old documents from the Stoddard files – letters with instructions, previous rental records, and so on. It was confusing but seemed to be legitimate."

"Did you see the envelope for the recent letter from the United States?"

"I did. It had an American stamp and a recent post mark."

"Excellent. Pray continue."

"After making sure that I had eaten on the train, Mr. Stoddard suggested that we depart. He had a small dog-cart rented and waiting around the corner, and we set out. It was an amiable enough trip as we traveled west, the miles rolling away and the weather much like today. We wandered down ever smaller and narrower roads until we finally crossed the river and reached a ragged drive, turning and winding out of sight between two mossy pillars.

"As we proceeded down the overgrown lane, covered with fallen leaves and identifiable as a roadway only by its relative straightness and slight elevation from the surrounding woods, I had my first view of the house. It's a rambling structure, just two stories tall with an attic, but quite wide, with a sheltered landing that surrounded it on several sides. It looked incongruous there, like something I've seen in photographs of homes in the American South. The dark grounds, choked with black-trunked trees and wild abandoned shrubbery, slope down toward the river, and there is

56

the suggestion that the scene should have swags of the Spanish Moss that grows in America, hanging from the trees.

"The house itself is in great disrepair. It is of a light-colored stone, but stained with mildew. Mounds of leaves and other detritus from the surrounding trees have piled along the foundation, and I could see a number of dead limbs protruding from over the edge of the roof high above us, remaining where they had fallen, possibly years earlier. We approached the front side of the house, as indicated by the imposing door centered there and the nearly obscured walkway approaching it from the drive. It has a heavy black door, quite wide. All of the window shutters were closed, but some were hanging loose from their hinges, and one was knocking against the wall in the slight breeze from the river. There are a number of dormer windows lined across the attic, and they are just high enough to catch some of the rare sunlight that penetrates the thick canopy of the trees, which themselves seemed fancifully to me as if they were somehow angry at having been disturbed from their long and ponderous isolation."

I glanced at Holmes, and I saw his mouth purse slightly. If I had been relating these events, he would have long before snapped something to the effect of sticking to the facts, or "Cut the poetry, Watson." However, he was striving to remain polite, and I for one appreciated the sense of the place that Hayden was constructing.

Our visitor, however, was not unaware of Holmes's reaction, and he strove to come back to the point. "It was then, looking at the overwhelming neglect of the house and grounds, that I began to have further questions, and just a few qualms, about whether this inheritance would actually be of any benefit to me. I hadn't really thought much about what to do before that point. Mr. Stoddard had explained that there was a small cash income associated with the house for its upkeep, but otherwise there would be no additional inheritance forthcoming.

"I was aware from our conversation that there was a bit of land along with the building, and when I saw the house and its condition, I began to calculate whether any buyer might be found to take this heap off my hands, in the condition in which it stood. It was fairly certain that the funds that Mr. Stoddard had described for upkeep were probably just enough to pay the taxes, and possibly hire someone to check the place a few times per year to ascertain that it hadn't burned. There was no way that I could fund a full restoration on my own, and I have grave doubts that I could find employment in that area, allowing me to abandon my current profession, move down from London, and set myself up as some sort of country squire.

"After we stopped, we walked a bit here and there, while I obtained different views of the house. It was in the same state of neglect upon all sides, and I suppose that my despair was becoming obvious, as Mr. Stoddard tried to cheer me up, saying that he was certain things would work out. He neglected, however, to specify exactly how that might be accomplished.

"Finally we arrived at the front door, which he opened with an age-stained key. We stepped inside, and if our eyes hadn't already been accustomed to the tree-darkened approach to the house, we wouldn't have been able to see the interior at all. As it was, I could dimly make out the hallway and stairs in front of us, and various doorways on either side. However, the smell of neglect was enough to bring tears to our eyes, and any view that had been initially obtained was quickly lost.

"We lit a couple of lamps, standing conveniently beside the door and apparently left by the irregular caretaker, and began to explore. I was happy to see that the place still benefited from the quite solid construction of the previous century. The floors were sound, and amazingly, there was no sign of leakage on the upstairs ceilings or down the walls. I quickly became confused at the upstairs layout, and was glad to find my way back down to the entry hall.

"I felt that I had seen all that there was to see, when I was shocked to find Mr. Stoddard standing in the entry way, holding a basket and telling me that he must leave, as night was approaching, and that he had brought enough food to see me through until morning. I recalled then that I had seen that same basket in the dog-cart, but I had paid it no mind.

"'Whatever can you mean?' I cried, for it was plain that he meant that I should remain there while he planned to depart.

"He apologized, saying that he thought he had mentioned that – although I knew that he had not. 'A requirement of the will,' he explained. 'Mr. Helverton stated that you must take possession of the house immediately, or it will be auctioned, with the proceeds turned over to a charity. I have consulted with my uncle,' he added, 'and we felt that some leniency in the interpretation of the document allows for you to claim the house by simply spending one night here to serve as your tenancy. Afterwards, you can declare your intent to return, an event which can be delayed indefinitely.'

"He said it all so matter-of-factly that I didn't see a way to disagree. I pointed out that, in spite of his basket of food and drink, there was nowhere for me to sleep. He seemed to think that easily solved, and led me to a side room, where the furniture was covered, and pulled a dusty sheet from a deep chair. Then, with the comment that it was getting dark and that he would be back for me in the morning, he bustled outside, ignoring my ill-formed arguments against remaining there. He pressed the old key into my hand – " and with that, Hayden pulled it from his waistcoat and handed it to Holmes, who looked at it and then placed it on the table beside him – "telling me not to lose it, as it was the only one. Then, with a warning to stay indoors, he stepped outside, pulling the door shut behind him.

"I immediately followed Stoddard to the door, opening it to see him already jumping blithely back into the dog-cart. With a wave, he turned the horse smartly and was gone.

"As you can imagine, I was stunned at how quickly this had occurred. I had gone from the despair of seeing the condition of the house and grounds to being abandoned there in the space of a few short minutes. After a time, while I stood in the doorway and considered simply trying to walk back to town, pondering that I would simply have to follow each smaller road to a larger, I realized that I hadn't paid attention to the turnings. I could certainly get out to the mossy pillars that marked the edge of the estate, but after that, I might end up walking farther from Chudleigh, and as Mr. Stoddard had pointed out, night was coming. Of course, I could always throw myself on the mercy of a neighboring farmer, provided I came across a house in my wanderings, but I couldn't even be sure of that.

"In the end, I decided I must stay. I picked up the basket and set it onto a nearby table. Opening it, I saw that it was filled with a generous supply of food – various tins and jars, a cold woodcock, a few bottles of water, and another of wine. I never eat a heavy meal in the evening, and, feeling neither hungry nor thirsty, I decided to explore the house a bit more. Taking up the lantern, I began a more systematic evaluation of the place. Some of the furniture was actually quite nice, when one ignored the dust. Upstairs, I was able to work out the initially confusing arrangement of the rooms, and I even went up to the attic, which was filled with additional old furniture, as well as numerous boxes and trunks. I heard the rustle of mice, which was not surprising, but everything seemed to be salvageable, and I was curious about what might be found amongst all the abandoned items, and frankly, how much I could get for it.

"I went back downstairs and made a light snack of some of the basket's contents. There was much more than I could eat, and I confess that I didn't open the wine, as I am a teetotaler. I glanced at my watch and saw that it was actually a bit later than I had thought. I considered pulling one of the dusty books off a shelf in the room in which I'd eaten, but first I decided that I wanted to get a breath of fresh air.

"Disregarding Mr. Stoddard's warning to stay inside, I stepped out onto the porch and pulled the door shut behind me. I'd left the lantern in the side room, not wanting to spoil my night vision, and I noticed that the heavy drapes in that room, combined with the closed shutters, prevented any of that light from leaking outside.

"Although it is October, it hasn't been cool yet, and the leaves on the trees are still quite thick, and just starting to turn. The moon was shining out on the river, and I took a few steps that way, the better to get a view of that romantic aspect. I stood for a few moments, inhaling deeply, and then, realizing that my eyes had adjusted quite a bit, I moved laterally along the river, staying an even distance away from the house. I was very quiet, without really intending to be, but it was fortunate, as it may have saved my life.

"I had come past the far end of the house, the river behind me, when I saw a movement near one of the abandoned outbuildings that we'd passed earlier. I've read that in darkness, one's peripheral vision is stronger at sensing motion than if one stares directly at an object, so I paused in the shadow of a thick tree trunk and generally cast my vision in that direction without looking too hard, if you catch my meaning. I was rewarded, as I saw the movement once again. It was a man, and he was moving slowly toward the front door of the house.

"A feeling of terror swept over me as I recalled the warning that Mr. Stoddard had made before he left, advising me to stay inside. What had he known? Was there some sinister association with this house that made living here dangerous? I was willing to believe it, when the man that I watched passed through a bar of moonlight, and I realized that it was Mr. Stoddard himself.

"With a sense of relief, I was about to hail him when I saw that his hands were not empty. In one, he appeared to hold something very much resembling a gun, and in the other – and upon this point there could be no mistake – he carried a hatchet.

"I watched as he progressed, thinking at first that he was hunting whatever the danger was that permeated these woods. But then I realized that he paid no attention to anything around him. He was focused on the front door, which he approached in a most stealthy manner, as if the enemy were within instead of without. At that point, I understood with vivid clarity that he was not protecting me, but attempting to reach me.

"He stepped to the doorway and fumbled for a moment before producing what could only be a key – another key, in spite of his recent statement that the one he had left for me was the only one. I tapped my own pocket to assure myself that it was still with me. He bent to the door, but with a barely audible sound of surprise, he discovered that his efforts had been unnecessary, as I'd left it unlocked. He opened it, so very slowly, and then slipped silently inside.

60

"I realized with a shock that I'd come down to that part of the world without informing anyone, upon this man's instructions, and that the only person in the entire world who knew that I was there was now approaching where he thought I waited, carrying both a gun and a hatchet. I didn't understand anything about what might be in back of all of this, but it didn't matter. All I knew then was that I needed to be somewhere else.

"Creeping along the river, staying in the trees so the moonlight wouldn't show me, I made my way back to the other side of the house, and the narrow lane leading out to the road. I could imagine Stoddard, finding the lantern and the basket, and wondering where I was. He would explore the house, trying to locate me, but eventually he'd realize that I wasn't there, and then he would look elsewhere. Seeing as how he'd approached the house without a light, I suspected that he wouldn't use one when he searched the grounds, and every step I took was with the terror that he would step out in front of me, a shadow only identified by the shine of moonlight on the gun and the blade.

"I may have sobbed with relief when, about halfway up the lane, I came upon his dog-cart, tied to a small tree. I'd loosened it and hurried the horse up the road before I even had time to think what I was doing. I reached the pillars at the main road, turned the way that seemed familiar, and kept going. Here in the open, with the moon high in the sky, the route was clear. Wherever there was a road that was wider than before, and seemed to be in the direction of Exeter, I took it. Soon I was on the main road, which I recognized, and I finally reached the outskirts of Exeter, where I found an inn of middle quality. I obtained a room, and asked that they stable the horse, with the instruction that it not be left where it could be seen. No doubt they were a bit suspicious, especially as I had no bags with me. I was fearful that the innkeeper was friends with Stoddard, would recognize the dog-cart, and somehow get word to the man, leading him to show up in the middle of the night. I don't think I slept a wink, hearing every creak and settlement in the old building.

"In the morning, I silently departed, leaving the cart, and wandered in a stealthy manner until I found a cab. I was then deposited at St. David's Station. It was still a bit before the London train, so I had a bite of breakfast in the Great Western Hotel, where I watched the doorway in fear and trusted no one, not even the old man dozing at a nearby table. My face, reflected in the mirror on the nearby wall, was ghastly. Finally it was time for my train and I departed. Along the way, I relaxed enough to fall into casual conversation with the man in my compartment and, upon learning his profession, told him my story. He suggested that it was odd, and while no crime had actually been committed, it might be something upon which you could advise me. Thus, here I am." And he spread his hands as if to demonstrate that, indeed, he was actually sitting in our basket chair.

I had felt a thrill of terror as he described the events of the previous evening, the dark and sinister isolation of the abandoned house, the moonlight and the river and the looming trees, and the sudden identification of the man who had invited him there, holding instruments of murder, moving silently toward where our visitor was thought to be innocently waiting . . . .

"The wine!" I cried.

Jerrold Hayden looked surprised and confused, but Holmes nodded. "Very good, Watson. My thoughts exactly."

"I'm sorry, but . . . ." said Hayden.

"I believe that Watson has worked out that, if you had chosen to drink the wine list night, you might have soon found yourself sleepy, or at least in such a fog as to be unable to defend yourself, making your end – for that is what we will suppose was planned by Mr. Stoddard – to be that much easier."

"You mean that the wine was drugged?"

"Possibly. He could have used a hypodermic needle to add something to the contents through the cork."

"Then why not the food or the water?"

"Any number of reasons. Perhaps what he used would have been noticeable when used in that fashion. Perhaps some of the food *was* drugged. Did you sample all of it?"

"I did not. I simply opened one of the potted meat tins and ate it with crackers."

"Of course. Both items are purchased unopened. Your lack of appetite may have saved you. Was the water sealed?"

"Yes, with a metal cap. No cork." He looked uncomfortable. "So you agree that there is something sinister about this business?"

"On the face of it, how could we not?" replied Holmes. "And yet, you say the documents, and the office itself, were legitimate enough." He leaned forward. "I will investigate this matter, although today being Saturday complicates things a bit. Do you have somewhere to stay, in order to avoid going home?"

"I . . . I can get a room at a hotel, if you recommend it."

"I do. When you are established, send word around as to where you can be reached. I cannot stress enough that you should avoid your lodgings. Where are they, by the way?"

Hayden provided an address near Moxon Street. Holmes noted it on his cuff, and then stood, indicating that the interview was over. A bit puzzled at this abrupt shift, Hayden rose as well, thanking us and moving

62

toward the door. In moments he was gone, and Holmes was consulting one of his reference books. Then, with a snap, he shut it and replaced it on the bookcase.

"Stoddard and Stoddard is indeed an actual firm."

"Was there a doubt? I thought that the description of the old office, the framed documents, and so on, was enough to convince you."

"Confirmation, especially when it is so easily obtained, should never be ignored."

I shifted, as if to stand. "Shall I make arrangements to go with you down to Exeter?"

He smiled. "This cake isn't quite baked yet, Watson. I'm afraid that you might need to plan on substituting for Dr. Weaver for just a bit longer." He shed his dressing gown, pulled on a coat, and reached for his Inverness and fore-and-aft cap, which he wore in both town and country, indifferent to convention. "I shall likely miss supper." And then he was gone.

I did not see him that night, but he returned the next evening, looking rather worn. As usual, he didn't provide any information as to his activities since his departure on Saturday. He glanced at Hayden's temporary address, delivered to our door the previous night, and wrote a message, which he handed to our page boy. Then, hungrily attacking the remains of the cold dinner provided by Mrs. Hudson, he asked if I could make myself available for a journey to Exeter the next day. I confirmed it, frankly happy to be free and rescued from my obligation to Dr. Weaver's grim practice, and set about making arrangements with a young physician of my acquaintance who had taken over my duties in the past. While I was doing so, Holmes said goodnight and retreated to his room.

And so on Monday, I found myself on the late morning Great Western Railway train out of Paddington, in the company of my friend, along with Jerrold Hayden and Inspector Youghal of Scotland Yard.

The inspector had a jovial smile, and seemed to appreciate being included. "I knew that you could make something out of this, Mr. Holmes. I knew it as soon as Mr. Hayden here told me his story."

"I'm still in the dark," said Hayden. "Am I to understand that you know the circumstances behind the events of last Friday night?"

I wished to know the details as well. Fortunately, Holmes began to explain.

"On Saturday, after you departed, Mr. Hayden, I found a location from which to observe your rooms. I soon learned that I was not alone."

"Stoddard?" asked our client with shock.

Holmes nodded. "If your Mr. Stoddard is about five feet, eight inches tall, with broad shoulders and a squarish head, blonde hair cut rather

63

longish in back, and a habit of standing with one foot flat and the other leg bent and resting upon a pointed toe."

"Yes, that sounds like him. He did that several times while we were talking last Friday."

"He wasn't there when I arrived, but showed up soon after, finding a place in a doorway across the street. He stayed for several hours before giving up, shifting back and forth impatiently but never trying to enter the building. He kept watch up and down the street, becoming more alert whenever someone approached."

"And he didn't see you?" asked Hayden.

Youghal laughed, and Holmes smiled. "He did not, for I did not wish to be seen." Then, the smile dropped away and he continued. "Eventually, he gave up and made his way to a small nearby hotel – fortunately, not the same one where you chose to stay! When he was in for the night, I arranged to have the place watched in my absence, and made myself useful elsewhere."

I was certain that assistance had been provided by those lads, and sometimes lasses, who made up Holmes's Irregular force. They were always willing to help, and the promise of payment was only part of the attraction. Their respect for Holmes, who valued them when often no one else did, made them very loyal allies indeed.

"I caught the late train to Exeter," Holmes said. "I had wired ahead to arrange an appointment with Fenton Stoddard, the surviving partner, and Ethan Stoddard's uncle. Although it was quite late by then, I felt that the matter would progress with a greater chance of success if I was able to make my investigation while Ethan, or so I believed the man I had observed to be, was still in London. Upon arrival at St. David's Station, I made my way to the home of Fenton Stoddard, who had waited up for me. I had revealed just enough in my message to rouse his concern. I didn't want to specify too much in my wire before I had ascertained that he wasn't in on the plot."

"Holmes," I said. "You were taking a chance. If the uncle was involved in this affair, you were placing yourself in the same position that Mr. Hayden had just a day or so earlier – traveling to Exeter and walking into the lion's den without letting anyone know where you had gone!"

Holmes smiled. "I took the precaution of arranging for covering fire, so to speak. You may recall that Thad Flatcher lives in Exeter. He and his brother met me at the station, and both of them waited hidden outside of Stoddard's home to see what would happen, and if I reappeared – which I did."

My thoughts flashed instantly to the man to whom Holmes was referring. If not for my friend's assistance, young Thad would have been

64

hanged in late '81 for a crime he didn't commit, wherein the theft of an ancient Devonshire Charter, and the hidden message it contained, had played such an unfortunate part in the brutal and unnecessary murder of old Dr. Chambers by the wicked Pennington Gang.

"After offering refreshments," continued Holmes, "the elder Stoddard clearly wished to know more of my assertions, as I had only wired that there was a matter of grave and confidential concern regarding his practice. Now, in his presence, I related your entire narrative, Mr. Hayden, along with showing him the letter you received last Tuesday. Needless to say, he was shocked, and I was convinced of his sincerity – but only to a certain degree. After all, while he might only be discovering the plot as I related it, he might still see some personal benefit to it and make a move of his own to support it. Therefore, I remained wary.

"Following his initial reaction, he shook his head sadly, as if it wasn't so great a surprise after all. 'Ethan has always been a wrong 'un,' he explained. 'He is my sister's boy. She married a man with a temper who died young. He had a way of believing that the world owed him something, and he passed it on to Ethan. When I became ill a few weeks ago, Ethan came down to help, although he was never put in any kind of permanent position, as he implied to your client. I should have known better.'

"Old Mr. Stoddard called to his servant, asking for his coat and for the carriage to be made ready. I was careful to note that at no time did he have a chance to write or pass a message, verbal or otherwise, to anyone that might be relayed to Ethan Stoddard in London. This did much to build my trust of him. Outside, he was helped into the carriage, and I joined him, surreptitiously signaling to Thad that he should follow, in case there was still some move to be made against me.

"My fears were groundless. We arrived at the Stoddard office and made a systematic search. All of the papers relating to Clark Helverton's estate were easily found on Ethan Stoddard's desk, and his uncle's examination of them revealed something both surprising and obvious." His gaze focused specifically upon our client. "Mr. Hayden, the details of the Helverton estate, and the amount apportioned to you as the only designated heir, was very much misrepresented by Ethan Stoddard. You did in fact inherit the remote house and grounds located along the River Teign, as described. But additionally, you are the sole recipient, upon providing proof of your identity in person to the Helverton legal representatives in New York, of a fortune totaling nearly a million pounds."

This startling statement was followed by silence from all parties, with only the steady thrum of our westward train, or the occasional London-bound roaring past on the adjacent track, providing any intrusive noise.

Hayden opened and closed his mouth, swallowing several times, and once his eyes widened as a thought occurred to him. He started to speak, but Youghal interrupted with a prosaic summary.

"And so this Ethan Stoddard has some plan to steal the inheritance."

"It would seem so," agreed Holmes. "Fenton Stoddard removed my last doubts of his own character and possible personal interest when he unhesitatingly summoned a local policeman of his acquaintance, making the matter official. He also sent some wires to the attorneys in New York, who could provide confirmatory information, even if it was early Sunday morning.

"Leaving the old man and the policeman to await responses to Stoddard's wires, Thad Flatcher and I, using the address listed in the Helverton papers found in the file on Ethan Stoddard's desk, found our way to the abandoned house on the river. It was as described, and the door was unlocked, although I was prepared to use the key that you had provided to me, Mr. Hayden, if we found it otherwise. The food basket provided for you was still there, as the stranded Ethan Stoddard had apparently been unwilling to carry it with him as he made his way back to town without benefit of his dog-cart. I retrieved the unopened wine bottle, as well as some of the food stuffs, and was able to obtain access to a local laboratory, using Fenton Stoddard's influence. I easily verified that the food was perfectly fine, but the wine bottle contained a possibly toxic amount of chloral hydrate. Close examination revealed the mark of a hypodermic needle through the wax and the bottle's cork where it had been added."

"So he did mean to kill me," muttered Hayden, finding his voice.

"Undoubtedly," replied Holmes. "To sneak in and shoot you if you were still conscious, or to simply dispose of you if you were fully unconscious or perhaps already dead. The dosage of chloral hydrate added to the wine was quite strong, and would have been undetectable if you had imbibed. The fact that he carried a hatchet lends further terror and grim possibilities to the speculations. Your body might never have been found, as the house and grounds are as lonely and abandoned as you described."

"Then," I said, "it was Stoddard's intention to somehow replace Mr. Hayden and assume the inheritance."

"That's how I read it," said Holmes. "He spoke the truth when explaining how he recently moved to Exeter to help with his uncle's practice, which seemingly does manage the affairs of just a few well-to-do clients, mostly in England, but a few with American connections. Only a few days after his arrival, as shown by documents on his desk, the information about the extent of Mr. Helverton's estate appeared – a fact completely unknown to Fenton Stoddard, I might add. These papers explained the true amount of the assets, the identity of the heir, and the conditions for claiming the inheritance – namely, a visit in person to the New York offices handling Helverton's fortune, with substantiating proofs in hand.

"While Thad Flatcher and I had been to the house, and then the chemical laboratory, Fenton Stoddard had received replies from New York, indicating that they had been told that the heir was found, and would present himself within a few weeks, providing proper documentation of his identity. Specifically, the heir was described to them as appearing very much like Ethan Stoddard, and *not* like you, Mr. Hayden. You will have observed that you are physically quite different from one another. This description of the heir was backed and certified by the good reputation of Stoddard and Stoddard, who had handled Clark Helverton's affairs in England for decades, and therefore it would have been completely accepted by the New York lawyers, as they indicated in their wire.

"We'll know more specifics when he is interrogated, but Ethan Stoddard realized as soon as the first letter arrived from New York that the requirements were just vague enough that he, a young man of the same approximate age, could take Mr. Hayden's place. However, rather than simply stealing documents that he could use to assume the true heir's identity, he apparently decided to make sure that any stray loopholes caused by your continued existence, Mr. Hayden, would be closed. He had quickly researched you and found that you were an orphan without living kin. After you were removed – "

"Killed," interrupted Hayden, with a catch in his voice.

"Yes, killed," amended Holmes, "with no one of your acquaintance knowing anything about your trip to Exeter, he would have broken into your London rooms, found what he needed to allow him to assume your identity, prepared whatever supporting legal documents that he would need to be sent or carried from England, and then made his way to New York, after convincingly winding up his affairs here. Who could challenge him? He would have sent word to your employer and landlord that you had departed in such a way that your absence would be regretted or resented, but quickly forgotten, and also provided some story to his uncle before he himself left, while preventing the old man from ever learning about the Helverton inheritance.

"He would have sent specific information to the New York offices managing the estate from Stoddard and Stoddard to make sure that nothing else was ever sent to Exeter that might undo his story. He might have even undertaken to use more of the chloral hydrate to remove his old uncle from the picture, effectively closing the Exeter practice completely. It was an opportunity that literally fell into his lap, and he saw that he could

67

manipulate both ends of things without it ever being discovered. He is the sort of crafty person that saw his chance and cobbled his plan together within days. The simple and unpleasant fact that you didn't drink the wine, Mr. Hayden, was the grit in the machine that saved your life and started the unraveling of his scheme."

"So what happens now, Mr. Holmes?" asked Youghal. "When I first heard of this on the train last Saturday, there was nothing criminal in what had occurred – yet. Mr. Hayden saw a fellow with a gun and a hatchet sneaking around in the dark, but no attack had actually occurred, and proving intent is sometimes impossible, as you know. Even now, we might make a case of fraud, based on what he told the New York lawyers, but Stoddard can rightly claim that he did find the correct heir, and that he still intended to present Mr. Hayden here at the proper time. Your theories about what he intended cannot be completely proven, and he can blow up any case we might make with legal tricks about making us provide proof."

"I believe that a bit more will come to light," replied Holmes cryptically. "When I left for London yesterday, Fenton Stoddard was curiously going over the books at his office, and he seemed to have found something more tangible. Additionally, he's been in touch with Ethan Stoddard's former employers in London, and I think they have something to say as well." Youghal waited, but Holmes didn't elaborate.

"When we arrive in Exeter," I said, filling the silence, "we will confront him."

"Yes," agreed Holmes. "Ethan returned to Exeter last night, accompanied unknowingly by Wiggins and a few of the other lads. They, along with the Flatcher brothers, have watched him continuously since then. Long before Ethan arrived, Fenton Stoddard returned to his own home with the plan to exaggerate his illness, in the unlikely event that his nephew tries to communicate with him in the meantime. He is genuinely outraged at the breach of trust enacted by his nephew, and he will let us do what is necessary. I expect that Ethan Stoddard is in the office now. We left the Helverton documents as we found them, so that he would not be alerted."

"Isn't that a risk?" I asked. "If he does think that his plan is coming apart, he might destroy something."

"Not too risky. He certainly knows nothing for certain except that Mr. Hayden disappeared from the river house on Friday night, along with the dog-cart that he left tied on the road. To his knowledge, Mr. Hayden never returned to his London rooms, and has seemingly vanished. Ethan may panic due to the uncertainty, but I think he's made of sterner stuff than that, and will wait to see if he has another chance. After all, he's playing for a very fine prize indeed. And even if he destroys documents in his possession, the information is still available at the New York end, as well as the testimony from those attorneys as to what fraudulent information he has already relayed to them – namely, that the heir has been found, along with a false description. Finally, as I said, the Irregulars and Thad Flatcher are in place if Ethan bolts, and the last wire I had from Exeter, an hour before we departed, reported that he had returned to Exeter yesterday evening – I likely passed him on the up train during my return – and after spending the night in his own rooms, he opened up the offices at eight o'clock this morning, the usual time."

Youghal nodded. "A workmanlike job as usual, Mr. Holmes. I look forward to speaking to this young scoundrel."

The inspector's wish was granted, and the rest is soon told. Holmes had nothing further to report and, refusing to speculate without further data, he smoked his pipe the rest of the journey while Hayden, Youghal, and I discussed the case. Hayden alternated between struggling comprehension of the sudden unexpected fortune and just how close he had come to disaster.

Upon our arrival at St. David's Station in Exeter, we were met by Wiggins, who informed us that Ethan Stoddard was still at the law practice, where he had been since that morning. Holmes then led us across to the Great Western Hotel, where Hayden had eaten breakfast just two days before. Waiting inside were several people, including a local inspector named Hanks, Thad Flatcher, and a wizened glowering old man, who, as expected, turned out to be Fenton Stoddard. Although his recent illness was apparent, he hobbled toward Holmes with vigor and shook a packet of telegrams. "Just as you thought, Mr. Holmes! It is beyond the theft of the inheritance. I have been nursing a viper to my bosom!"

Holmes quickly read through the flimsy sheets, one after another, before handing them to me. Some were from New York, confirming in greater detail the misleading statements and assertions made by Ethan Stoddard regarding the Helverton heir. There was no doubt that a case of fraud could be clearly proven. Another was from Stoddard's former employer in London. Unknown to his uncle, the nephew had been let go from his previous position in Lincoln's Inn Fields for suspected theft just weeks before being summoned to Exeter. "But even worse," said the old man, holding out a second sheaf of papers, "he has been moving against me here, forging my name to documents, and apparently cleaning out my own accounts before his departure for America."

Holmes looked at the papers and nodded. "He would have only done this, Mr. Stoddard, if he knew that you would not be around to discover it. Clearly, as I theorized, your death was part of his plan. Doubtless, you would have seemingly died in your sleep, with the story spread that it was

69

a relapse from your recent illness. He would have quietly closed your practice, with the assets already spirited away through his earlier forgeries, and then departed these shores, with no one the wiser, ready to assume Mr. Hayden's identity. What a pity he turned such a quick-thinking mind to crime."

With a scowl and a clearing of his throat, Mr. Stoddard signaled that he didn't share my friend's somewhat misplaced admiration. Holmes announced that there was no need to put off confronting Ethan Stoddard any longer, and we piled into cabs summoned from the nearby station. Then came the slow ascent up St. David's Hill, across the Iron Bridge, and eventually left into the High Street, with the Cathedral looming over us just a block away. Parking around the corner from Stoddard's office, we assembled a short distance from the legal practice, with Holmes and Wiggins providing assistance to the old man.

We approached the doorway by crowding near to the building, so as not to be seen from the windows. The old man had informed us that his nephew was likely at his desk upstairs. From nearby, Thad Flatcher and the Irregulars made themselves known.

After silently entering the ground floor, we gathered out of sight, away from the foot of the stairs, and Fenton Stoddard called out sharply, "Ethan! Come down here!"

Overhead, we heard a chair scrape, followed by a surprised, "Uncle?" Then we heard footsteps cross the room above us and start down the stairs. "I had no idea you were well enough to come into – " He was unable to continue the thought, as his appearance in the room corresponded with both arms being grabbed by the two inspectors, who quickly handcuffed him.

He fought for a moment and then, seeing Jerrold Hayden standing before him, fists clenched at his sides, he sagged in defeat. Later, under the combined questioning of Inspectors Youghal and Hanks, Ethan Stoddard would attempt a half-hearted defense, ignoring the offer of counsel and the initial warning that his statements could be used against him. He only dug himself deeper and deeper, straight into a substantial prison sentence.

The elder Mr. Stoddard, with a combination of unnecessary guilt by mere association to the affair and a lifetime of advising a few select wealthy clients, took Jerrold Hayden under his wing, and in future years, we were to hear of the exponential growth of the original Helverton inheritance, a great deal of which was used to fund charitable activities on both sides of the Atlantic, not the least of which was an orphanage of great renown in a formerly abandoned mansion on the shores of the River Teign.

More immediately satisfying to me upon our return to London was learning of the next day's arrangements to visit Hornchurch and dig up the treasure identified in Morgan's palimpsest. I wasted no time in seeking an extension of my physician friend's services at Dr. Weaver's practice. Apparently this worked out well for the both of them, as Dr. Weaver, having met a dancer in Cannes, decided to sell the practice post-haste, and for some reason the location appealed to my own temporary *locum*, who scraped up enough money to buy it.

On the following day, Holmes and I made our way northeast of London to find the treasure. Of course it wasn't that simple, and before we were finished, I'd had a dunking in an overgrown pond, one man had lost his freedom, and another his sanity. But that is another story . . . .

The Carroun Document

I regretted that it was too early in the day to decently adjourn to my club.

While certain members would doubtless already be in their fixed places – and indeed, many spent more time there in their favorite chairs than at their own hearths – I didn't want to cause undue comment, or start down that slippery slope wherein I, too, preferred to hide in that comfortable womb of favorite beverages and the latest periodicals and rounds of billiards rather than face the stark shades of reality.

But when Sherlock Holmes was in one of his moods, I was sorely tempted.

When my friend returned to London in April '94, after a three-year absence when he was believed to be dead, he found that he had become something of a mythological figure, in part because of my efforts to memorialize him by publishing a number of accounts of his adventures in a relatively new periodical. When he again took up the reins of his practice, those who had known him of old – either on the side of the law or otherwise – simply resumed their acquaintance in the previous manner. But those who had never encountered him except in the pages of a magazine now believed that he was someone larger-than-life – or worse, a fictional character.

Our rooms began to receive a certain amount of unwanted attention in the same manner that Dickens' homes had. Casual passers-by and tourists with much more specific (and dark) purposes of their own would stop and stare, standing upon the pavement across the way for varying lengths of time. And worse, we occasionally had visits from those simply wishing to get a look at the famous Sherlock Holmes, finding excuses to visit us on those routine mornings when Holmes's had his version of office hours.

That day, following visits ranging from that of a cabinet minister to a char-woman, there had been a few moments of silence while Holmes researched some fact or other in his scrapbooks. But soon the doorbell rang, and not long after Mrs. Hudson opened the door to reveal a mother and son. They appeared to be members of the comfortable middle class, with the woman sensibly dressed and the boy, about ten or twelve years of age, wearing some sort of school uniform. The woman introduced herself as Mrs. Burley and fumblingly apologized for taking up Holmes's time. I cringed inside, as I spotted what was held in the lad's hand: A dogged blue-covered journal – undoubtedly an issue of *The Strand*.

I realized why they were there, even as the woman explained that her son was quite taken by my stories – here she gave a cursory nod in my direction. But it was clear who they were here to see.

The young man simply looked at Holmes, his mouth slightly agape, and I couldn't tell if his expression denoted stunned amazement, satisfaction, or disappointment. His nose twitched, possibly from the pervasive smells of chemical experiments and pipe smoke.

Holmes listened politely for a few minutes, his lips becoming both tighter and straighter. It was when the woman asked if he might provide her son with some little souvenir, possibly one of his pipes, that the limit was reached. He rapidly led the way to the door, thanking them for dropping by while the woman attempted to keep talking, becoming louder and more ill-tempered as their visit ended. When the door was finally shut in their faces, Holmes stood glaring at it, listening first as the woman muttered darkly on the other side, and then as she and her son descended the stairs, closing the front door behind them. Only then did he begin that same litany that I'd heard so many times before.

"You see, Watson," he began, spinning in my direction, "why I was so reluctant to allow this foolishness? When you first cooked up the idea of 'publicly recognizing my merits', or however you phrased it, it was with the *caveat* – or should I say *threat*? – that if *I* didn't do it, *you* would. I rue the day that I didn't take charge of my own affairs then, instead of allowing you to do as you like."

"Really, Holmes – " I countered, all too familiar with these fits of pique regarding my writings. I made reference to how his practice had only increased following my efforts – particularly since he had returned from supposed death earlier that year. I pointed out that I had only written and published the majority of the narratives during that time when I believed him to be dead – and then I paused, withholding what else I was tempted to mention, related to my still-simmering resentment that he had allowed me to believe that he had died at the Reichenbach Falls.

Holmes continued to make point after point. It had all been discussed before: How my writings had degraded his serious work into a series of cheap tales. How he would lose any credibility if his reputation were to continue to be based on my inaccurate and romanticized scribbles. How he couldn't work as effectively if all of his methods were revealed as common knowledge. And of course he referenced Mrs. Burley and her son as the latest examples of how my efforts led directly to his valuable time being wasted.

It was at that point when I seriously considered bolting for my club. But before I could do so, there was a knock at the door, and Mrs. Hudson brought in a letter. While she handed it to Holmes, she gave me a look of sympathy. Clearly our discussion had carried beyond the sitting room.

Holmes thanked her shortly, took the envelope, and then examined it for a moment before slitting it open and withdrawing a single sheet. As he looked at it, I could see the tension of our recurring argument slough away as he became intrigued with the possibility of a new investigation. In a moment or two, he handed it my way as if there had been no rancor between us whatsoever. "This may interest you, Watson, if you wouldn't mind delaying the visit to your club."

I didn't bother to ask how he had divined my plans. No doubt my intention had been quite obvious. Rather, I glanced at the missive. It was a single sheet of ordinary paper. The script was formed from blue ink, rather thin and watery, using a pen with a worn nib. It was written by a right hand, at leisure, since the lines were evenly horizontal. There was nothing else that I observed of importance. It read:

Mrs. Raymond Oakshott
117 Brixton Road

Dear Mr. Holmes,

You may recall meeting my brother around Christmas-time several years ago. I don't mention his name here, but if I tell you that the matter involved a stone and a goose, you will certainly know of it.

As you know, after your leniency in the matter, my brother fled the country. Although we've corresponded since then, he hasn't been back to England. However, just this morning I received a letter threatening his life, and I don't know where else to turn. If you can visit me at my home – which I am unable to leave at present due to a family illness – it would be most appreciated, and I can provide any further details that you might require.

I look forward to seeing you very soon.

She concluded by again identifying herself as *Mrs. Raymond Oakshott.*

No. 117 Brixton Road was one of a row of very tidy houses on the east side of the street, three stories with dormer windows peeking from the attic above. I confessed to myself that it was quite different than I had imagined. I recalled several years earlier, when I had stopped in to visit Holmes on a cold morning two days after Christmas – and coincidentally deliver the first of my narratives of his cases to be published – only to find him studying a hat that had been found in the street. From that unlikely beginning, we had become involved in a matter of a stolen jewel – the stone to which Mrs. Oakshott had alluded in her letter – and a trek across London while evening fell around us. On the way, we had encountered Mrs. Oakshott's brother, James Ryder, and invited him back to Baker Street. He had accepted, thinking that we would provide knowledge regarding the stone, which he had stolen and subsequently lost. Instead, his guilt had been exposed, and he had promised to flee England, if only he was shown mercy. It being the Christmas season, Holmes had agreed.

I had later written up the story for *The Strand*, one of those cases that were published during Holmes's supposed death. But when doing so, I hadn't felt the need to visit some of the scenes mentioned in Ryder's tale – for instance, his sister's house, here in the Brixton Road, where he had surreptitiously carried the jewel stolen from the Countess of Morcar at the Hotel Cosmopolitan.

At the time he was telling us of his actions, and how, in order to hide it, he had forced the stone down the throat of one of the geese that his sister was raising in the back-yard, I had vaguely recalled the area. I knew that this house was just north of No. 3 Lauriston Gardens, where I had joined Holmes in early March 1881 on our first investigation together. When preparing Ryder's story for publication, I had spent time making sure that my recollections of the Alpha Inn and nearby Covent Garden Market were accurate, but I hadn't really given much thought to Mrs. Oakshott's house. I suppose that, knowing that she kept geese, I had pictured a dwelling that was conducive to raising fowl. The rather fine house before us seemed much too resplendent to have gaggles of geese in the back yard.

The door was answered by a young maid who took our coats and hats. She then led us through to a small parlor, modestly furnished. Standing to meet us was a middle-aged woman who introduced herself as our correspondent. She had iron-grey hair tucked tightly against her scalp, and a pursed mouth giving an expression of what must be perpetual perturbation. She directed us to seats and, when we had declined refreshments, dismissed the maid.

"Thank you for coming, Mr. Holmes. Doctor."

"Your note said something of an illness," I said, before Holmes could begin his interview with the woman. "May I offer my services?"

She seemed surprised, and a bit uncertain. "Why, thank you, Doctor, but it won't be necessary. One of the servants has a bad summer cold. She has been seen by my own family physician, and is now on the mend."

Holmes, seeing that this topic was apparently ended, asked, "How may we assist you?"

She blinked twice, and then said, "I didn't know where else to turn. My husband – he mustn't know of this!"

"And he is?" asked Holmes.

"He is one of the supervisory clerks at Barings Bank. He doesn't want anything to do with my poor brother – he won't want any complications in our lives. He managed to weather the Argentine bonds affair a few years ago, and he was doing well until you published that story, Doctor." She frowned my way. "I hadn't told him anything of my brother's sad transgression before then, and he only learned of it when one of his supervisors asked why his home and his wife were mentioned in the new Sherlock Holmes story."

From the corner of my eye, I saw Holmes frown my way, and could only imagine that this would be new grist for him to use when circumstances allowed another volley at my writings. "I apologize," I said to Mrs. Oakshott, taken aback that the story had caused her difficulties. "I had understood through conversations with the police that, in the intervening years, your brother's identity had become known to them, and that no action was contemplated toward seeking him out or prosecuting him."

She shook her head. "I had hoped that the matter would be forgotten. It is fortunate that my husband avoided gaining any such attention for as long as he did. For a while, he faced some ridicule, and speculation about our situation – his brother-in-law implicated in a jewel theft. And he was called in to explain the fact that we had at one time raised geese in the rear of the house."

"Indeed," said Holmes. "And how did that activity come about? It is rather unusual that residents of this neighborhood would be dabbling in such a rural pursuit."

She lowered her head. "We . . . we were guilty, for a period of time you see, of living beyond our means," she said. "My husband had obtained his promotion at the bank, and we felt that we needed to reflect his position and newfound prosperity with a house to match. We moved here, not quite realizing at first the extra expenses associated with maintaining a larger home than where we had lived previously. For a time, we were forced to economize, and at one point I had the idea to raise geese for market. I am a farmer's daughter, gentlemen, so hard work isn't new to me, and it is nothing of which to be ashamed. I raised the geese, and contracted with a

76

man to sell them – a curious fellow who had stubbornly established his stall in the middle of a vegetable market. This unusual strategy did him well, and his prosperity was indirectly passed on to me. By the time my brother made use of my geese as a place to hide the stolen jewel, I had been associated with Mr. Breckinridge for three years.

"Since then, our situation has improved, and when questioned about my brother and your story, Doctor, my husband brushed off the association, and fortunately it never since been an issue. But now I've received this note threatening my brother's life, and my husband must not be involved in any way."

"Ah, yes. The note."

She looked at Holmes. "I wrote to you because I knew that you had been kind enough to help my brother several years ago."

"I don't know that we actively helped him," replied Holmes. "Rather, our response to his crime was passive, in that we allowed him to escape. I can assure you that, if events had played out differently and an innocent man were to be prosecuted for the crime rather than cleared, your brother would have arrested and tried, no matter where he ran."

Mrs. Oakshott's lips pressed together tightly, but she nodded. "I understand your position, Mr. Holmes. James was always weak, and we made allowances for it. Perhaps that is what turned him down the wrong path. I sometimes forget that others aren't as willing to give him the same allowances that we have."

"You said in your letter, and again just now, that there was a threat against his life?"

"Yes, and I don't know what to make of it." She reached to a side table, where a note had been lying throughout the conversation. Holmes took it from her and gave it his usual thorough examination inside and out before passing it my way. I noticed several facts, but kept them to myself, as long experience had taught me. What seemed to be most important was the message itself:

> Your brother James's life is forfeit. His crimes must be avenged. But you can pay the price instead. Be in Perham Down by sunset today for further instructions.

The message was written on common paper stock. The spelling and punctuation indicated someone reasonably educated. There was nothing else inscribed upon it, front or back. I returned it to Holmes, who set it aside on a small table by his chair. Mrs. Oakshott's eyes followed this movement, but she made no comment.

"Any envelope?" he asked.

"None. We found it pushed through the letter box this morning."

"Perham Down. A curious location. Do you know of any reason why it must be today, or why that chosen location?"

"No. I have never heard of the place."

"What crimes," asked Holmes, shifting his questioning, "– plural – do you believe this references?"

Her eyes widened. "I'm sure that I don't know. I had assumed that it was something to do with the jewel he stole while employed at the Hotel Cosmopolitan. Do you think that it could be related to something that has happened since?"

I thought it a rather naïve question, but before I could ponder, she continued. "Since James left England, we've barely stayed in contact with one another. I'm not even sure if he still uses his real name."

"Where did he go when he fled the country?"

"To France. In the south, I believe. After he – after you let him go that night, he came here. That's when he told me the truth – about how he had stolen the blue carbuncle, and then hidden it by forcing it down the throat of one of our geese. He explained how the goose was sold to Breckinridge's stall before he could retrieve it, and then how you became involved. He said that you had shown him mercy, and that he had to leave right away. I tried to make him stay – I didn't understand at first the seriousness of what he had done. But he made it clear that he might be facing a stretch in prison if he were to remain, and I saw the wisdom in letting him go. He is my baby brother, you see. I had to help keep him safe."

"Have you ever had any other messages like these? Demands to rescue him from some other trouble?"

"None at all."

"To your knowledge, has he *been* in any other trouble?"

"No. Or so I believe."

"Has he given any indication of how he is supporting himself in France?" I asked.

"Soon after he went there, he wrote that he had found work at a hotel on the southern coast. It was something that he knew how to do, you see. I've assumed that he continued in the same position."

"May I see some of his letters?"

At that, her open and frank expression changed suddenly, as if a candle had been extinguished. "Why?" she asked flatly.

Holmes's eyebrow raised in a most minute fashion, but it was likely unnoticed by anyone who didn't know him so well. "To see if I can gather any clues from them, of course. His whereabouts, for instance. Indications of how he spends his time, and with whom."

"There is nothing there. He has always been most careful to shield me from knowing too much."

"Why would he wish to do that?" I asked, becoming more curious by the minute.

She shifted a bit. "He is still a fugitive, you see. Possibly he doesn't want his whereabouts known."

"But you are his sister," I noted.

"The information might have been forced from me," she replied, as if that explained everything.

Holmes chose to let that assertion pass without comment, as if he were satisfied. "I would still like to see the letters."

She stood, clearly irritated. "I'll just be a moment." Then she walked from the room. We heard her go towards the back of the house.

I started to speak, but Holmes shook his head slightly and raised a finger to his lips. He had the barest hint of a smile, as if anticipating what would happen next. We didn't have to wait very long.

"I've misplaced them," said Mrs. Oakshott in tight voice. "In any case, I cannot see what they would have to do with this matter. Clearly whatever has happened to prompt that letter – " She glanced toward the table beside Holmes's chair, " – is here in England. At this Perham Down mentioned in the note."

"It is in Wiltshire," said Holmes, "on the edge of the Salisbury Plain."

"I didn't know," she said. "Is it a difficult journey?"

"Moderate," replied Holmes. "One must be rather lucky in terms of railway connections, but there is still time to be there by sunset."

"Then you'll go for me?" she said, with a hopeful and trusting tone in her voice, but – perhaps – also the slyest of casts to her expression. "I cannot go. I would be helpless in such a situation. And my husband must not know . . . ."

My surprise at her confident assumption of our willingness to make the journey was matched only by Holmes's response. "Of course, madam. I feel a certain responsibility for your brother, having taken it upon myself to rescue his soul. However, I must ask: Do you have the resources to pay what might be asked? I have a feeling that there is some sort of payment involved in this scheme. We know nothing of the reasons for these threats, or what crimes your brother may have committed. Are you prepared to meet the demands?"

"How can I answer that honestly, Mr. Holmes, knowing nothing about what you will discover? However, knowing is the first step."

Holmes nodded. "Will you be available throughout the day, should we have any questions?"

"I will remain at home, and instruct the servants to find me immediately with any message that you send."

"That is all that I could ask," he replied.

"Please," she added, taking a step toward him and laying a hand upon his arm. "Please start immediately. Every moment might matter."

As we stepped out to the street, Holmes began to look for a cab. Knowing that my back was to the house, I smiled and said in a low voice, "We're not going to Perham Down, are we?"

He looked at me. "No, we are not."

Something in the way he answered gave me an anxious start. "*We* aren't," I said, "but I hope that you aren't being exact, when you mean to say that *I* am going, while you stay here."

He shook his head. "My apologies, Watson. My exact response to your question was misunderstood. Neither of us needs to go on that wild goose chase."

I had expected so see some signs of amusement in his expression to match my own, but there was none. In fact, he appeared quite anxious – a trait that he had hidden quite well while still in Mrs. Oakshott's parlor.

"She was lying to us," I said.

"You saw it then?"

"Enough to be going on with," I nodded. "Besides the fact that the story of her servant's illness was suspect, it was the handwriting on the notes." I phrased it as a statement, but I was still marginally uncertain, realizing that Holmes had certainly seen more than I had.

"Exactly," he confirmed. "Although she had attempted to disguise the handwriting on the note, with the belief that using different and cheaper paper would be a distraction, it was clearly her own. I'm gratified to see that some of my little lessons on graphology haven't gone to waste. Whatever made her write both the note to summon us to today's appointment in her own name, and also the supposedly anonymous note purportedly threatening her brother in a badly disguised manner, is supposed to get us on a train to Wiltshire – which we will *not* do."

"But if we go there, forewarned as we are by perception of her deception, we can turn the tables on whatever awaits us."

Holmes managed to attract the attention of a west-bound hansom. It stopped by the curb, and we climbed in. Looking back, I could see Mrs. Oakshott, watching us from the parlor window. "Paddington Station!" Holmes called loudly for her benefit, and the cab did a smart turn and headed back toward cricket grounds.

"Nothing awaits us in Wiltshire but wasted time," said Holmes. When we were out of sight of Mrs. Oakshott's home, Holmes rapped on the ceiling and instructed the cabbie to make his way to Baker Street instead with all possible speed. The horse lurched into a respectable trot. "This seems to be an ill-conceived idea to take us off the London board. We have to ask ourselves why."

"It wouldn't be the first time someone has tried to distract you in this manner. There was the matter of the priest's hole in Piccotts End, for instance."

Holmes smiled. "Ah, Watson. It's kind of you to mention that – one of my little successes –and to refrain from reminding me of the matter of Moriarty's similar distraction and his attempted jewel theft at The Tower. That was a valuable lesson, and it took quite a bit to get back in Sir Ronald's good graces."

I wasn't being kind – That particular incident at The Tower had slipped my mind. There had been a number of instances when attempts had been made to decoy Holmes away from this or that affair. And those were greatly outnumbered by the times that someone had attempted the same thing with his clients – when Mr. Hall Pycroft was diverted to Birmingham, or the occasion when Miss Sarah Gaddesden had – against Holmes's express advice – used a railway ticket that had been delivered in an otherwise empty envelope to visit Caerphilly, where she encountered a figure from her past that left her reason destroyed forever.

"It isn't simply that Mrs. Oakshott wrote both letters," said Holmes. "There is also the fact that she wouldn't show us anything purporting to be from her brother and his new life."

"Why do you suppose she did that?" I asked. "The handwriting on the 'anonymous' notes was her own. It isn't as if we would have seen that it was her brother's."

"She couldn't show me his letters from France because she doesn't have any. I've kept my eye on Mr. James Ryder from the time he was allowed to flee, and while he did cross almost immediately to the Continent, he soon came back, taking the name of Bert Abel and settling in Margate. He's worked at a little seaside hotel there ever since, and has most gratifyingly stayed out of trouble. I believe that he's even married. It's possible that he knows nothing whatsoever about his invocation into this business."

"Then what could possibly have led Mrs. Oakshott to attempt such a trick?"

Holmes didn't answer, and we fell silent for a minutes. I came to myself as we turned northwest at the Camberwell New Road, suddenly wondering why we were returning to Baker Street. I assumed that Holmes wished to find some pertinent fact in his voluminous commonplace books, or perhaps change into a disguise before venturing out on some investigatory path which had suggested itself to him. I asked, and he shook his head. "Actually, Watson, I don't intend that we should enter the building at all – at least not yet. Rather, we shall observe for a bit – with the help of the Irregulars."

I raised an eyebrow, and he continued. "Consider: Someone who happened to have our rooms – as well as the inhabitants – under regular observation, would quickly identify the day-to-day habits of the household. Today is Wednesday. Does that suggest anything?"

It took me no time to realize it. "Mrs. Hudson and Mrs. Turner usually go to visit their sister, Mrs. Grimshaw, on the first Wednesday of the month – today."

"Exactly. And while that fact may be meaningless by itself, I have to consider it with the thought that someone went to a good deal of trouble – either Mrs. Oakshott herself, or at the behest of someone else – to direct us away from London on the very day that our good landlady is also away."

"Leaving Baker Street undefended."

"Indeed."

"But we've discussed this many times over the years – the perils of having a practice such as yours in a private dwelling, wherein your records, as well as various criminal relics and pieces of evidence, are relatively unsecured."

"Not only my records," Holmes replied. "Your accumulated notes now hold a number of dark secrets as well. However, what can we do? Should I rent an office with bars on the window and an iron safe? Should we convert our cellar, or the lumber room perhaps, into a strong-room? Would Mycroft provide me with a cubby in one of the Whitehall buildings in which to conduct interviews and hide my artifacts? The fact that his agents could root through my records at their leisure is as unsettling as the thought of having them rifled in Baker Street."

I smiled. "I propose a room for you in one of the turrets at Scotland Yard – one with a view of Westminster Pier. Surely they wouldn't mind if you displaced the current occupant."

Holmes snorted, but his amusement quickly faded as he fell to pondering why someone might want to lure us away. As we were crossing Vauxhall Bridge, he turned his head as a thought crossed his mind. "Perhaps," he said, almost speaking aloud to himself, "it's related to the Carroun murder. As you know, that case is coming to trial in a couple of weeks."

"It's possible, but why would anyone think that you have retained anything of importance? Gregson assembled all that he needed, at your direction, months ago."

"And yet, there is the note what, while having no direct effect on the matter, we suppressed. We suspected that the lawyer, Chartridge, overheard us discuss it."

"But what does that case have to do with Mrs. Oakshott? Or her brother for that matter."

Holmes settled back with a sigh. "Nothing. Or everything. We don't have enough data. This could all be a shot on my part in the wrong direction, wherein no attempt will be made to enter our rooms. Or if someone does want to get at our papers, it could relate to any number of cases going back more than twenty years."

"Perhaps," I said with sudden alarm, "someone wants to burn the place, as was attempted by the Professor. Or possibly they are trying to blow the place up, along the lines of the explosive package sent by the Baron in the Eye of Heka matter."

Holmes nodded. "I've considered that, but if someone had those inclinations, would they feel the need to decoy us away? It's possible, of course. Something quite complex could be rigged within the building to detonate when we return. But for now, I'm going forward with the simplest assumption that this is simply an arrangement for someone to enter unseen. With any luck, we'll be able to spot whomever goes in and then follow them. If they've already been and gone, we'll have to hope that we can identify what's missing."

I shook my head. "The opposite of looking for a needle in a haystack. It would be like trying to find the one piece of hay that has been pulled out of the rick and carried away."

"We can only take comfort in the fact that we were to be lured away for a full day or better. Hopefully that means the player on the other side doesn't want to enter the rooms in daylight and hasn't been there yet, and we'll be in place for his nighttime assault." He knocked his stick against the ceiling of the cab. "Faster!"

A few hours later, we were sitting in two straight-backed chairs and, although they were not as comfortable as one might have hoped, it was a considerably better situation than how we had waited in this very same room just a few months earlier.

That morning, we had crossed the river and threaded our way north through the area around the Palace, and then Mayfair. At Portman Square, Holmes had signaled to the cabbie to pull over. After settling the fare, we walked up Baker Street to the Bazaar, where it didn't take long to find one of the Irregulars, that informal band of lads who served as Holmes's eyes and ears. Instructed to gather as many of his comrades as he could find, the lad scampered and vanished into the crowds. Then we walked at a more sedate pace, belying Holmes's growing impatience, with the intention of meeting them in the Paddington Gardens.

Five minutes or so later, we gathered in the shade underneath one of the trees on the southeast side. There were a dozen or so of them, with one of the Wiggins brood taking nominal command, as was typical. Holmes explained that they were to form a net around our lodgings, remaining completely invisible while making certain to observe anyone entering the building – either by day or night. If someone did make his or her way inside, they were to be allowed free passage to both come and go. If an intruder was seen to be making away with something from inside, no hindrance would be offered.

Most imperative, Holmes explained, was that once the person left, he or she must be followed, and on no account could the trail be lost. "Recruit additional help as you see fit. There is a chance that the intruder has already been inside and gone, but I sense that the assault will come after dark. Watson and I will be across the street in Camden House. When you report, enter by the back way."

The boys dispersed, and Holmes and I walked through the side streets. A thought occurred to me. "Do you suppose that someone is at Paddington, waiting to see if we actually leave for Perham Down?"

"That had occurred to me. However, I felt that it was more important to get our forces in place here, rather than take the time to be seen boarding a train, and then departing a few stations down the line to return. If nothing comes of this, I'll think of something else."

We stopped and sent a wire to Mrs. Hudson at her sister's home, indicating that she should delay her return until she heard from us. "Of course," said Holmes, "there is the slightest chance that she has already returned early today – a change of plans, perhaps, or an unexpected illness. We'll only know if we see signs of her presence while we watch – stepping out on an errand perhaps, or if she lights the lamps tonight. We can't take a chance on approaching the house to deliver a message."

We reached the back of Camden House, and only then did I recall that it was now occupied, having been leased earlier in the summer. Holmes knocked, and the door was opened by the young mother whose family had recently taken possession of the place. She seemed surprised to see us, but we were quickly allowed inside. We followed her to the front of the building, taking care to stay back from the windows, where her husband sat in a comfortable-looking chair, looking puzzled.

We knew the couple slightly, and in our previous encounters, they had always seemed to be a bit in awe of my friend – not an uncommon occurrence. Holmes explained that we were expecting some sort of intrusion into our lodgings, most likely that night, and asked permission to

84

wait and watch. He also related how we would be receiving messages by way of the back door from the Irregulars. They enthusiastically agreed, and soon we were seated in the very room where, just months before, we had captured the murderous Colonel Moran when he attempted to murder Holmes by shooting through the sitting room window directly across the street. Then, this room had been empty. Now it was fixed into a parlor of sorts, and felt much more crowded and small. I recalled Holmes's struggle with the murderous colonel, and how, as the man seized Holmes by the throat, I had struck him with great satisfaction across the head with the butt of my revolver. That spot was now filled with a filigree table.

Throughout the day, one or the other of us carefully kept an eye on the street below, confident that the rear of our lodgings, and even the unlikely route across the roof, was well-watched. It had become apparent that Mrs. Hudson was not in residence – a fact that gave us comfort, should an intruder actually appear. While we waited, our hostess made every effort to keep us more-than-well fed, and yet she also seemed to realize that we didn't with to be bothered. Holmes became increasingly tense as he muttered about various documents and objects that might be sought by an intruder.

It was the time of year when the sun normally set very late, but throughout the afternoon, clouds from the south began to build, and it was unnaturally dark by half-after-five. The wind picked up, and occasional spatters of rain hit the window like shot, although the storm took quite a while to actually break. When it did, the heavens opened, and I felt mightily guilty about the Irregulars who were out in it. It seemed as if the rains were approaching the level of a tempest, and I imagined the gutters overflowing as waterfalls and the ditches running like small rivers. Our view from the window was completely obscured by viscous-seeming water sliding across the glass. At one point, Holmes raised the sash to try and look through the narrow gap, but so much rain immediately forced itself inside to puddle on the floor that he was required to shut it again.

However, the initial heavy downpour did finally settle into a steadier soak, and we were once again able to peer across the street, although in a rather smeared way. As the shimmering lights resolved themselves, I was thrilled to see that, in our distant sitting room, a single lamp had been lit. Even as I spotted it, a shadow moved from the left window to the right, toward the chemical corner. Someone was there.

Holmes had seen it as well, of couse, but there was no need for conversation. Just a moment or so later, we heard the back door open and close, and then footsteps approaching along the hallway outside the room where we waited. One of the Irregulars slipped into the room, informing us that a man of indeterminate years, dressed in dark clothing, had made

85

his way into our lodgings by way of the yard behind the building and through the back door, which he had apparently jimmied open. Assuming that the intruder would leave the same way, all routes from the back of the house had been more-than-adequately covered – including placing young Jim Byrne in the thickly-leaved branches of the solitary plane tree that grew in the yard – although the other possibilities of departure would also stay under surveillance until such time as the man's path was ascertained. Holmes made sure that the house would remain guarded even as we were led away.

It was a long wait, nearly an hour, before we saw the shifting shadows cease and the light in the sitting room vanish. Holmes and I stood, found our coats and hats, and made our way downstairs. The occupants of Camden House were still up, for it was not yet ten o'clock, and we thanked them profusely, with a promise to explain the outcome when we knew it ourselves. Then we let ourselves out into the mews to await a report as to which way we should travel.

Within moments, a little fellow named McGee skittered to a stop before us. "He left by the back," he panted. "He's circled 'round through Gloucester Place, and now he's headed down Marylebone Road, toward the Crescent." Holmes thanked him and we set out to follow.

The rains had nearly stopped, and the air was considerably cooler than it had been earlier in the day. Occasional puffs of breeze would buffet us unexpectedly, and I feared that another storm was following the first – and this time we wouldn't have the comforting protection of windows and walls. Yet, we were fortunate in that the winds seemed to take a different direction, and we had no further difficulties that night – at least with the weather.

We were lucky, I suppose, in that the fellow chose to walk rather than take a cab. Several passed by him along the way, and if he had wanted one, it would have been his for the asking. However, we would have been caught short if he had, for there wouldn't have been another anytime soon for us, and we would have been left standing in the street while he vanished into the darkness, trusting that the Irregulars would find a way to stay with him. I knew that this was on Holmes's mind, and once he muttered darkly when it looked as if our prey might choose to ride rather than walk. Fortunately, he stayed afoot, unaware that the silent pack of Holmes's juvenile agents were swarming silently all around him, dashing ahead on side streets and constantly anticipating his route, while we inexorably came along behind.

We stayed well back in the shadows but we needn't have bothered, for the fellow never looked behind him, or did anything to obscure his route. He kept to the well-lit main thoroughfares. As he passed beneath the streetlamps, we could see that he carried a case of some sort, first in one hand, and then in the other, as if he were simply a businessman returning home after an honest day's labors. He seemed to be a rather small fellow, and the weight of the bag pulled him to one side or the other as he progressed.

"It appears that I was wrong," Holmes said at one point. "Recognize him?"

"Surely it is James Ryder," I said. "Clearly whatever life he built in Margate is less important than involving himself in this business."

"Don't judge too hastily, Watson. He may have had no choice. This is a bigger scheme than his impulsive theft of the Countess' Blue Carbuncle. Somehow it involves his sister, and the plan to get us out of town is beyond Ryder's abilities. He reached the limit of his inspiration when he thought of using a goose as a temporary jewel box."

As our journey continued, we had traversed south and east before reaching New Oxford Street, and that was where we remained for quite a distance. In fact, if was only after that street became High Holborn, and we had passed the narrow entrance to Bloomsbury Court, that the object of our attentions began to look around him, scanning the house numbers. Then, he abruptly turned left into a door located just one building before reaching Southampton Street. We had time to see what had occurred and crossed the street accordingly before continuing in the same direction, but now we were across from where the man might possibly be waiting to see if he was being followed.

However, as we glanced to our left, there was no one hiding in the darkness of the doorway. We turned south at Newton Street, just across from the building in question, and then slipped into a convenient recess. In just a moment, Wiggins appeared at our sides and Holmes gave him instructions to have the building surrounded. "How many of you are there?" he asked.

"Seventeen now."

"Excellent. More than enough. Follow anyone who comes out."

As Wiggins slipped away, I looked around surreptitiously, noting that the structure in question, Number 130, was a narrow four-story building whose white color gleamed in the darkness in contrast to its darker-stoned neighbors. The ground floor was a closed and shuttered stationery shop, and beside it, to the left, was the plain door leading to the upper rooms where our subject had entered. The three windows across the first floor were lit, while the two floors above were dark. Even as I watched, a shadow passed across the illuminated drawn shades.

Holmes was quiet for a moment before reaching a decision. "I believe that we can force the question," he said preparing to step out. "The fact that that our rooms were burgled with such confidence indicates that they are certain we are off the board entirely. Our arrival will be unexpected."

"Should we summon the police?" I questioned.

Holmes paused a moment and then shook his head. "If they are after something of a secret nature, then it should likely remain secret. No, we'll handle this ourselves."

He started to move from the doorway, but just as he did so, a hansom pulled to a stop in front of the building. Holmes gave an intake of breath and retreated backwards. I couldn't see what was happening without leaning past him, but fortunately Holmes narrated in a low whisper. "One man. Stout, with a stick. He's entering the building. Ah!" Then I heard the sound of horse's hooves carrying the hansom away.

He straightened. "I owe you thanks for that, Watson. If you hadn't slowed me by a second or two to ask about the police, we might have already been walking toward the intersection, possibly to be seen by our new arrival. It may interest you to know that we're somewhat acquainted with the man. It is Clarence Chartridge, the lawyer."

"Then this *is* about the Carroun paper. But – " I was still brought up short. "In what way could Ryder and Mrs. Oakshott be connected to that affair?"

"That's what we will now determine. You have your service revolver?"

"Never without it."

"Then quick-march to the north!" And he stepped out into the lane, slipping along the wall toward the white building before us.

The door was locked, certainly by Chartridge following his entry, but that simply meant a delay of a few seconds for someone with Holmes's practiced skills and specialized tools – specifically one that he favored and called "the smoker's companion". The door opened silently and we passed inside, quickly shutting it behind us. We took a moment to listen, determining whether our entrance had been detected. Apparently not, as the low murmur of voices we had heard upon stepping inside continued overhead. Holmes moved carefully toward the steps, faintly lit from a partly opened door at the top. My eyes adjusted and I was careful to place my feet on the outer edges of those same treads where Holmes had stepped, knowing that he had a cat-like gift for understanding how to avoid those which might creak or groan and reveal our presence.

We reached the top successfully and I indicated that my revolver was ready. With that, the door, already partly ajar, was pushed fully open and we stepped into the lit room.

Holmes immediately shifted to the left, while I moved in the opposite direction, keeping the three men facing us covered. One, in his fifties, was seated in a plush armchair, a small table beside him supporting a bottle of whisky and a half-filled glass. An attaché case was between his feet and a sheaf of papers was clutched in his hand. To his left was the elderly lawyer, Chartridge, dropping into a somewhat ludicrous defensive crouch while pulling a much-less humorous revolver from his pocket. And to our far left, apparently dismissed once his task as a housebreaker and courier was complete, was our old acquaintance, the cringing little white-faced James Ryder.

Before we had a chance to speak, Ryder bolted, turning and vanishing into an open doorway behind him. It was a darkened room, and before I could consider passing by Holmes and following after him, we heard a window slide open and a scrambling sound as someone climbed through and scampered down the side of the building, landing with a muffled cry.

"Let him go, Watson," said Holmes. "The Irregulars will trail him. We have bigger fish to fry." He stepped closer to the fireplace, where a pair of gas-lamps on the wall above provided a dim yellow glow. Reaching up, he adjusted the flames so that the room was better illuminated. Then he nodded toward an empty chair behind the lawyer. "Sit down, Mr. Chartridge. I'll feel much more comfortable with our discussion if I'm not worried that Watson will have to shoot you, should you try to flee."

The man straightened and gave a tight smile, glancing at the gun in my hand, very similar to his own. "I'm too old to run, Mr. Holmes. And I'm most curious to hear your explanation for staging an armed invasion of a private dwelling."

Holmes laughed – a short bark that never boded well. "Shall we summon the police, then? If so, I would ask that the papers on your lap, Mr. Elliot, remain there until they can be examined by the authorities to verify that they were recently extracted from our rooms."

"Certainly you don't want that," said Randolph Elliot, the man in the chair. We had met him during our consultation into the death of his daughter. "I call your bluff. After all, I only had these . . . *retrieved*, shall we say, by Chartridge's shabby little agent in order to make them public anyway, you know."

"I don't believe that you've thought the matter quite through," countered Holmes.

"Oh, but I have, you see," said Elliot, standing up, his anger giving him strength to master his enfeebled limbs. "It's obvious that our ruse to divert you to Wiltshire was a failure. What gave it away?"

"The handwriting on the anonymous note, though disguised, was clearly Mrs. Oakshott's."

Elliot shook his head and glared at Chartridge, as if it were somehow his fault.

"How is she involved?" Holmes asked.

The lawyer cleared his throat. "She is my step-sister," he explained. "And Ryder is my step-brother." His mouth tightened in distaste. "I was tasked with finding a way for someone to get into your rooms and retrieve the document we knew that you'd taken with you when . . . when you investigated the death of Mr. Elliot's daughter's. I conceived the idea of having my step-sister seek your help. We decided to send you to Perham Down. We looked for somewhere that you would be able to reach by our deadline, if you hurried."

"But why Mrs. Oakshott?" I asked. "Why draw her into this business? Surely when we realized that the trip was for nothing, we would return and question her further, and look deeper into the business."

"When you came back with further questions, she would have simply begged for you to drop it. I involved her and James in order to keep the circle of those involved quite close. She frequently speaks of her ill-will toward you both, and I knew that she would be a willing distraction. She has never forgiven you, Doctor, for mentioning her in your story, and bringing unwanted attention upon her family. She was quite willing to take this little revenge. And as for James . . . Let us say that I have a bit of leverage over him. He'll never be the sort to keep to the strictly legal side of the street, even in such a quiet little place as Margate. He's had a few scrapes in the last few years, and – related to his continued liberty – he owed me."

Nodding and speaking in a lower tone, lessening the tension in the room, Holmes turned from the lawyer to the other man and said, "Have you had a chance to read those yet?"

Elliot glanced toward the documents, still gripped in his hand. "No, of course not. Ryder just arrived with them – as you well know." He nudged the case with his foot. "He wasn't quite sure what he was looking for, so he brought a whole assortment of papers and notes. I'm confident that what I seek is here, but it will take some examination to find exactly what I want." His gaze darkened. "I won't return them until I find it," he threatened. "Dr. Watson will have to shoot me first."

"That won't be necessary," replied Holmes, stepping away and drawing out a straight-backed chair from underneath a side table. "No need for the gun, Watson," he said. "Pull up a seat while we wait."

Elliot and Chartridge both seemed surprised. Following Holmes's lead, I put away my revolver and located another chair behind me. Placing it where I could face the two men, with Holmes at my left, I sat down and awaited developments. After a moment, Elliot lowered himself back into his own chair.

"You may put away your revolver as well, Mr. Chartridge. I assure you that there will be no violence upon our part."

The lawyer glanced at Elliot, who kept his eyes directed our way. Then, with a shrug, he slipped the gun into his pocket and found a chair for himself.

"Assuming that Ryder did manage to find and bring the correct document," explained Holmes, pulling out a pipe and tobacco from his coat, "I must tell you that you most certainly do not want to read it." He opened the pouch and began to push shag into the pipe. "That being said, I doubt at this point you will be dissuaded. We have no wish to shoot you in order to get it back, as you likely realize, so that form of inducement is useless." He struck a match. "I won't attempt to wrest the papers from your hand as if we were boys in a schoolyard – although there is no doubt who would be the victor." A puff or two and the pipe was lit. "But I really cannot let you violate the confidentiality of others whose cases are referenced in those additional papers that have come into your possession."

Elliot smiled, not without some tension, and sank deeper into his own chair. Chartridge looked rather unnerved by the conversational turn the encounter had taken. "Surely," said Elliot, "you don't think that, after all this time and effort, I'll simply hand you these papers and ask you to look through them for me, naively trusting that in the end you won't shrug and smile and tell me that Ryder didn't get what he was sent for."

Holmes turned his head slightly. "It has only ever been for your sake, Mr. Elliot, that I chose to suppress the facts that Watson and I discovered in that paper. We knew that Mr. Chartridge likely suspected its existence, but I had no indication that you would go to these lengths."

"You say that you hid the paper for *my* sake," said Elliot. "Explain."

Holmes closed his eyes for a moment, as I've seen surgeons do before making the first cut. "Tell me the facts of the case as you understand them," he replied.

Elliot raised his eyebrows. Then he swallowed and took a deep breath. "My daughter, Elizabeth – my only dear child – was murdered by my ne'er-do-well son-in-law, Alexander Carroun. He apparently left so careless a trail that even the police could have followed it – if that idiotic inspector hadn't been assigned to the case and tried to claim that it was one of the servants that did it. However, I knew from the first time that I spoke with him that he was going in the wrong direction, and I hired you to oversee the matter. I don't need to repeat your steps in tracking him." He glanced my way. "I'm sure that the doctor has already written it up for publication," he snapped with acid in his tone.

91

I started to speak, but realized that anything said in my defense would sound thin. In any case, this wasn't the time. I also knew that Holmes would most likely reference these events at some point in the future when discussing my writings, and I didn't want to provide him with additional ammunition.

"In any event," said Elliot, "you *did* find him, although you betrayed my interests by concealing additional evidence that will help assure his execution. Beyond that, I don't need further explanation."

"I, however, would like to know more," said Chartridge. "I only became involved after the man had been caught and brought back to London."

Holmes nodded. "Carroun had been missing for several days before the murder," he said, "and it was later verified that he'd spent that time in an opium den near The Tower – not an unusual occurrence. He came to himself and made his way home, as was his usual way, whereupon he began to argue with his wife – your daughter, Mr. Elliot. The conflict escalated, and he strangled her. The marks upon her throat matched his hands, and his signet ring, which had become twisted during the crime, had turned palm-inward. Its distinctive pattern was graven into the flesh of your daughter's throat. The truth would have come out, in spite of Inspector Jones's misstep, and without my involvement. The police surgeon would have quickly seen the marks on her neck."

Holmes had recited these facts tonelessly and without mercy, and Elliot became progressively pale as he listened, although what he was hearing nothing new.

"Carroun fled, and as you know, Watson and I were able to make use of several individuals who serve as eyes and ears around the capital, enabling the police to surround his hotel Canterbury. Later, he confessed that, upon his arrival at home and during the subsequent argument with his wife, he had entered and departed unnoticed by the servants, which perhaps explained why he wasn't initially identified as the killer when the body was discovered. The police were called. Inspector Jones jumped to the unfortunate conclusion that the murder had been committed by the groomsman, Kevin Silsoe. This assumption was based solely on the knowledge that Silsoe had lied about his past, failing to admit a conviction in his youth for robbery. It didn't help his case that he seemed to have become rather protective of your daughter, to the point of it being gossiped about below-stairs."

Elliot nodded. "From what I understand, Silsoe had heard one of the earlier fights between Elizabeth and my . . . my son-in-law, and had lurked nearby to step in and protect her if needed, fearing that violence might ensue. I owe him a great debt . . . ."

"More than you know," I thought to myself as Elliot's voice drifted off. Holmes continued. "After you summoned Watson and me to the scene, I was able to piece together Mr. Carroun's presence in the room and discover the elementary evidence indicating the placement of his hands around your daughter's throat. As I mentioned, Watson and I quickly traced him to Canterbury, where he had most ineffectively gone to ground. We were on a following train, and were able to speak with him at some length in his hotel room. Following our discussion, he left with us, surrendered himself to the police, and was arrested. He then made his confession and is now awaiting sentencing."

"There is some talk," said Elliot, "that he will simply spend the rest of his life in prison, with the possibility of parole, instead of receiving what he deserves. Chartridge was around the corner the other day and overheard the two of you mention something about a letter that had been given to you by Alexander when you found him in Canterbury."

Chartridge had the decency to look ashamed. "I felt that it was my duty to continue to listen, gentlemen, even as I realized that I was eavesdropping. When you paused around the corner from me that day in the Old Bailey, I heard you mention a paper that Alexander Carroun had given to you when you met with him, and that it must not be revealed. I became . . . suspicious. I conveyed my thoughts to Mr. Elliot, and he became convinced that it might somehow provide an excuse for leniency at Carroun's sentencing. I don't entirely agree with him – after all, you are hiding it, and seem to wish to continue to do so, and if it would somehow mitigate Carroun's punishment, you are already preventing that from happening by concealing the existence of the paper. But . . . well, Mr. Elliot *is* my employer." He glanced at the older man, who kept his stony gaze upon my friend. "He fears that if the paper is allowed to continue to exist in any form, it still might come to light at a future time. He tasked me – "

"I told him," interrupted Elliot, "to come up with a scheme to find the paper, and bring it here so that I could destroy it. And here we are."

He glanced toward Chartridge, who continued. "I was able to learn fairly quickly about the habits of your household, Mr. Holmes, and the fact that you seem to keep materials like that close at hand. A ruse was required. I made use of my luckless step-siblings, one of which had been in your rooms once before, and – as Mr. Elliot has pointed out – here we are.

Holmes frowned but nodded. "This is a valuable lesson, and Watson and I will have to take more care in the future to prevent such indiscretions . . . and intrusions. In the meantime, I would urge you, Mr. Elliot, not to press forward on the nature of the paper. Would you instead accept my solemn word that such a document does not serve to lessen your son-in-law's guilt in any way, and that it will never be made public, based upon a prior agreement that I have pledged? That, in fact, I have promised to destroy it myself, upon your son-in-law's death."

Elliot shook his head. "No, Mr. Holmes, I won't be satisfied with that. I must read it and destroy it myself." He shifted in the seat and raised the sheaf of papers that had never left his hand. "Watch them, Chartridge," he said.

The lawyer looked toward us uncomfortably, and with some embarrassment. Holmes nodded, and an understanding seemed to pass between them that we wouldn't prevent Elliot from making his examination. "It's the oversized cream-colored sheet – your daughter's personal stationary. I can see it there in your hand.

Elliot didn't seem to listen, as he proceeded to turn the sheets one by one, giving a brief glance at each. He didn't find what he sought after five or ten sheets, and so he set those pages aside, before continuing his journey through the clutch of papers in his hand. It was only a moment later that he reached the sheet described by Holmes, either unheard or ignored. Seeing his daughter's monogram, he gave a slight cry and teased out that single sheet from the stack, casting the others leaf-like to the floor.

It was just a page among many. The gaslight from over the mantel revealed where it had originally been folded thrice, to be placed in an envelope. Holmes had noticed that crumpled and torn envelope on the floor near the murdered woman's body, and had theorized that there was some document related to the case, most likely carried away by the murderer. In his cheap hotel room on a shabby Canterbury street between the Cathedral and the Great Stour, Carroun had reluctantly admitted this to be true while pulling the letter from his pocket.

It was a holographic document, unquestionably written by Elizabeth Carroun *née* Elliot, and dated from the morning of her murder, outlining to her husband why she'd grown to despise him, and listing in great and graphic detail every unfaithful and vengeful infidelity that she had committed against him over the years as her initial love turned to hatred. She spelled out names and dates of her illicit affairs, her handwriting sharp and jagged as she wrote with incredible anger, as if she were stabbing her husband with every word.

Possibly her most damaging thrust had been to inform Carroun that the young son whom he had believed to be his own had in fact been fathered by another – Kevin Silsoe, the young groom who had befriended her in the preceding months when her husband had drifted away into a life of drunkenness and debauchery.

Carroun hadn't denied that he killed his wife. He had shown us the letter – which Holmes had deduced had a better-than-even chance of already having been destroyed – to demonstrate what had driven him to a killing rage. He didn't use it as an excuse, but rather only as an explanation.

The man was broken when we found him, and had subsequently offered no defense, having sworn us to secrecy, as he did not want any further stain on the young boy whom he still considered to be his son, in spite of his wife's declarations. The one rock that he seemed to cling to was that she was lying to hurt him, and that the boy was really his. However, Holmes and I had met Kevin Silsoe when we first visited the house, and having seen both him and the child and their strong resemblance, coupled with Elizabeth Carroun's vicious letter, there was really no doubt. However, we chose to let Carroun hold onto his illusion, for what else did he have in the little time that remained for him?

Holmes and I had agreed to keep the secret, for the sake of the child. However, Holmes – who had a horror of destroying documents – had resisted my advice to burn it immediately. We had unfortunately, and carelessly, discussed the matter without making sure that we weren't overheard, thus inadvertently negating our joint conclusion that the child's grandfather, Randolph Elliot, should be prevented from learning the truth about the child's heritage. However, he had maneuvered around us, and now the truth was in his hands. We watched as he read the letter, his eyes moving from top to bottom and back again, until such time as his tears made reading impossible. Still, he continued to stare at the sheet until Chartridge leaned over and took it from him. Then he read it for himself.

At this point, Holmes rose, stepped forward, and gently took the rest of the papers from the man's hand, as well as gathering those still in the case and what had fluttered to the floor. Then, with a nod to Chartridge, we made our way downstairs.

The air in the street felt cool and clean, and I breathed deeply, as if to expel the grief we had just witnessed. I tried to formulate thoughts into words, but before I could do so, we heard footsteps coming rapidly down the stairs, and in seconds Chartridge burst onto the pavement. He seemed most surprised to find us so close.

"I thought that you would already be away," he explained. "I . . . I wanted to thank you. For your discretion. You must understand – " continued Chartridge. "Mr. Elliot is a hard man. He has many secrets."

"Such as the use of this dwelling?" Holmes asked, nodding toward the building behind us.

Chartridge nodded. "Yes. He maintains it for his . . . private business." He cleared his throat. "It's his nature to react toward a problem in this manner. Losing his daughter . . . that has been the hardest thing he's ever faced."

"And will he lose his grandchild as well?" I asked. "Will he abandon the boy because his father is of the wrong class?"

"No," said Chartridge firmly. "I will make sure of it. Sometimes Mr. Elliot reacts too quickly, but I won't allow him to make that mistake – to do something that can't be undone. He will have his grandson, and the boy will have his family. His birthright. I've been with Mr. Elliot for a long time. I owe him a great deal, and I'll make certain that he has this – that he doesn't ruin it."

"That's all that any of us can hope for," replied Holmes. An awkward silence fell then, and after a moment, Chartridge nodded and slipped back inside, pulling the door shut behind him.

After a moment or two of simply standing there, I became aware that Holmes was shaking his head. "We must be more careful, Watson. Both of us."

"Yes. It was indiscrete to discuss the matter in public, even if we did believe that no one was nearby."

"Not just that. Your publication of the Ryder affair, and the naming of Mrs. Oakshott, was irresponsible."

I felt my hackles rise defensively, but seeing that it was so, Holmes raised a placating hand. "It is not only you, my friend. I trusted in the sanctity of our rooms for the filing away of Elizabeth Carroun's last letter. You would think that I would have learned my lesson long ago, after Professor Moriarty's clever intrusions."

"There was no need to think – "

"There was every need to think so!" he snapped, but then the scowl drifted away from his face. "That can be discussed later. For now, we need to find Ryder before he jumps on a whaler and is lost to a normal life forever."

He put his fingers to his lips and gave a shrill whistle, as if signaling a dog to turn the sheep. Within a moment, young Peake, one of the more regular Irregulars, appeared from Bloomsbury Court. Motioning us to follow, he led us through into Silver Street and then the King's Yard Arms, where we passed into the mews behind Elliot's building. There we found Ryder, lying upon a mound of sacks. "He fell from there," said Peake, pointing to a first-floor window. "He tried to shin down the drain pipe but lost his grip. I think he broke his leg. We didn't have instructions, so we waited and made him as comfortable as possible. Wiggins went and found some whisky."

I leaned down and saw that Ryder's ankle was turned at an odd angle. I stabilized it while Holmes summoned assistance, and within an hour or so poor James Ryder had been treated at Barts. Holmes spoke to him calmly at his bedside, in low tones so as not to attract the attention of the other men on the ward, letting him know that what he had just been forced to do was resolved, and that he should return to Margate and stay on the straight and narrow. The little man wept and was still thanking us both as we walked out of the room. As we made our way home, we decided that it was up to Ryder whether to let Mrs. Oakshott know that the affair was at an end.

After what came to be known between us as "The Carroun Document", Holmes instituted a series of improvements in the way that he stored and protected his papers and evidence, along with making some substantial changes to prevent unwanted intrusions into our Baker Street rooms. And I have become more discrete in how I identify individuals within my notes, be they tobacco millionaires or geese-raising sisters – should that ever again be necessary. Carroun was not the name of the doomed husband and wife, and a search for Elliot or Chartridge or Silsoe, or attempts to find James Ryder in Margate, will only bring disappointment. But I can state that Elliot – whomever he really was – raised the child of his daughter and the groomsman as well as he could, and the lad grew to be a fine young man indeed. Just last week I was in attendance at the ceremony where he posthumously received the George Cross for his exemplary efforts and bravery during an incident at the front, when, due to his efforts, not a single life was lost – except, tragically, for his own.

The Reappearance of
Mr. James Phillimore

The north wind was in our faces as we trudged homeward along Baker Street. It pushed dead leaves that danced with whispering rustles around our feet, along the pavement, and against the buildings. An October cold snap had descended on London several days before, along with brilliant blue autumn skies. We had enjoyed a refreshing change from the rains that had assailed us just days earlier, but now the clouds were building once again, and very shortly we would be inundated.

We had just reached the coffee house at the corner of Portland Mansions when we encountered a woman headed south. She had been walking with steady purpose, scanning passers-by with a peculiar intensity. When she spotted my friend Sherlock Holmes, she pulled up with recognition.

"Mr. Holmes!" she cried, causing several people nearby to look up and our way from their own inner distractions. "Your landlady said that you were out. It *is* you, isn't it?"

Holmes frowned – a not-uncommon reaction when called out by strangers in public. While it could not be denied that my literary endeavours of the late 1880's and early 1890's had substantially increased his fame, making him much more recognizable and enabling him to increase his caseload substantially, he still felt that my efforts had deprived him of a certain amount of necessary anonymity. And I had to agree – although it must be noted that any anonymity that he desired was also often undone by his own insistence upon wearing his Inverness and fore-and-aft cap in both the city and the country, all the year round. However he had justifiable reasons for this, rightly believing that he could not be kow-towing to fashion if the needs of a case suddenly called him into action. "This coat and hat enable me to instantly begin an investigation – to be dressed to follow someone, travel to high or low places, and stay out for days if necessary. Imagine, Watson, if I were sankoing down the street attired in a topper and tails when I suddenly caught sight of a wanted man. Could I drop everything and pursue him in those clothes? What if the merry chase led me to Limehouse, or Dartmoor – and I still in my formal-wear? Nonsense!"

He was right, of course, and this had been proven dozens upon dozens of times. It didn't hurt that Holmes cared nothing for fashion's – or society's – dictates. His was a Bohemian soul, and he wore what he wanted without regard to others' opinions. On this day, it was a fortunate thing, as he was both identified by a new client, and he was also properly dressed – better than I was – for the rains that were arriving, with the first drops hitting around us even as we paused to talk to the strange woman.

Seeing that we were at the door of the coffee shop, I suggested that we quickly adjourn inside. It was warm and welcoming as always, with the old wooden floorboards creaking as we passed across them. Behind the counter, Mrs. Brett, the owner, smiled our way. About our age, Holmes and I had both known her since she opened the shop nearly two decades earlier, around the time that Holmes was able to explain a small mystery that had vexed her. Now a settled and middle-aged wife and mother of three, she had built up the business with a skill to be admired. While Holmes led the woman to a quiet table, I said hello to our long-time friend and ordered three of her moderate blends – aware that some of the darker roasts might keep me awake for days.

Soon, with three hot mugs in hand, I joined the others and was able to see the woman from the street in better circumstances. She was around sixty years old, and rather matronly in a plain but pleasant way. She was moderately dressed, without any bright colors or noticeable jewelry. She carried a sensible bag, and her expression denoted intelligence. I was glad to see it, for her initial approach on the street had suggested that she was impulsive and overwrought. Clearly something was worrying her to have caused such a forward introduction.

I could hear the intensity of the rain increase outside, and I knew that we were in for it over the next few days. When this storm blew away, the last remaining bits of summer would have truly departed.

"While you were serving us," Holmes told me, "Mrs. Harlow introduced herself." I glanced at her ring finger, which was bare. A widow, perhaps?

"She hasn't related any other facts, however." He turned back to the woman. "How can we help you?"

Mrs. Harlow took a sip of the coffee and held the hot mug cupped in her hands for a moment, clearly enjoying the heat in her fingers. Then, realizing that the silence was becoming awkward, she squeezed her eyes shut, took a deep breath, set down the mug, and began.

"I live at Number 12, The Arbour, in Highgate," she said. At that, Holmes seemed to show a spark more interest, but perhaps only someone who knew him as well as I would have noticed.

"I bought my house there two years ago," continued Mrs. Harlow, "when my husband passed away. He was a supervisory clerk at a bank in the City, and he wisely maintained an insurance policy that paid quite handsomely when he died. Sadly, we were never blessed with children, and after he was gone, I began to feel the need for a change. A house agent who had been a friend of my husband's arranged for the sale of our old house and the purchase of the new one. I had considered traveling, but I realized that I'd like nothing better than to settle into my new home. And now . . . ." She closed her eyes again, and a tear suddenly ran down one cheek.

"There, there," I said, laying my hand on hers. "Whatever it is, I'm sure that we can help. What caused you to seek us out today?"

She dabbed at her eyes with a small handkerchief, produced from her bag. "After living so peacefully in my new home, I'm suddenly terrified of it. After . . . after last night, I didn't know what to do. I recalled you, Mr. Holmes, from when you once helped a friend of mine, Mrs. Horace Mortimer, and so I hurried around, without even making an appointment. When your landlady said that you weren't there, I turned away in despair. I . . . I believe that she called to me that you would be back soon and that I could wait, but I was so despondent that I simply needed to walk. Then I saw you both coming my way, and it seemed to be a miracle."

I could tell that Holmes was becoming impatient, but he'd learned over the years that often a story has to be told in its own way. I patted Mrs. Harlow's hand one more time and then withdrew my own. She was ready to continue.

"My little house is one of a row, not more than twenty years old. It consists of just two stories – a sitting room and parlor and kitchen on the ground floor, without a cellar, and a couple of bedrooms upstairs. It's cozy and comfortable, and I've filled it with objects that please me. Books, and interesting little curios that I obtain – selectively, I assure you – during explorations to various parts of London. I live a very quiet and satisfying life, with only my cat to keep me company.

She gave a small sob, and then continued. "It has been thus for many months, until . . . until five days ago, at which time I began to have . . . *visitations.*"

Holmes shifted in his seat and leaned forward, his hands resting on the table, fingers intertwined, coffee ignored. "What sort of visitations?" he asked. "Surely you don't mean to imply something along the lines of a spirit or ghost?"

She rocked a bit and chewed her lip before saying with a low cry, "Mr. Holmes, I simply do not know! I would have never thought that I could be afraid of such a thing, and yet – I have seen things that I cannot explain!"

Seeing that we were listening intently, she continued. "It began innocently enough, last Monday night – although at the time it was rather upsetting, as I didn't realize how much worse things could become. I was awakened by a noise in the night, in the hallway outside my bedroom. I sleep with the door closed, and my cat, Molly, was with me. I'm normally a light sleeper, and it was no wonder that such a sound would disturb me. It was a distinct thump, as if someone were walking in the darkness had inadvertently knocked against the small table standing outside my bedroom door.

"I gave an inadvertent cry, certain that a robber had entered the house. I was quite fearful and uncertain as to what I should do. But then, instead of hearing footsteps making a quick escape, I heard a moan, a terrible sound that started low, almost like the wind, but then grew in volume and intensity until it was nearly a scream. I didn't imagine it – it was no dream. Molly heard it as well, and instantly the hair on her back stood out while she cringed against me and hissed at the terrible sound. And then – it stopped abruptly, as if whomever – or whatever – had created it met with some great violence. Then, with another a painful groan, it vanished entirely.

"My heart was pounding, and I cowered in bed for the longest time. Molly seemed to calm herself after a while, but I never truly did. Morning light was beginning to peep through the windows before I managed to make myself arise. Only then did I remember that my door, while closed, had not been locked – for who locks themselves in their bedroom at night when living alone? Or perhaps that is a perfectly sound reason to do so, but it hadn't ever occurred to me before, and while the door had a lock, I'd never had a key for it, from the day that I moved there.

"I examined the hallway and saw no signs of an intruder. The small table was as I'd left it. I crept around the house for an hour or so, looking for evidence of a break-in, or half-expecting someone – or some*thing* – to jump out at me from every door or recess that I passed. It was a terrible feeling – this home that I'd loved from the beginning, and which was to me the coziest of havens – now suddenly an unfamiliar and dangerous threat.

"I was too ashamed to call the police, for even I could see that no one had broken in, and there was no sign of damage or proof that anyone had been there. Possibly you, Mr. Holmes, could have read much that was invisible to me, but I simply never thought of you. Instead, I relayed a message to the locksmith – I am on the telephone – and requested that he provide me with a key to my bedroom that very day. He seemed curious, and came around within the hour, but I provided no answers to his unvoiced questions.

"That day was so long, and it was dark as well – not quite raining, but with fitful and unceasing winds rattling around. I would look out the windows at the low clouds scudding by, my unease growing. I've never gotten to know any of my neighbors, and I've lost track of the few friends that I had when my husband was alive. I realized just how alone I was. I couldn't even go next door and ask if they had heard anything in the night – I had never met them, and they would think that I was touched in the head. Well, I suppose that I could have asked them, but it simply seemed impossible.

"And so Tuesday night came, and I followed my usual routine, cooking a small supper and carrying out the usual household chores. I tried to read, but every knock and thump from the rising wind outside distracted me. Finally, when I could avoid it no longer, I went up to bed.

"Somehow I fell asleep, comforted perhaps by my now-locked door. And yet, it was almost as if I'd known that the previous night was only the beginning. Around four in the morning, without any warning or preparation, my door was suddenly subjected to three very loud knocks – pounding, really, as if by a giant fist. And then, there was a low laugh – sinister, and slightly wheezy. It seemed to resolve itself into a repetition of sibilant whispers. Gradually they became loud enough for me to recognize their pattern: '*Get out!*' they hissed. '*Get out!*' Eventually they peaked in intensity before fading away.

"Once again, Molly beside me had been as frightened as I was. And yet, this time instead of cringing, she stood and walked down the bed, as if willing to fight. However, I was not so brave, making no effort to do anything but hide beneath my covers, weeping and wishing for morning.

"Wednesday was much the same, as has been each day since then. The daylight hours pass with a sense of dread and impending disaster, while the nights have been one terrifying incident after another. That night, nothing happened for so long that I began to believe it had ended – and yet, a sudden scream an hour or so before dawn woke me from a troubled slumber. After several moments nothing else happened, and I foresaw another wakeful wait for morning. Then I heard a terrible dragging noise on the door. It was over in seconds, and only when I exited hours later did I see that the woodwork had been damaged from the top to the middle, as if it had been raked by claws.

"Thursday night, I was awakened again by loud pounding on the door, followed by maniacal laughter. It was almost a comfort that nothing further occurred. And yet, when I went out in the morning, I found that a series of naked footprints, one after another, had been *burned into the floor*, leading from the top of the stairs to my doorway. I touched them and they were cool, but the floor where they lay was most definitely burned, and there was ash on my fingers. Likewise, at eye level on the wall across from my bedroom door was the word *Leave*, burned along the wallpaper.

"I know what you're thinking, gentlemen: Why in God's name was I putting up with this for so long? But I truly had nowhere else to go, and up until then I had feared approaching the police, as I had no real evidence – even the scratches on my door could have been made by me. My former sister-in-law had a mental affliction in which she made greater and greater efforts to inflict self-harm, pretending that she was being victimized by others, if she felt that she wasn't getting enough attention, and I saw over the years how she was treated and not believed. Even the footprints could have been something that I constructed in a warped effort to bring myself to someone's awareness. I only wish that I had gone yesterday morning, before this . . . this malevolent phantom escalated the affair to a new level!

"Last night, as I again prepared myself for another long night of waiting to see how I would be disturbed, I realized that I hadn't seen Molly for an hour or so. I went to the rear of the ground floor, into the kitchen, and saw that her food hadn't been eaten. I was more puzzled than I can say, and I searched high and low, calling her name. I knew that she couldn't have slipped out, because I hadn't opened the door in days – in fact, since the visit of the locksmith. Her absence made me more and more concerned, and angry as well, as if my willingness to fight back against this . . . this *thing* was finally awakening. Instead of going to bed last night, I lit all the lamps, found the largest knife that I owned and, carrying it into the sitting room, I placed myself in a chair, ready to confront whatever it was that was terrorizing me.

"Periodically through the night, I would pass through the house, terrified with every step and expecting to encounter the intruder, calling for Molly, and looking for anything unusual. But I never saw a sign of her, or my intruder. Eventually this morning came, and I was relieved – I seemed to have broken the cycle. And yet, it was a very hollow victory, for my only companion had vanished.

"As today wore on, I puttered about. I usually have very few chores, and so eventually I found myself back in the sitting room, reading a book, and becoming more and more sleepy. In mid-afternoon, I awoke with a start, with the vague sense that I'd heard a noise, like the sound of a door shutting in another part of the house. Rousing myself, for I'd slept deeply and I still felt as if I were halfway between wakefulness and drowsing, I picked up the knife and went to examine the house.

"I'd only reached the front hall, however, when I saw her – Molly – before me, on the floor near the front door. I dropped to my knees, the knife clattering to the woodwork beside me. She was dead – stiffened, and with a look of rage on her face, as if she'd fought whatever it was that killed her. The fur was bunched at her throat, and her head was . . . it was at an odd angle, as if her neck had been twisted and broken!"

103

At this point, Mrs. Harlow broke down, sobbing silently into her handkerchief. I glanced at Holmes. His gaze was intent, and there was an angry flame burning in his eyes that revealed his outrage at the circumstances faced by this poor woman.

"It was then that I knew I couldn't stay," said Mrs. Harlow. "I had remained for so long, but then I stood and fled, somehow remembering to grab my coat, hat, and bag. Thankfully I locked the house behind me, but I could have just as easily forgotten. I walked for quite a bit, only stopping to have a cup of tea and a bite to eat when I felt myself becoming weak. I was considering finally approaching the police when I thought of you, Mr. Holmes. I made my way to Baker Street, and then fortunately I saw you both on the street." Her voice faded away, as if every bit of her energy had been used up remembering the terrors of the last few days, and now she was trustingly placing the matter in Holmes's hands.

He thought for a moment, and then said, "I know that it will be difficult, and frightening, but can you return there, and wait for Dr. Watson and me to prepare ourselves?"

A look of terror filled her eyes. "I cannot! I can't be alone there. Can't you return with me?"

Holmes smiled and reached to pat her hand. "You won't be alone. Dr. Watson and I have something to do first, but in the meantime, we'll send you with a lad that I know, by the name of Philip Barsby."

Young Philip was one of Holmes's Irregulars, that group of lads – and occasionally lasses – who often served as his eyes and ears. I recalled passing Philip earlier as we had walked toward home. "His appearance," Holmes continued, "may not provide the greatest confidence, but there is no one more true and sure. But you must remember," he said, his tone changing, "that neither of you should speak to each other. Don't say a word. Whatever is in the house must believe that you have returned there alone. Do you understand?"

She nodded, uncertain, but willing to take the lifeline thrown to her.

"I don't believe that you will be in any immediate danger, but it's essential that the house be reoccupied as soon as possible. I assure you that we will settle this in a very short amount of time."

She nodded, and then her eyes widened momentarily. Tears formed, and I have no doubt that she was again seeing her poor cat lying dead in the hall where she had left it. So vivid had been her description that I could envision it there as well, and I felt her pain at being asked to go back. Holmes was not indifferent.

"I wouldn't ask you to return if there was any other way," he said. "But you may have left the place untenanted for too long already, and whomever wants you to leave must believe that you're still defenseless, and without aid, if he is to reveal himself."

"So," she asked, eyes wide, "you don't believe this to be some kind of monster?"

Holmes frowned. "Of course not. But if we have any hopes of putting a stop to this, we must hurry. You will return to Highgate with our young friend, as soon as I round him up, while Dr. Watson and I will repair to Baker Street and carry out our plans from there. Within the hour, the doctor will present himself at your home in the guise of a gas inspector."

With that, I raised an eyebrow, but Holmes continued without pause. "You will enter, Watson, making a great show of explaining that you are checking for leaks. Putter about, make some noise, and then return to the front door, where you will noisily say goodbye. But you will *not* leave. Rather, you will also remain in the house, quietly, and no further conversation will pass between any of you, whatsoever. That is most important. Mrs. Harlow, is there somewhere that the doctor and our young friend Philip can wait unobserved until tonight?"

She nodded. "The parlour, by the front door, is rarely used, and there is are comfortable chairs for reading."

"No reading, Watson. I'm afraid that you must both wait in darkness. And no smoking either, old fellow."

"I understand." And I did. It was rather like that terrible night in '83 when Holmes and I had hidden in a bed chamber where violent death had occurred before, knowing that the killer was waiting patiently in the adjacent room. There had been a ventilator constructed high in the wall where death would slip through, and any indication that we had replaced the room's regular occupant, as revealed by smoke from our pipes or cigarettes, would have ruined Holmes's scheme. The villain had never realized that we were there, and his murderous plot recoiled on him in a most fitting and satisfactory way – but not before Holmes and I had a few terrifying moments where our own deaths were entirely possible.

Holmes stepped outside to locate Philip Barsby, and I continued to speak softly to Mrs. Harlow, assuring her that my friend would soon find a solution. I didn't mention that he had seemed to recognize the address, and I looked forward to learning from him its significance.

In a moment, Holmes returned and waved toward us from the door. I nodded to Mrs. Brett behind the counter and then gave Mrs. Harlow my arm. Outside, Holmes introduced Mrs. Harlow to Philip, a bright boy of perhaps ten. He carefully instructed that Mrs. Harlow should arrive at the front of her house alone, and then let Philip in discretely through the back door. He made it quite clear that there should absolutely be no conversation between them to indicate that Philip was inside the house. I felt that the boy was trustworthy in this matter, but I wondered if Mrs. Harlow could remain silent. I assured her that I would soon join them, and that Holmes had a good idea of what to do. Then we put them in a cab and sent them away. Then, with the cold rain in our faces, we dashed for our rooms up the street.

I knew that Holmes already had some sense of what had occurred, but I didn't know yet how he came to any conclusion. I could only grasp with certainty that when Mrs. Harlow had stated her address, he seemed to show some additional interest, as if he'd recognized it. When we had entered the front hallway of our lodgings, and were shaking out our wet coats at the bottom of the stairs, I asked him to elaborate.

"Very good, Watson," he said as we started upstairs. "You see that this narrative, consisting of a series of events that are all self-contained within that small household, and with a very limited cast of characters, could have occurred anywhere. The only facts that might have a wider significance are the profession of the late husband or that specific address. How did you decide to ask about one over the other?"

"I hadn't given any thought to her late husband's job at the bank," I confessed, entering the sitting room and turning to face him. "Instead, I saw your interest when she mentioned her address."

"Ha!" he barked. "I must learn to guard against your growing observational skills," he said, "lest I become careless and give away other secrets before they can be dramatically revealed." He dashed into his room, only to immediately return carrying a shabby overcoat and a leather folder of the type used by workmen recording observations. "This shall be your disguise," he said. "Nothing too elaborate." I took the items from Holmes, who then said, "Make sure that you bring your service revolver."

I patted my coat. "As you know, I learned years ago never to step out without it."

"Good man. Be on your way soon. Don't look for me, but I will be nearby." And he walked toward the door, stopping to pick up his loaded riding crop from the nearby stand.

"But Holmes," I asked, "*why* were you interested in the address?"

"You'll find it in my commonplace books," he replied. "But don't dawdle – that poor woman is counting on you to join her soon. It's the Phillimore matter. You'll find it filed under '*F*'."

"Phillimore starts with a '*P*'," I called, but he was already gone.

His filing system was always more curious than could be comprehended by lesser mortals, but I suspected that he had listed it under '*F*' because he considered it to be a *Failure*. However, cases that he often judged to have unsatisfactory endings usually seemed, to me at least, to be astounding successes. Still, he would see something in those affairs that irritated him – a deduction made later than he would have liked, or his initial pursuit seemingly wasted time while he followed a false trail before comprehending the truth – and so forever after it would be labeled in his mind as a defeat. The Phillimore case of two years before had certainly been perceived that way by the public. When the man disappeared, Holmes had been consulted, and at the end he admitted that he had no solution. Afterwards, he'd accepted the good-natured chiding of the police, without revealing that he had in fact truly arrived at a solution, and rather easily at that. Yet he chose to hide it, rather than expose a man's carefully constructed secret.

I found the book for the letter 'F' and carried it to the dining table. I knew that every minute was important, and that Mrs. Harlow and Philip Barsby might, even at that moment, be entering her Highgate home. But I wanted to understand what Holmes had remembered, and he apparently felt that it was safe for her to return there, at least initially, if she could muster the courage.

Holmes's scrapbooks are not books at all, but rather a loose collection of documents somewhat enclosed in front-and-back covers. There are attached pages, but more are loose than not, and tucked between every leaf are other scraps of paper – photographs, receipts, handwritten notes, and brochures – along with other odd and unexplained items like feathers, or strips of papyrus with curious hieroglyphics upon them, or swatches of cloth. Each has a story, and relays some fact to Holmes that is often meaningless to others. In flipping through the sheets, I found his notes related to Phillimore, immediately after a small booklet describing the history of an ancient London church.

I scanned Holmes's neat handwriting and saw immediately why he had been alerted by Mrs. Harlow's story – the address that she gave us was the very same where James Phillimore had disappeared just over two years earlier, probably within a month or so before she purchased it.

The case was quite the nine-days wonder at the time, and it wasn't long until Holmes was consulted by our old friend, Inspector Lestrade. Phillimore, a bachelor who worked for a nearby wine merchant, had stepped outside one spring morning and called to a passing constable. He hurriedly made some explanation about a mysterious package that he'd received, and asked the constable to whom he should report it. Then, as a shower was about to begin, and before the constable could answer, Phillimore excused himself for a moment, indicating that he was going to step back inside for an umbrella. He turned and passed in, partially pushing the door to but not entirely closing it – and vanished.

After a few moments, the constable, Wilkins, became impatient, but rather than simply walking on, he knocked and called several times before entering the house. Inside, he found that James Phillimore had seemingly disappeared without a trace. Wilkins pushed the door shut, locking it and taking the key that was still in the lock with him while he searched the house, moving methodically from room to room. Wilkins was known to Holmes and me as being one of the more responsible of the bunch, and it was proven this his examination of the house was quite effective while he listened carefully to make certain that no one was moving around in places where he was not then occupying. The house was a small one, and I didn't take long to ascertain that it was mysteriously empty.

The windows were all locked, and there was a bar on the inside of the back door that absolutely could not have been replaced if Phillimore had exited by that route. Realizing that something was happening beyond his experience, Wilkins unlocked and re-opened the front door to blow his whistle. Within a few moments, several other officers had joined him, and before long Lestrade was there as well. A plethora of constables then swarmed through the place, and no sign of Phillimore was found.

Routine investigation revealed a number of documents left on Phillimore's desk, including a number of threatening letters that had been mailed to him at that address from central London over the preceding week, all written by a mysterious man named "Willoughby". Each was vague, promising that he would die for what he had done – without providing any details as to what exactly that might have been. Of this Willoughby there was no trace.

Phillimore, a quiet and anonymous man of around forty years, had led a routine life, moving from work to home and back again. He was engaged to be married to a middle-aged spinster named Sylvia Amherst, but the relationship had been long-standing, and there was no apparent urgency toward formalizing the arrangement. With no apparent clues, the public became fascinated with the story, especially as it somehow found its way into the newspapers, despite the efforts of the police to keep it quiet. Several anonymous letters to the editor were published, all calling for Holmes's intervention. With no other direction to turn, Lestrade summoned Holmes and me, and was immediately chided by my friend for waiting so long. He wasted no time in examining the entire house, which had remained locked and guarded since Phillimore's disappearance, while the inspector and I waited patiently in the sitting room off the front hall. We could hear Holmes exploring the building, upstairs and down, and then back again. Eventually he joined us, agreeing with Lestrade that Phillimore hadn't exited by the windows or the back door. With that, he indicated that he would continue his investigation, and we departed, leaving Lestrade markedly unsatisfied.

Over the next couple of days, Holmes built up a greater picture of Phillimore – a bland fellow, living life with a sameness that never varied from day to day and year to year. We met with Miss Amherst, and found her to be a singularly unpleasant person who gave us to understand that if we found her errant fiancé, she would quickly place him under a much firmer thumb than how he'd previously found himself. She let it slip through implication that it had only been through the threat of a breach of promise suit that they'd remained engaged as long as they had.

When we were back outside, both rather shaken at being in the presence of such a harridan, Holmes announced that it was time to settle this. He then hailed a cab and directed us to the Charing Cross Hotel.

In the lobby, a boy of ten or so approached us. It was young Abel Foster, one of Holmes's irregulars who often drew this sort of assignment, as he was from a middle-class home, and thus had both better manners and shoes. He informed us that Mr. Willoughby was still in his room, and how to find it. I started to ask how Willoughby had been located, but Holmes was already headed upstairs.

We knocked on the door of Number 412, which opened to reveal a rather plain middle-aged man with his brown hair combed low on his forehead. He peered at us curiously, but stepped back with a start when Holmes greeted him as Mr. Phillimore and asked if we could step inside.

Phillimore seemed to be trapped between amazement and nervous laughter when he realized that he'd been discovered, and that his use of the name "Willoughby" had been revealed. As expected, he wanted to know how he'd been found. Holmes explained that during his searches of the house, he'd found various footprints throughout belonging to Phillimore, as identified when matched with shoes belonging to the missing man, along with a number of constable's prints, along with the inspector's, the left of which had a marked inward twist. Oddly, some of those belonging to Phillimore had been mixed in with those of the constables in the ground floor entry hall. In fact, in a few cases these had lay *on top of* the constable's prints. Following some of Phillimore's tracks back from the front door, Holmes discovered that they had come from the closet underneath the stairs.

While Lestrade and I had waited in the sitting room, he had given the closet a more intense examination, aware that Phillimore couldn't have simply hidden there while Wilkins searched the house, as he would have been quickly discovered. Further examination of the space had led Holmes to discover that it had a false back, with room enough behind it for a man to hide, although just barely. This was confirmed by seeing that Phillimore's footprints were also there in the scattered dust.

Holmes had then realized what must have happened: Phillimore, planning to vanish, had waited until he saw a constable passing by. He called to him to obtain his attention, and then, with the excuse of retrieving an umbrella, he went back in the house, leaving the door open. He hurried to the closet, stepped inside and, closing the door behind him, he moved further back into the secret chamber. There, he had a constable's jacket and helmet hidden, and he put them on and waited.

Holmes revealed then that he'd consulted with the various constables who had been at the scene that morning and verified that no one had been allowed in or out of the house but the police. Lestrade confirmed that the house had been locked up tight since. With this in mind, Holmes was certain that the evidence of the footprints was unaltered.

With the testimony of the constables also confirming that no one else had been in the house that morning, Holmes knew that Phillimore had waited until the house was full of policemen searching for him. Then, disguised as one of them, he simply kept his head down and walked purposely out to the street, where he strolled away and vanished.

"Amongst the papers in your desk was a recent receipt for a theatrical costumer, located near your place of employment. The clerk there verified that they had rented a constable's coat and helmet to a man named Willoughby, and that they were returned later the same morning that you disappeared. Very conscientious, Mr. Phillimore, since you could have simply dropped them in any convenient alley. Perhaps more responsible of you was when you provided a required address – which turned out to be this hotel. You could have lied, but you had to tell them something, and this was what suggested itself to you. And then there's the use of the name Willoughby – not very imaginative, I'm afraid – using it to rent the costume, as well as your room here at the hotel, and also on the threatening letters that you forged to yourself. Though disguised, the handwriting is unmistakable as your own. What significance does the name Willoughby hold for you? I was able to ascertain that as well. As James Phillimore, you've slowly but surely been emptying your bank accounts, making regular payments – never large enough to attract attention – to the accounts of someone named Willoughby."

"That was my great-uncle's name – Thomas Willoughby," Phillimore replied with a rueful smile. "When I concocted this plan, it seemed fitting somehow to use that name, both on the letters, and as my new identity. Several months ago, you see, I received a rather substantial and unexpected inheritance from him. Realizing the freedom from responsibility that the funds now provided, I found that I had the itch to break out of my routine and see the world."

"But why this complex subterfuge?" I asked. "If you could now afford it, you could have simply quit the shop, sold the house, and bought a ticket."

Phillimore shrugged. "What can I say? I wanted to set forth as a different person – to be reinvented as an entirely different man. And Sylvia – that is, Miss Amherst . . . . ." He drifted off.

"Yes," Holmes nodded. "She is rather unpleasant."

Phillimore stared for a moment, as if feeling that he should defend her, before nodding. "She has always threatened to bring action against me if we should part. She is quite a . . . vengeful person. She would never have rested. Rather than that hanging over me, wherever I went, I decided that it was simply another reason to vanish entirely. Besides, I can assure you that she would much rather go forward as a jilted and broken-hearted fiancée – chewing on the grievance will sustain her for years!"

He smiled as he said it, but then a silence descended upon us, and his face settled into that bland forgettableness that was certainly its normal state. After a few minutes, Holmes glanced at me with an interrogative expression. "Well, Watson? No crime has been committed here. Do you think my little reputation can stand a bit of tarnish if we let this one remain unsolved, allowing Mr. Phillimore – that is, Mr. *Willoughby* – to follow his own path from here on out?"

"I think so," I agreed, "if you do."

And so, with Phillimore – as I continued to think of him – showing quite a bit of relief, we took our leave, and the matter played out for several more weeks in the press before fading and joining those other cases that are seemingly solution-less, but in actuality do have an explanation, if only one knows where to look and whom to ask.

Holmes's short written *précis* of the affair didn't deviate from my recollection. Yet, as I was about to close the scrapbook, I noticed a second sheet tucked behind the first, headed *Phillimore – Continued.* On this was only one cryptic sentence, written in Holmes's distinctive hand: *House at Number 12, The Arbour, Highgate Sold 17 October, 1895.*

That corresponded to the approximate date that Mrs. Harlow had purchased the house, not long after Phillimore vanished. No surprise there – and yet, why did Holmes feel the need to document it?

Realizing that precious time was slipping away, I pulled on the shabby overcoat and, tapping my pocket where my service revolver rested, I walked down and out to the street, where one of the cabbies that we knew, Bert Deacon, was passing. He waved and seemed oblivious to the driving rain. Giving him Mrs. Harlow's address, I settled back for the journey up to Highgate.

111

Deacon dropped me at the end of the block. The rain had diminished a bit, but the wind was rising. I walked slowly toward the remembered house, admitting to myself that I'd only given the neighborhood cursory attention when visiting there with Holmes two years earlier. Now, with the cold rain falling steadily and in the dim evening light, I was even less inclined to spend any time looking at it with any great intensity from the outside. I stopped in front of Number 12, put my foot on the single front step, and rang the bell.

Almost before I could withdraw my hand, Mrs. Harlow answered, her eyes wide with fear. "Good evening, ma'am," I croaked in my best Cockney accent – not entirely a terrible effort, but not worth trying to recreate here within this printed record. "We're checking the gas connections in the neighborhood – "

"Yes, yes," she interrupted, a bit shrill, and pulling me forward. "Come right in."

Knowing that Holmes had put me in disguise for a reason, I'm sure that he thought that the house was being watched. Mrs. Harlow's nearly panicked welcome of me was far too sudden – she might alert someone that my visit was more planned than the business-like and unexpected intrusion that it was supposed to portray. I needed to calm her down.

Inside, she quickly shut the door. The entry hall, much as I remembered it from two years earlier, was lit by a small gaslight. As my eyes adjusted, I saw young Philip standing in the shadows to the left, in the door of the small parlour. I nodded to him, and Mrs. Harlow began to whisper, hissing, "When I returned, just a few minutes ago – "

I held up my hand abruptly, and she stopped speaking. Then, holding a finger to my lips, I finished my prepared speech, in case someone was already in the house, listening. After all, we knew that there was a secret space behind the walls of the under-stairs closet, and it hadn't yet been searched. "Good evening, ma'am," I growled. "Sorry to bother you so late in the evening, but we've a report of a gas leak in the neighborhood. Have you noticed anything unusual? Have you smelled any gas?"

She shook her head, and I said, to remind her to speak, "What's that, ma'am? I'm a bit hard of hearing."

"No," she said, her voice almost a croak. Her hand was still on my arm, and I realized that she was trembling. "Not a thing."

"Where are the pipes? I asked. "In the cellar?"

"No," she said, calming a bit. "There is no cellar. They are out back, in an area near the small garden."

"Ah, then," I replied, making a few heavy footsteps across the hall. "Let me just see if I smell anything." I took a quick and noisy turn toward the back of the house, and then returned to where Mrs. Harlow was watching. "Nothing inside then. I'll just give it a check outside and then speak to your neighbors. Sorry to intrude." And I opened the door before immediately slamming it shut – while I remained inside.

Then I put my finger to my lips once again and nodded toward the parlour, on our left. As she led me in, Philip stepped aside and I removed the heavy coat that had served to minimally disguise me. She took it from me and then stepped close, indicating that she wanted to speak. Leaning toward her, she breathed with a quiver in her faint whisper, "When I returned home, only a few minutes ago, Molly was gone!"

I immediately remembered that, when she had fled the house earlier, the body of her cat had been left behind on the hall floor. I wanted to ask further questions, and to return to the hall and examine the scene to see if I could observe any signs of how it had been removed, but I realized that I needed to follow Holmes's instructions. Therefore, I simply nodded, I hope reassuringly, and indicated that I would now be taking a seat in the darkened room, as planned.

She pursed her lips a bit, as if she'd expected me to rush to examine the scene, or to somehow notify Holmes of this development, or to at least ask questions in my own strained whisper. However, when it was apparent that I was going to stay in the parlour with Philip, she mouthed the word, "Tea?" and I shook my head. She then set my coat on a small divan near the front window and walked out – quite stiff as she passed from the room, as if expecting a blow to fall at any second from a figure lurking just outside, or fearing that someone would jump from the dim surroundings with a heart-stopping scream –or perhaps she was just irritated with me as well.

And so began one of those long nights of waiting for something to happen. I only spoke to Mrs. Harlow one other time that evening, whispering so softly that I barely formed words, telling her that she should repeat her typical nightly routine, going to bed and locking the door behind her. Holmes hadn't specifically mentioned this, but it seemed to make the most sense. And as for Holmes himself? I had no idea where he was or what he was doing, but I assumed, having known him for so long, that he would reveal himself when the time was best.

We heard as she made her dinner, and I regretted not eating something earlier, when I'd had the chance.

Around ten o'clock, Mrs. Harlow walked to the front door, ostensibly to check the lock, but actually to peer into the dark parlour and raise a hand, as if saying farewell to each of us. I acknowledged with my own wave in return, and then I heard her go up the stairs, her pace slow and her feet dragging, as if she were climbing a gallows. Philip and I sat in darkness. In a moment, from deeper in the house, came the muffled sound of her bedroom door closing and the lock turning. Seconds later, I heard the sound of a sob, as if she had finally given way to the terrible grief that had gripped her throughout the day.

But it occurred to me then that, while I was correct to hide as soon as I'd pretended to leave, as per Holmes's instructions, I hadn't been able to search the house, and that she might very well be in danger. Whatever had been terrorizing her had been content so far to do so at night when she was safely in her room, while it had the full run of the rest of the house. But she had been away today for an hour or so, and during that time, her bedroom was undoubtedly accessible. What if she was being attacked right now? The intruder, having hidden itself in her bedroom, could wait until she locked the door, believing herself to be safe, and then she would turn around, only to discover . . . .

Just the thought of it made me stand before I realized it. Philip glanced at me in surprise, but good lad that he was, he didn't make a sound. I was nearly on my way to pound up the steps, calling Mrs. Harlow's name and telling her to open the door, when I stopped myself. Creeping to the hall door, I held my breath, trying to calm my heart and ignore the blood rushing in my ears, hoping not to hear any indications that some type of violence was occurring just a few feet above me.

But the house was silent, without even the typical creaks and settlings that one so often ignores, but nevertheless occur steadily. Even the lady's sob had only occurred once. Finally believing that she was in truth safe behind her locked door directly above us, I crept back to my chair, nodding reassurance to Philip.

There was no thought that I would sleep, but I did wish again that I'd thought to provide myself with something to eat. I was aware that food was certain to be found at the rear of the house, just a short excursion along the hall to the kitchen. But of course there was really no question but that I would remain where I was. I had been hungry before, and I knew that I'd survive it, as would my young companion.

I had just checked my watch to see that it was a little after one o'clock when I heard it – a sound barely noticeable above the steady fall of the rain outside. At first I wasn't sure that I'd heard anything at all. Perhaps there had been a noise out in the street. But I became convinced that it was real, and that it had been inside the house – a low thump, such as what a door makes when it's closed.

I arose slowly, cursing as my knees cracked. However, I was certain that my aging joints couldn't have been heard even five feet away. I glanced at Philip, and he nodded – he'd heard the noise from the other part of the house too. Walking forward with careful steps, and grateful that the house seemed solid and that creaking boards wouldn't betray my movement, I paused at the hall door, the boy waiting behind me, looking warily around the door-frame at the stairs.

I nearly fell back, with the primitive part of my brain reacting in terror at the sudden and unexpected hellish vision before me. It was tall, well over six feet, but it would have been even taller if it had possessed a head. Arms dangled at the sides, flopping forward and backward as it came to the base of the steps from somewhere in the back of the house. Then it turned and started up, rising from one step to the next, making no effort to grab the bannister for support. The shoulders were very broad, and only served to emphasize the absent head. But the twisted and mutilated aspect of the figure was only the merest part of its horror. For as it climbed, a hideous moan was building from within it, a low tone to a shriek. Even as I watched, it progressed into a terrifying ululation that pierced my ears. And throughout, perhaps the most terrifying of all, it appeared to glow with an inner fire that rippled and shimmered across its surface with every movement.

And yet, this light didn't appear to illuminate the stairs around it. It was self-contained, as if the figure burned with its own inner radiance, seemingly pulling an unholy fire from some other dimension that only barely pierced our own. Altogether, it was a hideous sight, and I wondered what Mrs. Harlow would have thought if she'd actually encountered it, rather than simply hearing its scream and movement from the other side of a locked door.

And yet, this phantom climbed the stairs, an action wherein its physical being interacted with solid materials – Verily, it *had* to touch each physical step to propel itself upward. There was nothing supernatural about that. It didn't float above the floor, or choose to suddenly glide, or apparate from one place to another, appearing instantaneously outside the poor woman's door. It pushed itself, one step at a time, up from the ground floor, and as I watched it do so, I recalled a similarly glowing figure from nearly a decade before that had to run across the fog-shrouded wastes of Dartmoor in order to pull down its terrified prey, rather than simply materializing from the ether, as one would expect a vengeful spirit to do. That had been a real beast that could be killed – and this was certainly the same.

Yet, even as I felt for my gun, I saw another movement in the hallway beyond the stairs. The headless monster had just reached the top and had turned out of sight when a second figure appeared, also moving to the foot of the steps at a near run. While not nearly as frightening as what had just preceded it, the other was no less disturbing. It was a normal man, or at it was least shaped like one. But while the first had glowed with an unholy fire that seemed to undulate with every movement, the second was a black void, a darker darkness against the lesser of the unlit hallway. It mounted the steps lightly and ascended two at a time. Believing that I dimly understood, I followed, motioning Philip to stay back until the danger had passed.

What I saw as I reached the top of the steps and turned to face down the hallway filled me with dread. The tall headless figure, still producing the nerve-tearing shrieks, had somehow managed to wedge its hands into the doorframe itself, and was lunging back and forth to the sound of cracking wood. Meanwhile, I was shocked to see that there appeared to be a second set of arms hanging from the creature's shoulders, swaying each time it tugged at the door. An entry was quickly being forced, and inside I could hear the terrified moans of Mrs. Harlow.

Then the door broke free and flew back into the room on its hinges. The figure made no move to enter, but rather stood there, swaying and moaning, it's horrible cries gradually coalescing into understandable words: *"Get out! Get out!"*

I raised my revolver, intending to shoot it down, intent on stopping that hellish shrieking and hoping that my bullets could destroy it, even as we had once fired on and killed the deadly Baskerville hound. Only then, just before I pulled the trigger, did I notice the black figure standing between me and the monster. It had planted its feet and, shoulders thrown back, and it yelled in a well-recognized voice, "Enough!"

As if a door had been slammed on a terrible storm, the sudden silence was shocking. The tall monster froze, both sets of arms dangling down from its great shoulders, while beyond in the bedroom we could hear the quiet weeping of our client.

"Watson," said Holmes, revealed now to be the figure in black. "Come forward. But keep your distance from this villain. He is a cornered rat, and might very well try anything." As I moved nearer, Holmes shifted slightly to the left, and I saw that he held his riding crop. Reaching forward, he prodded the broad shoulders of the creature, only dimly outlined by the light coming from the street window past him at the end of the landing.

"Mrs. Harlow," called Holmes. "We are here, and we have a gun trained on your persecutor. He is nothing other than a very evil man. Please light your lamp." The creature shifted then, as if planting its feet to either dash past us desperately, or even to throw itself through the window behind it and out to the street.

"Halt!" cried Holmes. "Watson, if he moves again, shoot him in the leg."

The figure settled back then – a collapse of apparent defeat, and with a very definite movement, but an action with a better intention than escape, and therefore I didn't shoot him. Without being told, the intruder dropped a metal pry bar at his feet. Light appeared from the bedroom as the lamp was lit, better illuminating the tall shape, and suddenly negating the unearthly glow that had been spread across its clothing, revealing instead a series of dull whitish stripes – some sort of luminescent chemical smeared onto the cloth.

Holmes took a cautious step closer and, making a more forceful jab this time with his riding crop, he pushed again at the figure's shoulders. With the sound of rubbing cloth, the whole structure started to slide, falling to the floor and revealing a rather harmless looking plain man, half-turned in our direction, and blinking rather stupidly in the dim light.

"Phillimore!" I said, nearly lowering my revolver, before Holmes snapped in response.

"Not James Phillimore. Rather, his cousin, Edward Harding."

Moving closer, I could see that, in spite of whatever name that he was called, this was the man whom we had located two years before, in a room at the Charing Cross Hotel.

Beside me, Holmes was dressed entirely in black, and I could see that he had darkened his face as well, so that he would be nigh invisible in the darkness. He reached into his coat and pulled out a police whistle. After several long bursts, I heard a curious thump, and within moments we were joined by Inspector Lestrade and a brace of constables as they scrambled up the stairs.

"Is she all right?" was the inspector's first question.

Holmes nodded, wiping the lamp-black from his face with a handkerchief. "I don't think that he intended her any permanent harm – at least not yet. Convincing her to abandon the property was his goal. Isn't that right, Harding?"

"I have nothing to say," said the man whom I had believed to be James Phillimore, quite a bit more surly and harsh than his previously portrayed personality would have suggested.

"No matter," said Holmes. "I know most of the story, and we'll soon have the rest of it out of you. Constables – please remove him to the sitting room downstairs. We'll join you shortly."

The officers moved past us and took Harding into custody. Kicking the construct that had fallen from his shoulders out of the way, they quick-marched him in front of us and down the stairs. I moved past Holmes and Lestrade to the bedroom, where I found Mrs. Harlow nearly in hysterics. However, she soon understood that she had simply been harassed, although to a remarkably terrible degree, by a man and not a monster, and she rallied most satisfactorily.

She asserted that she was feeling strong enough to join us in a moment and hear the explanation from the man being held downstairs, and we left the room to wait for her while she dressed. As her door closed, Holmes lit one of the lamps standing on a side table and then leaned down to pick up the item knocked from Harding's shoulders. In the light it was obvious that it consisted of a headless construct simulating broad shoulders, attached to a set of straps that had held it onto Harding's frame, fitting over his own head and giving him the illusion of great height. It was draped in an oversized shirt and dark coat, and the arms hanging from the sides were tied off at the wrists and filled with what turned out to be sandbags, causing them to dangle and swing in the odd way I'd observed when he'd climbed the stairs.

"Devious," muttered Holmes, tossing it aside once more.

"Mr. Holmes," said Lestrade, "Who is that man?"

"All will be revealed," replied my friend vaguely. Before he could be asked to elaborate, the bedroom door opened, and Mrs. Harlow joined us. I looked to see that Philip was standing at the top of the stairs. I hoped that he had stayed away when there was a chance of gunfire, but I doubted it.

Downstairs in the sitting room, we found the constables standing on either side of the man identified as Edward Harding. Two more had joined them, and another was standing by the front door. The prisoner was in a straight-backed chair, and I was glad to see that his hands were now manacled.

"There's really no need for you to explain much of anything, Mr. Harding," said Holmes. "I've waited quite a while to make your acquaintance once again, but I didn't expect that it would be in this fashion, or so fittingly at this location." He turned to me. "Would you care to enlighten the Inspector, Watson, as to our first encounter with the gentleman two years ago?"

I then related how, at the time of the mysterious disappearance, Holmes had tracked the man that we believed to be Phillimore from his hiding place behind the closet to the Charing Cross Hotel . . . and let him go. Lestrade exhibited a variety of emotions as the story was revealed, from surprise and wonder to frank irritation when learning that Holmes had discovered the solution but hadn't bothered to share it with him. While agreeing that no crime had been committed, he was properly resentful that the case had been allowed to remain open on Scotland Yard's books for so long, being logged as something of an embarrassment to them.

"And to you too, Mr. Holmes," he added, although like me, he certainly realized even as he said it that such a consideration would be of no consequence whatsoever to the consulting detective.

118

"I didn't see the harm in it then," replied Holmes with a frown. "Men disappear all the time, and there is no law against it. I'll grant that this method seemed eccentric, and overly complicated, but people's motivations are often that way. But it was only later that I realized that I'd been duped."

"How so?" I asked.

"It was when I recalled that the man we believed to be Phillimore was still legally the owner of this house. Did he simply choose to walk away from his investment here, or did he somehow have a plan to sell it? Out of curiosity, I checked the records and saw that it had sold quite soon after his supposed disappearance. But if he had truly disappeared, how could any legal affairs such as sale of the property be carried out? There was no body to prove that he had died, so in the eyes of the law he *wasn't* dead. There were no apparent heirs to have him declared deceased in order to take possession of the house. And yet . . . the house *had* sold.

"I did a bit more research, learning that the woman who bought the house – *you*, Mrs. Harlow – had no connections to Phillimore, so it wasn't a legally contrived transfer. I also found that, in fact, ownership of the property had been transferred to one Edward Harding – this man – some three weeks *before* Phillimore's disappearance, and it was he who sold you the house. The arrangement was accomplished through an attorney in Southwark named Shaplow. I arranged an appointment with him, only to discover that he was quite infirm, although stubbornly refusing to give up his practice – the perfect man for such a scheme.

"I managed to convince him to reveal to me that he'd never actually met James Phillimore – the man had never visited his office – or witnessed any signatures, but instead he'd simply filed, for a substantial fee, a set of signed property transfer papers that were presented to him by his client, one Edward Harding. These being legal documents, they had to be recorded under the true names. Therefore, Harding was the owner of Phillimore's house at the time of the man's disappearance, and it seemed quite probable that Phillimore had no knowledge that his house had just been stolen out from under him before he vanished.

"Old Shaplow could only provide the vaguest description of Harding, and it was of no practical help whatsoever. When I subsequently searched for more about the elusive Mr. Harding, it was as if he no longer existed – as if he had disappeared too. I could prove through various records that he'd been born, and I discovered that he was Phillimore's cousin, the son of the missing man's late aunt. He had no other living relatives besides Phillimore. Harding himself had seemingly vanished two years before Phillimore's disappearance, following his near-arrest in connection with an extensive embezzlement scheme, but there were no indications as to his current whereabouts.

"It was then that I suddenly looked at Phillimore's disappearance from a slightly different perspective, and realized that there was no proof, other than the acknowledgement that Watson and I received at the Charing Cross Hotel, that the man we had confronted there *actually was James Phillimore*. There were no photographs in Phillimore's house to show his appearance – if there had been, Harding had removed them so that there could be no positive identification – and if any images of Phillimore had existed in Miss Amherst's possession, no one had thought to retrieve them from her. To be certain, I did revisit her soon afterwards, and she confirmed that she had no photographs of her missing fiancé. I made certain during that visit to obtain her description of him, but it was singularly vague and unhelpful – it could have been the man that we met at the hotel, and it could have been the attorney's client, Harding. What I learned from Phillimore's former co-workers was just as useless. They could have been describing any medium-sized man with brown hair and plain features. Harding looks very much like their representation of Phillimore – hardly a surprise, considering their family connection.

"I felt then that I could piece together the situation quite well by that point. Phillimore had come into an unexpected inheritance from his great-uncle Willoughby – a man who was also *Harding's* great-uncle. Harding, who had already fled from his previous identity to avoid prosecution several years earlier, was apparently disqualified from receiving a share since he'd vanished, and couldn't legally claim it without reappearing. He conceived of the idea of taking what his cousin had inherited by arranging things so that Phillimore would seem to have vanished.

"After he cleverly arranged the disappearance to seem as mysterious as possible, he would leave a trail for me to follow, especially prepared with the types of clues that I'm known to observe – the footprints in the dust, for instance, and the costume shop receipt for the constable uniform, which laid a clear trail to Willoughby at the Charing Cross Hotel. Harding additionally made sure that I was involved by repeatedly writing anonymous letters to the editors of various newspapers regarding the disappearance, in spite of the police efforts to keep the affair quiet, and then he further specifically demanded that I be involved. There was really no way that I wouldn't examine the house and see what I was supposed to see. I would find him, blindly following the trail that he had constructed, and then he would hope to convince me with his seemingly harmless story that he – as Phillimore – just wanted to start anew, and that he should be allowed to stay hidden with the assets that he'd already transferred to different accounts under the name 'Willoughby' – again without his naïve cousin's knowledge through the use of forged documents.

"There was always a chance, of course, that I'd simply wash my hands of the matter and notify the police that Phillimore had been found, in which case he could still hope to flee. No doubt a plan was already in place for that eventuality as well. If nothing else, he'd simply return to whatever identity it was that he'd held since vanishing as Edward Harding – which is likely what he's done over the last two years, sinking back into that life when 'James Phillimore' was found at the Charing Cross Hotel, and I trustingly fell for his scheme like a fool, giving my blessing that his version of Phillimore should be able to go away and start over fresh, leading a brand new life. I allowed him to slip away, with the stolen inheritance and other resources that he'd siphoned away from his ignorant and trusting cousin." He turned to the prisoner. "When I realized that I'd been fooled, Mr. Harding, I set out to find you, but you had truly vanished. You had gone down a hole and pulled it in behind you. Yet, I've never stopped looking. Imagine my surprise when you reappeared here, at the house where it all began!"

"But Mr. Holmes," said Lestrade, puzzled. "If what you say is true, then we still don't know where the *real* James Phillimore is located."

"Ah, but I fancy that we will shortly." He turned to Harding, who had listened the entire time with his lips so tight that they appeared to have vanished. "Would you care to share the rest of your cleverness, or shall I?"

The man seemed determined to stand mute, and so Holmes continued. "It really is a unique tale, and I'd think that you'd be quite proud of the discovery. I only became peripherally aware when I was looking at the records of the sale of the house. I saw that it was built in the mid-1870's, upon the ruins of a much older church that had stood here in Highgate since the middle ages. I – "

"The brochure!" I interrupted. "In your scrapbook, next to your notes on the Phillimore investigation!"

"Exactly!" cried Holmes. "You didn't think to read the brochure when you refreshed your memory, thinking it was simply adjacent to my notes, but it was actually a part of the case. When looking into the records of the previous ownership transactions, I saw that this property, and the other houses around it, were built on what had originally been a church, and I was curious enough to obtain further information. As I assembled various facts, I learned that the crypts of the church still exist, underneath this row of houses. In fact, they can still be entered from a locked gate at the north end of the block. You stated, Mrs. Harlow," he said, turning toward our client, "that the house has no cellar."

She cleared her throat. "That's true."

"Not exactly," Holmes countered. "It wasn't constructed to have a cellar as such, but the crypt is located directly beneath us. In fact, I've only discovered tonight that the hidden chamber behind the closet wall itself opens yet again to a further narrow stairway, obviously constructed around the time that the house was built, leading down into the spaces below. When someone was able to get in and out despite the locked doors, I theorized another entrance, and thought that the hidden chamber behind the closet might have an additional opening – something that I should have seen two years ago." He turned to Harding. "How long have you known of the crypt?"

Still the man refused to answer, but his expression had become more calculating and watchful, as if he was concerned as to which direction Holmes's explanation was taking.

"You've certainly been using it to get in and out of the house this past week. I wonder if your cousin knew as well, or if it's something you figured out later. Apparently," Holmes continued, "you remained in contact with the real James Phillimore, even after disappearing as Harding and taking on a new identity. How did you explain to him why you had disappeared – or was he even aware of it? Your crime wasn't widely reported at the time. Did you remain in touch with him after you fled as Harding, or did you only re-establish relations later, after he received the inheritance from your mutual grand-uncle, when you decided to take it away from him? No matter. You were clearly the man whose footprints were in the closet, and who wore the rented constable uniform, and who left a trail for me to find from this house to your room at the Charing Cross Hotel. That will be enough to hang you."

Lestrade cleared his throat. "Yes, Inspector," Holmes continued. "I will explain. When I heard Mrs. Harlow's story this afternoon, giving this address, and specifically how someone was gaining access to it, in spite of locked doors, I immediately recalled what I had incidentally learned about the crypts while trying to track down the truth behind Phillimore's disappearance of the last couple of years. It reminded me that one might be able to get into the houses by way of that route. This evening, after Watson and young Philip returned here to keep guard, I found the builder who first constructed these houses twenty years ago. He confirmed that such an entry was possible, if someone had discovered the existence of the crypts and had made alterations in one of the houses to access them.

"The builder and I entered the crypt, exploring under this row of houses until we found the crude wooden steps that had been built to lead up to the foundations of this very address. That was when I summoned you and your men, Lestrade. After that, Watson, we placed the crypt entrance under observation. As expected, a man surreptitiously made his way in a little after midnight. We followed and watched as he, ignorant of our attention, climbed the steep steps up and into the bottom of this house. He was carrying something – which turned out to be that contraption that he'd strapped on to look like a giant headless monster. He ascended the crude steps into the space built into the back of the hidden closet. We immediately followed, and I pursued him the rest of the way up the stairs while Lestrade and his men came through and then waited downstairs in the hall. I was in time to see Harding carrying out his most bold and threatening move yet, attempting to force his way into Mrs. Harlow's presence to terrify her into abandoning the house – at least long enough for him to carry out an adequate search."

"But for what?" asked the lady herself, now quite recovered, and clearly very angry at the prisoner seated before her. "What is it that he seeks? And why now, after I've lived here for two years?

"That specific answer still eludes me," replied Holmes, "although it may have something to do with the man who first owned this house from the time that it was built in the 1870's. You'll have heard of him, Lestrade. Elias Bates."

I saw a light of recognition pass across the inspector's face. Sensing my confusion, he answered, "Bates was a most notorious fence, Doctor – made all the worse by the fact that he simply couldn't be caught. We knew what he was up to, but his methods always proved too much for us. Do you mean to say, Mr. Holmes, that this was *Bates'* house? And that he was the one who first built the secret closet, and the passage behind it, in order access the crypt, and then use it for his own illegal purposes?"

"Undoubtedly."

Lestrade nodded and sat back, as if all now made sense.

"When age overtook Bates," continued Holmes, "he simply closed up his operation, retired, and moved away. As you know, he died in Surrey several years ago, having never once been jailed. Years later, long after Bates had left London, the house was purchased innocently enough by James Phillimore, and it seems that he somehow discovered both the closet and then the access behind it to the crypt below while in the process of making himself at home. He foolishly shared that knowledge with his cousin Harding, who then made use of it over the course of the past week to enter the house while attempting to intimidate Mrs. Harlow into leaving." He glanced at Harding. "Now, having circled back to the lady's question, would you care to explain why you would do such a contemptible thing?"

Harding licked his lips, darting his eyes from Holmes to Mrs. Harlow and back, before speaking for the first time. "It started out innocently enough. I had some of James's papers, after he . . . disappeared, but I had never took the time to look through them. When I finally did, I saw something – a diary from this Elias Bates fellow. James must have found it in the house, likely left behind, and tucked it away. It was quite old, and reading between the lines, so to speak, it seemed to reference a cache of jewels that Bates had hidden here – or so it seemed to me. James had never mentioned this diary to me while he was – before he disappeared. After reading it, I decided that he must have been trying to find the jewels himself. They may not even be here – Bates may have taken them with him when he moved away – but there was always a chance that they could still be hidden somewhere about, if only someone took the time to seek them. I decided to see if I could find them. But the diary was vague, and I had no idea just where to look. And this woman here – she never seemed to leave or go anywhere so that I could get in and search the house! Or if she did go out, it was at random times, so that I could never count on getting in and being allowed any peace.

"I didn't want to hurt her, but I was getting frantic. I have . . . I have some debts that are due. The other night, I decided to sneak in after she'd gone to bed, and look all night if necessary. I came in through the crypt, just the way that James had discovered when he'd moved here, and I set about exploring, looking for some clue. But I accidentally bumped the table outside of her bedroom, and when I heard that she'd awakened, I froze. Then, not knowing if I could get back downstairs and out through the passage before she came out of the bedroom, I made as if I were some sort of ghost. Hoping that she was too scared to investigate, I then escaped down and out through the passage.

"After I'd had a chance to think about it, I realized that I might be able to scare her away for a much longer period of time, and I began to try more and more elaborate attempts each night. And yet, she refused to budge, no matter what I tried. Claws on the door. Flammable chemicals painted in the shape of footprints, and written as a warning. Nothing worked – she never went anywhere!"

"So," said Holmes coldly, "you escalated the stakes and killed her cat."

"I did. I left the closet slightly open during the day, and lured the cat in with some food. Then I caught it and killed it. I would have brought it back out that night, but she never went upstairs. So I waited and waited until I heard her sleeping the next day and then crept out, leaving it where she'd find it in the hall." He licked his lips in a curiously reptilian fashion. "It worked," he said, showing no apparent remorse. "She left."

Without a word, Mrs. Harlow rose and stepped forward. Then she slapped him, the force of it creating a loud *Crack!* and turning his head violently. Before he could react, both constables pushed down forcefully on his shoulders, apparently preventing him from rising if Mrs. Harlow wished to give him another. Instead, however, she sobbed and stepped back, turning away from him.

"I wonder if your cousin knew what he was letting himself in for when he shared the secret of the crypt with you," said Holmes. "He probably did it innocently enough – I've found no evidence that the real James Phillimore was as reprehensible as you are, Harding. The poor man never knew that sharing that curious knowledge would eventually lead to his death."

"Now hold on," said Harding, holding a hand to his face, still red from the vicious slap. "James planned his disappearance on his own. After he received the inheritance, he felt trapped – just as I told you when I pretended to be him in the hotel room. He knew that I had changed my name and taken a different identity, and he decided that he wanted to do the same thing. He asked my advice, and he arranged everything – including the payments to Willoughby."

"Then why were *you* the man who carried it out?"

"He . . . he was afraid. That he couldn't bring it off. He was never bold like me. He asked me to take his place in the house and pretend to be a constable."

"Then why the rest of it?" I asked. "Why leave clues leading to the hotel, and arrange that Holmes be involved at all. Why not simply vanish through the secret stairs and into the crypt?"

"We . . . wanted a witness, someone eminently trustworthy, and sympathetic, in case something ever came up, legally, to verify that someone had seen James *after* he disappeared – that he was still alive, but without giving away the secret. To testify if needed that he hadn't truly vanished."

Holmes nodded. "Strangely, that part makes sense. I learned that there were some irregularities with your great-uncle's estate, wherein the sales of various additional properties had to be arranged after the initial inheritance. In case Phillimore's legal participation was required, you could discretely contact the attorney handling the estate, show up to sign whatever was necessary, a summon me there to verify that *you* were actually James Phillimore, and that I was still keeping your secret and that all was above-board – even if you were choosing to live in anonymity.

Harding nodded. But then Holmes asked, "Where, then, *is* the true James Phillimore? After you staged the disappearance, your part was finished, and he was free to assume his new life. But how could he do that, as *you* had arranged for control of the accounts where his inheritance had been placed, and *you* were now the owner of this house?"

125

Harding was startled. "Oh, yes," Holmes continued. "You took over ownership of this house. Where does that fit in your explanation of selflessly helping your cousin?"

Harding again licked his lips, glancing from one to the other of us in rapid succession. He seemed to be coming apart before our very eyes. He began to speak, talking faster and faster, as if drowning us in words would make his story more believable. "He fell soon after we made our plans. He hit his head. And I realized that the inheritance, and everything else that he had, would be lost. I couldn't reveal myself as his cousin to make a claim on his estate as his only living relative – not without resuming my identity as Harding. And even if I did, the family relationship didn't seem strong enough to establish me as his heir. His plan for a new identity was already in place, and I simply took advantage of it."

Holmes shook his head with a smile. "You should have simply stood mute, Mr. Harding. Now you've opened the door. No, no, it really won't do. Certainly your cousin died, and I expect when we examine the body – and we will – we'll see that he did die from a blow to the head, but I seriously doubt that he fell. You forget, I had already long ago worked out your plan to take everything he had, and that you had done so several weeks *before* his disappearance. You had already taken ownership of this house, through the forged papers at the attorney's office. Your cousin James was still among the living then – he was still going to work every day, and he was still affianced, however unhappily, with Miss Amherst. He had in fact spent the entire day prior to his disappearance at work, and showed no signs of agitation. He was clearly a man who didn't realize that he'd been fleeced of everything that he owned, and that he was living on borrowed time.

"He may have come up with the original idea to disappear, as you say, but once you realized that what he intended, you saw a way to make it work to your advantage. You killed him and took his place."

Harding made a growling noise in his throat and tried to lurch to his feet before being slammed back once again by the massive hand of one of the constables. Holmes ignored him, turning instead to Lestrade. "Inspector, you're as aware as I am of just how difficult it is to dispose of a human corpse. I would advise that a thorough search be made of the crypt below. That seems to be the most likely place. I suspect that you'll find Mr. Phillimore buried somewhere, either in a shallow grave, or tucked in with one of the other permanent residents. Perhaps he'll be hidden behind or underneath some rocks. But be careful – it's possible he's been covered in quick-lime, and I'd hate for any of your men to accidentally plunge their hands into it, or stir it up and breathe the dust."

Lestrade waited until morning before sending a team into the crypt, armed with digging tools and powerful torches. They entered through the gate at the end of the street, as directed by the builder who had assisted Holmes the previous evening. He led them down into the dank passages. Holmes and I, on the other hand, walked along the street to Mrs. Harlow's house, where she let us in and joined us at the closet door beneath the steps. We left her there, standing in the hall, while we passed through and down the rude stairs into the chamber below. Holmes pointed out some aspects of their reinforced construction, obviously added at some point after the house was initially built. Then we stood there, watching the police lanterns moving this way and that through the forgotten crypt, but ever closer, in the distant darkness, waiting for word about the discovery of James Phillimore's body. It wasn't long in coming. Within a quarter-hour, the poor man had been found, buried under a loose cairn of stones seemingly borrowed from other graves, his head crushed by a far heavier blow than could have never come from a simple fall. The autopsy would reveal a twisted and broken neck as well. As expected, the corpse was covered underneath the rocks in quick-lime, in the mistaken belief that it would hasten decomposition – although it did do a great deal to prevent any signs of decay that might reveal the body's location.

Harding's arrest and reappearance under his own name set off something of a frenzy, as one past crime seemed to lead to another, like peeling the layers of an onion. The capital crime, however, superseded the lesser, and he met his fate on a cold morning a few months later at Newgate Prison, after his pathetic attempts to claim insanity were quickly disproven.

If Elias Bates hid a cache of jewels in either the house or the crypt, it was never found, although I understand that intruders are regularly caught trying to conduct illegal treasure hunts underneath the row of houses where the ancient church once stood.

Mrs. Harlow, despite the week of terror that she'd been forced to endure, recovered quickly, along with the realization that she needed to find friends and interests away from her home. She began to interact with her neighbors, and from there her influence began to spread, eventually leading her to establish the highly respected mission in the East End for which she has since become well-known. More importantly, she took an interest in young Philip Barsby, orphaned at a young age, and eventually adopted him.

I ran into her a month or so later, not having seen her since the events of that terrible October night. She informed me that her cat was doing well, as if I would know of what she spoke. Seeing my ignorance, she laughed and said that she wasn't surprised. She'd had a feeling, when Holmes had brought her a kitten just days after Harding's arrest, that he wouldn't be advertising the fact.

As she walked away, I considered how I would address this act of kindness when I saw Holmes that evening. But then I reconsidered. Obviously he hadn't wanted it to be known, and I found that just the knowledge of his gesture was satisfying enough, without making him aware that I knew. Sometimes friendship is allowing someone else to keep his secrets.

The Keadby Cross

"We're closed! Go away!"

The man on the other side of the locked tavern door said something that we couldn't hear, but his expression gave us to understand that he was not pleased. He grabbed the door handle one more time, gave it an angry shake, and turned away, joining and then vanishing into the other passers-by in the street. My eyes stayed drawn to the door and surrounding windows for a moment, looking at the sharply etched scene in the bright morning sunlight while our friend continued to speak.

"They wake up thirsty," said Isaiah Clark, "and take no account of the time. He'll have been drinking until three or four in the morning, and now here it is, not yet ten o'clock, and he's ready to start again." He shook his head with pity. "Poor old sot."

"Wasn't that Alfred Penrith?" asked Holmes.

Clark nodded. "He was of some help to us, if you'll recall."

I remembered the name, and couldn't believe that the man was still alive. He had provided a valuable bit of information during our pursuit of the Whitechapel Killer, and more important, Penrith had later roused himself from an alcoholic stupor when one of the Rippers attempted an ambuscade in Hanbury Street, distracting the man long enough that Holmes was temporarily able obtain the upper hand and send the murderer's blood-stained bayonet clattering onto the pavement. Our attacker had escaped into the warren of allies and passages that surrounded us, eluding even my friend for a time, while I'd remained behind to treat Penrith's wound, a cut along the length of his arm that was fortunately minor. It was then that he remarked that he'd received worse while in the service, and he mentioned a few details of his bravery with Wolesley at Amoaful, and the medal that he'd won there.

As I'd finished binding up the poor vagrant's wound, I had considered that I could have ended up in the same situation as Penrith – wounded in battle, returned to England, and left adrift and without purpose and a head too full of terrible memories. Just weeks after the *Orontes* had put me ashore on the Portsmouth jetty, I was already drifting toward profligacy and starting to pass my empty days with drink, a tendency that had devastated my poor brother, when a chance encounter with an old friend led me to the laboratory at Barts Hospital on New Year's Day, 1881, and thus my introduction to Mr. Sherlock Holmes. He and I had agreed to share a flat in Baker Street, and doing so immediately improved my behavior, decreasing my alcohol consumption in – as I see now in hindsight – what had been an attempt not to give this new acquaintance the impression that I was an incipient drunkard. Then, as I became more involved in his investigations, both my health and my aimlessness improved, each in their own way.

I have no doubt that this chain of my thoughts was apparent to Holmes, who glanced my way with a smile as I came back to myself, still standing by the bar in the Ten Bells in Spitalfields, while the owner, Isaiah Clark, continued to speak.

"There are so many like old Penrith," he said, "and some of us attempt to do what we can. I attend St. Mary's, and while the minister had some initial reservations about the owner of a pub like me actually having a soul, we've come to an accord. I'm in an odd spot, gentleman – something like the eye of the storm. Selling drink all day long, making my living from it, and yet trying to help those who are broken by it. It was through these efforts that I met Father Tim."

He was interrupted by another rattle at the door, this time from a heavy-set man in a long tattered coat and a battered bowler. In spite of his location, standing in the shadowed doorway, I could see that his nose, above a large and shaggy mustache, was oversized, misshapen, and discolored, either from *rosacea*, or chronic abuse of drink, or both. I have no doubt that Holmes could tell that and a dozen other things besides, such as whether the man was a retired Sergeant of Marines, or instead a former eye surgeon who had once served on a whaling ship before losing his practice following an adulterous relationship with the daughter of a friend while his own wife was dying of consumption.

The man looked through the door, rattled it once more, and then drifted away. "Let's go upstairs," said Clark, picking up the metal box that had rested on the bar while he spoke. "They'll never leave us alone down here."

He led us to a back corner of the room and then up the narrow stairwell to the first floor, consisting of a square space the same size as the bar below, identical in both its dismal lack of color and decoration, and presenting the same plain walls and ancient wood flooring. The only difference was that this chamber was empty except for a few rickety tables and chairs, while the downstairs contained the great square bar that filled the center of that room.

Clark led us to one of the tables by the tall front windows looking out onto Christ Church, just across Fournier Street, and then south along Commercial Street. Not far along I could see the corner of Dorset Street, leading to nearby Miller's Court, which will ever be associated with poor Mary Kelly. I shook my head. All around me, the East End was waking up, and the bright day with its brilliant blue skies might almost make one forget the horrors that had happened here six years earlier. And yet, as soon as Clark resumed his story, I realized that even though the truth of the Ripper murders had been discovered, though only known in its entirety to a few men such as Holmes and myself, the stain would never completely fade from this blighted place.

"I met Father Tim three years ago," said the big man. "He walked in one day, in a black suit and collar, and I didn't need to be you, Mr. Holmes, to see what his calling was, or that he was new at it – his clothes were new, the priest's collar was clean, and his hair was very neatly cut. He looked bright, like a new penny, – nothing about life seemed to have marked him. And yet, when I talked to him, I could see that there was a pain in his eyes – something haunted him. I never did find out anything about him – his past, anyway. He never even shared his last name. That isn't necessarily unusual around here – many men have secrets in Whitechapel and Spitalfields – but I did wonder sometimes. Yet it wasn't my place to ask.

"He explained that he'd rented rooms in New Broad Street, near the station, and that he wanted to help those in need – he said it just like that, without any specifics, and apparently without any kind of plan. I was busy, and I'd seen other do-gooders show up here before, taking a look around for a few days or so with upturned noses before wandering back to where they'd come from, thinking that they'd seen and learned enough in that short time to have a complete understanding of the poor unfortunates, and with material to color a lifetime of sermons. But he stayed, and I saw that he was actually out there amongst those who needed help – finding them shelter, helping them to get home at night, locating food or warm clothing, and most of all, simply talking with them, and listening in return.

"Like so many others around here, we became used to him, and began to trust him. He and I would talk sometimes of a morning – about the same time as we are now, before things get busy – and I soon learned that while he'd discuss people that we knew – those that needed help, or those who might provide it – he was very quiet about his own past. He didn't seem to lack for money, as he always had coins to give to those who needed help, but he didn't spend anything on himself. His black suit seemed to be his only one – I could tell because of a mended rip on the sleeve that was there day-in and day-out – and when that poor coat finally reached the end of its existence, he replaced it with a similar garment from one of the used clothing stalls in Petticoat Lane.

"And so it went, and the days passed, and soon he was as much a part of this little community as any of us. Over time, we became friends, of sorts. I might have been his only one. It was early this year that his landlady brought a message to me, saying that he was sick and asking for me. He didn't seem to want help from any other.

"I went to his rooms, and a plainer sight you've never seen. He had the fever – the Black Formosa Corruption – that was sweeping through the docks then. Possibly you remember it, Doctor? It was before you returned, Mr. Holmes. We hadn't seen it that bad since late '87. In any case, by the time that I arrived, Father Tim was out of his head, raving as the fever took him. I found one of the doctors from the ladies' shelters that would consent to see him, and he gave the landlady and me some medicine, but both she and the doctor seemed afraid to be in the same room with the poor man, so it was up to me to nurse poor Father Tim through the worst of it.

"One night, he was crying out and fighting to climb out of bed, but he was weak as a kitten. He kept calling for Lydia, and apologizing to her – he was weeping and wailing, and just when he'd drop off it would start again. Then the fever broke, and he fell asleep.

"He mended quickly after that, and I didn't mention what he'd said – we all have secrets down here, you know. Within a few weeks he had his strength back, and things resumed as they were, although we were perhaps better friends than before. Possibly that's why, just a couple of weeks ago, he spoke of something that was different from our usual conversations.

"We were sitting right here at this very table. 'I have an item that I wish for you to hold for me,' he said, and then he pushed this very metal box across the table. 'I mean to write a letter to go with it,' he said, 'explaining what it is, but . . . but I just haven't been able to find the courage to do so quite yet.'

"I know that I looked surprised. I generally keep an even expression when dealing with the public downstairs, but I suppose that I'd let down my guard around Father Tim. Something like this was unexpected, and I showed it. He hurried to explain – but he didn't really explain anything.

"'I assure you that there is nothing wrong here,' he said. 'What's in the box belongs to my family – to me. It's simply . . . something from my past that . . . I couldn't leave it behind. I've had it hidden in my room, underneath a floorboard, and in the three years that I've lived there, I've never had any reason to worry about my hiding place being found. But a couple of nights ago, someone went through several rooms in the lodging house. It was one of the other tenants who had become desperate enough to do that, seeking money for drink. I don't believe that he had any idea that my box was hidden there – I haven't taken it out since I first put it under the floor, and one cannot tell that such a hiding place even exists. But since my room was entered, it's been on my mind, and I decided to see about putting it in a safer place. I suppose that I could go to a bank, or leave it with a lawyer, but I'm disinclined to do so. Instead, I thought of you, my friend. You have a safe. Could you keep it there for me? I should really just let it go, but I can't bear it. And soon I'll put a letter with it, so that if should something happen to me, you'll know what it is . . . .'

"He drifted off then, as if lost in his memories. In the meantime, I was naturally curious, but he was my friend, after all, and as you can see, this little box wouldn't take up much room. I agreed, and he looked relieved, and when we finished talking about other things, he went downstairs with me to my office below street level and saw it placed into my safe.

"And I thought no more about it, until two days ago, when he was murdered."

Holmes nodded. "I saw the reports in the press. It seemed like a rather senseless crime of violence – he was struck terribly in the head and found very close to here, I believe."

Clark nodded toward the window. "Just on the other side of the church there, across from the graveyard where the lane opens into Harriot Place – not much more than a mews, really, running through to Fashion Street."

"Is there any idea why he would have been there – in the middle of the night as I recall?"

"No, but it wasn't unusual, either. All of us here use the alleys and cut-throughs to get where we're going, and in Father Tim's case, he could've had business anywhere, checking on someone that needed his help."

"And at any time of day," Holmes added.

"That's right. A lad had taken some food to his father who was working nights at the chocolate and mustard mill on Wentworth, and had come back by way of Brick Lane, and then along Fashion before cutting through Harriot. It was just a random decision on his part, he said, to go that route on his way back home, and if it hadn't been him who found Father Tim, then it would have been someone else soon after, I expect. It may get dark here in the East End, but it never actually goes to sleep."

"I confess that I noted the matter," said Holmes, "but haven't seen anything reported since then."

"Because there hasn't been much to report," said Clark. "I'm surprised that it was in the newspapers at all. Probably they only mentioned it because he was a man of the cloth."

Holmes nodded. "And you don't think that any progress has been made?"

"None at all that I've heard. I spoke to the sergeant that was sent around from the Bishopsgate Station the next morning, but no one has been by since then. But," he added, "the sergeant did mention that a witness had been found – John Llanfair, an old drunk who claims to have heard the attack. He was lying in the cemetery when he heard an argument in the direction of where the body was found. The sergeant was inclined to dismiss this story – he wasn't even sure that old John even knew which day was which – but there was one part of the story that makes it seem true. John mentioned that Father Tim cried out the name 'Lydia' during the argument."

"Did you tell the sergeant that you'd heard that name before – when you were caring for Father Tim earlier this year?"

"I did, and after that he seemed to credit John Llanfair's story just a wee bit more.

Holmes's eyes dropped to the table. "But you didn't tell him about the box?"

"No. Truth be told, at first it didn't occur to me, and then, thinking how Father Tim had acted and his story about his rooms being searched, I decided to ask you about it first, in case there's some connection."

"I see that the little lock has been cut."

Clark nodded. "I felt that I ought to. Father Tim never came back to leave a letter as he'd said he would, but I thought that there might be something inside that would be helpful – the name of a family member, for instance. Someone who might like to know what had happened to him. Instead, I found this . . . ." And drawing the box toward him, he raised the hasp and lifted the hinged lid. It was a small tin box, about six inches square and three deep. From where I was sitting, the interior wasn't visible, but Clark reached in with his thick blunt fingers and pulled out a handful of sparkling fire.

Or so it seemed as the morning light from the high windows beside us lit it up. It was an object in the form of a cross, encrusted with a vast number of gems – at first glance there didn't seem to be any metal showing whatsoever, with every surface faced with some jewel, either large or small. But then I saw that there were some plain surfaces here and there, highly polished, and catching the light as strongly as the stones.

Saying "May I?" Holmes reached for the object. Clark handed it to him and then sat back, as if he had transferred a burden. Holmes looked at it this way and that, and then again with his glass. He held it at different angles to the sunlight and then walked to the window. I noticed that he was careful not to simply hold it up where it would be visible to anyone looking up from the street one floor below. Then, having seen all that he could during that examination, he returned to his seat, handing it to me, saying, "It is most unique, and no doubt worth a fortune – not simply for the jewels themselves, but because of its apparent age and most unique craftsmanship. There is certainly some fascinating story associated with it. Besides the great artistry involved, the metal seems to be platinum, or some related alloy – and as I understand it, platinum is extremely difficult

134

to adapt for this type of purpose. I seem to recall reading something long ago about such an item, and the rumors of a lost process that went into its construction." He shook his head. "The facts elude me for now, but they can be located easily enough."

While he had been speaking, I'd continued to examine the piece, and quite frankly I'd never encountered anything so elaborate, yet perfect in its simplicity. Perhaps that is a contradiction, but seeing it that morning, and recalling still after so many years, I cannot puzzle together a different description. It was in the shape of a Celtic Cross, about five inches long, and covered along the front, back, and sides with jewels. The larger stones were along the main faces of the cross, and there were many smaller stones located along the sides and within the curve of the ring. The stones were arranged in an orderly fashion, and the simple color choices were most pleasing, with rubies running along the main upright and crosspiece, and emeralds around the faces of the ring. Smaller diamonds served to accentuate them, cunningly placed so that when each caught the light, it seemed to reflect back toward the adjacent stones. It was tempting to keep staring at the piece, turning it this way and that as if an even better and more pleasing angle could be found with just one more fractional turn. Sensing that I had looked at it long enough, I returned it to Clark, who held it without the same interest while Holmes turned his attention to both the tin box and the small cut lock beside it. Seemingly there was very little to be found there, for he quickly finished and said, "Nothing useful."

He handed the box to Clark, who replaced the jeweled cross inside. Then he immediately closed the lid and pushed it back across to Holmes. "You'll be needing this, and I have no use for it."

Holmes took the box, saying, "After Father Tim left it with you, did he mention it again? Check on its welfare, or ask to verify that it was still in the safe?"

Clark shook his head. "He did not. I saw him a few times after that, but we only talked about the things that had always passed between us – those in need, and efforts by some of the local churches and their effectiveness."

"And you wish me to locate to whom this object is connected?" asked Holmes.

Clark smiled. "I like how you put that, Mr. Holmes. There's a lot left unsaid when expressing it that way. I don't know why Father Tim had this, or how he came by it, or if it was even completely his, in spite of what he told me. Do you think that he was killed because of it?"

Holmes shook his head. "These are early days. We really don't know anything – but there are a number of threads to take up, and I shouldn't be surprised to know a lot more within just a few hours."

He asked a few more questions, such as where Father Tim's lodgings were located in New Broad Street, the name of the sergeant who had been by the morning following Father Tim's murder, and how to find John Llanfair. Then by mutual accord we stood and adjourned downstairs.

As we descended, Clark asked if we'd like anything to drink, but we declined. We entered the bar, and I was surprised for just a second when the room suddenly darkened. However, I realized that a large dray wagon with barrels of beer was pulling to a stop on Fournier Street just outside the corner doorway of the pub and blocking nearly all of the morning sunlight. Clark seemed apologetic as his attention was now needed elsewhere, but we said our farewells, stepped around the burly horses waiting patiently at the front of the wagon, and then walked across toward the steps of Christ Church, where we could talk relatively uninterrupted.

There was some sort of bazaar taking place on the church's front lawn, and several women looked suspiciously at Holmes as he walked through the displayed clothing without a glance. I nodded and attempted to appear friendly, but after we reached the steps, I glanced back and saw that we were still the subject of glares from several irritated organizers.

"Thoughts?" asked Holmes succinctly.

"Father Tim had a secret past," I speculated. "He showed up without any explanation. His choice of lodgings and clothing were humble. He had no obvious source of income, yet he seemed to have funds available. He was somehow able to pay for food and his rent. And of course there is his possession of this object." I nodded to the box in Holmes's hands.

"Ah, but anyone might seem mysterious under certain circumstances, and no one is obligated to simply provide an explanation about themselves – and in a location such as this, such explanations especially aren't expected. It isn't necessarily sinister that he chose not to share his past – or even his full name. And his possession of this object could be completely legitimate." Only then did he slip the box into the pocket of his Inverness. "As I said, there are several paths to explore, none any better than the others. As it's the closest, I suggest we start where the body was discovered – although I don't expect to find anything useful there."

He was correct. Leaving the bazaar behind, we walked around the front of the church and along the graveyard to the opening of Harriot Place. Holmes then slowly explored along the pavement for several moments, sometimes bent at the waist to see better, but never actually dropping to his knees and crawling as he did in some circumstances. A few times he would lean and touch something with his finger, including one spot about the size of a dinner plate that looked suspiciously like a dried blood stain. Finally he rose and brushed off his hands. "The body was there," he said, indicating the stain. "He was certainly struck down at this spot, for this is

136

where he bled as he died. But there is nothing else that I can see. Let us see if Mr. Llanfair is where Isaiah thought."

We crossed Commercial Street and into the Spitalfields Market, where Llanfair was indeed earning a few coins unloading boxes of produce for one of the stalls. The owner frowned when Holmes asked to borrow him for a couple of minutes, but he became more receptive when a few coins changed hands.

In the end, Holmes paid Llanfair as well, but he had nothing of substance to add to what we'd already heard.

Two nights earlier, the night had been quite fair, with a waxing moon high in the sky. Llanfair had acquired a bottle and made for a spot that had sheltered him before, alongside one of the larger ornate gravestones beside the church. It was there that he'd fallen asleep, and where he'd later awakened to hear an argument nearby, in the direction of Harriot Place. There were two men, he said, and their voices rose for several minutes before the sound of a terrible blow ended the argument – no other words were spoken.

"Did you go to see what had happened?" said Holmes.

The old man shook his head with a shamed expression.

"And you reported to the police that you heard Father Tim say 'Lydia'."

Llanfair shook his head. "That's not right. It was the other voice – the angry-sounding one – that said it. He said it twice, just before I heard the sound – well, it must have been when he did for Father Tim. They showed me the body, and I believe that's what I heard – when his head was crunched in."

The man had nothing else to offer, and we thanked him and left the market, with our next stop being the Bishopsgate Police Station.

We walked down Commercial Street, and then along Dorset Street. I sensed that Holmes had chosen this route specifically, but I was unsure of his motivations. It was almost as if he had decided to do so in order to show that the place had no power to intimidate him, but I rather felt as if we were whistling past the graveyard, as they say in America. We soon passed the narrow entrance to Miller's Court on our right, and my best intention to blithely ignore it quickly failed as I glanced that way, looking into the dim and hellish passage, recalling those terrible events of the early hours of 9 November, 1888, when the Ripper's maddened butchery reached its apex. My physical wounds from that night had healed, but I still carried the scar, and I knew that neither Holmes nor I would ever forget what we had seen in that cursed room, which in itself was only the tiniest piece of the overall catastrophe making up that nightmarish autumn.

Exiting the other end of Dorset Street felt as if we were emerging from a dank crypt, having outpaced creatures in the dark who would have pulled us down like wolves in a dark winter forest. The equally poverty-stricken streets of the remainder of our journey – Raven Row, Artillery Passage, and Widegate Street – seemed almost festive in comparison. Soon we were in the bustling Bishopsgate Road near Liverpool Street Station, and then walking into the stolid Bishopsgate Police Station.

Asking for Sergeant Corby, we were kept waiting in the lobby until a tall man in his thirties appeared from somewhere in the rear of the building. We had worked with Corby before, most recently in the curious affair of the brewer's murder, where Holmes had been trapped with a madman in the lost tunnel running underneath Pall Mall to St. James's Palace. The matter had begun with a rich man's strangling and finished with the recovery of a lost relic – and the sergeant's marriage to the brewer's daughter.

Corby was glad to see us, and after a few questions back-and-forth as to one another's welfare, and with the glad news that his wife was expecting, he led us back to a cramped little office where we could discuss the murdered priest. After confirming what we'd been told about the discovery of the dead man and Llanfair's story, Corby responded to Holmes's question as to the body's current location.

"He's in St. George's Mortuary, in Cannon Street Road. We thought when the body was found that there might be more of an uproar than there was, him being a priest and all, and we wanted to put him out of the way, so to speak. It turns out," he continued, "that there hasn't been much interest at all – which is sad, considering the good works that the man accomplished."

"Has anyone from any of the churches stepped forward to claim an association?"

"No, and in spite of him wearing priest's clothing, I can't find much else to corroborate it. There was nothing related to any formal ministry in his room. There isn't much information about him anywhere. There have been no responses to our inquiries outside of London. I haven't been able to find anyone else who saw or heard anything the night of his murder either, or who knows anything about this 'Lydia'. His room was remarkably empty – no letters or photographs, or even a magazine or newspaper, and there was nothing on the body except for this worn testament." He opened a desk drawer and pulled it out. Holmes took it and looked through it with great care, but finally returned it to the policeman with tight lips. "Nothing," he agreed. "Only a few months old from the looks of it – probably bought to replace another in the same way that he replaced his suit when it wore out."

"From what I've been able to determine," said Corby, shutting the drawer on the small black book, "the man had no enemies, and never had more than a few coins on him at any given time – so there was nothing to steal. Of course we all know that just a few coins that are nearly worthless to some are a treasure to others. Still, it was probably just an encounter with one of the drunks or disturbed men that are everywhere here – either home-grown, or a sailor that has already left port. Something was said, and the killer's temper flared . . . ." His hands, which had been folded on the desk before him, parted as he shrugged. "We really don't have any ideas where to look next." He refolded his hands. "Might I ask your interest?"

"We were approached by his friend, Mr. Clark, the proprietor of the Ten Bells." He didn't mention anything else, leaving that explanation to stand for itself.

That seemed to satisfy Corby, who knew Holmes and understood that my friend would say what he meant and no more. The officer nodded and stood, ending the interview. "Well then. Of course we'll appreciate any information that you find." Thus dismissed, he led us back to the lobby.

Outside, the street had become quite busy with the noon-time traffic. "I noticed that you chose not to share the contents of the tin box with the sergeant."

"It may or may not be a factor in the man's death, and if not, then it doesn't necessarily need to be brought to the attention of the official force. We may be dealing with two different questions."

I indicated that we ought to next examine the dead man's rooms, located just around the corner, and Holmes agreed. We found a rather tidy building, unusual in that particular part of London, and when we spoke to the landlady, Mrs. Carpenter, it was apparent that her strict influence was the reason why. She recognized both of us, stating that she'd been at the funeral of one of the Ripper's victims six years before when we had both been in attendance. She led us up to Father Tim's room, first floor rear, and stood in the doorway with me while Holmes made his examination.

"He knocked on my door three years ago, in the summer, responding to a sign that I'd put in the window just that morning about a room to rent. One of my long-timers, Mrs. Wittering, had passed away from a kidney complaint – we thought it was cancer, but the doctor only gave her some pills. It was terrible to watch her fade, and so fast, putting all her hopes in that useless medicine. No offense intended I'm sure, Dr. Watson."

I nodded and she continued. "Father Tim moved in with not much more than the clothes on his back and started helping with the poor from the first day. I asked which was his church, but he said that he was simply a minister of the streets."

She fell silent as Holmes systematically continued his investigation around the room. She watched with a sharp focus as he crawled along the floors and baseboards and, while still on his knees, lifted the thin and worn mattress, turning it this way and that to see if something might have been concealed within. After finding nothing, he stood and remade the bed before falling to his knees once again, quickly locating the floorboard where the tin box had been concealed. I glanced at Mrs. Carpenter and noticed her surprise when it was revealed, but she withheld comment.

Holmes replaced the flooring and then moved to the rickety deal bureau, looking behind and underneath before opening each drawer and then removing it, checking to see if anything had been hidden behind or concealed within the framework of the piece. He poked through the few items of clothing that were there before he finally reassembled the drawers, asking, "What was Father Tim's last name?"

She seemed surprised, and then she had to think. "Smith, I believe. I think that's what he said when he introduced himself – but really, there was never any need to use it after that. We always just thought of him as Father Tim."

Holmes shut the last drawer and looked around at the rest of the room to see if he'd missed anything. It had a small cot-like bed, a chair and plain table, and the bureau. There were a couple of ratty curtains hanging by the sole window, and the blanket on the bed was worn but clean. There were no decorations in the room whatsoever, and from the fact that Holmes had removed nothing from the bureau or the cavity in the floor, I knew that neither of them had offered anything of importance.

"Did he have any friends?" I asked. "Did anyone help look after him when he was sick earlier this year?"

"Ah, you heard of that? Then you've talked to Mr. Clark of the Ten Bells. He was the poor man's only friend. Other people liked Father Tim, but he never let anyone get too close, if you know what I mean. But Mr. Clark does a lot of work for the poor, and that put him and Father Tim pulling in the same direction more often than not. When Father Tim was so sick, no one wanted to be around him. I confess, I had qualms myself. I have a friend whose brother knew someone at the docks who worked with a man whose cousin died of the Black Formosa Corruption! It sounds dreadful!"

"It is. Was there anyone in the building," I pressed, "with whom he talked? Anyone to spend his spare time of an evening?"

"He didn't really have any spare time," was the answer, "and while he would take evening meals here, he would usually go back into the streets afterwards to help the unfortunates. Up early, out late – that was

Father Tim. Day in and day out – except for the days when he'd go away altogether."

"Indeed?" said Holmes. "And when did that happen?"

"Every few weeks, I suppose. Once a month for a few days at a time, actually."

"And was this his habit from the beginning?"

"Oh, no, only since last spring. He came in one afternoon, quite in a hurry and flustered he was, and said that he'd be back in two or three days. He didn't say where he was going, but he returned as he'd promised."

"And what was his mood when he told you that?"

"Hurried, as I said. Maybe a little anxious, as if he was trying to be away as soon as possible."

"Did he tell you every time that he went after that?"

"No, just the first two or three occasions. Not the more recent times."

"This is October. How often did he go away?"

She counted to herself, and then said, "Six. He started in April."

"That covers the six months. Hadn't he gone away this month as well?"

"No, not yet, although now that you mention it, it was just about time for him to go. He always went in the middle of the month – just for a few days. I remember, because it was always soon after that the rent was due, and he'd pay me before he went away. He was never late with that."

I asked her the amount of the rent, and it was quite modest – not surprising in this part of London. Meanwhile, Holmes pinched his lip as if searching for a reason for the priest's behavior, or why it occurred in the middle of the month. Then, seeming to set it aside for the time being, he thanked Mrs. Carpenter and allowed her to take us back to the street, chattering all the while.

"Well," I said as the door shut behind us and we walked up the narrow lane, "the groundwork is laid, and the routine examinations have been made: Talking with a friend, looking at the scene of the murder, questioning both a possible witness and the police, and then examining the dead man's lodgings. I suppose that next we take a look at the body."

"Yes. We progress, Watson – although to what end I'm not yet sure."

As it was farther than we wanted to walk, we finally found an unoccupied hansom in Brick Lane and set off to St. George's, the mortuary where the body had been taken. "What do you expect to find from an examination of the corpse?" I asked.

"Not much, I'm afraid," said Holmes. "This mysterious figure shows up from out of nowhere three years ago in a new priest's suit, and then seems to keep barely any more than that clothes on his back thereafter, replacing them only when necessary. He lives an apparently blameless life, well-known in the community but without any close associations – even Clark wasn't in his total confidence – and then he meets his death violently in an alley across from a graveyard within feet of a major thoroughfare – without explanations or clues. The name 'Lydia' has been mentioned twice, but we have no context, so for now that fact is of no use. His room showed nothing of interest – not a hint of a motive, and nothing about him as a person."

"There was obviously nothing in the bureau. I take it that the cavity hidden beneath the floorboard was empty as well."

"Not even a helpful scrap of paper or a pinch of strange dust."

We grew silent then, each with our own thoughts. I know now what Holmes was considering, but I was thinking about the streets around us, where we had spent so many nights patrolling through the autumn fogs, hoping to prevent additional murders while trying to pick up any threads that might lead us farther along toward a solution to the tangled Ripper killings.

It seemed no time at all before we arrived at St. George's. The fine old church presided over a brutal neighborhood, just a couple of blocks north of the London Docks. The smell of them was in the air – a different scent from the pervasive rot and filth that always hangs over Whitechapel and Spitalfields, even on that clear October morning. Sensing the change, I realized how easy it was to reacquaint myself with those odors without conscious thought. It's the same for a surgeon, who quickly becomes familiar with the mephitises produced by the human body, or for the engineers who maintain the London sewers – or so one of them has told me – in that the offensive vapors of the sanitary pipelines become easier to tolerate with time.

We ignored the main entrance to the church, instead walking to the side in order to approach the small area used as a mortuary. The last time that we'd been here was on the morning of 30 September, 1888, following the murder of Elizabeth Stride in nearby Berner Street. I noticed it in more detail now, as that visit had occurred quite early, and there had been many more things on my mind than cataloging details regarding the building and its surroundings.

The mortuary, too, had its own smells, long familiar to both me and my friend. We identified ourselves to an attendant and were led to the sheet-covered body, one of three or four in a row on slabs at the back of the low-ceilinged room.

Father Tim was in his mid- to late twenties, likely a little over six feet, and thin. In fact, his body, while lanky by nature, was nearly emaciated. There was a scent of ketosis about him, in addition to the expected early signs of decay.

"Holmes," I murmured. "He's been starving himself."

He simply nodded and continued his examination.

The young man had reddish hair and was clean-shaven. The wound on his head would have been instantly fatal – the left side of his frontal lobe was completely caved in. It could tentatively be assumed that he'd been struck by a right-handed man from the front. The blood had been washed away, and while Holmes would have preferred to examine the injury *in situ*, it was more visible that way.

The dead man's hands were rough, but there were no scars, and the nails were even, with no signs of nervousness, as would be shown if they were bitten down. His feet were quite calloused, as if he did a great deal of walking, and he had the beginnings of a bunion – he hadn't bothered to invest in the proper shoes.

Holmes and I both noted the scar on his lower right side of the young priest's abdomen, and then Holmes moved to an adjacent table, where a basket held the dead man's clothing. I could see that it was the plain and worn black suit as described to us, and Holmes's examination was quick, as there was clearly nothing to find. I could tell that the suit had an unwashed scent about it, as if Father Tim, whose body was itself clean, would bathe and then re-wear the same clothes.

With little left to find, we thanked the attendant and returned to our cab. "The surgical scar showed great skill," I said as we settled ourselves. "Most likely from an appendectomy. Could it indicate that Father Tim came from a comfortable background, with access to proper medical attention and a good doctor?"

"It's possible, although it doesn't firmly establish the fact. Poor men can also obtain medical treatment, even surgery, and a well-stitched scar doesn't have to be placed only by an expensive surgeon. It's indicative, but we can't make any firm conclusions from it."

With that, I didn't see that we had learned all that much, but the proper procedure of examining the body had been carried out, and there was still another avenue to explore. "The cross?" I asked, and Holmes nodded. I wasn't surprised that he directed the cabbie to an address in Hatton Gardens. I briefly considered intruding a thought about finding something to eat, but there would be time enough for that later, after every lead had been explored. We passed through Aldgate and circumnavigated the narrow streets around Barts to end our journey at the residence of Silas Hull, a retired jeweler who owed more than one debt to Holmes.

By then, Hull was not the famous figure that one recalls from the seventies and eighties. He had attached himself in those earlier days to many of the flamboyant figures that were regularly mentioned in the press. This practice had nearly ended with his imprisonment when he was implicated in a string of jewel thefts carried out by the younger son of Lord Byington. When questioned by the police, the arrogant lad had tossed out Hull's name, along with a number of others, in an attempt to confuse the issue. Over the years, Hull had made enemies, as he discovered to his surprise, and when his name was associated with the thieves, however falsely, many were quick to believe the accusations and use them to undercut his position in society. A year or so before this had occurred, Holmes had recovered some stolen objects for Hull, and thus it was because of this that the jeweler sought my friend's help in his time of jeopardy. Hull's innocence was established following a tense confrontation in a Mayfair drawing room. A careless comment by Lord Byington's sister had brought forth the truth, fortunately overheard by Inspector Lestrade, who had allowed himself to be folded and concealed behind a heavy sofa in order to record the confession from the true culprit.

We found Hull in poor health, smoking cigarette after cigarette while his browned fingers turned the cross over and over, muttering all the while. He wheezed and coughed, pulling himself upright each time to find capacity for the breath to do so. He had quite caved in during the months since we'd last seen him, and I feared that he was not long for this world. In truth, he lived another twelve years, never leaving his apartment throughout, before finally setting his bedsheets afire with a carelessly tossed-aside match.

"It is the Keadby Cross," he wheezed almost immediately after his gnarled fingers closed upon it. However, having identified it so easily, he continued to examine it. "Not seen in a generation at least. Where did you find it?"

"There is no doubt then?" asked Holmes, parrying Hull's question.

"None at all," the old man sighed, sounding like a collapsing and leaky bellows. Then he reluctantly he handed it back to Holmes, who replaced it in the tin box, and that into his coat pocket. Lighting a cigarette from the old one that had been smoked to the nub, Hull continued. "It is unknown when it was made, or where. The method of working the platinum is unknown – lost. That kind of thing happens more than you might realize. Only now are we starting to understand how to use platinum in jewelry. This is an ancient process – an ancient piece. The jewels are unusually cut – not a modern method or style at all. They are especially fine and pure. The cross was brought back from the Crusades, but as to its history before? Who knows?"

"And to whom does it belong?" asked Holmes.

Hull gave him a curious look. "You don't know? Well, that's interesting. It belongs to the Keadbys, of course. It was Sir Ashton, back in the first Crusade – sometime around 1100 A.D. – who carried it home,

144

and it's been in the family ever since. Or so I thought. The fact that you have it, and didn't know whose it was, is most interesting . . . ."

He left the statement hanging, but Holmes asked another question. "Keadby. Would that be the family from Sparsholt?"

Hull nodded. "It would, it would!"

Holmes frowned, as if that fact provided a darker aspect to the matter.

Hull clearly wanted to know more about the cross, and when it became obvious that no further facts were forthcoming, he tried to interest us in other bits of London gossip in a rather pathetic attempt to keep our attention and lengthen our visit. We stayed and talked for a few more minutes to be polite, but when Hull started slyly delving for the true details of the Hinstock thefts, and what had really happened with Lady Ava's suicide which had so recently been reported in all the newspapers, Holmes stood and thanked the old man for his help. I glanced back at Hull's disappointed visage as the door shut, watching him lighting another cigarette with shaking hands.

Outside, Holmes hailed a cab, giving the address of a club in St. James's. My mouth tightened – I knew that he was seeking further information regarding the Keadbys, and where we were going to obtain it.

As I stepped from the cab, I looked up at the bow window of the club where Langdale Pike spent his days, and saw the languid man watching us. Even from that distance, and with the morning light playing tricks on the glass, his smile at our arrival was obvious.

During my time in the army, and also during certain of Holmes's investigations, I'd had the opportunity to visit the warm climes where reptiles are far more common than Britain. There are some that crawl out on rocks each morning to absorb the sun's warmth, only moving when necessary, to feed or carry out other basic functions before returning to their lairs at night. I didn't know exactly where Pike's lair was located – in his club perhaps, or in a nearby building – but his daily settlement in the bow window, where he gathered those bits of random stories, tales, and tittle-tattle that earned him his bread-and-butter, always reminded me of the actions of those cold-blooded creatures, and I never approached him without feeling the same sort of distaste.

He and Holmes had known each other for many years, and I knew that my friend felt much the same as I did, but Pike was one of the useful tools in Holmes's drawer, and he had his purposes – such as this case, where he almost certainly held some knowledge of the Keadbys.

"Holmes! Watson! It's been too long," said Pike, attempting to right himself from where he'd been sprawled on a purple divan. Thank heavens there were solid and sensible chairs sitting nearby. I imagine that Pike had learned early on to supply them for his informants. "I haven't seen you since you called about that business last June in Whittesley Street. Did matters end satisfactorily? I confess that I've been unable to ferret out exactly what happened next."

"The Duke fled," replied Holmes succinctly. "With his wife's blessing." He leaned forward. "What do you know of the Keadbys of Sparsholt?"

Pike's watery eyes widened, and a wily smile turned up a corner of his mouth. "Now that is an interesting tale. Do you want something to drink?"

We settled for tea which was soon delivered, and Pike tipped something into his from a pocket flask. I sipped mine gratefully, but Holmes pushed his aside. "It's rather a sad story," Pike explained. "The Keadbys were once a great family, but are now down to the very last of them – should he even still be alive. Still a lot of money, though."

Holmes didn't comment, and after a sip, Pike continued. "Five years ago, Sir Brent Keadby died. If you recall, he owned a number of mills in the north, all managed by very competent managers and lawyers, leaving him free to live the life of a country gentleman. He had been widowed for many years, and upon his death, he left behind two children, twins, both in their early twenties: A son Timothy, and a daughter Lydia. These two couldn't have been more different. The boy was always a disappointment to his father – considered weak by the irascible old man, who was well into middle-age before the children were born. Timothy had no interest in business or the family affairs, being instead a scholar of sorts – fascinated by religion, as I recall. He would have been happy to hide away at some university, wandering through the libraries for the rest of his washed-out life. His sister, however, was much more direct about her necessities, and she always got along well with her father, having seemingly inherited his brusque traits. In spite of their differences, the two twins were always close, even though they went along very different paths. Lydia remained in Sparsholt while Timothy went away to school."

"You acted as if one of the twins was still living – 'should he still be alive'," I said. "Yet you also mention both of them in the past tense."

"Yes. About four years ago, not quite a year after Sir Brent died, a man – Stephen Lett – began to pay court to Lydia. His family has something to do with the docks in Southwark, and apparently they met when both were in Portsmouth on unrelated business. You know the type – suave, mysterious, intriguing, and clearly after her fortune. I suspect that she knew it, but it's likely that she saw something useful about him – or so she thought – and she probably believed that she could control him. She should have done a little research. He's at least twenty years older than she was, and he'd had two previous marriages that ended in the unexpected

146

deaths of his wealthy brides. In any event, he moved quickly and married her – it was a nine days' wonder – and took possession of the house in Sparsholt, as well as making himself free with his wife's half of the fortune. From what I heard, she quickly realized that she had opened her door to a scoundrel, but as is always the case, it was too late.

"The marriage was tense from the beginning, as would be expected, and Lett soon resented being trapped in Hampshire for so much of the time. My little birds were quite informative, and they willingly shared, for a few coins here and there, how the arguments escalated when the marital familiarity bred expected contempt. There were rumors of cries in the night, and bruises upon the young lady that weren't really explained by her stories of a sudden clumsiness that had never previously affected her.

"Timothy, who had been pursuing studies in Durham, came home to try and stand up to Lett, and that's where the story becomes a bit more murky. I've had the statements from three people who were there, and they are in agreement, but what they've related to me only tells part of the tale. On the night that Timothy arrived, there was a tremendous row between him and Lett – with a great deal of shouting from the both of them, and Lydia as well, all behind the locked doors of the late Sir Brent's study. It went on for hours, long into the night, but at one point things fell abruptly silent, and eventually the servants went to bed, realizing that the evening's entertainment was at an end.

"The next morning after the fight, the servants were told by their mistress that Master Timothy had departed in the night to return to school. But a few weeks later, one of the maids saw a message Timothy's school in Durham, inquiring as to his whereabouts, as he'd never returned after his visit to Sparsholt. Of course that only fed the fires of rumor. Later, when months went by and no word was ever heard from Timothy, the whispers below stairs ripened into open belief that Lett must have killed young Timothy in the heat of the argument, with his sister's apparent approval, but that seemed to be no more than sensational speculation.

"After Timothy's departure, Lydia seemed to have forgiven her husband for whatever stood between them. And yet, soon after the night of the argument, Lett began to act more agitated. He was seen on a regular basis searching the house for something, but he wouldn't reveal what it was and reacted angrily when any help was offered. Over time, whatever warmth that had reignited between husband and wife cooled, and again there was a pall over the house, while Lett continued to run through his wife's inheritance. She resumed having unusual bruises, making no effort to hide or excuse them, and then she began to drink more heavily. Of Timothy there continued to be no sign at all.

147

"And so it went, with Lett dividing his time between the Hampshire house and London, until last spring, when Lydia was found dead, apparently stricken by some sort of seizure in the night. Lett was home at the time, and found her. By all accounts, he was most dramatically grief-stricken. A doctor-friend of his quickly certified the cause of death as related to Lydia's ever-increasing alcohol consumption, and she was buried within days. Since then, Lett has spent most of his time carousing with his cronies at Sparsholt, with regular trips to London. Too regular, some would say . . . ."

"What do you mean?" asked Holmes, leaning forward. "Would these trips perhaps be around the middle of the month?"

Pike smiled and crossed his legs. "It would be lunacy to suggest otherwise."

Holmes slapped his knee, a smile on his face. "Of course – the fact that I couldn't recall! For the past six months or so, the full moon has occurred in the middle of the month!"

"Hold on for a moment," I interrupted. "Are you saying that Lett's trips into London are somehow related to the full moon?"

"And why not?" asked Pike. "Lett wouldn't be the first to feel such a pull. By all accounts – and I've heard that this has gone on for a few years – he becomes restless during the week before the full moon, and while his wife was alive, that was the period when the worst of their difficulties took place."

"And you have all of this information from the servants?" I asked.

Pike nodded. "It is well-known where such information may be delivered, and the messengers earn a small bit of financial gratitude."

"It strikes me," I said with a great deal of acid in my tone, "that you are only a few steps sideways from that bloated spider, Milverton. Doesn't he use the same methods?"

Pike's normally indifferent and slightly amused expression darkened in an instant, his lidded eyes flashed, and his voice hardened in a way that I'd never heard before. "The difference between that villain and myself," he said, his normally even-tones harsh and clipped, "is as divided as black and white. I would never use what I learn to injure anyone, and never to inflict pain through blackmail. The information that I gather is used to help in ways that you don't even realize, Doctor. If you only knew what happened to my parents while I was at university, you would never – "

He stopped suddenly, as if his throat had closed, and glanced toward Holmes, who was lost in his own thoughts. Then, by conscious decision, he settled back into the familiar Pike of the bow window, passing the day by watching the world slip by. Only now did I realize that the man whom I had seen all these years might very well be a façade of someone much more capable – and perhaps dangerous. Recalling that he and Holmes had known each other since their college days, and seeing how Pike had looked at Holmes when mentioning the misfortune of his past, I suspected that my friend had in some way assisted the gossip-monger at that time, but I was also aware that it was likely a story that I would never be told.

"In any case," I said to smooth the waters, "I don't disagree with you regarding the effects of the full moon. As any medical man will tell you, there is a demonstrable relation between the moon's phases and agitated behaviors, although some of the theories as to why this occurs are utter nonsense. We simply don't understand enough of the ways of the human mind to provide a full explanation."

Holmes had ignored this last exchange and appeared to be considering how to proceed. After Pike and I fell silent, we sat there for several minutes. Then Holmes spoke. "Watson and I are investigating a murder," he began simply, and then he told what we had seen and heard that morning, how Father Tim was certainly Timothy Keadby, who departed from his family home following the argument with Lett and showed up in London soon after, wearing priest's clothing to which he had no right, and devoting himself to the poor and downtrodden of eastern London. He finished by letting Pike hold the Keadby Cross.

"I would posit that after the argument with Lett concluded," Holmes stated, "Timothy Keadby was so mentally wounded, possibly by his sister's betrayal in taking Lett's side rather than his own, that he fled, convinced that he couldn't return to his former life. However, before he departed, he retrieved the family heirloom from wherever it was kept in the house, feeling that it couldn't fall into Lett's hands. He vanished into the warrens of Whitechapel and Spitalfields, apparently content to remain there."

"And meanwhile," said Pike, "after the suspicious death of his latest wife, Lett, now off the leash, began journeying up to London in the middle of each month – around the time of the full moon – either because of the city's opportunities to satisfy his peculiar tendencies that were absent in Hampshire, or the anonymity to partake of them, or both."

He emptied his teacup and rang for more. "I've gathered reports of some of Lett's activities while he's sojourned here in the capital. The signs of violence that were evident upon his poor wife in the months before her demise have appeared on a number of young women here as well. These unfortunates aren't of a social class to be able to successfully accuse him of anything, and yet they do have a certain amount of protection, and it is only his ability to reward them financially afterwards that has prevented his arrest."

The attentive waiter arrived with another pot of tea, and Pike and I accepted refills. Holmes waved away an attempt to replace his still-full and now-cold first cup.

"I'm glad that you sought me out," said Pike. "I've accumulated quite a dossier on Stephen Lett since he came to my attention, but I didn't yet feel that I had enough to notify anyone. The death of Timothy Keadby – and it is almost certainly him – adds a new layer to the affair. If we can establish that Lett was in London two nights ago when Timothy was murdered – "

" – then we still won't have enough to bring charges against him," finished Holmes. "It is nothing more than a supposition, a coincidence. But perhaps we do have enough of an idea to focus the investigation more intensely, with the result that we can uncover additional facts, and perhaps rattle Lett into making a mistake." And then he added, "I would advise a Council of War with the official force."

And so messages were sent to Sergeant Corby and our old friend Inspector Lestrade. It was decided that Pike's club was as fitting a location as any for a meeting, and while awaiting the arrival of the policemen, we had a late luncheon in the facility's well-appointed dining room. Holmes toyed with his food, as was to be expected, but I enjoyed mine, and found my attitude thawing toward Pike, who related a few facts that I hadn't heard about Milverton the blackmailer. Clearly he was accumulating them with the idea that they would be useful upon some future date when Holmes finally confronted the evil conniver.

We had resettled ourselves in the bow window when the policemen arrived. Holmes explained to Corby that the nature of our findings had necessitated a higher level of authority. Then he outlined our involvement, including both the facts that we had told Pike, and also what we had subsequently learned from him. Corby was stunned that Holmes had identified the priest in such a short amount of time, but Lestrade waved this away, saying that if he continued to work with Mr. Holmes, he would soon get used to it. Then the inspector leaned forward, asking, "What should we do now? I agree that there is almost certainly a direct connection between this Lett and the murdered man, but there is a gap between that and establishing Lett as the killer."

"As Pike mentioned before your arrival," answered Holmes, "we first need to find out whether Lett was in London two nights ago."

"Easy enough," said Lestrade, rising. "I assume that this club has a telephone?"

Pike gave him directions and, while we waited, Corby asked additional questions about the Keadby Cross. This led to the topic of the First Crusade, and Holmes related the curious history of Baldwin of

Edessa, the first King of Jerusalem, and his more well-known brother Godfrey, the defender of the Holy Sepulchre, and the curious letter related to both of them that Holmes had once secured from the collection of a Prussian poisoner because of certain damaging facts that it contained which cast dark implications upon the British Crown itself.

Lestrade returned, telling us that, "According to the local constable, who verified the information by way of his brother the station-master, Stephen Lett left on the up-train to London two days ago, was away on the night of the murder, and returned the following morning – that is to say, yesterday. He looked much the worse-for-wear, as he often does following one of his jaunts, but most curiously, he left again this morning on the London train."

Holmes nodded. "Today is the full moon – when he regularly visits the metropolis due to its strange influence upon him."

Lestrade frowned and shook his head. "One of those."

"It would seem so," was Holmes's reply. "But two nights ago he came to London because he was searching for his brother-in-law – and the Keadby Cross."

"That seems to be rather a leap, Mr. Holmes," said Corby.

"Not really," replied Holmes. "Consider: Timothy Keadby began leaving his lodgings in April – around the same time that Lett first began coming to London during the full moon after the death of his wife. It's safe to assume that somehow Timothy saw Lett and wished to lay low in order to avoid him. Possibly he was aware of his brother-in-law's lunar proclivities, or else he asked around and determined when Lett was showing up in London.

"In any case, he was successful at avoiding the man for half-a-year, but somehow Lett finally found him. He didn't just encounter Timothy by chance two nights ago near the cemetery. No, he was in London during a time when he would normally be in Hampshire. It was an intentional trip. He had a good idea about how to find Timothy. They argued, and no doubt Lett demanded the Keadby Cross, which he had sought ever since Timothy liberated it. But Timothy, probably certain that Lett had killed his sister, and yet terrified of the man, refused to turn it over, so Lett killed him. Only through Timothy Keadby's foresight in leaving the cross with a friend are we able to follow along and make sure that justice is served."

We formulated a plan over the next hour or so, with both Holmes and Lestrade slipping away at regular intervals – Lestrade to use the telephone, and Holmes to find and instruct one of his agents. Additionally, a police vehicle was sent to fetch Denholm Waitrose of Barbican, the long-time solicitor to the Keadby family, and when he arrived, he was able to provide valuable insight confirming how Lett had gained the trust of Lydia, and more importantly how Waitrose alone had known of Timothy's residence in London, being the source of the funds that the young man had used to pay for his meagre life.

He explained that when Timothy had originally returned to the family home at Sparsholt with the intention of protecting his sister, he had found that she was completely under Lett's spell. As the argument waxed and waned over several hours, it had become apparent that Lydia had been turned against her brother, body and soul, which broke his heart. Always quite sensitive, he couldn't conceive of returning to what he suddenly saw as an empty existence, duly attending his classes for no apparent purpose, and that very night he came to London, recreating himself as the priest who spent the rest of his life ministering to the unfortunates there. Until we told him, Waitrose hadn't known that young Timothy Keadby was the man murdered in Whitechapel – he was quite upset about it – and he'd also had no idea that the Keadby Cross had been carried away by Timothy when he fled Sparsholt, as no word about it had passed the young man's lips or had reached him by way of Lydia or Lett.

After the lawyer was thanked and dismissed, we debated a few final points, including whether our efforts would result in anything that would lead to Lett's arrest. "I believe," said Holmes, "that he has tasted blood, so to speak, less than forty-eight hours ago, and that he will find it easier to do so again. He is feeling powerful now, and arrogant."

"You speak as if you know this, Holmes," said Pike.

"Watson and I have encountered this man's type before," replied the consulting detective.

"As have I," concurred Lestrade. "If he's as affected by the moon as it sounds, there's a good chance that he'll be looking to kill again tonight."

While the inspector said this, Corby glanced at him, and I was glad to see that, despite his younger years, he was willing to listen and learn.

Finally, with our plans and facts and assumptions in place, we stood, prepared to commence our campaign. Pike shook our hands and gave us to understand that his contributions were limited to what he could provide from his divan, and that he expected to hear the end of the story – hopefully within the next twenty-four hours.

The resources of the officials were able to establish through questioning at Waterloo that Lett had arrived in London on the up-train from Winchester. The cabbie was located who had conveyed him to a small private hotel in Dysart Street, near Finsbury Square, and one of Holmes's Irregulars confirmed with the hotel's owner that Lett stayed there whenever he visited, like clockwork, in the middle of the month for at least the past six months.

The bright blue day had darkened as the hours passed, and by the time we concealed ourselves around Lett's hotel, there was the hint of dampness in the air that indicated fog. I dreaded it, recalling too many nights spent in this same manner, keeping an individual under observation, waiting for hours until he came out and moved around (if he came out at all), and then furtively and frantically following while ever-hoping that the rolling mists wouldn't provide him with cover just long enough to allow him to step out of sight and vanish.

I shrugged deeper into my overcoat, thankful that I had it, and also for my service revolver in my pocket – something that I had learned long ago never to leave behind.

Luckily we didn't have long to wait, as the pull of the full moon, still visible at times through the thickening clouds, exerted its attraction to our quarry. Just after six o'clock, he emerged.

We had circulated a description of Lett, as provided by Denholm Waitrose. Holmes had quietly confirmed it with the hotel manager, so it was easy enough to recognize the tall man who stood for a moment underneath the gas-lamp at the corner. High cheekbones on a thin face, with a rather thick and unpleasant mustache. Even from my position across the way, ostensibly reading a newspaper under the opposite gas-lamp, I could see that his unusual eyes matched their description: Very light, with a great deal of white showing around the pupils. In the dim light, it looked as if his pupils didn't exist at all, and that he was some reanimated lych setting forth in search of prey. I shivered.

He ambled off to the east, and his gait was unsteady, as if he had already been drinking heavily. He passed through Finsbury Market by the stationery works, and then set his steps to a public house on the corner of Vandy Street. Moments later, he was followed inside by Lestrade. My post was in the street, and I found a sheltered doorway in which to tarry for a while.

Lestrade later reported that Lett stood at the bar, tall and moving unnaturally as if he were supported by unseen wires that were being plucked randomly and from different directions. He looked around while consuming two pints in a quick manner before apparently deciding that what he sought wasn't there. He left quickly, and our group followed him as he again headed east – a mixture of plainclothes policemen, Holmes's band of irregulars racing ahead on the side streets, and of course my friend and me.

He walked alternately fast and slow along Market Street, turning into Appold Street just long enough to reach the passage underneath the wide expanse of railway tracks, and then he was soon in White Lion Street, just a few blocks north of the Spitalfields Market. At Commercial Street he

153

turned south, and within moments we were passing by the Ten Bells, where these events had started just that morning. He didn't spare a glance at the pub, but very soon, just after passing Christ Church, he turned into the graveyard, and then stopped at the entrance to Harriot Place, where Timothy Keadby had been murdered two nights before.

While it was entirely possible that Lett could have simply decided to visit the site where his brother-in-law had died, this was highly unlikely. Until that afternoon when Holmes connected the missing Keadby with Father Tim, no one knew the background of the dead man. In my mind, Lett's visitation of this spot proved his guilt.

He didn't pause there for very long. Back into Commercial Street, he crossed and went along Whites Row. The hour was early enough that there were still a number of people on the streets, and he attracted no attention – and more importantly, he didn't notice the crew that was following him. When he reached Bell Lane, he entered another pub, and this time Holmes followed him inside. The sense that I had jumped six years into the past, and the Autumn of Terror in 1888, was becoming rather overwhelming. All that had occurred in those intervening years – my marriage and subsequent widowhood, and Holmes's presumed death and reappearance – might not have happened at all. Here I was, once again tracking a killer through the streets of Whitechapel, the air cool with the approach of winter, and the poverty and despair of the district still as overwhelming as it had ever been. For a moment I wished that it was 1888 once more. I would make a number of different choices, and also provide words of warning for my friend, so that he never even considered approaching the dread ledge above the Falls of Reichenbach.

But I was forced back to the here and now when the pub door slammed open, causing a spill of noise to rush my way as sounds of the raucous crowd inside spilled forth. Stephen Lett was moving once again, and Sherlock Holmes was not far behind.

Our path roamed up and down the streets for the next half-hour. Lett paused when he saw a pair of unfortunate women loitering near Toynbee Hall, as if he wished to approach, but something prevented him from doing so. He visited two more public houses, leaving each soon after entering, before he spotted a solitary woman of the night near the public wash house in Goulston Street. He approached her with confidence, and apparently an agreement was reached quickly, for they set off together, turning into the darkness of Elison Street, and so into a mean little building squatting on the north side.

Once the door had shut, we collected nearby and quickly assigned posts for the various troops, some guarding the front, and some the back. Then Holmes, Lestrade, Corby, and I entered the building.

154

I had some misgivings about where to look, but immediately after ascending the stairs as quietly as we could to the first floor, we heard a woman's cry, fearful and then immediately silenced. Without hesitation, Holmes approached the doorway and kicked it open.

Thank heavens she was not dead, but it was a very close thing. Lett had the garments at her throat bunched in his left hand while the right held some sort of short-bladed knife – I would later learn that it was originally a specialized instrument used by farriers for popping stones from out of horses' hooves, but the end had been ground and sharpened to make it lethal. The woman was bleeding from a blow to the head, and appeared rather dazed and senseless. As the door slammed open and the four of us crowded in, Lett seemed confused, but also as if his senses had fled. His light eyes appeared to be blank and empty, and I didn't sense that he understood what was happening. Then, as if his compulsion controlled him, he pulled back his hand to accomplish is intention of killing the poor woman.

"Lett!" cried Holmes. "The cross!"

He had pulled the Keadby Cross from his pocket and was holding it before him, approaching the madman slowly. Any thoughts of murder temporarily seemed to slip from Lett's mind as he focused on the jewel-encrusted object, able to catch even the dimmest light in that room and reflect back an unnatural shimmer of winking fire. He let go of the woman's clothing, and she sank to the floor with a moan. If I'd hoped that he would drop the knife as well, I was mistaken. He shifted his grip and stepped toward Holmes, his eyes only on the cross, and reaching for it with his left hand even as his right was extending toward the unarmed detective.

We have argued since then who stopped him first. I maintain that my bullet was obviously faster than Holmes's own actions. And yet, when he pivoted to avoid the thrust of the knife while jamming the end of the cross deeply into Lett's left eye, he moved faster than I could follow. Perhaps it was just a trick of the light, but I didn't realize that he'd done it, until the man cried and pulled back, the five inches of metal still impaled into his eye socket. With a groan he collapsed, his blighted soul having already departed, and it was only later that the two bullet holes were found at his heart. Lestrade, it turned out, had fired his own pistol as well.

When Lett's personal effects were examined the next day, a trove of diaries and hideous souvenirs confirmed that he was a murderer many times over, and that his descent into madness had begun long before his joining with the Keadby family. Details of the deaths of his first two wives, as well as that of Lydia and a number of other unfortunate women, made for disturbing reading – and yet, what was seen in those papers proved to be quite useful in training others in later years to recognize that particular type of madness. One could only wish that such knowledge had been available when hunting the various members of The Ripper Cabal during the autumn of '88.

There hadn't been much time for Lett to record the details of Timothy Keadby's killing, but what little there was seemed to confirm that during one of his trips to London under the influence of the full moon, he'd spotted his missing brother-in-law – and he himself had been spotted in return. He had continued to return to London's East End each month to satisfy his peculiar and escalating impulses, while also seeking Timothy as a means to locate the Keadby Cross, an obsession that only increased with the passage of time. Timothy had clearly left the area during those times, hoping to avoid a further encounter with Lett, but finally on one dark night, the two met. Lett threatened Timothy angrily, eventually striking him down, but without learning the location of that which he sought. This frustration only served further to drive him into insanity.

With none of the Keadby family left, and without any relatives or heirs connected to Stephen Lett, the status of the entire Keadby fortune was suddenly the subject of much discussion throughout London. The facts related to Lett's murder of his brother-in-law, as well as his own dramatic passing, only added fuel to the telling. Eventually Denholm Waitrose, the Keadby family attorney, managed to cut through the complications that threatened to strangle the dispersal of the estate and, working with both Isaiah Clark and – surprisingly – Langdale Pike, a charitable trust was established for the poor of Whitechapel and Spitalfields. Among the first to receive aid was the sad woman who had nearly been killed by Lett, saved only by our intervention. She herself became an advocate for the poor, and served admirably in this role until her death.

The Keadby Cross was gifted to the British Museum, where it vanished into the vaults and hasn't been seen publicly again. And except for this narrative, it's unlikely that anyone has given any thought to it in the two decades that have passed since these events occurred.

The Rhayader Legacy

The heat was already stifling when I stepped outside that morning – a Tuesday, as I recall, in late July – but it was nothing like what I'd experienced a decade earlier in India and Afghanistan. As I don't find those conditions particularly unpleasant – at least at that time of day, and not long after breakfast – I decided to walk instead of hailing a hansom, which was never a problem that close to Paddington Station.

In my pocket was a letter from an old school chum, only just recovered from nearly ten weeks of debilitating brain fever following the shocking loss of a naval treaty that had been left in his care. I recalled him quite well from many years before, although our contact since then had been quite minimal. However, he knew of my connection to Sherlock Holmes – likely learned by way of his own position within the office of his uncle, Lord Holdhurst – and as soon as he had regained his senses, he'd sent a letter to me, begging that I obtain Holmes's assistance.

My wife and I agreed that there was something quite pitiful in his plea, and I resolved to bring it to Holmes's attention immediately. After arranging that my friend and neighbor Dr. Anstruther cover for me, I set out for Baker Street.

The doors were thrown wide for some early morning meeting at the Baptist Trinity Chapel, and as I passed I nodded at the minister. He did the same, but with a certain wariness. Although he seemed to respect me as a physician, we'd had an uneasy accord at best since the night that I'd helped Holmes force the church's side door to prevent young Alice Welwyn from hanging herself in the vestibule, convinced while drugged by her step-father that her death was the only way to save her reputation and expiate her sins – while simultaneously giving him control of the vast fortune left to her by her real father. We had only been just in time to prevent the tragedy, but the minister would probably never forgive himself for losing his temper when he learned the story, revealing to Holmes and me his own violent (and poorly suppressed) tendencies when he temporarily forgot the tenets of his faith and beat the step-father within an inch of his worthless life.

A turn along Chapel Street led me into the bustle of Marylebone Road, and I made my steady way, nodding here and there to strangers and the occasional familiar face. Soon I reached Baker Street Station and turned toward 221. As I walked, I considered how to place the matter before Holmes in such a way as to gain his interest. I knew well that he loved his art, and that usually he was as ready to bring his aid to a client as the client was to receive it. But there was always the possibility that he was already engaged.

And this concern seemed to be justified, as I observed upon my arrival. Letting myself in with the key that I'd retained at both Holmes's and Mrs. Hudson's insistence, I climbed upstairs to find my friend seated at his chemical table, absorbed in some investigation. He was clad in a dressing gown, and I wondered if he'd been up all night. Then I observed his dirty breakfast dishes on the dining table and concluded that he'd only recently become involved in his chemical research, as he would have otherwise ignored the food if he was carrying out his experiments when Mrs. Hudson brought it up.

I tried to see what he was doing, but the arrangement of glassware on the deal table was indecipherable. A large curved retort was boiling furiously in the bluish flame of a Bunsen burner, and the distilled drops were condensing into a two-litre measure. Holmes hardly glanced up as I entered, although he waved in my direction, and I seemed to have an indication that he would be finished shortly. I dropped into my old armchair, watching as he swirled the container around with one hand while drawing up a few drops in a glass pipette with the other. Eventually he stood, a test-tube in one hand and a slip of litmus paper in the other.

I could see that he looked rested, again confirming that he hadn't been up all night. Whatever he'd been doing hadn't taken much time.

"You come at a crisis, Watson," he said, as if we were in the middle of an ongoing conversation, instead of having not seen each other for a couple of days. "If this paper remains blue, all is well. If it turns red, it means a man's life."

He dipped it into the test tube and it immediately turned red. There was no doubt – whatever was in that test tube was acidic.

"Hmm," he said. "I thought as much!" Then he looked for a few more seconds at the paper before adding, "I will be at your service in an instant, Watson. You will find tobacco in the Persian slipper."

He placed the test tube in the rack on his chemical table and then stepped to his desk. After shifting through the various stacks of documents and journals, he found a pad of telegram forms and proceeded to scribble on several of them. Then he went to the landing door, threw it open, and called for the page boy. After handing over the slips of paper with instructions as to their disposition, he threw himself down into the chair opposite and drew up his knees until his fingers clasped round his long, thin shins.

Acknowledging my inquiring expression, he smiled and said, "A very commonplace little murder. You've got something better, I fancy. You are the stormy petrel of crime, Watson. What is it?"

I then handed him the letter from my old school chum, which he studied with great care.

I've recorded elsewhere the events of Holmes's subsequent recovery of the naval treaty, and the saving of the career of my friend Percy Phelps, as well as the great service that was performed for the country. As usual, Holmes was able to perceive the truth where it remained hidden from the rest of us, successfully revealing the stolen document and exposing a scoundrel in the process. And it was just two mornings later that Holmes and I, along with Percy, were back in that same room where the matter had first commenced.

As the three of us sat around the breakfast table, Holmes was able to explain the truth to a startled Percy. It had been a wearying couple of days, and during that time we'd made two trips to Briarbrae, Percy's family home in Woking, had interviewed several people of vastly diverse social stations in London, and Holmes had received a nasty knife cut across his knuckles. Now, with the treaty again in his possession after a long ten weeks, Percy would – in theory – be able to return to his position at the Foreign Office, under the aegis of his noted uncle.

When Holmes had revealed the truth of the matter and seen the treaty into Percy's hands, the nervous fellow had been beside himself, not knowing whether to rush home and tell his fiancé of his good fortune, or instead notify Lord Holdhurst that the treaty had been found. I advised the latter, going to Whitehall immediately to deliver the document back into responsible hands. I considered accompanying him, but instead felt that Percy should take care of this business on his own. And in truth, I was a bit raw and weary from having cared for him since the previous day while Holmes carried out his investigations.

I watched Percy's cab trundle down Baker Street and out of sight before climbing back upstairs to thank Holmes. Surprisingly, he had poured a bit of brandy for each of us, although the remains of breakfast were still on the nearby table. I raised an eyebrow.

"It seemed," he said, "that you could use this after so many hours spent with your quarrelsome and jittery friend, and I find that the pain in my knuckles is a bit more than I let on. I need a bracer before you look after the wound."

Although I didn't have my medical bag with me, there were sufficient supplies still in Baker Street to adequately fix up the cuts across a couple of his knuckles. They were clean with no underlying damage and would heal well. When I was finished, I poured another brandy for each of us and we retired to our chairs by the empty fireplace to discuss those features of the case which would have held no interest for Percy Phelps.

By then it was the first day of August, and the heat was already quite noticeable. It was the beginning of a long hot month in which the capital would feel like an oven, and the sunlight on the bricks would be painful to the eye. I was considering whether to rise and open the windows to a greater degree in order to catch the morning breeze. Yet even as I set down my glass to do so, the front doorbell began to ring with great ferocity. This was followed immediately by someone pounding upon the door.

Holmes raised an eyebrow, but he seemed tired and willing to wait for whomever had caused the commotion to come to him. I was more cautious, recalling past times when these rooms had been invaded by men – and the occasional woman – with an angry score to settle. I remembered one such only six years earlier, when a giant of a man – who had less than a day to live at that point, although we didn't know it then – had charged into the sitting room in a most abusive way. The brute had grabbed the iron fireplace poker, bending it and tossing it aside as an example of what he would do to Holmes if he didn't step out of the case. Holmes, in a rather amazing bit of strength of his own, had retrieved the ruined poker and straightened it back out – not perfectly, of course, but at least to a level of functionality. As we heard Mrs. Hudson and another voice speaking downstairs, I confirmed that I had my service revolver with me, as always, but I also glanced at the misshapen poker, still standing beside the fireplace, and considered whether I should take it up as well.

We heard the sound of one person ascending to the sitting room, indicating that Mrs. Hudson (by methods known only to her) had reasoned that her presence wasn't required. The footsteps were light and quick, and clearly those of a young woman. While that in itself didn't lessen any possible danger – as there were quite a few ladies who wished for an end to Holmes's life, and not quite as many (but some) who felt the same way toward me – I felt that the extra use of the poker would not be required.

There was a quick knock and then, without waiting for a reply, the door was thrown open to reveal a girl who appeared to be in her early twenties. (We were soon to learn that she was in fact only nineteen, but quite poised for her age.) She had neither hat nor gloves, as if she had just left home without preparing to properly pay a visit. She was angry, as evinced by her expression and stance, and her words quickly confirmed this observation.

Identifying Holmes immediately, she cried, "You have destroyed my father!"

We both stood, but Holmes didn't seem to feel threatened in any way. I, however, didn't immediately lower my guard.

"I'm sorry," replied Holmes. "You seem to have the advantage of me, Miss – ?"

160

"Natalie Rhayader," she replied, her tone filled with contempt. "Walter Rhayader is my father."

An understanding look crossed Holmes's face and he nodded. "Miss Rhayader, I'm very sorry that my conclusions implicated your father, but the experiment simply verified the official idea that the substance painted onto the metallic fittings, causing them to break loose and fall on Oswald Scampton, held traces of hydrofluoric acid – and your father was apparently seen painting near there a short time before. As I understand it, he admitted that he had been working nearby. I did nothing more than confirm what the police already suspected, and made my conclusions known to them day before yesterday."

She took a step closer. "And they arrested my father soon after they received your telegram. I've only just this morning learned that you were involved in gathering the evidence against him. I rushed over her to ask if you might investigate further, rather than simply sending a telegram and then washing your hands of the matter. He'll die, Mr. Holmes – long before his trial! He isn't well – He hasn't been for years! – and he's an innocent man, placed there because of your misreading of the evidence."

I thought back to the morning that I'd arrived two days before, waiting as Holmes finished his chemical experiment before telling me that the result might mean a man's life. The litmus paper had turned red, indicating the presence of an acid, and Holmes had then sent his wire to the Yard. Sadly, with my own story to tell, and in the rush to help my friend Percy Phelps, I hadn't given any more thought to that other "commonplace little murder", nor to any of the implications involved. Now this young lady stood before us, desperation and anger emanating from her in equal parts.

Holmes glanced my way. "Dr. Watson isn't aware of the facts of this case, Miss Rhayader. Won't you sit down while we discuss it? Perhaps I can clear up some of the confusion surrounding the matter."

She struggled with her decision – whether to remain standing in outrage, or capitulate and join us. Finally she did neither, instead saying, "Will you come with me? To speak with my father? He's being held at Scotland Yard."

Holmes glanced my way to see if I was free. I nodded that I was, for I hadn't known how long Holmes might take to resolve the matter of the missing naval treaty, and I had arranged with Anstruther to look after my practice until he heard otherwise.

Miss Rhayader said nothing, simply watching with her mouth tight while we retrieved our hats. Then we went downstairs, and soon we were in a growler headed south.

"Have either of you read of the case in the newspaper?" asked the young lady when we were underway. "There is a full account of it in yesterday's *Times*."

I shook my head. "We've been involved in another matter, and my time over the last day or so was spent caring for our client, who was ill. Mr. Holmes has been in Woking, related to the same affair."

"I did read *The Times*," Holmes stated, "as I had a number of empty hours yesterday as I waited for nightfall, and was able to examine several newspapers. From my understanding of the case, based on what has been reported, I had already intended to involve myself further in the matter. From the limited information conveyed to me by Inspector Gregson two days ago, your father is employed at the family glass factory in Hoxton, where the murder occurred."

"That's correct," replied Miss Rhayader. "The company was started by my grandfather."

"Three days ago," continued Holmes, "on July 29th, in the late afternoon, one of the long-time employees, Oswald Scampton, died horribly when a load of iron fittings, to be used by him in the framing and construction of industrial windows, fell from where it was suspended above him, killing him instantly."

"Oswald had worked there his whole adult life," Miss Rhayader said. "He was trained to do any task, but he had specialized in the last few years in the design and assembly of heavy windows with metal framing. He was fitting together one of them at his work table when the chain holding the iron works broke loose and crushed him. He should have known better than to leave them hanging there like that."

"May I ask," I interrupted, "if it was typical that he should be working in such a dangerous location?"

She closed her eyes. "Oswald was . . . willful. He often cut corners where safety was concerned. We have a series of tracks with rollers suspended from the ceiling throughout the factory which can be used to hoist and then shift various materials from one location to another. Earlier that day, Oswald had arranged to have the metal forms that he required chained together and loaded onto the hook. They were then pulled to his station, but he must have decided that he didn't need them quite yet, and they were left hanging while he worked on something else. They were directly above him when they broke free."

"At first," said Holmes, "it was believed that the chain simply snapped."

She nodded. "But my cousin, Brian Rhayader, who owns the factory, insisted that such a thing was impossible. The police had been called because of the accident, and when they examined the broken chain, they found a great deal of unusual corrosion."

"The chemist from the Yard suspected hydrofluoric acid," added Holmes, "but knowing that I had done some research in that area, he asked for me to confirm it. That was the limit of my involvement, I'm afraid. I had meant to follow up and ask a few additional questions, but then the other matter presented itself, and Dr. Watson and I have only completed it shortly before your arrival. The newspapers indicated that your father, Walter Rhayader, was arrested the day after the death occurred – on July 30th."

"That's right," she said with obvious bitterness. "That morning, soon after your wire arrived."

"The press accounts stated that a witness placed your father on the suspended walkway above the dead man's work area just an hour or so before the chain failed. He claimed to have been painting a rusty spot on the railing – one of his regular chores around the factory."

"If that's what he said he was doing, then that's what he *was* doing!"

"Did the police give any indication as to what they believed your father's motive would be for committing such a crime?"

"They said . . . they learned that my father and Oswald had been arguing. It has been going on for several weeks."

"What about?"

"I . . . I would prefer not to say."

"Miss Rhayader," I said gently, "we can easily determine from the police whatever motive is ascribed to your father. Your reluctance to discuss it will not prevent it from being discovered."

"It's not that it's a secret. It's simply that I find it . . . distasteful. You see, Oswald – that is, Mr. Scampton – had been pressing a case to ask for . . . to ask for my hand in marriage."

"I see. And your thoughts on that were – ?"

"It was ridiculous!" she snapped at me. "He's twice my age, and he thinks . . . *thought* . . . that simply because he was a valuable member of the business and a key employee, and that he had known me since I was born, that he had some special connection that would make him a legitimate suitor."

"And do you already have someone in your life to hold such a position?" I asked.

"I do. A major in the Army. He's out of the country at present, in Gibraltar, but I assure you – "

She stopped herself suddenly. "What, Miss Rhayader?" asked Holmes. "What were you about to say?"

"Only that if Thomas – that is, Major Stroud – were here, he might have . . . he would have already thrashed Oswald Scampton quite soundly long before things came to this point!"

She fell silent, her mouth tight with anger, and Holmes chose to leave off questioning her for the present. We continued to make our way south and then east. Our pace was steady, but not so fast that I couldn't observe the various people going about their business on the partially crowded streets. They moved with lethargy as the air grew warmer. Throughout our passage, Miss Rhayader didn't say another word.

We traversed Trafalgar Square, still somewhat empty at that time of morning. The spray of the fountains danced in the morning light, and the heat of that first day of August continued to build. When we entered the shade of the eastern side of the square, the morning sun was blocked by the tall buildings, and the sudden feeling of coolness was both palpable and welcome.

Turning along Northumberland Avenue, our cab soon released us within that warren of streets and buildings layered around Scotland Yard. At that time the men (and occasionally women) who made up the Force were still several months away from their planned move to new digs at the large handsome building beside Westminster Pier, but already there was a sense that plans were afoot to transfer elsewhere – for instance, there were boxes and crates standing in hallways between office doors that weren't normally left there. I wondered how all of this sprawl would somehow manage to fit into the new building.

Holmes and I were both well-known at the Yard, and we had been given unofficial free run of the place for years. We nodded at acquaintances and friends as we moved ever-deeper into the building, headed for the bank of modest offices which housed the various inspectors. We passed Lestrade's closed door and heard him reading the riot act to someone, his words indistinguishable through the aged oak door, but his tone unmistakable. A turn around the next corner and we found ourselves at Gregson's office, where the door was standing open.

The big fair-haired inspector looked up from a stack of papers and, when recognizing us, he stood and gave a smile of welcome. His eyes narrowed a bit when he identified Miss Rhayader, but he was no less gracious, seeing us all to chairs, inquiring if we wished for tea – we did not – and then closing the door with his large hands and reseating himself, asking how he could assist us.

Miss Rhayader took a breath, seemingly ready to voice a list of grievances, but Holmes spoke first. "Following my incidental involvement in the Scampton murder, by way of my chemical experiment a couple of mornings past, Miss Rhayader has now approached me with some dissatisfaction in regard to her father's arrest. I decided that, with your agreement, I would add a bit to what I've since learned by way of the newspapers."

Gregson leaned back, his aged chair complaining. "I'm not sure that discussing this in the presence of the suspect's daughter is wise, Mr. Holmes, but I can give you a limited amount of information – none of it is secret, after all. The iron that crushed Scampton was foolishly left suspended over his work station – specifically over the very stool where the man was laboring. Apparently he was often careless that way, regularly having materials loaded onto the hook that he'd pulled there, although he didn't necessarily always leave them directly over where he would be working. In fact, the men who chained the iron onto the hook swear that they left it positioned to one side of the work table, and that someone – possibly Scampton himself, or – (Here he cast a glance at the young lady.) – someone else pulled it further along the suspended track so that it was directly over where the dead man was working.

"We checked, and both track and hook were well-maintained, and loads hanging from them are easy to move, and can be done so silently. More importantly, they can also be moved easily by anyone standing on the suspended iron walkway that runs beside the track, so that someone could have come along there, reached over, and pulled the hanging iron-works directly over Scampton and – with the continuous hellish noise in that place – he might not have even been aware of it.

"There were a half-dozen of the iron frames chained together, comprising nearly half-a-ton of metal. As you know, when the load fell and killed Scampton, the first officers on the scene found signs of unusual corrosion on the remains of the chain wrapped around both them and the remnant suspended from the track." His scowled. "Constable Naughton handled the chain quite a bit before someone told him to stop."

"Oh no," I breathed, and Holmes shared my grim expression.

From her gasp, it seemed that Miss Rhayader understood the implications as well. Hydrofluoric acid can be absorbed by the skin, and while not immediately damaging to surface tissue, it can cause cardiac arrhythmia or pulmonary *oedema*, and other irreversible internal damage that can lead to death within days.

"How much of his body touched the acid?"

"Both hands – he had tugged the chain loose from the iron pieces for a better look before some of the workers could stop him."

"I assume that he has been treated with calcium gluconate injections or calcium chloride infusions?"

"He has. But – " Gregson added, "if the constable dies, an additional charge of murder will be laid upon . . . " Looking at Miss Rhayader, he finished, ". . . upon the person who tampered with the chain."

He shifted forward, twining his large fingers and placing his hands on the desk before him. "The owner of the factory is Brian Rhayader – your cousin, I understand, Miss?"

She nodded. "He and my father are both about the same age, but strangely my father is Brian's uncle. They are of the same generation, but not cousins as one would expect, due to the vast difference in years between when Brian's father and my father – brothers – were born. Brian is the only child of my grandfather's older son, while my father was the younger of those two sons. My grandfather . . . didn't feel that my father was capable of helping run the business, or even inheriting a share of it, so he instead left everything to his older son, Brian's father.

She lowered her head. "My father is . . . simple. He never had a head for business. His father – my grandfather – Bryn Rhayader, came from Wales and founded the business seventy years ago. He recognized my father's weakness and never expected anything from him, although he loved him in his own way and took care of him. When he died, his older son, Rhys – Brian's father – continued to do so.

"Somehow, twenty years ago, my father met my mother, and they married in secret. A year later I was born, and my mother died in childbirth." She said it without grief – a simple fact that had always been part of her life, and something sad that happened to someone whom she had never met. "Her death caused my father to further retreat from his responsibilities. He cared for me in his own way, but I was raised by a fine woman hired by my Uncle Rhys. Through my whole life, my poor father has simply been like a pleasant ghost. He's been interested in me, to be sure, but he is . . . distracted. When Oswald Scampton asked for my hand – " She stopped herself suddenly, afraid to give fresh emphasis to the possible motive that her father would have for committing murder.

Instead, she continued, "My cousin Brian has continued to care for my father since his father passed. He allows my father to carry out small jobs in the factory. It keeps him happy, and makes him feel useful."

Gregson nodded, but one could see that the history of the Rhayader family held no interest for him. "Brian Rhayader," he said, "was the one that told us that the metal looked as if it had been eaten through by acid, and that hydrofluoric acid is used a great deal in the factory for glass etching." He glanced at Holmes. "We had a good idea of what had happened, but Dr. Mayes in the laboratory wanted your opinion."

Holmes nodded. "Would it be possible to speak with Miss Rhayader's father?"

166

Gregson unlaced his fingers, and a pained expression crossed his face. "Umm, he is in the infirmary at present." Miss Rhayader gasped, and Gregson quickly raised a hand to placate her. "Purely precautionary, I assure you, Miss. He became rather . . . agitated after you left this morning, and considering what you'd told us about his health, we felt that it would be safest to move him there and sedate him."

Miss Rhayader rose to her feet. "I demand that I be allowed to see him immediately!"

Gregson stood as well. "Of course. I understand that he's asleep, but you may sit with him." He turned toward Holmes and me. "I suspect that you wished to question him, but I'm afraid that will have to wait."

"We understand," I said. Turning to Miss Rhayader, I added, "I personally know the physicians here at the Yard, and can vouch for every one of them. Your father will receive the best of care."

Holmes added that we would be in touch, and Gregson summoned a constable to take her to her father. Then, when she was gone, Gregson said, "It appears to be cut-and-dried, Mr. Holmes – although we both know that I've said that before, and you've revealed that it wasn't necessarily so. I'll be happy to hear whatever you learn. I admit that I'm of two minds – it seems likely that Rhayader did do something to the chain. A couple of witnesses place him on the metal walkway an hour or so before, although he says that he was painting – doing touch-ups is one of his duties – and several people knew that he and Scampton have been overheard arguing of late. It's fairly certain that Walter Rhayader gambles, and that Scampton had a hand in it – possibly placing bets for him, and no doubt skimming a hefty cut off the top.

"It wouldn't be too difficult to do. As you've gathered, the girl's father is rather simple-minded – a gentle-seeming soul, but just the type that might react stupidly and violently if he thought that he had a grievance. I talked to him last night, and one can see why his own father, the founder of the company, left him out of the inheritance. He'd be no use whatsoever at running a business.

"Now that other one, Brian Rhayader, unlike our suspect, is a right canny fellow. He only inherited the business a year or so ago, and even though his father Rhys was quite capable, the new owner has already doubled the production, and has a number of expansions planned. It seems that he had a lot of good ideas that he was prevented from implementing until his own father passed away."

"I believe then that Mr. Brian Rhayader is the next person that we should visit," said Holmes. Gregson agreed and wrote the address for the glass-works on a slip of paper. We thanked him and then wended our way

167

back to the street, where we settled into one of the many cabs that are always waiting in that quarter.

Holmes was quiet as we traversed London, making our way toward Hoxton. I glanced his way. "Do you see anything definite that leads you to believe that Walter Rhayader is innocent?"

"It's too soon to tell, and I would certainly like to hear his story. But this certainly reminds me that I need to have all of the data before making conclusions."

"But you did what was asked of you as a consultant – you verified the presence of hydrofluoric acid. That was the extent of what was requested."

"True, but obviously there is more to it than simply watching a piece of litmus paper change color and declaring that a man's life depends upon it. By agreeing to conduct the test, even if only to verify another's conclusions, I attached my reputation to the outcome. I did so without any thought to the bigger picture. I called it 'commonplace'. Now that I understand the case better, I realize that something isn't right. For instance, hydrofluoric acid wouldn't eat through a chain like that in such a quick manner. Instead, it would form an upper layer of iron fluoride and free hydrogen. If those chains failed, then there was something else going on besides the mere application of acid."

He became silent again, and I left him to his thoughts. Once as we moved along Farringdon Street he shifted his position, and I thought that he might have decided to say something else, but instead he simply settled a different way and continued to brood.

The steady pace of the horse, the rocking of the cab, the tedious monotony of the city around us as we passed through it, along with the absence of engagement from my companion, all acted upon the lack of rest that had defined my previous night when Percy Phelps, recovering from his brain fever and attempting to sleep without the benefit of his medication, had kept me from sinking into a steady doze. I must admit that I fell asleep sometime past the halfway point of our journey, and when I awakened, I found myself in a very unpleasant place indeed.

We had pulled to a stop alongside a plain gray factory building, the same as any number of others up and down the narrow and dark street. There was a steady cacophony coming from every direction, although it took different forms depending upon which direction one focused – here was a loud metallic pounding, while there was the high whine of some kind of saw, ululating in terrible shrieks when the teeth encountered some kind of resistance. But worst of all was the smell – a mixture of chemicals, heat, and burning, and a terrible rotten stench that one usually only encounters along the worst parts of the Thames. It was exacerbated by the rising August temperatures. Only a little later did I learn that we were amongst the factories lining the west side of the Wenlock Basin.

I visited there another time several years later in connection with another case – the sad affair of the misplaced newborn and the midwife's crab sleamery – and had a chance to observe the place in greater detail, approaching that time in a state of wakefulness. Running south off the Regent's Canal and not far from the Islington Tunnel, at the very western edge of Hackney and almost in Hoxton, the basin is a thousand feet long, but only forty or so feet wide. Just to the west is the larger City Road Basin, and surrounding the two are a number of very busy factories, all contributing to the disagreeable noise and stink of the region. We were standing in the Wharf Road, which runs between the two canals, and nearby were several iron and zinc foundries, a couple of sawmills, and perhaps most objectionable, a gutta percha factory, which took up many hundreds of square feet and was probably responsible for a great deal of the terrible odor hanging in the air. However, as bad as it all was, the overhanging reek coming from the canals was worse, a miasma that settled most in the back of one's throat and made one's eyes water. It was almost a relief to enter Rhayader's glass-works and shut the door behind us. The mephitis and clamor were awful here too, but relatively it was more pleasant within than without.

We immediately had to step back as a couple of cursing and sweating laborers pulled a large piece of glass past us, wrapped in padded fabric-covered chains and hanging from a pair of hooks. These in turn were attached to a pair of heavy chains that led up to a wheeled track system suspended from the ceiling. Here, then, was the same type of device that had been used to place the iron window pieces above Oswald Scampton's work space. I could see over us that a network of tracks was spread all across the underside of the building's roof and support beams, allowing workers to move loads, by clever manipulation, from here to there nearly anywhere in the building in the same way that a specific train car could be shunted and routed through a crowded yard, ending up exactly where it needed to be.

A wizened fellow passed us, and we managed to catch his attention and convince him to lead us to Brian Rhayader's office, which was actually quite close, in a suite of rooms to our left, tucked along the front wall of the building. As we reached the door, I heard a mighty crash of broken glass somewhere behind us in the vast structure and wondered if some new tragedy had occurred, but our guide showed no concern, and I began to realize that such sounds were probably heard all day long in this place, and simply an expected cost of doing business.

At the door, our guide turned and departed without a word. Inside the offices it was marginally quieter, and a man behind a desk near the door nodded when we asked for the owner and led us back through a short hallway. He knocked and opened a door, stating as he did so, "More police."

We hadn't identified ourselves, but we didn't bother to correct the man's assumption until the door had closed and we introduced ourselves to Brian Rhayader. He was a solid fellow of around forty, wearing an expensive-looking suit that somehow didn't fit with these surroundings. His hands were square and blunt, and his dark features were topped by hair that was black and rather shiny. It was combed back in a sleek flatness that gave him the appearance of a sly otter. He seemed distracted, which was to be expected, and waved us to a pair of chairs before his desk.

We introduced ourselves and he nodded, saying, "I take it that Natalie has hired you." He had a sour expression. "Well, I don't blame her, I suppose. But it was only a matter of time until Walter did something stupid like this. I only wish that he'd thought of a way to do it so that it didn't happen here at work, but he's always been impulsive."

"We learned from Inspector Gregson that there were disagreements between your Uncle Walter and Oswald Scampton."

"First I'd heard about it was when the inspector mentioned it to me, after the body had been taken away. He must have learned something from the men on the floor. It was probably about money, though. Walter has had a weakness for gambling the last few years – nothing substantial, you understand, as he doesn't have that much money of his own – and Oswald encouraged it."

"Miss Rhayader – your cousin – stated that Mr. Scampton had been pressuring her father to allow the two of them to be married.

"Indeed. Well, that's news to me as well. Did she want to? Marry him, I mean?"

"Apparently not."

"I wouldn't think so. Oswald was fifty if he was a day, and I believe that Natalie has been flirting with some army major for a year or so."

The more he spoke, the more I found myself disliking Mr. Brian Rhayader, but I held my tongue. I could see that Holmes agreed with me, although to anyone that didn't know him, he appeared to be unaffected by the factory owner's unpleasant mien.

"What can you tell us about the factory?" said Holmes, changing his questioning into a seemingly unimportant direction. It might have been to simply have a greater understanding of the business, or perhaps he was backing away from some point to be explored, lest he show too much interest in it and give away something that he wished to remain hidden for the present.

"Hmm? Let's see." Rhayader seemed to relax, as if he were more willing to have this discussion instead of what he'd expected. "The business started by my grandfather, Bryn Rhayader, seventy years ago – 1819, as a matter of fact. He'd come here from Wales, and there's some rumor that Rhayader wasn't his real name, although we've never bothered to find out. He was around twenty years old and had just two coins in his pocket, but he was blessed with quite a bit of physical strength. He never told anyone where he learned to work with glass, but he started in a small loft in Whitechapel, and by the time the basin here was constructed in 1826, he was ready to locate his own building here – this very factory.

"My father, Rhys, was born in 1830, and Walter – grandfather's only other child – wasn't born until twenty years later, around the same time as me. It's been fairly well accepted in the family that Walter wasn't planned – or wanted. He was always rather – well, weak and simple, but good-hearted enough. Or so we thought until the other day. My own father was invaluable at growing the business, and it was his pride and joy, but he always went out of his way to make a place here for Walter, his very much younger brother. Walter married about twenty years ago – he somehow found a girl willing to have him – but she died when the baby was born. I didn't really know Walter's wife, as he and I have never been close, but I suppose that Natalie takes after her mother – she's a smart girl, and nothing like her father.

"I grew up working here, like Walter, but unlike him, I was groomed to take over some day – which happened just a couple of years ago, when my father passed suddenly, and far too soon. He was only fifty-seven. I kept Walter on as father had done, paying him a good living, but not too much, as he wouldn't know how to manage it. I see now that letting him handle his own affairs was a mistake. He allowed his own problems grow until he tried to do something about it, and he did it here at work, which is unacceptable. Oswald Scampton will be difficult to replace."

Holmes chose then to pivoted back to Scampton's death. "The chain was compromised by use of hydrofluoric acid," he said.

"That's seems to be right. We use it here for etching the glass. When I saw the corrosion on the chain links, I suspected what might have happened. Then a couple of our workers remembered that they'd seen Walter on the walkway where the chain was hanging, just a few hours before it broke. He confirmed that he'd been painting that morning – it's one of his little jobs that gives him something to do – and there was fresh paint on the railing at that spot."

Holmes asked if we could see Scampton's work table where the death had occurred, and Rhayader seemed happy to be rid of us. He called to the man in the outer office and instructed him where to take us. Then, without another word, he returned to the papers on his desk.

We were led through the factory and along a round-about path to a wide work-table, about eight-feet square, near the rear wall. Overhead was an iron walkway, and above that was a track where the chain-and-hook system could pass overhead when necessary. Holmes asked where the hook was now.

"The police took the corroded chain that fell," replied our guide, who had introduced himself simply as Morrison, "and had a few of us cut off the other part still hanging from the track." Holmes nodded and then turned and made for a set of nearby stairs leading to the iron walkway. Morrison started to object, but then desisted, seeing that Holmes was only working his way slowly to a spot ten feet or so directly above us.

Holmes looked carefully at the railing. When he was finished, he rejoined us.

"Before the iron fell, had anything unusual happened that day? Any unexpected visitors?"

"Not a one. There are about fifty of us that work here, and we're told to keep an eye out for anyone uninvited."

"How often did Walter Rhayader's daughter visit him?"

"Occasionally, but I don't think she'd been here in weeks."

At Holmes's urging, we were introduced to several of the workers who might have relevant testimony – the two men who had seen Walter on the walkway, and another who had been first on the scene after the iron fell. The former confirmed that Walter had been at different locations that morning, painting as he sometimes did, but they couldn't place him for certain at the exact spot over Scampton's table. The man who had first found the body clearly enjoyed telling his version of the gruesome story, and had likely had a great deal of practice in the past few days in order to have so colorfully embellished the details of Scampton's terrible death in such a short amount of time.

At that point Holmes seemed satisfied and, with nothing further left to see, nor any other individuals to meet, we were taken to the front door and released.

It was quieter outside to a certain degree, but not necessarily more pleasant. "Let us walk for a few minutes," said Holmes, leading me north along Wharf Street, and so across Regent's Canal to the north bank. There he turned west along the tow-path, and we ambled as the stink and noise of the basin and the industries that had leeched onto it faded. The canal itself was none too clean, but compared to the Wenlock Basin, it was a like a pastoral brook.

"What did you find on the upper walkway?"

"Some evidence of recent painting – just a dab. Black enamel, to match that already there."

"Which confirms Walter Rhayader's story."

"Possibly. But the spot showed no signs of requiring additional paint. And that doesn't negate whatsoever the idea that he could have also been up there to spread acid on the chain – and to do whatever else was done to cause the fall of the iron-works – for hydrofluoric acid alone wouldn't have destroyed that chain so easily." He tapped his lip with a finger. "I feel as if something is missing – that there is some unknown fact."

"But surely it's too soon to know that. You've barely begun to investigate. And perhaps it's exactly as it looks – Walter Rhayader decided to kill Oswald Scampton, and he did so with a very poor and obvious plan, thinking that no one would actually notice him or investigate the damage to the chain."

"By all accounts he may very well be that naive. And yet, I observe that this crime not only removes Scampton from the board, but Walter Rhayader as well, and I have to wonder whom that benefits, and how."

We had reached the end of the towpath, where the canal continued west through a brick archway and into the dark Islington Tunnel. From somewhere inside we could hear the echo of calling voices, and then the sharp sudden peal of a woman's laughter. It stopped as suddenly as it had begun, with an almost hysterical quality, as if its effort to quell the nervousness and possibly terror that some might feel in such a place had failed suddenly and completely. We stood there at the end of the path for a moment, both frozen and alerted by some atavistic impulse when hearing a woman express fear. We waited for several long minutes to see if a boat would appear, but it never did, and we eventually came to the mutual unspoken conclusion that our concern was unfounded, and we retraced our steps back to a point where we could make our way up to Danbury Street and so find a cab.

Holmes directed its course toward the Strand. When we reached Somerset House, he disembarked, telling me that he had some facts to ascertain, and would it be possible to meet in Baker Street at seven o'clock that night. I agreed, and then requested that the cabbie take me on to my Paddington home.

My wife, having not seen me for two days, wanted to know all of the details related to Percy Phelps' difficulties. I found that I had to force myself to remember specifics, as my mind was already distracted by the current problem related to the curious death of Oswald Scampton.

I spent a portion of the afternoon conferring with Anstruther to learn whether any of my patients had special concerns, and then I made my rounds, planning my route so as to end up in Baker Street at nearly seven o'clock. As I approached the front door of No. 221, I noticed a hansom cab waiting nearby. In the early evening light, I identified the cabbie as Bert Deacon, the former Houndsditch ramper who had been proven innocent by Holmes of a murder seven years before. Since that time, he had been part of a steady group of cab-drivers that were generally available when Holmes had need of them. We nodded to one another and I looked up to see that the sitting room windows were lit. Using my key to let myself in, I climbed the stairs, where I found Holmes looking rather grim.

"You're just in time, Watson. Word has gone out that Walter Rhayader is not long for this world. Do you have your revolver?"

He knew that I did, as I'd learned long before never to leave home without it. I often wondered at the curious dichotomy of carrying out my duties as a physician while armed, but as I'd done the same in the army, nothing had really changed except the location and the sorts of enemies that I regularly encountered.

"What has happened to him?" After our recent encounter with Percy Phelps, the thought of brain fever was at the forefront of my thoughts. "We've heard nothing of any serious health problems. Did he have some sort of attack?"

"I shouldn't worry. I understand that he'll make a full recovery very soon. But be sure to wear your best concerned-doctor face."

Within moments we were ensconced in the hansom and to my surprise, Holmes directed Bert Deacon to make haste to Charing Cross Hospital. Then, in contrast to the quiet stretches that had characterized our earlier trips across the city, Holmes began to speak, but instead of explaining why we were going to the hospital, he said, "As I mentioned, I found it curious that the death of one man also effectively removed another as well, with the arrest and likely conviction of Walter Rhayader for the murder of Oswald Scampton. From the little we've heard, it didn't seem likely that Walter would be able to provide an adequate defense, and if someone was framing him, it would proceed without hindrance.

"But who might do such a thing?" I asked. "If we assume that Walter is innocent, then there is someone still unknown to us who wished to kill Scampton for entirely different reasons. Walter Rhayader would make an excellent scapegoat. We know from his daughter that Scampton was pressuring Walter regarding arranging a marriage with her, and that he also had some kind of leverage over him, if the story of Walter's gambling problem is true. It's likely that these facts are more commonly known than

174

is believed, and they would serve to incriminate Walter and deflect attention away from some other motive."

"But it's equally possible," Holmes replied, "that someone with a reason to get rid of *Walter* made use of his dealings with Scampton. Thus, Scampton's death was for no other purpose than to except incriminate Walter."

Holmes turned somewhat to face me. "You are correct – the facts of Walter's gambling, and Scampton's pressure upon him to encourage a marriage, are rather well known. And Walter Rhayader does have a problem with gambling. I verified it. At one point this afternoon, after my earlier researches were complete, I disguised myself and returned to Wenlock Basin. You may have noticed a rather shabby pub near the glass factory, just on the other side of one of the saw mills. I arranged to be there at the end of the work day, garbed as a workman from one of the nearby factories, and managed to ingratiate myself with a number of the employees who stopped there for a quick pint before continuing homeward. For the price of a few drinks, I quickly confirmed all that we'd heard – Walter is a known gambler, and Scampton served as something of a middle-man for him, all the while manipulating Walter terribly. The men in the factory didn't like it very much, as they feel no ill-will for Walter, but they also considered it none of their business if the uncle of the owner loses money to someone smart enough to take it from him – namely Scampton. I also found along the way that the employees don't like Mr. Brian Rhayader very much at all – although being liked is certainly not a part of his job.

"Well, I can understand that, as I didn't like him either, but what were their reasons?"

"They feel that he's been reckless with the business – taking on debt to expand while concurrently making excessive requirements of the employees in the process – increased output, longer hours for the same pay, and so on – in order to give the impression that the business is a greater success than it actually is. It is their perception that it's all being done to overvalue the business in order to obtain loans – and if something in Brian Rhayader's house of cards goes wrong, their livelihoods will be at risk."

"How would the employees know of this – these maneuverings to increase the company's resources? That isn't the sort of thing that is common knowledge among factory workers – or so it seems to me."

"That fellow who showed us the factory – Morrison – appears to pick up a lot of details from his position in the office, and he subsequently uses what he learns as currency amongst the workers, trading private information for whisky. I saw him in the pub, letting several men buy him

175

drinks while he blithely chattered away about various business-related facts that were probably not anyone's proper concern."

"So is Brian Rhayader financially unsound?"

"Unquestionably. That fact was verified by a few simple telegrams."

"But what does that have to do with Oswald Scampton's murder? Unless Scampton were blackmailing him somehow, I don't see how that the man's death could benefit him at all – or why he would frame his uncle for the crime."

"Ah, but Watson, you forget that before I went to the pub, I mentioned that I had undertaken some 'earlier researches'. When we parted in the Strand, I made my way to Somerset House, where I was able to take hold of one end of a thread that revealed a most interesting motive indeed.

"You'll recall that we heard several times that Walter Rhayader is around the same age as his nephew, Brian – both around forty. It was an easy assumption to picture Walter, the uncle, as the elder of the two, even if only by a small amount. But we also had an intimation of Walter's age when Brian stated that his own father was born in 1830, and that Walter was born 'twenty years later', or in 1850. That could have been an approximation, or it might have been precise. I was able to verify without any difficulty that Walter *was* born in 1850, and therefore next year he will turn forty."

"And since you've gone to the trouble to explain it, I'm sure that you will tell me the significance of it as well."

Holmes smiled. "Indeed. I looked at old Bryn Rhayader's will. The founder did leave the factory to his son, Brian's father Rhys, as well as the bulk of his fortune. But what hasn't been mentioned – and what no one may know except Brian – is that Bryn also left a substantial amount in trust for his second, much younger, son, Walter – an amount that, through careful investment by an independent financial counselor, has grown tidily over the previous decades to nearly three-quarters-of-a-million pounds."

I believe that my jaw had literally dropped open in amazement. There had been no mention of this factor, which led me to believe that –

"Is it possible," I said aloud, "that Walter isn't aware of this inheritance?"

"He didn't know it, and his daughter didn't either. I asked them when I stopped by the Yard. He was awake, and they were completely unaware that upon his fortieth birthday, in less than nine months, both the principal and accumulated interest that has been held in trust since the old man's death will be released to him, without strings or strictures, and he will go from being a tolerated and rather pitiful handy-man on the periphery of his own family's business to a fellow who is soon-to-be vastly more wealthy than his nephew – that same nephew who is now financially leveraged to the hilt, and who is quite aware of this possible source of future revenue, on the horizon and drifting ever closer to him."

"So," I said, "if Walter were to die before the designated age . . . ."

"Once again, Watson you have put your finger on the heart of it. The trust was set up by old Rhys care for the younger son whom he perceived as 'slow', and to make sure that he did in fact receive his share of his father's fortune, but only if he lived to the designated age – otherwise it reverts to Bryn's line of the family. One of the requirements was that Walter be given employment in the factory – which has been done. Thus, keeping him around was not simply an act of kindness by Brian or his father before him. Likewise, a small salary is generated by the trust for Walter's employment – and I believe that when this is settled, we'll find it quite likely that Walter never received the full amount of it that was designated for him."

"So Brian has an excellent reason for removing his uncle from the board – to gain control of the fortune that was so far out of reach. But why kill Scampton in the process? Why frame Walter for that murder, and then hope that Walter would be executed, rather than simply killing Walter?"

"I'm not yet certain. Perhaps the keepers of the trust are canny folk, and Brian was afraid that they would be suspicious if Walter were to simply die so close to coming into his inheritance. And knowing that Oswald Scampton was pressuring one Rhayader, isn't it likely that he was doing the same to Brian for some reason as well? He had worked at the glass factory his entire adult life – that's over thirty years – and he would have known Brian's father Rhys, and possibly old Bryn Rhayader as well. He would have kept his eyes and ears open, and if Brian was up to anything dodgy with his finances while trying to expand the business, who better than Scampton to notice – and then try and use that knowledge to his advantage? An excellent reason for him to die."

I raced to piece together what I had learned. "So it was well known that Oswald Scampton had leverage over Walter, apparently because of gambling debts, and also that he was trying to use this to marry Walter's daughter. While she is certainly attractive, is it possible that Oswald also had another reason to become her husband – Perhaps he had knowledge that in a few months the girl's father would become a rich man, and therefore as Walter's heir, perhaps she would eventually inherit that wealth."

"That's one way that I read it. In any case, Brian saw a way to take down two birds with one shot – he could kill Scampton before he somehow pressured Walter into approving of the marriage and diverting the fortune another way, although in truth the young lady would never have gone along with it, and more importantly he could frame Walter, and get it done now, months before the inheritance was to be released. He had to do it before Walter turned forty, or after Walter's death it would next go to Walter's daughter, and thus be lost to Brian forever, one way or another."

"Diabolical," I muttered.

"And subtle. Ah, but we've arrived."

Bert Deacon had brought us along a route through various byways to avoid the crowded main streets, depositing us at the front entrance of the hospital on Agar Street. Gregson and two constables were waiting just inside the door. Holmes looked expectantly and the inspector nodded.

"We sent a constable to retrieve him, timing it so that you could be here before he arrived."

"And Miss Rhayader?"

"On her way with her father from the Yard. He's improved quite a bit – especially after you spoke with us a few hours ago. She wanted to come along now and perform in your little drama, but I could see how angry that she was, and I believe that she would have given away too much."

I started to speak, but Holmes smiled and raised a hand. "Watson and I didn't have time to discuss the plan. Mr. Brian Rhayader has been told that Walter is near death, and has been transferred here, to the hospital. A constable was sent for him – as a courtesy. When he arrives – ah, but you shall see, for that is them I see now, walking in the door." I glanced over and saw an officer following the nattily dressed factory owner, who recognized us immediately and quickly stepped our way. Remembering Holmes's earlier warning, I put on a grave face, as if ready to impart grim news.

"Is he . . . is Walter . . . ?"

Holmes shook his head sadly. "I'm afraid that he passed ten minutes ago."

Rhayader glanced my way, and I added, "The stress of his arrest brought on some sort of attack."

I might not have seen it if I wasn't prepared to look, but the flash of triumph that seemed to cross Rhayader's eyes, if only for the briefest of instances, seemed too definite to ignore. And yet, it was immediately replaced by a look of profound sorrow. "This is terrible. He had such a sad and . . . unfulfilled life in so many ways, and for it to end so abruptly, and so soon . . . . If only he hadn't chosen to resolve his conflicts with Oswald in such a violent manner."

Gregson nodded and cleared his throat. "So true. Tell me, Mr. Rhayader, were his affairs in order?"

"What? I suppose so. There wasn't much to manage, and either I or his daughter did what was necessary. I paid for his lodgings, and for the housekeeper who essentially raised Natalie."

"We'd uncovered some mention of gambling debts, you see," added Gregson. "I wouldn't want you to be bothered about those, now that your uncle has passed."

"Thank you, Inspector. That's very kind."

"And did he have a will?" Gregson continued, glancing toward the door where a man with a crutch was being helped inside, as if the question held no great interest for him.

"No, he didn't. He'd never had any true assets to dispose of, you see."

Gregson nodded. "That tallies with what his daughter told us. But before he died, he became quite alert, if only for a little while. He wouldn't rest until he'd written a will. It was a very simple thing – he left everything – every last asset – to his daughter. It was properly fixed up by a lawyer associated with the Yard that we hold in high esteem. It was signed and witnessed not a quarter-hour before he died – although as you say, he had nothing to pass onto the girl, so getting it fixed up really did no more than give him a little piece of mind."

As Gregson said this, a slight frown pulled down Brian Rhayader's brow. I could see his thoughts racing – Did this affect anything? Would he still be able to take control of the trust as he'd planned, thinking that his Uncle Walter would die without a will before his fortieth birthday, or did the circumstances now send the fortune down a different track, forever out of his grasp?

While the man was still distracted by these questions, Holmes spoke. "I was wondering about the use of acid for etching glass," he said, in a conversational tone, and rather loud when discussing the recent death of a man. I noticed that he'd taken a step toward Rhayader, just a bit too close for the man to feel comfortable. "You use hydrofluoric acid, I believe?"

Rhayader looked at him, as if only then abandoning his worries about the will and noticing that Holmes had stepped so close. "Hmm? Yes. It's dangerous stuff, but we're careful and get good results."

"And of course that's what was used to corrode the chain holding the iron window pieces above Oswald Scampton."

"That's right."

"How much would one need to use in order to eat through a heavy iron chain like that?"

"I'm . . . I'm not sure. It's very destructive, you know. Intentionally applying it to the chain in that fashion was quite malicious."

"Indeed." Holmes edged even closer to the factory owner. "I'm something of a chemist, and generally the reaction between iron and hydrofluoric acid is rather topical – the reaction forms a paste that can be wiped away. I was curious about that, and went back and reexamined the

179

corroded chain, which was taken was taken as evidence by Scotland Yard."

Holmes shifted another inch closer. "Were you aware that one of the constables who initially arrived on the scene mistakenly touched the chain coated in acid?"

"I . . . I heard something of the sort."

"Do you know what happens when hydrofluoric acid is absorbed into the body?"

"Of course. It doesn't initially burn, as would happen if handling hydrochloric acid."

"Correct. By some curious property, the acid passes through the skin intact, penetrating and spreading through the body and, only when located in the dermis does it separate into free hydrogen and fluoride. After some time passes, and the victim begins to think that possibly he will emerge unscathed, the fluoride combines with other chemicals in the body to destroy tissue in a most terrible manner, almost liquefying it while causing extreme pain. Death follows – almost as a blessing."

Rhayader's voice cracked. "Why are you telling me this?"

"Why, simply because whomever slipped up there and painted the chain with hydrofluoric acid is now also responsible for the death of Constable Naughton, who passed away this afternoon. That's three deaths on someone's conscience."

"Three?" asked Rhayader, his slicked hair now looking somewhat ragged and a nervous sheen on his face. "But Walter only killed Oswald – and now, I suppose, this constable . . . ."

"No, the killer wasn't your uncle. He was another victim. This crime was beyond him. Knowledge that the acid wouldn't have caused the damage needed to make the chain break made us go back and reexamine the corroded links. Underneath the resultant material formed by the acid and the iron, we found evidence that the links had been filed part-way through beforehand. And there's no indication that your uncle would have had the opportunity to carry out something with that added complexity. But *you* could have."

Rhayader started to back away, only to realize that one of the constables was quite close behind him. He whipped his head around, and then back again toward Holmes.

"Several of your employees have been questioned. It was common for you to be seen on the work floor, so no one would have particularly noticed if *you* were the one to pull the iron works over Scampton's work space. No one else acknowledges doing it – "

"He did it himself!" Rhayader interrupted, but Holmes ignored him.

"You could have filed the chain ahead of time, even the night before. The acid wouldn't have been enough by itself, but applying it to already weakened links did guarantee a failure. A dab of paint on the railing above the work space – in a spot that clearly didn't need it – would be enough to imply that your uncle had been there. And you were the one who told your uncle to touch up the paint around the factory that day."

"What? You can't know that. The only one who knew was – "

"Your uncle? Yes, that's right. That's what he told us." And Holmes raised a hand, signaling a pair of constables who were now standing off to one side to open a door, allowing a tall man, his arm gripped by Miss Rhayader, to make his way awkwardly in our direction.

Brian Rhayader turned as white as a ghost. It's a literary cliché to use that expression, but in this case it was completely true. Except for his widened eyes and slight nervous twitch, he might have been a corpse pulled from the Thames.

"How – ?" he asked. "You said – "

When Miss Rhayader and the man who was clearly her father were quite close, she dropped his arm and took the remaining couple of steps to her cousin. Then with a mighty swing, she slapped him, the resounding crack echoing across the room.

"Mr. Holmes told us of grandfather's will!" she cried, and would have slapped him again, but Brian Rhayader took a stumbling step backward and tripped on his own feet, landing before the constable standing behind him.

Instead of responding to his cousin, he stared up at his uncle. "You're alive?" he said, not with wonder or joy, but barely concealed anger. "Walter – how?"

The other man, nearly the same age as Brian Rhayader but looking twenty years older, provided a gentle smile. I could see that the gravity of the situation didn't affect him. "Thank you for saving Natalie from marrying Oswald," he said, "but you didn't have to kill him. I had a plan. I would have taken care of things in my own way . . . ."

His voice drifted, and his daughter turned her attention from the man on the ground before her to her father, her expression changing from anger to sadness in an instant. Brian Rhayader used that time to scramble to his feet. Whatever he'd intended was arrested by the solid hand of the officer standing behind him.

"You can't prove I did anything!" he snarled. "Anyone might have killed Oswald. Walter here could have done it, just like you first thought. He just admitted that he intended to!"

"It isn't just Scampton's murder," rumbled Gregson. "We prevaricated about Mr. Walter Rhayader's death, but not so about

Constable Naughton. He apparently received a worse dose of the acid than we'd first known. He died today in agony. And while we don't yet have every duck in a row in terms of a case against you, Mr. Brian Rhayader, thanks to Mr. Holmes we know exactly how to start rounding them up. You're under arrest for the murders of Oswald Scampton and Constable Thomas Naughton." He turned away as if he didn't trust himself, his great hands clenched. "Get this Son of Cain out of my sight."

We chose to walk home, and we were somewhere on along Wardour Street, avoiding the busier thoroughfares, before either of us felt like speaking. Then a thought occurred to me. "Miss Rhayader's fiancé – the major from Gibraltar. Have his whereabouts been verified?"

Holmes shook his head. "He is still out of the country. I confirmed it early on. But I see that you're thinking he might have made his way back to England surreptitiously kill the man who was pestering his bride-to-be – somehow managing to sneak into the factory and inadvertently implicating his own future father-in-law. Rest assured – he had no involvement in the case."

We paused before crossing a street, and Holmes continued. "It's an ugly business, and it went on for far too long. Rhys Rhayader apparently kept the knowledge of his brother's inheritance a secret long before the son, Brian, chose to do so as well. They both withheld funds from Walter, and also knowledge and necessary assistance, in spite of giving the impression that they were generously providing for him. I've seen evidence this afternoon that Walter's young wife need not have died, but she didn't receive any help from Rhys, even when Walter asked for it.

"Both Rhys and then Brian cared for Walter in the same impersonal way that they would have nurtured an investment, with the certainty that someday when needed they could collect his inheritance. Perhaps Rhys loved his brother just enough not to go ahead and kill him, but as the event of Walter's birthday came closer, and Brian found himself in dire financial straits after over-extending himself to build the business, he decided to find a way to make sure that the fortune came to him. Hearing of Oswald's own machinations simply gave him the excuse to remove Walter. I expect that if Walter hadn't been convicted, Brian would have found a way to poison him, perhaps during a prison visit, in such a way that he would still die without ever knowing what his father had left for him."

"Still," I said, "it was such a clumsy plan. Why didn't Brian simply strike Walter down some night, as if he'd been attacked by a stranger in the street?"

"He couldn't risk the kind of attention that might bring to Walter's background. If he was killed outright, the police would begin to investigate

182

his past with an eye as to who might have a motive, possibly discovering the large inheritance that was coming his way. Better that Walter should be implicated in killing someone else, so that his death – by execution or simply the inability to survive arrest and imprisonment – would be the cause. Oswald Scampton made it easy for him."

In the coming weeks, the resources of Scotland Yard were able to gather a substantial case that was more than strong enough to convict Brian Rhayader without any difficulty whatsoever. Near the end, in some sort of attempt at easing his conscience, he signed over all rights to the business to his cousin Natalie. I understand that she consulted with her new husband, the major, but he had no interest in running a glass factory, so she sold it lock, stock, and barrel. The she and her husband, along with her father, departed from England with her father, gone long before Brian Rhayader was hanged in Newgate Prison.

I became aware that the unpleasant heat of the day had faded, and that there was now a pleasant-enough breeze from the south, carrying a curious spiced scent with it, possibly from as far away as south of the river. The sun was dropping in the sky, causing long shadows and giving the light a sentimental and brassy aspect. I'm not sure why, but instead of turning aside and continuing to my own home in Paddington, I continued to walk with Holmes toward Baker Street. We had both returned to the silence which had marked the first part of the journey, and I was unprepared when Holmes suddenly spoke, as 221 Baker Street came into view.

"Ho! What's this? I wonder what events have transpired to bring *this* particular visitor to my door. You don't recognize the crest on the carriage door? Well, no matter. Come upstairs – all we be explained soon, I expect."

In truth, I did not recognize the smart little brougham parked before the door, pulled by a pair of fine horses. The crest did look familiar, and yet the name of the owner escaped me.

The question was soon answered when we reached the top of the stairs and Holmes threw open the door of the sitting room to see a man pacing along the bearskin rug placed before the empty fireplace. I recognized him immediately. We had met with him only two days before, and his thin, tall figure, with sharp features, thoughtful face, and curling hair prematurely tinged with gray, was instantly recognizable. It was Lord Holdhurst, uncle of Percy Phelps, and the man ultimately responsible for the stolen naval treaty which had just been recovered that morning.

"Mr. Holmes!" the man cried. "I have been waiting for over an hour. Your landlady had no idea how to reach you, and could only say that she expected you back tonight, but with no guarantees. I need your help!"

Holmes calmly divested himself of his fore-and-aft cap, worn year-round in both the city and countryside with complete disregard to society's fashion requirements. Standing calmly before the revered nobleman, he asked, "What is the problem, sir?"

"It's that damned treaty!" cried the man, his clenched fists shaking before him. "It's been stolen from my own office, not eight hours after it was returned to me!"

"And Percy Phelps – ?" I asked, concerned for my old friend.

"Completely uninvolved," was the reply. "I had sent him home for more rest, He was obviously completely wrecked." He turned back to Holmes. "Can you help me?"

"Yes." Then Holmes glanced my way.

I nodded. "I'll send a note to Mary. And to Anstruther as well . . . ."

> *Holmes was seated at his side-table clad in his dressing-gown and working hard over a chemical investigation. A large curved retort was boiling furiously in the bluish flame of a Bunsen burner, and the distilled drops were condensing into a two-litre measure. My friend hardly glanced up as I entered, and I, seeing that his investigation must be of importance, seated myself in an armchair and waited. He dipped into this bottle or that, drawing out a few drops of each with his glass pipette, and finally brought a test-tube containing a solution over to the table. In his right hand he held a slip of litmus-paper.*
>
> *"You come at a crisis, Watson," said he. "If this paper remains blue, all is well. If it turns red, it means a man's life." He dipped it into the test-tube and it flushed at once into a dull, dirty crimson. "Hum! I thought as much!" he cried. "I will be at your service in an instant, Watson. You will find tobacco in the Persian slipper." He turned to his desk and scribbled off several telegrams, which were handed over to the page-boy. Then he threw himself down into the chair opposite and drew up his knees until his fingers clasped round his long, thin shins.*
>
> *"A very commonplace little murder," said he. "You've got something better, I fancy. You are the stormy petrel of crime, Watson. What is it?*

– Sherlock Holmes
"The Adventure of the Naval Treaty"

The Cliddesden Questions

Editor's Note: *As mentioned in the Foreword of* Sherlock Holmes and The Eye of Heka, *I was fortunate to stumble across a vast cache of Watsonian Manuscripts while in London my second Holmes Pilgrimage, having boldly knocked on the door of Watson's former Queen Anne Street lodgings and finding a distant descendant living within. This person, assured of my sincerity by my deerstalker hat and knowledge of Watson's life, has since given me access to these various accounts – of which I've only scratched the surface. Among those papers were a number of Holmes's documents as well, and presented here are several selected letters from April 1891, just weeks before Holmes would encounter Professor Moriarty atop the dreadful Reichenbach Falls . . . .*
– D.M.

5 April, 1891

Dear Holmes,

I hope that this finds you well. I was quite surprised to learn this morning that you were out of the country. But more of that in a moment.

I'm writing for advice regarding a curious matter that's fallen my way. This morning (being Sunday), I arose with no definite professional expectations before me, other than to check on a nearby patient who has been pestered with a chronic cough – possibly from the typical London springtime weather, or more likely from living too near to some of the Paddington air vents.

In any case, I left Mary asleep – you'll be happy to hear that her health seems to be on the mend – and slipped downstairs. The servant girl was already away to church, and even though Mary insists on fixing our breakfast on Sundays, I preferred to go hungry rather than disturb her sleep. Having prepared my own tea and then excavating a hard roll, I was walking to my study when I perceived an approaching shadow through the frosted windows beside the front door.

Rather than let the bell ring, I jumped forward and had the door open in time to startle a young man who had just placed himself there. After a few seconds of confusion upon his part, I was able to explain in a soft voice who I was and why I'd opened the door so abruptly. Then, cautioning him to be quiet, I led him inside and to my consulting room.

He is a tall thin fellow in his mid-twenties, and his back is rather stooped, as if he's already spent too much time bent over a book instead of walking or working upright. He is quite pale, and the nails at the ends of his long bony fingers are bitten to the quick. As I watched him during our conversation, the fingers of one hand constantly plucked at the other, doing so for quite a while before reversing, the picking hand now being picked, for no apparent reason except a nervous temperament.

He gave his name as Walter Pencombe and he said that he'd been directed to my door by one of the officials at Paddington – that same fellow whom I cured of the painful and lingering disease. (He never wearies of advertising my virtues, and he regularly sends to me every sufferer over whom he can gain any influence.) Naturally when the man's name was mentioned, I thought that young Pencombe was at my door seeking medical assistance, but in fact there had been a misunderstanding. He'd recently arrived from somewhere near Basingstoke and had been securing a cab to take him to see Sherlock Holmes when my acquaintance interjected himself into the conversation, referring him to me and telling him how to locate my practice within walking distance, without properly conveying that you wouldn't be found here.

After that was cleared up, I offered to provide him with tea but Pencombe declined, and then – after hearing his story – I decided to take him on to Baker Street to seek your counsel. Once there, I learned from Mrs. Hudson that you're out of the country, and she didn't know when you would be back. She wrote down the address to which I'm sending this, with the assurance that you're settled there for at least the next week or so, and thus there's a good chance that Pencombe's story will reach you.

It seems that he's the younger son of an army major who was killed at Ali Masjid in 1878, when the boy was twelve. His older brother died a year or so after that from a fever, and he and his mother were destined for penury when the lady was hired for the household staff at Pellington House, in Cliddesden. Without going into great detail, Pencombe explained that Lord Barnesbury, the master there, was a lonely widower who found himself quite taken by this comely lady now living with her son in his great house. Over the course of the next year or so, this admiration grew and he paid court to her, and was eventually his affection was returned. About ten years ago they married.

Of course, this rather scandalized the household, and there were several months where certain members of the staff were purged before things settled out. Some who had previously befriended Pencombe's mother were happy for her, while others of the servants were resentful, and a peace of sorts only returned only when these latter were finally gone. However, the situation was never idyllic, especially due to Lord Barnesbury's other step-children.

186

It seems that his previous wife had also been a widow when he met and married her, and she had brought with her a couple of children by her earlier husband, who had been some sort of banker in the City. Pencombe didn't know the details, but he believed that the fellow, named Selborne, had come under something of a cloud in the mid-1870's and blown his brains out rather than face prosecution and certain incarceration. In any case, the two children from that marriage, Jeffrey and Estelle, were both quite resentful of their step-father's new bride, and also her surviving son.

While Pencombe's mother had lived, there was an uneasy truce amongst them, and she tried to serve as a mother to the other children as well as her own son, but after her death the previous year, Jeffrey and Estelle seemed to believe that all requirements in terms of polite behavior toward my visitor had been lifted. However, Pencombe didn't really care, as his Oxford education had been financed by Lord Barnesbury, and he had left Cliddesden and eventually followed a calling into the ministry.

"I'd always had a fascination for it," he explained, "but little did I realize that my focus was misguided. I've found that I'm not cut out for it at all, really. Scholarly pursuits – that's what interests me, in the way that some doctors are better suited for research in a laboratory than seeing living and breathing patients. The study of the ancient texts is my calling, and the history of religion, and its effect on the people of the world – and how these people in turn use religion to achieve their own ends.

"But it was too late, I feared. My step-father was very proud that I'd entered the ministry, and he had funded my education, so that was that. I had an obligation that I couldn't abandon, and I couldn't ask him to do more, so I was rather stuck in the life I'd found. Or so I believed."

Here, I thought, was the crux of the matter.

"My step-father died at the end of last month," he continued, his hands worrying at one another, more frantically than before, as he dug little bits of cuticle and sometimes meat loose from around each nail, dropping them unknowingly (or uncaringly) upon my rug. You would find him a curious study. "I knew that I would receive a substantial inheritance – he'd promised my mother that it would be so – that would allow me to pursue my interests without disappointing him, or worrying about where my bread and cheese are to be found. But of course there is a snag."

Here he paused and leaned forward. I took the opportunity to hand him a cloth to wrap around his now-bleeding fingertips. He thanked me in an embarrassed way and resumed.

"At the reading of the will last Friday, there was a . . . condition. The old family attorney, Mr. Gerald Hobbes – long a crony of my step-father – stated that there would be a series of clues for each of the three of us – for Jeffrey and Estelle are the other two heirs – to solve, and upon doing so, we would then each receive our shares. We were all quite puzzled, and then Hobbes handed each of us sealed envelopes and sent us on our way.

"Outside, my two step-siblings made cutting remarks toward me, essentially letting years of anger reveal itself. I let it roll off, having learned patience a long time ago. Instead of engaging with them, I simply removed myself back to Pellington House and made my way up to my old bedroom, where I examined the contents of the envelope.

"It was a series of typed questions, and all of a biblical nature. They were extremely complex and rather obscure, and I felt that I'd be quite challenged to answer them in the time allotted. I set the letter aside to consider it further later. As I hadn't been back to Pellington House since beginning my ministerial service, there was something of a dinner affair planned for that night. Old Mr. Hobbes was set to join us, staying for the weekend, along with several more of my father's friends. I seem to have drunk too much wine during the evening, and it was in the middle of the night – or rather early yesterday morning – that I awoke, back in my room and with no memory of having gone up to bed. It was then that I noticed that the letter with the Biblical questions, which I'd left on my desk, was missing. It had been there when I'd gone down to dinner, of that I'm sure, and as I had no memory of returning to my room, I didn't know when it could have vanished. I never lock the door to my bedroom, so it would have been easy for someone – certainly Jeffrey or Estelle, or both of them – to have come in and taken it.

"Later that morning, I spoke to the family lawyer, Mr. Hobbes, and he was aghast. He stated that while there was no proof that one of the others had taken it, the conditions of the will are very strict: I must answer the questions, with my answers written on that particular sheet, and no other. Failure to do so means that my share of the inheritance will pass to Jeffrey or Estelle. Mr. Hobbes has no other copy of the text, and between us – for he briefly saw it when my step-father first delivered it to him several months ago – we couldn't recall all of the questions. In any case, remembering and then answering the questions alone won't help, for I still don't have the sheet itself, which is one of the will's requirements.

"I confronted Jeffrey and Estelle, but they angrily denied everything. Still, there was smugness about them that couldn't be ignored as they realized that they might gain my share of the inheritance. There is a time limit – one month – and precious days have already been lost, for answering those questions will not be easy. After looking around the house rather ineffectually throughout yesterday, it finally occurred to me that I should speak to Mr. Sherlock Holmes, who was of some service to a school chum of mine, Archer Kincaid, in that scandal two years ago involving the French gambler and the three wax heads."

I vaguely recalled the affair, something that you handled not long after my marriage. Thinking that this affair would be of interest to you, we then journeyed to Baker Street, where I discovered that you were in France – possibly related to that matter earlier this year for the French Government. In any case, a few days from now I'm going to arrange for Anstruther to cover my practice and go down to Cliddesden and Pellington House to see what I might find. Of course I'll have Mary forward any messages.

I hope that your ongoing work is successful, and let me know if I can be of assistance.

Best,
Watson

* * * * *

8 April, 1891
Cliddesden, Hampshire

Holmes,

It was good to hear from you, and glad that I could help in connection to your investigation in Narbonne – although ascertaining the color of Everett Tarbonnet's sole waistcoat does seem to be a most curious piece of the puzzle. One day I'll tell you about the risky ten minutes that I spent explaining to his laundress what I was about after I was caught, and I plan to hold you to your promise to tell me, when you're back in London, why this single fact was so important.

In the meantime, I can fill you in on more recent events in connection to Walter Pencombe and the curious missing document related to his legacy.

I was unable to get down here on either on Monday or Tuesday. Per your suggestion, my first stop was to meet with Lawyer Hobbes. I found him to be a corpulent and rather unpleasant old fellow, but he did seem to know the law, if one believes that he's read all of the old and worn law books filling his office. He has no clerk, and the desk where one would have sat is dark and dusty. I get the sense that his practice, while once successful, is winding down – not surprising, as he is advancing in years.

He was quite forthcoming in explaining to me the conditions of Lord Barnesbury's curious will. It was full of the usual bequests to various charities and servants, leaving the bulk of the sizable estate to be distributed equally among his three step-children, each carefully identified by name so that there would be no confusion, and with the added requirement near the end of the document that each should pass a test related to their own abilities and knowledge within one month of his death. As he died on March 26th, time has already become somewhat pressing.

Upon being questioned, Hobbes explained that Pencombe's test related to questions that were answered from any Bible, or other well-known and related scholarly works, while Jeffrey and Estelle Selborne's questions were connected to their own hobbies and interests – opera, and matters of Royal lineage, respectively. Hobbes had his own opinion about the requirements necessary to certify the inheritances. "Poppycock!" he wheezed. "I told Steven so – " (Steven being Lord Barnesbury.) " – but he wouldn't listen. He came in on the morning that the wills were to be signed, proudly showing me the little 'tests' that he'd contrived, and then sealed them in the envelope along with the signed will. Had some foolish idea that each of the three children would somehow come together with the 'fun' of solving his 'little puzzles' – as if the Selbornes might make friends with Walter after all these years in the same way that children playing at a church picnic overcome their differences and separations in the heat of a game. Steven always had a blind spot toward all of those children – especially the two from his first wife."

I asked him to elaborate, also asking if was there something about Walter Pencombe, implied in his comment, that was also objectionable and had been overlooked by his step-father?

"No, not in any definite sense. But the lad was never really suited to working toward a goal. Walter settled on the ministry, but it has always been clear there is no real interest on his part in either the good God Divine or His children. Rather, he simply wants to study and read and ponder ideas and follow one rabbit trail to another, seeing how this thought leads to the next one. Oh, if he finds his fortune by way of this will, he'll be happy for the rest of his life, and spend it all upon furthering his studies, but don't expect these studies to accomplish anything useful for the rest of us poor sheep. He'll simply keep digging through old texts, one after another, deeper and deeper, while his back grows more bent and his fingers more ragged. He'll grow old and won't even notice. He certainly won't be finding a way to turn whatever thoughts he develops towards assisting his fellow man as the Lord requires – or using the money in that way either."

This view of our client – if I may call him that – gives me added insight into the facets of Walter Pencombe, but in spite of the less-than-positive characterization, it's no reason to withhold assistance, particularly when his rightful inheritance is being cheated away from him somehow by the loss of his document, quite possibly by the actions of the other two potential inheritors.

Hobbes stated that he'd already conducted research to determine if the will and its odd requirement can be broken, and it is the opinion of several of his most learned colleagues that it's a very well-crafted document. "And so it should be," he grumbled. "I wrote it myself. Not quite ethical to be asking around concerning how to undo the wishes of my own client, you know, but I advised Steven at the time not to handle things this way – even though neither he nor I could have imagined it working out quite along these lines."

When asked if I could see the will, he frowned and then shuffled around on his desk, pulling out a document and handing it to me. "As I told you," he said, "it's all very straightforward." It was a typewritten copy of the original, consisting of several sheets, and the first page confirmed what I'd heard about the various bequests, and also the condition that each heir must answer a set of specific questions. The answers to these were to be submitted in the heirs' handwriting on the original question sheet, and if any of them failed to do so, his or her share would be divided amongst the others. If none of the three completely and correctly answered their questions, or if they failed to return them on the original sheet whatsoever, then the estate was to be liquidated and the funds distributed to charity. Before I could think about the will more closely, or look through all of the sheets, Hobbes spoke again.

"I think that Steven wrote the questions to show that he'd had an interest in their lives. He did love them, you know, and he thought that their filling out the sheets would indicate to them that he'd been paying attention to what they discussed with him over the years." He slumped back a bit. "Or perhaps – and this has occurred to me over the last few days – he did it as a way for them to choose whether they actually *want* to receive the inheritance. Steven naively seemed to believe that all three are more altruistic than is actually the case. They could decline to answer and thus refuse the money – although Jeffrey and Estelle would never choose that path. Perhaps Steven thought that Walter might refuse it, believing that his interests were more selfless. I'm afraid that knowing Walter as I do, Steven would have been very disappointed indeed. Walter obviously wants that money quite as much as the others – your presence here, Doctor, shows as much." He gave a sour grimace.

Realizing that I needed more time to study the document, I asked if I might borrow this copy long enough to make some notes. Hobbes frowned and harrumphed, but in the end he agreed. I folded it and placed it in my pocket, rising to depart. I thanked him, and he asked me my further plans, whereupon I explained that I intend to visit Pellington House tomorrow morning, having arrived too late to do so today. He confirmed that I'm staying at the nearby inn, and said that he might see me on the morrow, as he is a frequent visitor at the house.

I'm at the inn now, and I've had a chance to look more closely at the will. It seems to be in order. As I mentioned, it's a typewritten copy, without signatures. The initial paragraphs of necessary legal jargon give way to very straightforward bequests to favored staff and friends. Only near the very end of the first page are the three step-children addressed, with a simple paragraph indicating that each will receive a document with questions related to their interests, which they are to complete and then return to Hobbes. Failure to do so by the defined date will mean forfeiture of their share of the inheritance.

The subsequent sheets contained a list of various holdings and properties, and it seems that Lord Barnesbury was quite a wealthy man indeed. Also included with the will – to my surprise – was another typewritten sheet containing what appears to be the answers to the three sets of questions, although the questions themselves aren't there. I suppose that Lord Barnesbury provided this to Hobbes so that he can check the tests that each of the step-children complete and submit. I'm sure that the questions could be determined from the answers, but without the original document, these answers won't help Walter Pencombe at all. In any case, I'll need to specifically return this sheet to Hobbes tomorrow, as he probably didn't mean to give it to me when he loaned me the copy of the will.

I intend to go downstairs soon, walk around a bit, and mail this to you, and then I'll find something to eat. I'm sure that I'll have more to report tomorrow.

Watson

* * * * *

9 April, 1891
Cliddesden, Hampshire

Holmes,

With so much more to relate after my report of last night, I feel that I should have waited and sent a longer and more comprehensive letter, but I didn't know then what was to occur at Pellington House today. Hopefully this letter will arrive after the other so that you can follow the events in proper sequence, but should they not, suffice it to say that yesterday afternoon, I visited the family lawyer, Hobbes, who loaned me a copy of

192

the will, as well as inadvertently including the answers to the questions related to the inheritance. However, having them is useless without the original document to fulfill the will's requirements.

Following my meeting with Hobbes, I retreated back to the local inn, a rather sprawling and dilapidated affair left over from the coaching days, with many wings and passages that have been added to and altered over the last few hundred years – thus one follows a narrow hall over rising and falling floors, creaking with age, before taking a short turn, and then going off in another direction. Only then does one (hopefully) find one's room.

I mailed last night's letter to you, ate dinner, and then wandered about the tiny but picturesque village for an hour or so. Upon returning to my room, I found that it had been burgled – and rather clumsily. The door had been forced – although in truth the lock and fittings were in very poor and aged condition – and my bags had been opened and rifled, although some attempt had been made to restore them in the hopes that I wouldn't notice. As near as I could tell, nothing was missing.

It occurred to me, especially given the attention that was paid to the contents of my various notes and jottings, that someone may have been trying to find the answers to the will, although how they would have known that I had them was more than I could puzzle out. In any case, they were safely folded in my coat pocket, and to take them, the burglar would have had to physically attack me. I notified the management of the inn about what had occurred, and with many effusive apologies I was moved to another (better) room which could be safely locked. This morning, I received permission to have the documents received from Hobbes locked in the hotel safe, so that if I'm personally waylaid while in Cliddesden, before I can return them, the aggressor will receive nothing for his trouble but a view of my service revolver.

Upon arriving at Pellington House, I found the place in an uproar. It seems that there has been an intruder there in the night as well. Jeffrey Selborne was found in his room by a servant bringing his early-morning hot water, apparently hit over the head and unconscious. (I say "apparently" because we've seen this before – remember Ellicott in Filey who self-wounded himself so thoroughly while trying to deceive us that he permanently lost the hearing in his left ear?)

After I conveyed my name and purpose to the butler, I asked what had happened. Upon learning of the attack on Jeffrey Selborne, I offered my services, and was led up to his bedroom. He wasn't what I expected, instead being pleasant enough, and down to earth.

As I checked over the wound on his head, still a sizeable lump on the back of his skull, he related to me that he'd stayed up late last night, reading in the library and sipping more brandy than he should have done.

Then he'd made his way through the darkened house toward his bedroom along the rear of the first floor. He'd passed one of the hallways leading to another wing when he was aware of a nearby footstep – a creaking of the floor. There was a blow to his head, and then nothing until he was prodded awake earlier this morning, discovered lying on the floor of his own bedroom.

There is evidence on the old hallway carpet of where he was attacked and then dragged the short distance to his bedroom. (The backs of his heels also show evidence of dragging, as matched by the marks on the carpet and bare spots on the ancient wooden floor.) His room has been searched, and I was able to discover from the servant who found him that Jeffrey was lying tumbled on top of a number of disrupted papers scattered across the floor, indicating that he'd been deposited there *after* the rest of the room was ransacked.

"It didn't do him any good to search the room beforehand," said Jeffrey to me after I'd examined his wound, a painful lump with broken skin. "What he wanted was in my pocket – and he got it, blast him!"

He then explained that he'd been carrying his copy of his questions with him, glancing at them throughout the evening and trying to figure a way to start answering them. "I have no idea about some of them, or where to begin to find the answers." Hearing that the questions were taken from him in this way, and assuming that he's telling the truth, made me glad that I'd left those in my care securely locked in the hotel safe.

As mentioned, Jeffrey Selborne actually doesn't seem to be a bad sort of chap – quite unlike what I'd expected. I suppose that I'd expected him to be some sort of spoilt man-brat, but I found him, along with his sister, to be rather pleasant and well-spoken. It turns out that Jeffrey writes for the local Basingstoke newspaper, and his sister Estelle is a teacher. They both plan to continue in their positions after receiving their inheritance – as much as anyone, I suppose, can plan for that sort of thing before they actually have such potentially life-changing money in hand. Such a thing can't help but alter a person. In any case, it seems now that Jeffrey too has lost his chance, with his original document having been stolen as well. I suspect that whomever has taken it has put it – along with the one taken from Walter – into the nearest fire.

That leaves Estelle as the sole heir, providing that she can answer her questions. It turns out that she and Jeffrey are twins – which was not mentioned to me! – but except for sharing a birth-date and similar rather pleasant dispositions – at least when not having been recently attacked – they are nothing alike in terms of appearance. Jeremy is dark and stocky, while Estelle is fair and fine-boned, with her blonde hair shaded red in certain light. I had a chance to talk with both of them at Jeffrey's bedside, just the three of us, after the local constable and Lawyer Hobbes had been shooed out. (Walter, after initially offering his own concern, had quickly departed.)

The twins have a long-standing antipathy toward Walter Pencombe, seemingly and solely based upon his arrival in the house as a child, slightly younger than the two of them, more than a decade before. They are quite willing to believe that Walter is the one who attacked Jeffrey in the night after first unsuccessfully searching his room, taking his sheet and ruining his chances for a share of the step-father's estate. They both insist that Walter's own sheet isn't really gone – that in fact he's only establishing an alternate set of facts in order to seem innocent until the last minute when he submits his own answered test at the end of the month, as demanded in the will.

Estelle lowered her voice and said, "I've heard of you, Dr. Watson, and Mr. Holmes as well. I don't believe that you will help Walter in whatever he plans – You are honorable men and will both do the right thing, wherever the facts lead. That's why I don't mind telling you – my room was searched as well!"

Jeffrey sat upright in involuntary shock before giving a gasp of pain. Then he sank back against his pillow while his sister fussed over him, and I asked her to explain further.

"When I returned to my room after dinner last night, I too found that my room had been overturned – just the way Jeffrey's looks now. I was angry, and immediately set about straightening up. I quickly discovered that the intruder must have been after my own sheet of questions, for they were gone!"

"So," I said, "all three of you are now eliminated from the inheritance, as no one can provide a completed document."

"Walter still might," growled Jeffrey.

I was about to respond when Estelle smiled in that way women have when they reveal the winning card. "Don't count me out yet, Doctor. What the intruder stole was a copy. You see, I can use the typewriter – I keep a machine in my room, for preparing letters, and also for notes that I compile regarding a book that I'm writing regarding the history of the Plantagenets. In order to have a working copy of the questions, I had recopied them, in identical format, and safely hidden the original. When the thief found and took the sheet that was underneath some other papers on my desk, he didn't realize that he wasn't leaving with the real thing – *he stole the copy*!"

And she then removed from one of the pockets in her dress a folded sheet of paper. Handing it to me for examination, I saw that it was of a standard size and weight, covered with ten densely complex typewritten questions related to royal history.

"How difficult are these questions?" I asked.

"Very," was her reply. "Extremely. And Jeffrey said the same about his opera-related questions."

"Walter indicated that the Biblical questions were also going to require a great deal of thought and research," I added. Jeffrey started to say something, probably questioning the veracity of anything that Walter Pencombe said, but before he could do so, I continued. "I have to ask – is there any way of verifying that this sheet in my hand is the actual original, and not the copy?"

Estelle's eyes narrowed. "I suppose so, but I don't know how. Perhaps Mr. Hobbes knows a way – he was given the originals by our step-father. In any case, what are you implying, Doctor?" She stood. "Are you trying to say that I hit my own brother and stole his paper, cutting him out of the inheritance, along with Walter?"

I raised my hands to placate her. "Nothing like that. I was simply wondering more about the document itself, rather than any motives you might have. As I said, I wonder how the document's authenticity can be verified when the time comes. Whomever has stolen all three of them – two real and one false – now believes them to be out of play, and they are all likely destroyed. If I had gone to that trouble, that's what I would have done. What will happen when in due time you reveal this one? Will this person – whomever it is – be forced to try and discredit it? Or does that person already know a way to verify that your copy that he stole last night is different from the other two – should he still have Walter and Jeffrey's questions for comparison.

"There are defined ways, you know, to identify typewriting – from the shape of the letters and spacing and punctuation marks themselves, which vary between machines manufactured by different companies, to individual defects that show up on each letter, often becoming worse over time through normal wear. And even an individual's typing style can be identified from the darkness of certain letters as related to strength in that corresponding finger when the key is pressed."

I believe it was my knowledge of such, as well as my association with you and your reputation, Holmes, that helped me to convince Estelle to let me have her original sheet of questions so that I could keep it safely. Then I warned her. "Whomever searched your rooms and took the questions – both real and the copy – may notice that yours *is* a copy. I assume it's well known that you can use a typewriter?" Estelle nodded. "Then if the copy is spotted, this person will know that you still have the real set, and may make a try for them again. I believe that we should make it known that I have them now, simply to remove any danger that might hang over your head and draw it to me."

They understood the logic of this, and Estelle assured me that she was now familiar enough with the questions that she could continue to work without the actual sheet in hand. The upshot of our discussion was that we went downstairs, where I called together Walter, Mr. Hobbes (who was sipping a brandy, despite the early hour), and most of the staff, explaining what had happened in the night in the thinnest of detail. Then I elaborated, indicating that the letter stolen from Estelle's room had been a typewritten copy, and that I now had the original in my pocket, with intentions to return to London and keep it safe there. After the servants were dismissed, I had a few further words with Walter and Hobbes. The former was rather concerned that his step-siblings believed him to be responsible for Jeffrey's injury and the search of their rooms – I hadn't told him this, he'd just perceived it based on their past history. Then, with a promise to keep them informed as to further developments, I departed, leaving the young man and the lawyer in quiet conversation.

Although I had intended to return the copy of the will and the answers to the questions to Hobbes sooner rather than later, I decided to keep them for a while longer, in case they might prove useful. Retrieving my bags and then the documents from the hotel safe, I walked safely to the nearby station. I was soon back home in Paddington.

Since then, I've looked at the documents – Estelle's set of questions, and the answers for all three sets – and I'm left with a numb sense of ignorance. I don't know the questions from Walter and Jeffrey's sheets, but from studying the answers in hand, indications are that they too must have been terribly obscure and difficult. What was Lord Barnesbury thinking?

While I doubt that any attempt will be made to retrieve Estelle's questions now that I have them safely in London, I've arranged to have them safely protected, and Mary and I are being more cautious than usual – which is always considerable in any case – to maintain the security of our home.

I look forward to hearing from you.

Watson

* * * * *

13 April, 1891

Dear Holmes,

Your suggestions as to the truth proved to be correct, and the events of today certainly ended in a dramatic fashion. I'll relate them now, while they're still fresh in my mind.

After returning to London last week, I was rather at a loss in terms of which way to turn. The next day, I was visited in the late evening by Walter Pencombe, who seemed quite as perplexed as I was. He accepted my offer of a whisky and settled in to speculate for the next three-quarters-of-an-hour about who might have done what. The gist of his thoughts ran along the lines of suspecting that Jeffrey and Estelle Selborne are up to something in an attempt to cheat him out of his inheritance – the same belief, of course, that they have about him. I let him ramble, trying to get his measure, and in the end decided that Hobbes had described him correctly. I had to agree with Walter's own initial self-assessment that he didn't belong in a ministerial position, for he has a bitter streak of misanthropy that reveals itself with certain comments. Whatever the resolution of this affair, I don't see him and his step-siblings ever finding a common bond of fealty and friendship.

The next day (Saturday), I received your letter, but found that the man you'd instructed me to consult was away for the weekend, and therefore I was unable to visit him until today.

I'm constantly amazed that you – who describes yourself as essentially friendless (myself exempted) – has so many friends scattered around the capital – nay, the country, and the Continent as well – who think so highly of you. You really do yourself a disservice, Holmes, by believing that you are a solitary creature. But that is a discussion for another day. This morning found me knocking on Aaron Kincaid's door in King's Bench Walk, as you advised, and he couldn't sing your praises any higher. I am now in possession of the entire facts related to the Limping Verger and his Objectionable Tool, as well as the Singular Affair of the Thrice-Antagonized *Delincuente*. I suspect that he would have told me about several others if I hadn't reined him in – in spite of my inclinations to hear more! – and asked about the documents.

It was only a matter of minutes for him to examine them and provide his conclusion. You were correct – the copy of the will provided by Hobbes, the set of answers to all three tests, and the original sheet of questions given to me by Estelle Selborne were all composed on the same typewriting machine.

With a dim understanding of what this meant, my next stop was Scotland Yard. Gregson and Lestrade were both away, but Lanner was there, and in fine fettle, and still in a grateful mood for when you pulled his chestnuts from the fire last February in regard to that lecherous xylographer. I explained the situation, and he thought that a day in and around the Basingstoke countryside wouldn't be too objectionable.

Although we didn't know where to begin, there aren't that many lawyers in that part of the country, and even less in Cliddesden. We were discrete, and it didn't take long to determine that none of them had been consulted regarding breaking Lord Barnesbury's will, and that doing so might not have been a problem anyway.

Our next stop was Pellington House, where Walter Pencombe, as well as Jeffrey and Estelle Selborne, were waiting to meet with us. I explained how Hobbes had given me a copy of the will, along with accidentally providing a copy of the answers, and how at your suggestion, I'd had them – along with Estelle's set of questions – examined by a typewriting expert who determined that all three were produced on the same machine. They were quick to understand the significance, and I could see that there was some sort of thaw between Walter and the others, as they all realized how they had been duped in the same way. I doubt that they will ever be close, but perhaps this will be enough.

Walter produced a routine typewritten letter from Hobbes, and even with our amateur status and abilities we could all agree that it matched the three documents related to the inheritance.

Lanner and I then visited the local police station, where we obtained the assistance of a burly constable – the same fellow who had been out the morning of Jeremy's attack. Hobbes's office wasn't far away, and I believe that I saw him framed in his window as we approached, although he wasn't standing there when we arrived – if he had truly been there at all.

What followed was unpleasant, as the surly old man lost his temper, refusing to acknowledge the charge, and insisting that the documents that he'd given to me, as analyzed by the expert, had been somehow switched, and that I was attempting to destroy his reputation for reasons that he couldn't explain, since I'd never heard of him before last week. Possibly, he ranted, I was in collusion with Walter Pencombe to steal the entire estate. At one point he was so angry that I feared for his health, expecting some sort of apoplectic seizure, but Lanner and the constable seemed less concerned, and the lawyer was taken into custody.

After Hobbes was removed, a search of the papers in his office revealed several of interest. First, in spite of my belief that he would have destroyed them, the very difficult questions, in their original form, stolen from both Walter Pencombe and Jeffrey Selborne, were found in an unmarked file – along with three very different sets of questions in what turned out to Lord Barnesbury's handwriting, apparently those that were originally intended to be included with the will. They were much simpler, and contrived to convey the man's affection for his step-children. For instance, one of those on the sheet intended for Walter asked, *"What is Proverbs 23:24?"* A search through a Bible ironically found on the criminal lawyer's desk revealed the answer to be: *"The father of a righteous child has great joy; a man who fathers a wise son rejoices in him."*

I suppose that Hobbes has that typical lawyerly fear of destroying documents – a similar trait seems to hang around your neck, Holmes! – and rather than burn the originals, along with those that he stole, he kept them, which will only add further evidence of his machinations to clumsily steal the estate.

I believe that I understand why Hobbes wrote the much more difficult questions – the will only said that questions must be answered, and that they must be on the original sheet, so he knew that he could substitute impossible questions and no one would realize what had occurred. If the heirs had received the actual questions contrived by Lord Barnesbury, they could have filled them out in five minutes and put them right back into Hobbes's hands, so he came up with a much longer set of very difficult questions in an effort to prevent them from being answered quickly – or at all. Then, while they tried to sort through them, he would have time to steal the original required sheets at his leisure before the end of the one-month deadline. He had to type them, as he couldn't duplicate Lord Barnesbury's handwriting.

My only question is why did Hobbes go to the trouble of typing up a list of answers to the much harder questions in the first place? It seems very much a waste of time.

I look forward to hearing your thoughts, and I hope that your current endeavors conclude successfully.

Best,
Watson

* * * * *

16 April, 1891

Watson,

Many thanks for your timely report, and I'm glad that the matter was resolved satisfactorily. You really handled it very well, and I have no doubt that, given a little time to ponder it on your own, you would have reached the same conclusions regarding the significance of the typed documents – although you wouldn't have known about the expert assistance that could be provided by Aaron Kincaid. Now that you've met him, he will be another resource at your disposal.

My suspicions were first alerted when you wrote that an attempt had been made to steal the copy of the will from you just hours after it was put into your hands by Hobbes. What would this accomplish? The will wasn't a secret. Was it instead an attempt to get the answers to the questions that had also been given to you? As you pointed out, without the original question sheets, having the answers made no difference. But at that point, the Selborne twins still presumably had their question sheets, so it would benefit them to have the answers. And possibly Walter Pencombe had lied, as the twins later suspected, and still had his set too.

And yet, how could they have known that you had the answers, and so soon after you had received them? They had apparently been given to you inadvertently. Hobbes had no clerk who would know that you had either the copy of the will or the answers. Hobbes alone knew that you had the copy, and he may or may not have realized after you left that you also now had the answers. But why would he want to steal them from you? It might have been to get them back in case you subsequently offered provide the answers to one or more of the heirs, but he could have found you at the inn – where he knew you were staying – and simply asked you for the sheet, explaining that it had been provided to you by mistake.

It was your next letter, explaining that attempts had been made to steal the other sets of questions, that made me ponder a bit deeper. You had related how Hobbes stated that Lord Barnesbury briefly showed Hobbes the questions, and then sealed them in the envelope with the will. As you also stated, he had presumably provided the list of complex answers to Hobbes so that the lawyer could verify whether they were correct.

I considered again what you had told me of the reference in the will to the questions. It was vague, and gave no indication whether the questions would be easy or difficult. It occurred to me that this vagueness would serve to the advantage of someone who wanted to make answering the questions much more difficult than might have been originally intended – possibly to the point where they couldn't be answered at all. But who would benefit from such a course of action?

The obvious answer was Hobbes, the man in control of the estate, and how it would be disbursed to the various charities if the questions weren't answered correctly – if it was disbursed at all. And related to that, who would be the one man who would be able to swap more difficult questions for the easier versions, again making it nearly impossible for the conditions to be fulfilled? The answer was also Hobbes.

Possibly he originally intended to simply make the questions as difficult as he could, so that they couldn't be answered. And yet, they would have to be legitimate questions, and if some challenge were made when the heirs read them, he, as the administrator of the dead man's test, would be expected to have the answers.

He probably began to doubt himself. What if one of the heirs did successfully answer the questions before the deadline? Perhaps the three heirs were more knowledgeable than Hobbes realized. What if the substitute questions that he'd researched and assembled, thinking them to be nearly impossible, were in fact mere child's play – common knowledge to anyone that was an expert in his or her field: Religious texts, or opera, or Royal lineage.

So his doubts may have continued to gnaw at him, and when Hobbes had the chance on the very night that the will was read, I suspect that it occurred to him that he could avoid that matter entirely by acting sooner, rather than simply stealing the original sheets, which fortunately for him had been designated in Barnesbury's will as being required to fulfill the conditions of the inheritance.

Walter Pencombe's list was probably the easiest to steal. Hobbes simply went to his room and found it lying there. You indicated in your letter that Walter said he'd left it out before going to dinner. (You also indicated that Hobbes is a regular visitor to the house, so he would know his way around, and how to creep about unobtrusively. His presence would cause no comment.) Walter's drunken unconsciousness and subsequent awakening in his own room the next morning may have had nothing to do with the theft at all.

But it would have been more difficult for Hobbes to get at the twins' lists of questions, and Hobbes had certainly convinced himself by then that he needed to do so for the same reason that he'd taken Walter's – what if they actually provided him with the correct answers?

When I understood that Hobbes was likely the one to take Walter's list, I asked myself why he would need to also presumably steal back the documents that he had loaned to you – an attempt that occurred even before he took those belonging to the Selborne twins later that same night. What made it necessary for him to take the risk of entering that rambling old coaching inn and searching your room? That was dangerous, but possibly not as much as we might think – No doubt he knows the old building's layout very well. Still, there was more peril doing that than when he stole the documents in Pellington House, where he was a frequent and expected visitor.

I decided that some factor related to the different documents in your possession must have been his motivation to do something that might reveal his actions. What could that be?

The documents you held that night were the copy of the will and the list of answers. Based on what I knew then, the copy might have been made by Hobbes after the original was opened and read. The answers could have been the original document provide by Lord Barnesbury, or it could have been a later typewritten copy, also prepared in Hobbes's office. There is no reason that Hobbes shouldn't have made working copies of both, with the originals safely put away. But if they were both copies that had made in Hobbes's office, then they would have likely been typed on the same typewriting machine.

But recall that at that time, both twins still had their own original lists of questions. What, I asked, if Hobbes feared that somehow you would get a look at those when you went to Pellington House the next day, and realize – with your experience over the last decade in a number of criminal investigations – that they were *all* typed on the same typewriter – even the list of supposedly original (and very difficult) questions?

For if the "original" questions in the heirs' possession were typed on the same typewriter as that in Hobbes's office, then they wouldn't be the "original" documents after all, even though they were supposed to have been written, delivered, and sealed by Lord Barnesbury with the will. And if they weren't the original documents, then who could say if they were the original questions?

From there it was fairly easy, and that's why I advised you to see Aaron Kincaid, who has made several notable studies upon evaluation of typed documents. By then you had in your possession the copy of the will (certainly typed in Hobbes's office), the list of answers (which might or might not have been typed there), and Estelle's supposedly "original" list of questions, which was supposed to have been prepared by Lord Barnesbury himself, before he arrived at Hobbes's office, and placed almost immediately in the sealed envelope with the will, where it had supposedly remained until the will was read. As you no doubt saw, and as Kincaid confirmed, Estelle's "original" list of complex questions was also typed on Hobbes's office machine, with its own unique set of characteristics and defects, meaning that Hobbes had typed the document given to Estelle that he'd claimed was the one prepared by Lord Barnesbury.

It all fell into place. Hobbes hoped to remain in control of the estate – and it's very doubtful that the charities named in the will would ever see a fraction of what they might expect otherwise. It's an old story. To accomplish this, he created and substituted the list of very difficult questions. Then, upon uneasy reflection, he'd decided to commit assault and burglary to get his hands on the documents before they could be either examined or completed.

It was a pretty little problem, and shows how a man can quickly dig himself into a spot where he can't properly see the right way out. It sounds from your description as if Hobbes doesn't have too many more years left, and he could have likely continued to maintain an adequate living managing the estate and its affairs for the three heirs. Instead, he saw in Lord Barnesbury's vague will, and its reference to questions, a chance to hijack the estate entirely. He somehow talked himself into thinking that the plan would work, and that no one would recognize that he alone had ended up the sole beneficiary, in control of the disbursal of the funds, by way of a dodgy will. When he became aggressive and tried to take back the sheets, he only accelerated his downfall.

I appreciate the distraction that this provided. I plan on moving on to Nimes in the next day or so, as this business seems to lead from one strand of the web to five others. I'm not sure when I'll be able to return to London, but I hope to see you one way or another in just a few weeks. I'll be glad when this whole problem is finally over – the Professor is a nimble opponent – and I think that when he's finally locked away or hanged, I'll be able to rest for two or three years, and look back upon a job well done.

Ah, but that's wishful thinking, and as we both know, I would soon be hungry for another distraction.

My best wishes to you and Mary, and I remain,

Your friend,
Holmes

The Affair of the
Mother's Return

It was in the first year of my marriage that I received one of those laconic messages from my friend, Mr. Sherlock Holmes, requesting my presence at our old lodgings in the northern end of Baker Street. As my practice was never very engaging, especially that day, and my wife's health was causing no concern that day, I decided to go. Shaking off my mid-morning drowsiness, and donning my coat against the autumn chill, I departed.

The walk from Paddington was unusually pleasant, and I had time to ponder our recent trip to Edinburgh, and that little matter of the Robert Burns Cameo at the recently opened Scottish National Portrait Gallery, wherein an innocent substitution of an obviously inferior copy had led to a suicide, a wedding, and a promise to the Lord Advocate that Holmes and I would never again return to the Gallery again without a specific invitation.

Letting myself into the entryway at No. 221, I paused for a moment to listen. The house was quiet, and I decided that Mrs. Hudson must be out, as she was normally quite alert as to the comings and goings through her front door.

I began to climb the steps, aware that if Holmes were upstairs, he would hear me and recognize who I was from my characteristic limp – although now much less noticeable than when I first mounted these steps years earlier. Pausing for a moment on the turn of the stairs, I looked out the landing window into the rear yard, and the plane tree growing there. It hadn't ever been a very healthy fellow, even at the best of times, and it had never quite recovered from when Holmes had poured the end results of one of his chemical experiments into the dirt nearby, indicating that the contents, used to poison a banker, were far too foul for London's sewers.

With a sigh, I shook my head and continued up the steps. Knocking on the closed sitting room door and then turning the knob without waiting for a response, I stepped inside to find Holmes curled into his chair, his head wreathed in pipe smoke. With a languid wave, he silently gestured toward my old armchair.

I settled into the well-worn cushions and glanced around the room. As usual, it was filled with relics of my friend's cases, an ever-changing collection of the bizarre, the random, and the unexplained. Since my last visit, only a few days earlier, I observed the addition of some sort of tribal figurine, stalwartly but ineffectively anchoring a slumping pile of papers on the floor beside the dining table, and a bottle of reddish liquid, in which there're floated what suspiciously resembled a severed human great toe. I wanted to ask about the significance of these new items before Holmes had the chance to progress to some new bit of business, thereby losing interest in them. Before I could clear my throat to speak, however, he was straightening in his chair and tossing me a letter.

Reaching for a pinch of tobacco, and without a word of greeting, he said, "I would value your insight on this little matter."

I picked up the sheet that had landed perfectly in my lap. It consisted of a single leaf of thick and somewhat expensive stationary. Noting that it had been folded once, I asked, "Was there an envelope?"

"Good, Watson!" replied Holmes. "You are examining all aspects of the item before jumping to conclusions. Our friends at the Yard would have simply read the thing."

"Not altogether unreasonable," I said wryly. I glanced at the sheet. It was a short message, written only on one side, with a broad-tipped pen. Right handed, with a very calm and even line, showing no signs of hurry or emotional distress. I tilted the paper back and forth toward the fading afternoon light from the window behind Holmes. No watermark, and it was a true black ink, not something watered down that one might find at a bank, hotel, or other public location. I checked – there was no odor, such as tobacco or incense, to provide any information. The stiffness of the paper, as well as the apparent quality of the ink, indicated a person who was not necessarily of means, but comfortable.

"The envelope?" I repeated.

He picked it up from the small octagonal table by his chair. I had already seen it there, and suspected that it matched the missive in my hand.

This time he leaned forward to hand it to me, perhaps not trusting his ability to repeat the perfect toss of the letter, possibly due to the envelope's flap disrupting its aerodynamic symmetry. I glanced at him as I took possession of it, and saw a slight smile on his face, and I knew that he knew what I was thinking.

The envelope resembled the stationary, and the address on the front was written by the same pen, and with the same hand. There was no return address or postage stamp, indicating that in some way the message had been hand delivered.

Finally I turned my attention to the contents of the letter.

Dear Mr. Holmes, (it read)

I am taking the liberty to request an appointment with you today at 10 a.m. (I glanced at the mantel clock – ten minutes until the hour.) *to lay a matter before you concerning my parents. Perhaps you have heard of the unfortunate Leland and Sarah Cole. I had believed the affair to have been long settled, but recent events have served to arouse my curiosity.*

Unless I receive word to the contrary, I shall plan upon laying this matter before you.

Very best regards,

Andrew Cole

"And how was this letter delivered?"

"A commissionaire. Mrs. Hudson didn't recognize him. If it becomes important, we can certainly track him down. However, the fellow will be here in just a few moments, and the question will likely be answered in due course."

I glanced toward the envelope. "How did he expect to receive word if he didn't provide his address?"

"Quite right. He is young."

"You know him, then?"

"Rather, I know of him by knowing of his parents.

"The letter is so calmly written. It's curious he didn't notice that error."

"It is calm, but I suspect that the emotions related to the situation run deep."

"And his parents?"

He reached toward one of his scrapbooks, standing against the mantel beneath his Persian slipper. I had noticed it there, but had credited it no importance in relation to this matter, as there were so many other haphazard items scattered hither and yon about the room. Handing it to me, he added, "The page is marked."

Describing it as a "page" was charitable. Holmes's scrapbooks were collections of news clippings, brochures, programs, labels, and photographs, mixed in with the occasional indiscriminate glassine envelope of ash, tissue, or a hundred, nay, a thousand other possibilities. Residing on a sagging shelf mounted to the wall between the fireplace and Holmes's bedroom, these commonplace books were the primary annex to Holmes's brain attic. He spent a great deal of time updating them, culling articles from newspapers, and making annotations throughout about this or that item, or an individual who had come to his attention and was marked down for greater things, in the sense that the person was putting his first steps on a path leading to the gallows.

After having a small packet fall to my lap containing what appeared to be a fine collection of mismatched small animal claws, I found the items to which my attention had been directed: Namely, a clipped and tidy stack of newspaper articles, now yellowed with age, relating to Leland Cole.

Taking them out, I closed the book, such as it was, and stood it on the floor beside my own chair. "You could have simply handed me the clippings," I said, beginning to quickly read through them.

There were half-a-dozen, all from mid-1880, except for one dated early the following year, specifically February 1881. Although presenting different perspectives, the facts of the case were rather clear. Cole had been a rising constable with Scotland Yard when the Turf Fraud Scandal of '77 led to the formation of the CID the next year. During the reorganization, he had been promoted to Detective Sergeant, a position held until he was forced to resign three years later. Apparently, he had been implicated in the theft of a great deal of gold coins from a group of bank robbers who were all found dead in a Bermondsey lodging house. The gold was never found, but it was suspected that Cole had been in league with the men, killed them, and then taken the loot. While no firm proof was ever found, his credibility within the Force was shattered, and he was released from his position.

The final article from 1881 simply indicated that no new clues had been found, either toward identifying and locating the killer or the stolen money, although there was the obligatory statement that "*the police are following certain leads*".

"The evidence must have been quite strong against the man," I said. "'*Innocent until proven guilty*' didn't save his job."

"I understand that the feeling was that his connection to the matter was well established, if not proven. As you know, I was out of England during that portion of 1880, so I had no opportunity to consult on the matter. When I arrived home later that autumn and set about catching up on all that I had missed, this came to my attention, and I mentioned it to Lestrade, but he was quite understandably reluctant to open old wounds."

"Even if it meant resolving the question?"

"Your confidence in me is noted, Watson, but in those earlier days, the official force was much more inclined to see me as a useful amateur rather than a prized confidante."

I tapped the letter from Cole with a finger. "You say that Cole is young?"

"Yes. He would have been about sixteen at the time of the murders, as I recall."

"Making him about twenty-six or twenty-seven now. Not so young. I was nearly twenty-eight at Maiwand, and you were also already well established by that age."

"True. Perhaps I did err in crediting his epistolary *faux pas* to simple youth and inexperience. Another question to ask him, as I hear the bell ringing. Excuse me, Watson, while I go let him in. Mrs. Hudson is visiting her sister, and I am left alone to pilot the domestic ship."

And so saying, he made his way downstairs. I heard the usual business of the door opening and closing, removal of a coat, murmured conversation, and then the return of the detective with his client.

We were introduced, and I had a chance to observe Andrew Cole as he settled into the basket chair across from the fire. He acknowledged the lack of available tea or coffee, and waved away an offer of something stronger. He was in his mid-twenties, as expected, a big fellow with longish blonde hair, almost Byronic in its style. He was broad-shouldered, but seemed to have inherited it rather than developed it from hard work. His hands were well-manicured, and maintained for work with pen and paper, rather than tools. He had a frank open countenance, but it was marred by worry lines between his brows, and he sat forward on the chair instead of relaxing. He glanced at his note on the table beside my chair and, looking back and forth between us, began to apologize.

"I realized just moments after it left my hand that I had neglected to provide a return address, should this appointment be inconvenient." He glanced toward me. "Mr. Holmes explained downstairs that this time is acceptable, but I never meant to foist myself upon you so impolitely."

"We *had* noticed that you had neglected to tell us where to reach you," replied Holmes, his fingers steepled before his eyes.

Andrew Cole nodded. "I wrote and rewrote what I would say before carefully copying the final missive, but I never thought about something so basic."

"It is of no matter. You are correct that I recall the matter of your father, but I didn't know of any related involvement by your mother, as mentioned in the letter."

"I'm afraid that there is more to the affair than was ever made public, and my mother's reputation must have been as compromised as my father's, if only by association."

Holmes gestured at Cole to continue.

209

"As you may remember, my father was a Detective Sergeant in 1877, and those were good times for us. We had a small home, and while there was never much to spare, to be sure, we were warm and well-fed, and I felt safe. Then came the troubles.

"I'll admit that I was ignorant at the time of much that occurred. I was aware of a tension that hadn't existed before, and my mother and father, who had previously been much devoted to one another, now shared harsh words, often in whispers as they tried to protect me from knowing exactly what was happening. Only later was I able to force my father to tell me the story – at least, his version of it, as I'm sure to this day that he held back many important facts.

"According to him, on the night of the incident he had finished his duties and was returning home. It was quite late, and as he passed by a building, one of many in a row of darkened structures, his instincts as a former constable were aroused when he saw an unlocked door, standing partly open. (Much was made at the time that the building where this occurred was nowhere near the direct route between the police station where he worked and our home, and he never adequately explained exactly why he was actually in that area.)

"He knocked and received no answer. Entering the building, he perceived a single light coming from a back room, when the rest of the building was in darkness. Proceeding cautiously down the hallway, he entered a kitchen, lit by a single gas-lamp. He told me that the harsh light horrifyingly highlighted the three bodies lying on the floor, each of them dead and with their throats cut.

"As you'll recall, it was later determined that all of them had apparently been made unconscious by an opiate that was found in the stew that all three had eaten. The pot was still on the stove, and it contained more than enough of the narcotic to have put a dozen men to sleep. Apparently whoever had done so had then taken the opportunity to kill them unhindered.

"My father instantly recognized the three men as members of the Oak Ridge Gang, as all of them had been sought for the past couple of weeks following the robbery of the funds being accumulated by the Close Brothers for the formation of their bank."

Holmes nodded. "I recall that the theft wasn't widely reported, as the victims didn't want to undermine confidence in their upcoming financial endeavor."

"So I understand. In any case, the gold was never recovered."

"And your father," added Holmes, "was accused of taking advantage of the situation at best, and possibly of being involved in the theft."

"Yes. The official theory, although he was never charged, was that he was somehow in league with the Wards, the father and two sons, and that he had gone to meet them at that out-of-the-way house at the end of his working day. As you probably know, by the time he sounded the alarm, it was several hours after the end of his shift, and he was unable to account for either his time in between or his reasons for being in that area."

"And it was thought," I said, catching up, "that he went there for the meeting, put the men to sleep, killed them, moved the gold, only to then return and sound the alarm."

"Exactly, Doctor."

"But that makes no sense!" I exclaimed. "If he had no known connections to these men, he could have killed them and gotten away with the money without ever returning and sounding the alarm, thus trapping himself in that gyre."

"The reasoning power of the Yard," said Holmes wryly, "especially in those days, left a great deal to be desired. You've seen it a hundred times yourself, Watson. How often do they seek the simplest solution, bending facts to fit their theories?"

"Sometimes the simplest solution *is* the best," I said. "You've referred to Occam's Razor yourself, Holmes. And I've found in medicine that rare is rare and common is common."

"And stupid is stupid. However, in this case, it would have been uncommonly stupid indeed for Mr. Cole to have allowed himself to become more involved than he already had to be, even assuming that he was guilty." Holmes turned to our visitor. "Do you have any more information? Such as what happened after your father was drummed out of the Force without more substantial evidence of his guilt?"

"Nothing for certain, Mr. Holmes. As I said, at first I wasn't even aware of a problem. I have no recollection of the specific day when this would have happened. Back then, I slept quite soundly through the nights and hadn't many cares in the world. It was only over the course of the next days and weeks that I became aware of the increasing tension. My father and mother began to argue, although trying to hide it from me. It escalated to the point that finally, after a few weeks, my mother declared that she was leaving. Only then, when she was gone, did my father explain, in a very simplified way, what had happened and what was suspected of him. He was a broken man, and the fact that his own wife apparently believed the accusations against him only served as the final nail."

"And your mother left you there with him?" I asked, somewhat shocked.

"Exactly, Watson!" cried Holmes. "Quite unusual. Unheard of, as a matter of fact. That alone raises this matter to a different level." Turning back toward young Andrew Cole, he asked. "Why, now? What has happened that you've decided to consult me, after all this time? Has some new development occurred?"

"It has, Mr. Holmes. I have seen my mother!"

"And that is unusual because . . . ."

"Because I hadn't seen her since she left, back in 1880."

"What?" I asked. "You've had no contact with her whatsoever since that time?"

"No, Doctor. Following her departure, my father lost his job with the Force. He was able to obtain work as a groom at the estate of Lord Belving, in Surrey. My father had once done him a good turn, and it hadn't been forgotten. I spent the rest of my childhood, what little there was of it, there on the estate. Lord Belving, having no children of his own, took an interest in me and saw to my education. Upon reaching adulthood, I was able to obtain a scholarship to university, and upon completion, I entered a position in the City – again through Lord Belvin's influence. It was there, yesterday, that I happened to see my mother, in the most unusual manner imaginable.

"I was part of a group of three young men accompanying my supervisor into a meeting. We were standing in the hallway, waiting for our client, when a door to a nearby room opened. As the group inside exited, one of my companions nudged me and nodded toward a woman in black. 'That's the Countess of Houghton,' he said. 'Her husband just died. Worth millions, she is.'

"As this woman stepped into the hallway, speaking to one of our representatives, she glanced my way. The recognition between us was immediate and certain. She was literally rocked back on her heels, and I believe that I was as well. She said something to the men around her, quickly lowered her veil over her face, and set off quickly down the hallway, her companion hurrying to keep up.

"I hurriedly excused myself from my puzzled associates and went after her. I caught up with them in the great hall near the door, calling for her to stop. She turned to me, for just a moment, and I couldn't read her face, although I could see the sparkle of her eyes under the veil. There was so much that I wanted to ask, but I found that my throat was closed. Before I could find the words, she murmured, almost angrily it seemed, 'Leave me be!' and turned away. Her companion, whom I now realize was likely a solicitor, took her elbow and hurriedly directed her toward the door. Before I had sense to follow, she was gone."

"And did you relay this story to your father?" I asked.

Andrew Cole shook his head. "Sadly, he passed two years ago. He had always been a broken man, and gradually he simply seemed to lose interest in the business of living. It was almost a blessing."

"And you never," asked Holmes, "found out any other details about the stolen gold?"

"I did not. I'm convinced of my father's innocence, but he was quite reticent on the matter, and as I said, I always felt that there was more to the story."

"What do you wish from us?" asked Holmes, gesturing in my direction. "Although it might bring you some piece of mind, finding the gold now wouldn't bring your father any comfort, although it might clear his reputation. However, the facts of the matter could end up being as damning as it has always been assumed."

"I want to know the truth. I always have, and this meeting with my mother, however brief, has sharpened that to an urgent degree. I could not sleep last night. But as you say, dredging things up now might make matters worse for all concerned. My mother has apparently made a new and successful life for herself, although I know not how. What if my own clumsy and amateur investigation were to spoil that for her somehow? I thought of you, Mr. Holmes, and realized that you could apply your talents with the skill of a surgeon. Will you look into the matter?"

Holmes was quiet for a moment, his gaze far away, and then he seemed to pull himself back to the present. "I will, Mr. Cole, on the condition that you leave matters in my hands entirely. As you say, there is the possibility that this old business could have fresh implications and most unsatisfactory results."

"Then I shall be satisfied. I'll return to my place of business – here is my card – and will await your report."

With that, hands were shaken, and our young visitor departed. Turning to me, Holmes asked, "Do you have a few hours free, Watson?" I suspect he already knew the answer, and when I replied affirmatively, he responded, "Excellent!" Rubbing his hands, he set about getting ready, and in just a few moments, he was locking the front door behind us while I whistled for the third empty cab to pass by. Soon we were heading toward Whitehall and New Scotland Yard.

The streets weren't crowded, and it wasn't long at all before we were seated in front of our old friend, Inspector Lestrade, explaining our mission. A pained look crossed his face, and he stood up, looking from his window toward the Westminster Pier down below, a location which I shall ever associate as being the initial point of departure for what ended up being a dangerous river chase down the Thames, ending near the Plumstead Marshes.

"Leland Cole," muttered Lestrade, "is a blot upon the Yard's copy-book."

"Would you care to elaborate?" asked Holmes.

The inspector shook his head. "It's distasteful, Holmes. We were just a few years past the scandals, and all of us were working to build respect for our profession. And then Cole goes and murders a pack of robbers and steals the gold."

"Which has yet to be found," I added.

"That's right," said Lestrade. "Which only makes it worse. The entire case is still on the books as unsolved."

"I believe we understand the basic facts – the men were put to sleep, and then killed when they couldn't resist. They had obviously been hiding in that house ever since the theft. Were there any other facts that were not related in the press at the time? Something that the police held back, as you often do?"

Lestrade ran a hand over the lower part of his face, glancing again out of the window. "No, Mr. Holmes, it was very straightforward. The food was analyzed, especially when someone asked how three men would have sat there patiently at table and allowed their throats to be cut. We know that they had the gold – they were identified, as you may recall, by an eyewitness during the theft – and there was no coin found with them. Obviously whoever went to the trouble to kill them, silence them, took it, and it hasn't been found since."

"Was there anything that would have made the loot identifiable?" I asked. "Were the coins unusual, for instance?"

"No, Doctor, nothing about them stood out. And there wasn't a flood of them suddenly appearing to indicate that they were being spent. They simply vanished, and have remained that way for nearly a decade."

Holmes frowned. "If there was nothing unusual about the murders – if one can say that the poisoning was normal – then what about the robbery of the gold itself?"

"It occurred two weeks before. It was being loaded into wagons, carried in chests from the basement of Drummonds to be moved to Close Brothers. The transfer was carried out in the evening, in order to minimize interest, in the mistaken belief that not attracting attention to it would make the move more successful. Only later was it determined that the Close Brother's receiving carriage was not manned by their employees, as planned, but rather by the Wards, who had tied up the actual bank employees some hours earlier and left them in an empty room in Cheapside. It was only by accident that a passer-by identified Marcus Ward as one of the men loading the carriage and was able to put us onto their identity. We wasted a lot of time looking for them around their home in Oak Ridge, near Woking. That's how the press named them the Oak Ridge Gang. However, we had no signs of them until we were notified – by Leland Cole – of the discovery of their bodies a couple of weeks later."

"And there was no other clue? Nothing else about the robbery itself?"

"Nothing, except that we decided that it had to have been planned with inside information, someone at one of the banks, so that the Wards would know how to arrange to take the place of the actual guards in order to receive the money."

"And were there any clues as to who this inside person was?"

"None. All of the employees at each bank passed muster." He frowned, and after a moment added, "Except . . . ."

"Hmm?"

"It's nothing, I'm sure, but there *was* a cleaning woman at the time, at the Close Brothers building, who was unaccounted for after the fact. Simply stopped coming to work in the evenings, and we couldn't trace her. But that probably meant nothing. After all, people like that leave and change jobs all the time."

"No doubt," said Holmes, rising. "Thank you, Inspector. You've provided us with a great deal of help."

Lestrade gave him a canny look. "I trust that you'll let me know where this leads."

"I am always on the side of justice, as you know," replied Holmes. I believe that Lestrade understood the unspoken implications of that statement as well as I.

Outside, Holmes led us west toward Parliament. "I must send a few wires, and then, while we wait for replies, what do you say to a restoration of the inner man?"

I agreed, and we strolled toward a nearby telegraph office, where Holmes composed his messages, and then informed the clerk that we would return in an hour for replies. Then, as if by mutual agreement, we made our way round and about to Northumberland Street, and so into a fine pub of our acquaintance, where we passed the time with a late lunch.

About two o'clock found us back at the telegraph office, where Holmes's replies were waiting. One was from Andrew Cole, stating simply that, during the months leading up to the incident, his father has worked a shift spread over the afternoon and into the late evening, and that his mother hadn't worked at all. The second was from Langdale Pike, that cesspool of societal gossip, indicating that the Countess of Houghton was currently residing in her Mayfair home. There were various other facts about the lady's background in the lengthy message. I confess that as I read through her *vitae*, I couldn't understand how such a woman could have once been Cole's humble mother. Holmes waved Pike's wire in the air. "I think I see a bold venture in our futures, Watson. And as they say, *'Nothing ventured, nothing gained.'*" Hailing a cab, we set out for Bruton Place.

Fifteen minutes later, we stood before a well-kept but discreet multi-story house. A ring of the bell resulted in the appearance of a man in his fifties, opening the door with a quizzical expression. We presented our cards and were invited inside, to wait and see if the lady of the house was at home.

I knew but little about the Countess, having never heard of her until a few weeks earlier, when it was reported in the press that her much older husband had died of a coronary thrombosis while traveling with her upon the Continent. I knew that we were treading dangerously on bad form by visiting a recent widow in such a manner, but I had long ago learned to swallow discomfort in such situations when in the presence of Sherlock Holmes. He had no patience for such societal contrivances, and as had often proven to be the case, he was correct in his beliefs.

The butler who had initially greeted us showed us into a formal sitting room, and in just a moment, the lady herself entered, accompanied by a silky man in his thirties. Like the Countess, he was dressed in black, and he hovered near her, his hand darting toward her often – not quite touching her, but almost. I wondered if this was the man that Andrew Cole had thought to be her solicitor.

"Gentlemen?" he asked. "What is the meaning of this intrusion? Surely you are aware of the Countess's recent loss. There are better times and ways to pay your respects."

"And you are – ?" asked Holmes.

"I am Milton Crane, a close friend and advisor to the Countess."

"I see," said Holmes. Turning to the lady, Holmes said, "Madam, do you think it wise to discuss your personal business in front of this gentleman?"

She lifted her veil then and gave a tight smile. She was a handsome woman in her mid-forties, well kept, and still quite lovely. In her younger days, she would have certainly been a beauty indeed. "I have no secrets from Milton," she said. "Won't you be seated?" She gestured toward a grouping of chairs, and – under Milton Crane's disapproving gaze – we all found our places.

"As you wish," said Holmes, "*Mrs. Cole*."

The lady's eyes widened, clearly surprised, as I was myself. Holmes had apparently decided to cut through the politeness and subterfuge and proceed to the heart of the matter. Milton Crane started to make some sort of squawk, but her raised hand was enough to instantly silence him.

The Countess smiled tightly. "I see that Andrew didn't wait long at all before setting you upon my trail."

Holmes nodded. "Your son – "

"*Son!*" exclaimed Crane. "The Countess has no son!"

"Do be quiet, Milton," she said, without vexation, or really without any emotion whatsoever. "You surely knew that I had a life before I married Eustace."

"But a *son*. Why, I never had any idea. Why wasn't I told – ?" Another wave of the hand, and he sank and subsided back into a chair, a puzzled look filling his smooth face.

"I was glad to see Andrew looking so well," she said. "I had quite lost track of him. Although to be honest, it was intentional. Once, soon after I had married Eustace, we were invited to Lord Belving's house in Surrey. I knew that Leland and Andrew were living there by then, and I had to feign an illness in order to avoid attending."

Holmes leaned back and crossed his legs. "Your son," he said with a disarming smile, "mentioned that he slept quite deeply, back around the time of your first husband's tribulations."

"First husband?" said Crane.

Her eyes narrowed, her expression wary. "What of it?"

"Oh, nothing, I suppose. Perhaps it's simply a coincidence that he was sleeping so well, at around the same time the three men were drugged with opiates."

"You really aren't making any sense, Mr. Holmes."

"I suppose not," he agreed. "I wonder if anyone at Close Brothers remembers the cleaning woman who suddenly abandoned her post, all those years ago. She worked in the evenings, I believe."

Except for a flaring of her thin nostrils, there was no reaction. Crane was looking back and forth between he lady at his side and Holmes, uncertain as to what was happening. "*Nothing ventured*," I thought to myself, having almost caught up. However, having caught the ship, I was now struggling to stay on board, in spite of having had the benefit of seeing Langdale Pike's wire.

Turning his head, Holmes asked, "Mr. Crane, when did you meet the Countess?"

"What? Oh, three or four years ago, at Ascot. Since then, our circles have intersected more and more often, and we became . . . better acquainted. Then, when the Count passed several weeks ago, I was able to, you know, make myself useful."

"Indeed. Fortunately, the Countess, *nee* Mrs. Cole, has indicated that she has no secrets from you, so we can discuss matters in a frank and forthright manner. Do you agree, madam?"

He had pivoted his hawk-like gaze back toward the black-clad lady, who was watching him as a small animal ponders a snake – afraid to move, and afraid to run.

"I really don't know why you're here, Mr. Holmes. What you refer to happened ten years ago." Turning to Crane, she explained, "I was once in much less fortunate circumstances than when you first encountered me, Martin. I was rather common, you see, and married to a *policeman*." She said it the same as if she'd said *leper*. "He got himself mixed up in a crime – probably not for the first time, since that was in the days of the various police corruption scandals – and I really had no choice but to get away from him."

Crane nodded, apparently looking for any way to excuse her past actions. I interjected, "But your son, madam! Your own child! How could you abandon him as you did, leaving him with a man that you believed to be a criminal?"

She frowned, and her cold façade seemed to crack in the very slightest way. "You don't understand. You cannot. To be trapped in that life – that *slattern* that I was forced to be was not the person that I truly am. I had always known that I belonged in better circumstances – that I could do so much more with my life. Marrying . . . marrying Leland was a mistake. I didn't think so at the time. I thought that it would make things better, more complete. That it would be a step up. They were always telling me to settle, to accept my place. As if it were my fate!"

She became more agitated as she spoke, and I asked again, "But your child?"

"*Child!*" she snapped. "I never wanted a *child*! Being a mother was simply another part of the role that I had to play, being the wife of a common policeman. I suppose at the time that I believed that it might help. I saw all the other women finding purpose and meaning with their children. It seemed to be a way for them to escape from their lives by having such distractions. But I never understood. I tried, for years and years I tried, but I just couldn't. Andrew only reminded me every day of how the coils of that life were slipping tighter and tighter around my throat!"

Crane was looking at her now with something like the way that one sees a complete stranger. The sudden change in her had shocked him. His fluttering motions toward her, constant up to this point, had ceased as he folded his hands tightly in his lap, as if he were protecting himself.

"And so you went off to the Continent," prompted Holmes.

She nodded. "When Leland had his . . . troubles, it seemed like a heaven-sent opportunity. I tried to stay with him, to reason with him, after the killings, but he wouldn't have any of it. He could have come with me. We could have even taken Andrew. We could have started over together. But instead, he kept clinging to the idea that we could go on as we had."

"You left them then, and made your way to the Continent. Did you never wonder about them? About the husband and son that you had abandoned?"

"I did. At first." She was trying to give the appearance that none of it had mattered, but emotion was altering her voice, roughening it as she spoke more urgently. "God help me, I wanted to cut the cords, but it wasn't as easy as I thought it would be. But as time passed – "

"As time passed," interrupted Holmes, "you accustomed yourself to your new lifestyle, and you met and married the Count, and discovered that you had finally found the life that you'd been missing for all those years."

"Yes!" she hissed. "Yes. I was finally *happy!*"

"Did you know that your first husband, Leland, died two years ago?"

Her eyes widened. "No – No, I didn't. I – I stopped keeping track of them at some point."

"Did you ever actually divorce him?"

Crane was, by this time, leaning forward intently on the edge of his chair.

"I – no, I – that is to say, not officially."

"So your marriage to the Count was bigamous."

No answer.

"Mr. Crane," snapped Holmes.

Surprised. "Um, yes?"

"How much was the Count's fortune?"

"Well, it was – that is to say, it is five million pounds."

"Who are his heirs?"

"Why, the Countess."

219

"No one else?"

"No."

"She was named in the will?"

"I believe so."

"And now that we know that she is *not* his wife, who are the other heirs?"

"Well, there are some estranged children, from a previous marriage."

"Estranged? How so?"

Crane glanced at the Countess – that is to say, Mrs. Cole – with a sour look. "They were close to the Count, until he married the Countess. Um, until he *thought* that he was marrying his current wife." He turned back to Holmes. "Until he married this woman." He swallowed and continued. "Mr. Holmes, I have some association with the legalities of the Estate. Can you prove any of this?"

Holmes fished out Pike's telegram. "Yes." Without handing it to Crane, he turned back to Mrs. Cole, who was now hunched forward, looking decidedly less attractive than she had before, her eyes fixed on the slip of paper. "What would an autopsy reveal, madam, regarding the Count's death?" Glancing my way, he said, "A coronary thrombosis can be *caused*, can it not, Doctor?"

"Yes."

"If such an act were deliberately induced, would it be noticed in an elderly patient?"

"Not necessarily."

Holmes nodded. Turning back to Mrs. Cole and holding up the telegram, he asked, "Was it difficult to establish yourself when you first arrived in Nice, ten years ago?"

"What?" she asked, clearly off balance and trying to change directions from her thoughts about the Count's death. "What?"

"Ten years ago. When you arrived in Nice with the stolen gold. Your history is well established afterwards, but nothing before. You appeared out of nowhere, it seems, wealthy, but with a certain, shall we say, *crudity* unbefitting a lady accustomed to old money. However, you were a quick study, and apparently spent your funds wisely in terms of both clothing and choosing where to appear. It wasn't long before you had made the Count's acquaintance, was it?"

She shook her head, as if something were buzzing around her ears. "Mr. Crane," asked Holmes. "How did the Count's first wife die?"

"Why, she fell from one of the cliffs during a nighttime walk."

Glancing at the wire, Holmes said, "And that would have been in the spring of 1881, I believe."

A look of enlightenment and shock passed across Crane's face. "I think that's right."

Back to Mrs. Cole: "Just a few months after your arrival in Nice, and just a few months *before* your quick marriage to the Count."

She shook her head. It was appalling to see how fast the lady had fallen from the confident creature that had first walked into the room.

"I doubt if you've changed all that much in ten years – you've likely worked to preserve yourself. So I have to ask," said Holmes, "isn't it likely that the staff at Close Brothers will recall when you worked there as a cleaning lady, while your husband was at work, and when your poor son was at home, drugged and sleeping deeply from the same opiates that you would later use in the Wards' food?"

I had seen Holmes do this before – battering someone with facts from so many different directions, the same way that he kept a bare-knuckle opponent off balance by gracefully dancing from side-to-side, throwing punches from one direction and then the other, seemingly at random, but in fact scientifically calculated to crumble any resistance.

"No," said the lady. "No, they wouldn't know me. I changed my appearance."

"Good," said Holmes. "No need to follow that up, then." She looked up, almost happy that he was agreeing with her, too confused now to realize what was happening. "We progress. And the Wards? How did you become involved with their scheme?"

"I knew Marcus, when I was a girl. We grew up together. There was some understanding that we would marry, but I couldn't – I just couldn't do that. I settled for Leland, thinking that path would be a better way. I didn't see Marcus for years, but then I ran into him one day in the street. We began to talk, and we kept meeting. It wasn't anything to me, just a way to avoid the terrible monotony, but he believed it was becoming something more.

"He told me about the gold. He had heard of it from one of his friends. He and his two sons from his earlier marriage were prepared to try and steal it, but they needed to know when it would be moved. He helped me get a job with the Close Brothers. I would slip some of the powder into Andrew's food – Marcus gave it to me for just that reason – after Leland went to work, and while the boy . . . while my son slept, I would clean the offices and read their papers. They never worried about putting them away or covering them up – they never paid any attention to us at all."

"And then the Wards stole the gold."

221

"That's right. And Marcus wanted me to run away with him. But that would have been trading just one kind of despair for another."

"And what happened the night of the murder?"

Apparently, she couldn't stop herself now. Perhaps the secrets had cried out too long for confession. "I had decided what I needed to do. To get the money. But I didn't know that Leland was scheduled to get off from work early that night. He arrived in our street and saw me leaving. Without telling me, he followed. I went to where Marcus and the others were hiding and . . . and poisoned their food. I started to just take the gold then and disappear, but I realized that I would never be able to stop looking over my shoulder. So . . . so I did it. I killed them."

Crane stood up then and took a step back, knocking into his chair. Mrs. Cole didn't notice.

"I took the gold and left. It was heavy, but I could just carry it in two leather cases. I took it home and buried it in an abandoned shed near where we lived, so it wouldn't be found. Leland, who had seen me go into the hiding place, let me go without revealing himself, and then went inside to see why I had been there. I had shut the door behind me when I left – he only said that he had found it open as a reason for him to enter. He discovered the bodies inside. He recognized the Wards, and he told me later that he put together the fact that I was the missing cleaning lady. Being a good policeman, he couldn't just walk away. He sounded the alarm, not realizing that he was implicating himself, as he couldn't satisfactorily explain why he was in that neighborhood.

"After several days of not speaking about it, his will broke. He confronted me, and I confessed. I tried to get him to go away with me – I really did. I was willing to include him and the child in my new life, but he wouldn't have any of it. As the days went on, he fell more and more under suspicion, but of course he couldn't give me up. The anger between us grew, and finally I couldn't stand it any longer. I retrieved the coins and left them. And he . . . he kept my secret all these years. And now . . . now you tell me that he's dead?"

Finally, at this point she seemed to run down, and a single tear tracked along her cheek. "Watson," said Holmes softly. "Summon Lestrade."

Later, we were back in Baker Street, and I asked to see Langdale Pike's telegram once again. It was all there – the raw facts that had allowed Holmes to see the invisible threads that connected them. "She had appeared out of nowhere in France at about the same that Mrs. Cole had disappeared. This only confirmed that the woman Andrew Cole saw yesterday, a Countess, as in fact his humble mother. When this woman arrived in Nice ten years ago, she was clearly wealthy. Where had the money come from to finance this life? Pike, though curious, of course had no knowledge about that aspect, but the connection is obvious to us, who can see both sides. We know that the woman who surfaced in France was also married to a policeman who was accused of stealing a fortune in gold which had never been recovered. Lestrade's fortuitous mention of a missing cleaning woman, along with Andrew's offhand reference to sleeping deeply at around the same time that men died because they were given opiates, was enough to cause the idea to coalesce in my mind. The only real challenge was to pick at different threads throughout her whole construct until enough of them weakened and it all came apart, letting her fall through."

At that moment, the bell rang, and Holmes went downstairs to let in Andrew Cole, recently summoned. After Holmes brought him up, the young man resumed the seat that had held him that morning. Trying to sound jovial, he asked, "News already? That was fast, gentlemen." Then, seeing our rather grim expressions, his wan smile dropped, and he said flatly, "Tell me."

And Holmes did, laying it out linearly and simply. When he was done, the young man thought for a moment and then stood. "Thank you, Mr. Holmes. Dr. Watson," he said simply. "I don't know what to think, really. She ceased to be my mother a long time ago, but I am glad to know the truth about my poor father, who kept her secret to the end. He must have loved her all the way."

"Yes," I murmured.

"Inspector Lestrade will be in touch," said Holmes. "Your father did have knowledge that he held back about a crime, but there were . . . extenuating and understandable circumstances. I believe that he would like to discuss it with you."

"Certainly. You can tell him where to find me. And please send your bill to the same location. I believe that I gave you my card?"

Holmes nodded and stood. I followed. We each shook Andrew Cole's hand, and the young man passed out of our lives and back into that throng of four millions all jostling each other within the space of a few miles. We were destined to meet him again, but that is another tale.

Smoking quietly, we passed a solemn hour until it was time for me to arise and walk back to Paddington. Holmes, deep in his own meditations, looked up and gave a nod, which I returned. Then, letting myself out, I returned to my wife, very fortunate indeed in knowing that I had the truest treasure of them all.

The Painting in the Parlour

That August had been cooler than typical, for which I was grateful, and my evening walks were more pleasant because of it. On that particular night, with the apparent sunset occurring unnaturally early due to the heavy clouds overhead, I was met at my door upon my return by my faithful housekeeper, who handed me a telegram.

As she shut the door on Queen Anne Street, I opened it to discover a terse communiqué from my old friend, Sherlock Holmes: *Available tomorrow for epilogue to old case.*

It was no surprise to receive such a laconic message. In fact, I had the manuscript of one of our old investigations, relating to the strange events of nearly twenty years before in the home of Professor Presbury, lying on my desk upstairs, to be submitted at some unspecified point in time to *The Strand.* It had begun with just such a message from the famous detective, summoning me to his side with the certain assumption that I would join him. My only question about the current communication was whether my friend meant to end the seven words with a question mark, or if it was a declarative assertion. I suspected that it was sent exactly the way he intended.

No time of arrival was given, but if he was traveling up on the usual train from where he'd lived since his retirement, in a "villa" near Beachy Head, I knew when he would likely appear.

I was correct, and my bell rang promptly the next morning at the expected time. I made my way to the door to greet my friend, who had already been admitted by the housekeeper.

"No bag?" I asked.

He shook his head. "I'm only up for the day. A coda related to an old case." He followed me into my study. "In any event, I have had enough traveling for a few weeks."

"And how was Dublin?"

"Wet and cold, the same as here. What an unusual August."

I knew that he had been in Ireland earlier in the month for the formal transfer of Dublin Castle to the Irish Republican Army. The Empire would probably never know what he had accomplished when unexpectedly involved at the last minute in that tense and frustrating imbroglio.

Holmes explained that we had time for a cup of tea, and we chatted about the old days. He informed me that his brother Mycroft, who had remained at his post even after the War, finally intended to retire the next month. We both agreed that it would truly be the end of an era, except for

224

the fact that he would not truly retire, no doubt continuing to provide his unique skills as a fixture at the Diogenes Club until they carried him out.

Finally, Holmes stood and said it was time to go. "Are you game for a walk?" he asked. When learning that we only had to make our way to Montague Street, I let him know that I was more than able.

We wound down into Wigmore and Mortimer Streets, and on across Tottenham Court Road. The morning was still cloudy but not unpleasant. We trod near that house close to the corner of Gower and Keppel, which I shall always associate with the murder of old Mr. Raines. Finally, passing behind the Museum, we entered Montague Street.

As usual, the short street was very quiet, considering how close it was to Russell Square on one end and Great Russell Street at the other. Our footsteps echoed off the stone faces of the houses. On the right, the edifice of the British Museum loomed over everything. Holmes and I had strolled in companionable silence for most of the way, and I wasn't surprised when we stopped at No. 24, where he had lived when first coming up to London, now nearly fifty years before.

There was a handsome brougham parked in front, and as we had approached, a portly man in his late sixties, a contemporary to Holmes and myself, hefted himself with a grunt onto the pavement. I recognized him at once.

"Watson," he said. "Good to see you. And Holmes," he continued. "How long has it been?"

"Two years, Sir Clive. The matter of the fraudulent McGander."

"That's right. That *was* a snorter." He waved his stick toward No. 24, now joined with No. 23 next door, and part of a hotel. "Shall we go inside?"

Still ignorant as to the reason for our visit, I followed them up the short flight of steps. We rang the bell, and in a moment a girl answered with a curtsy. Sir Clive stepped in and we followed him into the hallway. Apparently we were expected, as no explanations were given or required.

At the very back of the hall on the left was the door to the parlour. Beyond it was a narrow passage to the kitchens beneath us, and then the very narrow and steep stairs leading up to the lodger's rooms. I recalled that Holmes had occupied a room on the top floor front when he first came up to London, although he had finally been able to afford something a bit larger, lower down on the first floor, in the year before he had moved to Baker Street.

"They think they've identified the painter," Sir Clive said to me, turning to make this whispered comment.

Making our way to that curiously curved parlour door on our left, Holmes said, "Officially, then? We established that fact to our own satisfaction almost half-a-century ago." Sir Clive harrumphed.

Stepping through the door, I still had no idea what this was about, but I certainly remembered the painting to which he referred.

"Yes," answered Sir Clive, "but Richardson, from around the corner in Russell Square, has been doing some research lately, and he wants to write something up for the journals. And then there's talk again of removing it and selling it to a collector. They asked me to be here today, and I thought of inviting the two of you. "

"Remove it?" scoffed Holmes. "Impossible."

Entering the oddly-shaped room, squared at the front windows but rounded at the back, we encountered a grouping of three other men, standing opposite to us beneath a tall and wide painting, about six feet square, affixed above the fireplace. Strangely it didn't hang there, as it was painted directly onto the plaster. I had seen it before on the few occasions when I had visited this address, most notably to investigate a murder on the top floor in Holmes's old room that had taken place a number of years earlier.

"Richardson," bellowed Sir Clive to a scholarly looking fellow, thus identifying for me the man in question. "Still trying to nail down the provenance of this old painting?"

The man responded good-naturedly. "You know how it is to get a bee in one's bonnet, Clive," he said. "I have some fresh correspondence from the Duke of Bedford that almost makes it certain that the painter was James Ward."

"I've told you that it was Ward for the last forty years. I knew it when I first saw it, and we had additional confirmation from Abel Granger's people, who had hired Ward to paint a very similar painting. The man," said Sir Clive to me, "was rather specialized in what he liked to paint."

"Anecdotal evidence is certainly valuable," sniffed Richardson, "but one's case is always so much more solid with the written word." He reached into his breast pocket and pulled out a packet of folded yellow papers. "Letters, Sir Clive!" He waved them about. "The proof!"

"I don't need any such proof," said one of the other two men. He was a cadaverous looking fellow with unhealthy dark hollows under his cheeks. Speaking with an American accent, he added, "I recognized it for a Ward from the minute I saw it. Those letters will simply make it even sweeter when it's hanging in my own little museum in Pittsburg."

"And I can't make it any plainer than I already have, Mr. K--------," said the third man, whose origins were clearly British, "that the painting cannot be moved. It was applied directly onto the ordinary plaster surface

226

above the mantel. A massive and expensive effort would have to be undertaken to remove it, and even then it's likely that you would fail. We would need to construct a special steel underpinning and frame, and after all of that, it would likely crumble to pieces."

Sir Clive gestured with his thumb toward the third man. "Grigsby. British Museum."

The man nodded, looking curiously at Holmes and me, obviously wondering why we were there. Sir Clive made no move to introduce us.

The American shrugged his too-heavy coat up around his thin shoulders. "Don't care. Whatever it takes. Money is no object. And keep looking for that canvas version as well."

"It was lost nearly a decade ago," said Grigsby.

"Money's no object," K-------- repeated, and then, with a quick and hungry look toward the painting, he turned and stalked from the room. Grigsby looked with frustration to Sir Clive, and then hurried to follow.

We three and Richardson were left in front of the fireplace, naturally turning our gazes upward at the object under discussion, I had seen it before, of course, but had never given it more than a passing glance. Now, I studied it more carefully.

It was a landscape, done in rather unpleasant yellows and browns. The upper two-thirds portrayed a brassy sky, with sour-looking and strangely lit clouds mostly hiding the light but dull blue that peeked through in just a few places. On the ground beneath them was a rural and timeless scene, tedious in its plainness and, frankly, lack of imagination. In the center, taller than almost anything else in the painting, was a figure seated on a downtrodden white horse, both man and beast with their backs to the viewer. The rider, in a brown hat and matching brown clothing, was holding out a hand to a boy at his right. The lad was wearing a blue coat and red pants – the only unusual colors in the whole artwork. The man on the horse seemed to be reaching for a hat that the boy was offering, in spite of already having his own hat upon his head.

Incongruously, there were three cows spread around them, all of apparently different breeds (or so it seemed to me, as I know little of cattle), two lying down and one standing, facing indifferently away from the men and beasts. To the left, the land dropped off to a dark hollow and distant forest, while on the right, set back at what seemed to be a couple of hundred feet, were some ill-defined trees, with the lop-sided roof of a two- or three-story house barely showing amongst them. It was competently painted, no doubt, but not – to my view – anything that would inspire a collector to declare, "*Money's no object.*"

"It was the cows," said Sir Clive, to my obvious confusion and his amusement. "That's how I first knew it was a Ward, you see. The old Duke of Bedford, who owned of all the property around us, including this house – and the family still owns it, by the way! – took Ward under his wing over a hundred years ago. Ward, you see, was the most popular painter of cattle of his day."

"Cattle?" I said. "Are you serious? That was a specialty?"

"A most sought-after specialty," asserted Sir Clive. "The early 1800's was a period of romanticism, a reaction against classicism, wherein people wanted paintings that glorified nature and invoked an emotion, sometimes with a solemn and mysterious feel." He gestured at the painting and glanced toward Holmes, who had remained strangely tacit the entire time. "Of course, we know what the mystery connected to the painting was. Eh?" Richardson, who had been pondering the illustration, silently glanced toward Sir Clive, who continued, "In any case, the Duke of Bedford hired Ward to paint this picture for this particular house, although we never did find out what the significance of *this* house was. According to the records, this house wasn't built until 1808, and by then Ward had become somewhat separated from the Duke's sphere of influence, having long since departed from the Bedfordshire home of his lordship, where he stayed for quite some time."

"Old news," Richardson snorted, his patience fractured. "I must be about other business. Good morning, gentlemen!" And he turned and left without a backward glance.

Sir Clive gave a short bark of a laugh – "No great loss!" – and shook his head.

"You obviously have researched this subject," I said. "And this painting is connected to the old case that you mentioned, Holmes?"

But my friend was staring fixedly at the bottom right corner of the painting, where the brown hill rippled as it dropped towards us, away from the subjects, cattle and otherwise. There was a slight crack there, and that corner appeared to be on a somewhat different plane of plaster.

Sir Clive followed his glance at the corner of the painting as well. "It will be gone in another ten years, I'm afraid."

"Yes," said Holmes. I leaned in to see the object of their comments.

Low in the corner, near the simple wooden frame that had been constructed around the painting, were a faint series of vertical marks, three rows of them. Each row was quite small, no more than a quarter-inch in height, and there appeared to be no pattern whatsoever. They looked to be composed of some sort of flaked metal, golden colored, that had been pressed on top of the paint.

"Is that – ?" I asked.

"Yes," replied Holmes. "Gold leaf. Although there is less of it there now than there was back in 1875."

"Is there gold under the painting? Is that why Mr. K-------- desires it?"

"No, no. Those markings were put there in 1811, not long after the painting was made, by a man who was staying here in this house at the time."

"But why was gold leaf applied onto a painting such as this, with its otherwise unpleasant brownish tones?"

Sir Clive laughed with surprise. "You haven't told him, then?"

Holmes shook his head, replying, "I thought that it would make for an interesting narrative later today. Can you join us 'round the corner?"

Sir Clive shook his head. "Much as I would like to, I must get over to Ratham's. The old scoundrel is auctioning a widow's estate, and I promised that I would stop by." He glanced at me. "Just when you thought you'd heard them all, Watson, it's time for another one!"

With a last glance at the artwork, he turned to go, leading us back out to the street.

"Until we meet again, gentlemen," he huffed as he fit himself back into the brougham. Then, with a lurch, it set off toward Great Russell Street, and so to the right and out of our sight.

Holmes gestured in the same direction, and I agreed. We set off at a leisurely pace. Mere moments later, after passing in front of the gates of the Museum, we were seated in the back of the Alpha Inn. It was a bit early in the morning for it, but we bravely faced the pints of the landlord's excellent beer in front of us.

After taking a swallow, I cleared my throat and said, "I believe there was mention of an interesting narrative? Set back about 1875?"

Holmes nodded and fished in his coat. Pulling out a packet of folded and worn slips of paper, he flattened them and then tossed two upon the table, retaining the third. "What do you make of these?"

They were each three or four inches across, and the paper was quite worn. I picked them up. "They are old," I said.

Holmes gave a short laugh. "Be careful how you toss around someone else's dates so easily, my friend," he smiled. "These are all that I have left of an odd little mystery that took up a day or so when I was but twenty-one, and had only been up to London for less than a year."

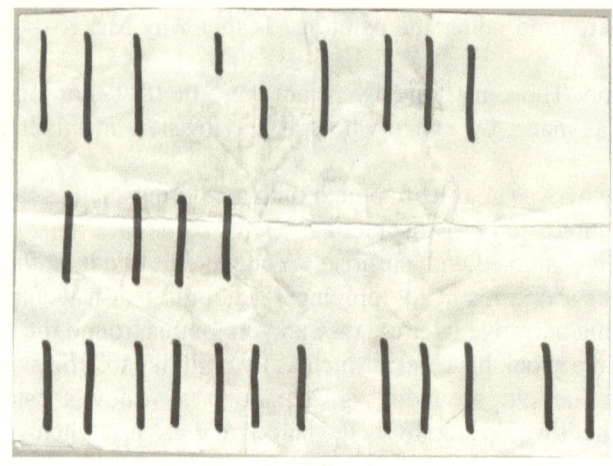

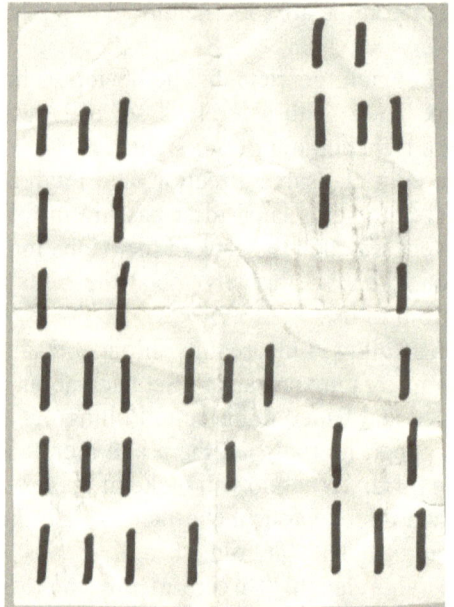

"You brought them with you today when Sir Clive asked you to drop around at Montague Street."

"Obviously. I still look back with fondness at this little case, and when I heard that someone else was considering, yet again, the purchase of the Ward painting from the No. 24 parlour, it seemed to be the perfect opportunity for a bit of reminiscing."

I tapped the scrap on the left. "This looks like the gold leaf markings on the corner of the painting." I lifted the sheets and examined them. "I assume it's some sort of code. What about this other sheet?" I recalled what the American had said. "Were these other markings on the missing canvas version of the painting?"

Holmes, in the act of swallowing, lowered his glass and smiled. "Very good, Watson. You are correct. Shall I tell the entire tale wrong-way around, or would you like to hear it from the beginning?"

I returned the squares of paper to the table and nodded to for him to tell it in his own way. He was correct. This wasn't some potboiler, after all, to be revealed just for the drama of the thing.

Settling back, Holmes began. "It was in the fall of '75. I had been in London a little over a year, having settled into Montague Street and working to master my new craft. My landlady, the wife of one of my father's cousins, had several other lodgers, and she'd grudgingly taken me in as well. There were only a few of us regulars there, as more often than not rooms were taken by nearby University students who soon found better or worse accommodations, depending on their prospects, before moving on.

"It was a late afternoon in early October when there was a knock at my door. I opened to find a man in his thirties, well dressed, and trying to catch his breath from the steep climb to my top-floor rooms. I had observed him on several occasions since his arrival earlier in the week. He was what I considered to be a short-timer, as there had been no indication that he had moved in with more than what would be needed for a few days in the capital. No matter what time I had arrived or departed during the recent days, he had been in the parlour, staring at the painting that you and I were admiring just a quarter-hour ago. I had been curious about the object of his fascination – you have seen that it isn't the *Mona Lisa*, after all – but it had been none of my business.

"'Mr. Holmes?' he wheezed. Clearly, climbing six flights of stairs was not part of his normal routine.

"I observed that he was left-handed, smoked Trichinopoly cigars, had attended Corpus Christi College at Cambridge, hunted with a bow for sport, had written letters both the previous evening and again that morning, as shown by the overlapping ink spots on his fingers. He suffered from digestive complaints, was unmarried but with sweetheart, had a slightly built-up left shoe manufactured by Tundell's off the Strand, and that he was from north of London. In his hand, he carried a rolled canvas.

"I nodded to indicate that he had found the right man and motioned for him to enter. He dropped into my sole visitor's chair near the front window, standing the painting, for it was unrolled just enough to see that that was what it was, beside him."

"'Early 1800's, I'd venture,' gesturing toward it.

He glanced toward it in surprise. 'Why yes? How did you know?'

"'I've made a study of both canvas and paints. I can tell from the portion of the sky revealed there that it is from that general period. Does it relate to the painting that you have been pondering so steadfastly downstairs for the past week?"

He looked at me as if I were some sort of necromancer and nodded. Then he bent and unrolled it upon the floor between us. The setting sun hadn't quite yet fallen behind the Museum, and there was still enough light to pick out the details. I slid from my chair to the floor, kneeling to lean closer. It was clearly by the same painter as the one downstairs in the parlour, and in many respects, it was the same scene, though perhaps the better of the two. This painting did not have the dingy yellow-browns of the other. Rather, it was brighter, with the clear blue skies giving it a more fresh feeling. However, the man on the horse, the boy, and the cows were practically identical. Yet the background was different – this was a bluer sky, as I said, and instead of a distant dark grove of trees on one side and an old house on the other, there was a manor house in the distance, more centered behind the horseman, as if he had been interrupted by the boy while on his way there. Instead of a hat in the boy's hand, the rider was curiously handing him a knife. Ignoring the safe way to do such a thing, the man on the horse had retained a normal grip on the handle, leaving the boy to reach for the blade. In the foreground was a stream with various rocks piled along its banks, looking as if they had been cut and arranged there long ago by masons to prevent the bank from eroding.

"'Interesting,' I muttered, then looked up. 'I suppose there is some reason that there are two of these paintings. Perhaps a message?' He nodded, and when I added, 'A treasure hunt?' he clapped his hands together.

"'That's it exactly!' he cried. 'They told me that you were some sort of detective, and that you know things that others do not. I can see I've come to the right place!'

"I had, in truth, seen a few things already, but I needed to know more. Returning to my seat, I said, 'What is the history of these paintings?'

"He nodded, as if that were a fair question, and began. 'My name,' he said, 'is Edward Cavenham, and my people have lived near Bishop's Stortford since beyond memory.' He pointed toward the painting on the floor. 'That's the family house there in the background. It doesn't look much different now than when that was painted – '

"'The year being – ?'

"'Early 1800's. That fits with the story I'm going to relate, as we have learned from letters handed down within our family. In 1810, my grandfather, Richard Cavenham, was serving in the Royal Navy, against the wishes of his father, Lloyd. He was at the battle of Grand Port, when the French forced the British surrender following the failed attempt to blockade the Isle de France. He was taken prisoner, but because he was an officer, he was treated with dignity, even being entertained in some of the finer French homes.

"'While there, he became immediately enamored with his host's daughter, Lisette Duvelle. Within a few weeks, they had wed. It is not recorded what Lisette's father thought, although there seems to have been no objection, but the upshot was that my father's release was negotiated, and he returned with his new bride to the family home in Hertfordshire, hard upon the Essex border.

"'The fine treatment that Richard received in France was not reflected in England. Lloyd was outraged that his son had married without his permission or influence, and worse – that he had married a French girl to boot. Before long, things became intolerable, and Richard and Lisette departed, indicating that they were returning to France, where their union had been received with acceptance.

"'However, when he left, Richard took with him his father Lloyd's most prized possession, a jeweled dagger that one of the Cavenham's had received from Charles I after helping the king escape from the Siege of Oxford in 1646. Richard left a note for his father, informing him that he had taken the dagger to pass along to his own child, now being carried by Lisette, as nothing else could be counted upon from Lloyd.

"'Lloyd was beside himself, not with rage, but rather with the sudden realization that his narrow-minded reaction had driven his own son, and now future grandchild, from his home. He sent agents to France to look for Richard and Lisette, assuming that they would immediately return to her family's residence. What Lloyd did not know was that Richard and Lisette had actually first come up to London for a time while they figured out what they wanted to do. In fact, they stayed right here, at No. 24 Montague Street.

"'It was while here that Richard encountered a painter who had been commissioned, by the Duke of Bedford, to create the painting that you see down in the parlour. He struck up an acquaintance with the fellow, and then he had a second painting made – ' and here he pointed toward the canvas unrolled at our feet – 'this one.'

"'An interesting story,' I said, 'but how do you know of all this?'

"Cavenham removed a few folded sheets from his pocket. 'The story has come down through the family through my great-grandfather Lloyd, who wrote down what he learned after the fact. It seems that, after Richard had the canvas painting made, he sent it, along with a cryptic message, to his father Lloyd. Then, he and Lisette left Montague Street and continued their delayed journey to France, where they did return to live with her family – although *after* Lloyd's agents had initially searched for them there, thus missing them.

"'However, Lloyd had previously convinced Lisette's parents of his good will, and that he was truly penitent for his earlier reactions. They secretly sent word to Lloyd of the arrival of Richard and Lisette. But this was the spring of 1811, and Anglo-French relations were even worse. The British had defeated the French at the Battle of Lissa just a few months earlier, and it was difficult for Lloyd to arrange passage to France so that he could apologize in person. When he finally arrived, he found a newborn grandson, and also that his son Richard had recently passed away due to a sudden fever.

"'Amazingly, Lloyd was able to convince Lisette to leave her family and return with her baby to England with him, where he would be raised in the house of his ancestors. That child was my father, William Cavenham, and he grew to be a very fine man indeed. His own grandfather, Lloyd, accepted them completely, and he was raised with every advantage. And yet, throughout his life, the circumstances of his own father Richard's departure, and the question of where the jeweled dagger was, hung like a shadow over our house. It still does, to the present day. For when Lloyd found Lisette, he learned that she did not have the dagger, and it wasn't discovered in Richard's effects. They came to believe that perhaps the painting sent to Lloyd, along with the cryptic letter, gave some sort of clue to the dagger's location. It has haunted my father William throughout his life, even now as he approaches his final days.'

"'May I see the documents from your great-grandfather, as well as the message from Richard?' I asked. He handed them to me silently, and I flipped rapidly through them. They were quite old and faded, a mixture of Lloyd's own summary of events, as well as communications between Lloyd Cavenham and Lisette's parents, all confirming my client's story. I set them aside and looked at Richard's communication with his father.

"It was a quarto-sized sheet on cheap rag paper. Both it and the faded ink were consistent with that manufactured in the early nineteenth century. The message consisted of four stanzas. This is a copy I made at the time." He pushed the third folded sheet toward me, joining the two already on the table. I read:

Top to bottom
Side to side
Bitter old man
Family divide

Treasure loved more
Than faithful son
Now lost both
'Til puzzle is done

For future heirs
Right under your nose
Preserved for them
From time's flows

Not to be found
'Til divide is combined
The paintings are key
The treasure you'll find.

Top to bottom
Side to side
Bitter old man
Family divide

Treasure loved more
Than faithful son
Now lost both
'Til puzzle is done

For future heirs
Right under your nose
Preserved for them
From time's flows

Not to be found
'Til divide is combined
The paintings are key
The treasure you'll find

I raised an eyebrow. "Treasure hunt indeed."

"Exactly."

"It mentioned *paintings*, plural. Had they never questioned that fact before discovering that there was a second painting?"

"It had apparently escaped them."

"And how did the paintings relate?"

"That is what I attempted to find out from my visitor. 'This painting,' I said, pointing toward the floor, "was sent with that message.' He nodded. 'How did you find out about the one downstairs? I assume that you only recently learned of it, which explains why you've come up to London to study it.'

"He looked surprised that I had determined this, but said, 'That is true, Mr. Holmes. For years, the poem and this painting have been in our family, as we've all had a go at trying to figure out Richard's intentions. Of course, old Lloyd died long before I was born, but I still remember how my grandmother Lisette would puzzle over it. Quite frankly, it's haunted my father, William, his whole life. Obviously, Richard meant for *his* father Lloyd to be able to solve it, taunting him to recover the dagger. He must have hidden it somewhere, since he didn't have it in France when he died, and Lisette knew nothing about it. The poem says that the painting is the key, but we could see nothing in it that would tell us anything. What could we discover from a man on a horse, or a boy, or three cows?

236

"'But just a few weeks ago, we had a man that came down to work on some of the gas jets, and he happened to notice the canvas painting lying out on one of the desks in the library. I confess that I've often studied it and the riddle over the years, trying to get behind Richard's thinking, and more so recently, since my father's health has started to fail. I'd dearly love to find the dagger and restore it to his hands before he passes. He hasn't been well, you see.'

"'And this man saw the painting, and remembered where he had seen one very much like it.'

"'Exactly. He mentioned it to the cook while taking some refreshment in the kitchen, she told the butler, and he told me. I questioned the workman, and he said that the other painting was here, just a stone's throw from the British Museum. I quickly decided to come up to London and see it for myself. I've stayed longer than I initially intended, hoping each day to find a clue to the dagger's location. But I have no idea where the setting in the painting downstairs is located, and there is no more to be learned from the man, the horse, the boy, or the cows in that painting than there is in this one.'

"I confess, Watson, that up to that time, I hadn't paid much attention to the painting in the parlour. It isn't very attractive, as you'll agree, and in general, my time in that room was generally spent in deep thought when I could no longer stand to be in my top-floor chambers. I felt that further study was required, and also a second opinion was needed. I sent word –"

" – to Sir Clive," I interrupted.

He nodded. "Just Clive Bartleby then. A relatively new acquaintance that I'd made at the Museum while carrying out my diverse studies. Even then, he was making a name for himself. I sent a message around to his office, asking him to step over if convenient."

"And not if inconvenient, come all the same?" I asked with a smile, recalling my friend's message from the day before.

"It was implied," Holmes responded. "Cavenham and I were in the parlour, looking at the painting, when Clive bustled in. After introductions were made, under the baleful glare of my landlady, we explained in hushed tones – for there were several other boarders enjoying the cool October breeze coming in from the tall open windows – about the two paintings, the message, and the long-lost dagger. Clive unrolled the painting, held it wide between his outstretched arms, and compared it from different angles to the larger version above the mantel.

"He nodded and muttered for some time, and he was clearly onto something. I knew better than to interrupt, but Edward Cavenham was

237

becoming increasingly impatient. Luckily, at the moment Edward was about the burst, Clive was ready to speak to us.

"'Clearly, it's by Ward,' he said, lowering his arms. "Funny that it's been so close, and no one has bothered to identify it before now.'

"'What?' asked my client. 'Who?'

"Clive went on to relate what he explained earlier this morning, as to how James Ward had been commissioned by the Duke of Bedford to create a number of paintings in the early 1800's. 'Obviously, he was hired to create one here as well, although there's no telling why in this particular house without further research. The Bedford Estate has owned this property since the mid-1600's, long before the houses were built. No doubt, the Duke simply wanted to provide a painting for whomever lived here then, or to give Ward another job, or both.'

"'Perhaps the Duke of Bedford was friends with Richard,' said Edward Cavenham, almost hopefully. 'Possibly that's why Richard and Lisette came here to stay before going on to France. They may have intended to stay here permanently.'

"'You forget your own evidence,' I pointed out. 'The letters indicate that this was simply a stopping point along the way. Lisette apparently gave no indication that they knew anyone at this location, or that there was anything special about it.'

"'But the painting!' he cried, pointing at the wall. 'You can't deny that connection between this painting in this house, and the painting sent to my great-grandfather Lloyd.'

"I turned to Clive with a little idea that had been in the back of my mind. 'Is it possible that the dagger is concealed *behind* the painting?'

"He shook his head. 'Oh, I shouldn't think so. This one is painted directly onto the plaster. I can't imagine that destroying a work of art would have been an acceptable price to pay in order to retrieve the dagger. After all, according to what you've told me is recorded in the letters, Richard Cavenham struck up an acquaintance of sorts with Ward while they were here, getting him to paint the second picture that was sent to his father after this one was finished. I don't believe that Ward would have been party to anything that might lead to the future destruction of his work, should someone have to remove the plaster to get at the dagger.'

"Edward looked at the painting on the wall. 'I know that my painting is of our family estate. Where is the setting shown in *that* painting? Could the house beyond the trees be the location of the dagger?'

"'No,' Clive answered with certainty. 'The plaster painting is clearly the meadow lands near Camden Town, with the northern heights in the distance – at least how they looked sixty-five years ago.' He shook his head. 'I've seen something of the sort before.'

"'But perhaps the house in the painting . . . .' Edward added hopefully.

"'Not likely. If it was a real house, it looks as if it was headed for collapse, even then. And that area is greatly built up since those days. It certainly would have been pulled down long ago.'

"Edward looked as if the wind had gone out of his sails, but I had noticed something on the painting on the wall."

"The little vertical lines in gold leaf in the right hand corner."

"Ah, Watson, my bag of tricks is truly emptied. You see right through me. I can remain in Sussex, and you can take over here in London."

"That role is already being capably handled by your protégé in Praed Street, not to mention our Belgian friend in Farraway Street and Thorndyke in King's Bench Walk. No, I was able to see where this was going from years spent getting events down in my journal in a linear manner."

Holmes smiled, drank the last of his beer, and continued. "As Clive and Edward had talked, I began to notice, in the last rays of sunlight streaming through the high windows, the glint of the lines to which you referred. Stepping closer, I saw, well, I saw this . . . ." And he put a finger on this sketch:

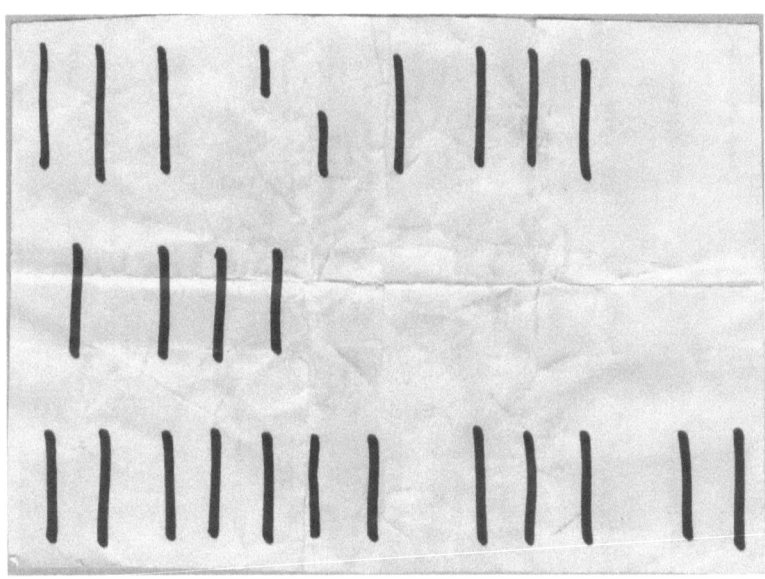

"Calling Clive over, I asked him what he thought. He leaned closer, and then stepped back, scanning the entire painting. 'No, it only appears in that corner. I wonder what it could mean . . . .'

"A sudden thought occurred to me. *'Top to bottom. Side to side.* I wonder – " Stepping over to one of the residents sitting in a deep chair underneath the window, an unhealthy looking student obviously from Aberdeen with three sisters and a secret shame that he wasn't hiding very well, I asked to borrow a few sheets of paper. He nodded wordlessly and handed me these very sheets you see before you, upon which I sketched the lines and copied the little verse.

"Clive and Edward looked puzzled, but I reached and took the canvas painting, stepping to a side table. They quickly caught my intent, and joined me, each looking for matching gold-leaf lines on that picture as well. As it was much smaller, only about two feet square, it quickly became obvious that there was no golden glint whatsoever. But I did see another set of lines, the lines copied on this other sheet of paper here. Not in gold, but in blacks and browns. And not *vertical*, like in the mantel painting, but rather *horizontal*."

"*Side to side*," I said.

"Yes. On one of the rocks that were lining the stream." He rearranged the sheets on the table, turning the second that I'd also placed in the vertical position on its side. "So now they looked like this from the parlour painting . . . ."

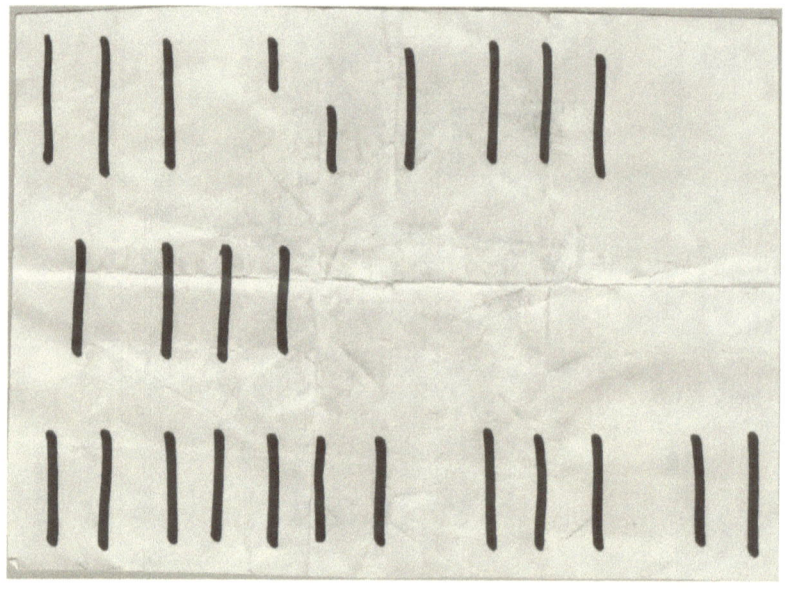

"And this from the canvas painting . . ." he continued, placing the other beneath it.

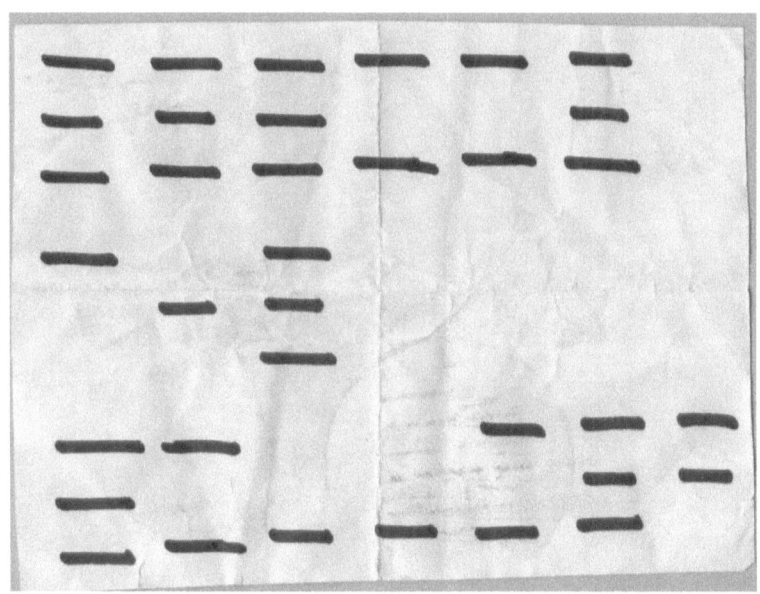

"They almost line up," I muttered.

I examined them again, realized after almost grasping it that none of it yet made sense, and admitted as much. "Ah, Watson, remember the poem. It was the only clue that Richard sent to his father. There had to be enough there to solve it. Perhaps there was some shared reference point between the two in their past that Richard thought his father would understand. The first stanza clearly refers to the lines in the paintings – *top to bottom* and *side to side* – and the feud that had sprung up between father and son. The second and third elaborate on Richard's division from his family and the taking of the dagger. But the last stanza – that was the answer."

I read it again, aloud. *"Not to be found 'til divide is combined. The paintings are key. The treasure you'll find."* And suddenly it made sense. *Top to bottom, side to side . . . combined.* Holmes smiled when he saw me catch up, and leaned back with a satisfied sigh when I picked up the two sheets and carried them over to the window. It wasn't as bright as I would have liked out in Museum Street, as the morning light had still not quite illuminated it. But it was enough. Laying one sheet atop the other, I pressed them up against the glass and read the message, formed when the vertical and horizontal lines combined.

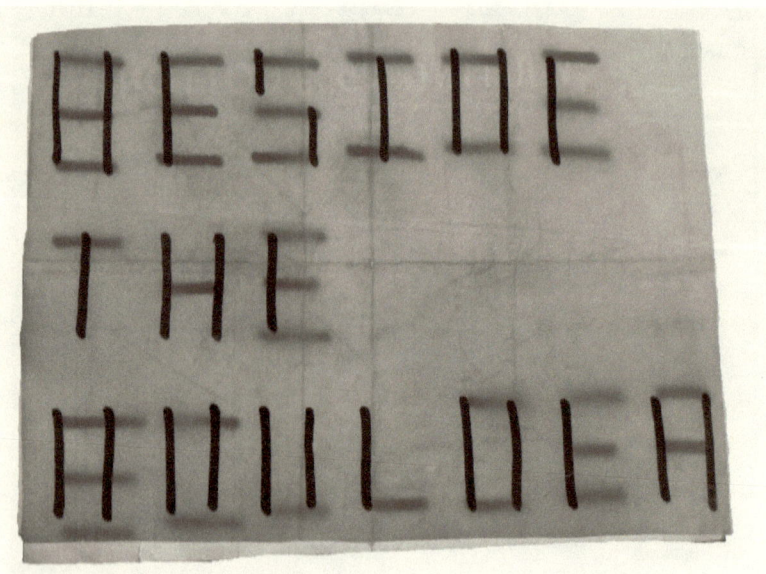

"'*BESIDE THE BOULDER*'."

"Precisely."

Turning, I asked, "And did you hold the sheets up to the parlour window when you figured it out?"

"The sun had already set behind the Museum at that point. I positioned them in front of one of the lamps."

I returned to the table, folding the three pages. Offering them to Holmes, he waved them back to me. "For the archives, Doctor."

I resumed my seat, wondering about another beer. It was later than before, and listening was thirsty work. Not to mention following in the footsteps of Sherlock Holmes.

My friend must have divined my thoughts, for he stepped to the bar, returning in a moment with two fresh pints. "Shall we adjourn in a bit for lunch at Simpsons?" he asked, checking his watch, and I agreed.

Wiping my mouth, I said, "I think I understand. Was it the boulder shown beside the stream in front of the manor house?"

He nodded. "Yes. In the canvas painting, where the horizontal lines are marked across the stone."

"Without knowing about the second painting in Montague Street, in spite of the reference to paintings, plural, they never had a chance of solving it."

"I expect that Richard intended to give his father further clues. Perhaps it was his unusual way of keeping the lines of communication open. Or possibly it was done in anger, to taunt him. But before he could elaborate, he died of the unexpected fever. Lloyd brought Lisette and the child, William, home, and they never knew that there was any more to the riddle. Only a chance visit by a gasfitter provided the link that brought Edward to London."

"I presume that the dagger was found."

"Yes, that night. Edward did not want to wait, and truth be told, neither did I. Clive, certainly an interested party by that point, would have put it off until morning, but he was outvoted. We caught a late train from Liverpool Street Station, and were standing on the bank of the stream before midnight.

"While we were traveling, a band of rough weather had been moving in, and by the time we arrived, the wind was moaning through the trees. You would have quite enjoyed the atmosphere, Watson, and could have certainly described the mood better than I. Nevertheless, we equipped ourselves with a brace of dark lanterns and crowbars from one of the out-buildings, set off across the estate toward the stream, and soon found the stone in question, right where it was memorialized in the painting. There is no doubt whatsoever that Clive had been right, and we should have waited until morning. But in spite of the wind and threat of rain, and finding no other way but to wade into the stream, it was a relatively straightforward procedure, once we found the rock in the dark, still covered with the horizontal markings, although somewhat effaced by sixty years of stream flow and weathering."

"The stone was leveraged out with ease, and Edward had the honor of reaching into the resulting void, giving a satisfied gasp as his fingers closed upon something."

"Not exactly '*Beside the Boulder*', was it? More like '*Behind the stone*'."

Holmes grinned. "Richard was working with letters that would translate into vertical and horizontal components. The letter '*n*' in '*behind*' and '*stone*' would have been problematic."

He took a sip and continued. "As I was saying, Edward reached into the cavity and pulled out an oilskin packet, tied with rotting leather thongs, somewhat less than a foot in length. He started to open it right there, but then stopped, insisting that it should be his father who did the honors. There was no question but that we would join him, so we trooped back to the house and, in spite of our muddy and wet clothing and the old man's nurse's attempts to stop us, woke William up. Edward explained what had happened and how, and then, with reverence, placed the bundle in the old man's hands.

"William Cavenham's hands shook as he started to untie the thongs, whether from age, illness, or excitement, I could not tell. The old leather quickly crumbled away, and he proceeded to unwrap the cloth, first bound up over six decades before by his father, whom he never knew. There, in the flickering lights of his bedroom, quite likely the very bedroom where old Lloyd Cavenham had slept so many years earlier, the dagger was returned to the family.

"It was a curious thing – about nine inches in length, made of some dull alloy, and with a few awkwardly cut jewels pressed into it here and there with no apparent pattern. Ugly and plain as it was, however, it held a certain fascination nonetheless, simply knowing as we did whose it had been and some of the curious events surrounding it.

"It's still there," Holmes added, "if you want to see it. I'm sure they would be glad to show it to you."

"And the canvas painting? What became of it? Grigsby said that it was lost."

"It was destroyed in 1915, during a zeppelin attack that leveled Edward's London house where he kept it. Sadly, Edward was also killed in the attack as well. He was in town, advising the Admiralty. Fortunately, his wife and son were at the country house in Bishop's Stortford, and they were spared."

We sat silently for a moment, recalling the terrible losses of just a few years before. I had never known Edward Cavenham, had in fact never heard of him until this past hour, but I was saddened at his passing nonetheless.

"'*From time's flows . . . .*'" Holmes said, returning me to the present.

"What? From the poem?"

He nodded. "Obviously, it was a play on the fact that Richard had hidden the dagger beside a stream. He must have slipped back to bury it there while he and Lisette were staying in Montague Street. Not only did he commission the canvas version, along with adding the gold leaf to the plaster version, but he also chiseled the clue onto the rock. All of that effort, and for what? To tweak his father? To jeer at him? To use it as a lure so that they could reconcile?

"Imagine how his actions rippled the flows through all of those lives. He went to all of that trouble. He was right there at the manor house when he went to hide the dagger. What if he'd simply gone inside and talked to his father instead? The family might have been reunited right then. If he hadn't gone to France, he mightn't have caught the fever and died early, leaving his son to grow up without a father." He shook his head. "Suppose the squabbles between the English and French hadn't been so fierce just then, and Lloyd had been able to reach France sooner? And generations later, if a stranger hadn't noticed two similar paintings in different houses, the mystery still might not be resolved. Each man's path leads to so many possibilities, and they are so often fraught with perils."

I had seen Holmes spiral around these maudlin thoughts of fate before. I recalled once when he discovered the identity of the murderer, only to find that the man had really had no other choice than to kill. *"God help us!"* Holmes had said at the time, after letting the man go. *"Why does fate play such tricks with poor, helpless worms?"*

I could see that his thoughts were leading him that way again. But, I decided, *Not this day!* I finished the beer and set the glass down firmly. "Any number of alternatives can always be spun out. What if I hadn't been shot at Maiwand? Or what if the bullet had been an inch to the right or left? Your foot might have slipped on the ledge at Reichenbach. The *Titanic* could have sailed fifty yards to the south and been spared. Perhaps things would have been much different if Franz Ferdinand's car hadn't taken a wrong turn, placing him in Princip's sight. Who can know?

"That type of thinking," I continued, "is a pointless path that should be avoided." I stood up. "No one can know the end results of all the turns of his or her life. One can only make the best choice possible from all the available data, and then face forward bravely, and be willing to adapt as well as possible when the time comes." I gestured toward Museum Street, now starting to brighten as the noonday sun illuminated it and the last of the clouds burned away. "It is too beautiful a day to ponder one's missteps or might-have-beens. I believe that you mentioned lunch at Simpsons?"

He pulled his thoughts back from wherever they had been going, looked up, smiled, and nodded. Joining me, we stepped away from our table and out through the side door. I took a deep breath of the summer air. Beside me, Holmes pulled on his ever-present deerstalker, worn year after year in spite of season and social convention. Then, gesturing ahead of him with his stick, he said – as he had done on that night so many years before when we'd stood on this very same spot, that time on the path of another man's poor choices and a Christmas goose – "Faces to the south, then, and quick march!"

NOTE:

The painting in the parlour at No. 24 Montague Street, now a part of the Ruskin Hotel, is still on the plaster wall above the fireplace mantel, where it has been located for over two-hundred years. Sadly, as Sir Clive Bartleby predicted, the vertical gold leaf markings on the bottom right have long since flaked away. Fortunately, Watson's notes upon the matter have survived.

"The Painting in the Parlour"
Photograph taken by David Marcum
while staying at
No. 24 Montague Street,
September 10th, 2016

The Two Bullets

My friend, Mr. Sherlock Holmes, has never been particularly reticent about the nature of his gifts. He rightly feels that to hide one's light under a bushel is as disingenuous as falsifying data in a chemical experiment. "I have never," he has frequently told me, "felt modesty to be one of the virtues."

Therefore, it came as a surprise to me, one morning in mid-1881, when Holmes seemed reluctant to offer his assistance in what appeared to be a matter that would require little effort upon his part, while remunerating him handsomely – and this in the days when the rent money to Mrs. Hudson was dear and always of great concern to both of us.

I had returned late that morning from Barts, where I worked upon occasion when not filling in as a *locum*. Pausing at the bottom of the steps leading to our sitting room, I allowed a girl of about twenty to pass and depart. Upstairs, I found Holmes seated by the fire.

"A client?" I asked, dropping into my own chair.

He waved a hand. "The usual. Her mother has lost an article which was loaned to them. Fearing that it may have been stolen, she consulted me. I was able to offer a few words of advice."

That was the way in those early years, when Holmes would be visited by a number of different individuals – servants and nobility, policemen and criminals – on a daily basis. In most cases he never had to leave his armchair in order to arrive at a solution. A suggestion would be offered and he would pocket his fee. Only occasionally did he feel the need to arise and move about in order to determine the truth.

He reached to the side-table and lifted a small note. "Are you free this afternoon?"

I said yes, and he handed me the missive. It was a curt invitation from an Edgar Jessup, saying that he would send a carriage for Holmes, if that was acceptable. "Edgar Jessup?" I asked. "The textile king?"

"The same."

"I notice that I am not included in this invitation."

"Nevertheless, your assistance would be invaluable. Although," he added, "I am myself of two minds regarding this matter, and not at all sure that I wish to accept Mr. Jessup's summons."

I looked at the note. "Why ever not? There's money in this case, Holmes, if nothing else." I must confess that, in those days, fear of penury was always a motivation for the both of us. "He simply asks for your opinion on the measures he has undertaken to protect his art collection."

"True, Watson. But I recall too well another recent encounter between the two of us, although we never spoke a word."

This interested me greatly. Bear in mind that at that time in our friendship, Holmes had chosen to tell me almost nothing of his past. I had yet to learn where he attended University, or very much about his earlier days in Montague Street, or that he even had a brother, seven years his senior, who sometimes *is* the British Government.

"Just a few weeks after that Jefferson Hope business," Holmes began, "before you were quite so involved in my investigations, I was consulted by Inspector Plummer regarding a series of shop burglaries taking place in the area north of Bloomsbury. It was initially thought to be a routine affair, involving a local smash-and-grab gang that seemed to have formed spontaneously, as they do. You will know the place. The incidents were centered around shops near Woburn Place and Tavistock Square. The thieves always worked the same pattern, breaking a window and dashing in to steal the cashbox, and whatever else they could lay their hands upon. They were never in the shops for more than a moment, and gone before the inevitable alarm could be sounded."

"I remember reading something about it," I said, "although I had no idea that you were involved. It sounds as if they were rather foolhardy."

Holmes nodded. "Oh, they were. It was clearly the work of a group of ignorant thieves who were full of their own previous successes, and heading for a fall. In fact, they became more bold and careless as time went on. Eight shops had been hit over the course of a couple of months when the incidents finally caught the eye of the press. '*Crime Ring!*' proclaimed the headlines, as you may recall. A few of the shopkeepers were interviewed, and one, owner of a small bauble shop, foolishly proclaimed that the thieves had been so careless as to miss the cashbox in his store, along with a valuable sculpture that he kept on his front counter. As you might think, two days later, the man was robbed again, in the same manner, his newly repaired front door smashed, and the cashbox and statue taken this time before anyone could arrive on the scene."

"How could they do such a thing at the front door in a well-travelled street?"

"Not so well-travelled at three in the morning, my friend. Before I was ever involved, it was theorized – correctly as it turned out – that the gang consisted of only a few individuals – one or two to commit the robbery, and one or two others to serve as lookouts, keeping watch as to when the street was deserted."

"It appears to have been a routine police matter," I said, "in spite of how long it went on. Why did the inspector involve you?"

"It was by way of a referral. The last shopkeeper to be robbed, the same braggadocious fellow who had thoughtlessly informed the thieves what they had missed on the first visit to his establishment, had been a former client of mine, in a little matter regarding a cursed curio."

"Holmes," I interrupted while leaning forward. "Without derailing the current narrative, I would also love to hear an account of that one, to get a record of it for my notes."

He smiled tolerantly. "Perhaps another time." Then the smile faded. "Although considering the outcome of the case, one might almost believe there was a curse after all."

As I settled back in disappointment, realizing that he wasn't going to elaborate, he continued. "After he was immediately robbed a second time – as one might expect – this shopkeeper, an opinionated man named Mr. Silas, insisted to the police that I should be involved in the investigation. Knowing that he might have further dealings with the press, wherein Silas would shame the police if they didn't take his advice, Inspector Plummer was deputized to approach me. It didn't hurt at all that Plummer and I had worked successfully together on a few affairs in the past, when I lived in Montague Street.

"I examined the shop, and also several of the other more recent burglary sites, but could find nothing of any use. It seemed as if my contribution wasn't going to bring any credit to me at all. Mr. Silas, however, remained confident in my abilities, and the inspector was not unmindful of past instances when I had accomplished a thing or two.

"It was Mr. Silas who decided that if the thieves could be goaded once, it could be done again. I had my doubts about this, for who would be witless enough to return a third time, but I was to be proven wrong – unfortunately for Mr. Silas. He delayed an order that he had placed for new bars for his windows and door, and then reached out to the press once more, this time to suggest a story that once again the thieves had missed items of importance. As I said, I thought it unlikely that anyone would fall for it, undoubtedly sensing the trap, but I was mistaken.

"Working with Inspector Plummer, I helped to draw up a battle plan to keep the shop under observation during the nighttime. Some of his best officers, former military men, were selected from the Force to keep watch in the deepest hours of darkness. For the first two nights after Mr. Silas's latest pronouncement appeared in the newspapers, we arranged ourselves as planned, but nothing happened. Then, on the third night, tragedy struck.

"The fog was unfortunately quite thick that night. Plummer and I had planned for such an eventuality, but it still was not to our liking. The handpicked men drew in to closer positions, as they had been told to do, and we hoped that either the criminals wouldn't notice them, should they fall for the bait, or that they would postpone their efforts for another night. This, I may add, was also an unwelcome option, as the nights of lying in wait were becoming quite tedious.

"It was therefore with a mixture of surprise, relief, and anticipation when we heard the crash of breaking glass, indicating that the trap was being sprung. I had been hiding across the street in the Square with the inspector, and we both dashed toward Mr. Silas's shop. To my left and right, echoing in the fog, I could hear the heavy boot steps of constables running to join us.

"As we neared the shop, there was a combination of sounds that changed everything – two gunshots, one after the other, followed by an abbreviated scream that ominously stopped abruptly.

"We arrived in front of the shop just as two men stepped out of the doorway, straight into the arms of the policemen. Watson, if I am ever too critical of the official force, it is because they so often fail to show any imagination. On that night, however, it was this same 'failure' that let those brave men fearlessly disarm the two prisoners, without a thought to their own safety.

"Much as you would imagine, for a few moments there was a great deal of confusion, made up of the milling constables, the futile attempts by the prisoners to escape, and my effort, along with Inspector Plummer, to make our way past them all and into the shop in order to see who had screamed. I feared that I knew the answer, and I was correct.

"The plan had been for Mr. Silas, a widower who lived alone over his shop, to withdraw upstairs on each of the nights that we undertook his plan to capture the burglars. As we had known nothing about those responsible for the past violations, there was no way to ascertain just how dangerous the men might be. Mr. Silas had agreed willingly enough, but apparently it was only for show, as he was there in the shop when the two men broke open the door, and he had likely been hiding there on the previous nights as well.

"We found him on the floor, halfway behind the counter, and half into the main part of the shop, a shallow area stretching six or eight feet back from the front door. One of the constables lit the gas, and it was quickly determined that the man had died nearly instantly, the scream that we heard being his last sound on this earth.

"There did not seem to be any question as to what had happened. However, that was before we had a chance to interview the prisoners, whose stories muddled the issue. They were pulled into the shop, where the dead owner was quite visible to them, lying accusingly at their feet. Both men were in their mid-twenties, not much younger than we are, and upon seeing the body, one of them gave a great cry of grief and would have collapsed, had he not been securely in the constable's grip. The other prisoner looked at him in disgust.

"'Here now,' said Plummer to the distraught man, who now had tears running down his face. 'You're fair caught, and it's a hanging matter. What's your name?'

"The man swallowed and said, 'Edward. Edward Jessup.'

I must have shown some recognition, as Holmes nodded. "Exactly, Watson. The son of the same Edgar Jessup who has requested my presence today." He tapped the note from the man, lying on the table beside him. "The name meant nothing to us then, and the inspector continued his questioning. 'And you?' he asked the other man. 'Your name is – ?'

"'Abbott,' came the sneering reply. 'John Abbott.'

"'Well, you're both under arrest for the series of burglaries, along with murder.'

"At that instant, Jessup started. 'Oh, no!' he cried. 'I didn't murder him!' He looked with loathing at his companion. 'No! It was Abbott here. He's the one!'

"Abbott attempted to lunge at him, but the big officer holding him pulled him back and shook him like a terrier snapping a rat. 'Noon o' that,' he said in a broad Devonshire accent.

"Jessup raised his arms pleadingly. 'I admit to the burglaries. At first it seemed like a lark – something to do, a game almost. But as time went on, he became afraid.' Jessup pointed toward Abbott. 'The last couple of times, he insisted that we carry guns. I didn't want to, but somehow, I couldn't say no.'

"'Shut your mouth,' growled Abbott, trying again to step forward. 'I'm warning you – '

"'Go on,' said Plummer, sensing he could get the full story and a confession if he just let the man talk.

"'I didn't want to come back here, but John insisted. I thought it seemed like a trap, but he said that the old man couldn't help bragging. It would be just like before – that we'd be in and away before anyone knew a thing. But when the glass smashed and we stepped in, that man – ' and at this, he glanced toward Mr. Silas's body on the floor, ' – he rose up from behind the counter. John . . . John raised his gun then, and fired a shot.'

"Abbott growled and lunged ineffectively, whereupon Plummer said, 'We heard *two* shots. What of the other?'

"'That was my gun,' said Jessup. 'After John shot the poor man, he backed up into me, knocking my arm. I was so surprised, my own gun went off.'

"A sly expression crossed Abbott's face. 'You lie,' he said. '*You* were the one who shot him, and then backed into *me*, making *my* gun go off.'

251

"Jessup's face looked possibly more stricken than before. 'No!' he said. 'That isn't the way of it at all. You killed him! It was you!'

"A thought occurred to me then, although I supposed the question was moot in the end, as either way, one was a killer and the other an accomplice, and the law would treat them the same, no matter which name was associated with the actual death. 'The guns?' I asked. 'Where are they?'

"One constable answered, 'This one is on the ground, where I knocked it from that one's hand.' He nodded his head toward Abbott.

"'And I have the other,' said an officer beside me. 'In my pocket. I took it from him.' And he indicated Jessup.

"I nodded. 'Please keep them separate. It is important to keep track of who held which gun.' At that point, I asked everyone to remain still for a moment as I moved around and between them, observing what I could upon the floor. The prisoners' footprints were clearly identifiable, having tracked in the damp of the night fog, and each had a different pattern matching their shoes. It was evident that they had only proceeded a few feet into the shop, as there was no evidence that either had approached any closer to the counter. Of course, this did not contradict that part of their stories, or what we had heard at the time of the crime, when the breaking glass was followed so quickly by the two gunshots. The prints were too muddled to see who had advanced further into the shop.

"Additional examination quickly revealed one of the bullets lodged in the soft plaster, off to the right side of the counter. Clearly, this weapon had been aimed at a very different angle from that of the shot that killed the proprietor. Stepping behind the counter, I used my pocket knife to dig out the projectile, wrapping it carefully in my handkerchief.

"Plummer gestured toward me and, pulling me outside, asked what I was doing. 'It may or may not be important,' I answered, 'but I have been doing some research of late that may determine which of the two men fired the fatal shot.'

"He shook his head. 'It's obvious that it was Abbott. He is just claiming Jessup's version of events as his own in order to save himself, or to confuse things.'

"'I agree. However, if it is possible to settle the matter in a more exact manner, I expect that we should do so.'

"Plummer agreed and, after the two men were removed, he made sure that the two weapons were clearly identified and saved for my later examination.

"What," Holmes then asked unexpectedly, "is your knowledge of firearms, Watson?"

I pursed my lips. "As much as any common fellow's, I suppose."

"Are you familiar with rifling?"

I nodded. "I am. The placement of spiraling grooves within the barrel of a gun, running from back to front, so to speak, that put a spin on the bullet, thus allowing it to have a longer and straighter course."

"Exactly. Invented in the sixteenth century by the Germans, who have always had some skill with these matters, it vastly improved the performance of earlier weapons, such as the aptly named 'smooth-bores'."

"But what has such a thing to do with this investigation?"

"Well you might ask, as the inspector did at the time. I had been doing some experiments with firearms, having observed that this rifling action marks a bullet as it passes through the gun barrel.'

"What of it? I would be surprised if it did not."

"Ah, Watson, an idea should not remain thoroughly unexplored simply because something has occurred as one expected it to. Not long before the incident in Mr. Silas's shop, I had researched the nature of these marks upon bullets, and whether a projectile could be identified by the markings of a particular gun in a particular way, thus showing that it was fired from that same gun."

"But surely, Holmes, a bullet moving at such high speeds would be damaged in a different way from another bullet coming from the same gun, regardless of the permanent rifling marks. And what of the differences that already exist in the bullets themselves?"

"Those differences are there, to be sure. But a microscopic examination of the rifling marks on the soft lead of bullets are very sharply defined, I assure you, and in fact are reproducible time and again on different bullets fired from the same gun."

"I see where you are going with this. You hoped to establish conclusively through these rifling marks that it was Abbott who held the gun that matched the fatal bullet."

"Absolutely correct, my dear Watson. I set myself up in one of the labs at Barts, where I still have an arrangement, as you know. Following the autopsy, Plummer arranged for me to receive the bullet from Mr. Silas's body, and I set about examining it under a microscope, along with the other bullet removed from the wall. Luckily, both objects were in excellent shape, the one from the wall having simply imbedded itself into the soft plaster, while the one from the body hadn't been deflected or deformed by impact with a bone.

"First I examined the bullets fired on the night of the crime, and sketched the markings that I observed. The murder bullet, as I shall call it, had a full set of rifling marks, while the wall bullet had only 'false' rifling markings from what appeared to come from the tip of the muzzle. Then, I fired additional test bullets from each of the guns – both Webleys by the way, same caliber, different models – in order that I might see comparative examples of each. The bullets were fired into a great wad of bedding, to protect them from any deforming damage.

"When these were also examined and sketched, it was easy to see that the test bullets had markings matching the two bullets from the crime, and it was definitive which gun had shot which. I had conclusive evidence as to whose gun had fired the bullet into the shopkeeper, and whose had shot at the wall.

"Needless to say, the inspector was with me throughout the process, and saw what I saw in the microscope. He agreed with my sketches completely. 'One question, however,' he said when we had finished. 'We now know for sure which gun fired the bullet that killed Mr. Silas – it was Abbott's, as we suspected all along. But who's to say that Abbott won't claim that Jessup still fired first, intending to hit Silas but *missing*, and then, when backing up, he nudged Abbott, who then accidentally fired and hit Silas by mistake?'

"I saw his point. We were both certain that Abbott had undoubtedly been the first to fire, and intentionally at the dead man. However, how to prove the order of events? And after our efforts, what did it matter anyway? In any case, Plummer was loathe to bring this new and unproven ballistic science into court, especially as the defense would raise the very questions that he had just shared.

"In the end, the inspector sat down with Abbott, using my sketches, and was able to overwhelm the man's defenses so well that a confession was inevitable. He was subsequently convicted and hanged."

"And Jessup?" I asked. "He would have been considered an accomplice – also a capital crime."

Holmes nodded. "He was convicted, although the appeals process was much more extensive in his case, due to the influence and resources of his family. It was argued, bolstered by Abbott's confession, that he was not responsible for the murder, and that it was only due to his weak character that he had allowed himself to be coerced into participating in the earlier robberies – a poor defense at best. However, in the end, it was indisputable that he had been present at the crime, carrying a firearm, and he was convicted and sentenced to death."

"And was the sentence carried out?"

"It was. Last month. Inspector Plummer sent a note asking if I wished to attend. I did not."

We both fell silent for a moment, pondering the unexpected choices and twists and turns in a man's life that can lead to such a bad end. Knowing nothing of Abbott, I could imagine his past, perhaps a steady decline until the unsurprising conclusion, terminating upon the gallows.

But the other, Edward Jessup – he had been of a good family, with every opportunity. What could have happened? What turn left when he should have gone right had taken him to the same tragic destiny?

"I understand your reluctance at meeting with the boy's father," I said. "But do you think that he even knows of your involvement in the matter?"

"Without doubt. As a witness, I was called to testify in court. As expected, the evidence of the ballistic rifling was not used, but my testimony as to the first statements of the accused when arrested was considered useful. I well recall the expressionless stare of the man in the courtroom as I was questioned. It hasn't been long enough for him to forget."

"Do you intend to see him, then?"

With a sigh, Holmes stood. "I suppose so. When I chose this profession, I never expected that every encounter would be dripping with bonhomie and good cheer. Will you join me?"

A part of me did not want to go, as the circumstances sounded rather grim indeed. But I could sense that Holmes wished for me to accompany him and, as his friend, I could do no less. "Yes, of course," I agreed.

So that afternoon, Holmes and I found ourselves in the textile king's well-tricked carriage, making our way toward the man's home near Berkeley Square. My companion was silent, pondering his own thoughts, while I inhaled deeply, not looking forward to the upcoming encounter.

At the Jessup home, we were shown in by a cadaverous-looking butler. I could sense that this was a house of sadness. We were taken through to a sitting room, and within moments Mr. Jessup entered.

Both of us had remained standing. When the man entered the room, I could tell that Holmes was exhibiting some reserve, although anyone that knew him less might not have noticed it. He was as surprised as I when Mr. Jessup reached out and clasped his hand warmly.

"Mr. Holmes, it has been far too long. I apologize."

I rarely see Holmes speechless, but that was one of those times. Finally, as the man continued to grasp his hand, he uttered, "I beg your pardon?"

"I apologize. For taking so long to thank you. It has been . . . difficult." Releasing Holmes's grip, he turned to me. "I am Edgar Jessup." To me he also offered a hand, which I accepted out of reflex. "I understand that you are the doctor that assists Mr. Holmes in his investigations."

I started to speak, but Mr. Jessup continued. "Please. Don't be surprised. I have done some checking into Mr. Holmes's career. Since . . . since the arrest and conviction of my son, Edward . . . ." He gestured toward a grouping of chairs. "Please, have a seat. Collins!"

He called the butler over to see if we would have something to drink, but we both declined. With the departure of Collins, Holmes began to speak.

"Mr. Jessup, I understand that you wish to consult me about your collection – "

"Yes, yes, we'll get to that in a moment. But first, my apology. And you must forgive me, you see. I've wanted to thank you for quite a while, but . . . ." His voice faded, and he swallowed. Then, more softly, he said, "Since Edward's . . . death. My wife is still not over it – she may never be, you understand. He was our only . . . our only . . . ." At that point, his emotions overcame him, and for a moment he could not speak. Then, composing himself, he continued.

"All this time, Mr. Holmes, I've wanted to thank you, but the wound was too fresh. I suppose it still is, but when I needed someone to advise me upon the security of my collection, and your name was suggested, I realized that I might never have a better opportunity."

"Thank me? For what, Mr. Jessup?"

"Why, for proving my son did not shoot the owner of that shop."

"How do you know of that, sir?"

"The police inspector informed me."

"But Mr. Jessup, I'm afraid that my efforts did nothing to help save the life of your son. He was convicted as an accomplice of the crime."

"True, Mr. Holmes, true. But the statements of that . . . Mr. Abbott, attempting to lay the blame upon my son, might have made things more ambiguous than they would have been otherwise. My son's reputation, there at the end, would have been further destroyed, much more so than it was. My wife and I . . . we would have known the truth, but to others, there would always have been some doubt.

"My son and I had been estranged for a time before his death. I blame myself now. It was this that let him fall under the evil influence of John Abbott. But after his arrest, and during the time of the trial and the appeals, he and I were able to become much closer. I like to think that it would have been the same regardless, Mr. Holmes, but truth be told, the fact that you were able to clear him of the murder helped my peace of mind as he and I faced those last terrible days together."

He swallowed again before gaining control of himself. "You didn't have to do that, Mr. Holmes. He was caught, and conviction was certain, whether or not he pulled the trigger of that fatal shot. But you went to the effort to discover the truth anyway, and for that, I shall be forever grateful."

"But Mr. Jessup – " said my friend.

"That is all that needs to be said!" interrupted the textile king, showing the force of will that had gotten him to that successful perch he occupied. "But know this, Mr. Holmes. You have a friend. Whatever I can do to help you in your career, you have but to ask."

I didn't know what to expect from Sherlock Holmes. Perhaps he would don that mask of cold aloofness he often wears. Possibly he would dodge the issue by explaining that he'd arrived at his solution more for the sake of science than to prove young Jessup's innocence. Instead, he responded with that grace and tact which have always been his hallmark, replying with a simple, "Thank you."

We proceeded then to discuss Mr. Jessup's art collection, with valuable advice provided by Holmes. On that day, the consulting detective acquired a patron of sorts, one of many that would line up on his side as the years went by. Very rarely would he draw upon this well of good will, but he always knew that it was there, should he need it. My friend has many gifts, and he has never felt the need to hide them under a bushel, but it is a testament to his integrity that he is uncharacteristically modest about this, that large and disparate group of people that owes him so much.

The Coombs Contrivance

When leaving our rooms in Baker Street, it is sometimes necessary to slip out in disguise, or through the rear entrance and across the small yard where a sole plane tree keeps vigil, hoping to avoid whomever might be observing the house. Other departures might be more forthright – when keeping an appointment or catching a train, or simply stepping down the street to the tobacconist.

On rare occasions, I am sometimes able to convince my friend, Sherlock Holmes, to take a stroll in the evening, stepping out occasionally after a day of being immersed in the stultifying and poisonous atmosphere of one of his a chemical investigations, only to return and find a client or policemen, anxious to tell a story and draw us away again. Holmes will glance my way with a feigned frown, indicating that my insistence upon his physical well-being, fresh air, and good walk, has come dangerously close to depriving him of a new case.

But whatever the reason for going away, there was never a guarantee of a calm return.

I had walked back from Paddington that afternoon, having visited the medical practice that I had recently purchased. It was few weeks before my marriage, and I was in that odd mental state of anticipating a change while feeling rather melancholy about what I would be leaving behind. However, I was certain that I would continue to be involved in Holmes's investigations.

But upon opening the door, I recalled some of the dismay associated with that same situation. I entered to find Mrs. Hudson, tensely standing at the foot of the stairs, her back protectively against a waist-high plinth that supported a white ceramic jug. I smiled.

"The Irregulars?" I asked.

She nodded, her frown staying in place.

It was no great deduction upon my part. The various boys – and a few girls – that Holmes employed as his eyes and ears throughout the city, going places and seeing things that others would miss while themselves being ignored, were, by necessity, occasional visitors to our rooms – much to the dismay of our landlady. She had a stern mien with them, though it was realized by all that she a soft heart underneath her exterior. At times, however, that exterior could be especially tart and thorny – as we had discovered the previous year when a number of the Irregulars, as they were called, had come barreling down the stairs, each richer than when they had arrived, and turned loose upon some unknowing subject. Young Abel

Peake, no more or less enthusiastic than his friends, had knocked against the plinth as he left the stairs for the ground floor hall, causing the vase that had rested there to tumble and shatter into a million pieces.

It was an accident that could have happened to any of us, and Mrs. Hudson knew it. The vase was a cheap piece of crockery that she had purchased from the shop and factory of a distant relative, Morse Hudson, in the Kennington Road. Nevertheless, she had given young Abel a memorable scolding until she saw the chagrined expression on his face. He would have been free to go after that, if she hadn't taken him aside to give him a slice of cake and some tea. Nevertheless, he and the other Irregulars had been much more careful after that. Still, when they were inside the house, Mrs. Hudson became nervous and, until they had left again, she would stand guard at the foot of the steps to protect the vase's replacement, an unfortunate and ugly jug, purchased at the same source, that mysteriously seemed to appeal to her.

"How many of them?" I asked her.

"Nearly two-dozen," was her grim reply. I raised an eyebrow – a substantial number indeed. But then again, this was an important case. It was at that moment that we heard muted and boyish laughter from upstairs, punctuating her concern – any high spirits might result in a temporary forgetfulness regarding the fate of the last object to be in danger. She stood a little straighter, as if renewing her resolve to protect the domicile.

Hiding my smile, I nodded and went upstairs. Opening the door to the sitting room, I found it crowded with Irregulars – on the chairs at the dining table and the desks and at Holmes's chemical corner, on the settee, and on the rug before the fire. A score of them – not quite the two-dozen estimated by Mrs. Hudson, but certainly capable of causing destruction as their tide washed out to the street.

"Keep to your positions," Holmes was saying, nodding my way as I entered and closed the door. "Clayton must not know that he is being watched. Some of you remain near his lodgings, and others in Covent Garden. I will be along at different times. Whatever my guise, you will know me by a red bandanna. Now . . . *Dismissed!*"

He said it with a cry and a twinkle in his eye, and – as if a starting gun had been fired at a horse race – the lads scrambled into motion and surged toward the door. "Slowly . . . slowly," I cautioned, tapping a lad here and there on the shoulder as they stepped out to the landing. I could hear them pounding down the steps – faster than I would have liked, but still slower than it might have been otherwise.

I closed the door and turned back to question Holmes about the boys' report when I saw that one of them hadn't left.

259

Sitting in my desk chair, turned around sideways with his feet not quite touching the floor, was young Levi, who had been indispensable to Holmes on several recent investigations. Not long a member of the Irregulars, he was the son of pair of well-meaning parents who worked too hard to support their growing family. Levi had been recruited by Wiggins himself, the leader of the group, and following a small service that Holmes was able to perform for Levi's father soon after, the boy's parents had felt no concern regarding his continued association with the Irregulars or the detective.

Holmes had his back turned while he packed tobacco into his pipe. And yet, he revealed that he was aware of the boy's presence by asking, "Is there something else, Levi?"

The boy appeared nervous, which was unusual, as he was usually brimming with a cheerful confidence. However, he waited no more than an extra second before replying, "I saw something."

Holmes turned then and dropped into his chair. With a hand he waved toward the basket chair facing the fire. "Move closer and tell us about it."

I found my own seat as well while Levi climbed into the chair situated between us. He tried sitting all the way to the back, but his legs were at an uncomfortable position, so he shifted forward again and let his feet dangle toward the rug.

"I was one of them that you had in Covent Garden," he began. "Watching when the cab passed."

Holmes simply nodded. Levi glanced my way, but he knew Holmes well enough by now and was not intimidated by the silence. "I was standing near the two sisters' stall. Where they sell the cakes."

"I know it," said Holmes, who then glanced my way.

I nodded. "The Coombs sisters. They've been there selling pastries to market-goers since before I was in medical school."

"I've been there three days," Levi continued, "leaning against that one corner. Wiggins thought it would be the best place when the cab comes by, because it has to go slow to get through the posts, and I can jump on the back if I need to.

"As he told you a few minutes ago, Clayton has been by there several times since we started watching, but he hasn't had the other man with him, so we've let him pass. I've had a lot of time to stand and think, and when you do that, you start to notice what's going on around you. You see what's regular, and what isn't.

"Every day, at about three o'clock, one of the ladies, the dark-haired one, brews up a pot of tea over a little lamp that they keep in the stall."

"You know the time from the clock across the court?"

"Right. The market has gotten quiet by then, since most of the customers have come and gone. All three times that I've seen them drink the tea, the other lady, the older one with white hair, has started to cough soon after, and then she seemed to get tired and had to sit down. It happened on the first two days, so today I was watching to see if it happened again. And it did. But this time I saw something else.

"After the dark-haired lady brewed the tea, she poured it out into two cups. She left them sitting on the counter to cool, and after a while, the older lady started boxing up the cakes that hadn't sold. She was still all right then. But once while she was turned away, the dark-haired lady reached under her shawl and pulled out a little bottle. She opened it very quickly and then poured something from it into the older one's cup. The older lady never saw her, but a few minutes later, when the tea had cooled off some more, she drank it all away, and then she started to cough and sat down like before, very fast, like she was out of breath."

He glanced back and forth between Holmes and me, to see if we comprehended what he was thinking. "I didn't see if she did it the first two days, but maybe the dark-haired one poured something into the tea on those days, too."

"And you're sure that she only started to cough and sat down *after* she drank the tea?" I asked, although I believed him. "Possibly the work had already wearied her, and it was only then that she gave into it."

"It was *after*," said Levi firmly. "The older lady had seemed fine-enough before."

"What about the younger woman's tea?" asked Holmes.

"When it was first poured, the two cups were side by side, no difference. The younger lady hadn't taken any, and then the older one picked a cup and moved it onto her side of the counter. Then the younger one took the other and had a sip. She was fine."

He fell silent, as if realizing that there was nothing more to relate. He had already learned to stick to the facts and let Holmes put together the pieces.

My friend was not long in coming to a decision. "The matter with Clayton is stagnant at the moment, until his brother comes down from Yorkshire and tries to kill him," he said, "and in any case, I'll be in and out of Covent Garden over the next few days. It won't hurt to devote a little time to this additional matter in order to see what we shall see." He stood. "Thank you for bringing this to my attention, Levi. I'll keep you informed of any developments."

The boy slid forward and off the chair, gravely nodding at the man more than twice his height. Then, he turned and made for the door. I wondered if Mrs. Hudson had kept count of how many boys had departed, realizing that one had remained behind, forcing her to stay on guard. She needn't have worried, for Levi slipped down the stairs at a steady pace, rather than in the manner of a Red Indian on the warpath.

"Do you think this is worthy of investigation?" I asked Holmes as he walked toward his bedroom.

"We have become involved in any number of serious matters that have begun with smaller incidents than this," he replied over his shoulder. I heard him rummaging around for a few minutes, and then he returned dressed as a common laborer – a favorite guise. I knew that it didn't matter what personality he portrayed when he left, as there was a good chance he would return as someone else, following a visit to one or more of the various hidey-holes he had scattered throughout the metropolis.

He adjusted the red bandanna which would identify him to his troops. "Should word come from Yorkshire that Clayton's brother is on the move, get a message to Wiggins. He'll be able to find me. I also have some ten or twelve other little matters on hand at present, but none with any features of interest, and therefore they will wait."

With that, he departed, leaving me to my own devices. I resumed the ongoing planning for my impending move. When Mrs. Hudson brought up my evening meal, I saw that she carried nothing for Holmes, so he must have given instructions to her on his way out that he would be away. If she hadn't been told, she would have optimistically fixed something for him as well, always hoping that he would eat this time, rather than risk – as he put it – diverting essential blood-flow from his mind "toward the purely animalistic activity of digestion".

Early that night, a telegram arrived from Mycroft Holmes indicating that Clayton's younger brother had departed for London, as expected. I stepped outside and relayed the information to one of the lads always waiting nearby, instructing that it be delivered to Wiggins, and thence to Holmes, straightaway. Then I went back upstairs and so on to bed.

We had met John Clayton, of 3 Turpey Street in the Borough, the previous year, when he had driven the cab that was used by a very bad man to dog the footsteps of our client through London. At that time, Holmes had noticed that Clayton was wearing a pin with a unique coat-of-arms. Curious about him, it only took a few hours to subsequently learn that cab-driver Clayton was actually of the nobility, but of a socialist turn – thus his renouncement of family and title so that he could drive about London, unencumbered of both wealth and responsibility, leaving the care of his Yorkshire estate in the hands of his disreputable younger brother. Holmes had turned the occasional eye toward the man over the next few months, mostly due to simple curiosity. But a week earlier, Holmes's brother Mycroft had summoned us to his office in Whitehall, seeking my friend's assistance. Clayton's son, of the Colonial Office, had been lost at sea the previous year, his young wife perishing with him. With the cab-driver's legitimate heir removed, Mycroft had caught the vaguest of hints that Clayton's younger brother, still residing in Yorkshire, intended to take steps to remove his socialist-leaning sibling and then assume the title and all that went with it for himself. Holmes's job was to protect the elder brother until such time as the younger could be warned off by Mycroft's agents. However, to avoid a premature accusation, the younger brother had to be allowed to make a play first. A plan involving the Irregulars was quickly devised, and the waiting game began.

I saw no more of Holmes until late afternoon the next day, when he entered, dressed as some sort of clerk. I could discern something of my friend underneath the hair parted on the wrong side and combed low across his forehead, and the underslung jaw resting upon a frame several inches shorter than normal, giving his walk and very stance an oddly simian gate. He nodded and remained in character as he passed through the sitting room, returning in just a few moments as himself to join me before the fire, where he filled and lit his pipe.

After letting me know that Clayton was still being watched, as was his brother while he slowly made his way to London, Holmes said, "I had the opportunity to observe the younger Coombs sister, Portia, surreptitiously pour something from a small glass vial into her older sister's tea. Upon drinking it, the elder woman, Letitia, immediately began to cough and show symptoms of fatigue, as described. Portia was very solicitous, graciously offering to finish boxing up the unsold stock before they both left to make their way home."

"You know their names now?" I asked. "In the ten years or more that I've been aware of them and their stall, I don't think that I ever heard what they were called."

"And no reason that you should. But I know much more about them now than simply their names. Yesterday afternoon, while watching Clayton's cab pass on several occasions through Covent Garden, I made myself useful as the vendors were packing up near the sisters' stall. I learned that they live in nearby Langley Street, in a fourth floor room near the brewery. They rent kitchen space a block or two away, and they're up before dawn six days a week, constructing the cakes and treats that have made them modestly noted in that very small circle.

"Letitia, the older sister, is truly quite a bit older – some twenty years, as a matter of fact. Even though their stall identifies them as the Coombs sisters, they are regularly taken to be mother and daughter."

"An interesting set of characters, I'm sure, in a minor Dickensian way," I interjected. "But what does this have to do with the possible poisoning that Levi – and then you – witnessed?"

"An excellent question. A superficial observation of their assets is not encouraging, and the younger killing the older would, on the surface, gain very little. They have a rickety setup in Covent Garden, where they have operated for a number of years, and also the very modest shared lodgings to the north. They have no partners or assistants, and the labor – quite a bit of it, apparently – is shared equally. If one were to be removed from their joint harness, it's unlikely that the other could carry on without assistance. Oh, a helper could be found, and the baking could continue as before, but it is not a business with a great deal of wealth that could be shifted from one to the other if a death should occur – in contrast to the situation if John Clayton were to die, thereby enriching his younger brother's means considerably. Upon initial examination, there is no motive for Portia to murder her older sister."

"You neglect," I added with a tone of weary worldliness, "the motivation of simple dislike. Perhaps Letitia has complained incessantly for multiple decades about her sore feet, and Portia has finally had enough of it, deciding to rid herself of the drone of it all in the same way that the anonymous narrator of Poe's 'The Tell-tale Heart' vowed to remove the old man's staring and filmed vulture eye."

"Then surely," was Holmes's rejoinder, "there is a more decisive way to do so than whatever is being slipped into Letitia's tea, simply causing her to cough and feel suddenly weary. If that is the case, Portia is certainly playing a long game. Whatever trouble she went to in order to obtain the mysterious poison could have also been better purposed to finding a faster method of murder – saving her sooner rather than later from hearing further tales of tired feet.

"In any case," he added with a smile, "there is another factor."

"Ah," I replied. "There often is."

"There are rumors that the sisters have expectations of an inheritance."

I shifted in my seat. "This makes things a bit clearer."

"Does it? I wonder. Several of the nearby vendors with whom I spoke related that in years past, the sisters have occasionally referenced a rich relative, from whom they hope to be remembered in his will. It isn't a frequent theme, but on days when the weather is too cold or too hot, they are sometimes heard to mention that one day, selling cakes to the patrons of Covent Garden might no longer be their burden."

I rose and poured a brandy. Holmes declined. "Is there any way to determine the nature of this inheritance?" I asked.

"An excellent idea, Watson! I'm happy to report that an examination of the matter has already been undertaken. After I learned of this factor, I visited Marchmont and set him on the trail. It was really no challenge for him, as he already knew of their situation. Apparently the story is well known."

Marchmont was a solicitor in Gray's Inn, for whom Holmes had performed several investigations. Their complete and satisfying success had converted Marchmont into one of those many individuals scattered around the capital who would do anything for Holmes in gratitude. The fellow was stout and pleasant, and I had used him myself for a few of my own legal matters.

"Letitia and Portia Coombs," Holmes explained, "are the nieces of old Silas Coombs."

It was suddenly clear to me, as rumors of the man's impending death had been reported for weeks. A miser who had made a small fortune during the expansion of the railways, he was surely well beyond seventy now.

Holmes saw that I recognized the name. "Old Silas outlived two wives before his third, dying in the process, presented him with a daughter, Susan Coombs, who should have been his only heir. She never married and spent her entire life taking care of her father – when not helping the London poor. In a fit of anger several months ago, jealous of the time that she was spending assisting the less fortunate instead of catering to him, he disinherited her, directing that his fortune should go to his two nieces, Letitia and Portia – with whom, I might add, he had never maintained any association whatsoever, having long since separated himself from the rest of his own family.

"However, before he could correct that error, he suffered an aneurism, leaving him unable to function. Soon after, in one of those terrible turns of fate, the daughter Susan dropped dead from a long-standing heart problem, and the two sisters, living in conditions barely above penury, are now in line for a fortune, as soon as the old man shuffles off. Yet, according to Marchmont, the twist is that both sisters have to inherit jointly, according to the terms of the will. If one dies before the other, all is forfeit to The Society for Displaced Communards – apparently chosen at random by the old man out of spite."

"But that makes no sense!" I cried. "If they have to inherit together, then why is the younger trying to kill the older?"

"Ah, but is she?" He pinched the bridge of his nose. "Do you trust Levi's judgment, Watson?"

I considered. "For an eight-year-old, he's remarkable perceptive – as much as any of the other Irregulars who have assisted you. The Wiggins family, or the Peakes, or Thorndyke, before he went away to university."

"And yet, he is young. When I watched the sisters today, I had the impression that Portia was looking to make sure that none of the neighboring vendors at nearby stalls saw her action, and not her sister. She seemed indifferent as to whatever the itinerant strangers, such as myself, might observe."

He set down his pipe. "We need to determine the nature of the liquid being poured into Letitia's tea. If a crime is taking place, it might be enough to warn Portia that all is known, but without definite facts . . . ." He was silent for a moment, and then, "I will have to devise some method of examining the tea. I can think of seven separate stratagems that might serve the purpose, but – "

At that moment, the doorbell peeled, and within moments, Wiggins himself had appeared at our doorway. Clayton's younger brother had arrived in London and revealed himself. Without further comment, Holmes and I donned coats and hats and joined the Irregular in a quickly obtained four-wheeler.

I gave no further thought to the Sisters Coombs until early the next day, when we wearily sank into our chairs before the sitting room fireplace. Holmes's pipe and my brandy glass were exactly as we had left them at the time of our abrupt departure. John Clayton's younger brother had indeed attempted to kill him, but Holmes had cast his net so well around the man that his effort was an exercise in futility. Following his exposure, the younger brother had ranted at us, and my friend most of all, but he was interrupted by an intercession of Mycroft Holmes's agents. An astonished John Clayton, his younger brother, and the government agents who had assisted us had all climbed into suddenly present cabs and had then vanished within moments like wraiths into the fog, leaving Holmes, the Irregulars, and myself, standing in the silent empty street. The matter was now out of our hands, and Holmes gave a barking laugh – he has always been amused by the most unusual aspects of situations.

The situation was recalled eighteen months later when John Clayton was actually murdered. Holmes, hearing of the event, summoned me to join him, and his investigations had only begun when his brother Mycroft made it very clear that the matter was to remain unsolved at the behest of the Crown. I'm aware that Holmes ignored the request, and determined to his satisfaction the true killer – the identity of which would surprise no one who knew the facts of the case. However, the younger brother did indeed become the new Duke of G--------, and a century must pass before my notes can reveal the truth of the matter. As I write this now, in May 1910, the current Duke's son is presumed lost at sea, in a cruel parallel to the fate of his long-lost cousin, and I'm aware that the Duke has approached Holmes, now retired, to see what facts, if any, might be learned. Holmes

266

had previously done another reluctant service for the Duke in 1901, when this same son who is now lost at sea was kidnapped as a boy while attending school, and his distaste for the man, still evident then, has not subsided even now. I don't know what his decision will be as to whether he will provide assistance in the current occurrence.

But on that early morning in April 1889, John Clayton still lived, though under a grim cloud for a time, and Holmes and I both had a feeling of dissatisfaction and business unfinished. I was considering pouring a new brandy when he began to speak again of the Coombs sisters, and I needed a moment to shift from the sordid affairs of the Clayton family and back those of the sisters and the possibility of sororicide.

"I will need your assistance, Watson," he said. "I should have it all arranged by this afternoon."

"Hmm. Pardon me?" I said, confused.

"The Coombs sisters. While we were busy saving John Clayton, I had Layton Rathe burgle the Coombs sisters' rooms, but he couldn't find any of Portia's mysterious liquid. I've decided that I must instead get a sample of some of her tainted tea.

Rathe was one of Holmes's agents in the underworld, a barely reformed burglar who was nearly as good as Holmes himself at that craft. "And how will you do that?"

"There is a method that has worked well for me in several cases. The Arnsworth Castle business, and the Darlington Substitution, along with that business for the King of Bohemia a couple of years ago."

I laughed. "As I recall, this method involves making a woman believe there is a fire or something of that sort, forcing her to reveal where she has placed what she values the most. You mentioned once that a married woman will grab her baby, and an unmarried one her jewel box. Neither of the Coombs sisters has baby or jewels. How is this scheme relevant?"

"This," he said with a smile, "will be a variation. I don't need for them to show me where something will be hidden. Rather, I simply need for them to be distracted while I get a sample of the tea."

"Why not simply try to obtain the vial itself?"

"I certainly could, but there are social considerations to follow. Pickpocketing a woman is not an optimal plan. In any case, it would be missed and raise suspicions. A sample of the tea will suffice."

And so it was that, in the middle of the afternoon, we found ourselves scattered around Covent Garden. Holmes was again disguised as the loafer of a few days earlier, and he had insisted that I look the part as well. Thus, I was in one of my own quite worn suits, saved for just such an occasion as this. Along with several Irregulars, Levi had joined us, as Holmes felt that he'd earned a place as well. I also recognized two or three of Holmes's other agents.

Glancing around from where I leaned against a stained wall, I saw that a quiet had descended upon the market. The fruit and vegetable vendors, so busy that morning providing their wares to restaurants and homes, had mostly emptied their booths, and some were starting to clean up or close.

Nearby was a salesman that I recognized named Breckinridge – unusual in this vegetable and fruit market, he was a purveyor of fowl. Holmes and I had once had a passing interaction with him. I knew that he kept his books well, but he was abrasive and a gambler. It wouldn't be long after these events that he would go out of business.

Shifting my gaze around the market, I turned toward the Coombs sisters' stall which, like a number of others that peripherally catered to the customers lured there for produce, had seemingly come to the end of its working day. Without being too obtrusive in my observations, I saw that the dark-haired sister, Portia, was making tea.

It went just as Levi described. She was a handsome woman of around forty, and moved with sureness as she lit a small spirit lamp and then boiled the water. Taking out two mugs from beneath the counter, she fixed the tea leaves, and then poured the water when it had come to a boil. Leaving it to steep, she turned to help the older woman in the packing up of the remaining cakes.

After a few moments, the older woman selected one of the cups, raised it to her lips, blew across it, and took a hesitant sip, afraid of burning her mouth. Then she set it down and turned away. In a moment or two, but not immediately, the younger sister reached beneath her shawl and withdrew . . . something. I couldn't see clearly, but she twisted at the top with her other hand, lowered the object to the other's teacup and tipped something into it. Then she had replaced the cover and tucked it out of sight.

Alerted by Holmes, I tried to see if she was more interested in hiding her actions from her sister or the other vendors, but it happened so quickly that I couldn't tell. I glanced at Levi to see if he had done anything to give away the game, but he was simply reclining where he had been before, looking here and there in a bored manner. There was nothing that would cause anyone to give him a second glance.

I had asked Holmes beforehand whether we would wait for the older sister to take another sip, after the second liquid had been added, but he indicated that our plan would move forward immediately. So, as I had several years before while then standing in the twilight outside of Briony Lodge, I waited for Holmes's signal. When it came, I pulled a plumber's smoke rocket from beneath my coat, looked to ascertain that I was unobserved, activated it, and tossed it at the foot of the sisters' stall.

"Fire!" came the cry immediately from half-a-dozen boys and adults scattered around the court. "Fire!"

The sisters turned quickly, looking here and there and, seeing that the thick smoke was billowing from their own stall, made as if to run from behind it and learn more about the impending disaster. But a rush of humanity pushed toward them, forcing them back and away from the smoke. I saw that a stout matron named Hilda Stanholt, one of Holmes's acquaintances, had shepherded the two sisters over to the wall near Levi. An Irregular loped forward carrying a bucket of water, which he used to dowse the smoke rocket. Another slid by so quickly to pick it up and carry it away that one would be hard-pressed to see what had happened. And through all the confusion, Sherlock Holmes, in his guise of a loafer, stood at the stall counter with his back to the sisters and calmly poured some of the altered tea into a vial of his own. Then he was away, and the crowd began to disperse. None was the wiser, and the sisters were left with a mysterious fire that had no apparent origin and produced no damage. The entire drama had started and finished in less than half-a-minute.

Holmes and I were a block or two away when we heard a woman's voice call from behind us. It was Hilda Stanholt, and she waved Holmes back with some urgency. "A moment, Watson," he said, taking a few steps to join her. She whispered something to him which caused his eyebrows to raise. Then, with a half-smile, he thanked her and rejoined me. I tipped my hat to her, but she only scowled, having distrusted me ever since I had inadvertently ruined one of her schemes in Charing Cross Station.

"A possible twist, Watson," he said. I knew that he would tell me if he wanted, or more likely withhold it until he had both verified it and could then present it in that dramatic way he so favored. I resolved to maintain my patience.

Back in our rooms, we resumed our regular attire, and then Holmes spent only a quarter-hour at his chemical table analyzing the tea. With a satisfied grunt, he closed the flame of his Bunsen burner and sat back on his stool, one arm across his chest, and the other resting on it to cup his chin. He was looking toward the window and the houses opposite, but I knew that he was seeing something far different.

When he stood up, it was to move around to his own chair, where he sat and reached for his pipe. Seeing that something – either Hilda Stanholt's information or the results of his chemical investigation – had given him a puzzling new aspect to consider, I went about my business. I had thought that the poison would be identified and the younger sister confronted, or perhaps arrested. It seemed that it was to be a bit more complicated than that. Knowing that it might be a two- or even three-pipe problem, with the resulting poisonous atmosphere that accompanied it, I absconded for my club.

When I returned, I met Holmes as he was leaving. "I believe this will be easier to arrange in person," he said. "Will you be available tomorrow morning?"

I averred that I would be, and he nodded and departed. Later that night, I received a wire to be at Marchmont's office at ten a.m. I heard nothing more before retiring.

I presented myself at Marchmont's office promptly the next morning, where his taciturn secretary showed me into his large meeting room. I hadn't been there for over a year. I recalled that day, which had begun as a rather routine appointment, just hours before the dreadful incident on the street in front of Simpsons, related to the terrible affair of the Heka idol.

Already seated around the table was a gruff looking man in a fine suit, another man in more modest clothing – I took him to be a gardener, correctly as it turned out – and a heavy-set older woman who appeared to be in domestic service of some sort. I nodded, but no introductions were made. I was just finding a seat when Holmes joined us. Following him through the door were two women, being shepherded in by Hilda Stanholt. One was Portia Coombs, while the other was unidentifiable in a dark veil, although it was more than likely that this was her sister, Letitia, as verified by her white hair.

"They didn't want to come, Mr. Holmes," said Hilda Stanholt.

"Nevertheless, here they are."

"It's the busiest time of the day," complained Portia Coombs, her voice rough.

"You'll be free to go soon," explained Holmes. "Provided that I have a full and satisfactory understanding of the situation."

With that, he gave a nod, saying, "Thank you, Mrs. Stanholt." Marchmont's man appeared, allowing Hilda to pass by him before he pulled the door shut.

"Please sit down, ladies," said Holmes. "This won't take long."

Portia started to speak again, and then nervously took her sister's arm and led her to two adjoining chairs.

"This is unnecessary, Mr. Holmes," said the well-dressed man. His voice was gruff and angry, but I thought that he looked a trifle uneasy as well.

"I think that it is," replied Holmes. "Watson, this is Sir Edwin Bales, Silas Coombs' doctor. Beside him is Mrs. Gates, the housekeeper of the Coombs estate, and Samuel Morton, the groundskeeper."

"Sam," wheezed Mr. Morton. "You can call me Sam."

"Thank you," replied Holmes. He looked at the three of them. "I suppose that I could have summoned all of the staff as witnesses, but you two, along with the doctor, will suffice."

He turned his head. "And this, Watson, as you certainly know, is Miss Portia Coombs. With her is – "

"Letitia," interrupted the dark-haired woman. "This is my sister, Letitia."

"It's no use, Portia," growled Sir Edwin. "He knows."

"That's right, Miss Coombs," Holmes said, speaking not to Portia, but the other woman. "I do wish that you would remove the veil."

With some hesitance, and her masked features turning from Portia to the doctor, she reached up and unfastened the veil.

Her face was strangely young, and quite familiar somehow.

"And the wig, as well," added Holmes.

With lowered eyes, she reached up again and tugged away the white tangled mane, revealing instead hair as dark as that of Portia Coombs beside her!

The two women looked at one another, and I was stunned to see that they might have been twins. Both of the same approximate age, their features and builds were nearly identical. Portia reached for the other's hand. Before I could find an explanation on my own, Holmes smiled and said, "*Cousins*, Watson. May I introduce you to Susan Coombs, the daughter of Silas, and not quite as deceased as the world has been led to believe."

He walked to the side of the table where he could equally face all of those seated. "It isn't a new idea. Sidney Carton substituted himself for the look-alike Darnay in *A Tale of Two Cities*. There was something like it in America – the Driscol case Missouri I believe, in the earlier part of this century, where an inheritance was obtained through a swap. But perhaps this matter is more similar to the tale of Isaac and Esau, wherein Isaac disguised himself to obtain the elder brother's birthright from their father, Jacob."

"It's nothing like that," growled the doctor. "It was all my idea. They didn't want to do it, but we all knew how evil old Silas really is! There would have been no justice if his fortune had gone to those drodded Communards!"

"He treated her something terrible," added Mrs. Gates, her voice an outraged squeak. "She's an angel, is our Susan, and she wasted her life taking care of that old devil!"

Susan Coombs looked at the old woman with warm affection.

"My idea," repeated Sir Edwin. "I'll take the blame."

271

"Blame?" asked Holmes. "We're here to determine facts, not to affix blame." He shifted to the two women, now sitting huddled together, tightly gripping one another's hands. "Please, ladies. Tell us the story, so that we may know the truth."

"It's really very simple," said the woman who had pretended to be Letitia Coombs. Her voice was much smoother than that of her cousin. "My father has always been beastly, but it was my duty to care for him. And yet, he became enraged one day. He ordered me from the house and altered his will. He might have changed his mind, but his illness prevented it.

"At first, my emotions overwhelmed me. I left the house, not knowing where to go. Then it came to me to throw myself on the mercy of my cousins, Portia and Letitia. I barely knew them, having been separated from that side of the family since I was a child. But I remembered that they had a baking stall in Covent Garden, and when I showed up there, they took me in."

"She is family," said Portia grimly, holding her cousin's hand tighter.

"Soon after, Father had his attack, and when it was determined that his condition was hopeless, I returned home and began to care for him again. He couldn't speak, but I could see that he appreciated it – at least, I have convinced myself of it. Then . . . just a few days later, cousin Letitia suddenly died."

"Heart problems," muttered Sir Edwin. "Family trait." He glanced toward Susan, and then away quickly, a pitying look upon his face. He sat up straighter. "That's when I thought of it. There was no way that the will could be changed by then – Silas was too sick. We might try to break it in court, but what if we failed? The estate would bypass Susan. Now, with Letitia dead, the ridiculous requirement that both sisters should jointly inherit would be the final nail. Rather than see it all go to a pack of French fanatics, I broached the idea of Susan taking Letitia's place – at least for a time. Take the chance while we have it. It . . . it won't be long until Silas passes."

"But you had a spare body for which to account," said Holmes."

"Indeed. It didn't take long to decide that we could say that it was Susan who had died instead of Leticia. We hired undertakers who wouldn't know the difference. Silas has always held the world at arm's length, so that most everyone now is a stranger to him. We sent word to the mission where Susan volunteered that she had passed, and that there would be no services, hoping she would be mourned but quickly forgotten – as was the case. Then we interred Leticia in the family crypt."

"Under a false name," added Holmes.

"Not so, Mr. Holmes," said Portia Coombs. "Her middle name *was* Susan. It was our grandmother's name. So she is buried correctly."

Holmes turned to Morton. "This is why I wanted you here, Mr. Morton. By all accounts, you are a solid British citizen – a jury of one. Can you confirm that the body was buried with respect in the family crypt?"

The groundskeeper cleared his throat. "I can, sir. Very carefully, and with dignity, and with the blessing of a minister that we know who understood. Nothing shady about it." He glanced down. "You can call me Sam."

"Thank you, Sam." He shifted his gaze to the housekeeper. "You are also honest, Mrs. Gates. Do you affirm this story?"

"I do! Mr. Silas is a beast, and this girl is an angel!"

"Thank you. And so," continued Holmes, looking back at Susan, "you became Letitia and joined your cousin, Portia, in Covent Garden, helping with the baking and the selling. Why not simply remain at your father's estate?"

"We knew," answered Portia, "that people might be aware of my connection and . . . and Letitia's to Uncle Silas. If we let it be known that Letitia had died, or if she simply disappeared, it might raise questions. Better to wait until the inheritance was settled, and then quietly fade away, with no suspicions." She frowned. "But how did you get onto us?"

"Someone saw you pouring medicine into your cousin's tea – presumably for the same type of heart condition that affected Letitia." She nodded. "After drinking the medicated tea, Susan evinced a period of coughing and weakness. It raised suspicions." He looked at Susan. "You knew, of course, what she was doing."

"I did. I've always been a bit forgetful about my medications, so I asked Portia to remember it for me."

"And to preserve the medication's effectiveness, you poured it in after the tea had cooled?"

"Sometimes," replied Portia. "Not always."

"You did so on each of the days that you were observed, and it seemed suspicious. I see now that we had too few data points to make definite conclusions. In fact, you were hiding it from the neighboring vendors."

Portia nodded. "Nosy busy-bodies. It was none of their business. We didn't want anyone being too curious or concerned, only to start a conversation and realize that Susan wasn't Letitia."

"What's this about coughing and weakness?" asked Sir Edwin. "I prescribed that medication, Mr. Holmes." Looking back at the cousins, he said, "There should be no coughing or fatigue. Just how much have you been giving her, Portia?"

"Just a tip in the afternoon, and another at bedtime."

"A tip? Good Lord, woman! She's only supposed to receive a few drops at a time!"

"I . . . I didn't know . . . ."

"I'm sure it will be all right," said Holmes. "I am not a doctor, but after an analysis the other day of the tea and my identification of the medication, I believe that no long-lasting effects will have occurred."

"The tea . . . ." said Susan, and then, with a sudden enlightened expression, she smiled. "The fire! That was you! When it was all over, half of my tea was gone. You managed all of that just to take some of it!"

"That's correct. And at the same time, the woman who blocked your path happened to notice that you were wearing a wig – a fact that she wasted no time in relating to me. After I analyzed the tea and discovered that it was dosed with medication and not poison, I realized that the matter required further thought. Then, I realized that, with the odd terms of the will, a substitution of sorts had almost certainly taken place. It was no great leap to realize that Susan, who had no chance to inherit, was likely pretending to be Letitia, who was no longer in the picture. It was unlikely that Portia would have killed her, although she might conceivably done so a fit of anger. More likely that she died by natural causes. The rest was easy to verify, and I thought it best to clear things up here, in this private setting."

"I didn't kill my sister," Portia murmured.

"We know, dear," whispered Mrs. Gates, glaring at Holmes.

"So what are your plans now, sir?" grumbled Sir Edwin. "Exposure? A miscarriage of justice, allowing these girls to be punished by one evil old man's temporary whim?"

Holmes smiled and shook his head. "I'm an unofficial agent, Sir Edwin. I was drawn to examine this affair because there seemed to be some slight chance that a murder might be committed. I'm satisfied with your explanations here today – especially because I have already confirmed so many of them independently. But – " and his smile faded and he took on a steely aspect, " – I wanted to make you aware that all is known, should any other irregularities be planned."

He looked at the two women, so alike in appearance, watching him while holding one another's hands. "I would advise that you both go carefully. What has been observed before might be noticed again. I understand that Mr. Silas Coombs will pass soon. May I ask your future intentions?"

The two women looked at one another. "We'll gradually fade from Covent Garden, as we said," replied Portia. "Then, Susan wants to keep helping the poor – but we can't do that here, because she is known, and

274

believed to be dead. Likely we'll go to another town where we'll start a mission of our own."

Holmes nodded. "As I expected." He looked around the room. "Then I see no reason to keep you here any longer." He gestured toward the door, while those around the table expressed surprise at the quick finish to the affair. Then, they slowly stood and made their way out. Both of the Coombs women quietly thanked Holmes. Sam Morton kept his head down, but nodded in passing, and Mrs. Gates peered at him when she went by, as if he were a zoo animal. Sir Edwin looked as if he wanted to stay and discuss something further, but in the end he simply departed.

Thanking Marchmont for the use of his office, we stepped outside. Holmes felt like walking back to Baker Street, and I concurred. Making our way along High Holborn, the morning sun at our backs, Holmes stated, "I believe that you plan to publish again."

Puzzled, I replied, "Possibly. I was dissatisfied when my first effort appeared in that throw-away Christmas journal. I've written up many cases, but I'm hoping that Doyle will next find a place for the matter of the Sholtos."

Holmes smiled. I was surprised, as I knew he hadn't been pleased with my initial effort. "That will be satisfactory. Whereas this affair," he said, the smile fading, "and the matter of the Claytons as well, must join that ever-growing collection of narratives in your tin dispatch box that will not be seen by this generation – the Clayton investigation as a matter of State secrecy, and the Coombs sisters' contrivance to guard their secret."

I replied, a bit stiffly, "I would naturally treat them both with such discretion. Additionally, I wouldn't wish for anyone to know of our own collusion in this matter of subverting a dying man's wishes, however willing we might be."

"I would rather having something like this on my conscience than to know that these women were prevented from accomplishing their good works by an old miser's spiteful impulse. And," he added, revealing his ever-pervasive distrust of human nature, "their awareness of our oversight in the matter will prevent any temptations to accelerate natural events."

And so it was. When Silas Coombs died a few weeks later, Holmes and I satisfied ourselves that he had indeed passed at his proper time, without a gentle push. As planned, the two cousins accepted the inheritance and slowly withdrew from Covent Garden, reestablishing themselves in Portsmouth, where they continue provide great comfort to that city's poor and downtrodden.

The True Account of the Bushell Street Killing

Sherlock Holmes and I had returned to London that morning after departing late the night before from the Lizard, in Cornwall, having fulfilled our responsibility in relation to the loss of the *Mohegan* just two days before. When word had reached the capitol of the terrible tragedy and the significant loss of life, we had been as interested and horrified as the rest of our stunned countrymen. But within hours we found ourselves rushed onto a special train leaving Paddington Station and headed west with a grim and urgent mission, delivered into our care by Mycroft Holmes himself, a man whom I had repeatedly observed as someone who sometimes *is* the British Government.

Several generations must pass before the truth of that journey can be told, and the reason that Holmes – with my humble assistance – was drafted to quest on such a fool's errand to the far coast. Yet against all odds, Holmes was able to identify the party responsible for the terrible loss, and to retrieve an object which should never have been on the ship. We had just finished leaving it in the care of a special curator at the British Museum, where it would be returned to a secret room deep in the bowels of that vast institution, before wearily crossing through London to Baker Street, only to learn that we had a visitor.

Mrs. Hudson met us at the bottom of the steps as we divested ourselves of coats and hats, explaining that the girl, who had given her name as Patience Moran, had seemed to be quite determined, and was willing to wait for our return, no matter how long that it might take. She had initially refused refreshment, but after the first hour, she'd meekly accepted some tea and a little something to go with it. I smiled to myself, well aware of just what made up Mrs. Hudson's idea of "a little something".

At the top of the steps, Holmes gave a little knock upon the sitting groom door, of the same sort that I myself as a physician had demonstrated countless times before entering an examination room. We walked in to see a woman in her mid-twenties, rising from the basket chair before the fire, and turning our way.

She was of average height, with dark brown hair in a rather tight and practical style. Her clothing was well-kept but modest, and I didn't need my friend's skills to see that she was of the serving class.

276

"Miss Moran? I am Sherlock Holmes, and this is Dr. Watson. How may we assist you?"

We stepped closer as she nodded an acknowledgement, not speaking until we had all found our seats. Then she said cryptically, "I remember seeing you both when I was a girl, but you'll have no memory of me. It was in 1889, not quite ten years ago. Just before Midsummer, when you came to Boscombe Valley after old Mr. McCarthy was killed."

Holmes raised an eyebrow as he tried to place her, but in this case I was the one who remembered. "You were the daughter of John Turner's lodge-keeper," I said. "I believe that you provided some sort of testimony to the investigators."

She nodded. "I was picking flowers near Boscombe Pool when I saw the two McCarthy's – father and son – having a quarrel. I ran to tell my parents, but before we could inform anyone else, young Mr. McCarthy came stumbling out of the woods, blood on his suit, saying that he had found his father dead by the water."

Holmes replied, "I recall that there was some question regarding the time element – that is to say, you were uncertain as to how much time had passed between when you saw the quarrel and when the young man came to the lodge to report that he'd found his father's body."

"That's right," answered Miss Moran. "The police insisted that there was practically no time between the quarrel and when he said someone else had killed his father, and that Mr. McCarthy's story about finding the body must have been false. But they didn't want to take into account that I had quite a distance to travel from the pool back to the lodge, and that I hadn't rushed straight home. Rather, I'd hidden several times in the woods, for I was fearful that . . . well, that young Mr. McCarthy might have followed me. So there was time for the two of them to have argued and separated, and then someone else to have killed the older Mr. McCarthy. You'll recall what the son said that after their quarrel – that he had walked a few hundred yards away, at which point he heard his father's terrible cry and rushed back, where he found the body."

"Indeed," replied Holmes. "And it turned out that the young man's story was true."

"That's right. I was glad for him, as he always seemed to be such a nice sort."

Holmes shifted in his seat. "This is interesting, of course, but does it have anything to do with your reason for consulting with us?"

"Indirectly." Miss Moran glanced my way. "It was only later, when your story appeared in *The Strand*, Doctor, that we realized the whole truth of it – how old Mr. McCarthy had actually been killed by Mr. Turner, and that you, Mr. Holmes, had let him off the hook, as he was a dying man."

Holmes maintained a neutral expression. He and I had discussed this matter before. At the time of the crime's solution, Holmes had obtained a written confession from old John Turner, and he had promised that it would "never be seen by mortal eye, and your secret, whether you be alive or dead, shall be safe with us", as long as it wasn't needed to free James McCarthy from a charge of murder. It hadn't been needed, as Holmes had raised a number of other objections to the accusation against young McCarthy, and the crime was officially left unsolved. And yet, just a few years later, I had revealed the whole and unvarnished truth in the pages of a popular periodical.

"Do you have some additional information that was not considered at the time of the investigation?" Holmes asked the young lady. "Something that casts a new light on the known facts?"

"No," was her reply. "All that I knew then fits with what was later explained. This is about old Mr. Turner."

"Turner?" Holmes asked. "What does he have to do with it?"

She frowned. "He was sick when the murder occurred. When he killed Mr. McCarthy. He died several months later of the diabetes."

"That's right," I said. "We received a notification from his attorney."

"Then tell me this," she countered. "Tell me how he could still be alive? Because I've seen him this very day, here in London, and as quick as any of us."

Finding that I wanted some myself, I offered refreshments, and she accepted brandy with a nod. As I poured it, along with some for Holmes and myself, my friend unexpectedly changed the subject.

"I see that you have been in London for a few years, working as a hotel maid."

"That's right. My mother's cousin is a housekeeper here, and found me a place at the Milton Hotel, nearby in Boston Street. My father had died, and mother didn't want me to waste my life in the country."

"You show signs of having received an excellent education."

She nodded and took a sip of the brandy. "We had a good teacher, and since I've come to London, I've been attending classes at night to better one's self, taught by a young professor at the University of London."

I didn't need to be Sherlock Holmes to see the slight blush when she mentioned the professor. I wondered if he reciprocated her interest.

"The class meets several nights each week," she continued, "and we discuss things that we read – novels, philosophy, news of the day, and so on. One can't help but speak a little better if one reads, I've discovered."

"That's not always the case with everyone," countered Holmes, "but clearly you have been able to successfully take advantage of the

278

opportunity." He set his glass aside, untouched, and leaned back. "Now tell us your story, and we'll see what sense we can make of it."

She closed her eyes, composing her thoughts, and began.

"A week ago, in the course of my duties, I was on the second floor of the hotel, sorting the linen closet, when the porter, Abel French, led a man past, down the hallway and to a room. This happens with such regularity that I gave it no real notice, but when the man asked Abel to have extra towels brought in, his voice sounded familiar. A moment later, Abel was at the linen closet, relaying the request, and so I gathered a couple of extras and knocked on the man's door.

"He opened it almost immediately and, without really glancing my way, thanked me and took them from my hands. But before the door shut, I was able to study his face – even in that short fraction of time – and see that the voice that I'd remembered matched his features. There was no doubt. It was Mr. John Turner, who died in January of 1890." She looked at me, and then Holmes. "Or so we were told."

"What makes you certain that it was him?" asked Holmes.

"His voice. His accent, which was always an odd mix of British and Australian. The shape of his face, and the old hooked scar on his left cheek. I'd heard him say once that it was from a knife fight when he was young, and that he was lucky that it missed his eye. He's a big man, you'll recall, even though he is elderly, and he still has strong arms and long legs. He also still has the same tangled beard and eyebrows, and wild hair as well, although now it's even whiter than it was before.

"I was very surprised, but I don't believe that I showed it. After taking the towels, he shut the door and I returned to my tasks. Later, I found an excuse to look at the registration book, and he had signed in as "John Tanner" of Hythe. Do you know where that is?"

"It's along the coast of Kent," I replied. "Near the edge of the Romney Marsh." Holmes and I were both fully aware of the location, having nearly died there in the early eighties when we had been cornered by a band of naval mutineers who had fled there and were hiding in an abandoned smuggler's shack inland between there and Dymchurch. Never had we been so glad for the presence of our friend Inspector Lestrade and his often under-recognized but steadfast bravery.

"You say this was a week ago," Holmes interjected. "Have you learned anything else?"

"Not directly," replied Miss Moran. "In my position, I can only find out so much. He has nothing of interest in his room except for a few changes of clothes and his traveling items. He sleeps late every morning before going out around mid-day. I believe that he lunches nearby and returns soon after, sitting in the parlour with a stack of newspapers. Then, around four o'clock, he folds them all and places them on a side table, stands up, and departs, only to return very late – or so I'm told by Mr. Wells, the evening man at the desk."

"Does he show any signs of illness?" I asked, recalling the one time that we met the man, at the conclusion of the Boscombe Valley affair, he had given every appearance of someone that was dying – his face ashen white, his lips and nostrils a faint shade of blue. The fact that he was still alive over nine years later countered all that Holmes and I had observed and had been told on that day in June 1889.

She shook her head. "He's older, of course, but seems quite fit."

"What you tell us is certainly of interest," said Holmes, "but I fail to see the relevance. If Watson and I were deceived a decade ago, and this man evaded justice, we can certainly explore it. However, there must be some other reason that you have waited to talk to us, after knowing for a week that Mr. Turner was still alive."

She nodded. "It was late yesterday afternoon. I was asking Mr. Wells a question when Mr. Turner – or Tanner, as he calls himself – came out of the parlour for his usual departure. He stopped and stared at me. Perhaps he recognized my voice, even though it's been years since we saw one another. Although he was the master and my father was his lodge-keeper, we had very few dealings back in those days. Still, his estate was really a small place after all, and he certainly knew who I was. When the murder occurred, I was only fourteen, and I've changed some as I've grown, but there is more about me that it the same than is different.

"When he stopped to stare, I'm afraid that I looked back, and he must have certainly seen that I recognized him – there was no way that I could hide it. However, he set himself back in motion and on out to wherever it is that he goes every afternoon.

"I don't know why, but I found myself suddenly frightened. I'd never had anything to fear from him in the old days, and yet, he did commit a murder, even though – from what I read in your story, Doctor – he was driven to it, and from what I read, he was no stranger to violence when he was younger.

"This morning when I arrived at the hotel, the morning man, Mr. Tenlevy, told me that one of the guests had been asking about me. He said it in a rather smarmy way, as he does with everything out of his mouth, as if implying that someone had taken a romantic interest in me. Although I already suspected the answer, I asked who, and sure enough, it was Mr. 'Tanner'. So now he knows my name, and if he didn't recognize me before, he can now be certain that someone from home knows that he's still alive.

"Today is my half-day, and I begged to leave a bit early, before Mr. Turner normally comes down, as I couldn't be certain that otherwise I wouldn't accidentally encounter him in the course of my duties. I came around here, and your landlady was very kind to let me wait until I could share my story. I know that I have to be back at the hotel tomorrow, and I'm not sure what you can do to help me, but I needed for someone to know, if nothing else."

Holmes was silent for a long couple of minutes as he considered. Then he said, "If you were to miss work for a couple of days, feigning an illness, would your position be in jeopardy?"

She shook her head. "No. When I begged to leave early today, I implied that I didn't feel well. And the managers, Mr. and Mrs. Milton, are a very nice married couple, and they know that I wouldn't abuse their trust by missing work for no good reason. And this is a good reason – although I won't be telling them that."

"Where do you live?" I asked.

"With my mother's cousin, in Upper Bridport Street."

"It would be advisable to go straight there – We'll put you in a cab when we're finished – and you should stay there until you hear from us. Send a note 'round to the hotel explaining that you will be absent – claiming an illness will suffice for a reason."

She nodded. "Do you think that you can help me? What will you do? Confront Mr. Turner and discover why he is still alive after all this time, after allowing everyone to believe that he died?"

"Perhaps, but not immediately. First, I'd like to get a sense of what is occurring – Why he is in London? Where does he go? And most important, what were the details of his supposed death in early 1890?"

Holmes stood then, indicating that the interview was at an end. He asked for the young lady's address in Upper Bridport Street, and then I escorted her down and to the street, where I hailed a hansom driving by a cabbie of our acquaintance. Miss Moran baulked when I handed him some coins, but I refused to take no for an answer, and in moments she was away for the short drive to her home.

Back upstairs, I found that Holmes had reseated himself, a frown on his face. His legs were crossed, and on his knee was an open blue-backed journal. I didn't need to peer over his shoulder to recognize an issue of *The Strand*, and it was a safe assumption that it contained the narrative of "The Boscombe Valley Mystery", published in mid-1891, only a few months after his presumed "death" at the Reichenbach Falls. I considered obtaining another brandy, decided to forego it, and then dropped with an inner sigh into my armchair, awaiting the inevitable criticisms related to my publication of Holmes's cases.

Holmes had long objected to certain aspects of my efforts to chronicle his investigations, wishing that I might cleave myself to basic facts, rather than, as he put it, sinking to the level of relating his investigations as "common tales" – said in the same way that a prudish minister might be forced to use some vile phrase only heard in the city's lowest quarters. In this particular case, I had written up the affair at the time that it occurred, in June 1889, soon after our return from Boscombe Valley. I'd wanted to record it quickly, both because the facts were fresh in my mind, and also due to the curious nature of the truth that we had discovered.

Holmes had asked me to accompany him to the picturesque setting near Ross, in Herefordshire, to investigate the brutal killing of Mr. Charles McCarthy, supposedly murdered by his son, James, following an argument along the shore of Boscombe Pool. Our old friend Inspector Lestrade was already on the scene, and had settled on James as the killer, based on very credible evidence. Holmes had been summoned by John Turner's daughter, Alice, to clear young James, as she had an obvious romantic interest in him.

The murdered man and his son had been living in the area for a number of years at the apparent invitation of John Turner, the richest man in the district, and an old friend of Charles McCarthy's from their younger days in Australia – or so everyone thought. Years before, Turner had returned to England, rich from his long years overseas, and made quite the success of himself, marrying and having a beautiful daughter. Widowed since the girl was young, he was quite surprised when Charles McCarthy and his son had showed up – surprised and dismayed.

For as we learned later, Turner and McCarthy had both spent their younger days in the 1860's in Australia – Turner as a bandit known as "Black Jack of Ballarat", and McCarthy as a wagon-driver. During a daring robbery of a gold convoy passing from Ballarat to Melbourne, Turner had encountered McCarthy and, against his better judgement, spared the driver's life, never expecting to see the little man again. However, long after Turner had repatriated to England, McCarthy returned as well. After a chance encounter in one of London's main thoroughfares, McCarthy had proceeded to fasten himself onto John Turner like a leech, blackmailing him, and living at Hatherley Farm, Turner's best property, rent free. Years passed, and Turner gritted his teeth, allowing the *façade* of a friendship between himself and McCarthy to be presented to the little community. But finally McCarthy had decided to take the game to a new level, demanding that Turner allow his only daughter, Alice, to marry McCarthy's son, James. And that John Turner could not abide.

On the day of the killing, Turner and McCarthy planned to meet at Boscombe Pool to discuss the blackmailer's continuing demand for the

282

marriage. However, when Turner arrived, he heard that James McCarthy was already there, arguing with his father about that very matter. James was resisting the marriage – for as Holmes had learned, the young man had already gotten himself snared in a previous marriage to a Bristol barmaid. Turner had to listen as the elder McCarthy, unaware of his son's prior obligation, ranted and raved, referring to Turner's daughter in a most unseemly manner. This only served to enrage Turner so that, when James McCarthy walked away, Turner then stepped forward and killed Charles McCarthy with a stone in cold blood before running back into the surrounding forest.

James McCarthy, hearing his father's cry, returned to find his dying father. He was subsequently arrested, but Holmes's evaluation of the dying man's final puzzling utterance, as well as the physical evidence at the scene, were enough to reveal the truth – to the two of us at least. Holmes sent a message to John Turner, who then visited us at the inn near his estate where we were staying. There, the old man, realizing that the truth was known, told us his strange and tragic story.

He'd insisted that he would have never let young James McCarthy come to true harm, but I had some doubts about that as, in spite of the young man's innocence, old John Turner seemed to feel that he was beneath contempt simply because of who his father was. Still, Turner had arrived to tell us the truth when he realized that Holmes already knew a great deal of it, and he was willing to sign a confession. He'd informed us beforehand that he was a dying man, not expecting to live another month. Holmes assured him that he'd keep the confession a secret unless it was needed to free James McCarthy, and that he would only use it if absolutely necessary. Otherwise, John Turner's daughter need not know what her father had done. James was indeed acquitted, mostly due to points raised by Holmes.

My friend had discovered that James McCarthy's supposed wife from Bristol was actually already married to another, so the union was spurious, allowing James to marry Alice Turner as soon as he could. Apparently John Turner gritted his teeth and allowed it, fearing that prevention of the marriage might bring to light his own secrets. Turner lived another seven months – or so we had been told – before dying of the diabetes that he had described on the day he met with us at the inn. We learned of his death after receiving a curt note from his attorney, who had been tasked by his late client to notify us.

As I finished recalling these events, Holmes closed the magazine and placed it on the octagonal table beside his chair. I felt as if I were still in school, having just watched as my teacher grimly read through my essay, finding it sorely lacking.

283

"You're aware," Holmes began in an even tone, "that I have various objections to these narratives, although we have yet to schedule a series of conversations that will address each of the efforts individually. I had assumed that the first two from your pen – the Jefferson Hope affair, and the events of your introduction to Mary by way of the Sholtos – would be rather unique. Although you have always kept extensive notes, and threatened over the years to publish your own accounts of the investigations to 'set the record straight', I confess that I was surprised to discover, not long before my return, that you had finished and published a round two-dozen more of the them – including this one. In considering the whole of your collected *oeuvre*, I have neglected to evaluate them individually. In this case, I now have to ask how, with my promise that Turner's written confession would be kept – how did you put it – ?"

He retrieved *The Strand* and flipped the pages until he found what he wished to quote:

> "*I will keep your confession, and if McCarthy is condemned I shall be forced to use it. If not, it shall never be seen by mortal eye; and your secret, whether you be alive or dead, shall be safe with us.*"

He set the periodical aside once more, and repeated, "*Never seen by mortal eye*'."

I cleared my throat. "It was in the middle of '91, not long after you were believed to have perished. As you know, I had long declared that I wanted to share the true story of many of your investigations – to make public the truth of those times where the police claimed the credit, or simply because the world needed to know what you did, and of the profession that you were creating. I already had a number of finished narratives in my files, and time to write more, but I was uncertain as to how best to get them published. Based on past associations related to the two earlier published works, I approached Doyle for advice. He was frustrated with his practice and had been seeking an inroad to the literary world He felt that associating himself with my writings would be something to add to his *curriculum vitae*, thus giving him more clout when he tried to publish his own historical novels.

"Now, not long before, Doyle had met George Newnes, the magazine publisher. They had been talking, and earlier that year, in January I believe, Newnes had started *The Strand*. Doyle arranged for us to meet, and 'A Scandal in Bohemia' was chosen as the first of your cases to appear in the magazine. I'm not being humble when I report that the response was rather electrifying.

"The next month we chose 'The Red-Headed League', and within a few days of its appearance, I had a visitor. It was Alice McCarthy, neé Turner, now the wife of James McCarthy, who informed me that she had traveled to London for the sole purpose of meeting with me, having arrived just moments before at Paddington Station, down Praed Street from my practice. In her hand was the latest *Strand.*

"After she was seated, she confirmed that I remembered her, and then I asked, 'How did you locate me?'

"She was rather vague, explaining that she had queried some of her father's old business friends, with whom she had remained in touch following his death the year before. Then, she held up the magazine. 'I understand that you have started publishing some accounts of Mr. Holmes's cases.'

"Thinking that I understood her concern, I was quick to reassure her. 'I have many hundreds of accounts to choose from,' I said, 'dating back over ten years, and I can promise that I won't make any reference to the affair of two years ago.'

"She shook her head impatiently. 'You misunderstand me, Doctor. I'm here to encourage that you *do* relate the affair – and as soon as possible. The *entire* story, including the fact that my father was responsible for Mr. McCarthy's death.'

"I was confused at that point, but before I could raise my questions, she continued. 'I'm aware of the meeting that you both had with my father, and what he told you – about what he did at the Pool, and why. I also know of the confession that he signed and left with Mr. Holmes, should it have been needed to free James from the false charge of the murder of his own father. My father told me everything, and he was clearly provoked by Mr. McCarthy. I hold father blameless – as does my husband.'

"'But,' I had to ask, having my doubts about that last statement, 'what purpose could be served by telling this story now? It would only serve to open up matters to public scrutiny that have ceased to be important.' And I didn't add that it would place you, Holmes, in a bad light with the police – even posthumously – having solved the case and yet withheld the solution from the authorities.

"'We have had no true peace since that man's death,' whispered Alice McCarthy. 'By not having a definite guilty party upon whom to fix the blame, cruel whispers have persisted that James actually did kill his father, and only escaped punishment through legal tricks and technicalities. My father is gone now, and he is beyond any damage that might be done to his reputation. And truth be told, I am rather proud of how he handled it. While James might not feel quite the same as I do in that particular regard, he does agree that with the truth revealed, the suspicions that have hovered around him – around us – ever since will ease and eventually dissipate. I suspect that it would be too much to ask that my father's actual confession, left in Mr. Holmes's care, be somehow circulated or published in its entirety, but the next best thing, as I realized when I ran across your most recent story, would be for you to relate the whole story and let us get on with our lives.'

"I had some initial reservations, but I discussed it with Mary, and she thought that shining a light on the affair might in fact give the young couple a better chance at finding happiness. Doyle, of course, was most insistent that it be published from the moment that he heard about it, but that sort of impetuosity is quite typical of him, as you know, so I didn't immediately trust his opinion. Finally, I met with Lestrade and revealed the truth of the affair in confidence. I had expected some sort of irate reaction, but he surprised me, indicating that he'd suspected something of the sort all along, and then he proceeded to lay out several points of his own to back this up, showing me the steps that he'd used to come to the truth by his own route. It turned out that he agreed with the way you handled it, Holmes. His feelings towards a blackmailer such as McCarthy don't deviate a jot from yours or mine, although he doesn't have the freedom from duty that you do.

"And so I polished up my manuscript, and later that fall it was published. And to be honest, I haven't given it very much thought at all since then."

Holmes sat and pondered my explanation, pinching his earlobe between thumb and forefinger. After a few moments, apparently deciding to proceed without providing any comment on this latest question related to my writings, he glanced at the clock. The time was now half-after-two. He stood and walked toward his bedroom.

"I have time to change my appearance and get into place at the hotel, in order to follow Turner and see what he's up to – assuming that he keeps to his schedule, now that he realizes he's been recognized by Miss Moran. Will you be available later?"

I indicated that I would be, and he nodded, passing into his bedroom. I stood and retrieved the *Strand* beside Holmes's chair, and then crossed the room and replaced it carefully with its brothers, on that little shelf containing my few published works.

Within moments, Holmes was departing, his appearance now altered to represent what appeared to be a provincial gentleman wearing poorly fitting and out-of-fashion clothing. He had done something to his hair which implied a whole change of shape for his head, and he wore a distracting little *pince-nez* on the bridge of his nose. I was reminded of that character Ichabod Crane, who had featured in a story by Washington

Irving, read in my youth. I hadn't seen this disguise before, and I tried to remember the details as Holmes waved and departed, since I knew that there was a good chance that he would be rearranged to look a different way when next we met.

After I heard the front door slam shut, I busied myself with catching up on notes related to several past investigations. While all of them had been remarkable in differing degrees, and would seem to be unforgettable, I'd learned over the years that each new affair tended to crowd out the details of those that have come before, so that recording the specifics in my journals while the details are still fresh is essential. Fortunately, my writing has become habitual in my free time, and I've become rather skilled in my abilities to construct accurate accounts of Holmes's many cases for my future reference, with very few errors. I had finished recounting the little research into Miss Beckwith's school in Clowne, and what the students found under the decagonal flagstone, and had moved on to the more subtle matter of the Long Eaton Cacodemon when a great weariness overtook me, the cumulative result of our fast dash and subsequent return from the West Country. Laying down my pen, I crossed to my chair. I was soon fast asleep.

I awoke with a start when Mrs. Hudson entered the room. She was carrying a small tray, and I could tell that she hadn't intended to be quiet. From the wan light through the windows, I realized that it was late in the day.

Seeing that I was awake, she started to pour a cup of tea from the pot that she carried while saying, "Young Morton was just around with a message." Morton was one of Holmes's Baker Street Irregulars, those lads and lasses who served as his unofficial agents, seeing that others did not, and going where others could not. "Two messages, actually," she continued. "One for me, telling me to wake you, and the other for you to join Mr. Holmes at the butcher's shop on Dorchester Street near Boston Street as soon as you're able." She handed me the cup. "But you'll have this first, as well as the biscuits."

I blessed her thricely, drank the tea, quickly took a few obligatory bites of the snack, and then made my way outside. The October air was brisk, and there was a fog building, although it was nothing as compared to some that had choked the city in times past.

The butcher's shop had several customers, but I didn't see Holmes – and in spite of his abilities to disguise himself, it was clear that none of the patrons were him. The butcher, a man named Dunleavy who owed the life of his daughter to my friend, caught my eye and nodded toward the back of the shop. I passed beyond the counter and into a small room set up as an office, where Holmes, now looking like himself once more, was waiting.

"Ah, Watson. You are well rested, I hope?" Without allowing me to affirm or deny this assertion, he continued. "The Irregulars are up the street, ready to follow Mr. Turner when he departs, and when we are informed that he's in motion, we shall join them. In the meantime, I'll apprise you of my day.

"I began by sending various wires to agents that I trust in in the neighborhoods of both Hythe and Boscombe Valley, in order to determine what could be learned of the supposedly deceased John Turner, and the newly discovered John Tanner. From the west came the curious fact that that Mr. Turner's death in early 1890 was a very private affair. In fact, only his daughter and son-in-law were in attendance, the servants having been sent away a day or so before, and the death was verified by a very elderly village doctor – not the regular family physician – who died himself not much later of old age. Soon after, it was announced that the body had already been sent to London for cremation, although my agent can find no one local that was associated with its transport.

"Interestingly, a week after John Turner's death, Mr. John Tanner's story begins. With no established antecedents, he arrived in Hythe, offering a London address that turns out to be a small hotel in the Strand. He stayed in the local inn for a week while examining local properties with the assistance of an agent, and then he selected and purchased one, where he has lived to the present, attracting very little notice. He has a part-time housekeeper and a man – her husband – to take care of the grounds of his little house, and except for the occasional overnight trip – ostensibly up to London – he does nothing more than read, take long walks, and visit the local pub, where he sits quietly, seeming to enjoy the company there without unduly mixing with them. All in all, a comfortable and friendly arrangement. He's respected, left to himself, and doesn't seem to be short of funds."

"And for the last week," I added, "he's been away on one of his London trips – although quite a bit longer than what is typical."

"Exactly. Which brings us to this afternoon, where I hope to learn more about the man whom he has been following every day since his arrival, Silas Peasemore."

"You have been busy," I said. "You have already learned the man's name."

"It wasn't too difficult. Tanner – or Turner, as I will continue to call him – hired the services of a local cabbie on a daily basis. It was no great feat to locate him, based on a few well-placed questions directed toward the neighbors of the Milton Hotel, located just around the corner from here in Boston Street. It turns out that the cabbie, a fellow named Chilton, is a former soldier who worked as a guard in the detention barracks at Aldershot, and therefore feels a sense of duty in terms of those who flout the law. After identifying myself, and mentioning that there was some reason to question Mr. Tanner's actions, Mr. Chilton related a very simple tale: Every afternoon about four o'clock, his client enters Chilton's cab, and he is conveyed to a shabby lodging house in Bushell Street, near the Hermitage Basin, on the steam wharf end. Then Tanner simply sits in the cab until a man leaves the house – Silas Peasemore, as I determined – and Tanner gets out, usually following the man, but once entering the lodging house in his absence."

"To search his room," I said.

Holmes nodded. "Most likely. It's what I would do after the man left if I had the opportunity. In fact, it's similar to what I *did* do today, while Turner was downstairs in the hotel lobby reading his newspapers, just as Miss Moran described. I entered the hotel, where I saw the man himself sitting off to the side – and it is unquestionably John Turner, older and grayer, but surprisingly quite a bit more vital-looking than when we met him in 1889. In my disguise, I rented a room on the same floor as Turner's and, within five minutes of being left up there, I was down the hall and seeing what might be seen. As Miss Moran indicated, he is living a Spartan existence, with no significant personal possessions except a worn bag marked with the initials '*J.T.*'. But cleverly concealed within the lining of said bag was a small packet of letters.

"Reading them in chronological order really lays out the whole matter rather simply. Several weeks ago, according to the postmark of the earliest, addressed to John Tanner of Hythe, Alice McCarthy wrote in the cheeriest yet quite brittle of tones, explaining that she'd had a visit from a Mr. Peasemore of Australia. She refers to him as an old acquaintance of her father's, writing to seem as if 'Tanner' were a totally different man from 'Turner'. She says no more than that, but it is enough to serve as a warning – especially when taken with the next letter, also sent to Tanner in Hythe just a day later, but in a much rougher hand.

"'*I know you're still alive*,' it says, '*and as you can see, I know where you're hiding. Tell your daughter to pay what I ask, and keep paying, or do it yourself. It matters not to me.*' And it was signed '*Silas Peasemore*'.

"There was nothing else from that quarter, but three other letters from daughter Alice completed the little collection, each apparently acknowledging responses from her father. The first said that she had sent the payment as requested, to a certain post office in London. The second was of greater length, explaining how she'd come down to London and mailed the payment here, and then waited at the post office, in disguise, to see Peasemore claim it, whereupon she followed him to a lodging house in Bushell Street. Quite her father's daughter, is Mrs. McCarthy. The third said that she'd had another visit from Peasemore in Boscombe Valley, and he'd made a vague threats against her, indicating that on second thought he wanted more money than he'd received so far. That letter was dated two days before Turner traveled up to London."

"He's going to kill him," I reasoned. Holmes nodded, and then I asked, "Why has he waited so long?"

"I suspect that he's getting the lay of the land first. After all, he went to a certain amount of trouble to arrange his 'death', and then establish his new life in Kent. Why throw that all away now?"

"Rather careless of him, then, to register at the hotel under his new name," I said. Then I was silent for a moment while another thought occurred to me. As usual, Holmes knew my thinking. "You wonder if, knowing what we know now, we shouldn't simply withdraw and let matters take their course."

I frowned. Life is precious, and the law is the law, but Holmes and both had little sympathy for blackmailers, those parasites who fasten onto the innocent – or in this case those who might not be quite so innocent after all – and proceed to make their lives a living hell. There is no recourse within the law, so often the victim has no other choice but the handle the matter in whatever way they see fit.

"And yet," I said, knowing that had followed my reasoning as if I'd spoken aloud, "now that we know, how can we not act? Perhaps there is a better way."

"Perhaps. That's why I asked for you to join me."

"Surely Turner will be moved to do something soon – he's had a week to examine things, and besides that, he now knows that he's been recognized by Patience Moran."

"Yes, and that's another reason not to simply walk away. I'd like to think that John Turner has been forced to do what he is considering, and to give him the benefit of the doubt as to his intentions. But we really don't know just how black his heart is, or what he did in those far off days of his outlaw youth. If he was pushed to settle matters with McCarthy – even after so many years – and now Peasemore, what else might he do? Does the life of a young woman who has knowledge of his secret hold any special value if he's trying to protect that secret? No, we must involve ourselves, if for no other reason than to let him know that his secret is known after all, and that he must restrain himself."

At that moment, the door opened, and Morton Thatcher, one of Holmes's Irregulars, leaned in. "He's in the cab."

290

Holmes stood, and I joined him. "Are the other lads along the route?" Holmes asked. Morton nodded, and Holmes tossed him a shilling. Then he led me out, nodding toward Dunleavy the butcher, and so on to a waiting cab in Upper Dorchester Place, manned by a cabbie of our acquaintance.

"Why did you not simply have me meet you in Shadwell, at Peasemore's rooms?" I asked.

"I considered it, but what if today is the day that Turner goes a different way? No, it's better that we follow him." He was looking intently toward the right of the street, and in a moment I saw one of his Irregulars, a girl named Emilie, catching his eye and point in the direction that we were headed. Over the next fifteen minutes, we passed three more Irregulars, each doing the same thing.

"I had the route from Chilton, Turner's cab driver," Holmes explained, "and posted the children along the way as guideposts, to make sure that he doesn't deviate. Chilton promised to travel it as usual, unless given some other instructions. And it appears that Turner is indeed headed toward Peasemore's lodgings along his regular route."

And so it was. The prosperity of our surroundings waxed and waned as we crossed through the different sections of London, with a gradual decline as we made our way further east, ever closer to the Thames. Finally, at what I correctly assumed was a block or so from our final destination, Holmes signaled the cabbie to stop and wait while we proceeded on foot.

As we slipped through darkening streets and filthy alleys, Holmes indicated that his research in this area had been carried out from afar, and that he hadn't had time to personally visit the environs of Peasemore's lodging house. And yet, his encyclopedic knowledge of the capital led us unerringly to a spot across the street, a narrow alley where we could watch unseen. Holmes informed me that the back of the house was similarly covered by the Irregulars. He kept looking to our left, toward the river, explaining that per Chilton's description, Turner's cab was usually parked to the south, in the High Street by Acorn Wharf, and that our subject would thus be approaching from that direction. As we had followed him across London at a matching rate of speed, but had parked closer and reached our hiding spot more quickly, so it was no surprise that we were in place when Turner was spotted coming in our direction.

Holmes gripped my wrist, but there was no need to alert or warn me – I had seen the man as well. He was moving with confidence, as if he belonged there, making his way to the very house where Peasemore resided, while not calling any attention to himself with suspicious furtiveness.

"There is no need to search his room twice," muttered Holmes, almost to himself. "There must be a meeting planned between them – or a reckoning. We are just in time, Watson."

He continued to watch, and we have discussed several times since that terrible afternoon what might have happened if we'd stepped out at that moment to confront Turner with the knowledge that we knew he was alive. Instead, we held our ground, in the shadows, our eyes focused on the approaching man, even as we saw him stop for just a moment before unexpectedly breaking into an awkward shambling run in the same direction as before. I became aware of the sound of another set of footsteps off to our right, on the opposite end of the street. They were light and quick, and I glanced that way to see that they were being made by a small woman, her features obscured by the ever-increasing fog. I started to speak, telling Holmes that I thought I recognized her, even as I suspected that he surely did too. Then Turner called out.

"Alice! Don't!"

But the young woman only ran faster, and it was clear that she would reach the entrance to the building before the old man. He was still fifty feet away when she mounted the step, opened the front door, and vanished within. Turner increased his speed, awkwardly lurching as best he could, and he had also just reached the door when Holmes stepped out, also running in that direction. "John Turner!" he thundered. "Wait!"

The old man turned and saw us both crossing the street. With a curse, he pushed his way inside. Even as we saw the darkness of the entryway swallow him, there was no mistaking the sound of a gunshot, curiously muffled and dead in the lowering fog.

I had my weapon drawn as we entered the building. From above came angry but unintelligible tones, and Holmes took the stairs two at a time. I followed as best as I could, reaching the first floor and perceiving light from an open door toward the back of the building. Holmes reached it only a second before I did, and I was in time to see Turner wrenching a smoking gun from the hands of his daughter. Beside them on the floor lay the body of a ratty little man in very poor clothing, a surprised look on his face, and a bullet hole on one side of his head, matched on the other by a much larger and terrible exit wound. Peasemore, as we quickly determined, was beyond my assistance.

Turner had by now pushed the petite young woman aside. He started to raise the gun, but seeing my own weapon aimed in his direction, he lowered slowly lowered it again. However, despite my order to do so, he didn't drop it all together.

"Sherlock Holmes, is it?" he snarled, his voice cracking with age and anger. "Butting into my business again!"

"Drop the gun, Turner," I said again. Behind me, I could hear people gathering in the hallway, other lodgers alerted by the gunshot.

"The constable is coming," one voice informed us.

Turner took a couple of steps back, circling behind the body and increasing the distance between himself and his daughter. I kept my gaze locked on the gun in his hand.

"We know nearly everything," stated Holmes in a low voice. I doubted that building's other residents, foolishly in the doorway behind me, could even hear what he said. "How you faked your death and relocated to Hythe. How this man Peasemore showed up to blackmail you, and how you came to London, probably to kill him. But I don't know how he found you."

"I made a mistake," growled Turner. "I made a trip to Ross, to see my daughter. I thought that I'd be safe enough if I kept away from my usual haunts, and was discrete about showing myself. But Peasemore had come back to England, and saw me there. He and I ranged together in the old days, and he knew that I was supposed to be dead. But instead of confronting me, he laid back, knowing that there was something that wasn't right, and then he followed me back to Hythe. After making sure what I now called myself and where I hung my hat, and that I was keeping a secret, he made his move, visiting Alice, and then sending a letter to me, asking for money.

"I know that there's only one way to get out from under a blackmailer. I learned it the hard way. After I came back to England, I tried to live a good life, to atone for what I'd done all those years ago. And then McCarthy fastened onto me and bled me dry for what seemed like a lifetime. He kept pushing and pushing, and you know what I finally had to do. What I learned then was that I should have struck him down from the day he first accosted me in Regent's Street and saved myself years of heartache. And when this foul beast tried to do the same thing – " He nodded toward the dead man on the floor. " – Well, this time I knew how to handle it."

"And yet," countered Holmes, "your daughter was the one who killed him."

Turner gave a queer smile. "You're mistaken. I shot him."

To our side, where she had stood in silence, Alice McCarthy gave a small sob. She made no move toward him, but Turner snapped anyway, "Stay away, Alice."

Holmes frowned and was silent for a moment before replying, "So that's how you're playing it?"

"It is. I'm an old man – "

293

"And is it a question this time as well of whether you shall live just a month?" Holmes asked.

Turner shook his head, almost smiling as he recalled what he'd told us so many years ago when offering his first confession. "I won't try that on you again. But I *am* old, and have been living on borrowed time all these years. Alice has her whole life in front of her. In fact, she's with child – that's why I went to see her in Ross, when I fell under this dog's power. I couldn't stay away." He licked his lips and said softly, "Do we understand each other, gentlemen?"

We heard a noise behind us, and I glanced away long enough to see a young constable – tall, thin, eyes wide, and with an Adam's apple as big as his considerable nose – pushing his way into the room and looking past us at the dead body and the old man with a gun. I looked back as Turner addressed him.

"I killed this man, Constable. Do you understand? I shot him. These two men here arrived right after I did it, and can confirm it." He then looked back at the both of us, one and then the other, his gaze searching. Finally, Holmes gave an almost imperceptible nod. Turner saw it and gave one in return. His daughter, as if understanding something then, screamed and lurched forward, making as if to grab Turner's arm, but it was too late. He shoved a stiff arm in her direction, and she was flung away. Then he had inserted the barrel of the gun in his mouth and blew off the top of his head.

Later, in Baker Street, an awkward conference was held. Alice McCarthy was there, in shock at the violent suicide of her father. Patience Moran had been summoned as well, and had taken charge of seeing to the comfort of her former mistress, sitting beside her on the settee. Making up the last of the party, in addition to Holmes and myself, was Inspector Lestrade. Although he had known nothing of this business until summoned, having not yet heard of the death of the two men in Shadwell, Holmes felt that he deserved an explanation – especially as the original truth had been hidden from him nearly a decade earlier, following our visit to Boscombe Valley.

Mrs. Hudson brought in tea, and when everyone was situated, I recalled the events immediately after Turner had shot himself. Almost as soon as the man had fallen, Alice fainted away. Concerned about her condition, I took charge of her, arranging to remove her from that room of death and into our cab, still waiting on a nearby street, in spite of the young constable's protestations. She awoke on the way to Barts and suffered a fit of quiet hysterics, but she had composed herself by the time we reached the hospital. Nevertheless, I insisted that she be examined to make sure that there was no physical damage from the incident, after what she had been forced to witness.

I had spoken quickly to Holmes before we separated in Bushell Street, and he indicated that I should bring her back to Baker Street when we were finished. There, she sat quietly sipping tea on the settee until the rest of the group assembled. Then Holmes explained briefly what had happened, indicating that Alice should share her portion of the story.

She did so, somewhat to my surprise, confirming what Holmes had already determined.

"My father did believe that he was dying on that day he spoke with you, Mr. Holmes, when he signed the confession. Surely you know that you would have seen through any attempt to deceive you by falsifying the symptoms of his illness. But contrary to all expectations, his health improved. Perhaps it was knowing that he was free of the malignant grasp of that reptile who had haunted his every step for so many years.

"Not long after James was released, Father told me the truth of what happened, and I shared it with James. Then, in spite of Father's disapproval, James and I married. Father was accepting enough after the fact, and he only lost his temper about it once, stating that I was blackmailing him with what I knew in order to marry, in the same way that he's been under old Mr. McCarthy's power.

"I was sorry that he felt that way, but my father had no choice – he had to accept my marriage. Still, he didn't like it. Oh, he had nothing against James, except for the unfortunate fact that my husband's father had tormented him for so many years. As months passed, and his health began to improve, he began to fret that you would suspect that he'd lied to you to avoid prosecution, and that at any moment you would return to Boscombe Valley and reveal his crime. Finally, he decided to falsify his own death and start a new life elsewhere for whatever time that he had left.

"It wasn't a hurried process, and we – that is, he and I, for I was a close partner in the process, and James to some degree – had time to plan carefully. We found a place where he wanted to go, and picked an old doctor who could certify his 'death' without suspecting a thing. We were fortunate that the doctor passed away soon after, and that no one was able to question him."

I had to wonder if John Turner had taken it upon himself to close that loop, but we would never know for sure.

"I had already been serving as my father's agent for quite some time during his illness, and it was no difficulty to step in and continue doing so after he departed. Things were as happy as might be expected, except for the continued suspicion in the village toward James about his father's death. Finally, after seeing your stories, Dr. Watson, and consulting with my father (who, by this time was well-established in Hythe), I visited you about telling that really happened that day by Boscombe Pool. And so the truth came out, and the cloud lifted from my poor husband.

"After that, the time passed, and we were happy, except that we seemed unable to have a child. Then, after so many empty years, I found that a miracle had occurred. My father came to Ross to share in my joy – and it was there that he was seen by this man, Peasemore.

"Not long after, Peasemore made an appointment to see me. He was a terrible little fellow, crude and leering. My guard was up as soon as I met him, and he quickly let me know that he not only knew a great deal about my father's past, but that – to my horror – he had traced him to his new life in Kent. Then it was just the same old story – he wanted money.

"Father and I exchanged letters, and we agreed to pay the man until we could figure out what to do. I came up to London and mailed the second payment from here, and then waited to see Peasemore retrieve it. He was a stupid man, and it was easy to follow him. Now we knew where he lived." At this she fell silent, and Holmes continued for her.

"Peasemore made another visit to your home," he said. "He threatened you." Alice McCarthy looked at him with a puzzled expression. "I've read your letters to your father," Holmes explained. "In his room at the hotel. You wrote to him about Peasemore's new demand. What was his response?"

"There was none, at first. And then he sent a telegram yesterday, stating that he'd been recognized." She glanced at Patience Moran, who had been sitting quietly beside here, her expressions ranging from fascination to astonishment. "He said that you had seen him at the hotel, Patience, and knew that he was alive. That he was running out of time."

"So you traveled to London yourself," prompted Holmes, "arriving in Bushell Street just ahead of your father."

She nodded but didn't elaborate on what had happened next – how she had entered the building first, and how we'd heard the gunshot that killed the blackmailer while her father was still passing through the front door. I wondered myself just how much further Holmes would push her to comment. He was at the very limit of what could be truthfully be revealed in front of Inspector Lestrade without explaining what had really occurred – exactly who had pulled the trigger, killing the blackmailer, and the subsequent tacit understanding between Holmes and Turner – and myself as well, I suppose – to let the father take the blame for Peasemore's death.

Lestrade had followed the conversation with rapt attention, and he seemed as if he wanted to ask a question, but he was interrupted by Patience Moran, who took Alice McCarthy's hand and stated firmly that the poor woman had been through enough, and that the little gathering was at an end. She bundled the small fair-haired Alice into a cab, intending that she should stay at her own lodgings in Upper Bridport Street until able to return to Boscombe Valley.

After they had gone downstairs and out to the street, Lestrade made his way back to the basket chair, where he had previously sat listening to the strange tale. I was surprised that he hadn't departed as well, and I moved to pour something stronger than tea for the three of us. Then we all sat silently for some time, sipping and thinking our own thoughts. Finally the inspector spoke, in a surprising way.

"After that matter of the killing at Abbey Grange," he began, "early last year, Hopkins asked me my opinion – after the likely suspects were determined to already be in custody in New York during the time that the murder occurred."

I recalled the incident well. The death of Sir Eustace Brackenstall had been particularly brutal. Holmes and I had been summoned to the dead man's manor in Kent by Inspector Stanley Hopkins. His examination of the evidence had seemed to indicate that the crime was carried out by the three-man Randall gang, a father and two sons who were known to be operating in the area, having pulled off a particularly brutal job a fortnight earlier in Sydenham. After it was proven that these three men couldn't have committed the murder, Hopkins had asked for a hint, and Holmes had told him that some of the aspects of the case were a blind. However, Hopkins had missed the point – as Holmes had intended – and had continued his hunt for a different but similar gang. The truth later came out, privately, in something of the same manner as the solution to the McCarthy murder in 1889 – the real killer had had excellent provocation against a vile man who had no place in society.

Lestrade seemed to be following my thinking. "I went back over the evidence, and what Hopkins said about your suggestion that it was a blind. And it occurred to me that the murder at the Abbey Grange might have something in common with the events in Boscombe Valley long ago – not in terms of the same criminal, mind you, but in the way that there seemed to be no official solution when it was over – and after your involvement."

Holmes smiled. "Indeed." And then he took a sip of whisky, and a great silence filled the room until Lestrade tipped up his own glass, finishing the contents and setting it on a side table. He stood up.

"A policeman learns," he said, looking intently at Holmes, "that it's sometimes best not to ask too many questions. I never know for certain what had happened in Boscombe Valley until Dr. Watson shared it with me, before it ended up appearing in *The Strand*. I don't know what happened at Abbey Grange either – not for sure, anyway –but I went down to Kent a day or so after the two of you had been there, and I saw the bruises on Lady Brackenstall's arm, the same as you likely did. It didn't escape my notice that you let Hopkins keep chasing after the mysterious gang while you withdrew from the case. I also made it my business to pay attention when the lady married that sea captain a few months ago – a captain who had been in London at the time of the murder, and who knew the lady from a previous sea voyage, and who only returned after a long absence following the murder in time to wed her."

Holmes lifted an eyebrow and raised his glass for another sip. Was it simply a trick of the light, or did he tip his glass first toward the inspector in some kind of salute?

Lestrade apparently thought that he saw it as well, for he gave a small nod, adding, "It also hasn't escaped me that Mrs. McCarthy's story ended today at her arrival at the house in Bushell Street, following her sudden trip to London, just moments before the blackmailer was killed and her father took his own life after pointedly confessing to the first constable on the scene." He stepped to the door and donned his coat. Holding his hat in one hand and opening the door with the other, he said, "I wish you both a good evening." And then he departed.

We were quiet long after we'd heard him go down the stairs and out the front door. Then, taking the last sip from my own whisky glass, I had to ask, "Is it ever a burden, Holmes? Deciding when to play God? When to excuse a crime for the greater good? Can the greater good even be determined?"

He was silent for such a spell that I wasn't sure if he would answer at all. Perhaps my question had contained some unrealized offense. It was unintended, but I did have a few doubts of my own. After all, I also knew the truth of who had killed Peasemore that afternoon, and I'd remained silent while her father took the blame – more than that, while he took his own life. As usual, Holmes followed my thoughts.

"Would it have been better to denounce her?" he asked, his tone surprisingly harsh after the recent moments of quiet. "To have her father's sacrifice count for nothing, while she – and her unborn child – were subjected to a trial? The press would have made it a circus, and while it's doubtful that she would have been hanged, how much would her life, and that of her husband and the child, have been ruined – all to satisfy the requirements of justice for killing a man who himself deserved very little pity."

I started to speak, but he continued. "Perhaps it *was* a mistake. We let John Turner go for killing his blackmailer ten years ago, and then the public continued to unfairly believe that James McCarthy was the real killer – a situation that was only rectified when you published the true account a couple of years later. We allowed the true murderer to escape following the events at the Abbey Grange in January '97, and so far our decision has been justified, but the case is still officially open. What happens if, in a year or so, Hopkins arrests some other gang of three, all innocent, and we are then forced to tell the truth in order to save them?

"Or what if this, or this, or this? Can we mere mortals see the interconnections of every twisting thread, stretching off into the darkness far beyond our own awareness? Will freeing Alice McCarthy from the responsibility of her crime today lead to a happy outcome? Or is she in fact some conniver who has fooled us and manipulated events, and will go on to commit other crimes that would never occur otherwise if she were punished today? Will her child be somehow tainted by what has occurred, or by her family's bloody history, and himself carry out some atrocity years from now that would never have occurred otherwise?"

He closed his eyes. "I sometimes feel that by exposing the guilty, I've done more harm than good, but at other times, I've likewise protected the guilty for what I felt was the greater good. Was I right? Was I wrong? I suppose only time will tell, but it's a burden that sometimes weighs on me, Watson. It weighs heavily."

I said nothing – not sure of what could be said. But then I rose and retrieved the whisky decanter from the sideboard, refilling his glass, and then my own. Then, instead of replacing it, I set it on the table by my chair. I sat back down, took a long sip, and looked into the fire. I knew that this could be along night, and it was likely that, in spite of Holmes's current silence, he might need to talk some more before morning.

The Polmayne Puzzles

28 March, 1887

My Dear Holmes,

I hope that this letter finds you well. I've done what you asked, as confirmed by separate wire, to serve notice at Baron Maupertuis' banks that his accounts shall be frozen – but *only* at your notification, and not before. Old Flanders at the Capital and Counties gave some trouble – as you had predicted – but a word from Lord Halsted reminded him of his obligations and he was soon silenced.

I'm writing today with something of a different matter, although I realize that all of your attentions and energies are currently engaged in thwarting the Baron's colossal schemes. However, I thought that perhaps, considering the urgency of a request that was brought to my attention only today, you might find a moment here and there to give me your thoughts and provide a bit of guidance from afar.

I was in my consulting rooms this morning when a visitor presented himself. He stated that his name was Edward Polmayne, a junior solicitor – "most junior" he wryly asserted – associated with the firm of Ames and Notting in Lincoln's Inn Fields. Using your methods, I could see that the fellow was a bachelor in his early twenties, a very tentative smoker of Trichinopoly cigars, and someone who stays inside far too often for his own good – likely connected to his efforts to rise in his profession. He is the beneficiary of healthy ancestors (as reflected by his general size and well-being), and someone who is interested in his appearance, although living within quite limited means, as befits his low position at his place of employment.

He explained that he had been by Baker Street not half-an-hour before to lay his problem before you, but Mrs. Hudson explained that you are out of the country. Apparently when she observed his urgent disappointment, she sent him 'round my way to tell his story.

In short, he is a young man with a difficulty who has a limited amount of time to solve it. He related that he is an orphan whose parents died when he was but nine years old. He was taken in by his paternal grandfather, Martin Polmayne, his only living relative. He had been raised well and wanted for nothing growing up, having been brought to London from his parents' home in Cornwall at the time of their death in a railway accident. His grandfather owned a comfortable – if somewhat gloomy – old house

300

at one end of Gloucester Terrace, and it was there that the lad spent his formative years.

It was made clear from an early age that his grandfather thought that he should be seasoned, and able to function on his own as an adult. Thus, Edward Polmayne had learned early to work hard and persevere. His grandfather Martin had made his own fortune when he was young, and he was loathe to simply pass it on to his grandson unearned.

Edward Polmayne went on to relate some of the curious history of his grandfather, which I suspect may be relevant to the young man's problem. Martin Polmayne was born in Truro in 1805. Martin's father had been a craftsman – a woodworker – helping to build the cathedral there, and when Martin was grown, he was expected to follow in his father's footsteps. However, he had instead run away to sea, obtaining a berth as a ship's carpenter. He was part of the British and French fleet that defeated the Greek pirates at Grambusa in 1828, and his bravery during the battle earned him a commission. He rose from triumph to triumph, eventually becoming a ranking officer.

Seeing which way the wind was blowing, he took advantage of the Pax Britannica and left the service, investing in shipping and slowly accumulating a tidy fortune that enabled him to retire and purchase his home in Mayfair where he and his wife lived. (She died in the 1860's.) After taking in his grandson fifteen years ago, Martin was firm but fair, never spoiling Edward, but caring for the boy as if he were his own child. He assisted him through university and then into a chosen career in the law offices of his old friend, solicitor Clayton Notting – but always with the *caveat* that the youth be his own man.

And so it was until just a few weeks ago. Martin Polmayne, whose health had remained fairly good for his whole life, took a sudden turn and began to decline. Sensing that his end was approaching, he visited solicitor Notting's office – without Edward's knowledge – and curiously revised his will, along with leaving a letter for his grandson, to be delivered upon his passing.

A day or two after the old man's funeral, Clayton Notting summoned Edward into his office, explaining about the changes in the will, along with the instructions that the letter be delivered posthumously.

This letter, which I have read, states that Martin held the greatest affection for his grandson Edward, but as had always been his intention, the old man wanted the younger to earn his fortune, and not simply have it handed to him. "Seeing as how you never had the benefit of physical labor, as did I and my father before me," Martin states in his letter, "I will test your mind instead. Follow the steps of success, and you shall not fail." And with that cryptic instruction, the letter ends.

301

Notting explained that unless Edward could work through a series of messages devised by his grandfather within a month, the man's accumulated wealth, along with the house in Gloucester Terrace, would be donated towards maintenance of the Truro Cathedral. "One final hint," said the old attorney, with a suspiciously knowing look in his eye. "I was told that you must begin your search in the house in which you were raised." And with that, he would provide no further comment or instruction.

Edward Polmayne then spent the next fortnight frantically searching through the house before realizing that he was in over his head. Knowing that he had squandered precious time, and that the deadline is April 13th, he called in Baker Street this morning, and thus on to my door. Knowing that his opportunity was quickly growing short, and that your assistance might not be so easily obtained, both due to distance and more pressing concerns, I joined the young man in going around to the old house posthaste.

It's a grim pile, much darker in color and ambience than its neighbors. I can almost hear you telling me to "Cut the poetry, Watson!", but I feel that the nature of the house is relevant to reveal the nature of its owner, and the chore that he has set. Edward explained that his grandfather had maintained a number of servants in days of old, but as time passed, they departed or passed away, until only two were left, a butler-of-many tasks named Silas Hayes and his housekeeper wife. They had been given a substantial gift at Martin's death – £1,000 – enough to settle them comfortably, and sent on their way.

Edward had known nothing of this at the time, he explained. He maintained his own lodgings near his place of work, and had been unaware of his grandfather's final illness until the very end. In fact, he only had time to see the old man once before he died, and no relevant information was passed between them then.

Edward led me inside the empty house, and the immediate darkness was overwhelming – as was the mustiness of the place. This was understandable, given that the old man had gradually withdrawn from society, relying only upon the two servants who were apparently as old as he was.

We took a quick tour, and I understood Edward's initial sense of being overwhelmed. Luckily the place isn't filled with a lifetime of collected detritus, as the old man had apparently (and sensibly) divested himself of many of the items that one accumulates over a lifetime – anchors and weights that become chained to one's self as inevitably as did the those burdens fastened to Jacob Marley when he appeared before Ebenezer Scrooge.

You and I have seen many houses filled to the brim with jumbled and useless treasures. (I'm reminded of that old Buck woman's house near Armathwaite, where the journal with the lost literary treasures was found in a box of old ledgers, along with the three torn pound-notes.) Martin Polmayne's house wasn't like those of a hoarder. Rather, it was clean and trim, as one would expect of a man who had risen from the bottom to the top during much of a life spent at sea. Many of the upstairs rooms were in fact completely empty, and all that was left downstairs were a few tasteful items of high quality. If the house had been brighter and less dusty, it might have almost seemed cheerful. As it was, the lack of warmth and light only contributed to a sense of gloom – and a rising sense of frantic despair as Edward Polmayne looked around and was overwhelmed yet again by the scope of his assignment.

I tried to step back and see the house as you would, and to keep the little that I knew of the old man in the front of my thoughts. Surely he would not want to completely deprive his grandson of the inheritance by making the undertaking an impossible one. And yet, there was so little to go on.

Glancing around, I saw that the very lack of material possessions might almost indicate an added importance to the few that were left. It was then that I questioned Edward more about the items still there. Edward pointed to a favorite chair of his grandfather's in a rear study – and without destroying it, we examined it, but to no avail. (Afterwards, Edward told me that he had already looked at it, but he wished for my fresh eyes to also see what they might see.) There was a great standing clock in one corner of the parlour, a massive beast that Edward said the old man had proudly acquired when he bought the house. There was nothing inside it. Other pieces of furniture were equally disappointing. Martin's desk, while containing some documents related to the household, was surprisingly empty – which Edward indicated had also occurred within recent months, as the old man apparently simplified his affairs.

Finally – and I really must think that you'll be quite proud of me, Holmes – I recalled the old man's instructions, by way of the solicitor: *Follow the steps of success, and you won't fail.* To what else could this refer but the massive staircase in the front hall?

Edward led me there with a look of admiration for my insight. Surely this must be what we sought. It's a wide and ornate stairwell of perhaps two-dozen solid steps rising from the front door to the first floor. It is truly a tribute to the craftsman who constructed it. We began to look up and down, crawling and prodding and poking, thinking perhaps that there was some hidden cavity that might be opened to reveal the secreted fortune. For after all, hadn't Martin Polmayne been a ship's carpenter in his youth?

Edward assured me that contriving such a hidey-hole would have been well within his grandfather's skills.

I asked for more light, and Edward carried in a number of lamps. As they were placed, it was he who noticed what we sought. For as the shadows played about the stairwell, we could see dark carvings – grooves in the original wood – that were suddenly noticeable on the upright risers – darker than the old wood upon which they were etched.

Edward assured me that he had never seen them before, and that they must have been placed there recently. Although dark like the rest of the wood, their newness was confirmed when we knelt to examine them, only to discover that they had been stained recently – the odor was unmistakable, and rubbing a finger across one left a smudge on my skin that was difficult to remove.

Calling for paper and a pen, I carefully recorded the marks, as shown below. I'm certain that, with their recent addition to the steps, they must be the clue to the next step in the puzzle, but for the life of me, I cannot perceive what it might mean. They occur on the bottom seven risers. The carving on the lowest riser is thus:

The second from the bottom is:

The third is:

. . . and the fourth:

304

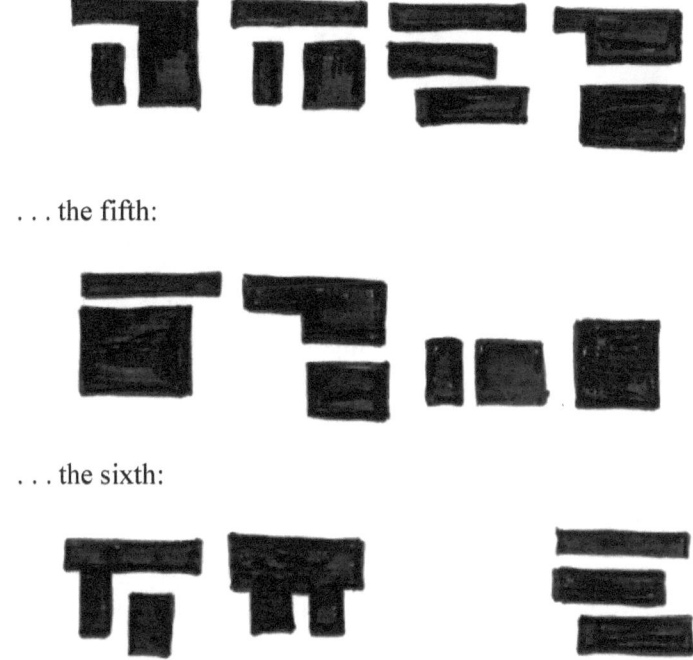

. . . the fifth:

. . . the sixth:

. . . and the seventh and final mark, which is to the right, with the left side apparently blank:

After our initial discovery, Edward seemed as filled with gloom as before, if not more so, especially after I could provide no guidance. The best that I could promise was to send this information to you, along with the records that you have requested regarding the Baron's property holdings. I am dispatching both by a fast messenger tonight, and this should be in your hands by tomorrow. Any thoughts that you might have will be most appreciated – especially as the time before the gate closes upon the young man dwindles with each day.

I look forward to our insight, and I await further instructions.

Very best,

Watson

* * * * *

1 April, 1887

Dear Holmes,

I have set the hounds loose at Somerset House, and the search is on for details regarding Baron Maupertuis' dubious birth, but Alderson assures me that what you request cannot be found within the time limits that you have set. Based on the assumption that he is exaggerating yet again – as we learned he is likely to do during that matter with the four leather targets – I held firm and informed him that I'll be back for the documents tomorrow. He made a half-hearted show of resistance, but Lestrade's pointed warning and reminder that knowledge of his gambling debts is known seemed to sharpen his focus. (Lestrade plays The Game very well when he needs to.)

In the meantime, I wanted to provide an update to you on the Polmayne Affair. Your wire was most timely, and we found a new clue in the search exactly where you suggested – but it only revealed a different puzzle, and the search continues.

But first, I must tell you of a curious incident. After I received your reply yesterday regarding the mysterious carvings on the steps – and you really must tell me someday what they mean, and how you knew exactly where to direct our attentions! – I summoned Edward to my consulting rooms. Before I could explain your suggestion of where to search next, he informed me that he had been walking just that morning along High Holborn, returning from an errand for his employer, Mr. Notting, when he encountered Mrs. Hayes, his uncle's former housekeeper.

He was quite surprised, as he'd understood (by way of a comment from Mr. Notting, who had delivered their £1,000 legacy) that both Mr. and Mrs. Hayes had departed London for Chelmsford as soon as old Martin Polmayne was laid to rest. Apparently Mr. Hayes has a sister who moved years ago to Essex, and with no reason to remain in London, the butler and housekeeper had decided to join her.

Edward explained that he hurried forward, hoping to have a word with Mrs. Hayes, and to again express his thankfulness that she and her husband had cared for his grandfather so well over the years, and especially during his final days.

And, he admitted to me, he hoped to question her about the matter of his grandfather's hidden fortune – for after all, hadn't they been in the house during the old man's last months? Not to mention during that time

306

when the old man had carved the mysterious runes on the stair risers that served as the first clue towards locating the missing estate.

Calling her name, he had the sense that she heard him but chose to keep walking. He increased his speed and caught up with her, whereupon she had no choice but to acknowledge his presence. She seemed quite flustered, Edward said, and immediately created an awkwardness between them when none need have existed. He thanked her, as had been his intention, and she nodded, a genuine tear forming in the corner of her eye. They talked for a moment then with a bit more friendliness – for after all Edward had known her for much of his life, and if she was not a mother to him, she had still been something of a friend and confidante during his formative years.

With that in mind, Edward attempted to shift the conversation from details of Martin's final days, (when the grandson was not even aware of the old man's illness – based upon Martin's express orders, Mrs. Hayes was quick to assert – and general ponderings about how fast a man of health could decline,) to specifics related to this unwanted treasure hunt upon which our client – for such we must consider him – has unwillingly found himself. And that was enough to make the old woman go silent. And in fact, more-so, in a somewhat dramatic fashion.

When Edward mentioned the carvings upon the stairs, her eyes widened and she took a step back as if he had raised a hand against her. Shaking her head, she whispered, "Not yet! Not this way! I was told – " Whereupon she turned and ducked into the passing throng.

Edward was tempted to follow her, he told me, but he was stunned, and also realized that whatever she knew was apparently a secret that caused her great anguish – and just then he was not prepared to force more of the same upon her. Instead, he returned to his office to find my message, whereupon he obtained leave from his employer – who again seemed to have some sort of knowing glint in his eye, indicating that he knows more than he is telling, I'm bound! – and came around to my rooms.

It was there that I showed him your cryptic wire – "Examine the clock". As I said, I'm sure that someday you will explain to me just what you saw in those odd carvings that led you to suggest that, but in the meantime, we departed immediately for Gloucester Terrace – for there was only one clock that you could mean: The massive beast towering over the parlour.

As I mentioned in my last letter, Edward said that his grandfather bought the clock when he acquired the house – or so Edward had always understood. He really knew no more about it, and feared that if there was some family legend connected with it that would be necessary to solving the riddle, he didn't know what it would be. He wracked his brain as we

307

traveled, hoping to recall an anecdote from his youth that he had foolishly ignored, but he could remember nothing.

Back inside, the house was as dark and gloomy as I recalled. However, we ignored it as we made our way directly to the clock, which stood over us a good seven feet from top to bottom. We had looked through it the other day, but it was clear that there was nothing hidden inside, and nothing that could be a hidden cavity – although I was wishing that you were there, because I trusted your ability to make certain of that fact far more than mine.

However, as I looked the thing up and down, I noticed upon the floor some minute scratches where it had apparently been pivoted to turn it away from the wall. Perhaps, I thought, something was hidden <u>behind</u> it – or possibly there was a receptacle or safe in the wall, hidden from sight.

I pointed to the scratches, and Edward immediately understood. He helped me shift the clock, which really wasn't that heavy at all, considering its size. (This really wasn't a surprise in hindsight, as it's mostly filled with empty space.) We eagerly looked behind it, to find . . . nothing. The space between clock and wall was empty, and no seams or openings in the wall indicated a place to conceal anything there.

And then . . . I noticed fresh scratches in the wood at eye level, in the dark varnished wood of the clock's smooth rear face. I glanced at Edward, and he at me, and then he gave a rueful laugh. We both understood immediately that – once again – this was beyond us.

Here, for your consideration, is the latest message:

O I C V I I O X I C V I I I O V I I I O V O V I I I O I C X I I I O V C V I I

As before, I'm forwarding this message tonight, along with the documents that you requested from your scrapbooks about the Baron's former servants. Please let me know whatever I can do to assist, and any thoughts that you might offer about Polmayne's problem will be much appreciated – as the time to solve the riddle is rapidly coming to a close. In the meantime, I'll turn my attention to this cypher – although we both know that the chances are likely that the solution will most certainly be provided through your understanding rather than mine.

Very best,

Watson

* * * * *

6 April, 1887

My Dear Holmes,

I saw in the morning newspapers that you had been attacked two days ago in Paris. Reading between the lines, I'm sure that it was the Baron's men – much as they attacked you in the same way in Great Coram Street before you journeyed to the Continent. I wasn't surprised that you've made no mention of it, but I am concerned that you didn't send for me to provide assistance. Please take care, and let me know if I can do anything to help, other than what I've been doing here in London.

Your wire this morning was most appreciated, and I felt that I must share with you the day's events, as we seem to be no closer to a solution of Polmayne's problem than we were when I first wrote to you about it. I am truly curious as to what these various messages mean, but I understand that your attentions are elsewhere, and that an explanation must wait for some time when events are not quite so pressing. I am simply grateful that you've been able to direct us from one step to the next, and I know that Polmayne feels that way to an infinitely greater degree.

Based on your suggestion, I traveled this morning to the office of Ames and Notting, where I gained permission to speak to Polmayne. He seemed quite surprised to see me, but when I showed him your telegram, advising us to speak to the Hayes couple, he wasted no time in seeking an audience with old Mr. Notting.

I found the fellow to be quite curious indeed. He is a small man with great upswept eyebrows, and a knowing look in his eyes as if everything amuses him. I suspect that it is a useful method of disconcerting his opponents, and more than compensates for his slight stature, which was almost comical as he sat across from us in a very high chair behind a great empty field of a desk.

He nodded knowingly when Polmayne asked for the Hayes' address in Chelmsford, but I don't know if he expected the question or if it was just his way. However, he wrote the address on a slip of paper – without seeking the information elsewhere, it should be noted, as if he already had it in his head should it be needed – and used a small forefinger to push it across the desk. Polmayne obtained permission to be away for the rest of the day, and when it was granted, he went to gather his things. Half-an-hour later we were in a train departing Liverpool Street Station for Essex.

Hayes and his wife had settled in with his sister in her comfortable house in Sandford Road, Chelmsford, which was not so far from the station. We stopped for a moment at the edge of the curved street to make sure of the address, and I noticed an upstairs curtain flick. We had been observed.

Our knock brought old Silas Hayes himself, who greeted us with a marked lack of surprise. He led us into an open room which seemed to fill most of the ground floor. Seated near the front window were two old women, introduced to us as Hayes' wife and his sister.

As I walked toward them to introduce myself, I noticed a telegram lying face up on a side table. While Edward greeted his grandfather's former servants, I contrived to bend and read it. It was from Clayton Notting, sent that morning as soon as we had left his office, informing Hayes that Edward was on his way to Chelmsford. Clearly this lawyer's actions deserve some scrutiny!

I looked up to see Silas Hayes scowling at me, but I resolved to ignore it. No good would come from antagonizing him when Edward needed information – as directed by his late grandfather in the clue from the clock (which you somehow determined).

Throughout our visit, the sister remained silent, and in fact seemed rather pleasantly confused, as if she were in the early stages of elderly enfeeblement. Mrs. Hayes seemed flustered, apologizing about her reaction days earlier when she had encountered Edward in the street. When prompted, she answered Edward that she and her husband did have something for the young man, as directed by his late grandfather. "But," she explained, "we were told that you would visit us, and only then could we reveal it. I was afraid that you wanted it that day in the street, and that wasn't how it is to be given."

Edward assured her that he'd had no notion then that he should even ask for a message, and the old woman seemed relieved. Without prompting, Silas Brown stepped to another room and returned with a most curious object – a fiddle made out of tin.

Edward's eyes lit up, and he explained to me that it was an old souvenir from his grandfather's travels – an instrument constructed by a convict in the Antipodes. His grandfather had taught himself to play it, and how to read music as well, and had spent many a happy and entertaining hour. When it was missing from the house, Edward had assumed that it had been sold or given away.

Edward asked the Hayes what it could mean, but their puzzlement was as great as our own. He turned it over, and then passed it to me. I knew that we both wondered if some coded message might be scratched upon it, as had been on the stair risers and then clock, but there was nothing. However, as I rotated it for myself, I heard the whisper of something moving loose inside.

310

With the loan of a hairpin, we were able to snag a rolled piece of paper and pull it through the F-holes. It should come as no surprise that it was yet another coded message – which I reproduce here:

With nothing further to add, the Hayes seemed content to visit with Edward for a while, and they obviously cared about him a great deal. Vows were made to stay in touch, and then we departed for London.

And so once again, Holmes, I commend this into your capable hands. I have no doubts that you will furnish us with our next destination. In the meantime, please find me,

Your friend,

Watson

* * * * *

12 April, 1887

Holmes,

I have much to report, as events have crowded fast and thick upon us. By now, Baron Maupertuis' castles have started to crumble, and more than one man across London is pondering the inexorable fate, tied to his own associated corruption, that is trundling his way. Only moments ago, I received a message from Lestrade that Sir Martin Rhofer has shot himself

– most certainly related to his previous unwavering support of the Baron. It is likely that other solitarily engineered solutions will follow.

In the meantime, I will take a moment to relate the latest in the Polmayne matter. Your wire, with the solution to the code of the music staff, was most instructive. You will be happy to learn that I had actually puzzled out a piece of it myself, realizing that our next journey would be to the Royal Observatory at Greenwich, and to the Prime Meridian – although until your clarifying telegram stating to go there and "See A. Bede", I had no idea how to proceed.

Polmayne and I made our way east and across the river, arriving mid-morning. The blue sky illuminated the impressive buildings of the Royal Naval College, and once again I found that I can never go there without recalling so much of the proud history of our Empire.

Our carriage made its way up the hill, with the parkland dropping away from us and London shining in the distance across the river. The beauty of the morning, however, was in direct contrast with young Edward's mood. He had initially been happy and then intrigued by the solution to the latest of his grandfather's messages, but he feared that our destination would simply reveal another puzzle – and I began to absorb much of his mood as well, when a full realization of how little time was left recalled itself to me – for the deadline is tomorrow!

We reached the top of the hill and stepped to the ground. It was then that I saw something which I must relate to you, Holmes, although it has nothing to do with the current matter. Across the way, having an intense conversation with Sir Pelton of the observatory, was a certain mathematical professor of our acquaintance. He didn't see me, and to Edward's surprise, I took him by the arm and pulled him quickly into a nearby building. Although whatever business Moriarty was on certainly had no intersection with mine, I knew that it wouldn't do for me to be seen. I would have dearly loved to determine just what his game was, but there was simply no way to get closer and eavesdrop. I had to watch in frustration as, through the rippled glass of the old window, I saw him enter his own coach and slowly depart down the hill.

Edward was still puzzled, but he quickly forgot when I asked a passing chap if he could direct us to "A. Bede". Without a question or comment, we were led through a series of hallways to a small door on the south of the building. It was marked modestly with the legend Albert Bede. A knock brought forth a call to enter, and we opened the door to discover a portly gentleman, clearly in his eighth decade. He looked up puzzled for a moment, and then he seemed to recognize Edward, and a wide smile broadened his face. "So you found me, then," he chortled.

He invited us to sit, and then looked questioningly in my direction. Edward was tongue-tied, so I introduced us both, explaining our mission. Bede replied, "Nothing against seeking help. In fact, that's a sign of intelligence, if you ask me." Edward seemed puzzled, and the old man continued. "Your grandfather and I were great friends. When he set this quest before you, he asked if I would be a part of it. My pleasure, my pleasure."

Edward's eyes widened, and he seemed to straddle both hope and despair. "Please, sir," he managed to say. "Tell me what you must, and pray that it isn't another one of these dreadful puzzles!"

Bede laughed and slapped his desk. "I imagine that one would weary of them," he said, "and that's a fact. Well, not far to go now. You only have one more task – to travel back to Notting's office and tell him just one word: 'Truro'."

Edward raised his eyebrows, and then, after a long pause, said, "And then – ?"

The old man shrugged. "Success? Satisfaction? I suppose then, after all is said and done, it will be up to you, my boy, to determine just how your life will play out. I wish you well. Come back and tell me about it sometime."

And so we soon found ourselves in Lincoln's Inn Fields, and sitting before Notting's desk. He smiled knowingly and placed two documents before him on the desk.

"Here," he said, tapping the one on the right, "is the will giving your grandfather's estate to the Truro Cathedral, provided you could not solve his tests. And this," he said, putting a finger on the document on the left, "is another document, carefully dated after the first, giving the estate to you."

"So," I asked, "am I to understand that the estate went to Edward in its entirety regardless? The later will supersedes the first, whether or not he solved the puzzles?"

"It does. I convinced Martin that his puzzle game was both unfair, and probably wouldn't stand up to legal challenge. In fact, I had some ethical concerns about even making myself a part of it. But Martin left specific instructions that the quest should be carried out nonetheless, in order to see if Edward had the gumption to work it out for himself." He smiled fondly at the young man. "I was against it, but at the same time, I could see your grandfather's point of view. And you did it my boy! Congratulations!"

Edward seemed rather stunned. Then, he finally spoke. "I'm not sure that I did it, actually. I had the help of Dr. Watson, and through him Mr.

Sherlock Holmes, who guided us from the Continent, where he is currently involved in another investigation."

"Indeed," said Notting. "I thought that Dr. Watson seemed familiar. And I've been following Mr. Holmes's activities in the newspapers. Why, the news has just broken that Baron Maupertuis has been arrested – in Lyons, as a matter of fact. He was attempting to flee when the Sûreté frustrated him, so to speak."

It was my turn to be surprised. "I haven't even heard that news yet," I said. I turned to Edward. "I'm very glad that all has worked out for the best, and you must come and tell me what happens next. Besides, I know that we both want to know how Holmes solved these various coded messages. But for now, I must depart. My help will be needed elsewhere!"

I shook hands with both of them and rapidly made my way home, where I now await your instructions. To fill the time, I'm writing this to record as much as possible, and I'll send by way of the same messengers that we have so recently used.

In the meantime, many congratulations, my friend, on yet another victory!

Watson

* * * * *

14 April, 1887

My Dear Watson,

I write these lines courtesy of Baron Maupertuis, who thankfully bolted prematurely, thus acknowledging his guilt and placing him in the sure hands of the French police. His scheming is at an end, although I fear that the reverberations will ring for quite some time as the rot we uncovered is rooted out (to mix my metaphors.)

While I enjoy my well-earned relaxation, and every comfort that the Hotel Dulong can supply, I will take a moment to reply to your most recent letter and explain my solutions to the various puzzles in relation to your acquaintance, Edward Polmayne, and his inheritance.

The insight into the initial message being related to the stairway, and the subsequent discovery of the new carvings upon the stair risers, was quite useful, as it gave me an indication into the thinking of Mr. Martin Polmayne. I pondered over the various meanings of the curious line figures, even for a moment considering some obscure variant of the Ogham language. Then, I considered the arrangement on the rising and subsequent steps, and it occurred to me to rotate the sketch ninety-degrees clockwise, to view it the way one tilts one's head to read titles on the spines of books, lined up across a shelf.

You had presented the carvings in your letter in reverse order, with the top step copied first and so on to the bottom, when it fact the first carving that you drew should have been presented on the right, at the end of the message (which actually records lines of text.) Removing the separating spaces between the carvings necessitated by the physical placement of the stair treads revealed something like this . . .

. . . and filling the edges produced something more legible (as well as using a great deal of my ink!) This, with some imagination, can be read as *Tempus Fugate Magna Fortuna*:

I'm uncertain of my Latin to know if this is the correct form, but it is what Martin Polmayne intended. <u>Time Flies Great Fortune</u>. It might have been simply a warning that the puzzle had a limited time to be solved, but if so, that wouldn't advance young Edward a single jot toward the solution. Thus, I chose to take "time" more literally, and recalled the great clock which you had described in the otherwise mostly emptied house.

Following my advice, you examined the clock and sent me the curious message made up of *O*'s, *C*'s, *X*'s, *V*'s, and *I*'s. After consideration, I realized that, except for the *O*'s and *C*'s, the other letters were those used as the basic units for smaller Roman Numerals. Specifically, these numbers were connected with the numbers associated with clocks and telling time. "I" for one o'clock, "II" for two o'clock and so on. After the a.m. (or daytime) twelve-hour period, the numbers start over at night, running from one to twelve again, or *I* to *XII*.

This of course gives us twenty-four time periods – a number which is close to the twenty-six in the alphabet. This realization gave me the suspicion that this was a simple substitution code. But then what did the O's and C's mean? Suddenly it was so simple. The O represented the sun, or day, and the first twelve time periods – or the first twelve letters of the alphabet. The C was then the moon, or the second twelve time periods, and naturally the thirteenth through twenty-fourth letters of the alphabet.

With that in mind, the code becomes:

$$A – OI$$
$$B – OII$$
$$C – OIII$$
$$D – OIV$$
$$E – OV$$
$$F – OVI$$
$$G – OVII$$
$$H – OVIII$$
$$I – OIX$$
$$J – OX$$
$$K – OXI$$
$$L – OXII$$
$$M – CI$$
$$N – CII$$
$$O – CIII$$
$$P – CIV$$
$$Q – CV$$
$$R – CVI$$
$$S – CVII$$
$$T– CVIII$$
$$U – CIX$$
$$V – CX$$
$$W – CXI$$
$$X – CXII$$
$$Y – CXIII$$
$$Z – CXIIII$$

(Presumably, if the twenty-fifth and twenty-sixth letter of the alphabet – Y and Z – were needed, they could be written as shown, which I worked out from the message itself, or in some similar way.) Using this, I saw that the O's and C's served as natural breaks to indicate where each letter began. Thus, the coded message –

– was easily be deciphered as "*Ask the Hayes*".

The musical clue was quite easily explained. The notation at the top was possibly placed there to imply (to someone who didn't know better) some sort of tempo marking or instruction to the player. However, the Italian phrase "*Via A*" – loosely translated as "*Go to*" – followed by a series of numbers that could very well be coordinates – *Latitude 51.48*, and *Longitude 0* – could only lead to just a pair of places on earth, and since you didn't need to the ocean between Cape Town and Antarctica, it must mean the Prime Meridian at Royal Observatory at Greenwich. (My congratulations upon also perceiving this!)

The musical "composition" was quite straightforward as well. The first note to sound, a whole-note "*C*" in the base clef, is solitary by means of the quarter-rest above it. It is held throughout the two-measure piece, tied to a similar "*C*" in the second measure. In the treble clef, the quarter-rest is then followed by an "*A*". Then another quarter-rest, implying a space and indicating that the "*A*" stands alone, before the notes "*B*", "*E*", "*D*", and "*E*" are indicated.

With these various pieces identified, the message clearly reads: "*Go to 51.48 – 0. See A. Bede.*"

While all of this was an elementary child's play of deduction, it did serve as a much-needed distraction from the cut-and-parry work as the Baron attempted to squirm out of the trap, and for that I'm grateful.

I appreciate your letter telling me of the happy ending of the affair. Now I find myself rather weary. I cannot make the staff here at the hotel understand just what kind of tobacco that I desire, and the knocking upon my door by various officials who either want to ask questions or congratulate me is becoming quite tiresome. I believe that I will save this letter to deliver personally into your hands, and send a wire inviting you to join me here. Assuming that you accept, I look forward to your arrival, Watson, but for now I believe that I will attempt to sleep.

With very best regards,

Holmes

The Curious
Cardboard Boxes

I had seen less of my friend Sherlock Holmes in the recent weeks following my marriage – although less is certainly a relative term. Even as I settled into my new domesticity, as well as working long hours to build up the Paddington practice that I'd recently purchased from old Mr. Farquhar, it seemed that I remained quite involved in Holmes's investigations. In recent weeks he had requested my assistance in various quarters of London and the countryside, including a visit to Herefordshire in connection with the vicious McCarthy killing. More recently we had looked into the matter of the three-sided coin, and the subsequent terror-filled entrapment of Miss Sarah Wentlow. Another time, Mr. Farquhar himself had turned up at my door, having learned of my association with Holmes, and in dire need of help in disentangling himself from a grasping and conniving nephew. And soon after that, we had dashed up to Birmingham to clear away the mess in which young Hall Pycroft found himself.

I was passing through Baker Street several days later and decided to stop in for a few minutes and see what was on Holmes's docket. There had been some talk that he might be called to the north to look into a dispute between two landholders with conflicting charters – "Nothing that would interest you, Watson," he'd said – but I found him at home, in conference with our old friend, Kirbishaw, the lawyer. I believe that they had known each other since some case from Holmes's Montague Street days, although neither had as yet shared the circumstances of their first meeting. I began to excuse my interruption, but Holmes waved me in, calling at the same time down to Mrs. Hudson for more tea.

"Kirbishaw is just explaining a little law to me about Mr. Pycroft's status," Holmes indicated, preparing a cigar. Kirbishaw and I had both refused. "I believe that his position is once again secure after his misguided fiasco."

Kirbishaw nodded. He was a heavy-set man, probably in his late-fifties at that point, although his love of rich foods and wine had aged him up a bit. He was always quite jolly, however, and a good companion with whom to while away an hour or two in pleasant conversation.

"Nothing that unusual about it, actually," said Kirbishaw. "There was something similar in one of the City banks – now long defunct – back in the sixties."

Mrs. Hudson arrived then and, after Kirbishaw took a sip of his fresh tea, he continued. "Something a bit more interesting came my way earlier today. Thought I'd mention it to you – to see if you're interested."

Holmes didn't literally sit up in the way that a hound is suddenly alert when catching the scent, but he didn't fool me. I had known him for too long.

"Indeed," he said laconically. "Pray – share with us."

Kirbishaw shook his head. "I can't tell it as well as the verger – it's his story, you see, and he shared it when our paths crossed this morning. If he's free tomorrow, can you drop by my chambers and meet with him?"

Holmes confirmed that he could and, when it was arranged that I could be there as well, our conversation turned in other directions.

And so it was that on the following afternoon, Holmes picked me up in a cab and we made our way across the city to the Inner Temple. I had hoped to finally see Kirbishaw's chambers in King's Bench Walk for myself, having heard about them before from Holmes, but it was not to be. Holmes explained that he'd had a message from the lawyer that it was more convenient for the verger to meet with us at Temple Church, where he carried out his service.

I had been in the church the previous year, when Holmes and I were summoned by Inspector Youghal of the Yard to get to the bottom of the affair of the shifting of stones in the church's cellar. But at that time, we hadn't been introduced to the verger, Clement Mason. He was about Kirbishaw's age, but where the lawyer was well-fed and settled, Mason was tall and thin. Yet there was nothing delicate him. Instead of being stick-like and fragile, he gave the impression of being weathered and toughened, with a whip-like energy about him. In truth, he suggested to me what Holmes himself would look like at that age.

With him was a man in his mid-thirties, closer to Holmes's and my own age, introduced as Mason's nephew, Aaron Todd. I didn't need to be Sherlock Holmes to recognize that the fellow was a cabbie.

The verger ushered us through the majestic Round Church and past the knights' effigies, and so on until we were ensconced in a small but cozy office. The smell of old books and tobacco was quite comforting and, after tea was poured, the verger began.

"Thank you for joining us today, gentlemen," he said. "When I related this curious affair to Kirbishaw yesterday, as we passed the time while strolling in the Temple Gardens, it was fresh on my mind, and he felt that something like this, Mr. Holmes, would be right up your alley.

"Yet," he continued, "it's really my nephew's story first. Aaron?"

The younger man cleared his throat. "Well, sirs, as you probably know, cabbies like to keep to a certain patch, unless directed to go further.

I stick to Clerkenwell, stretching as far as St. Pancras and Euston at times on a normal day. I have my routes, and I know those of the other cabbies, like they know mine. We're not in competition, strictly – there's enough to go around for all of us – but we do have our regulars too, and we don't poach.

"One of my friends, another driver named Claude Wells, has a regular job that he does for a man that lives in Hardwick Street, near the corner with Garnault Mews. But Claude was hurt a couple of weeks ago – a wheel ran over his foot pretty badly – and he can't drive for a while. Rather than lose that job, he asked me to take it over temporarily. So I went around to the house and introduced myself on the next day that Claude was to drive for him. The man, a Mr. Montfield, seemed a little suspicious, but I convinced him that Claude had sent me. Then, he handed me a cardboard box, about a foot long on each side, sealed up and tied, and addressed to the Weights and Measures Office on Roseberry Avenue. He counted out some coins and told me to take the box and leave it in the lobby, making sure that I didn't speak to anyone there, inside or out. This was square with what Claude had already explained to me, so I didn't think too much about it.

"Claude had said that he'd been doing things like this for Mr. Montfield for the better part of a year – picking up similar-sized boxes and leaving them in different businesses and buildings all over that part of London. He's always careful to get away before anyone asks a question. At first he was a bit leery of it all – thinking that the man might be boxing up some sort of infernal devices to be left where they could cause mischief – but he never heard of any problems connected with it. No fires broke out, nor any explosions, and so he didn't object when the work stayed steady – twice a week, like clockwork.

"I stopped in to see Claude that night, and told him where I'd been sent. He nodded and said that he'd been there a few times as well. Then he asked me if I'd seen the watching man. I asked him what he meant, and why he hadn't mentioned it before. He explained that not long after he'd started, he'd seen a man standing across Hardwick Street, in a doorway, watching him intently. If the man hadn't been focused on him so strongly, he might never have been noticed. But he was, and once Claude saw him that first time, he noticed him again – not every time, mind you, and not every week, but often enough, and in the same place – enough so that he became suspicious. Sometimes the man followed him in another cab.

"After two or three months, Claude finally asked Mr. Montfield about it, although he'd held off before then because he didn't want to do anything to disrupt this steady task. Mr. Montfield's only response was to smile and nod, as if this made sense to him, and pleased him.

"While Claude has been healing, I've carried on for several more trips, going to the Corporation Buildings off Crawford Passage, and St. Peter's Chapel near the Clerkenwell Road, and once all the way to a lawyer's office in the Raymond Buildings. I saw the watching man a couple of other times, always in the same place. Then, two trips ago, on Tuesday when I was going to Ridler's Hotel in Holborn, I realized that I was being followed – another cab was sticking to me like glue, like Claude had said. On a corner, I could see that the passenger was this same man. It made me wonder how many times that I'd been followed before and hadn't realized it.

"I knew that cabbie somewhat – a shifty fellow named Akins – and cornered him the next day in the cabmen's shelter. It turns out that he has something of the same arrangement – every week or so, on a Tuesday or Thursday, or sometimes both, this man hires him to wait around the corner while he slips into Hardwick Street to watch Mr. Montfield's house. Then, after Claude – and now me – picks up the package, this man runs back and jumps into Akins' cab, and they follow to wherever it's addressed that day. From what he said, it's been going on for nearly as long as the packages have been being sent.

"Claude will be well enough to return to work in a week or so, but I'd planned to keep doing this until he's back, rather jealous of the easy work. And then, yesterday, Mr. Montfield handed me a box addressed here, to Temple Church. I know that I'm supposed to slip in and out without speaking to anyone, and just leave it tucked against a wall somewhere, but I thought that as long as I was here, I might take a minute and say hello to my uncle. I did, and after we spoke for a few minutes, I explained why I was here, and – well, my uncle can tell the next part better."

Mason, the verger, cleared his throat. "I was amazed, frankly, to see that my own nephew was delivering these packages, as they have been such a mystery over the last year. They are always the same size, as Aaron said – about a cubic foot – and simply addressed to *Temple Church*, in plain handwritten script. The first one that we found caused some confusion, but no great concern. But when they continued to irregularly arrive, it became something of an amusement, and then an irritant."

"And what is in these mysterious boxes?" asked Holmes – a question uppermost in my own mind as well.

The verger turned in his chair, leaned forward, and then made some effort to lift a box from the floor behind him. "See for yourself. We've disposed of the others, but this one brought by Aaron yesterday morning is typical."

Holmes and I stood up while Kirbishaw simply leaned back and sipped his tea, watching with a smile. Instead of directly opening the box,

322

Holmes peered at it closely, walking to different sides of the verger's desk in order to see the entire thing. Then, pulling his lens from his pocket, he studied the address – simply *Temple Church* as described. Finally he leaned forward and smelled the box before opening it.

To say that it was disappointing would be an understatement – for it appeared to be filled with old copies of *The Times*, folded awkwardly to take up the entire space.

"Is there anything else underneath?" I asked.

The verger shook his head. "Just the newspapers. That is the way of it every time. A box full of someone else's trash."

Holmes began pulling the various issues out, looking at them closely. "Hmm. Multiple copies of the same issue, neatly folded and seemingly never read. The date is only four days ago. These have apparently been purchased directly from a vendor. I wonder – is the date significant?" He looked up at the verger. "Did the previous boxes also contain clean copies of *The Times*, only a few days old?"

Mason nodded. "Usually, although once the box contained copies of *The Star*. However, those were also unread copies, only a few days old."

"And the other boxes?" Holmes asked Aaron Todd. "Did they seem to be the same weight as this one?"

"They did. Same size box, too, exactly as Claude described."

"It's a standard cardboard box," muttered Holmes. "It doesn't seem to have been previously used. There is no evidence of a prior shipping label, and the sides are relatively clean and unscuffed." He looked back at Mason. "There was a string?"

The verger pulled open his desk drawer and the handed a twine tangle to Holmes. I could see that it had been cut, preserving the knot – a fact that I thought would please Holmes. Yet he shook his head. "A very common and amateur knot. It can tell us nothing."

"But wait – " interjected Kirbishaw. "I can add my own brick in this wall. You see, when I heard Mr. Mason's story, something about it – specifically the name 'Montfield' – sounded familiar. After my visit to Baker Street yesterday, I asked a few of my colleagues, and learned a most curious story.

"You may have heard of Lucius Montfield, the American millionaire. He grew up in New Hampshire, the younger son of a munitions manufacturer. Instead of joining the family business, he became a doctor, and after their Civil War, when the family had greatly increased their wealth, he became disgusted with their role in the war against the Confederate traitors, and how little mercy was being shown to the South during the Reconstruction. He came to England and bought the house on Hardwick Street – a rather frugal house for a man of his means, for he had inherited a sizeable amount of his father's fortune. His wife had died years before, so it was just him and his two sons – twins, yet as different in temperament as can be.

"I have all this from his Montfield's attorney, Marchmont, who shared as much as he could without violating a confidence. Montfield lived a retiring life and kept to himself, sometimes venturing out to a concert, but more often staying in. In truth, it seems as if he was changed somehow by the war, becoming withdrawn as he aged. This had a curious and opposite effect on his sons, as they become rather generous, assisting charities when they are able, and lending their efforts to good works. Yet strangely they only feel enmity towards one another, to their father's despair, right up to when he died.

"No one knows how it started, this feeling between the brothers, and often these things cannot be explained. But if one of them, Peter for instance, favored a certain charitable cause, the other, Jonathan, would actively turn his attentions a different way. While this is essentially harmless in and of itself, and certainly benefitted the respective charities, their bickering vexed their father to no end. When he sickened suddenly and neared death a year ago, he called them both to his bedside and told them something – whatever it was Marchmont would not reveal, and quite right too! – and since Lucius Montfield's passing soon after, they have carried out a most bizarre series of activities.

"Peter, the elder, was allowed to remain in the Hardwick Street house until such time as some requirement is fulfilled – Marchmont wouldn't tell me exactly what that is. Since then, Peter, living on a most meagre allowance, has refused to leave the premises, presumably searching for something inside and using the butler, in the family's service since the twins were very small, to run errands and have most of the dealings with the outside world. Meanwhile, Jonathan, cut off from any income until the condition has been fulfilled, has taken a job at a nearby hotel, but he spends much of his free time loitering and hiding in the street, watching the house – Lord knows for what!" Kirbishaw leaned back. "How this relates to these mysterious and useless packages delivered all over London for nearly a year is beyond me, and Marchmont didn't seem to have any ideas either, even if he could have answered more of my questions."

We were silent as Kirbishaw's narrative wound down to silence. I think that we could each think of questions of our own, but they would have booted no useful response, as none of us knew the answers. Finally, it was Holmes who effectively ended the conference. "I'll look into it," he said, "and report as to what I discover." He took a moment to verify with Kirbishaw where Jonathan Montfield was employed, and then stood, nodded, and left in that abrupt way of his when he is finished and ready to turn his attentions elsewhere.

I tendered my goodbyes as well and followed, joining him as we walked up Inner Temple Lane to Fleet Street. "What do you intend?" I asked in the quiet of the lane, just before we reached the bustle of the thoroughfare.

"I believe that I shall cultivate the acquaintance of Mr. Jonathan Montfield, as his brother Peter – ensconced as he is in the Hardwick Street house, might be much harder to meet by accident." He hailed a hansom. "Return home, Watson, and I shall be by tonight or tomorrow. Sadly, today is Friday, so it will be several days before the next performance by Peter Montfield and his cab-conveyed packages. But perhaps that it is a blessing, allowing me to gather as many facts as possible before next week."

Then, seeing that I had secured the cab, he touched the brim of his fore-and-aft cap, which he wears throughout the year, city or country, turned, and vanished into the throng.

As I returned home, I pondered what we had heard, and wondered what Holmes might discover from the younger twin, who spent his free moments spying on his former home, now in the hands of his brother. I suspected that Holmes was making his way to one of his hidey-holes throughout the city where he stored clothing and other accoutrements and appurtenances to aid in his disguised transformations.

My wife had listened to my tale with great interest during dinner, and was as intrigued as I when Holmes arrived not long after. I was rather surprised that he was there so soon, and also that he was dressed as himself, rather than in the guise of a groom or defrocked clergyman, or any of the other dozens of identities that he was wont to assume during an investigation. He noted my reaction, and, after Mary had excused herself, he began to explain.

"I did consider taking on some other personality, so as to win Jonathan Montfield's confidence," he said, "but after quickly visiting the hotel where he works, and asking a few well-placed questions that established the good-natured character of the fellow, I decided that the direct approach might be best. He was willing to talk with me when his labors ended for the day, and we met in a nearby pub. I truthfully explained how I came to be interested in the matter, and offered my services to clear up whatever stands between him and his brother.

"He shook his head ruefully. 'It is a shame that the two of us cannot get along. We could accomplish so much pulling in tandem. But no matter our best intentions, we soon fall to fighting, and not long after that hateful words are being hurled at one another.'

325

"He went on to explain how bad it had become in the year or so before his father's death, and to what degree it had pained the old man. He'd tried several times to heal the breach between his sons, but to no avail, and finally at his deathbed, he'd called his sons together, where he showed them a sheet of paper.

"'This,' he explained, 'contains the riddle to receiving my inheritance. You must each solve it. Peter, as the oldest, will keep possession of the house until the solution is presented to my lawyer, Marchmont.' He carefully tore the paper long-ways down the middle, giving one side to Peter and the other to Jonathan. Then, taking both their hands, he looked from one to the other and said, 'I love you both. God bless you, and God bless the United States! *E pluribus unum!*' And so saying, he lapsed into a coma from which he was never to awaken, and died the next day.

"They'd each met separately with Marchmont, and he seemed to know what it was about. He enforced that Jonathan should move out, without an allowance, until such time as the riddle was solved. In the meantime, Peter stayed in the Hardwick Street house, but subsisting on only the stingiest of funds, until he could present a solution.

"Jonathan had studied his own half of the sheet, and had made a few efforts at a solution, but when he presented them to Marchmont, he was informed that he was incorrect. He had the sense that the same had happened for Peter. In the meantime, he kept watch on the house to see if Peter was looking for the inheritance, as he'd intimated a belief that the solution was hidden within the building. It wasn't long before Jonathan saw that his brother was sending out the mysterious packages. He has no idea what is in them, but he's certain that it has something to do with the inheritance. He's able to watch the house on Tuesdays and Thursdays only, in relation to his scheduled employment, and doesn't seem to realize that these are also the only days in which the packages are sent – which seems to imply that brother Peter is only doing this on days that he knows that Jonathan will be watching."

"How curious," I said. By this point we were sitting before the fire, each enjoying a pipe. "But this riddle?" I asked. "What did you make of that?"

"Ah, yes," he said, pulling a folded strip from his pocket and handing it to me. "He lent me the original," Holmes explained. As described, it was a strip of paper, torn top to bottom from a larger sheet. The writing on it was rather feeble, as if done by a dying man. Jonathan's was the right side of the paper, and the words consisted of only a few lines along the ragged left edge:

326

Carefully watch
to find my fortune.
Your Brother
someone who will
be
your enemy
untrustworthy. Your ally is
always there to
be your guide.
Take this sheet, and
lay it before my lawyer, and
when he sees it,
will you obtain
my legacy.

I handed it back. "I hope that Lucius Montfield was an adequate doctor. He was certainly no poet."

Holmes smiled. "I think that he tried something when he was near death, hoping that it would work, and did the best that he could."

"What does it mean?" I asked. "Is it a cipher? Should we count every third word, as in the matter of that old escaped convict who remained hidden for so long in Norfolk?"

"By no means. This is easily settled. I've arranged for Kirbishaw and the two brothers to meet tomorrow morning at Marchmont's office – if that's convenient, of course."

I wouldn't have missed it for the world, and said so.

The following morning found us at Marchmont's office at Gray's Inn. He had done some legal work for me before, and I had last seen him the previous year during those terrible events connected with The Eye of Heka. He greeted us and led the way back to an inner office with a large table. Kirbishaw was already seated there, along with Jonathan Montfield, a pleasant looking fellow who rose to shake my hand, and then Holmes's. We were getting settled when the door opened and a man who looked very much like Jonathan entered, a suspicious look upon his face. This, then, was older brother Peter. He apparently knew why we were there. He was friendly enough to all but his brother Jonathan, to whom he did not speak or acknowledge.

"Let us begin," said Holmes, pulling out Jonathan's half of the sheet. After identifying it, he read the curious message aloud before laying it in the center of the table, asking, "What do you suppose that it means?"

Marchmont was silently watching with a gleam in his eye. Kirbishaw, having heard the lines for the first time, looked puzzled. "It's a warning –

advising Jonathan that his brother is untrustworthy. But his seems counter to what we heard about their father wishing to unify them. And the second part refers to some ally who will serve as a guide. And finally, the sheet advises that it be laid before '*my lawyer*' – Marchmont, I assume – to obtain the legacy." He looked at Marchmont. "Well, there it is. Does that satisfy the requirement?"

"No," said Marchmont firmly. "It does not."

"I've brought it to him before," added Jonathan, "but it did no good."

"Is there some code involved?" asked Kirbishaw. "If so, I don't see what it could tell us."

Holmes smiled and shook his head. "Watson asked the same question. No, when considering all the facts, the meaning is quite clear." He turned to the older brother. "Did you bring your sheet, as requested?"

I had been watching Peter Montfield as he heard the lines on his brother's sheet. His face had become more and more puzzled, and without a word, he pulled a similar document from his pocket, the left side of the torn sheet, and handed it to Holmes, who unrolled it and read aloud:

> *Search diligently*
> *to find the treasure*
> *Trust*
> *the man that is*
> *always*
> *your ally, and not*
> *your brother. He is not*
> *someone who will*
> *be your strength;*
> *Take this paper, yes*
> *present it to my lawyer*
> *Only then*
> *will you receive*
> *my fortune*

"Why, it's the same!" said Jonathan.

"Not quite," said Holmes, "although it follows essentially the same format – 'Search diligently' versus 'Carefully watch'. A warning about the brother and a recommendation to trust an ally. Present the paper to the lawyer. Did you also present this to Mr. Marchmont?"

Peter Montfield nodded. "It did no good. He told me to keep thinking."

Holmes nodded. "Can you tell us why you were sending packages all over London?" He then looked at the rest of us. "I've already told Mr.

Peter Montfield, as part of my invitation here this morning, how we learned of this matter, based on the cab-driver's testimony."

Peter lowered his eyes before sheepishly replying, "It was simply to discourage Jonathan, and to fool him into thinking that I was making progress at finding father's legacy. I knew that he was working at a nearby hotel, and when I noticed him watching the house – "

" – To see if you were tearing it part looking for treasure!" interjected Jonathan.

Peter nodded. "I decided to give you something to watch, to make you think that I was actually accomplishing something, even as I tried to puzzle out Father's last message. I had Beeton – he's our old butler – keep a steady supply of boxes and newspapers in the house, and I arranged to have them carried all over London." He smiled, but there was no animosity in it. "It was amusing to watch you follow the cabs as they carried away boxes of useless newspapers."

Jonathan smiled too, as if the joke wasn't lost on him.

"And yet," Holmes said, "in a year, neither of you has solved the riddle." He looked at Jonathan. "Could you repeat for me again your father's last words?"

"He said that he loved us, and he blessed us, and the United States as well. He was always a great patriot, and it broke his heart to see how the country turned after the War."

"No, what did he say exactly?"

"Well, it was, 'I love you both. God bless you, and God bless the United States! *E pluribus unum!*'"

"Exactly. And what does that final phrase mean to you?"

"I'm not sure," replied Jonathan. "We didn't study Latin. It's something of an American motto, I believe."

Holmes turned to the elder brother. "Do you agree?"

"Yes. Father often said it when he discussed his experiences during the War, and the reunification of the States."

Holmes then asked Marchmont, "Would you care to translate for us?"

The lawyer shook his head. "I cannot."

"Cannot, or will not?"

"It's all the same," said Marchmont with a smile.

"Oh, for heaven's sake," growled Kirbishaw. "Let's put an end to this silliness. It means '*Out of many, one*'."

Holmes tossed Peter Montfield's sheet on the table. "I see that you're caught up as well, Kirbishaw. Would you care to do the honors?"

"Gladly," he replied, rising and leaning forward, placing the two sheets together so that Peter's left-hand portion lined up once again with Jonathan's right-hand segment. "Out of many, one," said Kirbishaw.

Around the table, the rest of us – less Marchmont – stood as well, leaning forward to read:

> *Search diligently – Carefully watch*
> *to find the treasure – to find my fortune.*
> *Trust – Your Brother*
> *the man that is – someone who will*
> *always – be*
> *your ally, and not – your enemy*
> *your brother. He is not – untrustworthy. Your ally is*
> *someone who will – always there to*
> *be your strength; be your guide.*
> *Take this paper, yes – Take this sheet, and*
> *present it to my lawyer – lay it before my lawyer, and*
> *Only then – when he sees it,*
> *will you receive – will you obtain*
> *my fortune – my legacy.*

Holmes faced Marchmont. "Does that fulfill the requirement?"

"I'm not sure that Lucius meant for an outsider to intervene before the boys could learn their lesson – " Marchmont said, but with a smile.

"Does it?" interrupted Kirbishaw, also smiling. "They're here together, and the meaning of the sheet is revealed."

Marchmont nodded. "It does." But then he looked sternly from Peter to Jonathan. "But I hope that you understand what your father was trying to teach you, even if you didn't exactly work it out on your own. Together you will be one another's strength and guide. Forget these silly differences of personality. Work together, and fill one's weaknesses with the other's strengths, and you can achieve some really good things."

And so it proved. The wealth left by their father was far greater than either had realized, and the two young men learned to value their differences as they went on to do a great deal of good for the fortunate citizens of London.

As we left Marchmont's office that morning, not yet realizing how well the brothers would be able to reconcile, I started to ask what Holmes had gotten from this. He'd had no real client, after all. But when I saw the newfound reunion between the two brothers, laughing at their activities over the past year in the matter of the cardboard boxes, and Holmes as he watched them, I realized that he meant it when he sometimes averred that the work is its own reward.

The Bizarre Adventure
of the Octagon House

. . . with Solar Pons and Dr. Parker,
and others . . .

Editor's Note: *The following narrative involves Solar Pons, "The Sherlock Holmes of Praed Street", and his friend and biographer, Dr. Lyndon Parker. For those unfamiliar with Pons and Parker, I urge you to correct that mistake at your earliest opportunity . . . .*

* * * * *

". . . time had been pressing heavily on [Solar Pons's] hands since the bizarre adventure of the Octagon House."

– "The Adventure of the Frightened Baronet"
In Re: Sherlock Holmes
Early October 1922

W hile I had awakened quite early that morning, I discovered when I came down to breakfast that Sherlock Holmes had awakened earlier still.

"Ah, Watson!" He pushed an empty plate back and reached for his coffee cup. "Were you able to sleep?"

"A bit. In addition to last night's physically taxing activities, the things that we saw – " I shut my eyes for a few seconds. "Well, as you know, they don't make for pleasant dreams."

"Indeed. And the thought that haunts me is that even as we cleaned out that one singular nest of suffering, there are others – Ten? Twenty? A hundred? – spread across the city that will continue today as they did yesterday or fifty years ago, and as they will tomorrow, and we cannot do a thing to locate or stop every one of them."

With that, my housekeeper pushed open the door and delivered my breakfast. I found that I was hungry, and the hot coffee was a godsend. As I ate, Holmes drank the last of his cup, and appeared to be in a pensive mood.

We had been up quite late the night before, watching as the Stockwell Slayer, Ethan Rowan, made his stealthy way to one of those shabby and sagging little houses lying just east of where Regent's Canal joins the Limehouse Basin, between the iron works and the Commercial Road. He'd knocked on the door that Holmes had identified beforehand, indicating that the information he'd received was reliable.

I was surprised that Rowan went straight to the door instead of trying to sneak in, considering his agenda, but perhaps he had a plan of some sort – likely involving violence, considering his peculiar skills. After a period of time that stretched until we didn't think there would be an answer, the door slowly opened, but we couldn't see who stood inside, as the room beyond was in shadow. Then, to the surprise of the Stockwell Slayer and also that of whomever was just inside the house, fourteen constables and three inspectors rushed from where they were concealed in nearby alleys, their loud and intentionally confusing roars causing extreme confusion for Rowan and the immediate occupant of the building, if only for the moment required to overwhelm and disable them. The official force then surged through the door and stormed past the rest of the building's considerable defenses before any effective resistance could be mounted, and more importantly before the young women being held there could be permanently silenced.

It was over almost as soon as it had begun, and the sounds of police whistles in the street calling for a procession of Black Marias to assemble outside caused countless neighbors to peep from behind pulled curtains – but only for a moment before the curtains flicked closed again, lest one of the watchers be observed and somehow drawn into this affair.

A dozen men displaying signs of a variety of foreign backgrounds were dragged from the house, under arrest. Somehow in the initial confusion, Rowan broke loose and fled deeper into the house. He was a brutal killer, having the deaths of eight women held against him, and yet he was discovered sobbing like a child beside a shackled girl of no more than fifteen years of age. It was his sister, Lily, taken by the slavers who had been ensconced within this filthy house. It was an unnerving sight.

Only three days before, Holmes had been tasked with tracking Rowan in order to prevent him from carrying out yet another of those bizarre murders that had so captured the imagination of the public and press during that long summer. While ostensibly retired and living the life of a reclusive Sussex apiarist, enjoying his well-earned rest after the end of the War over three years earlier, he could be lured back to London for the occasional investigation, especially if particularly requested by one of his old friends at Scotland Yard – and in this case, the man asking for Holmes's help was Superintendent Alec MacDonald, now retired, but still with his finger in more than a few official pies.

Holmes had quickly identified the patterns behind the killings, and through the use of those contacts that he still maintained within the capital, he was able to cast his nets in several carefully chosen directions, taking only a few days to identify Rowan as the man who had been sought by the official force for the past four months. It only required a little longer to determine where Rowan was hiding, and to begin carefully following him. But Holmes wasn't satisfied with simply having Rowan arrested – the man's actions as he lurked in Limehouse seemed unusual, for that was far from his usual hunting grounds. It quickly became apparent that something else was going on, as Rowan was paying particular interest to that house just east of the Regent's Canal locks.

Holmes was staying with me in my Queen Anne Street lodgings during the time he was in London, but he didn't involve me any more than necessary, as I had my practice to maintain – limited though it was at that point. I would turn seventy that August. After the War, I had reduced my obligations, seeing only certain long-time patients while still putting in a few hours a week at Barts. Therefore I wasn't with Holmes on the morning that he met with Denis Nayland Smith at Scotland Yard to ask him some questions.

Holmes had simply wished to obtain the latest updated information about Limehouse in general, but the mention of the address that seemed to fascinate Rowan had instantly alerted Nayland Smith, who had made such a careful study of that region, and particularly of the Devil Doctor who permeated its every crack and crevice like a deadly and mephitic miasma. Suddenly the question of why Rowan was acting unusual took on a great deal more gravity.

Over the next day or so, Holmes gained further understanding of the situation by way of his own agents, who carefully canvassed Limehouse while asking guarded questions, and additionally he conscripted Solar Pons and Dr. Lyndon Parker into the affair, for they, like Holmes and me, had previously crossed paths with the Limehouse Doctor. Holmes and I also took a morning to visit our friend the Belgian consultant at 14 Farraway Street, who was even then, following the marriage and move by his friend Captain Hastings to Argentina the previous autumn, in the process of stepping up his own early initial investigations into the Doctor (later named by his biographer, with the most understandable motive of obfuscation in mind, under the sobriquet *Li Chang Yen.*)

Nayland Smith and our friend Dr. Petrie insisted on being in at the kill, and so we found ourselves that night walking through the filthy house, in the wake of the army of policeman who had just stormed the place, examining the dreadful conditions forced upon the prisoners, and doing what we could to help those poor young women chained there, none of whom had even been reported as missing. The Doctor and his agents had done their work very well, carefully identifying those whose absence would not be noticed, and then quietly removing them from their normal lives as the first step in a long chain of events that would end in their deaths, but only after the intervening months when their existence would have been worse than death. Yet somehow they had foolishly taken the Stockwell Slayer's sister along with the rest. Likely they had believed her as alone and disconnected as the others, not realizing that Rowan had severed connections with her after his return from the War, when he started to understand the terrible desires that were overtaking him, and which could only be sated by the spilling of blood.

When his beloved sister was abducted, his own animal cunning and unique skills had soon led him to the slavers' door, but even with the deadly methods that he'd learned during four terrible years on the Continent, it was doubtful that he could have rescued his sister alone. It seemed that he wasn't thinking clearly, and we never did learn what he'd hoped to accomplish once he entered the house. Only the sheer good luck of Holmes's involvement in the matter at the right time to observe Rowan's unusual behavior had led to a better ending.

The constables dragged Rowan away from his sister, and I made him understand through his wracking sobs that she was not dead, but only sedated, and that she would make a full recovery. He finally comprehended what I was saying, but then became frantic yet again when he wasn't allowed to stay with her, instead being taken away to be charged with his own crimes. Parker, Petrie, and I did what we could to help her and the others, working as quickly and efficiently as if we were back in the field hospitals where we had served only a few years before. We made the various young women ready for transport to Barts, and I despaired to see that some were in a terrible condition. Although I hated to believe that such violations could occur in England, I truly wasn't surprised.

As the various physicians labored to provide comfort to our patients, Holmes, Pons, and Nayland Smith ventured into the tunnels beneath the house, but they found nothing of any use. The passages ran back towards the Basin and also in the opposite direction, deeper into Limehouse. Holmes later described the brick and stonework, indicating that some of it was quite ancient, possibly Roman, while other sections were more recently constructed. However, the age was irrelevant when considering the terrible and vile crimes that were trafficked there on a regular basis.

There was no one to be found in the tunnels, and before very much exploration could occur, the sound of muffled and distant explosions occurred in several directions. Someone was systematically destroying the tunnels. For a few moments, there was the very real fear that explosives might also have been set in the chambers where we were caring for the mistreated girls, and Inspector Jamison, in charge of the police, efficiently started evacuating much faster than before. Maiwand was over forty years before, and on a hot, dusty and bloody plain instead of a dank shadowed Limehouse tunnel, but the urgent feeling of being a physician in battle during those few moments felt very much the same.

Dirt fell from the bricked arches that formed the chambers in which we labored, and I feared that the roof might collapse from sheer age or shoddy workmanship, rather than deliberately planted explosives. A moment later a rolling wave of dust came toward us from the tunnels, and it was only then that it occurred to me to be concerned for our friends who had been exploring that nest of villainy.

Holmes and the others had been pressing deeper into the earth when the explosions began. There was no question as to what was being done, and Solar Pons yelled for everyone to flee back the way they'd come. They hadn't gone far when the choking dust overtook them, and Holmes later told me that having an electric torch in hand proved to be useless – the light couldn't penetrate any distance whatsoever, and it was only useful as a tool to judge if one was about to immediately walk into a tunnel wall.

Soon the dust cleared, however, and Holmes, Pons, and Nayland Smith, along with several policemen who had accompanied them, found that they had kept the same pace during their retreat, and ended up in approximately the same location. As they discussed the likelihood that cave-ins now blocked the tunnels in every direction away from the chamber with the rescued prisoners, one of the constables began to wander a bit from the group. It was only Pons's keen eye – which noticed when the officer's torchlight passed for a just fraction of a second across a trip wire – and his quick lunge that pulled the young fellow abruptly back from where he'd nearly broken it, that prevented that portion of the ceiling with thousands of pounds of rock and dirt from blowing to pieces just over our heads.

Later, as we stood outside and we three physicians were informed about what had been found underground, Pons stated, "When interest in this house has died down – in a week or a year – the Doctor's minions will certainly be set to work reopening the tunnels – working in the dark and in secret, and above-ground there will never be a hint of what's going on. They will clear them in the same way that ants rush to rebuild their mound when a careless passing heel crushes it. In the meantime, the Doctor will simply shift what he needs from here to elsewhere."

Holmes nodded. "We've won a battle, but the war isn't over."

Nayland Smith agreed, and then he proceeded to horrify us with a succinctly related list of the Doctor's other ongoing plans. We were frankly a bit overwhelmed with the knowledge provided by the admirable gentleman. With that, the night's work seemed to be complete, and we all went our different ways.

The next morning, Holmes seemed disinclined to discuss the matter, and I could tell that his thoughts had turned toward returning to Sussex. I expected that he would take the mid-morning train from Victoria and, while it wasn't worth confirming, I began to say something along those lines when the doorbell rang.

Never one to rely completely upon servants, I stepped that way myself to find a shiny-faced constable on my doorstep. "Dr. Watson?" he asked with a bit of bright-eyed anticipation.

I agreed that I was, and he asked in the same tone if Mr. Holmes was available. Without speaking, I nodded him in, and then led him through to the dining room. Holmes, his coffee in hand, raised an eyebrow inquiringly.

"A message from Inspector Jamison, sir," he said. "About the killer, Rowan. It seems there's a bit of a complication."

"Indeed?" asked Holmes. "In what way?"

"He's admitted to all of the killings, except one. He swears that it wasn't one of his, and he won't take the blame for it. Seems to think that having one less on his bill of sale will somehow give him a credit and that we'll turn him loose to check on his sister." He shook his head.

"And which murder does he disclaim?"

"What? Oh, the girl from Twickenham. Sir Geoffrey Colsworth's daughter."

As I tried to recall details of the girl's murder, Holmes asked, "Did MacDonald send you?"

"He did, along with Inspector Jamison. They're at the Yard – "

"Tell them that we'll be along shortly."

The constable touched his helmet with a finger. "Very good, sir."

I shut the front door behind the officer while Holmes, standing behind me, turned and reentered the dining room, pouring us both some more coffee. I sat down across from him. "Sir Geoffrey's daughter was the fourth of Rowan's victims to be found."

"That's right. Back in May. Like the others, she was strangled, and then the body was left at random in an alley – that time in Bloomsbury. As I recall, it was a particularly brutal example of the Slayer's compulsion."

I deferred to Holmes's familiarity with the case. Of course I'd been aware of the murders. The first, a shop girl from Stockwell and the sole support of her aged mother, had seemed like just another terrible London killing. She was found against the ruins of the Roman wall, not far from the Underground entrance near the Tower. There was some question as to whether she was killed there, or hauled from somewhere else and left in the middle of the night. Another murder had followed a week later – a nurse returning home from her shift at Bedlam. Strangled the same as the first, she had been found in an alley not far from the hospital – which was an unusual fact, in that the other victims were all discovered a great distance from where they should have been when the killer caught them. It was this curious incident that gave Holmes a starting point toward identifying Rowan as the strangler, as he'd been a patient for a short time at the hospital after the War, which was where he'd met Betsy Hicks, the nurse who had died.

Apparently he'd fixated upon her, and his initial killing of Sarah Bates, the shop girl, had been some attempt to bleed off the pressures that were building within him in relation to the rebuff that he'd received from his former nurse. (We learned all of this, of course, after the fact, when the police interrogators and alienist had finished with him.) After killing Miss Hicks, the compulsion was still upon him, and he killed again and again – eight young women in all.

Oddly, the series of murders never seemed to panic the capital in the way that the Ripper's crimes had done thirty-four years earlier. I'd theorized about this as more bodies were discovered, speculating that it was possibly due to the fact that the murders were less brutal than the terrible butchery of '88, but more likely it was simply because we were still weary from the horrors of war, and these killings were just one more thing that had to be endured for a while. It was terrible to realize that fact, but likely true to a certain degree, nonetheless.

Only the death of Sir Geoffrey Colsworth's daughter had stood out during the series of crimes, for her body had been much more brutalized than the others. From what I'd understood, reading the files following Holmes's involvement in the matter, each of the other victims had been found strangled, but their faces were untouched, usually with a look of surprise upon them, as if this was not how they had expected their stories to end. In the case of Lady Eva Colsworth, there had been a great deal of damage, as she had clearly fought back, likely enraging her killer. Flesh, certainly scratched from the killer's face, had been found underneath her fingernails, and there were contusions along her head and shoulders where she had been pounded with something like a brick or a rock. Her face was nearly unrecognizable. No weapon had been found near the body – lying underneath a tree beside the road at 48 Doughty Street, one of Dickens' former homes. In spite of the damage to the corpse, it was this fact – that the body had been found far from any of her normal locations – that seemed to confirm that she was one of Rowan's victims. But now Rowan denied killing her, while he seemed willing to make his claim upon the other murders.

After Eve Colsworth died, the murders continued, returning to their pattern of strangulation and then abandonment of the body in an unexpected part of the city. While Holmes had narrowly missed catching Rowan after the eighth killing, he was finally in custody. Considering the passivity of the public's response, I wondered how much would even be addressed in the newspapers. I glanced at them, lying neatly stacked at the end of the table, but realized that I wouldn't have a chance to peruse them, certain that we would be leaving momentarily for the Yard.

And I was right. The day was filled with drizzle, and we had to walk to Harley Street, and so on down to Wigmore Street, before we could find a cab. After that, our progress was swift. Holmes was quiet throughout, and I had long ago learned that when he was pondering, it was best to leave him be.

The driver brought us to the river-side entrance of the Yard, and as we climbed out, I glanced over toward the Thames. In the misty morning light, it might have looked as it did half-a-century earlier, when I was a young fellow without a seeming care in the world, my worst problem being the soreness associated with rugby and getting thrown over the ropes and into the crowd at Old Deer Park. The boats on the river might be a bit bigger and sleeker, and their motors much more powerful and efficient, but when I gazed down at the Westminster Pier, it could have been that night in September 1888 when Holmes and I, along with poor old Inspector Athelney Jones, had set out to lie in wait for Jonathan Small, not realizing that just a little while later we'd face a much more sinister and unusual danger.

I was called back to the present when I sensed that Holmes had paused before entering, waiting for me to catch up. The smile on his face showed that once again he'd read my thoughts in their entirety. I nodded and joined him.

Scotland Yard had changed quite a bit since moving to its "new" digs just over thirty years before. It hadn't taken the Force long to settle in and quickly fill the space, but for quite a while the residents had helped maintain it with a sort of pride. Now, however, long after the original inhabitants who remembered the even older location in Great Scotland Yard were gone, the building was starting to show its age. It wasn't surprising, really. By its very nature, it saw hard and steady use, and the decades of grim business carried out there had taken their toll.

We made our way toward the area of the building housing the inspectors. I nodded to several that I knew, including Charles Parker (a distant relation of our friend the doctor), Stanislaus Oates, and of course the indomitable Jimmy Japp, whom had been with us in Limehouse the night before, and who had inherited Gregson's old office. Soon, however,

338

we progressed deeper into the building and arrived at a familiar door, but the plate no longer read *Inspector Lestrade.* Instead, the name *Jamison* was in its place.

We knocked and entered, finding the small space already crowded with the inspector, Solar Pons, Dr. Parker, and Spilsbury, the forensic specialist. It was he who had been speaking, standing at one end of Jamison's desk, and he seemed a bit peeved to be interrupted.

"Thank you for coming, gentlemen," said the inspector. "The doctor here was just explaining some additional facts regarding the death of Lady Eva Colsworth."

Holmes and I nodded to Pons and Parker and found seats in the cramped little room while Spilsbury continued. "Eva Colsworth was found early on the morning of May 14th, over two months ago in Doughty Streeet, by a passing laborer. She had clearly been dumped at that location after being murdered elsewhere – unlike the other victims who were simply strangled, there was quite a bit of damage to the body, particularly the frontal face and left side of her head, where she had been repeatedly struck by a right-handed person holding a blunt object while the killer's left hand grasped her throat, as well as the collar of her dress, which was ripped on her right side, corresponding to what I've described. There were also abrasions on her left shoulder. The dress there was ripped, indicating that some of the blows had missed the face, or hit the shoulder with the same swing.

"At the time –" Spilsbury paused, a small frown unusually passing across his face, as he was generally quite assertive and grimly confident. "At the time," he repeated, "there was no indication that this was anything other than another murder by that man whom the press began to call the 'Stockwell Slayer', curiously named for the place of residence of the first victim – albeit this killing was a bit more violent. That was put down to the lady's resistance, while the others had been too frightened or overwhelmed to fight back."

Spilsbury's mouth tightened. "I must admit that, while there were differences in this affair from the previous and subsequent victims, I did not – that is to say, I chose to forego additional investigation, having conducted the initial autopsy."

"Do you mean to say, Doctor," said Pons, "that you now have more information for us? I don't think that anyone here will begrudge that. You were correct to believe that Eva Colsworth's death was part of the same group of killings, in spite of the differences. It was what we all thought. Any new information that you have to help answer this new question as to whether or not Rowan is correct in denying his guilt in this one particular murder will only be appreciated."

Spilsbury swallowed. "Thank you, Mr. Pons. I . . . thank you. I fear that I became . . . complacent in this case." He turned towards Holmes. "I believe, sir, that you once faced a similar problem, when you told Dr. Watson here to whisper a word in your ear if it ever seemed that you weren't giving a case enough attention."

Holmes nodded. "Norbury – for the location of the investigation which turned out to not be a crime whatsoever, in spite of my initial beliefs. I assure you that Watson has had to remind me of it on numerous occasions. It is nothing of which to be ashamed."

Spilsbury nodded and lowered his eyes. I don't know when I've seen the man, rather known for his arrogance truth be told, seem so humble. I began to wonder just what he had seen or missed during the initial autopsy that was causing him so much doubt now.

"As I said," he continued, "the body was not killed where it was found – typical of these murders, and another sign that it was part of the same series. The violence was explained away, but I can say that I did complete a thorough examination, even if I didn't follow up on a certain clue that fell into my hands, as I wrongly deemed it unimportant."

I could see that Holmes was becoming impatient, and Pons too, but they both knew that Spilsbury was a professional who would arrive at the goal shortly. And he did.

"There were . . . smudges around the wounds. Mud streaks, essentially. I collected samples of each – all that I could retrieve, actually, since they would just be washed away by the undertaker during the preparation of the body. I also visited Doughty Street, where the body was found, and verified that this soil didn't match what was on the ground there." He paused and looked at us, as if awaiting questions.

Jamison frowned, and I could almost hear him about to growl, "Is that all this is, then?" but Holmes interrupted. "This could be useful. If we can find where she was killed, based on the soil sample, it might be possible to get on the trail of who actually killed her."

"From smears of dirt?" asked Jamison. "Isn't that searching in a haystack the size of London?"

Pons shook his head. "Quite a bit of work has been done on soil identification. Holmes here left me with his own notes when he retired, and I've done a bit of research since then – although not as much as some others." He looked at Spilsbury. "As I recall, the wounds were rounded, indicating that a rock, perhaps six or eight inches in diameter, had been the murder weapon. Is that correct?"

"It is, and no such rock was found with the body – another indication that it was dumped there in the early hours. I did check, of course, to verify that there were no indications of other shapes in the depressions that might

340

indicate a different weapon – no corners, for instance, that might have been from a board or brick, and no detritus like brick dust or splinters. The shape was definitely that of a rounded object, like a stone, applied repeatedly."

"She had time to fight back," added Parker. "She must have suffered terribly."

"Perhaps not," replied Spilsbury. "While the blows were terrible, she would have soon been unconscious, and the killer did finish her off by strangulation. The marks were vague, but they matched what we'd seen on the previous – and later – victims, so we had no reason to suspect a different killer. Perhaps," added Spilsbury, "for some reason that only Rowan could ever explain, he *did* kill this young lady as well, but in his madness, there is some reason that won't allow him to admit it."

"That is possible," said Holmes, "but just in case, we'll follow up to make sure that if there is another murderer, he or she doesn't escape by letting the blame die with Rowan."

At that point there was a knock on the door and Inspector Japp leaned in, addressing Jamison. "M. Poirot is here to give us additional information regarding that Aberystwith case, if you can join us."

Behind his desk, Jamison nodded. "I'll be there in a moment." Japp departed and Jamison stood. "Your help in this matter is much appreciated, gentlemen. As you know, Sir Geoffrey Colsworth is a pretty important chap right now, and this business of his daughter's murder has interest at the highest levels. It was bad enough when she was killed as part of a string of unrelated crimes of madness. But if there's something else involved – if someone saw that these stranglings were occurring and decided to hide her murder amongst them – we'll need to get to the bottom of it sooner rather than later. I understand," he added, glancing toward Pons, "that your brother has taken an interest. Please let me know what I can next do to help."

Pons nodded. "I believe that a visit with Sir Geoffrey will be of some initial help – along with obtaining further information about that soil." He looked at Spilsbury.

"Of course. I'll go retrieve the samples now, and meet you in the front lobby." He slipped from the room.

The rest of us stood, said our goodbyes to the inspector, and filed out toward the front entrance. It was as busy here as deeper in the building, but a different kind of busy, for it was there that the business of the Yard intersected awkwardly with the public – men and women arriving for interviews, or to hear facts about crimes which had touched their lives (either as victims or perpetrators), or to learn terrible news, or to report it. I was glad when Spilsbury joined us in a couple of minutes to give several glassine bags to Pons. Then with a nod, he returned to his gleaming rooms deep within the building, each of them shiny and sterile and well-lit, and with a sinister drain in the floor beneath gleaming metal tables on wheels.

Outside, Pons handed the bags to Holmes. "Can you see to these while we confer with Bancroft? I'd like to know a bit more about Sir Geoffrey. Then perhaps we can meet back at Charing Cross at about eleven, before going on to his house in Twickenham?"

We agreed and went our separate ways, Pons and Parker to the Admiralty, and Holmes and me heading north along the river. The rain had become worse, and it was cold for July. The drops sizzled on the pavement, and both of us, in the closed little worlds under our umbrellas, pressed forward without conversation. Soon, when we reached the Underground Station at the Embankment, we found a train ready to depart, so there was still no conversation on that part of the journey as well. Only when we climbed back to street level at Temple Station, finding that the rain had abated while we passed beneath the city, were we able to speak. "Can you really learn where the lady was killed from such a slender thread?"

Holmes nodded. "It's possible. As was pointed out in that unusual list you constructed of my 'limits' so long ago, I do have knowledge of soils from the different districts of the city – although it is certainly rusty right now. It's for that reason that I'm seeking a better opinion. The soils themselves haven't changed, but it's possible that my memory of them has – and in the intervening years, a great deal of additional research has been done. As you say – a slender thread, but it might be the only string to our bow."

By then we had reached the Embankment and were walking between the river and the gardens. After a steady progression along the way, we turned to our left, entering the Temple, and so wound our way to the north for just a little bit until we found ourselves in the wide opening that made up the lower end of Kings Bench Walk. We veered across the space, now covered in ugly pavement and dotted with parked automobiles where before it had been a pleasant place to stroll. We nodded to a few passersby and then entered Number 5, climbing the steps to apartment *A* on the first floor and knocking upon the heavy oak door. Within moments, our old friend Doctor Christopher Jervis had pulled it open and we were sitting beside the fire with enthusiastic welcomes from both him and Doctor John Thorndyke, who appeared from upstairs.

Holmes and I had known both of them for years, and we'd first met Thorndyke long before we became acquainted with Jervis. We'd been involved in the matter that had initially led Thorndyke to becoming a lawyer, in addition to being a doctor, and there at the first steps that led to him being of the most respected experts in matters of medical jurisprudence in the country, and ending up at 5A Kings Bench Walk, where he'd maintained his consulting practice for many years. Jervis was Thorndyke's old school chum who had gone to work for him sometime around the turn of the century, and like me, he was both a student of his friend's crime-solving methods, as well as someone who wrote them up and saw to their publication by way of a literary agent. Jervis and I had held many a conversation over the years since regarding the pros and pitfalls of such a course, and on several occasions Parker had joined us, listening with fascination as to the advantages and disadvantages of publishing narratives related to mysterious events and their solutions. I had no doubt that, at some point, Parker would be recording some of Solar Pons's exploits in a similar manner.

After the niceties had been attended to, and a very-much appreciated pot of tea was shared to fight away the rainy chill, Thorndyke invited us upstairs to his laboratory – much better than anything Holmes or Pons had constructed in the corners of their own sitting rooms. Thorndyke's, as a matter of fact, rivaled that of the Yard in some aspects, and while the official Force had its experts, nothing could equal Thorndyke's secret weapon: The very winning Nathaniel Polton, who greeted every challenge with happiness and most visitors with his crinkly smile.

Thorndyke passed the small bags to Polton and then, while the fellow got busy, spoke to us about research into the field of soil samples.

"I don't have to tell you," he said, glancing at Holmes, since clearly this was beyond my scope of work, "that soil typing can become very specific, and certain aspects can narrow down a sample to a very small and certain area. Your own notes, which were of such use to me when I was starting out, formed the core of a much greater collection that I've expanded over the years."

Polton, as Thorndyke talked, was doing various things to the samples, including preparing slides for the very nice microscope that stood upon one of the tables. Then he started pulling various maps and booklets from a cabinet set along one wall.

"Soil mapping in Britain has been hit or miss," continued Thorndyke, "but for the last twenty years or so, there have been better maps identifying surface texture and parent rock materials. I've only recently heard of work being done by Dokuchaev in Russia, involving soil morphology and the development of the soil profile, and Polton and I have been working to re-type the information that we've collected, along with the existing maps, to see if we can't bring the local knowledge up to date. I'd be quite surprised if we can't give you a location where the samples on the girl's body originated."

Polton indicated that he was ready to proceed, and he, Thorndyke, and Holmes, then went about various tasks in a workmanlike but mysterious manner, muttering to themselves, confirming what each other saw, flipping through maps and booklets, and generally behaving as alchemists trying to see if the smears of dirt had turned to gold. In the meantime, Jervis beckoned me out and back downstairs, where he offered me more tea, and we discussed what each of us had been about since our last meeting. Finally we heard footsteps coming downstairs, and in a few minutes Holmes and Thorndyke had rejoined us.

"Twickenham," said Thorndyke. "We can't be more specific than that. The soil is freely draining and slightly acid. Loamy and alluvial. Certain particles are firmly identified with that area of the riverbank near Eel Pie Island."

Jervis showed no reaction, and there was no reason why he should, but I understood the significance immediately. "That's near where Sir Geoffrey lives – in the Octagon House."

Thorndyke nodded. "Which could indicate that the girl was murdered near her home and the body carried to London – quite a ways – instead of her being killed closer to where she was found."

"It does open up a number of possibilities," agreed Holmes. "All the more reason to get down to Twickenham post haste."

"I had intended to offer you both lunch," countered Thorndyke, "but I understand your urgency. Be sure to send word when you get a chance of how things turn out."

Holmes agreed and we said our goodbyes. We met another old friend, Superintendent Miller of the Yard, climbing the steps as we descended, but he – like us – appeared to be in a hurry, so there was no time to stop and visit with one another. Soon we were retracing our steps – along the Embankment and thence to the Underground – and we made our way into Charing Cross only twenty or thirty feet behind Solar Pons and Dr. Parker, who had arrived just before us, but from the direction of Whitehall.

Inside, we agreed to find a quick bite of lunch before setting out. A small pub standing in the corner of the station was known to all of us for its fine cider and meat pies, so we crowded inside, where we were greeted by the holder of the lease, a little woman named Mabel Mathews. She owed Holmes a great deal for a matter long resolved, there in the station not twenty feet from the entrance to her establishment, when an encounter with her ne'er-do-well brother had almost gone terribly wrong. As always, in the years since her wrongful arrest for murder had been prevented, she tried to serve us for free, and as always we refused, reminding her yet again that if she kept trying to do that, then we'd have to stop placing our custom there, and none of us wanted that to happen.

344

Our inner fortitude replenished, we boarded the next train to our destination and settled back in a private smoker. When everyone was situated, and the window thankfully opened so that we didn't suffocate from the tobacco plumes, we began to share knowledge from our separate investigations.

Holmes related what Thorndyke had provided about soil type found on the body and the indications that the death had occurred in Twickenham. Pons glanced at Parker and stated that their own interview with Bancroft had tended to confirm that direction for the investigation.

"Bancroft was distracted, as usual," began Pons. "Ever since Irish agents assassinated Sir Henry Wilson in Belgravia last month, his department has been on alert. The assassins are to be executed in a few days, and he fears that something else – a rescue attempt, perhaps, or another assassination in retaliation – is in the works. But when we mentioned Sir Geoffrey and some questions related to the death of his daughter, Bancroft became more attentive.

"Ever since Britain ended the Protectorate over Egypt last month, there has been concern regarding how much the Egyptians plan to take on for themselves, and what we will retain. As you know, we reserved the right to maintain a controlling interest in four areas: Foreign relations, the military, questions regarding the Anglo-Egyptian Sudan, and communications. It's that last area that makes Sir Geoffrey of such interest to the government.

"His fortune was made acquiring patents and developing equipment in relation to radio. The military sees a great deal of importance in this type of work – especially after some hard lessons that were dealt to us during the War. Sir Geoffrey has always pulled in tandem with the official thinking – until a few months ago, when he seemed to lose focus on the mission. He's since been swayed into thinking that radio broadcasts might be of some value to the public in addition to their military possibilities. His company was involved in that radio broadcast in Chelmsford a couple of years ago when Lady Nellie, the Australian opera singer, caught the public's attention in such a way. Now there's a growing interest now in more broadcasts of the same type of thing – musical performances, and possibly plays. Reports of immediate newsworthy events and such. There are now upwards of a hundred applications for radio broadcasting licenses already making their way through the official channels – and the military is concerned."

He glanced at the three of us. "How familiar are you with the concept of radio?"

Holmes was proficient, I knew, based on some of his experiences before and during the War. I was quite a bit less so, and I suspected that

Parker was much the same. I indicated that Pons should continue his explanation.

"Radio waves cover a certain very specific width of the electromagnetic spectrum in which a number of cycles occur per second, and within this space, if too many radios are broadcasting, they can become crowded, and one can negate another, depending on distance and broadcast strength. Radio waves have a wider cycle than that of visible light – that which can be broken into various colors by a prism. Light such as we perceive it is somewhere in the middle of the overall spectrum. Röntgen Waves, and above that those emitted by radium and other materials such as those being investigated by Madame Curie, are much more dense and cycle quite frequently. In any case, the point of this is that radio waves hold a certain specific spot in the electromagnetic spectrum, and as it's only so wide, the military fears that overcrowding by too many of the civilian uses within that zone will prevent their own radio waves from working properly when needed."

"But what does this have to do with Egypt?" I asked.

"It seems that, when we agreed to end the Protectorate, it was with the secret understanding – all on our side, you see – that we would still retain a great deal of shadowy control. This could be accomplished in many ways, but one such instance is by way of radio – both for instantaneous responses to situations when necessary, and also by use of this same idea of broadcasts to the public, much like those which are gaining such popularity here, but in a way that public opinion would be swayed and even controlled with carefully selected facts and ideas."

Parker shook his head. He had spent a great deal of time in Egypt during the War, and had an affection for the place. "It's shabby treatment all the way around," he spat. "I was at least glad to see that Bancroft disapproved."

Pons nodded. "He has much influence, and had mostly negated a great deal of enthusiasm for this type of subtle manipulation of the Egyptian people. But then Sir Geoffrey, who was still deeply in the thick of supporting the plan, suddenly shifted his interests toward the notion of public broadcasts here at home – music, dramas, and such – over military reservation of the airwaves, and that pivot was enough to spook those who also still favored the idea into digging in and insisting even more more forcefully upon retaining military control – not only in Egypt, but now to a greater degree here in England as well."

I was shocked that such a thing might be considered, and I could see that Holmes was nonplussed as well. We both understood the basic passive nature of so much of the populace – sheep who could be nudged in any direction by a powerful motivator, or a subliminal notion beyond their general understanding, which would send them in the wrong direction without a single individual stopping to question or reason the advisability of such a course. Holmes had always said that the Press was a most valuable institution if one only know how to use it. If the public's opinions could be swayed so easily by this new form of communication, a plethora of untold problems was suddenly upon us that we hadn't even anticipated.

"So that explains the government's interest in Sir Geoffrey," I said, "and why Bancroft was willing to stop and discuss him. But what does any of this have to do with his daughter?"

"It seems," explained Pons, "that she held a great deal of influence over her father – more and more as he's aged. He's in his seventies now, she's the daughter of his second wife, who passed away a few years ago. It was a late marriage, and the girl wasn't born until Sir Geoffrey was about fifty. He had little interest in her until the last few years, when she reached adulthood. Since that time, he's turned to her more and more as something of an advisor and counselor. It was she who saw the possibilities for allowing radio to be used by the masses in a positive way, and it was at her urging that her father gradually changed his thinking."

"And now she's dead," said Holmes. "She was killed two months ago. Has that altered anything? Has Sir Geoffrey changed course to once again support the military use of the radio waves?"

"No," responded Pons, "in the sense that he hasn't changed his opinion. Rather, he doesn't seem to have an opinion now. The death of his daughter has left him as something of a broken man. His son has taken over the running of the old man's enterprises now – and he's the one who is willing to return to the original plan of allowing the military to develop their monopolistic control of the airwaves."

"A son?" I asked. "What about him?"

"Raymond Colsworth. The only other child, and now in his forties – son of Sir Geoffrey's first wife, who died thirty years ago or more. He spent his early years along familiar tracks – Eton, Oxford, a tour of the Continent. Pretty much of a wastrel until the War. Then he went to work representing his father's interests with a vengeance and seemed to find within himself previously unsuspected skills. He's rather cut-throat, it seems, and has spent the years since the War working to expand his father's interests, particularly in America. But he wasn't averse to lending a hand in Egypt when he got wind of that scheme, and he'd convinced his father to agree – at least until daughter Eva had a different idea."

Our conversation drifted to silence as we each pondered our own thoughts, and our arrival in Twickenham was unremarkable, although the rains seemed to have stopped. We found a cab that could hold all of us and were rattling on our way within minutes, back the short distance to the east toward the famed Octagon House where Sir Geoffrey resided.

I was aware of the structure, having read a profile of it several years before in *The Strand*. It had been built about two-hundred years before, in the 1720's, by a diplomat near the end of his political career. He'd settled in Twickenham and began construction there of a fine mansion. Commissioning one of the noted architects of the day, they embarked on a creative journey together that would take the next thirty-five years before the house was considered complete. In addition to the actual building, there were gardens of several sorts, elaborate canals, trails through which to wander, and even a grotto. But the most striking feature of the house was a large octagonal tower, as high inside as out, whose lofty ceilings oversaw countless elaborate parties, and even visits by the king himself upon occasion.

Over the years since the original owner spent the last portions of his life building and refining this masterpiece, it had fallen somewhat into mediocrity. Much of the land was sold off. The gardens fell fallow, and the canal was filled – its exact path was now unknown. At the turn of the current century, Sir Geoffrey Colsworth had purchased the place and he had moved there and set about restoring it to something of its original grandeur – though nothing as elaborate as in days of old. The *Strand* account hadn't given any personal details about the man, but now, having heard that the house was purchased around the time of the birth of his daughter Eva, I suspected that it was related to the man's second marriage.

Our route took us through busy Twickenham streets, quieter residential lanes, sometimes veering inland, and at others with the Thames in view. But always eastward. I knew that we were getting close when I could see Eel Pie Island off to our right, although the leaves were too thick upon the trees to get a good view of the hotel. I tried to recall when last I'd been there, and realized that it was over thirty years earlier, when Holmes had solved a rather complicated poisoning.

Just a few hundred feet past the island, the cab slowed, turned to the left away from the river, and approached the house. It was everything that I'd imagined when reading about it. The Octagon Tower dominated the overall structure, with its ornate baroque style, each of the visible walls having a tall arched window, topped with another round window just above it. I imagined that the inside of the room would be wonderfully lit. Each corner at the top of the eight-sided tower, probably forty or so feet high, had a rather plain rounded sculpture, and I was certain that the view from up there toward the river would be spectacular.

The Octagon House

The main entrance was twenty-or-so feet to the right of the tower, and we climbed the low flat steps and approached the high double doors. Holmes stepped forward and rang the bell, and then we waited – for an unusually long period of time.

The air was hot and damp after the recent rains, and much worse here, down near the river, than back in London. I knew that the eastern end of Eel Pie Island was undeveloped, as it tended to flood, and I wondered if the land around this house as well, not much more than an aggressive stone's throw away from the island, would be susceptible to the same problem. I saw no indications of it, but then again, there hadn't been any great floods along the Thames in quite a while – since November 1894, as I recalled. I wondered if that one had extended this far upstream.

Holmes rang the bell again, with no immediate effect, but we did see a curtain flick at a window to the right of the door. Then, a couple of minutes later, there was the sound of a heavy lock being turned, and the tall door was pulled back by a small man in his thirties, wearing ill-fitting livery – apparently the butler.

"Yes?"

"We are here to see Sir Geoffrey," replied Holmes, promptly stepping forward and giving the man his card.

"Sir Geoffrey is ill and does not receive visitors," came the reply. There was something unusual about the man's accent, but I couldn't place it. Without bothering to glance at Holmes's card, the butler stepped back and started to close the door.

I've been with Holmes countless times when he might have prevented something like this by sticking his foot in the path of the door and blocking it from being shut, but in this case, with the size of the door involved, doing so would have been foolhardy, likely risking an injury. Instead, Holmes barked, in a much more commanding tone than that which he'd previously used, "Stop! We are investigating the death of Sir Geoffrey's daughter, and have the authority of the Crown to do so. Your refusal now will mean our return within a quarter-hour with an army of policemen. I would advise that you step aside and let us meet with Sir Geoffrey immediately."

Upon hearing Holmes's tone, perhaps even more than the words, the fellow responded as if he'd had past military training, his eyes involuntarily snapping forward and staring into the distance even as his posture straightened and he came to something resembling standing straight, although his bulky coat, far too large for his slim frame, ruined the illusion.

Without another word, Holmes stepped around the man and so inside, and we joined him. "Now take my card to your master."

The man's eyes then looked again at Holmes, although they smoldered with suppressed anger. "I'm sorry, sir, but he really is ill. He's been in bed for the most part since his daughter died. I can, however, let you speak with his son."

Holmes nodded, and the man led us to the left side of the great but quite dark front hall. The house felt still and oppressive, likely due to the recent death. I tried to imagine how it had been just a few months before, when Lady Eva Colsworth was still alive.

We were taken into the famed Octagon Tower, and for a moment my breath was nearly taken away, as it was much more beautiful inside than the sketches in *The Strand* could convey. It wasn't overly large in terms of area – a gathering of sixty would feel quite crowded. The floor was made of large black-and-white tiles, arranged in a chessboard fashion, and I was reminded of an affair five years of so earlier, when we had encountered a similar floor at an old house in Northumberland, converted at the time to a home for recovering soldiers. The family there was burdened by an old ritual, similar to what the Musgraves had honored through the generations at their home of Hurlstone in western Sussex, and Holmes had solved the thing by having the family members play a living game of chess across the floor, according to the clues in the ritual's text. The game had led to a visit to the old family crypt underneath the house, and the revelation of an ancient land grant worth millions. The last I'd heard, the value of this document had gone a great way toward restoring the family's fortunes, and letting them make a number of improvements to the old house.

Similar repairs and improvements had been done here, although clearly in recent months the place had been ignored – surely related to the death of the mistress of the house. The tall windows were as beautiful inside as I had expected, but they were streaked and grimy. The intricate design painted on the high ceiling was astounding, but I expect that a closer examination would reveal that work was probably needed there as well. All in all, this magnificent room was as lifeless as the darkened front hall that we'd just seen. A couple of lamps were lit and placed on tables, but much was in shadow, in spite of the many large south-facing windows. I didn't need to be Sherlock Holmes – or Solar Pons – to see the neglect as evidenced by the dust on every surface.

We only waited for a moment before we were joined by a man in his forties – Raymond Colsworth, as I recalled from seeing his photograph in the newspapers. Remarkably, the servant who had met us at the front door remained within the room, leaving the entry to the dark hall open.

"I am Raymond Colsworth," said the new arrival. He glanced at the card. "I have heard of you, Mr. Sherlock Holmes. I see no reason why you or your companions need to be poking your nose into this business. My sister is dead – killed by that madman, the Stockwell Slayer. I understand that he had some sort of fascination for a nurse who was one of his victims, and once he'd killed her he got a taste for it and kept killing. My poor sister ended up being just another random target."

Holmes glanced at the man by the door. "If we could speak alone?"

Colsworth seemed frozen, making no effort to deny Holmes's request, or to enforce it. Pons walked to the door and, laying a hand on the butler's shoulder, propelled him into motion. The fellow seemed surprised to have been displaced so easily, and just outside the room he rounded to say something, but Pons shut the door in his face. Then, with a metallic clink, he pulled a small ring of lock-picking tools from his pocket, quite similar to the set regularly carried by Holmes, and locked the door. He returned to our group, saying softly something about not remaining standing in front of doors should someone decide to shoot through them. I was glad that I had my service revolver, and I was certain that Parker was armed as well. There was something dangerous here.

"You were notified that the man believed to have killed your sister was arrested last night," Holmes said loudly, apparently for the benefit of someone who might be eavesdropping.

Colsworth nodded and took a step toward us, all-the-while glancing nervously toward the locked door. From a closer perspective, his appearance was shocking. Having heard about him previously, I expected

351

a man of confidence and strength, even arrogance, but this fellow was anything but. He looked as if he'd recently lost a great deal of weight. His skin was blotchy, and his hair looked dead and lifeless. He came to rest before us, alongside a tall table, and he rested his nervous right hand upon it – having shifted direction slightly but intentionally so that hand would end up there, as his original path would have put the table on his left side. I could see that his nails were bitten to the quick, with a number of barely-healed wounds along the cuticles, and he nervously twitched his fingers over the marble table-top, tapping incessantly as he spoke.

"An inspector was out here this morning," said Colsworth. "He said something about how the killer admitted to every murder except for that of my sister. It sounded like nonsense to me – can the word of a man so insane be trusted? I . . . saw my sister's body."

His voice choked at this point, as if he were viewing her once again as she had ended, forever spoiling any memories of her life before her tragic death. His fingers began to tap at the table more insistently.

Suddenly, I noticed the look in his eyes as he turned his gaze from one of us to the other, as if willing us to understand something. That was the expression, I thought, of the man I'd expected to see – an inner strength that was there, but hidden behind the shabby and distressed outward appearance. Then I recognized the pattern of the man's finger-taps. It was Morse Code.

Of course – a man of his background would know that method of communication as well as his native verbal tongue. He was sending us a message, and he didn't want to say it out loud, in case the mysterious man in the butler livery – almost certainly still just outside the door and listening to our exchange – was listening. My Morse Code was rather rusty, but even I recognized a portion of the message. Every schoolboy knows *three shorts*, *three longs*, and *three shorts*. He was tapping out *S.O.S.*

I glanced at my companions, and both Holmes and Pons were nodding. Parker was looking at the floor, a pained look resting upon his features. I immediately recalled that his wife, Louisa, had died on the *Titanic*, that ship which had so famously signaled an *S.O.S.* some hours before sinking. How could he ever hear that now and not think of that tragedy, and specifically how it had changed is life so terribly?

Colsworth was tapping out something else now that he had our attention, much faster, and I couldn't follow. Holmes and Pons, however, had no difficulties, and Parker seemed to be caught up as well. Pons had served in the Cryptology Branch with great distinction during the War, so Morse Code was almost ridiculously basic for a man of his skills, and I expect that Parker had also made use of it during his relatively recent wartime escapades. And of course Holmes would have extensive knowledge of it too.

Holmes nodded and said, still with excessive volume to his voice, "We understand that your father is ill. Two of these men are doctors – they would be glad to examine him."

A fearful look crossed Colsworth's face for a moment, and then his eyes took on a steely resolve. Out loud he said, "I don't know, gentlemen. Father has been in terrible shape since Eva's passing." But as he verbally disagreed with the notion, he nodded vigorously in agreement.

"We insist," I said.

"It's our duty," added Parker.

Pons walked quietly but swiftly to the door, unlocked it quickly, and threw it open. The butler was standing there as expected, and we also heard the sound of someone else's footsteps skittering away, deeper into the house.

"One side," said Pons, pushing past the man. Parker and I followed, leaving Holmes with Colsworth in the Octagon Room.

Not knowing where to stay – with Colsworth and Holmes, or chasing after us as we started up the wide stairs – the butler chose neither and dashed past and underneath the stairs.

At the top of the landing, the stairs split. We didn't know where we were going, but there is a certain sameness to these great houses, and it seemed likely that we would find where Sir Geoffrey was located sooner rather than later. It was sooner, as we spotted a woman sitting beside a door at the end of the first long hall we tried, her chair pulled up near the door. The very unusualness of that seemed to cry out that this was our destination. Even as we started toward her, we heard a loud pounding and a repeated ringing of a bell behind us in the distance – seemingly someone at the front door demanding entrance – but we didn't pause.

The woman was dressed as a nurse, but something about her didn't appear to be very nurse-like. She was smoking a thin black cigarette, and there were several others mashed out on a piece of china placed on the floor beside her. When she saw us approach, she half-rose before sinking back into her chair, muttering a curse in Russian that I'd learned during the war – something that wouldn't be uttered by a true lady. Clearly she was unhappy to see us.

Pons said something back to her in Russian, and she only paused for a moment before nodding toward the door behind her. Pons in turn nodded to Parker and me and we went inside, even as the Russian conversation continued behind us.

The room was dark, and had a strong and sour odor of illness and neglect. Parker pulled the curtains back from the high window, causing a billow of dust that set us both to coughing. The additional light revealed a massive and ancient bed along the far wall. The covers were matted and twisted, and lying amongst them was an old man. He was alive, but in a terrible state of neglect. Even though we didn't have any of our typical medical accoutrements, Parker and I were able to get him fixed up and responsive rather quickly. Urging him to drink some water, and then eat a bit of the stale food found on his bedside table, enabled him to be more alert by the minute.

Pons had entered the room by then, bringing the woman with him, her arm tight in his grip. Clearly she was not a willing participant in our little gathering.

"They have been keeping Sir Geoffrey a prisoner," Pons explained. "Ever since they told him that his daughter had died."

"She isn't dead!" cried the old man, speaking for the first time. "I see her! She is sometimes here, in this room. She cannot speak, but she wants me to know that she is all right!"

I feared the old man's reason had fled, but Pons clarified. "He *does* see her. They bring her in at night in order to calm him down, or to force him to sign documents." He indicated the woman beside him. "Anna was quick to sense which way the wind is blowing and reveal their secrets."

"So Lady Eva isn't dead, then," said Parker.

"No. That's what her brother was trying to convey to us in his limited way downstairs. After his *S.O.S.*, he kept tapping *auto* and *stable*. I suspect that is the clue to where she's being kept, her death having been faked somehow to gain control over the family, and through them their radio interests."

Anna spoke. "She is being kept under one of the outbuildings."

"If Lady Eva is being held here," I said, "then there must be more of the Russians. We heard someone else in the hall with the man who answered the door."

Parker nodded. "The humbug butler, you mean?"

Pons nodded. "He's no butler. For a number of reasons – one being his blackened fingernails, stained by motor oil. He's more likely some kind of mechanic. And his accent, though of from a different region than our 'nurse' here – " he added, nodding her way, " – has indications of Russian origin as well."

I glanced at the old man, now somewhat recovered, but still quite confused. "We left Holmes down there with him – and whomever else is in the house."

"No need to worry about Holmes," said Pons. "But having said that, we need to rejoin him and figure out how to locate and rescue Lady Eva. We're a bit too near the river to be entirely comfortable."

I was uncertain as to his intent with this statement – did he think that they might escape with her by boat, to continue to exert influence over the Colsworth family from afar, or might they instead actually kill her this time, and put her body into the water?

Parker helped the old man to his feet, and Pons kept hold of the nurse, who showed no inclination to fight or flee. However, I am an old campaigner, and knew that, while she might in fact have given up and have no reason to resist, she could also be as suddenly dangerous as a swamp adder. While it was likely that Pons had ascertained that she had no weapon while they were still in the hallway, it was possible that she had any number of other deadly tricks at her disposal.

As we walked back along the hallway, I stepped out in front, my service revolver raised. I could hear the sound of a number of various voices calling in the distance throughout the house, all sounding forceful, but none displaying any indication of panic or anger. As we neared the top of the stairs, a figure from below rose in front of us. I couldn't immediately identify him, as he was a darker shadow against the dim downstairs light. I pointed my gun, calling for him to halt, but he responded immediately.

"Dr. Watson? It's Jamison. The house is secure."

A feeling of relief washed over me. I hadn't feared for our own escape, in spite of not knowing how many foes were awaiting us, but I had worried about finding Lady Eva before she might be harmed. Now, with official reinforcements, things were looking better. My questions about how they had arrived would soon be answered.

Downstairs, to my surprise, I saw a number of constables moving here and there, searching every part of the building. Amongst them were a number of dark-suited and much more dangerous looking men, almost certainly agents of Bancroft Pons. And standing in the center of the entry hall were Dr. Thorndyke, Dr. Jervis, and Superintendent Miller. At their feet was the butler, trussed with a rope apparently cut from a bell-pull and guarded by a couple of burly constables.

Their presence was quickly explained. When we had passed Miller that morning at 5A Kings Bench Walk, he had been on his way to urgently consult with Thorndyke about the very matter which had sent us there, but from a different direction. Apparently Bancroft Pons, now concerned after Pons and Parker's visit, had dimly perceived what might be occurring, and had ordered an emergency exhumation of the dead girl. Miller was notified to involve Thorndyke, and to make a determination as quickly as possible. Rather than being interred in Twickenham, the woman believed to be Lady Eva Colsworth had been placed in a crypt at All-Hallows-by-the-Tower in Byward Street, solely through the influence of her father, so obtaining access to her body was immediate, and the examination was made right at the gravesite.

"This is going to be a bit of an embarrassment for Spilsbury," said Miller. "He never bothered to make a full evaluation of the body. It was easy to see, once we knew where to look, that the dead girl could never have been Lady Eva." He glanced at Thorndyke.

"There were callosities upon her hands and feet – old ones. Those on her feet were from poorly fitting shoes. Her fingernails were broken and dirty. There was evidence of drug use in the form of both old and recent scars upon her arms. Any of this could have been true of Lady Eva – we didn't know enough about her to say for sure that she hadn't been a drug addict herself at some point, or that she didn't enjoy working in the garden or walking, giving rise to the callosities and dirty fingernails. But the wear on the dead woman's teeth indicated an older person, and the roots of her hair indicated that it had been dyed. A few other scars indicated that she'd had a slight case of smallpox in her youth. Clearly, this was not Lady Eva, but someone else killed in her place – with the face disfigured so as to hide her true identity – if one didn't look too closely.

"We immediately obtained an emergency warrant," added Miller, "and rounded up some officers and Government agents and came out here as fast as we could. A good thing, too."

"But where is Holmes?" I asked.

"He went with Colsworth to the garage," explained Jervis. "It used to be the stables. According to Colsworth, that's where they've been keeping her – in some old tunnels that run underneath the property, and are entered by way of the stable building."

"And here she is," added Holmes, walking in the front door at that moment with Raymond Colsworth and a tall blonde woman, quite mussed, but apparently otherwise in good health. With a cry, she rushed toward her father, and they fell into one another's arms with quiet sobs.

"I think that I understand," said Parker. "Lady Eva's interest in changing the focus of radio broadcasts went against the wishes of . . . someone, so something had to be done to force her father and brother back to the correct way of thinking. They didn't want to kill her, however, so they killed someone else instead, and made the murder look like one of a series of similar crimes that just happened to be taking place at the same time. But how do these Russians fit in?"

"Your explanation is partly correct," said Raymond Colsworth. "My sister *was* using her influence to make sure that radio would be used for the public good, and not just for military purposes. There were lots of heated discussions about it in rooms all over London, with many angry opinions directed toward us – those of the Government, and other leaders

356

in the industry who stood to gain fortunes from government contracts." He looked fondly at his sister. "Eva had convinced me 'round to her way of thinking as well. But in the middle of this, we had a visit from the Russians – but no. 'Visit' sounds pleasant, as if they simply came to make a terrible business proposal.

"The day of – the day of the murder of that young woman was when they arrived. It was the man who was in charge – clearly a Russian, although he called himself 'Smith' – and Sidorov here – " He nodded to the tied man at our feet. " – and a blonde woman of rather rough mien who wasn't introduced by name. This fellow Smith then made sure that no one was around – he looked in the hall and confirm that the servants were elsewhere – and then he explained what he wanted: For us to betray our country. My father was astonished, and flatly refused. Smith said that he'd already taken Eva prisoner and that we had no choice. It was then that, without warning, Sidorov pulled a muddy stone from his pocket, apparently picked up somewhere nearby, and began to hit the girl repeatedly about the head – violently killing her before we could stop him.

"Smith held a gun on my father and me, smiling all the while and holding his finger upright before his lips, indicating that we should remain silent. The poor girl never had a chance to cry out, although she tried to fight. Even after it was clear that she was gone, Sidorov continued to hit her, and then he strangled her dead body as well – I suppose to simulate the method used by her supposed murderer.

"Only then did Smith explain that they intended to leave the body in London, with Eva's identifying information to indicate that it was my sister who had died. He did this, he said, to gain control over me and my father. As mentioned, I too had been leaning toward a preference for civilian use of radio, and I was now instructed to throw my weight once gain into supporting the military's plan instead. These Russians then intended to use our connections to siphon off intelligence related to the military from the broadcast-side of things – not only obtaining information, but learning in greater depth how our system works, and all about our broadcast frequencies and codes, with plans to stay abreast of all of our activities, in order to be ready if needed to plan their strategy, or to shut our system completely down at some crucial moment, or take it over and broadcast their own messages and propaganda, leaving the military helpless at the worst possible instant. The possibilities were staggering.

"After Eva's supposed death, they took the dead girl up to London – she'd been recruited simply as a body to make the plan work. They had me dismiss all the servants – due to my 'grief' was the reason that was given – and then the Russians moved in. There have only been a few of them – 'Smith', the man in charge, Sidorov, who seems to be something of a mechanic and works on the boat tied by along the riverbank, and Anna, the nurse." He glanced toward the girl, now in the grip of a constable. "There were also a couple of men to guard Eva in the tunnel – now arrested. They kept her alive to control me and my father, but his mind was shattered almost immediately after what he'd seen and the knowledge of what was expected of him, and he took to his bed. They could have killed him, but they still needed him to sign documents, and he was useful to control me. The same for Eva – they could have killed her at any time as well, so I had to go along with them the whole way down the line to keep her safe. I was only allowed to meet with other people – military and industry leaders – in the presence of the Russians, here at the house, and I had no chance to pass any messages. My nervousness, manner, and appearance were put down to grief, while in truth it was fear for my family, and what I was being forced to do.

"I'd already instructed the attorneys to start the process to include several people with unknown Russian connections into our business dealings. By year's end, they planned to have entirely infiltrated the whole operation – our radio interests, and specifically the planned military applications."

Holmes turned to Jamison. "We have the Sidorov and the nurse, and the guards in the tunnel. Don't tell me that the head man, Smith, has escaped!"

Jamison smiled, shook his head, and called to someone named Presley. There was a noise in the Octagon Room where we'd initially spoken with Raymond Colsworth, and then two constables came in, dragging a short but fat fellow between them. He fought and cursed and spit, and when he was placed before Holmes, my friend smiled and nodded.

"Ah, Klopman. We meet again. I believe that the last time was twenty years ago, in Dartmoor, when we saw you safely into the custody of a former Belgian policeman of our acquaintance for the attempted murder of Count Von und Zu Grafenstein. I must admit my negligence – I lost track of you, and was certain that you had been taken back to the Continent and shot."

The man hissed and fought his captors, trying to lunge at Holmes, but he wasn't going anywhere.

"You will have noticed," said Holmes to the rest of us, "that our rather heavyset former Nihilist friend is in his shirtsleeves. Clearly he was the man pretending to be the butler. When he looked out and saw us – and recognized me specifically – he hurriedly dashed back into the house and

358

found Sidorov, putting him into the much larger butler's coat to answer the door."

At that point, one of the dark-suited men requested to speak to Holmes and Pons, and when they left the house, Parker and I made further examination of the girl and the old man. I set one of the constables to finding something for them to eat, and he only looked mildly intimidated as he went to locate the kitchen. Then I looked around until I located a more comfortable location than the Octagon Room, and Parker led the patients there, where they were able to sit an relax without fear for the first time in months.

Later, Holmes and Pons guided a number of us down into the tunnels beneath the old stable. They were ancient, much older than the house that had stood on this property for a couple of centuries. After going far in the direction away from the river without ever reaching an endpoint, and encountering a number of side-tunnels along the way, we returned and explored more closely the area near the entrance, in the mean little chamber where Lady Eva had been kept, and also where an extremely large cache of supplies was being assembled – food, bedding and similar gear, munitions of all types, and most unnerving, numerous crates of explosives.

"I suspect that in their research of Sir Geoffrey and the Octagon House," said Pons, "the Russians stumbled upon some reference to these old tunnels – likely Roman. It's almost certain that all of this was transported surreptitiously here by way of the river. Whether or not the initial plan was simply to keep Lady Eva here, or if they had already determined to also store all of this material here for the possibility of some future conflict, may not ever be determined. I doubt that Klopman will tell."

There was some talk of trying to mount an operation wherein the Russians would be fooled into thinking that their plan was still in operation, so that we could feed them false information, but in the end it was decided to be too cumbersome. It was uncertain as to which individuals were already bought-and-paid-for by the Russians, and the near-certain likelihood that a single one of them would get the truth back to his masters meant that the greater effort to fool them simply wasn't worth it.

After Lady Eva's rescue, the Colsworth family relocated to London. Sir Geoffrey quickly recovered, and there was no greater enemy working against the Russians within the British Government from that day forward. He found the whole property at Twickenham to be distasteful in the extreme and planned to have it razed to the ground. A good portion of the house was, in fact, torn down before he could be stopped, and was later

359

used for a time as a gravel quarry. However, wiser heads were able to step in and save the Octagon Tower itself as something of an important historic artifact, and it still stands to this day, although a shadow of its former self, abandoned and neglected beside a filthy open pit, the fine house that it showcased gone.

Not long after these events occurred, a number of us ventured back into the tunnels on the property. Holmes and Pons, with the backing of the Government and a few specific and highly motivated scholars, had carried out a great deal of research on the history there and had come to some truly startling conclusions. On a day a few weeks later, Holmes, Pons, Parker, and I, along with Thorndyke, Jervis, Nayland Smith, and Petrie, met in Twickenham and set forth to the now-empty Colsworth estate, each with specific assigned tasks to accomplish. Our friend Lord Peter had been invited to join us as well, based on his recent archeological interests, but an experience he'd had during the War, being buried alive in one of the front-line trenches, left him understandably reluctant. In his place we invited an adventurous American of twenty-two or –three named Jones who had recently completed his undergraduate degree at the University of Chicago and was soon planning to attend a graduate program (in linguistics) at the Sorbonne, in France.

One by one our party climbed underground by way of the stable entrance. We found ourselves quite glad that young independent Jones was with us, as he had quite a bit of natural luck which, combined with a few other most interesting skills, ended up saving all our lives.

Over the next forty-eight hours beneath the earth's surface, we made a discovery that might one day rock the very heart of this nation, should its existence be revealed.

But I'm informed by the authorities – specifically Bancroft Pons and a rather peeved Mycroft Holmes in a late-night meeting at the Admiralty – that this "one day" will be long after I've ceased to care, and the same is true for my companions who were also there during that momentous excursion. I'll have to be satisfied for now with the memory if it, and also with my apparently illegal decision to have recorded those details elsewhere in a separate manuscript, in the hopes that my own carefully concealed chronicles detailing the affair may someday be published. Knowing them as I do, I would suspect that my like-minded friends of a similar literary turn – Parker, Jervis, and Petrie – have done the same.

The Peculiar Persecution
of Mr. Druitt

13 October, 1881

Dear Holmes,

I hope that your investigation is progressing successfully, and I very much wish that I could have taken advantage of your kind invitation to join you. A trip to Edinburgh and a chance to revisit a number of my old haunts would have been just what the doctor ordered, but sadly I'm still having a bit of difficulty with the latest flare-up of my wound.

I've been making the most of my recovery, however, taking the opportunity to stay in and recuperate – but I had forgotten how beautiful and tempting London can be in October. (If you'll recall, I didn't arrive home last year on the *Orontes* until November, and then in the pouring rain.) After such a long time spent in the sere Afghan landscape, with its hot tan skies stretching overhead, as if one is walking underneath a Benares-crafted platter, every day lately has been a wonder. The heavens here are a blue that calms the soul – even if I only see a thin slice of them from our windows as I look out above the houses on the other side of Baker Street.

As per your instructions, I've made notes – some extensive, some less-so – of your visitors. Most are matters that would either hold no interest for you (or so I would judge, having consulted with you on several cases now over the last seven months), while others would seem to be of the sort where no urgency is required. These include a matter of an otherwise unimportant and previously ignored tree at the corner of a small cemetery that now seems to be "weeping"; a land surveyor who unexpectedly feels the need to take a mid-day nap (when he'd never been so inclined before) and who, upon awakening, finds that many of his survey notes have already been completed – for property which he has not yet examined; and a massive figure of a man with a completely hairless head – apparently from alopecia rather than by choice – who claims your prior acquaintance and wishes to give you further data regarding the "Tavistock Court ruction" – which he assures me can wait, as "that pot still has a ways to cook, Doctor."

However, there was one visitor an hour or so ago whose tale sounded a bit more intriguing and urgent, and I felt the need to forward those details your way.

Just before lunch, Mrs. Hudson knocked and announced a young lade of about twenty. (It always amuses me to try and determine when or why our estimable landlady will choose to climb the stairs and announce a visitor. I believe that she was showing some sort of approval of your new client, because she announced – without asking if it was requested – that she would return soon with tea. As you have remarked before, most of your clientele is usually not honored or acknowledged in this way.)

Miss Emily Hayes is pretty in a careworn sort of way – dark hair worn long, and a sweet smile. She informed me that she currently lives nearby in one of the Portman Mansions along East Street, and that she had been advised to consult you by Old Ted Farways, whom you will recall from that business back in June with the thrice-rolled cobble stone. She had barely introduced herself and found a place in the basket chair before the fire when Mrs. Hudson brought in tea, as well as a tidy mound of toothsome comestibles. After we were situated all over again, I explained that you were away, but that I was able to take down the details of her story and forward them to you. She nodded and then related her narrative.

"I was born and raised here in London, where my mother still lives, and until recently I was employed as a governess," she explained. "I lived with the Meltons – the naval captain, his wife, and two daughters, in Greenwich. It was a good arrangement, as my younger brother, Anthony, is a student at Mr. Valentine's boarding school in Blackheath, in Eliot Place and within walking distance of the Melton house. He's fourteen now, and has attended there for the past two years. We were very fortunate to get him in – Mr. Disraeli was a student there. Anthony is a legacy student, as our father attended there as well.

"While I lived in Greenwich, I was able to check on him regularly, but after the Meltons went out to India a month ago, my position came to an end, and I've since returned to stay with my mother. She has a small income from investments left by my father when he died. It gives her enough to maintain the house, and to pay for Anthony's tuition – which is augmented by a small scholarship set up by some of Father's former school chums.

"In spite of our six-year age difference, Anthony and I have always been close, and when I lived nearby, we contrived to visit regularly – meeting for walks or tea. Since my return to Mother's house, I miss him terribly, and I believe that he feels the same. We've continued to exchange letters – always little notes of news about our days, or something we've seen. But yesterday Anthony sent something with a different tone.

362

"The school isn't very big – it's in an old house which faces north, looking upon the various open fields that lead down toward the Greenwich Observatory and then the river. It shares something of a small park to the rear with the neighboring houses. While the students are encouraged to visit the grounds of the Observatory and the Prime Meridian, or to gain their exercise on the nearby athletic fields, they're discouraged from entering the park behind the house – it's felt that the neighbors don't want to have interactions with schoolboys, and the school itself would prefer to avoid attracting any attention, in spite of its fine reputation.

"Over the last two years, Anthony has told me quite a bit about his teachers – he has a comical but rather sweet way of writing that brings out their humorous aspects and foibles. But one teacher who started last year – a part-time law student named Druitt – has been rather different. He's a grim fellow, often falling into brown studies while staring into the distance. He's frequently the butt of jokes by some of the more cruel students, but he seems to be unaware of it. Unfortunately, Anthony has more to do with Mr. Druitt than might otherwise be expected, as part of his duties as a student involve his assignment as Druitt's sometime-assistant – sorting papers, cleaning the blackboards, and so on. In his letters, Anthony has tried to present the man in a light manner, in the way that he's done with his other teachers, but the fellow's oppressive moods have made that rather impossible.

"Over the few weeks, Anthony has noticed that Mr. Druitt leaves the building at odd hours, often late in the evening. He acts in a very awkward and suspicious manner, as if he doesn't want to be seen. It seems that only Thomas has noticed him so far.

"A few nights ago, Anthony decided to follow Mr. Druitt. If I'd known, I would have warned him not to – wherever the man is going is none of his business. But he wasn't seen, and he had no trouble keeping up. After a short saunter down Eliot Place, Mr. Druitt abruptly turned between houses, and so through and into the park – with Anthony close behind. After just a few minutes, his teacher entered a small grove of dense trees, where he simply waited for ten or fifteen minutes, standing beside a large stone projecting from the ground, before departing.

"This has been repeated on subsequent nights, and on the night before Anthony wrote to me, he stayed when his teacher departed, going into the grove to see what was to be found. He described it as a place with a bad feeling to it, although that may be simply because he was there at dusk, where he wasn't supposed to be. But he said that he felt a chill when he saw the stone – a long flat thing, like an altar. Rather freshly carved in the center, it's edges bright against the rest of the weathered rock, was this . . . ."

And at this point, Holmes, she showed me a sketch made by her brother of an eye centered within a triangle:

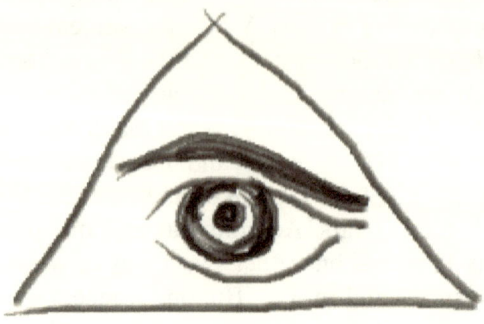

I'll admit that it gave me something of a chill as well, for I remembered where I'd seen that before – in your scrapbooks. She had nothing more to tell, except that Anthony had passed on the information, asking her opinion, and that she was disturbed enough to remember your name and seek your help.

I told her that I'd pass it along to you and see if you had any advice or questions. That satisfied her, and she departed soon after. Then I confirmed what I'd read – this symbol had connections to many religions and cults, including some of the darker aspects of Freemasonry.

Without adding any of my interpretations or concerns, I'll post this letter and await your response.

Very best,

Watson

* * * * *

16th of October, 1881

Dear Mr. Holmes,

Thank you for taking time to reply to my inquiries, and so quickly. Please let Dr. Watson know that I appreciate his help as well. He seems to be a very nice man, and I hope that his health improves. (Please don't scold her for being indiscrete, but your landlady took several minutes after I left the doctor to sing his praises and tell me what a hero he'd been in Afghanistan. She clearly has great respect and motherly affection for him,

364

and I hope someday to be able to introduce him to my fiancé, an Army major currently out of the country.)

The information that you related in your wire regarding the eye in the triangle was fascinating, and rather frightening. I'm not sure that I was able to adequately express to the doctor the dark aura that Anthony said seems to project from his teacher, Mr. Druitt – especially lately. Normally Anthony is a very chipper and positive-minded fellow – and he has been his whole life – but from the time Mr. Druitt came to work at the school an assistant master about a year ago, he seems to cast a pall over the building in general and lately my brother in particular. No one is quite certain as to how the man obtained the position, although there is a rumor that he's somehow related to the headmaster and owner, Mr. Valentine.

As I mentioned to Doctor Watson, Anthony was assigned as Mr. Druitt's assistant, and as such, he's required to work for him for an hour or so every day, in the late evenings before dinner. Generally this work is of no consequence – straightening the classroom, cleaning blackboards, carrying out the wastepaper, and so on. In spite of Mr. Druitt being present, there is never any interaction between them, as the man spends his afternoons reading a book, sometimes making notes, or occasionally writing letters.

The reason that I mention this is that Anthony has shared additional information with me, beyond the affair of following his teacher to the rock in the copse of trees, and the frightening carving that he found there. Anthony believes that Mr. Druitt's trips are related to a series of small slips of paper that are suddenly taking up a great deal of his time. As Anthony describes the situation, Mr. Druitt is receiving what appears to be coded messages, and his fascination with them is causing him to neglect his regular duties – such as whatever lesson preparations that he formerly did in the late afternoons.

Anthony first became aware of these papers when Mr. Druitt began examining them in earnest several weeks ago. The first time that Anthony was aware of them, his teacher entered the classroom in great haste, sat down at his desk, unfolded one of the pieces of paper, and began what only be described as decoding a message from it.

Since then, he has entered the empty classroom each day in the same way, in the late afternoon when classes have finished. He flings his books onto his desk and fishes in his pocket for one of the folded messages. Then he pulls out another worn and much re-folded sheet from within his case, finds a blank sheet of paper, and begins to slowly and laboriously decipher whatever is written on the slip onto the clean sheet by comparing it to the folded sheet. Then, when he's finished and without doing anything else, he will repack his things and leave without a word.

It was having seen this that prompted Anthony to follow Mr. Druitt in the first place to the carved rock. Additionally, he began to watch more closely, and he informs me that he's actually seen Mr. Druitt find these pieces of paper on several occasions. Twice, for instance, in the dining hall during lunch, Anthony saw Mr. Druitt lift his plate as soon as he sat down at the head table, where a folded slip could be seen hidden underneath. He hurriedly placed it in his pocket, and would have certainly dashed out to decode it then and there if his responsibilities hadn't prevented it. He has a full class schedule every afternoon, so the first chance he likely has to study the message is in his free period when Anthony is also in the classroom. It seems to be a laborious process for him, so he needs the uninterrupted period to accomplish his task.

Two days ago, during the great storm that passed through London, Anthony was cleaning the classroom as usual while Mr. Druitt performed his typical ritual with the slip of paper, the folded sheet, and the clean sheet. But suddenly Mr. Druitt was summoned to help with a small emergency related to rainwater entering at the back of the building. He stood and shoved the blank sheet (with the partial translation of the code) into his pocket and rushed out without thinking, leaving his other materials behind. Anthony immediately grabbed another blank sheet of paper and proceeded to copy both what was written on the much-used sheet and also from the latest slip of paper.

There was but one line on the oft-referred-to sheet:

Pack my box with five dozen liquor jugs.

The message on the slip of paper simply consisted of a series of numbers:

26-12-2-6_26-12-23-8-19-25_14-23-11-16-19-17

3-8-19-12-11-19-22-16_12-8_2-10-2-11-12

23-16-3-23-22-11-12-26_2-12_23-8-3-4

8-3-12_14-8-22-23-12-16-16-19_26-11-9_1-5

Soon after Anthony was able to copy these and return to his chores, Mr. Druitt returned, sat down, and finished his painstaking work, looking back and forth between the message and the document upon which he was writing his decoded results. Suddenly with a cry, he arose, glanced at the mantel clock, jammed all of the papers into his pocket, and fled the room.

Anthony followed along behind and saw him dash out the front door and into the storm.

With a bit more forethought, Anthony retrieved his coat and hat and slipped out as well. Of course he didn't know which way Mr. Druitt had gone, but he decided to see if the mysterious rock was again the man's destination. He crept up to it and, peering through the surrounding brush, he could see the man standing there, soaking wet and waiting for . . . something. He would look this way and that, as if expecting someone to arrive at any moment from out of the downpour. And yet, no one ever did.

Anthony said it was quite dark, and the rainfall and the storm were terribly noisy, so he's certain that he was never observed by Mr. Druitt. He wanted to wait and see who arrived, since an appointment was apparent, but he realized that he needed to return to the school to be ready for dinner, so he slipped away without any further enlightenment.

This affair, while not of great importance, is quite curious, as I'm sure you'll agree. I've given Anthony the address in Edinburgh that you've provided to me, as he indicates that he will write to you directly now with whatever he learns, as he feels that the added step of going through his sister may delay matters if something becomes urgent.

Thank you for your help, and indulging us with your interest. I hope that this matter has a happy ending, although there is a feeling of ugliness about it that makes me uneasy.

With best regards,

Emily Hayes

* * * * *

27 October, 1881

Dear Mr. Holmes,

Thank you sir for the telegram that you sent this morning. It's the first one that I've ever received, and it very much made me the most interesting person in school. The Headmaster, Mr. Valentine, summoned me to his office to receive it, and I could tell that he was very curious. He kept asking me questions about "A problem at home, Hayes?" or whether I needed to dictate a reply to him. I thanked him but didn't give away anything about your help.

I have given thought to your questions and tried to answer them as well as I can. Mr. Druitt arrived her a bit over a year ago to serve as the assistant master. From what I've heard, he's in his early twenties, and is reading for the law. He has this job by way of some family connection.

He always seems most unhappy, and I can't think of a time when I've seen him laugh or even smile. I barely had any dealings with him last year, but this year, as part of our regular chores, I was assigned to Mr. Druitt's classroom. I haven't had any of his classes, although my friends say that he is very morose, and often loses his train of thought in the middle of a lesson – sometimes in the middle of a sentence. He is an object of a great deal of ridicule by some of the boys, although I feel that they're being rather unkind, as they don't know what his circumstances are, or what thoughts are in his mind that cause him to lose track of things.

To further answer your question, there are three of the older boys in particular who seem to delight in making japes at his expense. I'm sure you know the type – the fellows who are always lounging about and making snide comments under their breath. One, Rance Conway, is rather small and ratty, the son of a PM, and he never lets anyone forget it. The other two, Sid Drake and Ralph Morgan, are big bruisers from middle-class families who follow Conway around as an ever-present audience to laugh at his jokes, and also somewhat in the fashion of bodyguards, as until recently no one was safe from Conway's bullying, and sometimes his victims were inclined to fight back. But after they began to taunt and tease Mr. Druitt, they seem to have left everyone else alone.

My father went to this school when he was my age, and I'm considered a legacy student – although that doesn't really make any difference about anything, except that I was able to gain admission somewhat easier than might otherwise have been possible. The only person here to whom it might matter is old Hadley, the man-of-all-work – he takes care of the grounds, does general maintenance, and the like. He and I have struck up a friendship, and a few days ago I felt comfortable in asking him if he had any thoughts on Mr. Druitt's persecution.

He agreed that Conway and his two troops have certainly had it in for Mr. Druitt of late, although he doesn't know why. Perhaps it's simply because Mr. Druitt doesn't seem to be all there at times, which makes him something of an easy victim. Fortunately, Mr. Druitt doesn't seem to realize a great deal of the time when Conway has made some subtle attack at his expense – but for the same reason, because he doesn't realize he's under attack, he makes no effort to defend himself.

The reason I mention this is because Hadley has confirmed Conway's connection to the coded messages, as he has seen some things as well. As I mentioned to my sister, I've observed Mr. Druitt find messages under his dinner plate on several occasions. I've also seen him reach into his pocket once or twice and find a message there, which he pulls out with great surprise. When I told Hadley this, he nodded and said he'd seen Conway leaving folded notes under Mr. Druitt's plate in the dining hall a couple of time – which is surely confirmation as to where the messages are originating! (Until I spoke to him, however, he was unaware of the rest of it, and hadn't felt the need to report what was happening to the headmaster.)

Hadley and I have become quite curious about this affair, and he was able to see if there was anything of interest in Mr. Druitt's room. While I was with Mr. Druitt in the classroom, even as he decoded his latest message, Hadley slipped into his room. He said that there were a great deal of books and pamphlets regarding Freemasonry, along with a numerous sketches of things that seem to relate to the Masons – including at least a dozen versions of the eye in the triangle!

Most of all, Hadley said that one of the coded messages was pinned over Mr. Druitt's desk, as if in a place of honor:

6-8-22_13-2-15-16_7-16-16-19_26-16-20-16-3-12-16-17_14-8-23

2_1-8-26-11-12-11-8-19_11-19_12-13-16_13-11-25-13

5-2-26-8-19_3-8-22-19-3-11-20_7-16_2-12_12-13-16

23-8-3-4_10-11-12-13_8-22-23_26-11-25-19_10-13-16-19

23-16-21-22-11-23-16-17_6-8-22-23_14-2-11-12-13_10-11-20-20

7-16_23-16-10-2-23-17-16-17_7-23-8-12-13-16-23

Hadley told me that, besides the coded message hanging on the wall above the desk, there was also a sketch of the eye and triangle!

In addition to that, I was able to copy Mr. Druitt's latest message. Last night, he was called out of the classroom just a few minutes after he'd arrived and set out his latest slip of paper for decoding. (He ignores me, so it never crossed his mind that I was still there when he left.) I quickly stepped across, saw that the original sheet with *Pack my box with five dozen liquor jugs* written on it – now looking much more ragged – was still in use. I copied what was on the small new sheet beside it:

7-16_2-12_12-13-16_23-8-3-4_2-12_26-22-19-26-16-12_8-19

2-20-20_13-2-20-20-8-10-26_16-15-16_10-16-2-23_19-8

3-20-8-12-13-16-26

Today Mr. Druitt seems much more distracted and upset looking than usual, and I wonder what was in this latest message to upset him. I feel as if things are becoming more serious, and whatever Conway and his lackeys are up to will only lead to disaster for the poor man.

Let me know if there is anything else that I can do, and thank you.

Sincerely,
Anthony B. Hayes

* * * * *

6 November, 1881

Dear Mr. Holmes,

I'm writing to thank you for your timely intervention in recent events that were occurring at my school, unfortunately completely unknown to me. I must confess to a great deal of embarrassment that such goings-on had progressed to this degree without my knowledge, and I can assure you that I will do far better in the future.

I also wish for you to know that the persecution of Mr. Druitt has ended, and the malefactors have been duly punished. While I could have notified you by telegram, in the same way that yours urgently requested my intervention, I feel that a longer response is justified, to explain the events as they occurred.

Your wire arrived on the afternoon of 31 October, as the school was preparing for a small All Hallows Eve celebration later that night. (A bit of fun is not a bad thing – in its proper place.) Frankly, I was puzzled by your message:

> *Prevent Druitt from disrobing at rock in park behind school at sunset Halloween. Further details can be provided by A. Hayes. Then question Conway et al. Further information to follow in person this afternoon.*

Initially, I was inclined to throw the message away, but for mention of Mr. Druitt, which alerted me that there might be a problem worth

370

investigating after all. He is a somewhat troubled young man, attempting to study to be a lawyer, but with a number of problems which don't need to be specifically elaborated upon in this letter. He is an old friend of my family, and I felt an obligation to provide a position for him. He has worked here about a year, and for the most part has been adequate in his duties as one of the two assistant masters.

I have noticed of late that he was more distracted and morose than normal, but I myself have been quite a bit busier than usual, and failed to follow up on the matter as I should have. As you suggested, I called in young Hayes and showed him your wire. He was rather reluctant at first to share with me the details of the matter, before finally revealing that he'd observed how Druitt has received a number of apparently coded messages, and the effect they were having upon the man. Hayes also explained how he'd recruited Hadley in the matter, and how between the two of them, they had established that Conway, Drake, and Morgan – three students already known for their decidedly conniving character – were the persecutors. Unknown to young Hayes, who was initially very reluctant to involve our maintenance man, I think the world of Hadley, and if he had established the involvement and guilt of the three reprobates, then I knew that the cause was just and the information reliable.

Of course, however, I called in Hadley, who confirmed every bit of Hayes' story. At that time, I was prepared to immediately summon Conway and his entourage, but Hayes then reminded me that you had promised more information to be forthcoming. I tabled the matter to await further word – which was not long in arriving

Not long after four o'clock, as the sun was setting, a visitor was announced. I confess that I expected you in person, but instead it was your brother, Mycroft Holmes, who was rather irate at being cajoled by your telephone call into making his way from an office – in Whitehall, I believe that he said? – to share information that was too complex for a telegram. (I confirmed to him that in any case the school did not have a telephone, whereupon your brother snapped that I should acquire one!)

However, despite his initial irritation, our conversation turned more congenial when he accepted a glass of Madeira, and he informed me how you had decoded the messages, and particularly what the latest message said: For Druitt to be accepted into some made-up Masonic society, he must disrobe and be at one of the rocks in the park behind the school at sunset. Clearly if the messages were being left by Conway in order to manipulate him, there was nothing good about the situation.

With that, I called in Conway, Drake, and Morgan. Your brother felt curious enough to stay, and I felt that his mysterious presence would provide a welcome addition of grim gravitas to the proceedings.

It went quickly. When I told Conway that I was aware of the messages – of course implying that I knew more than I did – and particularly about his plan to lure Druitt to the rock without any clothes, he broke down, trying to pass it off as simply a joke. He explained that he had been "bothered" by Druitt's "differentness", and it had brought out his spirit of good-natured teasing. (I expected this type of explanation from such a mean-spirited individual.) Having become aware of Druitt's fascination with Freemasons from snippets dropped into his lectures – and I suspect forays into Druitt's room, for how else would he know about the eye in the triangle? – Conway contrived a code for luring Druitt to disaster. Initially he sent an anonymous letter to his teacher, stating that he'd been especially noticed and subsequently selected for membership in an elite leadership cadre of the Masons. Along with this letter was the key to a code, with a promise of further coded messages carrying important instructions.

Then Conway began to send him messages. The first few were by mail, but when that became too much trouble, he started leaving them on Druitt's desk in his room, or slipping them into his coat pocket, or even under his plate in the dining hall, where Conroy had his student job – thus allowing him to be there early and leave the note before he might otherwise be observed.

Initially, the notes were simply promises to offer poor Mr. Druitt prestige and friendship, making him a part of some brotherhood. Then they decided to manipulate him further for their own amusement, sending him outside to wait for hours at various locations, often in the cold or during rainy weather. They fixed up one of the rocks behind the school in a copse of trees with a crude and cabalistic carving of the eye, supposedly a feature of the society who was sending the messages, and then directed him there on any number of occasions to wait for someone to arrive – always in vain, but also always observed from a distance, to their great and misplaced merriment.

This went on for several weeks, and then they had the idea to escalate the embarrassment to a much greater degree. As part of some supposed initiation, they would send Druitt out on All Hallows Eve to wait on the rock, completely unclothed. At first this was just to let him stand there in the cold, but then Conway decided that he would find a way to get the entire population of the school to go there and catch poor Druitt in the act. Only your masterful decoding of the message a few hours before the event prevented this from occurring.

If Druitt hadn't fallen for that plot, Conway planned to continue. He indicated that he had a new arrangement for Bonfire Night – last night – but I didn't hear the specifics, as by that point I was quite disgusted.

372

As I mentioned, Conway *had* a student job in the dining hall. I intentionally used the past tense, as he and the others are no longer welcome at this school. I summoned their parents and explained the entire situation. The families of Drake and Morgan seemed mortified, but Conway's parents seemed perversely proud of him, and I expect to read of that young man's hanging in the newspapers someday – that, or instead of his election to Parliament.

Needless to say, I found a way to prevent Mr. Druitt from going out to the rock that night without embarrassing him or letting him know that his secret was known, and the notes have stopped. I didn't share any of this with him. In his delicate state, I don't feel that I can. I expect that the mysterious and unexplained withdrawal of an offer of comradeship within this fictional branch of the Masons will devastate him, but hopefully he will learn and grow from it.

Now you know the story, if you hadn't heard from your brother already. Young Anthony Hayes has proven himself to be a young man of good character and willingness to act when necessary, and I've happily given him more responsibility and marked him for advancement, with a word in the right ears when the time is right.

In the meantime, I thank you again for your unexpected but very timely intervention.

I wish you well, and look forward to meeting you in person at some point in the future.

With very best regards,

George Valentine
Headmaster, Eliot Place School

* * * * *

4 December, 1888

My Dear Watson,

I hope that this finds you well on the road to recovery. I will never forgive myself for the injuries that you sustained last month following the terrible events in Miller's Court.

The clean-up of the Ripper Cabal continues, although I can safely say that the tide has turned, and most of the various factions have been eliminated to one degree or another. There still remains a further confrontation with the Prime Minister regarding the complicity of those who followed his implied directions and first set this hellish plot into motion, but after our meeting several weeks ago, he understands that my position is firm.

It may interest you to know that one of those who was involved with the murders – Mr. Druitt – has vanished. As you'll recall, he was a teacher at a boys' school in Blackheath, and he was dismissed last Friday. I had met the headmaster, George Valentine, seven years ago, when I performed a service for the school, but when I questioned him yesterday, he refused to provide any details, except to say that just before Druitt disappeared, he was dismissed from his position at the school, after being there for nearly a decade. I suspect that some of Mycroft's influence will need to be brought to bear in order to get at the full truth.

I'm aware that you're using your holiday back in Southsea to recuperate, but I also know that you're taking time to write up your notes about the Ripper matter, as well as some other past and unrelated investigations. (And your host, Dr. Doyle, must certainly be pestering you for details.) To assist in your efforts, I'm including a few letters that I received related to Druitt in Autumn 1881. Among them is one that you initially wrote to me on 13 October, instigating the matter following a visit from a Miss Emilie Hayes. I don't believe that that I ever told you what else happened with the affair, but read these letters and you'll understand the further association with Mr. Druitt. After you've had a look at them, continue with this letter for an explanation of the solution to the code, should you not be able to work it out for yourself . . . .

. . . I trust that your curiosity is now thoroughly whetted. While the matter itself is fully explained in the letters, I'm certain that the code is not so easily deciphered. If you've looked it through and have satisfied yourself that you cannot arrive at a solution, I'll explain.

From the little we know of Mr. Druitt – and considering that I knew even less of him in October 1881 – it's unlikely that he could have worked out a code on his own. That's why Conway, the villain of the piece, provided him with a key early on – to make sure that his manipulation could proceed successfully.

The sentence that was initially provided, and used so often by Druitt to decode the messages, was thus:

Pack my box with five dozen liquor jugs.

I instantly recognized this as a *pangram,* or a holoalphatetic sentence, which contains every letter of the alphabet at least once. (These have been used in recent years to assist in the training of those learning the typewriter. You may have heard of another – *The quick brown fox jumps over the lazy dog* – which contains thirty-five letters)

The sentence provided to Druitt is shorter, with only thirty-two letters. Of these, three are repeated more than once – *I* appears three times, *O* also three times, with *E* and *U* two times each. When the two extra *I*'s and *O*'s are deleted, along with the extra *E* and *U*, were left with the twenty-six letters of the alphabet, in this order:

Pack my box with f – ve d – z – n l – qu – r j – gs

By placing a number by each of the letters as it appears in this revised format: *1* for *P*, *2* for *A*, and so on – one comes up with a fairly simple substitution code, with each of the twenty-six letters represented by a unique number, according to where it falls within this pangram, after the extra six letters are removed:

P-1 a-2 c-3 k-4 m-5 y-6 b-7 o-8 x-9 w-10 i-11 t-12 h-13 f-14
v-15 e-16 d-17 z-18 n-19 l-20 q-21 u-22 r-23 j-24 g-25 s-2

Rearranging the letters alphabetically, it was easy to see which number stood for which letter:

A-2 B-7 C-3 D-17 E-16 F-14 G-25 H-13 I-11 J-24 K-4 L-20
M-5 N-19 O-8 P-1 Q-21 R-23 S-26 T-12 U-22 V-15 W-10 X-9 Y-6 Z-18

Thus, it was quite easy to decipher the few messages that were copied by Anthony Hayes and sent on for my examination.

If you review the messages in the enclosed letters, you'll see that the first one copied by young Hayes was:

Stay strong friend
Continue to await
recruits at rock
Oct Fourteen Six PM

That was the message that caused Druitt to glance at the clock and then rush out into the great storm, standing uncloaked at the rock while futilely waiting to meet someone from the supposed Masonic Brotherhood. That message had obviously been prepared with the sole purpose of driving the poor man into the rain.

Subsequently, Hayes sent me the message which was found in Druitt's room:

You have been selected for
a position in the high
Mason Council. Be at the
rock with our sign when
required. Your faith will
be rewarded Brother.

Without doubt, that message, with its promise of reward and inclusion, seduced poor lonely Druitt, sadly wallowing in his fascination with Freemasonry. Doubtless he looked for the rock with the carving of the eye, matching that which was on the message, until he located it in the nearby park.

On Halloween, when this all came to a head, Hayes had found the latest and last message:

Be at the rock at sunset on
All Hallows Eve. Wear no
clothes

One can only imagine what was planned for the poor fellow – public embarrassment at best, or possibly dismissal or arrest.

Over the years, I've kept my eye on Conway, who instigated the plot – you'll be pleased to know that he's already serving fifteen hard years in Dartmoor – but I'll admit that I looked away from Druitt. Perhaps that was a mistake.

I did feel pity for him after the letter from Valentine and sent the man a final anonymous coded message, encouraging him to seek out a legitimate Masonic organization – with the idea that he would find some purpose and fellowship. Sadly, we've seen how that turned out – he was used by them in a terrible way.

As we now know, he remained at that school as assistant master while trying to begin his feeble law practice at No. 9 King's Bench Walk. What occurred in those seven years to Druitt – already disturbed to some degree – to lead to his manipulation by the various groups that are coming to be known as under the single sobriquet of *Jack the Ripper*? When he reappears, perhaps we can ask him.

I'm sure that your holiday and recovery will continue successfully. Give my regards to Dr. Doyle, and I have passed along your last message to Miss Morstan.

I will write with more information about the Ripper affair as it becomes available, and look forward to your healthy return to London.

Very best,
Holmes

* * * * *

NOTE

The following was scribbled at the bottom of Holmes's letter of 4 December, 1888:

> *Montague John Druitt's body was found floating in the Thames off Thornycroft's torpedo works, Chiswick, by a waterman named Henry Winslade on 31 December, 1888. Stones in Druitt's pockets had kept his body submerged for about a month. – JHW 2 January, 1889*

The Service for the American Colonel

I had returned to Baker Street that morning, after finishing my regular rounds, to change the dressing on Sherlock Holmes's wound. He was up when I arrived, although I had expected that he might still be asleep, considering our late arrival in London the previous night.

He didn't appear to be in any remarkable pain, and the wound looked clean with no prospect of permanent damage. He'd earned it when defending a young woman against the sudden rage of a cornered nobleman carrying an unsuspected knife. Holmes had easily disarmed the fellow, but not before his upper arm was slashed. The well-aimed butt of my own pistol had put the deviant on the ground, but even so, he began to recover much sooner than one might have expected – no doubt related to some extra strength he drew upon in relation to his previously disguised madness.

It was no surprise that our talk had drifted to speculation on the man's fate. Throughout the series of murders which he had committed, there had been no signs of his insanity, but the gibbering and shrieking wreck that had been hauled away by Inspector Lanner would likely end up in the Broadmoor Criminal Lunatic Asylum rather than upon the gallows.

Our conversation had turned toward the concepts of criminal insanity and recidivism in general when there was a ring at the doorbell.

"As our discussion progressed, I neglected that we're expecting a visitor." He lifted a small note from the curious octagonal table beside his chair – a souvenir from one of those untold cases during his Montague Street days – and sailed it accurately in my direction. "This request for an appointment was waiting last night when we returned."

I recognized the stationery used by the Langham. There was nothing remarkable about Holmes's name and address scrawled on the front of the envelope – typical pen and ink. It was a man's handwriting, firm and confident, perhaps a bit elderly. I said as much to Holmes, adding rather inanely, "He is right-handed."

Holmes nodded, and as I heard steady solid footsteps beginning to climb toward the sitting room, I gave a quick glance at the note:

Mr. Sherlock Holmes,

I propose to call up on you at ten a.m. tomorrow morning if convenient to discuss a matter of fraud. Your name has been recommended to me by Inspector Lestrade of Scotland Yard, and also a man named Yves Paterson, from America.

Colonel H.B. Finn (Retired)

I looked toward Holmes. "Paterson was before your time, when I was in New York in '80, touring with Sasanoff. He was poisoning his wife with nutmeg – "

Before I could learn any more about that intriguing incident, and with the realization that like so many others of Holmes's early cases I might never convince him to share the details, there was a solid knock upon the door. Holmes bid the visitor to enter, and we stood.

Colonel Finn was a tall fellow in his early sixties, generally slim, but with wide shoulders, only just beginning to round a bit with age. His face was lined and long-darkened by the sun, and he had somewhat unhealthy circles under his eyes, as if a hard life was catching up with him, and he no longer lacked the strength to put up an opposing argument. He had big hands with large knuckles – clearly he had done much hard labor in his youth. His clothes were of an American cut, as were his boots, and well made – tailored and rather expensive looking. They weren't old, but obviously they were comfortable friends. Hanging from one hand was a wide-brimmed western-style American hat, such as I had last seen just a year before during an extended sojourn in the United States – particularly in San Francisco, but with forays into other areas of the North American continent as well.

As was so often the case, visitors to Holmes's sitting room inherently identified my friend as the man whom they were seeking. Finn glanced up and down Holmes's lean figure, a smile crossing his face when seeing that my friend was still in his dressing gown, although otherwise clothed properly to meet guests.

"Colonel Finn?" confirmed Holmes. "Excuse my casual attire. Watson here had just finished changing the dressing on a wound received last night in noble combat."

"Knife cut?" asked the American, his voice a growl, the accent containing a curious American twang. "I thought so. I saw the medical bag, open there on the table. You hold your arm as if it's tender, but there isn't any sign of a bulky bandage, such as one would pack around a bullet

379

wound, and anyway your color is too normal for a man who's been shot and lost a lot of blood."

Holmes smiled. "An observant man after our own hearts, Watson! Most who cross that threshold, Colonel, are not nearly so eagle-eyed."

"Nothing to it," the man said gruffly. "I've been cut a few times myself, and so have others that I've known. Just a matter of recognizing what you're seeing and making the right assumptions to be going on with." He glanced my way, and Holmes explained my presence.

"This my friend and associate, Dr. John Watson. He is often involved in my investigations, and is invaluable during an investigation."

Finn offered a hand to me and then Holmes. "That Inspector said you'd likely be here, Doctor. The more insight the better, I suppose."

Holmes gestured the visitor towards the basket chair facing the fire, and Finn nodded, removed his overcoat, and laid it and the hat across the settee. I offered him coffee or tea, but amended the statement when he glanced toward the spirit cabinet. "Or something stronger?"

"Whisky, if you don't mind," he said. "I've been in worse weather than what England can throw at me in February, but as I get older, I feel the cold worse and worse." He thanked me when I placed a glass containing a generous amount in his hand and settled into his seat. "Of course, I try and be careful – my own father was a drunk, you see, and I'm extra chary not to travel down that road."

I understood, for my own brother was of a similar nature, and watching his long and steady self-destruction had been an object lesson of incredible, though tragic, value.

"You mentioned fraud in your note . . . ." Holmes prompted, his tone encouraging elaboration.

Finn nodded. "Mind if I smoke?"

Holmes offered no objection, and decided to prepare a pipe for himself as well. (I declined.) Finn accepted Holmes's offer of tobacco, raising a curious eyebrow when it was presented in the Persian slipper kept on the mantel, but he made no comment. He packed his own pipe – a curious corncob construction that I had seen used before in more rural parts of the United States, and said, "I came to England to acquire a work of art – although it's more for sentimental reasons than it actually being any good. When I arrived, the dealer suddenly became coy with me – he didn't quite have it in his possession after all, he said, but he might be able to get it, though it was going to cost me extra. There was another bidder, and so on and so forth. He didn't know who he was dealing with, and rather than play his game, I walked around to the police. They've heard of the fellow – seems he has a reputation for this kind of thing – skirts right up to the edge of the law – but in this case he hasn't done anything illegal –

yet. But the inspector who talked with me – Lestrade – said that you might be able to get me some leverage."

"Who is this shady dealer?" asked Holmes.

"A kind of a man called Swadlincote. He has a little shop in a place named the Lowther Arcade, on the Strand."

Holmes smiled – not amused, but knowledgeable. "Mr. Lucius Swadlincote is in fact named Rufus Conger – a shining success story of sorts from the Rookeries near Seven Dials. It's possible he actually has the artwork which you seek, but this would need to be ascertained to your satisfaction. What is the object?"

Finn shifted and his eyes narrowed. He looked up and to the left, as if he could see what he recalled. "A drawing –fifty years old, give or take. It's – well, it's hard to describe, really. Most would say it's ugly, and amateur and raw, but that kind of thing has become popular of late. I first saw it when I was a boy, and over the years I never thought of it as anything but an unsettling peculiarity at best. In the last year or so, thought, things like that have become popular, and in spite of how bad it is, somehow this artwork became known and collectible.

"I'm getting old, and have more money than I know what to do with – my children are comfortable, and they don't need all of that burden settled on them. I've spent some of my fortune in some good ways, and some not so good, but the last few years I've had extra cause to be reminded of my misspent youth, and to become sentimental about it, and this drawing is a part of that. I decided that I could afford it – and other works by this dead artist too – and wanted to buy it, and the road led to the Swadlincote feller."

Something about the man's story sounded vaguely familiar, and I asked for additional information. "Could you describe the drawing?"

"I can, but perhaps I should lay a little more groundwork first." He raised his glass, let pipe smoke flow from house mouth across the glass of whisky, and took a sip. He licked his lips, and then judged how much of the amber liquid remained. Then he tightened his mouth as if making a choice and set aside what was left – more than half of what had been provided to him – abandoned on the side table. He didn't drink any more of it during the remainder of his visit.

"When I was a boy, just fourteen or fifteen, I was no account. I was raised in St. Petersburg, Missouri, on the banks of the Mississippi. My mother was long dead, and my father – as mentioned – was a drunk. The town drunk, as a matter of fact.

"I lived as I pleased, friends with some of the other children my age, while others shunned me. In fact, I was either hated or dreaded by all the mothers of the town, as they thought me idle and lawless and vulgar and bad. It was for this reason that I was admired so by the other children – they delighted in my forbidden society, and wished to be like me.

"I was always dressed in the cast-off clothes of full-grown men, and they were in perennial bloom and fluttering with rags. My hat was a vast ruin with a wide crescent lopped out of its brim, and my coat – when I wore one – hung nearly to my heels and had the rearward buttons far down the back. One suspender supported my trousers, and the fringed legs dragged in the dirt when not rolled up." He gestured at his current costume. "Not like now, you see. I came and went at my own free will. I slept on doorsteps in fine weather and in empty hogsheads in wet. I didn't have to go to school or to church, or call any being master or obey anybody. I could go fishing or swimming when and where I chose, and stay as long as it suited me. I wasn't forbidden to fight, and I could sit up as late as I pleased. I was always the first boy that went barefoot in the spring and the last to resume leather in the fall. I never had to wash, nor put on clean clothes – and I could swear wonderfully. In a word, everything that goes to make life precious I had. And I tell all of this to explain why I left St. Petersburg.

"I had lived wild and free for so long that when a local widow took me in and tried to 'civilize' me, I nearly couldn't stand it. Finally, when I had a chance to leave town and help a friend – and in truth, what I was doing was trying to help him escape to the north, for he was a slave of long acquaintance – I took it. We wandered from place to place, riding a raft when we were able. At one point we were separated for a few days, and I was taken in for a time by the Grangerford family.

"They were a curious bunch – wealthy enough for that area, and locked into some sort of blood feud with their neighbors. But they cared for me when I needed it, and for a few days I was able to live in their house and see their ways.

"They'd had a daughter who had died sometime before I arrived– Emmeline Grangerford. She was only fifteen years old at the time of her death, and she'd made quite an impression on the family when she was alive, because the whole house was a tribute to her now that she was dead. She'd written up all sorts of poems and produced a shocking amount of black charcoal drawings – all related to some sort of heartbreak or tragedy or death. I supposed that it was only fitting that such a one as she, who was so fascinated with dying, should be taken early.

He puffed the pipe, and then continued. "They called her drawings 'crayons', and had them hanging all over the house. They were different from any pictures that I'd ever seen before – blacker, mostly, than is common. One was a woman in a slim black dress, belted small under the armpits, with bulges like a cabbage in the middle of the sleeves, and a large black scoop-shovel bonnet with a black veil, and white slim ankles crossed about with black tape, and very wee black slippers, like a chisel, and she was leaning pensive on a tombstone on her right elbow, under a weeping willow, and her other hand hanging down her side holding a white handkerchief and a reticule, and underneath the picture it said, '*Shall I Never See Thee More Alas*'. Another one was a young lady with her hair all combed up straight to the top of her head, and knotted there in front of a comb like a chair-back, and she was crying into a handkerchief and had a dead bird laying on its back in her other hand with its heels up, and underneath the picture it said '*I Shall Never Hear Thy Sweet Chirrup More Alas*'.

"There was one where a young lady was at a window looking up at the moon, and tears running down her cheeks, and she had an open letter in one hand with black sealing wax showing on one edge of it, and she was mashing a locket with a chain to it against her mouth, and underneath the picture it said '*And Art Thou Gone Yes Thou Art Gone Alas*'.

"These was all nice pictures, I reckon, but I didn't somehow seem to take to them, because if ever I was down a little they always give me the fan-tods. Everybody was sorry she died, because she had laid out a lot more of these pictures to do, and a body could see by what she had done what they had lost. But I reckoned that with her disposition she was having a better time in the graveyard. She was at work on what they said was her greatest picture when she took sick, and every day and every night it was her prayer to be allowed to live till she got it done, but she never got the chance. It's this picture that I'm here to buy.

"After I left the Grangerford house, I re-established myself with my runaway slave friend, and we continued our journey. Eventually I ended up staying with a kind old woman for a while before I started to feel strangled again, just as I had when the widow had tried to adopt me, and so I lit out for the Territories.

"I did a lot of wandering out there, and made fortunes and lost them. I was in the Mexican-American War, and met a lot of those officers that would later be on both sides of the Civil War. A year or so later I was a Forty-Niner in California. That's where I got rich the first time. I was married for a time then to a widowed school-teacher who showed me the value of education in a way that I never grasped as a boy. Later, after she died, I drifted some more. I was with the anti-Slavers and abolitionists in Kansas in the 1850's, and by 1861 I had made it to Virginia City, Nevada, where I made my second fortune on the periphery of the bonanza at the Comstock Lode – I was too smart to mine, but I knew from my California days that money could be made supplying the miners. For a time there I was good friends with a former sea captain named Ben that I'd met years before in my travels – he'd since established himself near Virginia City with a massive ranch, which he owned and defended with the help of his three grown sons, each from a different mother, and all of them as different from one another as night and day. I used to go to his ranch often for the conversation and an evening meal – he had a most talented Chinese cook. It was at one of Ben's dinners where I was introduced to a newspaper fella who was working then in Virginia City.

"I became thick with that feller – name of Sam – and ended up telling him a whole passel of stories about my days as a youth. After that we lost touch with one another – he went his way, and I went back east and served in the Army – for the North to preserve the Union and free the slaves, mind you. That's where I picked up the rank of Colonel. It isn't an honorary thing – I did a fair bit to earn it in Knoxville campaign and the battle at Chattanooga. Then I went west again and settled in Santa Fe, where I took sides with the Mora Gunfighter. I still live there when I'm not gallivanting all over. Twelve years or so ago, Sam from Virginia City tracked me down again to ask more questions about the tales I'd shared, and he ended up writing a couple of books based on what I told him – with my permission, of course. The first of them came out in '76, and the other just a few years ago, in '84.

"It was that second book that had a bit about my descriptions of Emmeline Grangerford's peculiar artworks and poetry. Nothing came of it then, but last year when that other poet, Emily Dickinson, died, there was a sudden interest in that kind of poetry – a terrible fascination with death that woman had. Someone remembered reading what I'd said in that book by Sam and tracked down the Grangerford family, looking for Emmeline's old art and poems. By then, all the Grangerfords that I'd known were long dead, mostly killed by their neighbors, I reckon, if the War didn't get them, but what was left of the current generation still had all of that girl's scratchings stored away in a box, and they sold it lock, stock, and barrel to a New York art dealer. He worked up a real frenzy about all of it – a true nine-days' wonder – and when all that happened, my friend Sam sent me a letter, thinking I might be amused.

"I was, but more than that, I also became interested in buying some of it – and eventually *all* of it – more for sentimental reasons about my long-gone boyhood than any belief that there was anything good or talented about what Emmeline wrote and drew. I've read that some people thought she was a genius, cut down before her prime. And I recall at the time – when I was fourteen or so – that I thought that if she could make poetry like that before she was fourteen, there was no telling what she could have done by-and-by. They said she could rattle off poetry like nothing, and didn't ever have to stop to think. She would slap down a line, and if she couldn't find anything to rhyme with it, she'd just scratch it out and slap down another one, and go ahead. She wasn't particular. She could write about anything you choose to give her to write about, just so it was sadful.

"Every time a man died, or a woman died, or a child died, she would be on hand with her 'tribute' before he was cold. She called them 'tributes'. The neighbors said it was the doctor first, then Emmeline, then the undertaker – the undertaker never got in ahead of Emmeline but once, and then she hung fire on a rhyme for the dead person's name, which was Whistler. She wasn't ever the same after that, they'd said. She never complained, but she pined away and didn't live long, poor thing.

"Over the last year or so, I bought one of her drawings, and then another and another, and the poems too. I have all of those that I mentioned, and a number of others besides – the dealers and critics are calling them Emmeline's '*Alas*' series. I'm afraid that it's became something more than a hobby to me lately, filling up my time as I track down what I don't have. My last wife died a couple of years ago, and my children are scattered, so I have nothing much else to do, and as you'll know, gentleman, collectors are the strangest sorts of cats. How else to explain that I hope to acquire Emmeline Grangerford's complete works? And I'm very close to doing it.

"Word went out that I was the man to beat when collecting Emmeline Grangerford art, and that has led to the prices on what's left going up – knowing I can afford it – and me receiving messages from dealers all over offering items that I wasn't even chasing quite yet. One such was from a man here in London, a private individual named Potter, who had one of Emmeline's handwritten poems, "*Ode to Stephen Dowling Bots, Dec'd*", about a lad who fell down a well and drowned. When I learned about the drawing offered by Swadlincote, also here in London, I sent a message to him indicating that I was going to be over here anyway, and would like to purchase what he had for sale. That was a mistake, I guess. It let him know my interest, and gave him time to find out more about me – and just what I could afford. By the time I got here, he'd decided to chisel me for whatever else he could get. And so here I am."

Colonel Finn's story had been in more depth than Holmes will usually tolerate, but he seemed to be enjoying the story, and he's always had a unique fascination with and affection for Americans. For my part, suspecting who our visitor was, I was quite happy to hear the man's narrative.

"Tell us of the drawing you're here to acquire," said Holmes.

"Well, as I said, it was the drawing Emmeline left unfinished when she died. It was a picture of a young woman in a long white gown, standing on the rail of a bridge all ready to jump off, with her hair all down her back, and looking up to the moon, with the tears running down her face, and she had two arms folded across her breast, and two arms stretched out in front, and two more reaching up towards the moon – and the idea was to see which pair would look best, and then scratch out all the other arms. But as I was saying, she died before she got her mind made up, and afterwards the Grangerfords kept that picture over the head of the bed in her room, and every time her birthday came they hung flowers on it. Other times it was hid with a little curtain. The young woman in the picture had a kind of a nice sweet face, but there was so many arms it made her look too spidery, seemed to me."

I laughed, and Colonel Finn nodded good-naturedly. Holmes had a raised eyebrow, as if contemplating why such a work as described would ever solicit a single jot of interest, even for sentimental reasons. And yet, some of the items that he keeps – from a rudely framed and unfocused photograph of Charlie Peace on his bedroom wall, to the carefully shaved and shaped femur of a Neolithic man – which he desperately carved into a dagger as a boy to defend himself against an unexpected rabid dog (or so I'm told) – seem just as unusual when considered in the cold light of dawn.

Holmes set aside his pipe. "Your story has some features of interest, but I must honestly tell you that normally it wouldn't be the sort of case I'd take. Finding 'leverage', as Lestrade suggested I might do, for one man to use against another in a business dealing is outside the normal self-described limits of my practice. However, I am familiar with Mr. Swadlincote, and this is an excuse to pry into his affairs a little bit, for I've neglected him for too long. You're staying at the Langham, I believe?"

Colonel Finn nodded.

"Excellent. Watson and I should have something to report within a day or so. In the meantime, a message regarding any new factors connected to the problem will find us here and will be much appreciated."

Finn nodded again and pushed himself to his feet. "That's all that I can ask, then," he said. "I normally take care of my own business, but I'm a stranger here, and haven't had a chance to get the lay of the land." And with that, he offered his hand to both of us and made his departure.

When he'd gone, I tossed the remains of whiskey into the fire, causing it to blaze forth a satisfying but very brief flash before setting the glass on the dining table for later retrieval by Mrs. Hudson. Finn's story sounded quite familiar, and I wanted a chance to conduct a quick bit of research, but instead I asked, "What are your plans? Do you intend to see this Swadlincote in Lowther Arcade?"

386

"I don't think that would be advisable," was Holmes's reply. He had dropped back into his chair after Finn's departure, where he continued to smoke, an unusually concerned look upon his face.

"Is this more serious than I thought?" I asked.

"It is indeed. Swadlincote, originally named Conger, is one of the lower-tier agents of the Professor, and as such, I must be careful in how I express my interest in this matter."

At that time, in early 1887, Holmes had been aware for quite a while of the organization constructed by Professor Moriarty, later to have such an infamous reputation. But then, the Professor seemed to most observers to be living a quiet life as an army coach, having come down to London a few years earlier from one of the university towns, where he had been compelled to resign his chair after dark rumors gathered around him. Holmes had known him in his own university days, and initially he had been resistant to believe that his old math tutor could be responsible for the unifying criminal web that was slowly being constructed in the capital. Eventually, however, the evidence could not be ignored. And yet, he was still having a most difficult time convincing the authorities of the truth, while each day the web grew more complex and its grip tightened stronger.

In those days, Moriarty was not quite the notable criminal of just a few short years later, and neither was he yet as bitter as he would specifically become toward my friend. Then, it was almost as if they were playing some sort of chess game, constantly testing and trying to guess the strategy and resources of one another, although Holmes was never complacent or amused. Only after the professor's injuries a few years later following a fall from the Tower of London (when attempting to steal the Crown Jewels while disguised as a constable) did the game become grim and deadly.

"Swadlincote knows me," said Holmes. "I would prefer not to appear as myself in this matter. But perhaps, Watson, I could enlist you to be my representative?"

"I would be glad to assist in any way." Suspecting Finn's identity made me all the more willing to be involved in the affair.

"Then I see you acting as a competing buyer – having heard of this rather dodgy-sounding piece of art, you can present yourself at the shop and see if our man is open to a bidding war between you and the Colonel."

"Won't that have an adverse effect for your client?" I asked. "If the dealer believes there's more interest, he'll raise the price even higher, so that when Finn does complete the arrangements – assuming that this dealer even has the drawing – he'll have to pay an excessive amount beyond what's being asked now. It seems as if you're asking him to cover an extra cost just so that you can carefully probe the Professor's organization from a distance."

"Not at all. While you approach Swadlincote, I'll refresh my memory on his associations with the Professor, and determine just how deeply he's involved. We should be able to use the 'leverage' Lestrade mentioned to get the drawing for Finn while finding some new and useful fact that will be of use in the future. And there's always the chance that our sudden interest in Swadlincote, coming from an unexpected direction, will be like suddenly turning over a rock and sending what lives beneath it scurrying around helplessly in the bright sunshine."

"Shall I go over there, then?"

"Not quite yet. First, do a few hours of preparation. Go see your friend Lomax, and have him give you information about the current interest in this sort of art. Perhaps he can tell you more of Emily Dickinson, mentioned by the Colonel, to give you a frame of reference when talking over the Grangerford drawing. I've found that just a little knowledge of art can be spun into a lot of convincing moonshine, with the right attitude. In the meantime, I'll carry out my own inquiries, and we'll meet back here in a few hours."

And so I set off for St. James's Square, and the London Library, where I knew that Lomax, the sublibrarian, could be found, regardless of the season or the time of day. And so he was. I explained a bit about my mission, without getting into specifics, and that I needed to have some frame of reference when talking to the dealer. Like all good librarians, he let me ask about what I *thought* that I needed, and then, through a few intelligent and defining questions, discovered what I *really* needed. He had some knowledge of this new interest in the type of poetry that had been popularized by the recently deceased Emily Dickinson, but said that I'd be better off finding out about Susan A. Moore, an American whose volume *The Sentimental Song Book* had been published in 1876, and seemed to feature much the same type of verse as that of the long-deceased Emmeline Grangerford.

Of course, Lomax had made sure that the London Library's collection had acquired a copy, and he pressed it into my hand, noting that no one had checked it out since the book had been acquired over a decade before.

I stepped outside, where I read one of the pieces at random, entitled "*Little Libbie*":

> *One more little spirit to Heaven has flown,*
> *To dwell in that mansion above,*
> *Where dear little angels, together roam,*
> *In God's everlasting love.*

With an expression on my face that might seem as if I'd inadvertently walked through a floating miasma of passing sewer gas, I snapped the small book shut, muttered something about "Ineffable twaddle!", and walked into Pall Mall to find a hansom cab for the ride back to Baker Street.

I hadn't been gone as long as I might have thought, and so I settled in with a cup of hot *café noir* as provided by the indefatigable Mrs. Hudson and read through as many of the other poems as I could tolerate. One referred to a dead man sleeping and resting in peace in a cold silent tomb. I scanned down the six stanzas and decided that I had no need to reach the end. Another concerned the death of a girl – one of nine children – who was now waiting for her siblings in heaven. While it wasn't necessarily bad, it was doggerel of the type that I simply could not enjoy. And yet, I suspected that it was written at the time as a comfort to a family known by Moore who had lost a daughter, and it was surely heartfelt and sincere, if unpolished. Certainly Emmeline Grangerford's own poems, as described by Finn, had been written with the same intent – to act as "tributes" to provide honor and comfort to grieving families. In spite of my own failure to enjoy this type of thing, and even an initial impulse to ridicule, I couldn't fault the intent, and I found that I was apologizing a bit to Mrs. Moore, wherever she might be, for initially and harshly judging her work – albeit without her knowledge.

Holmes arrived an hour or so later, and I could somehow sense that it had gotten colder outside. I recalled seeing the high icy clouds pushing in from the west, and wondered if the morrow wouldn't bring some rather unpleasant weather.

After hanging his Inverness and fore-and-aft cap, Holmes poured himself a cup of coffee from the pot left by Mrs. Hudson, certainly cool by now, and joined me by the fire. Rather than tell me of his own efforts, he had me summarize a bit what I'd learned from Lomax. Then we began to discuss a strategy whereby I could present myself at Swadlincote's shop – ideally later that afternoon – and open my own fraudulent negotiations for the curiously unappealing Grangerford artwork.

Holmes was discussing how I could bluff my way into seemingly having enough knowledge of the subject to interest an unscrupulous dealer when the doorbell rang. Within a moment, we heard the steady and heavy tromp of boots regularly climbing the stairs, and both of us knew it could only be a policeman.

It was – Constable Wilkins, whom we both knew of old. "Gentlemen," he said, speaking formally and carefully while touching his helmet with a finger. "Compliments of Inspector Lestrade, he asks if you might return with me to the Lowther Arcade. There has been a murder, and the man who seems to be responsible – an American – is in custody there and asking for you both."

Holmes's lips tightened and he shook his head – not a refusal to accompany the constable, but rather an expression of irritation. It seemed that our plans had been disrupted, or negated completely.

Wilkins had a growler waiting, and we were soon making our way through the surprisingly busy streets. I asked about the weather, and the constable confirmed that a winter storm was on the way – perhaps explaining why so many Londoners were out and about that afternoon, as they took care of business before the need to possibly hide away for a day or so. I pulled my heavy overcoat tighter.

When the inane conversation was complete, Holmes leaned forward like a bird of prey and instructed Wilkins to provide particulars about the murder to which we traveled. Having known one another for quite a while, the policeman complied as if answering to one of his own inspectors.

"The dead man is an art dealer, Lucius Swadlincote. He has a shop about halfway through the Lowther Arcade. Inspector Lestrade said that he was asked about this very chap only this morning by an American – the same one who was found beside the body, unconscious, and with blood on his hands.

"Both of them were in the back room, which seems like a small office. The dead man was in his chair, his throat cut, and the American – a Colonel Finn – was on the floor beside the desk. The back of his head has a lump, and he was unconscious when we arrived – or at least he was pretending to be. Mrs. Swadlincote had been out – she sometimes serves as something of a clerk there, she explained – and when she returned from a visit to see her sister in Touchen-End, she found her husband dead and the American lying on the floor. She ran out screaming until Constable Wilson heard her. He whistled, and it wasn't long before the Inspector and I were there. After all, it isn't far from the Yard, is it?"

By then we had arrived. The driver pulled to a stop in Adelaide Street, by the path leading through to St. Martin's Church. We could see that word of the murder had already spread, as a motley crowd of loungers was clustered around the entrance to the Arcade. Several seemed to recognize Holmes, as they pointed and whispered. One man – a fellow named Alfred Bassick – was familiar to me. He was a trusted member of that small squad of Professor Moriarty's lieutenants, and when our eyes met, he awkwardly ducked his head and turned away, as if looking elsewhere, and then crept away. He knew that I had recognized him.

We passed through the crowd, and in the short space between the entrance and Swadlincote's shop, where a number of policemen were clustered, I shared that piece of intelligence with Holmes. He nodded, and then we were shown into the presence of Lestrade and a small taciturn woman, deeply grooved lines on either side of her bitter mouth, each standing by a counter, upon which several sheets of paper were spread. At the side of the room was our client, Colonel Finn, sitting in a chair while a constable stood behind him. He flashed a rueful smile on his face when he saw us, and he shrugged as if to apologize.

Holmes joined Lestrade, who led him to the office door to view the body, while I walked over to Finn. The constable behind him, Burnsall, had been along the previous autumn when Holmes and I had revealed the secret tunnel leading to the counterfeiter Malham's presses, so he wasn't concerned when I offered to check Finn's head.

"I'd been to the other dealer to complete the purchase of Emmeline's poem about that Bots feller, and even though I'd spoke to you and Mr. Holmes just an hour or so earlier, I didn't see any harm in sending a note that I'd be stopping by. I didn't let on about our earlier pow-wow. I just asked if he'd had any luck in tracking down the drawing. When I arrived, he said that he'd found the drawing – which would mean that what we discussed earlier didn't necessarily matter anymore – and then he took me there to his office. It's a small room, barely big enough for him to squeeze around and behind his desk, so I stood in the doorway. I was watching as he bent down to open a desk drawer when everything went dark. Someone hit me from behind while I was standing there. When I woke up, the police were here, the man was dead, and there was blood on my hands." He held them up, but I could tell that he'd since been allowed to wipe them clean.

I observed that, while Finn had a sizeable lump upon the back of his head, he wasn't in any serious danger, provided that we kept an eye on him for possible concussion. As I straightened up, I realized that the others in the room had fallen silent and had been listening to his statement.

Lestrade beckoned me closer. "Is it possible, Doctor," he asked *sotto voce*, "that the wound on his head could be self-inflicted? His story doesn't make any sense. He told us that when he arrived, it was only him and Swadlincote in this room, and it was just a moment later, only a few footsteps away, that he was standing in the office door when he was struck behind. He claims that Swadlincote was alive up to that moment, but he awoke to find us here, standing over him, and the dealer dead. And Mrs. Swadlincote says that when she walked in, she saw the door to the office standing open – it's normally kept closed – and the Colonel lying there. She could see her husband past him, dead in his chair. That's when she went out and summoned the police."

"He killed him!" the woman shrieked, surprising us all after the low tones from the inspector. "He's been pestering him to death about the awful drawing, and acting as if he didn't believe that Lucius was doing everything he could to find it. Now what will I do? How can a woman like me carry on with such a business? My livelihood is ruined!"

She evinced a hardness that left no surprise when she didn't seem to care that her husband was dead, other than how it affected her economic prospects. Holmes, however, only seemed to be half-listening. He looked my way. "What say you, Watson?" Could he have faked the blow to his head?"

"I don't see how. It appears to be from some object – and I trust that no such thing was found beside him, dropped by his own hand."

"No," agreed Lestrade, "but he could have hit himself with something – one of these knick-knacks on the shelves – and not knocked himself unconscious, but instead replaced it and then lay down on the floor until someone arrived."

"But why do that?" asked Holmes. "He had no reason that we know to kill the man, and if he did, why would he then stay and incriminate himself in such a manner."

"He knew that he'd sent a note telling that he was coming," said Lestrade, picking up one of the sheets on the counter. "This note, as a matter of fact." It looked to have a few drops of blood across it.

"Where was it?" asked Holmes.

"Lying on top of the dead man's desk."

"So again, the flimsy case you build makes no sense. The Colonel sends a note, and then subsequently arrives and is told that the drawing has been found – I believe that the drawing is also there on the counter, based on how it was described – and then for some reason he then decides to cut Swadlincote's throat. Instead of gathering up the drawing and the note indicting that he'd be visiting here, and then making his escape, he hits himself on the head with a curio, replaces it, and then lowers himself to the floor to await the inevitable arrival of the authorities. No, Lestrade, it won't do."

He turned to the dead man's wife. "Did you know of the note sent by the Colonel?"

"No," she answered, almost immediately by "Yes!" She seemed prepared to speak further, but Holmes nodded and then stepped into the small office to examine the body. I glanced through the door to see that dead man, originally named Rufus Conger, was leaned back in a chair behind the desk. The room was quite small, not more than eight feet square – really more of a storage closet. The room opened to the left beyond the door, with shelves on the right wall running to the back, and the desk pushed over against the left wall. There was a chair in front of the desk on the door side, and Swadlincote's own chair at the back of the room, with a number of boxes stacked haphazardly around it. The dead man was a balding and puffy man in his fifties, and he had a shocked expression on his face. The gaping wound on his throat, a terrible cut that resembled an upturned red smile, had spurted a gout of blood across the desk, and had then continued to flow down his shirt.

Leaving Holmes to his examination, I looked at the documents on the counter. Besides the note written by Colonel Finn, indicating that he would be by that afternoon to check on the progress in locating the dead girl's drawing, there was the illustration itself, about a foot high and nine inches wide, on thick yellowed paper, the kind often used for amateur sketches. Finn had said that the drawn figure appeared to be on the railing of a bridge, although I could not confirm it. She was on a railing of some sort, but if it was a bridge, the water was very high, as the posts seemed to be reflected into the water just beneath where she stood, and there was no indication of the bridge's deck. Something like a crescent moon was just above her head, but pointed up on each end in the way that a child would draw a smile. It terribly reminded me of the gash on Swadlincote's throat.

There was a dead-looking tree on the right of the picture, and quite a bit of hatching back-and-forth darkening the background behind the central figure, a young woman in a long white dress, with her tiny pointed feet sticking out beneath her on the bridge rail, and her long black hair hanging behind her and fanned out, visible on both sides. Her long weary-looking face was actually rather well executed, and she seemed to be looking up toward the sky – possibly toward the smiling moon that hovered over her. As Finn had described, she had three pairs of arms, one set held heavenward, one grasping in prayer across her breast, and the third hang hanging down. Around the entire thing was a rough and crude blacked-in border. I understood that the artist, young Emmeline Grangerford, had passed before she could complete it and choose which set of arms to keep, but in some way, all of the arms seemed to convey a message – although I couldn't quite express it. In any case, I was not repulsed, but neither was I interested enough to see it as any more than the sketching of a moderately talented child. I certainly couldn't understand the desire to collect it.

Beside it was third document, a sheet of old and yellowed copy-book paper. It was a hand-written verse with the curious title *Ode to Stephen Dowling Bots, Dec'd.* Picking it up, I looked toward Finn. He nodded. "That's the poem I came over here to buy from the other dealer. The inspector took it from me when I was searched." He scowled, and I held it a little more carefully, not quite sure what such an item cost, but certain that it was overpriced to the point that I ought not to damage it. Having seen Miss Grangerford's illustrative talents, I held it closer to read how she set about writing a poem:

> *And did young Stephen sicken,*
> *And did young Stephen die?*
> *And did the sad hearts thicken,*
> *And did the mourners cry?*
>
> *No; such was not the fate of*
> *Young Stephen Dowling Bots;*
> *Though sad hearts round him thickened,*
> *'Twas not from sickness' shots.*
>
> *No whooping-cough did rack his frame,*
> *Nor measles drear with spots;*
> *Not these impaired the sacred name*
> *Of Stephen Dowling Bots.*
>
> *Despised love struck not with woe*
> *That head of curly knots,*
> *Nor stomach troubles laid him low,*
> *Young Stephen Dowling Bots.*
>
> *O no. Then list with tearful eye,*
> *Whilst I his fate do tell.*
> *His soul did from this cold world fly*
> *By falling down a well.*
>
> *They got him out and emptied him;*
> *Alas it was too late;*
> *His spirit was gone for to sport aloft*
> *In the realms of the good and great.*

Having now seen and judged it, and as a man with a vastly different set of priorities about what was good and what was not, I replaced the sheet on the counter, uncoveted.

As I did so, Holmes stepped out of the office, carrying a bloody knife – looking something like a *kris* that I had seen in my soldiering days, and not an unusual artifact considering the similar items littering the small shop. "It was on the floor beside the body," Lestrade explained.

Holmes laid the knife, which he held delicately by two fingers, on the counter, a distance away from the three documents. I could see that the blood was still damp. Then he continued to the front door, where he spent a moment opening it and closing it, fast and slow, sometimes from inside, and sometimes in the Arcade, while a couple of constables standing out there watched curiously. When he was finished, he returned to stand beside us. Looking at the small bitter woman standing alongside the inspector, Holmes said, "Sadly, it's impolite to ask if I can inspect your shoes. May I instead have a look at your cuffs?"

Mrs. Swadlincote started to extend her arms, and then abruptly dropped them to her side. Holmes nodded as if it was expected. "No matter. I understand you'd been to visit your sister in Berkshire?"

"Yes," she said with tight lips.

"And when you arrived back here, you discovered the body? And once you saw it, you turned and left the shop, screaming for help?" Again she agreed, warily.

Holmes turned to look past her at Colonel Finn. "What time did you send your note to indicate you'd be stopping here?"

"Around two o'clock. I paid a lad at the Langham to run it over while I had a late lunch."

"Both facts that can be verified. What time did you arrive here?"

"A little before three."

"And you came by cab?"

"I did."

"It should be easy to locate the cabbie that brought you, fixing the time you arrived." Holmes turned back to Lestrade. "The cabbie is likely one of those who frequent the Langham. What time was the alarm given?"

"A bit after three o'clock."

Holmes nodded and looked back at Mrs. Swadlincote. "But the train from Touchen-End by way of Windsor arrived at Paddington around one o'clock, about two hours before you said that you walked in that door. Assuming that you actually visited your sister there as described," Holmes said, his tone becoming more clipped, "which will also be investigated, you returned to London well before your stated arrival at this shop to find your husband dead and the Colonel unconscious on the floor. What did you do in the meantime during those two hours?"

"I . . . I came straight here."

"Careful, Mrs. Swadlincote – you are on treacherous ground now. You haven't had time to see how these different threads are tangled. A moment ago, you seemed to have some confusion as to whether you'd seen the note sent by the Colonel. First you said no, and then yes. Which was it?"

She didn't answer, apparently trying to see the value or danger of each choice. Holmes glanced at Lestrade. "You say that the note was found on the desk in the office?"

"It was."

"And the first constable on the scene was told that Mrs. Swadlincote had arrived, saw the body, and then immediately turned and ran back into the Arcade to summon help – without entering the office."

Lestrade glanced at the woman. "That was her story. But what difference does it make whether she was back in time to know or not to know about the note and the Colonel's proposed visit?"

"Knowing ahead of time that the Colonel would be here gave her the knowledge that a suspect would be available for the police after she killed her husband."

The woman gave a shriek then, attempting to lunge across the counter for the bloody knife, but she was too short to do so effectively and, unable to reach it, she was pulled back by Constable Wilkins, who was joined by another officer. They each held one of her arms as she violently struggled from side to side before abruptly dropping to her knees with a sob.

"I have an advantage, Lestrade," explained Holmes. "You and I both knew that Swadlincote had criminal connections, but you may not be aware that he's part of a larger and growing organization. Today, when Colonel Finn shared his story with Watson and me, and that he'd had dealings with this shop, I sent Watson to some research while I visited one or two of my acquaintances in the criminal fellowship. They were reluctant to provide me with a great many details, as this larger organization of which I speak has a long arm and very little tolerance for those who reveal its secrets. But these individuals owe me a thing or two, and know that I can be trusted.

"As I hadn't previously shined too much light on Swadlincote, I was rather surprised to learn that he wasn't as important as I'd first thought – although I know for certain what sort of business has been carried out in this shop and its value to that organization. But it all made sense when my second source explained that the husband lying dead in the other room was simply a figure-head, and a rather stupid one, while his wife – this woman – is the actual brains of the business, and she was the one who had gained both the attention and the respect of the larger criminal organization.

"It seems that she's been marked down for greater things, and all that's been holding her back was her husband, perceived as something of a jelly-fish who could not be trusted. Things have been coming to a head of late, and today when the Colonel's note arrived – and she was certainly on hand to read it – she suddenly saw a way to rid herself of a useless husband and frame this American, afflicted with the collector's mania and rather bothersome of late as well. What she didn't know was that Colonel Finn had already chosen to involve me in the business.

"Mrs. Swadlincote came back early, as can be shown by the train times – if she really went to Touchen-End at all. Your men can ascertain that, Inspector. In any case, she was here in time to know about the Colonel's note, saying he'd be along about three o'clock. She left the shop sometime before he got here, but soon after he arrived, she slipped back inside. My investigations of the door just now show that, if one is careful and knowledgeable about its workings, that door can be opened silently." He looked toward Colonel Finn. "She wasn't here when you arrived, was she?"

"Of course not." The older man said, waving a hand. "As you can see, there's no place for anyone to hide. I would have known."

Holmes nodded. "Then she looked in from the outside – perhaps, Lestrade, you can find a witness in the Arcade who saw her standing there, peeping through the window. She observed where the Colonel was standing, slipped inside, and crept close enough behind him to knock him unconscious. Then, when her husband – seated in that cramped space behind his desk – asked what was happening and why she had done what she'd done, she stepped over the Colonel's recumbent form, approached her husband, likely as if to show him something, and then cut his throat, using a knife from the shop and dropping it by the body. How else to explain how he seemingly let someone approach in that cramped space without any signs of disruption? He certainly wouldn't have let the Colonel do so. Only someone he trusted could have stood so closely.

"I saw a few signs along the edges of the bloodstains on the floor behind the desk of a small foot. That's why I mentioned examining the lady's shoes. There was also a chance that a few drops of spurting blood might be on her sleeve, despite her care to avoid it or remove them before summoning the constable."

Lestrade seemed to have some questions as he struggled to understand, but Holmes pulled him aside and they spoke in low tones, no doubt explaining further details of Professor Moriarty's organization which he didn't wish to share with the entire room. At that time, there was some skepticism in the official ranks about what was perceived by the Yard as this peculiar "bee in Holmes's bonnet", and his apparent *idée fixe* on the mild-mannered mathematics professor, but to his credit, Lestrade had already seen first-hand some of the Professor's evil handy-work, and he took no additional convincing to understand what had occurred, and that the American colonel was simply a scape-goat drawn into the ugly business.

By the time Holmes and the inspector had completed their discussion, Mrs. Swadlincote had been led away, and her dead husband's body was being loaded for removal to the morgue. Colonel Finn was on his feet, indicating that he'd had much worse injuries in his long and storied past, and that a bump on the head wasn't going to slow him down, curiously adding that someone who was so incapacitated "might as well walk".

He stepped up to the counter to retrieve the handwritten document chronicling the unappealing *Ode to Stephen Dowling Bots, Dec'd.* He carefully replaced it within a long leather wallet held in his coat, and then asked, "What about the drawing? I haven't paid for it yet."

Holmes stepped behind the counter, where he retrieved a stiff folder lying there that would protect the artwork. "I believe," he said, putting the drawing inside, "that the Swadlincote enterprise is now defunct. Perhaps, if your conscious requires it, you can make a donation to the lady's legal defense in exchange for this drawing, but I have no doubt that it, based on your association with it from so long ago, should stay with you, rather than being carelessly examined and then likely destroyed by whomever empties this shop."

He glanced toward Lestrade, who looked surprised at being asked. The inspector raised a hand in agreement. "Take it, for your troubles. Mr. Holmes is right. If I was the one cleaning out the place, I'd throw it in the furnace."

Holmes re-opened the folder and gave the thing a closer look. Then he shuddered and handed it across to the Colonel.

Lestrade saw to the locking of the shop door behind us, and then he and Holmes set off for Scotland Yard to explore the further aspects of the affair. I located a hansom to take Colonel Finn and me to the Langham. As we passed through the lobby, I asked that the hotel doctor join us upstairs. Then, in Finn's room, I explained that the man had a possible concussion and arranged that he receive regular examinations over the next day or so. Finn growled about it, but agreed. After the doctor departed, I wanted to ask the American a number of questions, specifically related to his past, but I found that I was uncertain how to broach the matter, and more important, that I didn't necessarily want to know the truth from the ideas that I'd assembled in my head about the man. I was awkwardly reluctant to know the truth about someone whom I'd thought to be fictional.

For I was certain that I knew who he was. I think that he knew that I was aware of it, and he was grateful that I chose to leave the matter unexplored. I congratulated him on his possession of the recovered artwork, gave him some more medical advice regarding his injury that I doubted he'd follow, and then departed. But before leaving the building entirely, I sought out a hotel employee who owed me a long-standing debt, being paid over the years in tiny increments, and obtained a look at the hotel register. I was right – the Colonel's initials, *"H.B."*, represented exactly what I'd surmised.

A decade later, during the Queen's Diamond Jubilee in the summer of 1897, I was able to meet the American author, Samuel Clemens, when he was living in Chelsea, tarrying there after his world tour and living in temporary seclusion following the death of his beloved daughter the previous year. We had a chance during those days to have many a long and free-wheeling discussion, and I was able to confirm a number of other particulars regarding my suspicions as to the identity of the man whom Holmes always simply called "the American Colonel", although my friend never once gave any indication as to whether he was also aware the man's true and notable identity, and if he was, whether he realized its significance.

"These was all nice pictures, I reckon, but I didn't somehow seem to take to them, because if ever I was down a little they always give me the fan-tods."

Illustration from the original edition of
Adventures of Huckleberry Finn
by Edward Windsor Kemble (1861–1933)

With many thanks to Samuel Clemens (Mark Twain) for a lot of fun . . . .

400

The Rescue at Ypres

The crossing to Dunkirk had passed with no more incident than a queasy stomach, and the journey from there across the border into Belgium was nothing more than a formality. We were met at the other side by a short Belgian of our acquaintance, formerly a high-ranking policeman. He had been pressed into service against the invading Germans, and he now rode with us into Ypres.

"Ah, *mes amies*," said Monsieur P-----. "It is good to see you once again." He might have been comical with his short stature and egg-shaped head if one didn't know better. At times his accent had been known to grow droll with over-exaggeration, and he sometimes appeared to preen in a harmless sort of way, but it was only to lull and trick his prey – to make those criminals that he sought dismiss him as a fool – for he was a detective of rare and noted ability. There was none of that foolishness today. None of it was necessary for either Sherlock Holmes or me – we knew him well from olden days.

That day, P-----'s bright green eyes were sharp, and he evinced no more of an accent than any Belgian would when speaking English. I had greeted him fondly, despite the circumstances, and was about to say his name aloud, but he raised a hand. "*Non.* Simply call me 'Louis'. I am – how do you say – *undercover.*"

"Is that why you have shaved your moustache?" I asked – for if the man had been known for anything, it was the well-maintained and luxurious decoration that was so uniquely associated with him. Now it was gone – his bare lip marked only by a small scar. Seeing it that way for the first time, I realized why he'd likely grown the moustache in the first place as a young man.

He nodded, and gave a small shrug. "A sad sacrifice, but necessary. But soon, when these Germans have been put into their places, I shall regrow it, even more resplendent than before." There was a twinkle in his eye as he said it, and I was glad that it was there, considering what he and his country had been through in recent months.

We settled into the automobile and lurched into motion.

"The urgency of your journey robs me of the joy of seeing you again," said "Louis", and then he got down to business, relating the latest news that he and his men had managed to obtain from behind the German lines.

I should have paid more attention, but the sameness of the names of little villages overrun by the Germans in just the past few days began to sound meaningless to me. I was weary from unexpectedly being summoned to Whitehall the night before for instructions. My mind drifted back there, where I'd found a building humming with tense vitality. Even at that hour, the tense men (and women) were dashing here and there, flimsy documents in their hands. Others clustered in groups of twos or threes, whispering urgently as they leaned toward one another before breaking apart to step briskly from here to there. I was feeling my age, and couldn't help but notice the curious fact that those I passed were all so much younger than me. It was only as I penetrated into the depths of the building, where the decisions were made that would send so many of the young ones to their deaths, that I started to encounter old soldiers like myself.

I was guided to a conference room where I'd been many times before over the last thirty-odd years. Before his "retirement", when he began to carry out numerous tasks for the British Government to prepare for the unavoidable war, Sherlock Holmes's clients in Baker Street had ranged from beggars to kings, but a certain percentage of his cases even then had been in service to the Crown, one way or another, and that had occasionally included receiving instructions in this very room – and on one occasion unmasking a traitor. Ever since, I hadn't been able to enter the room without glancing to the spot where the broken man had jammed a pistol into his mouth and escaped justice.

Now the room was filled with military men, many of them in medal-covered uniforms like something from a Gilbert and Sullivan operetta, or resembling a few of the more pompous leaders from insignificant countries who had traveled to our shores in '87 for the Jubilee. But several of them didn't feel the need for such puffery, and I knew that they, at least, could be trusted to know what was what without making a right hash of things.

At one end of the long table, bent in close conference, were the Holmes brothers, Sherlock and Mycroft, and also Bancroft Pons, now in his early forties, and just as capable as Mycroft at keeping tabs on the quivers of every strand of the web which had slowly been forged toward protection of British interests over the last four decades.

Seeing me approach, Holmes had straightened his tall lean frame. Now sixty, he still seemed as vital and energetic as when I'd first met him in the laboratory at Barts, ebullient over his just-completed successful experiment that would aid in the forensic identification of dried hemoglobin. I'd seen him infrequently over the last couple of months, following our capture of the German spy Von Bork at a lonely Essex manor house. A couple of days after that, we'd been in London when the country declared war, and had spent a few quiet hours hiding in the pub on the ground floor of the Northumberland Hotel. [1] Since then, Holmes

402

had been busy in service to British Intelligence, while I was involved in rejoining my old unit, and overseeing the preparations for the medical needs there were soon to follow. Too many of the young ones thought that this glorious little exercise would be over by cold weather, but those of us who knew better stayed busy preparing for what might last for years – and this time on our very doorstep, instead of in far-away Afghanistan or on desolate South African plains.

"Your message said that they were being held prisoner," I said, uselessly repeating what they already knew.

Bancroft stood straight as well, his stout frame quite reminiscent of the seated Mycroft Holmes beside him. He looked up and down the room. "That's correct," he replied, his voice low. "According to our sources, 'Bridges' and 'Caesar' were captured behind the lines, with the threat that they could be shot as spies at any moment."

I recognized that he intentionally used the two agent's code names – which told me that even amongst the men in that room there was a certain level of distrust, and that someone there didn't need to know their true identities. I nodded my understanding.

Although knowing it really made no difference, I asked, "What were they doing when caught?"

"Caesar was playing the part of a minor German nobleman," answered Mycroft. "Despite his young age, he is a master at projecting the arrogance necessary for such a role." I nodded – this attitude was one of the reasons that Caesar had earned his code name when he first began working for Mycroft Holmes. On his various missions, he often took the first name of a Roman Emperor: Claudius, for instance, or Trajan or Nero.

"Bridges," continued Mycroft, "was playing the part of his military escort. Together, they were working both sides towards the middle, and came up with important information about the German's movements over the next few weeks."

"They were working with my contact when they were captured," added Holmes. "It was he who managed to send word about what happened." Seeing that I was about to ask, he continued. "A bit of bad luck – it seems that one of the aides to an officer who had stopped nearby for the night recalled Caesar from a year or so ago, when he was posing as a beer-swilling chef at a shabby inn. Unknown to our men, a cursory investigation revealed that there is no such noble house as the one claimed by Caesar. They were both put under arrest, and it's been decided that there's no time to waste with formalities like prisoner exchanges."

"How long do we have?" I asked.

"Just hours."

"And what is our plan?"

"We can't take a chance on trying to manipulate events from a distance," replied Holmes, "and there's no one there that we can trust to handle it satisfactorily. It isn't simply about saving their lives, but also retrieving the information that they were sent to obtain – if they got it, and if they still have it."

I nodded. "Then we have to go get them."

"As simple as that," rumbled Mycroft Holmes. He had lost some weight over the last couple of years as the war loomed inevitably closer – weight that seemed to have been acquired by Bancroft Pons. A number of responsibilities had also passed to the younger man, but Mycroft – in his self-created and wonderfully unique position – was still indispensable. If his calculating mind agreed that this was the best option, then it wasn't worth considering any other.

"We'll cross in a few hours, as soon as we reach the coast, and be behind the lines while it's still dark," said Holmes. "We must be there before dawn." He didn't need to add that we could not be late, arriving after the traditional time for shooting one's enemies . . . .

The front right tire of our automobile lurched into a muddy hole, and I was drawn abruptly back to the present, where Holmes and our friend, who I must remember to call "Louis" for the duration of this mission, were sitting in the rear seat, discussing what to expect. The auto was only a year or so old, a Berliet closed car, but it was the only one with enough capacity that could be found at short notice to carry the four of us, as well as our two friends following their rescue. Beside me, our driver – introduced only as "Andy" – skillfully pushed along the bad roads at high speed with confidence and skill, flicking the wheel this way and that with the minimum of effort. In spite of our velocity, and my awareness of what a vehicle of our mass would do if suddenly out of control on the muddy road, I felt no worries – at least about that part of the affair.

As the conversation behind me was proceeding without my involvement, I tried to find out more about our driver. I'd heard his name mentioned a few months before, a story about how he'd wrestled an axe-wielding German agent to the ground on the Flushing docks, but I'd never met him in person. I found that he was a taciturn Scot, and I had certainly known many of those throughout my life – my own father had been one. I asked him where he was from, and he simply growled, "Glencoe." I nodded, trying to remember if I had relatives from there. It was possible – Watsons were all over, but Glencoe was a long way from Stranraer, where I was born. I managed to tease a bit more out of him – he'd gone to Fettes, and then to Aberdeen to study engineering. With the coming of the war, he'd joined the Royal Engineers, but no sooner had he started to become accustomed to his post than he was pulled a different direction – into a group of agents with special skills being assembled by Bancroft Pons. He'd already been to a few "dances", as he called the group's missions, and this wasn't the first time he'd gone behind enemy lines. He refused to be drawn about the incident in Flushing, where I'd heard that he could have lost an arm.

At that point, seeing his reluctance to elaborate, there wasn't much left to ask him. To dig any more concerning his past would be impolite, and to ask further about his recent missions would be indiscreet and unprofessional. If he was the kind of man that I perceived him to be, he wouldn't tell me anything else anyway.

I suspected that he would be quite effective in whatever Bancroft required of him. He was about six feet tall, slim but strongly built, and from the little I'd seen, he moved with an easy grace. He had a mustache similar to my own, and his dark hair was brushed so that a thick comma of black hair fell above his right eye.

Not long after, Andy announced that we were close to the front lines, and would be crossing soon. A few minutes earlier, we pulled to the side of the road, and Louis gave us some different clothing to wear, taken from men recently deceased. I was happy to see that mine fit, and I pulled the heavy wool coat tighter around me and tried to further awaken myself. As I did so, I noticed the coat's markings, indicating that I was portraying a German officer, I felt a small surge of adrenalin when considering that Holmes and I could now be shot as spies, and that was enough for me to be fully awake.

As we climbed back into the vehicle, I considered the two prisoners we were going to rescue. Knowing that they were in danger, we really had no choice but to make the effort, regardless of the possible information that they might have obtained. Bridges (*for I will continue to use their field names in this narrative to protect their identities*) was the older of the two, now about thirty-four. He was the spitting image of Holmes in terms of appearance, temperament, and mental acuity. Born and raised in Yorkshire, he'd attended Oxford, and afterwards served as one of Holmes's apprentices around the turn of the century. He'd opened his own consulting detective practice in 1907, finding increasing success over the course of several years. However, he was dismayed that many people came to him expecting the services Sherlock Holmes. Eventually, he drifted into doing work for the Government as events ran down an ever-steepening slope toward an encompassing European War. Although he had particular skills in cryptography, he was also a master of disguise, and functioned with amazing success as an agent of the small organization controlled by Bancroft Pons.

The young man known as Caesar had a much different background, but had ended up being just as effective as Bridges. Born in 1892 and half-American, he'd spent much of his youth either touring with his mother, an occasional opera singer, across the Continent and the United States, when she wasn't living in Montenegro with her second husband, Count Vukčić, and her other children. The death of his mother in 1903 turned young Caesar's life upside down, and through a series of circumstances beyond the scope of this memoir, he came under the influence and tutelage of Sherlock Holmes. During that time, he became close friends with the older Bridges. He evinced a quite notable intelligence, and also an interest in Holmes's work, but always a distinct trait towards working alone.

In 1911, Caesar inadvertently became involved in a series of events that resulted in the defeat of a group that would have prevented the crowning of King George V. By that time, the nineteen-year-old young man had eschewed college, preferring to educate himself, learning more that way than he probably could have by attending any university. As a result of Caesar's service to the Crown, he was officially recruited into Mycroft Holmes's organization, where he and Bridges soon became a team that was unparalleled for its masterful successes in discovering information to aid the British government as the threat of war rolled ever closer.

Working together, the two young men criss-crossed Europe. Their exploits and antics during this time became something of a legend, and although they frequently vexed both Mycroft Holmes and Bancroft Pons to no end, no one could argue with their results.

Since the beginning of the war, just a few months earlier, they had been deep within German territory, working their way back along with the advancing German lines. In the rear seat, Louis was telling Holmes how his own network of agents spread across Belgium had already benefited from what the two had learned. He had been more than willing to assist in setting Mycroft's sudden plan for their rescue into motion – and so I, a sixty-two-year-old doctor, found myself knocking across the muddy Belgian pre-dawn landscape in a race against the sun to infiltrate a German camp and help effect an impossible rescue.

Sometimes I wondered where my life might have ended up if I'd passed on Stamford's invitation on that long ago 1881 New Year's Day to meet an acquaintance of his who needed a flat-mate to share expenses at a set of rooms he'd found in Baker Street. It's certain that I wouldn't have found myself in that automobile rattling a few miles beyond Ypres on 17 October, 1914 – but it's just as likely that I would have remained for a while in that small featureless room of a small private hotel off the Strand where I'd settled upon returning from Afghanistan, nursing my barely

406

healed injuries and spending my wound pension too freely, depending more and more on the artificial solace of drink, and fooling myself that in a few months I'd be healed enough for the Review Board to return me to my unit. When that didn't happen, would I have resettled in the countryside – perhaps obtaining a little practice and settling down to the life of a rural doctor? Or would I have continued to slide in the same way as my brother – into an alcoholic ignominy and an early death. I gave a little shake of my head. I had picked the correct path – even if the events of the next few hours led to sharing the same firing squad that would now be expanded beyond Caesar and Bridges to include Holmes, Louis, our taciturn driver Andy – and me.

I'm far too world-wearied to have naively thought that the front line would be some formalized location with a high sturdy fence stretching into the distance on either side, and a guard asking to check our papers, but I was surprised when we passed a group of German soldiers slogging in the same direction in which we were headed. I sat up straighter, realizing that we had, at some point, already crossed into enemy territory.

I suspected that we were approaching our destination when the roadway became more thickly peopled with German soldiers walking wearily in both directions, or standing in knots of twos and threes, talking and smoking. The occasional vehicle passed us, heading the other direction, and the road became narrower as we entered into the confines of a small village. Andy seemed entirely conversant with our route, and deftly guided us through several turns before pulling to a stop at a large tent that stood well away from the others, near the edge of the settlement. Not far behind the tent loomed a range of black trees, but in the early morning darkness, I couldn't tell whether it was just a small stand separating this cleared area from another, or if it extended for miles.

I glanced back to where Holmes had already brushed his hair forward to change his appearance. While that in itself would not have been enough, his inherent skills as an actor, and ability to seemingly alter his features and stance at will would complete the illusion. He pulled on his cap, and he'd already slumped, thickening his body and losing six inches. He looked like a different person.

I glanced back toward the tent, where a guard was squaring himself to attention. I took a deep breath and stepped away from the automobile, tapping the right pocket of my greatcoat as I did so, where my old and faithful service revolver was concealed.

While Andy remained behind at the Berliet, propped on the fender and smoking a cigarette, Holmes walked toward the tent as if he'd been there a hundred times before, with Louis and myself falling in line behind him, acting as anonymous staff members. Louis had assured us that that our clothing would completely pass inspection as authentic, as would the papers that he had provided to us – after all, just hours before, they *had* been authentic for the men who'd possessed them then. This was proven to be true when the sole armed guard before the tent snapped to full attention when perceiving Holmes's assumed rank, completely convinced of his authority, and ours as well by way of my friend's short but masterful performance. No identification was demanded, and we were waved forward and into the tent.

Although it was still dark outside, with only the promise – or threat – of false dawn in the cloud-tarnished east, it took a moment for my eyes to adjust inside the tent. Before I could truly see, I was assailed by a curious combination of smells – damp canvas, the pasture-like scent of churned mud and manure, trod underfoot into an inseparable muck, and unwashed men, and peculiarly the yeasty smell of bread. As my vision cleared, the first thing I saw was a low deal table near the central support pole, and as indicated, the substantial remains of a baguette lying there, alongside a jug of wine.

Then my eyes focused beyond that, to the two men seated on chairs near the back of the tent, their arms pulled behind them.

In the dim yellow light, I first recognized Bridges' high forehead, so like Holmes's that for a moment, I would have thought it was my friend who was tied there, as he'd looked a quarter-century before. I was glad that Holmes had taken the precaution of altering his own appearance before entering.

Beside Bridges was another man – Caesar – his thick brown hair brushed straight back from his own high intelligent brow. He was about an inch under six feet, and lean, although with his love of food, his figure would grow should he ever settle long enough in one place. Both he and Bridges were looking at us without expression or apparent recognition. On either side of them stood two grim German soldiers – big ones – with rifles held at the ready. But there was one other in the tent as well.

From the shadows to our left, where he'd been sitting on a folding camp chair, a tall man in what appeared to be an immaculate German uniform – or so it was my impression in that dark setting – uncrossed his legs and stood. Even in that front-line squalor, his pants were immaculately pressed, the cuffs sharp, and there didn't seem to be a spot of mud upon him. His boots had a gleam in the thin light that should have been missing after any time whatsoever spent in that location.

He took a step forward into the light, and I could see that his face held that Teutonic chiseled aspect so idealized by our German cousins. He was almost a cliché, with his monocle tightly fixed in his left eye, it's hanging black silk string perfectly and symmetrically balanced upon the right by a

408

thin white dueling scar running from the dark circle under his eye to his jawline. He had blonde hair, parted in a careful knife-thin line on the right side of his head, and his eyes were light – they looked blue in good light, as I knew from when I'd met him once, long ago, at a diplomatic conference in Berne.

At that time, he had taken a particularly surprising and unexpected position that threatened to disrupt a number of sensitive negotiations, to the consternation of both the British and his own people. Holmes had perceived that he was under some sort of duress and, with a very short amount of available time before a crucial vote had to be taken, a desperate investigation was undertaken which had resulted in the timely rescue of the man's wife from those who had taken her hostage in an attempt to sabotage the proceedings. The German, living under that threat and forced to disrupt the conference, had wept when his wife was returned to him, frankly unashamed to express his feelings. Then – knowing that Holmes and I were guarding his wife against any further last-minute attempts to reach her – he'd rejoined the conference, casting his vote decidedly in favor of the negotiated proposal, and putting a nail into his enemies' coffin.

It was this man who stepped into the light, looking from of us to the other. Then, in the clear and sharp voice I remembered, he turned to the two guards. "You will wait outside during our discussion."

The well-disciplined Myrmidons straightened, turned, and were gone in an instant, their intimidating miens somewhat negated by the sloppy squelching of their boots through the muck making up the tent's floor. After watching the tent flap fall and swing for a moment before shutting completely, the German stepped forward with an outstretched hand, his voice low and urgent.

"Herr Holmes," he said to my friend, shaking his hand urgently. And then he turned to me. "And Herr Doctor! I'm glad you made it. I was starting to fear the worst."

He spoke in English, with very little accent, and Holmes interrupted him. "We will speak in German, if you don't mind, Oberst Metz. Should anyone be listening, we don't want to confuse them by tossing around an unfamiliar diphthong."

Metz smiled. "Always the same, Herr Holmes. You never overlook a point. You are the fixed point in a changing age."

"I leave that honor to Watson, here." He then made a gesture toward our Belgian friend. "This is Louis. He knows the countryside. It was he who made the local arrangements and will arrange our departure." Louis and the colonel nodded to one another.

"I feared that you would be too late," continued Metz. "They have revealed nothing, but at the same time, their assumed identities could not be confirmed. They are to be shot within the hour, when the Divisional Commander arrives from Robaix."

"Then we haven't a moment to lose," replied Holmes, turning toward the prisoners.

"About time," growled Caesar, his low voice a bit impatient. "I'm getting hungry."

"I am sorry," said Metz, turning toward the small table. "I would have fed you if I could." He had the baguette in hand by the time Holmes had cut Caesar's bonds, and the young man stood and eagerly took it, tearing off a great hunk and then pulling a bite off with his strong white teeth. He masticated steadily while Bridges was similarly freed. When he was standing up as well, Caesar handed him the other half of the loaf and then stepped past us for the jug of wine. Bridges nodded, but instead of immediately taking a bite, he asked a question.

"How do we plan to depart?" he said. "We were initially caught when we encountered unknown German patrols to the northwest. They'll be further entrenched throughout that area now."

"He's right," said Metz. "I helped arrange these patrols myself."

"I don't suppose that you could get some of them to be redirected?" asked Louis. "When we leave here, it's very likely that the alarm will be given very soon after. My people are planning for us to loop deeper into occupied territory – that will be unexpected – but I was counting on the northwest being clear for a little longer."

Metz nodded. "I apologize. I had no idea what you would do after the men were freed. Notifying you of their capture – and fulfilling my old debt to Herr Holmes – is the best that I could do. Until this war is settled, we are still after all on the opposite sides. I can do no more to help, I'm afraid."

"Make no mistake," replied Louis, stepping forward. "We are most grateful for all that you have done, and all that you have risked. To inform us of the impending risk to the lives of these men – " He gestured to the two released prisoners. " – is more than we can ever repay. It is up to our own efforts and the Good God to manage our escape, now that we have freed them."

"Speaking of which," I interrupted, "after we all climb in the car and drive away, how do you, Colonel Metz, keep from being shot yourself? Those three guards outside won't waste any time in reporting the obvious: That you let us go, even if it appears that you were ordered to release the prisoners to our custody by the character portrayed by Holmes."

410

"I have thought of that," he replied. "After disabling the guards, one by one, you must take me with you as a prisoner as well. Then I will 'escape' before you cross the lines."

Holmes shook his head. "You're taking a terrible chance," he said. "It's unlikely that they'll ever believe it. Your credibility will be destroyed."

"Nevertheless," replied the German.

"And in any case," added Louis, "the available space in our vehicle is already dangerously tight. A seventh man may not fit – and might dangerously overload us. Should we burst a tire from the excess weight, or become stuck in the mud – "

His words were cut short when we all heard it – the approach of a vehicle, its brakes squealing as it pulled to a stop outside the tent. Louis cursed under his breath, and Metz's eyes widened in concern.

"It's too late. He's here – to shoot the prisoners."

"How many?" snapped Holmes, while I pulled my service revolver from my pocket, and Caesar and Bridges stepped to the far corner of the tent, where their possessions were apparently located. In the dim light, I saw them retrieve their guns, turning as one to face the entrance to the tent.

"Just the General – and his driver. The two men we just sent outside will be tasked with the executions."

"Five of them, then," said Holmes, "counting the guard outside when we entered. How far are we from anyone else?"

"Far enough," replied Metz, "if we're quiet. But any shooting will bring men from the further encampment at a run. There will be no escaping then."

"Right." Holmes looked around. "You heard the colonel. Be silent."

He made a gesture to Bridges and Caesar, and they immediately dropped back into their seats and held their arms behind their backs, as if still tied in the manner in which we'd first seen them. The only difference now was that their arms were free and they held deadly concealed firearms.

Through the dark canvas walls we could hear when the automobile's engine shut off, and the opening and closing of a single door. Then, after a short interval of boots mashing through wet ground, we caught hints of the murmur of guttural conversation between the new arrival and the three guards just outside the tent. We looked at one another – each was as prepared as possible. Then the tent flap drew back and a sole figure was silhouetted against the brighter near-dawn light. Short and squat, he still had to lean down to enter. I knew that his eyes were adjusting much the same as mine had, but he knew to turn his head first toward the prisoners, ascertaining as soon as he was able that they were still in custody.

"Metz," said the man in a snide tone, "I understand we have unexpected visitors. Here to watch the show, I imagine? Perhaps get in a little target practice? We can have a competition of sorts with my men – shots from a hundred yards – winner buys the beer."

Metz's mouth tightened in distaste, but he stepped forward and said, "They arrived unexpectedly, General – with new orders not to shoot anyone until the prisoners can be questioned further by General der Infanterie Kohl."

The newcomer raised an amused eyebrow. His form was stout and thick, and his shaved head appeared to grow directly from his broad shoulders, as if no neck was necessary in the construction of this model. The little knob of his chin-bone ballooned into a sagging skin sack that bulged over his tightly buttoned collar, and it said much for his own self-discipline that he hadn't unbuttoned it to save himself some discomfort when away from those who might expect otherwise, here in this odorous tent on the outskirts of an unknown village.

"Is that so?" he drawled. "Funny, when I left the general's quarters not half-an-hour ago, he seemed indifferent as to whether these spies lived or died. He believes – and I agree – that they are only here to see what they can see, and having prevented them from carrying home their paltry report, there's nothing that they can tell us in return. Who is this visitor who has delayed the proceedings?" He looked from me to Holmes, not seeing Louis, who had drifted back into the shadows near the prisoners.

Holmes stepped forward, still unrecognizable as himself in his improvised disguise. "I believe that Oberfst Metz has slightly misunderstood our instructions. We are not here to represent General Kohl, Count. Rather, we are from Berlin, making a tour of the front and on our way to see the general. Along the way, we have a roving brief to collect all spies for further interrogation, instead of short-sightedly eliminating them."

Upon hearing himself addressed as "Count", the man appeared more interested. "You know me, then?"

"I do. Count von Und Zu Grafenstein. We met in Berlin last year, although you might not remember our introduction."

I had to wonder – could there be an element of truth in Holmes's statement? He might have met the Count in Berlin in 1913. Anything was possible. Since 1912, he'd been spending most of his time traveling, helping gather data to prepare the nation for the upcoming war. A great deal of those months had been undercover in America and parts of Britain in the guise of the bitter Irish expatriate Altamont, but he'd also found time to return to his small farm in Sussex, making appearances as Holmes on occasion in order to give the impression that he was still a retired and reclusive apiarist. He'd also had missions elsewhere – some with my assistance, and some that would never be known to me. It was entirely possible that he'd been to Berlin and met Count von Und Zu Grafenstein while there.

But I knew that wasn't the first time that we'd met him. In 1902, the Count – who was also the uncle of the recently defeated Von Bork – was nearly murdered by a Nihilist named Klopman. I recalled the events clearly, and Holmes's capture of the criminal in the post office of the small Dartmoor village of Grimpen. More specifically, I also remembered that Monsieur P----- had been in attendance, and had departed with both the Count and the prisoner, Klopman, for the long train journey back to London. [2] The Count might not recognize Holmes in disguise, and doubtless I had never made an impression on him whatsoever, but P----- was rather unforgettable, and even in this darkened tent on the outskirts of a Belgian village, he – in his undisguised state and *sans* moustache – would likely be instantly recognizable.

And it was inevitable. The Count took a step toward the prisoners, and P-----, that is to say "Louis", surely knowing what was about to happen, made as if to shift in a different direction, keeping to the shadows along the tent wall. But the Count's gaze was attracted by the motion, and something about it seemed to alert him. He took a sudden step toward Louis, and then, being within range to recognize him, his eyes widened with understanding. One could follow his thoughts – the last time he'd seen "Louis" had been in connection to Klopman's arrest a dozen years before, and that event had involved Sherlock Holmes. With sudden enlightenment, he turned his head sharply, first toward Bridges, and then back to Holmes. There was no mistaking when he saw past the disguise. His expression changed – he tensed and opened his mouth to cry out, certainly to call to the guards outside. It was then that Metz took a step forward, coming up behind him, reaching around to cover the Count's mouth with his left hand while bringing up his right. The glint of a knife, the unforgettable fast slice of blade across flesh, a gout of black blood spraying across the empty space before the dying man, and then the body silently sinking to the mud.

There was no sound at all for a long moment as we all waited to see if any suspicions were aroused, and then one of the guards outside laughed – shockingly loud – and we were all startled. But silently. Metz turned to Holmes.

"And now you owe me one, I think, Herr Holmes."

My friend nodded, no making no further attempt to shorten himself or disguise his expression. "We must hurry. Caesar – take the Count's overcoat. Clean it as best you can. It will appear to be a uniform, and will cover your civilian clothing. Bridges – see if you can prop the body up so that it will look natural enough – if only for a moment – when someone comes in. Even if they find him in a chair, presumably asleep, it might give us a few precious seconds before the alarm is given if they're hesitant to disturb him."

Then, as Bridges helped Caesar wrestle the coat from off the corpse, Holmes interrupted. "Do you have the information?"

Metz's head whipped around. He had forgotten that there was more to this than simply settling a debt by arranging for the rescue of a couple of prisoners. These men had been on a mission.

"I do," said Bridges, and then he tapped his temple. "Up here."

"Good enough," said Holmes, who then turned back to the colonel.

"You have placed yourself in even greater danger," said Holmes. "Your idea of being taken as a prisoner, only to later escape or be released, won't work. It isn't plausible. But there is just a slim chance that you'll come out of this without being shot yourself."

Metz's lips tightened. "I understand."

"Would you rather be stabbed before or after I knock you unconscious?"

"After, I suppose. But please – let the Doctor do the stabbing."

"It will be bloody," I said, "but should heal easily if you keep it away from the mud."

"After this war is over," Holmes added, "I'll buy you a drink. Now turn around."

Metz did so, but not before he shook hands with Holmes and me. Then he spun, his military training apparent even in that setting and circumstance, and Holmes, using a woven leather blackjack removed from his picket, hit the colonel scientifically behind the right ear. Then, after helping to lower the unconscious man to the ground, I proceeded to pull back his coat and, using my own knife, cut through it and his shirt. After disinfecting the knife and thinking of my Oath and the greater good, I wounded the flesh on his right side above the hip bone. It was a messy injury, but negligible. As long as he played up the head wound, no one would question that he had been attacked.

By then Caesar was wearing the dead Count's coat, and the blood stains across the front didn't look too unusual, considering the circumstances in which we found ourselves – doubtless a number of soldiers were already wearing blood-stained clothing. Holmes whispered that we would try and take the guards one by one as they entered, assuming he could lure them inside that way. He then stepped to the flap of the tent and uttered a guttural command for one of them to enter. The flap pulled back, showing more light than just a few minutes earlier, and a dark head

414

cautiously looked in. Holmes, who had been prepared to use his blackjack once more when the fellow had fully entered, instead lowered his arm. The man at the entrance was Andy, our driver.

"I knew something had gone wrong," he said softly, joining us inside but holding the flap open while observing the seated and somewhat slumped body of the general, the colonel sprawled artfully on the ground, and the two figures of Bridges and Caesar standing nearby. "I cut the odds."

We looked outside and saw one of the guards, unconscious and somehow propped cleverly to that he couldn't fall completely flat.

"Where are the others?" asked Holmes.

"In the car. We can carry them in here."

"Are they alive or dead?"

"Some of both."

I was impressed – we'd never heard a sound, and Andy had somehow accomplished this feat by himself against four armed soldiers, and in such a way as to attract no attention whatsoever, either inside the tent or out. I was about to say so, when he himself looked around the tent once more and remarked, "I never heard a sound. Nice work."

We dragged in the three from the car – two deceased – and put them in the darkest part of the tent. We prepared to tie and gag the one that still lived when Andy offered a suggestion.

"Let me change clothes with him first. Then I'll stay here and slip way into the crowds. Perhaps I can accomplish something more useful over the next few days, instead of just being a chauffeur. I expect I can gum up the German works quite a bit in ways that they aren't expecting. Besides, that will be one less man in the auto."

It was agreed, and within moments the rest of us were all climbing into the Berliet, while Andy tossed a wave and walked away in the opposite direction.

"A brave man is young Monsieur Bond," said Louis. I raised an eyebrow. "Andy. Andrew Bond. He is quite capable. In the few days that I've known him, I've seen much to admire."

"Good thing he's on our side," said Bridges, who was now driving the car.

The rest of the trip was rather anticlimactic. We avoided the northwest, which had been Louis's original route of return to Ypres, and instead looped first to the east and then back around toward the border, holding to the smaller roads and farm tracks, and even crossing a pasture on one occasion, nearly becoming mired in the process. When we were back in safe Belgian territory, we pulled over and shed our German clothing, glad for the chance to avoid being shot a second time that day.

At the border, Louis took his leave of us, shaking our hands effusively and hoping that we would see each other sooner rather than later. In fact, it would be another two years before we would re-encounter him, after he'd been forced to flee Belgium after receiving a grievous wound. He settled for a time with a group of other Belgian refugees in Essex. The death of his beloved wife at the hands of the Germans soured him on ever returning to Belgium, and after the war, he gravitated to London, where he achieved a noted amount of success – such that his previous notable years with the Belgian police were all but eclipsed.

When we were back in France, Bridges disclosed the information that he'd carried in his head – he'd always had a good memory for that sort of thing – and then he and Caesar cleaned up, received new orders, and headed immediately back across the lines into occupied territory.

Holmes and I were in London by nightfall. If I'd thought that I was to immediately resume my duties, I was mistaken. Within a week, the two of us were on Tory Island, northwest of Ireland, when the dreadnought *HMS Audacious* was sunk – a fact that wasn't revealed to the public until November 1918, over four years later. I'm prevented to this day from revealing the truth behind that decision, but I can assert that Sherlock Holmes's bravery and abilities once again saved the country from a worse disaster than might be imagined. Hopefully one day the story can be told. It's my hope to tell all of what we accomplished during the war, but my days are likely too short to ever accomplish that task.

NOTES:

1. "Some Notes Upon the Matter of John Douglas"
2. "An Actor and a Rare One"

The Problem of the Hindhead Minister

The summer of 1883 brought a number of interesting cases to the rooms that I shared with Mr. Sherlock Holmes, and we found ourselves staying quite busy. By that time, my health had been restored to a remarkable degree, far beyond what I would have expected if asked even a year earlier, and I was able to accompany my friend on many of his investigations. My notes for that season fill several volumes, and in glancing through them, I see with fondness the little matter of the restoration of Miss Hayes to her position as headmistress to the school that she founded in Biggleswade, the terrible disappointment related to the Fawsley Cemetery Demon, and the sinister matter of the Five Red Ice-men. But I think that among them all, nothing seems as shocking as the sudden intrusion of Reverend Angus Blackthorn and his peculiar persecution.

Holmes and I found ourselves at home one afternoon, unexpectedly free from recent obligations. It was a rare chance to catch our collective breath and enjoy a quiet moment – or so we thought. We had been lazily discussing Darwinism and its societal relationship to execution for capital crimes. We offered contrary opinions, each taking one side and then dancing to the other as a new fact occurred to us. We had reached no clear consensus when suddenly the front doorbell began to ring urgently.

Holmes sat up, tossing the remains of his cigar into the unlit fireplace. A smile crossed his face as we heard a faint exchange at the front door between Mrs. Hudson and the visitor – a man, from the low rumbles of his voice. Then, the sound of heavy footsteps climbing the stairs was soon followed by a knock. Holmes called, "Enter," and the door was thrown open, revealing a towering figure with wild black hair and a long tangled matching beard of equivalent shading.

He wore a dark suit, quite rumpled, and his face had a frantic look. "Mr. Holmes?" he said, looking unerringly toward my friend. We had both stood as the man entered, and when he took a step forward and then collapsed to the floor, we were already moving to his assistance.

As I knelt beside him, I saw that his clothing was loose and ill-fitting, as if he had recently lost weight. His face had a gaunt look, and he evinced the peculiar and unmistakable odor of someone who has been starved. I picked up his wrist to check his pulse – steady, I was gratified to find – and saw that his nails had been chewed down to the quick. I glanced up to

418

see that Holmes had noticed this as well, and probably a dozen other things beyond my ability to observe.

We got the man to his feet, and I retrieved my bag from near the door. Soon I had examined him thoroughly, and he was awake and eating tea and biscuits from a tray, fetched by Holmes from Mrs. Hudson. Only when the man seemed well enough would I allow him to tell his story.

"Gentlemen, my name is Angus Blackthorn. I live in Hindhead, where I am the minister to a little non-conformist church."

Holmes and I had discussed the man's likely profession while he was still unconscious. Even I, still unschooled in Holmes's methods during those early days, had spotted the man's well-worn Testament, tucked in his breast pocket.

"We aren't a large congregation," Blackthorn continued, "and we don't seek new members. If someone hears of us, and our beliefs, they are welcome to visit, and join us if they would like, but it isn't part of our mission to proselytize, or to save everyone if they don't want to be saved.

"We – my son and I – live in a small rectory beside our church. The church building itself is quite old – it might even be called ancient – having been built nearly a thousand years ago, before the Norman Conquest. Gradually, as I have been told, the traditional church that occupied the grounds for so long withered and died as members moved on. Apparently the building stood empty for thirty years or more. When my wife died ten years ago, I felt the calling to remove myself from where we lived near Manchester and begin my work anew. I traveled the country a bit before discovering the old building in Hindhead. Arrangements were made, and my son and I moved south. Since then, we've attracted a small congregation that cares for one another, while preparing for coming tribulations."

"And what would those be, Reverend Blackthorn?" asked Holmes.

"The End Times," he said matter-of-factly. "I know in this day and age, many people don't believe in God's judgment, but it is coming nonetheless," he added. "One can see the signs every day – people forget about God and his Commandments. They pursue their own earthly and prurient interests. The only solution is to keep one's eyes upon the Lord."

I could see that Holmes was about to make some comment which would place the minister upon the defensive, so I interjected by asking, "You have a son," I said. "Is he your only child?"

"Yes. He is ten years old, and was born when I lost my wife." He lowered his eyes. "I realize that my beliefs are difficult for some to understand, and I do not try to force others to agree with me, and I also pray not to judge. It . . . it has been a struggle at times not to wonder if I

419

was at fault – that I had sinned in some way – to bring about my wife's death."

"Surely," said Holmes, "your God would not punish someone else for *your* sin," he said. "Do you not consider that the sin could have been credited to your wife?"

Blackthorn's eyes lifted suddenly, and I saw the quick intake of breath that dilated both of his nostrils, which suddenly went white. In that moment, he looked like an angry bull, about to charge. But then he closed his eyes and let whatever anger that had washed over him flow away. Then he gave a sad smile, and Holmes returned the look as if the minister had passed a test. "It is a question that intrudes on my own mind on nights when I cannot sleep," said Blackthorn, "and there have been many of them of late, Mr. Holmes. I believe in God as I am able to understand Him, and He expects obedience from me, but He also created me as I am, and that includes possession of a questioning nature. I must be aware of this, and accept it as a mortal flaw, and not give in to despair or temptation, no matter what doubts creep into my mind in the dark and lonely hours."

Holmes nodded. I knew he did not agree with someone such as Blackthorn, but at least it seemed to be clear that the man was not an unreasonable fanatic.

"What has caused you to hurry here so frantically this afternoon?" asked Holmes. "Apparently it is the culmination of a situation long-standing, if your physical condition is any indication."

Blackthorn nodded. "It is. It all began a month ago, when the first message appeared."

"Message?"

"I suppose it can be called that, although at the time I thought it was no more than harassment from a villager. It surprised me, because we have never been bothered by this type of thing before." He fished in his waistcoat pocket and pulled out a folded sheet, which he handed to Holmes. "This," he said, "is what I copied before wiping it away. It was written in chalk on the front door of the church."

Holmes unfolded the sheet, glanced at it, and then handed it to me. It could only be described as a skull-like face, with empty eye sockets and grinning teeth. Protruding from the smooth high frontal bones were two horns, each coming to sharp and devilish-looking points.

"You say this appeared a month ago. What did you do?"

"Why, after the initial surprise, I copied it and washed it away."

"Why copy it?"

"I suppose to have something to use as a reference if I determined who had done it."

"And did you have any suspicions?"

420

"None. We've been tolerated, if not completely accepted, within the village. As I said, we only seek to be left alone. Our beliefs call for us to prepare for the coming tribulations, and to be ready when they arrive. My son and I have lived peacefully since moving there, having little contact with the town except for the church members from the surrounding community – some shopkeepers and merchants, a few professionals, and a smattering of elderly folk."

"How large is your congregation?"

"Around thirty people."

"Did you ask any of them about the drawing?"

"I did not."

"Indeed. Did you make any investigation at all?"

"I . . . I kept an eye on the church, to see if anyone came back, but I never saw when it happened again."

"I take it that your investigations found no indication of the perpetrator. Did you hear of any similar desecrations in the village?"

"None."

"Clearly it worried you more than you let on. Your appearance indicates as much."

"This is true, Mr. Holmes. It has preyed on my mind as I sought to discover who would do this, and why."

"When did the next occurrence take place?"

"A week later to the day. I found the same drawing, but this time within the church, scrawled on the stone wall behind the pulpit."

"Did you copy that one as well?"

"There was no need. It was the same. Since then I haven't had a good night's sleep, and I cannot eat. I was never the same after my wife died, and the last weeks have been much worse. I can't get the matter out of my head, feeling that it portends something terrible. And then, in spite of my efforts to detect the next instance, it happened again the next week – last week."

"On the same day?"

"Yes. Thursday. Each time it has been on that day. Like today."

"But what happened today? What was different that would prompt your rush to London?"

"Because today my son was taken."

Holmes straightened in his chair. "Kidnapped?"

"Yes." He raised a hand. "But he was returned."

"Explain."

"Last night, I hid within the church, hoping to see the intruder, perhaps to capture him. However, the night passed without incident, and when the sun rose, I looked around the building, only to find that there were no chalk drawings. I hoped that was finally the end of it, but I suspected that in fact, my presence had been somehow detected, and I had scared the intruder. I went back to the rectory, intending to have a bite of breakfast, but first I went to awaken my son. I knocked, opened the door to his bedroom, and found his bed empty, the bedclothes thrown back, and the window open. Drawn in chalk on the wall above his bed was the symbol, the very same one, the skull with the devil's horns. But this time there was something different. Along with the skull, there was a word: *Abaddon*."

Holmes cocked his head. "The Hebrew word for *The Angel of Death*?"

"Yes, although sometimes the name is used to refer instead to a place of lost souls – Hell, if you will. Seeing such a . . . thing, an *abomination*, over my own dear son's bed – Why, I nearly collapsed, and I must have cried out, because Mrs. Beddowes, the housekeeper who comes from the village every day, came running in. She gave a small scream, somehow understanding immediately that something terrible had happened.

"I immediately searched the room, but found no clues that meant anything to me. It was then that I recalled you, Mr. Holmes. I've heard that you can see what is hidden from others. I resolved to seek your help, but it was at that point that I heard my son, Timothy, call from outside the window.

"I raced outside to find him, still dressed for bed, looking confused and standing beneath a nearby tree. I scooped him up, for he truly is the most precious thing in the world to me, and thanked God for his safe return. I quickly saw that he seemed to be in a fog, possibly drugged, and that he was unclear as to what had happened. He couldn't explain how he had ended up under the tree, or where he had been through the night."

"Did you call a doctor?" I asked.

"No, sir. I realized that this was the sort of thing that didn't need to become village gossip, and our doctor is the type who enjoys using little scraps of knowledge to enhance his own reputation. Instead, I remembered my earlier decision to ask for your help, Mr. Holmes, so I traveled to the station and made my way up to London."

"Where is your son now?" I queried.

"With Mrs. Beddowes. She stayed over last night as well to keep him, as I intended to hide within the church."

"Did she know about the previous drawings, or why you intended to keep watch?"

"I hadn't told her. She has commented on my state over the past weeks – my nervousness, sleeplessness, and lack of appetite. She was under the impression that I intended to pray all night, and I didn't disabuse her of the notion."

Holmes sat silently for a few moments, and then rose, walked around Blackthorn and me, and made his way to the shelf containing his indexes. He took one, flipped through it without apparent success, and then two or three more, returning each to its place when he was done. "The symbol you describe doesn't appear to be uniquely associated with any specific cult or religion," he said. "Clearly something like that implies a connection with the dark side of things, but even with the information that I've collected, I cannot identify any one group that might be associated with your persecution."

Blackthorn seemed disappointed, and Holmes stated, "Do not misunderstand me, sir. That little bit of research is not the limit of my assistance to you. We shall journey down to Hindhead immediately, assuming the good Doctor here is available to join us."

I confirmed my participation, and soon we were at Waterloo, boarding a train to Haslemere, the nearest station to Hindhead. I had thought that Holmes would continue to question Blackthorn, but instead he sat in silence, smoking his pipe and pondering. I prompted Blackthorn to tell me a bit more about his church and its beliefs. It seemed to be a rather strict group, something along the lines of a few of the more grim American churches. Their beliefs were rather narrow, with specific requirements as to what was and wasn't considered a sin. Dancing and music, for instance, were forbidden, but the group appeared to lack some of the other judgmental aspects so common to other religions. While achieving a rewarded afterlife was an impossibility if one disagreed with their beliefs, there was no attempt to shame or otherwise shun those who were not part of the chosen flock.

"If you don't increase your congregation," I asked, "how do you expect to survive?"

"It isn't part of our mission to grow, or even to serve as missionaries. We believe that everyone has their own responsibility to find the true path. If someone comes to us and agrees with our teachings, he or she is welcome. If not, then all we ask is to be left alone."

"And this open-door philosophy has given you a living?" I asked frankly.

Blackthorn smiled. "It doesn't hurt that one of our members, Mr. Hilton Frame, is one of the wealthier residents of Hindhead, and he generally provides more than his required tithe. For that I am grateful."

Conversation gradually drifted to a halt, and it seemed that I had only looked out the window and back at the beautiful Surrey countryside before

I discovered that Blackthorn had fallen asleep. Holmes noticed as well, but offered no other comment.

We had been fortunate enough to travel by express, arriving in Haslemere by late morning. Leaving the small station, Blackthorn retrieved his wagon, and we made our way north and slightly east to nearby Hindhead. The summer day was warm and not too hot, and the pleasant breezes and signs of idyllic country life almost made me forget the grim reason for our travels.

We came to a stop before an ancient church, a thick-walled stone building not more than four or five hundred square feet in size. It was tucked into the southern side of the Portsmouth Road and Hindhead Road intersection, hidden from the road by tall hedges and ancient trees. The land dropped away to the south, with a fine view of British forests stretching in the distance toward the Downs.

I was surprised to see that there was no cemetery. Blackthorn explained that there was one nearby, believed to have been associated with the church at some time in the past. At the time of the building's abandonment, decades before, it been deconsecrated, an act that was accomplished with greater ease than if it had been associated with a cemetery.

Blackthorn led us inside the adjacent rectory. The building consisted of a short hallway just inside the door, with two doors on our left and two on the right. I had the sense that this building hadn't originally been designed to be a residence, but rather some type of storage building in ages past. Blackthorn called to the housekeeper, who stepped out of the first door on the right, which proved to be the kitchen. She was followed immediately by a small boy who ran and jumped into the arms of his father. With eyes closed, the minister kissed the top of the little fellow's head, held him a moment longer, and then set him down, only to follow by dropping to his knees beside him. "Are you all right, then, Timothy?"

"I am, Papa. What happened?"

"I'm not sure, but these men are going to help us find out."

"Mrs. Beddowes won't let me go into my bedroom."

"It's just for a little while," said his father. Then, with an additional hug, he stood and spoke to the housekeeper. "Has anything else happened?"

"Not a thing. What does it all mean?"

"Mr. Holmes and Dr. Watson will help to explain it." His voice sounded certain as he gestured toward us, and I was flattered to be included in his trusting assertion.

Holmes asked to see the bedroom, and Blackthorn directed us to the room immediately opposite the kitchen, where Timothy returned with the housekeeper, who indicated that she would make some tea.

The room was a small one, but cheery nonetheless. The walls had been whitewashed, and there was a wide south-facing window. A small desk was underneath it, covered with sheets of colorful drawings, obviously by Master Timothy. A shelf containing books stood nearby. Holmes walked around, looking at the desk and the window before kneeling and examining the bookshelves as well. I only spared the slightest glance in that direction, as my attention was instead pulled toward the chalk drawing defacing the wall over the boy's bed.

As described, it was a skull, drawn in simple white chalk. The eyes had been filled in, with no pupils to give it any sort of living semblance. The teeth were sketched with terrible sharpness, but no attempt had been made to match them exactly to the number that would be found in an actual mouth. Rather, there were about a dozen jagged fangs, arranged to approximate an evil grin. The horns were long and tapered to a point, and these, unlike the simpler versions on Blackthorn's sketch, had a slight twist in the middle, pointing out to the sides a bit instead of straight up.

I sensed that Holmes was beside me, now studying the wall as well. "*Abaddon*," I said softly while he stepped closer, looking first at the wall, and then at and around the bed below it. "Isn't that also the same figure as the Greek *Apollyon*?"

"It is," answered Blackthorn from behind us, "although the word can mean different things. As I mentioned, sometimes it refers to the Angel of Death, and sometimes to a place very much like what has come to be known as Hell. Abaddon's function has been confused and conflated with that of Satan over the years."

"And where does he figure in your religion?" asked Holmes, straightening from his examination and moving nearer the doorway.

"He doesn't," said Blackthorn. "Not in this manifestation. I'm aware of him through my studies, and who am I to say whether he is truly a part of God's order? But our congregation doesn't refer to him in our teachings, and threats of him, like he's some bogey-man, aren't used to coerce our followers into better behavior."

"A sensible path," said Holmes absently as he looked around. I could see that this bit of approval pleased the minister.

"Let us speak again to Mrs. Beddowes," said Holmes, gesturing that we move in that direction.

In the hallway, Holmes nodded to the pair of closed doors at the end of the hall. "What are these other rooms?"

"That is a guest room," said Blackthorn, gesturing to the door on the left, on the same side as Timothy's room. "Mrs. Beddowes sometimes uses it, as she did last night when she stayed with Timothy." He made no move to open that door, but he did walk down the hall and reach for the knob upon the other, throwing it wide. "And this is my room."

It was on the north side of the house, and considerably darker – and smaller – than that of his son. There was a narrow bed, and also a desk underneath the single window. There were several tall bookshelves around the walls, along with a bureau and a desk. A bush outside the window further shaded the room. "I have it fixed up as something of a study," explained our host.

Holmes nodded but made no move to enter. Then he turned back toward the nearby kitchen. Blackthorn pulled the door shut and followed. I let both go in front of me, thinking it said much for the man that he gave his son the larger and cheerier room, while taking the rather monastic cell as his own.

In the kitchen, Timothy was sitting at a table eating a piece of bread smeared with jam. Blackthorn apologized. "I'm sorry that we don't have a parlor. The house is rather small – just the three bedrooms and this room. It suffices, but when we have visitors . . . ." His voice trailed off, but Holmes waved away.

The tea kettle was whistling upon the stove, and Mrs. Beddowes poured the hot water into the teapot. Soon we were all sitting around the table, while Holmes asked questions. He began by asking Timothy what he remembered, but it quickly became apparent that nothing useful was to be found from that quarter. He had eaten his evening meal, a soup prepared by Mrs. Beddowes, and had then gone to bed. He recalled that he was very sleepy the night before, and the next thing he remembered was standing under the tree outside as his father rushed toward him. Only after the minister had left for London did he start to feel like himself again.

Mrs. Beddowes had even less to tell. After Blackthorn had left the previous night to step next door to the church, she had finished cooking the soup, served the boy, and sent him off to bed. She cleaned up, sat around the kitchen for another hour or so, and then made her way to the guest room. She explained that, although she lived just up the road, she occasionally stayed over on nights when the weather was bad, or when some event was planned at the church the next day, requiring that she get an early start.

"You are a member of the congregation?" asked Holmes.

"Oh yes," she nodded. "Almost from the beginning. When the Reverend moved here with Timothy, who was just a babe then, he hired me to help care for the lad. I began to learn about his beliefs, and it seemed

426

to suit me – more than what some around here require." She frowned then, but her expression immediately cleared. "I became a member, and have helped convince a few others as well."

"Mrs. Beddowes is too modest," added Blackthorn. "She has brought several valuable members to our flock, including Mr. Frame, whom I mentioned earlier. I believe that some are members more from respect for her than anything that I can teach."

The old woman blushed and bowed her head with a small smile.

Holmes stood abruptly and excused himself, stating that he would like to look around outside. We made small talk while he was absent, chiefly consisting of my questions about the old church. Blackthorn gave further information about its abandonment many years before he and his son moved there. He surprisingly knew very little of its past, but that did not seem to interest him. He explained that when he had looked to move away from Manchester a decade earlier, he had decided to try Surrey first. In less than a day, he had come across the old church, and had been introduced with Mr. Frame, who was the owner. He attributed the ease in which it was located to a miracle. Frame had been willing to lease it to Blackthorn, who had a small amount of funds put aside. The man and his son had moved to Hindhead, hired Mrs. Beddowes, cleaned up the property, and had opened the doors. While not overwhelmed with members since then, the group had grown to the point that they considered themselves a tight-knit little community.

"Would it be possible to meet Mr. Frame?" asked Holmes, seemingly out-of-the-blue, stepping into the kitchen and resuming his seat.

Blackthorn's eyebrows raised, but he replied, "I don't see why not. But may I ask why?"

"I have questions about the church, and why it – and you – are attracting this sort of attention. As the owner of the property, he might possibly provide some relevant information."

This seemed to appease Blackthorn's curiosity, although I suspected there was more to it than this simple explanation. We stood, thanked Mrs. Beddowes, and then followed Blackthorn outside, where he asked if we would care to examine the church before we left.

Holmes replied that he had already been in during his earlier solitary exploration. I, however, wished to see it, and he waited patiently while Blackthorn took me inside. It was a typical building of the sort that I had seen a hundred times before – stone floors, mismatched chairs and pews, some decorations hanging from the walls. Blackthorn explained that there was no crypt. Rather, it was simply a square stone building, four walls and a roof, and there was nothing about it to attract attention.

We went outside and climbed into the carriage, which had been left in front of the church, the patient horse contentedly nibbling upon the rather unkempt grass surrounding the building. With a flick of the reins, the vehicle was set into motion, and we found ourselves out and circling behind the church, heading east on what was described as the London Road. It was not long before we had turned off into a meandering series of lanes, each narrower than the last. At one point I was aware of a great declivity in the earth, stretching away to the northeast. "The Devil's Punchbowl," explained our host.

"That sounds rather curious," I said.

"Nothing more than a geologic curiosity," said Blackthorn, "although there are any number of local legends about it. Some state that the Devil was so irritated about all of the churches being built around here – ours among them, no doubt – that he decided to dig a channel or a tunnel, depending which version you hear – from Hindhead to the sea, intending to flood us all. His efforts threw up the various hills in the area. Other stories state that the Devil battled the old gods, and that they threw soil from what became the Punch Bowl at him – or conversely, he threw the soil at them, creating the cavity. Others tell stories of giants who fought here, and that the soil from the punchbowl was thrown by one at another, but it overshot, and became the Isle of Wight." He shook his head. "It is confounding what the gullible will believe."

Holmes nodded. "Apparently someone hopes that you will be gullible enough to believe that the Angel of Death is threatening your son."

"Well, I don't believe it," said Blackthorn. "But I do know that some person is doing these things, and I want to know why, and I want it to stop!"

We rode along in silence for a few more minutes until Blackthorn turned the carriage between two tall and weathered gateposts, drawing up shortly before a sprawling manor house, surrounded by many venerable old oaks. I suspected that the property connected with the Devil's Punchbowl which we had recently passed. We approached the front door, which was opened before we reached it by a man, a butler most likely, who recognized the minister and let us in.

"Blake, can we see Mr. Frame?" he asked. The man nodded, stepped through a nearby door, and returned almost immediately to show us in.

It was a low-ceilinged room, with exposed beams running above us, revealing the age of the building. It was quite warm, as a fire blazed upon the hearth, in spite of the summer temperatures outside. An elderly man was sitting near the fireplace in an expensive-looking bath chair, a rug lying across his legs. Beside him stood a man in his mid-thirties, approximately the same age as Blackthorn, and several years older than both Holmes and myself. He looked at us with curiosity.

Blackthorn introduced the two of us, and then explained that the young man was Mr. Frame's nephew, Joseph Beddowes.

"Beddowes?" asked Holmes. "Any relation to your housekeeper, Reverend Blackthorn?"

"Her son," Blackthorn replied. "Mrs. Beddowes is the widow of Mr. Frame's brother." He fell silent then, as if uncertain how to proceed.

Frame filled the silence. "That's right," he said. "I've tried to convince her that she doesn't have to work, but she's a proud woman. Claims she would get old and die if she had nothing to do. And of course, she has a great affection for young Timothy." He shifted in the chair, and then continued, "To what do I owe the honor?" There was no impatience or animosity in his tone. He clearly held the minister in the highest regard.

When Blackthorn again seemed to hesitate, Holmes began to speak, relating that he was a consulting detective from London, and that I was his associate, summoned by the worried minister. He explained what we had only recently heard ourselves – the weekly appearances of the skull drawing at the church, and how, the night before, it had been drawn within the rectory itself, above young Timothy Blackthorn's bed, along with the name of the Angel of Death. Finally, he told how the boy had been found outside that morning, with no memory of how he got there.

Frame seemed to become rather agitated as the narrative progressed, and when Holmes had finished speaking, he asked several times whether the boy was truly all right. Blackthorn's reassurances helped to calm the man, and Joseph Beddowes stepped forward to fix the man's blanket and to pour him something from a decanter upon the nearby sideboard. He offered some to us as well, but we all declined.

Taking a sip of the amber-colored liquid, the older man asked, "How can I help you? You must think that I can, or you wouldn't have come here."

"That is correct, Mr. Frame," replied Holmes. "As the owner of the property, you may have some knowledge that would help explain why such harassment is taking place. Is there any fact that you can recall, any connection, that would provide an explanation about why the church, or Reverend Blackthorn's son, have been singled out?"

"I can't think of a thing," said the old man. "I purchased the property years ago, when I heard that there was some talk of increased railway activity in this area – this is the high point between here and Portsmouth, you know – and I started snapping up land. I held on to it for a while, and when the railway plans collapsed, I divested myself of nearly all of it. Broke even. But for some reason I still held the church, and when the

429

Reverend spoke to me about it ten years ago, it seemed like a good use of the place.

"I never bothered to learn about its history, and I don't know anything now either. But I did hear good things about the Reverend here from my sister-in-law, and I decided to attend and see for myself. Since then, I've come to be a full member, and I believe in the importance of Blackthorn's teachings. I'd like to do more to help him, if he'd let me."

Blackthorn smiled and shook his head. "If it's the Lord's will that we grow, then we will. No need to chase after people."

Frame shook his head with affection. "It's an argument we've had many times before. I've tried to get him to at least acknowledge that my offer to help could be the very manifestation of the Lord's will to which he refers, but he won't budge."

During this conversation, which continued in this vein for several more minutes, Holmes had begun to wander the room, looking at the paintings upon the walls and the books upon the shelves. He peered at a glass figure upon the mantel, and then, without realizing what was behind him, he backed into an ash bucket sitting beside the fireplace, tipping it over with a clatter and upsetting a spill of cinders across the floor.

He avoided falling down and spun around to see what he had done, a mortified look upon his face. The conversation between Frame and the minister ended abruptly as we reacted to Holmes's misfortune. Holmes quickly apologized, and dropped to his knees beside the mess, attempting to use a small shovel to pick up as much as he could of the disturbed ashes and return them to the now-righted bucket.

"Mr. Beddowes," said Holmes. "Do you have a broom?"

I saw that there was one propped near the fireplace poker. Frame gestured impatiently, indicating that Joseph Beddowes should step across and assist my friend, who was still awkwardly making excuses and explanations and apologies. Things only became more confused as Holmes, apparently not realizing how close Beddowes was, chose that moment to stand, awkwardly blundering into the man, both doing a confused dance around the spilled ashes before they found their footing.

Beddowes bent to reach for the small broom, but stopped when Holmes spoke, the chattering and embarrassed tone in his voice from just a moment before suddenly gone as he commanded, "That can wait, Mr. Beddowes. First, would you care to tell us why you have been chalking the marks upon the church and rectory walls, and more specifically, whether it was done with your mother's assistance?"

The man straightened abruptly, clutching the broom like a weapon. He looked back and forth from Holmes to Frame, and then at Blackthorn to me, before seeming to realize what he had done. Slowly, he bent and placed the broom against the fireplace. "I don't know what you mean."

"Really," replied Holmes, "it couldn't be clearer. I could spend a great deal of time asking questions in the village, and conniving a way to gain an understanding of Mr. Frame's financial situation, and finding a dozen other pieces of information that might be useful. Additionally, I can think of seven separate stratagems to press you specifically for information, but I believe the direct approach will wind this up as quickly as possible.

"An examination of Timothy's bedroom showed that the intruder must have come from inside the house. The boy's desk, covered with his drawings, is underneath the window. Although the window was open, there is no sign on the sill that anything has crossed that way, and the papers on the desk were undisturbed. No one stood on the desk to come in or out. The desk wasn't moved, as I determined from the dust undisturbed underneath. An examination outside showed the same – no one had recently stood outside that window.

"More importantly, the chalk drawing was directly over the bed, which has also not been moved. Clearly, the 'artist' had stood *on* the bed. While the Reverend and Dr. Watson were looking at the bizarre skull and the threatening name, I was looking at the sheets. There were several clear footprints still impressed there. The size of the shoes was clearly evident to someone who has made a study of such things, as were the various unique features on the soles, including a nail upon the right shoe that has been hammered in after being bent, and a crack along the toe box near the end of the left shoe. Once I found those shoes, it would be as clear to me who had stood on the bed and made the chalk marks as if I had a photograph of the man.

"My mind was still open as to what might be behind this harassment, and I really did want to know if Mr. Frame could provide any information about the church and its history. But the conversation here, revealing that you were Mr. Frame's nephew and that, through your mother, you likely had access to the rectory, quickly suggested the hint of another explanation. I observed that you were wearing the type and size of shoes that I sought. It seemed very likely that you were the man who had been in that bedroom and drew on the wall. Rather than go through excessive steps to contrive some other method of establishing your involvement, I decided to see if I could obtain your footprints in the spilled ash. I only needed to confirm the finer points, and by stepping in the ashes, you accommodated my wishes very nicely indeed. The features that I mentioned – the nail and the crack – are easily visible for all to see. So I repeat my question: Why?"

The room was silent for what seemed like a long time, while one could see the desperate thoughts racing across the man's face. Then, his patience at an end, Frame thundered, "Well? Explain yourself!"

Beddowes' gaze dropped, and he muttered, "It's true."

"Why?" asked Blackthorn, sounding puzzled.

"Because . . ." began Beddowes, and then he blurted, "Because every time you refused to take my uncle's money, he seemed more intent on finding a way to convince you. He's even begun to talk of changing his will to leave everything to your church."

Holmes nodded. "That is one of the facts that I would have had to ferret out over the course of a long and tedious investigation. Thank you for providing it so quickly."

"And your mother?" growled Frame, twisting to sit up straighter in his chair. "Is she in on all of this?"

"No," said Beddowes with an urgent tone. "She knew nothing. I stopped by last night as she was about to feed the boy, and when they weren't looking, I put a little something into the soup to make them sleep. She had told me that she was staying over while the Reverend prayed all night. I knew that he wasn't going to do that. Rather, I was certain that he was setting some sort of trap. I had been leaving the drawings on the same night each week, and he must have been expecting it to happen again. It had occurred to me that it would be a perfect chance to slip into the house while he was in the church, and do something that would truly frighten him away, since the drawings in the church weren't accomplishing anything.

"I left, and then waited outside while she put Timothy to bed and then put out her own light. Soon I could hear her sleeping, and I went back inside. The door was unlocked. I went to Timothy's room, scooped him up from the bed, put him into his chair, and stood on the bed to draw the picture. Afterwards, I took him nearby to the house I share with my mother, and kept him there until this morning, when I brought him back."

"And Abaddon?" asked Holmes. "What made you decide to drag in the Hebrew Angel of Death?"

"It was simply something I'd run across in one of my uncle's books. It seemed as if it would add to the threat. If the Reverend's son was in danger, he might decide to move away. I knew how he had picked this place at random ten years ago, and I thought that it would be easy for him to do it again somewhere else." He turned toward Blackthorn. "I am truly ashamed. Can you forgive me?"

Blackthorn's hands had been clenched through the entire explanation, but he sighed and let them drop to his sides. "Of course."

432

"But I cannot," growled Frame. "I want you out of this house within the hour. Do not darken my door ever again."

Blackthorn looked surprised, and moved to speak, but something in Frame's countenance stopped him. Instead, we watched as Beddowes fled from the room, leaving us with an awkward silence. Finally, Blackthorn spoke. "You should forgive him. He is your family. And no true harm was done."

"But there might have been," retorted the invalid. "The matter is beyond discussion."

"And yet," said Blackthorn, "you and I will discuss it. But later." With that, we departed.

Holmes and I found transportation back to Haslemere on our own, leaving Blackthorn to break the news to his housekeeper. On the train, we were silent for some time before I commented, "Blackthorn surprised me."

"And me as well."

"When he first walked into Baker Street," I said, "I was prepared, based upon his appearance, to believe that he would be some sort of pseudo-Old Testament prophet, prepared to rage with contempt against anyone who dared to disagree with him."

"Indeed. Which only goes to show how easily that anyone, including the two of us, can fall into the trap of making incorrect assumptions and judgments instead of giving someone the benefit of the doubt. I hope that things turn out well for Blackthorn – although I sense that this affair isn't over."

Sadly, Holmes was right. I heard at a later date that Frame's stubborn rejection of his nephew led to a falling out between the rich man and the minister, resulting in Blackthorn and his son moving to a new location somewhere near Chelmsford. I understand that his new congregation is thriving. Frame, however, became something of a bitter recluse following the removal of his ministerial advisor, and he eventually pulled down the minister's humble residence and the old church building entirely, leaving the property bare as if nothing had ever been there. Years later, a fine house was built upon the site, and the new occupants didn't realize the history until learning it from me. Holmes and I had been summoned there by the man who had built the new house, an old friend of ours, in connection to a particularly dangerous threat involving an Arctic whaler, long believed dead, who had returned seeking vengeance. But that is another adventure.

The Edinburgh Bankers

"Mr. Holmes, I'm not asking for myself. It's for the livelihood of all the rest us."

My friend did not seem to be convinced.

I watched with interest to see if our visitor – a nervous and bald-headed fellow who resembled a long-legged stork in a solemn black suit – might still be able to present his case in such a way as to raise Holmes's interest. It didn't seem likely, as we were due to return to London by way of the following morning's train, having just concluded a rather seamy bit of business related to a traitor within the ranks at Edinburgh Castle.

I filled my coffee cup, savoring the strong brew, and considering whether it would keep me awake when the sun set in a few hours. I decided that I didn't care. It had been a trying day, and I needed the jolt of *café noir*. I offered a cup to our visitor, but he declined, instead choosing to pack his pipe with a rather peculiar-smelling tobacco.

Sherlock Holmes and I had started the morning with a grim meeting that included representatives of both the military and the Crown, where Holmes explained the truth of the matter that had summoned us to the Scottish capital. The meeting concluded with an offer to the traitor of a revolver and one bullet, and five minutes of solitude to discuss the matter with his God before he had a tragic gun-cleaning accident. Within three minutes we heard, through the closed door, a ringing curse directed toward Holmes and then a gunshot. After determining that the first person to enter the room wouldn't fall victim to an ambush, we had then delivered the man's confession into the proper hands at Holyrood Palace.

We were now back in our tidy little hotel near the center of the Royal Mile, and ensconced in the small sitting room located between our two bedrooms. I'd believed the knock on our door to be our coffee, but in fact it was Ian Kilbury, who introduced himself as Head Clerk at the nearby Merchants Bank of Edinburgh, located where North Bridge meets South Bridge. (The coffee had arrived just behind him.)

Holmes was especially weary after the events of the last two days, particularly after we had trailed the traitor through the secret entryway and into the forgotten underground areas around Marlin's Wynd. I'd thought that Holmes was done for when our guide, Lieutenant Carfax, had been tripped by one of the traitor's traps and had fallen into a forgotten sewage chute, and then Holmes dived in head-first right behind to save him. I'd scrambled across the slick stones in time to see that Holmes was hanging on by his fingertips, while the lieutenant grasped his leg – all that prevented him from the terrible drop and certain death. I managed to get a hold on Holmes's coat and pull them both up far enough that they could save themselves. When the traitor saw Holmes and the Lieutenant walk into the castle the following morning, the look in his eyes betrayed that he knew his exposure was imminent.

Now we'd finished with that business, but twenty minutes too late to catch the train to London. Holmes had made a show of impatience, but I could tell that the idea of an enforced rest wasn't entirely unwelcome, and that he wouldn't mind a sunset walk up and down the Royal Mile. But then Ian Kilbury arrived.

Through our cracked window, I could hear the sound of bagpipes – probably the same busker who'd set up across the road about that time the afternoon before. I started to close the window, but then changed my mind – how often did one get to hear something like that?

Kilbury cleared his throat. "I'm the Head Clerk at the Merchants Bank, just to the east of here. You will have certainly passed us when going up or down the Royal Mile. We're at the corner of the High Street and South Bridge – a tidy little building of four stories, just across from the Currency Exchange. The bank was formed a century-and-a-half ago, and we specialize in financial matters related to linens."

Holmes simply nodded. He hadn't shut his eyes to listen, indicating that he was in a tolerant but not-engaged frame of mind.

"Our president and chief shareholder is Colonel Allen Corby, a direct descendant of our founder, who came up in the years following Culloden. The Colonel has always been a hearty and fit man, and he remains so, but he's in his early seventies now, and one cannot be unaware that he will not last forever. And yet, he seems to think that he will. When most men begin to make transitional plans and acknowledge their mortality, the Colonel seems to defy it. Instead of cutting back, he has recently spent a fortune to construct a massive home south of the city, and to hear him brag about it, one would think that he considers himself immortal, with a fitting place to spend eternity.

"If I'm to be completely frank, it has been this attitude that has prevented him from adequately seeing to the future of the bank. He has two sons, both of whom have worked there since reaching their majority. Neither was ever given a choice about their careers. It was expected that they would join the bank, although neither is adequately prepared to shoulder their additional responsibilities when the Colonel passes – and despite his attitude to the contrary, that day will surely come.

"I could provide further examples of the Colonel's irresponsibility, but I'm sure you have the sense of it. Without trying your patience, I'll now turn to the events which led me to seek you out, once I heard that you were here in Edinburgh.

"I'm often the last one at the bank each day, taking it upon myself to see that all is well and finish locking up. Last night about nine o'clock, I was checking the empty building. I started at the top, where we have a board room and a small apartment for the Colonel or members of his family if they wish to stay over. I made sure that all was well, and then started down the stairs, which are located along the eastern side of the building.

"As I descended, I could see through one of the tall windows and across the alley-way into the conference room of one of our competitors, the Lenders and Creditors Savings Association. Normally that time of night, their building is dark, but it isn't completely unusual for an evening or even late-night meeting to take place.

"I paused, with just a little professional curiosity, so see what – and whom – I might see. I was surprised to observe that this wasn't a typical meeting, but rather some sort of party – no, that isn't quite right. A party implies a social gathering with many guests, food, and mingled conversation. This appeared to be some sort of card game, with only half-a-dozen participants – with three playing and three watching.

"They were set up near the window, at a round table. There were cards before each player, and mounds of money, and also documents piled beside them or in the middle of the table. There were also a number of bottles of whisky and other liquors cluttering the playing area.

"I could observe everything quite clearly – we were really only separated by a matter of yards – and I have no fear that they were able to see me. They were in a lit room, and would have only seen their own reflections in the window-glass, while I was standing in the darkened stairwell. There is no mistake as to what happened.

"Sitting on the right side of my view was the Colonel's son Joseph, clearly drunk, and even as I watched, encouraged to drink further still. A hand of cards was in process, and one of the other two men threw down his cards. The betting then settled down between Joseph Corby and a devious and conniving man across from him, the president of Lenders and Creditors, Craig McCain. Standing slightly behind Joseph was another of the Lenders officers, Stafford Guinn, who moved here from Manchester four years ago.

"As I watched, Joseph pushed in all of the money piled in front of him, laughing and gesturing awkwardly, clearly quite inebriated. Behind him and out of his sight, Guinn – who had his eye fixed on Joseph's cards – shook his head 'No' and smiled. Then Craig McCain raised the bet.

"It was then that Guinn leaned down, whispered in Joseph's ear while laying a hand on his back in a fatherly way, and then put a sheet of paper in front of him. Another fellow quickly leaned in from the surrounding darkness with a pen, and it was but the work of a moment for Joseph to sign his name and toss the sheet into the pot.

"You know what happened next. Joseph lost, of course, and McCain raked in his winnings – including whatever Joseph had just signed. I continued to watch, aghast, but that seemed to be that. Having achieved this victory, the men of the Lenders and Creditors had no further interest in playing cards. Everyone stood up to leave, and Joseph was put into his coat, handed his stick and hat, and shuffled out of my view. As I stood considering what I'd seen, it was just a moment later that Joseph appeared on the pavement far below, looking around in confusion before shuffling away toward the west. If he went home – he and his brother live with the Colonel, despite both being well into adulthood – then he likely crossed North Bridge and found a cab at Waverly Station, but I have no knowledge of it.

"All I know for certain is that he was back at his desk this morning, hungover in a typical fashion, and giving no indication that anything untoward happened last night. In fact, he may not even remember it, but the fact is that he signed some sort of document, after what seemed to be a well-planned effort to lead him to that point. I am greatly concerned."

Holmes roused himself. "And you have brought us this story for what reason, exactly?"

Kilbury seemed confused, as if the answer was self-evident. "I am a student of your works, Mr. Holmes." He glanced my way, his brow bent with a shade of disdain. "I'm afraid that I must tell you, Doctor, that I'm in agreement with Mr. Holmes when I state that you would be better served by presenting accounts of his narratives in a more . . . *scientific* manner, so that a student such as myself could learn of the actual method of investigation, rather than contriving the narrative in such a way as to hide the process in favor of a dramatic solution."

I was not offended, but rather amused, and considered pointing out that Holmes himself often *contrived* his own narrative in such a way as to keep me in the dark until he could reveal the truth in a showman-like fashion. But I held my tongue, and Kilbury turned back to Holmes.

"As I stated, the Colonel cannot live forever. While I don't know specifics, I'm aware that his estate is a tangled mess, and if his older son has signed away a piece of it – and possibly of the bank itself – to our most bitter rival, all our livelihoods are in jeopardy. I need you to help me cut through the knot."

He looked hopefully at Holmes, but I could tell that my friend wasn't interested – a fact that he confirmed immediately.

"I am sorry, Mr. Kilbury, but I'm not quite sure what you would like me to do. If the Colonel's son signed a paper, it's beyond my skills to get it unsigned, even if he was tricked into doing so. In any case, Dr. Watson and I are leaving tomorrow morning for London – we would already be on our way now, but for a small delay in convincing a fellow to look into a matter of firearm maintenance." Holmes glanced my way, and I understood.

"I'm sorry as well, Mr. Kilbury," I said, rising and showing him to the door. "I do wish you luck in getting to bottom of the matter."

Kilbury stood and looked from one to the other of us, working his arms futilely as if about to take flight. The expression on his face indicated that he was considering some further appeal, but he likely hadn't reached his position as a Head Clerk without learning how to read people. With a nod of understanding, he wished us a good day and departed.

At times I have chastised Holmes for dismissing a case, and have cajoled him into reconsidering. Once or twice when he's sent a prospective client away, I've followed up myself, doing a bit of investigating on my own – with admittedly mixed results. But this time, I tended to agree with Holmes – there wasn't really anything to investigate, and we were both prepared to return to London on the morrow.

The next morning, we were faced with a torrential downpour, and I knew that the trip back would tedious at best. After an early breakfast, we sent our bags ahead and elected to walk the short distance across the recently rebuilt North Bridge and around and down to Waverley Station. It wasn't far, but in that rain, I immediately regretted the decision. While we mostly stayed dry by way of hats, overcoats, and umbrellas, the rainwater sluicing down the cobblestones threatened to soak through our boots and rush our feet out from underneath us. And yet, through small careful steps, and forward progression at times by mere inches, we traversed the steep slope downward, and so into the station.

We still had a few free minutes before the train was scheduled to depart, giving us time to visit a newsagent's stand. I was looking to see if there were any yellow-back novels that I'd yet to examine when I felt Holmes tap me on the shoulder. I turned, and he indicated one of the headlines on a local newspaper:

Ian Kilbury, Bank Clerk – Mysteriously Murdered

I left Holmes there to purchase whichever papers carried the story while I went to retrieve our luggage.

We were back at our small hotel, once again in the same sitting room we'd used for the past couple of days. If the manager had been surprised, he was too experienced and professional to display it. Holmes and I each settled in to go through the various newspapers, trading them back and forth until we knew all that had been publicly released.

The night before, according to Kilbury's wife and children – a son and daughter – the man had been most agitated, without providing a reason why. About nine o'clock, he'd suddenly announced that he was going out to the pub just across the way from their Picardy Place residence in order to meet a man about "something going on at the bank". This was highly unusual, and the family definitively stated that Kilbury had never done such a thing before.

Several people in the pub remembered Kilbury's entrance and his subsequent meeting with a cloaked figure in a dark corner. It wasn't unusual, said the barkeep, for the unknown man to have remained covered, as the rains had started by then, and several people had elected to do the same thing. Kilbury and the other man had each ordered a pint, but only the stranger drank his before leaving soon after. Kilbury followed almost immediately.

An hour later, a certain Constable Naughton had been passing through Northumberland Street when he heard the cry of "Murder!" Rushing up, he found two people, a man and woman, standing alongside a body. "It's Mr. Kilbury of the bank!" the woman cried.

Naughton leaned over and aimed his torch at the figure, finding a tall, bald man in his fifties lying there, face up, eyes closed and deathly pale. There was what seemed to be a pool of blood around his head, but no visible wound, and the blood was washing away in the rain even as he watched.

Before he could examine the body, Naughton was stunned to find that he suddenly had a blanket thrown over his head, apparently by the couple who had found the dead man. Naughton stated that both of them had seemed quite nervous – something he put down to their inexperience at suddenly encountering a corpse – but in hindsight he felt that they had acted that way because they were planning his ambush. Before he could free himself, they had wrapped him in a strap, holding the blanket in place. When he fought his way free, he found the street empty – not only of the two people who had waylaid him, but of the body itself. They had stolen and carried away the deceased Mr. Ian Kilbury.

It was at this point that I asked Holmes, "Is it possible that these are two different affairs? Kilbury was murdered because of the card game he'd witnessed, but then his body was stolen for different reasons? By a medical student and his girlfriend, perhaps? Are we dealing with another Burke and Hare, finding subjects for human vivisection?"

Holmes smiled and shook his head. "I think that if you consider the facts, Watson, you'll see that isn't likely." But he refused to be drawn further, and suggested instead that we present ourselves to the local police, ostensibly to offer our assistance and provide what facts we knew, but also to further our own investigation.

We located an old acquaintance, Inspector Dougal MacDonald – a distant kinsman of Scotland Yard Inspector Alec MacDonald. Whereas our London friend had elected to rise to fame within the Metropolitan Police, his Albannaich cousin had established his own strong reputation in the north. He had been present the day before when the traitor had withdrawn himself from further mischief, and seemed surprised to see us. When Holmes had related Kilbury's reason for visiting us the previous afternoon, MacDonald nodded.

"That fits with what the family said. He was worried about something going on at the bank. Apparently he's been in service there his whole adult life, and cares very deeply." He stood. "I have their story, but you should talk to them as well. Let's go visit them."

After making a telephone call to the constable who found the body, MacDonald led us outside to a four-wheeler. Holmes and I answered several questions along the way concerning the events related to Kilbury's visit the day before, but no moments of *Eureka*-like understanding seemed to result from our narrative.

The family lived in the upstairs apartments at 11 Picardy Place. I was surprised that the head clerk of a noted bank centered in the Royal Mile couldn't do better, finding a showier and larger place, but after meeting the man's forthright and no-nonsense wife, the idea that the family could have been anything but sensible and thrifty was pure nonsense.

Mrs. Kilbury's mouth was a tight line, holding back anger – and any comments. Her children were not so restrained.

"Father asked for your help," snapped his son, Brian. "He's admired your methods for years, Mr. Holmes. 'Logic and observation,' he would say. 'That man has refined logic and observation to a remarkable degree.' When he heard that you were in town, he believed that you would be able to gather evidence that some skullduggery was afoot at the bank and put a stop to it. When you refused, he said that he'd have to take care of it himself."

MacDonald frowned. "You didn't mention that your father had spoken to Mr. Holmes when I questioned you earlier."

The young man didn't answer, and his sister Tara spoke. "Father made a telephone call. He was going out to confront someone. He felt that it was important – whatever is happening threatened the bank, he said, and the loyal employees who work there."

"Do you know why he was in Northumberland Street an hour later?" asked Holmes, passing over asking further about the reason for Kilbury's departure. "That's quite a distance away."

All three shook their heads. "We've already answered these questions for the police," said Tara Kilbury with scorn. "What are you going to do about it?"

"Apply logic and observation, of course," he replied in a rather glib manner. I was surprised that he would take that tone with the deceased's family, but he indicated that he was finished and, offering our condolences, we departed.

Outside, we walked across the wide intersection to the pub where Kilbury had met the mysterious stranger the night before. Waiting for us was Constable Naughton, off-duty and holding a blanket.

"This is it," the big officer growled when we were settled inside, and after he had drunk a third of his dark pint. "They wrapped it around me while I was bent over to look at the body."

Holmes took the blanket and gave it a thorough examination, even taking a moment to sniff it. He smiled to himself and then said to Naughton, "And you recognized the dead man as Mr. Kilbury?"

"That's right," said the constable. "My father was a security officer at the bank. I've known Mr. Kilbury my whole life."

"Any idea why he was in Northumberland Street?"

"Nary a clue, sir. That's been my beat for several years now, and I've never once encountered him there."

"Could he have known that you would be found there?" I asked.

"Good, Watson," murmured Holmes.

"Perhaps he needed to ask for your help surreptitiously in this matter?" I added, noticing that Holmes frowned at this statement.

"It's possible, sir," said Naughton. "But what I can't figure is why steal his body in the way they did? He was lying there in the empty street, outside of an alleyway that leads to a whole warren of byways and side streets. Was he struck down there because that's where his killer caught up with him, or did he have business in the alley, or had he just come out of it?"

"Perhaps the true question is why did the couple scream 'Murder!'" asked Holmes, "attracting your attention, only to immediately attack you and steal the body – presumably escaping down the alley with it – when they could have simply taken it and never called you over in the first place."

"Aye," said Naughton, "that is a puzzler."

"And does the theft of the body even connect to what Kilbury observed with Joseph Corby?" added Macdonald.

"We'll talk to him next," said Holmes.

We thanked the constable and stepped outside. "Any need to visit Northumberland Street, where the body was found?" asked MacDonald. I could see that he wanted to steer us that way, perhaps to see Holmes in action, crawling around on the pavement, measuring between footprints to determine the killer's stride and height, or perhaps to see some fragment, placed carefully in one of the little evidence envelopes that Holmes habitually carried, that would rip the case wide open. But Holmes shook his head.

"The rain will have washed away any signs on the street," he said. "If there were any signs to see . . . ." He stopped speaking and looked across the street for a moment toward the Kilbury apartment, but there was nothing there except several passers-by going about their business.

"We might find the tracks of their escape through the alleyway," he continued, "but that would serve no purpose. No, we should next visit the Corby clan."

We had our driver convey us back to the Merchant's Bank, where we were taken upstairs to the apartment described by Kilbury, used by the family for their own private doings. There we had our first look at the Colonel, an old fellow, once obviously quite large, but now collapsed in upon himself. The few remaining strands of his wispy white hair were long and danced about when he moved his head. With him were his two sons, Joseph – the fellow who had lost at cards – and his younger sibling, Thomas. The difference between the two men was startling. Joseph was big and red-faced, loud and angry, and bald like his father, the skin on his damp high forehead bunched as if there were too much cloth ruched on a dressmaker's figure, while Thomas was dark and slight, and clearly twenty years younger than the other, not much past his thirtieth birthday. Yet he too was noticeably bald.

"A shame," growled the Colonel, rather insincerely. "Not sure what Kilbury was up to, but I've initiated a review of the books to make sure that he hadn't been stealing from me."

Joseph nodded and muttered something about a knife in the back. MacDonald countered the Colonel's statement. "We've seen no evidence that Mr. Kilbury was anything but honorable. In fact, he seems to have gotten himself into this by looking out for your interests. Mr. Holmes?"

My friend then recounted Kilbury's visit the afternoon before, and what he had told us. Joseph Corby began to bluster, but he wilted when his father turned a dark eye upon him. "What's this?" he said in a low dangerous voice. "Conniving against me, are you? What did you sign?"

Joseph Corby shook his head, speechless. I could see that he would ordinarily be an overbearing bully, but he had been caught out and had no immediate defense. His brother beside him had the faintest flash of triumph in his eyes.

The Colonel looked back at us. "No matter. I'll handle this myself."

"It isn't that easy," countered MacDonald. "It's very likely that Mr. Kilbury, in attempting to conduct his own investigation, reached out to one of the men involved, and as a result was killed for it."

"Nonsense. I heard his body was stolen. He was knocked in the head by some stranger and carried away. You need to look in the dissecting rooms at the medical school. That's where you'll find your killer."

"Colonel," said Holmes, "the likelihood that this occurred so soon after your son's meeting with your competitors, and Mr. Kilbury's subsequent involvement, makes it nearly certain that there is a connection between those events and the murder. We – "

"Then talk to McCain at Lenders and Creditors. We have nothing for you here."

He said it with finality and, as we knew when to pick our battles, we departed, retreating outside and stepping along the fifty feet or so to the entrance of the Lenders and Creditors Savings Association. Within moments, we were shown to the highest floor and a room very much like the Corby's apartment atop the Merchant's Bank. Facing us with a sneer was Craig McCain, and his chief factotum, Stafford Guinn. Each of them was as bald as a cue ball – so much so that I suspected they shaved their heads, McCain to look imposing, and Guinn because McCain did it.

I was rather unnerved to note that nearly every important figure that we'd met over the course of this investigation – Kilbury, the Corbys, and these two men from the Lenders and Creditors, were glabrous. Without meaning to, I reached up and gave a touch to my own full head of hair as a comfort.

McCain and Guinn were intentionally unpleasant, making it clear that they had no intention of helping us whatsoever. "Card game?" asked McCain. His skull was a curiosity – the front of his forehead bulged out, as if there was an extra lobe squatting upon the front of his brain. "Possibly. What of it? It isn't illegal. A few friends meeting and wagering."

443

"We've just come from the Merchants Bank," said Holmes. "The Colonel is aware of these facts as well."

McCain frowned and then shrugged. "What of it? Joseph Corby is a grown man – legally, anyway. He can make his arrangements, and the Colonel can go to blazes."

"This way out, gentlemen," sneered Guinn, stepping toward us from his post behind his master. Up close, I recalled why he had looked familiar to me when we'd initially arrived: With the way his ears lay flat against his head, he resembled one of those black-eyed serpents that one might encounter in the London Zoo.

Outside, the rains had finally stopped. We conferred for a moment with the inspector. He promised to wait at the station for word from Holmes – who had indicated that he saw a way forward toward a quick solution. Then saying goodbye to both of us, he walked off to the east, down the hill and toward the palace.

Nodding to the inspector, with a comment that doubtless we would see each other soon, I returned to our sitting room, where I ensconced myself with a late but very fine lunch and a nap. I was still so occupied when the door burst open to reveal Holmes, a smile on his face and color in his cheeks, exhorting me to be up and about, for we were due in the apartments atop the Merchants Bank almost immediately.

Within five minutes we'd been shown upstairs, where Inspector MacDonald waited with the Corbys, the Kilbury family, and the two men we'd recently met from the Lenders and Creditors. Each group sat tightly together, and the palpable tension indicated that we hadn't missed any revealing conversation before our arrival.

Our presence seemed to be what everyone was awaiting, and Holmes began. "This morning, Dr. Watson and I familiarized ourselves with the events of last night, and met the principal players in the drama that Mr. Kilbury first described to us yesterday afternoon. I already had some sense of the truth from the initial newspaper accounts, and what we saw afterwards only confirmed it, and cleared away some of the brush. This afternoon, after a rather brisk walk through the city, I arranged to meet with Colonel Corby in secret and explained my thinking."

The Colonel cleared his throat. "Most enlightening." He turned to glare at his older son, Joseph. "You're a fool. I notified McCain immediately what I intended to do, and he's smart enough realize that he lost this round." He spun back to face his competitor. "What did I tell you?"

McCain looked as if he'd bit into a wormy apple. "You're changing your will. Disinheriting your sons. The paper that Joseph signed is worthless."

"That's right," agreed the Colonel. Back to his elder son. "Thinking that you could pay a gambling debt with my inheritance? You're an idiot, Joe. I'm going to live for years, but putting something like that in writing was like setting a target on me. McCain would have me snuffed in a month."

McCain stood up angrily. "Here now! That's not true! I confirmed what I'd done, and what your son had signed – That's no reason to make such an unfounded accusation!"

Throughout this entire exchange, I happened to notice the sudden blanching of younger son Thomas, who had also apparently just lost his inheritance in one stroke, because of his older brother's irresponsibility. And curiously, another who seemed affected in was Tara Kilbury, suddenly slumped and pale, and staring at her hands as they twisted a handkerchief.

"I mentioned my walk through the city this afternoon," said Holmes, taking back everyone's attention. "I headed down the hill toward the Palace, taking a sudden turn into Bakehouse Close. I thought that more effort would be required, but it only took a moment to snag the man who had been following me. In fact, I had seen him several times already this morning – in Picardy Place when we visited the Kilbury house, and again when we exited the pub. Finally, he was outside the Lenders and Creditors, loitering across the street in a most amateur false beard." He raised his voice. "Constable Naughton!"

As the door opened, I recalled when Holmes had paused for a moment outside the pub, still as a statue for just a moment there in Picardy Place. I had only seen passersby, but he had recognized one as having appeared before, causing him to keep his eyes open for later appearances. When a tall thin man entered with Naughton, I realized why he should have caught my attention too: The thick black beard was patently false. To the surprise of many in the room – but not to the mother and her two children – the fellow removed his hat and the beard to reveal our initial client, Ian Kilbury.

"It's true," he said. "I was the man following Mr. Holmes. I faked my death last night to attract his interest before he and Dr. Watson left town this morning." He glanced affectionately at his family. "I had help, of course. After my meeting at the pub – " And here Kilbury glanced tellingly toward Thomas Corby, who looked at the floor. " – I made my way across town to Northumberland Street, where I knew that my old acquaintance the constable walked a beat. When he was near, I lay down and poured a blood-looking mixture on the pavement near my head. Then my daughter cried 'Murder!' When the constable arrived, she and my son wrapped him in a blanket, and we escaped down the alley-way together – for how could

I be murdered without leaving a body? Then a word to a friendly newspaper reporter of my acquaintance made sure that the word was spread by morning, ensuring that Mr. Holmes would become involved." He then moved to sit beside his wife, who looked considerably less grim than when I'd seen her before. As he took her hand, his son, standing behind the small sofa, squeezed his father's shoulder. However, Tara Kilbury still looked washed out and rather ill.

It did not go unnoticed.

"Mr. McCain," said Holmes. "You didn't come up with this scheme to acquire Joseph Corby's inheritance on your own, did you?"

McCain shook his head. "No. I should have stayed away and thought of something clever."

"Who gave you the idea?"

He tipped a head toward the younger Corby sibling. "Thomas."

At this, Kilbury half-rose to his feet. "Thomas? But it was him that I called last night to discuss the paper that his brother had signed. I wanted his advice. He never said a word . . . ."

The fellow in question then rose to his feet. I could see that he wanted to decry the claim – to say it was a lie. But instead he just looked at his father, who himself dragged himself to his feet.

"Is this true?" he rumbled.

The younger man could only nod. And then, astonishingly, Tara Kilbury rose and went to stand beside him. Her small hand sought that of Thomas, and they faced the assembly together. Any look of contentment that had been on Ian Kilbury's face following the revelation of his actual survival and explanation how he had involved Holmes in the matter faded. He chewed his lip with a great frown upon his lean face.

"Thomas and I conceived the idea together," she said. "To disinherit Joseph. It was always intended to make what had happened known to the Colonel sooner rather than later. Thomas approached Mr. McCain, and from there it was easily accomplished." She glanced at Ian Kilbury. "We didn't know that father would see the card game, or start his own investigation – or want to meet with Thomas about it. It . . . it has spiraled beyond our control."

McCain growled. "So you played me too, then?" He pulled a piece of paper from his pocket and tossed it at the Colonel's feet. "Here's the document. I was a fool to be involved. I'll do better next time."

The Colonel said "Ha!" as if he looked forward to it, while McCain stomped from the room, Guinn slithering along behind him. After the door slammed, the room was spiked into silence until Holmes finally spoke.

"I had realized from reading the newspapers how unlikely the events in Northumberland Street were – a cry of 'Murder!' and the constable summoned by the very people who then assaulted him – with a harmless blanket! – and then spiriting the body away. They could never have expected the blanket to hold him for long – certainly not long enough to carry away an actual dead body. I saw that it was carefully staged, and with Mr. Kilbury's active involvement – he simply jumped up and ran away with his children.

"When I heard that he had a son and daughter, I recognized that they were the likely accomplices. When we visited the Kilbury apartments, I made careful note of everything, not knowing when a confirming clue would present itself. And it did, not long after – the blanket used to wrap the constable. It matched one that had been in the apartment, and more importantly, it held the scent of a rather uniquely flavored strong tobacco – the same that Mr. Kilbury uses himself, and which permeates their living quarters.

"After luring Mr. Kilbury into Bakehouse Close and taking custody of the supposedly murdered man, I was able to clear my thinking and focus on the problem that had originally caused him to visit Dr. Watson and me. It was obvious that the document Joseph Corby had signed while drunk – and the victim of cheating – was some claim upon his inheritance. My own hurried investigations showed that he has no real funds of his own to otherwise draw upon. As I said, I met with the Colonel in private, explained my thoughts, and we realized that disinheriting his son was the only way to expose the truth and force Mr. McCain realize that his document was now worthless."

He turned to the Colonel. "It wasn't part of our discussion that he would say that he was disinheriting both of them – but his spontaneously doing so led to unexpected dividends: Namely, the exposure of his younger son's involvement, along with that of Miss Kilbury."

"Mrs. Corby," she corrected. "Thomas and I were married six months ago, but we knew that the Colonel would object – he would never let one of his sons marry 'beneath' him."

Her comment left the room was suspended in silence. Joseph Corby had sunk into a chair, lost in his own thoughts, his fingers picking at one another. The Kilburys were all staring at Tara, their initial shock at her involvement now replaced by a stunned wonder that she was married, and had been, and they had clearly never realized it. The police officers stood at the side with canny expressions, and MacDonald was likely wondering if any charges could be filed. Thomas and Tara stood hand-in-hand, facing the Colonel, who had in turn shifted to direct his attention their way.

I expected him to explode, to roar that the disinheritance would stand. But he surprised us all.

"Good thing," he grumbled. "You're a smart one, aren't you girl? Just what we need around here." He glanced toward Joseph and shook his head. "I probably would have said no, had you asked first. Good job – taking the initiative that way." Then he smiled. It was a terrible thing to see, but it was probably sincere and the best that he could do. "With you on our side, McCain doesn't have a chance, does he?" And he sank into his seat, chuckling and muttering.

Indeed, the infusion of Tara Kilbury Corby's rather shrewd intellect, and the contempt for the Lenders and Creditors Savings Association which had permeated her existence from birth, seemed to light a fire under the old man. Within a year, the Merchants Bank had completely subsumed McCain's organization.

I mentioned that fact some months later after I'd read in a newspaper where the Merchants had been named as a major source of funding for the construction of the new Midlothian County Buildings after the failure of the Lenders and Creditors. Holmes was indifferent. "Don't bother mentioning that affair to me until the newspapers report that the Colonel has died. Then we'll have to hie ourselves back to Edinburgh to investigate."

I raised an eyebrow. "You suspect that he will have been murdered? The fellow is in terrible shape – he seemed as if his heart would burst with every breath."

"True, but he has taken a serpent to his bosom with that daughter-in-law of his."

"Possibly," I said, "although I would think she will bide her time. In spite of his own beliefs on the subject, the Colonel can't live forever."

"True," countered Holmes. "But at what point will she decide that he's lived long enough?" He set aside the chemistry experiment he'd finished, arose, and walked toward his room. "We'll wait and see," he said darkly before closing the door.

Holmes has never had a high regard for the female of the species. "Women are never to be entirely trusted," he's said before, "not the best of them." Often I disagree with him, but considering the rather cold-blooded way that Tara Kilbury Corby had initiated events, I wondered if in this case Holmes might be right. Time would tell.

About the Author

David Marcum plays *The Game* with deadly seriousness. He first discovered Sherlock Holmes in 1975 at the age of ten, and since that time, he has collected, read, and chronologicized literally thousands of traditional Holmes pastiches in the form of novels, short stories, radio and television episodes, movies and scripts, comics, fan-fiction, and unpublished manuscripts. He is the author of over eighty Sherlockian pastiches, some published in anthologies and magazines such as *The Strand*, and others collected in his own books, *The Papers of Sherlock Holmes*, *Sherlock Holmes and A Quantity of Debt*, and *Sherlock Holmes – Tangled Skeins*. He has edited almost sixty books, including several dozen traditional Sherlockian anthologies, such as the ongoing series *The MX Book of New Sherlock Holmes Stories*, which he created in 2015. This collection is now up to 27 volumes, with more in preparation.

He was responsible for bringing back August Derleth's Solar Pons for a new generation, first with his collection of authorized Pons stories, *The Papers of Solar Pons*, and then by editing the reissued authorized versions of the original Pons books, and then volumes of new Pons adventures. He has done the same for the adventures of Dr. Thorndyke, and has plans for similar projects in the future. He has contributed numerous essays to various publications, and is a member of a number of Sherlockian groups and Scions. His irregular Sherlockian blog, *A Seventeen Step Program*, addresses various topics related to his favorite book friends (as his son used to call them when he was small), and can be found at *http://17stepprogram.blogspot.com/*

He is a licensed Civil Engineer, living in Tennessee with his wife and son. Since the age of nineteen, he has worn a deerstalker as his regular-and-only hat. In 2013, he and his deerstalker were finally able make his first trip-of-a-lifetime Holmes Pilgrimage to England, with return Pilgrimages in 2015 and 2016, where you may have spotted him. If you ever run into him and his deerstalker out and about, feel free to say hello!

451

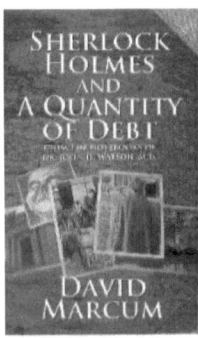

454

Edited by David Marcum
from MX Publishing
The MX Book of New Sherlock Holmes Stories
(MX Publishing, 2015-   )

"This is the finest volume of Sherlockian fiction I have ever read, and I have read, literally, thousands." – Philip K. Jones

"Beyond Impressive . . . This is a splendid venture for a great cause!"
– Roger Johnson, Editor, *The Sherlock Holmes Journal*,
The Sherlock Holmes Society of London

Part I: 1881-1889
Part II: 1890-1895
Part III: 1896-1929
Part IV: 2016 Annual
Part V: Christmas Adventures
Part VI: 2017 Annual
Part VII: Eliminate the Impossible (1880-1891)
Part VIII – Eliminate the Impossible (1892-1905)
Part IX – 2018 Annual (1879-1895)
Part X – 2018 Annual (1896-1916)
Part XI – Some Untold Cases (1880-1891)
Part XII – Some Untold Cases (1894-1902)
Part XIII – 2019 Annual (1881-1890)
Part XIV – 2019 Annual (1891-1897)
Part XV – 2019 Annual (1898-1917)
Part XVI – Whatever Remains . . . Must be the Truth (1881-1890)
Part XVII – Whatever Remains . . . Must be the Truth (1891-1898)
Part XVIII – Whatever Remains . . . Must be the Truth (1898-1925)
Part XIX – 2020 Annual (1882-1890)
Part XX – 2020 Annual (1891-1897)
Part XXI – 2020 Annual (1898-1923)
Part XXII – Some More Untold Cases (1877-1887)
Part XXIII – Some More Untold Cases (1888-1894)
Part XXIV – Some More Untold Cases (1895-1903)
Part XXV – 2021 Annual (1881-1888)
Part XXVI – 2021 Annual (1889-1897)
Part XXVII – 2021 Annual (1898-1928)
Part XXVIII – More Christmas Adventures (1869-1888)
Part XXIX – More Christmas Adventures (1889-1896)
Part XXX – More Christmas Adventures (1897-1928)
In Preparation
Part XXXI (and XXXII and XXXIII?) – 2022 Annual

. . . and more to come!

Edited by David Marcum
from MX Publishing
The MX Book of New Sherlock Holmes Stories
(MX Publishing, 2015-   )

<u>*Publishers Weekly* says:</u>

Part VI: *The traditional pastiche is alive and well . . . .*

Part VII: *Sherlockians eager for faithful-to-the-canon plots
and characters will be delighted.*

Part VIII: *The imagination of the contributors in coming up with variations on the
volume's theme is matched by their ingenious resolutions.*

Part IX: *The 18 stories . . . will satisfy fans of Conan Doyle's originals. Sherlockians will
rejoice that more volumes are on the way.*

Part X: *. . . new Sherlock Holmes adventures of consistently high quality.*

Part XI: *. . . an essential volume for Sherlock Holmes fans.*

Part XII: *. . . continues to amaze with the number of high-quality pastiches.*

Part XIII: *. . . Amazingly, Marcum has found 22 superb pastiches . . . This is more catnip
for fans of stories faithful to Conan Doyle's original*

Part XIV: *. . . . this standout anthology of 21 short stories written in the spirit of Conan
Doyle's originals.*

Part XV: *Stories pitting Sherlock Holmes against seemingly supernatural phenomena
highlight Marcum's 15ᵗʰ anthology of superior short pastiches.*

Part XVI: *Marcum has once again done fans of Conan Doyle's originals a service.*

Part XVII: *This is yet another impressive array of new but traditional Holmes stories.*

Part XVIII: *Sherlockians will again be grateful to Marcum and MX for high-quality new
Holmes tales.*

Part XIX: *Inventive plots and intriguing explorations of aspects of Dr. Watson's life and
beliefs lift the 24 pastiches in Marcum's impressive 19ᵗʰ Sherlock Holmes anthology*

Part XX: *Marcum's reserve of high-quality new Holmes exploits seems endless.*

Part XXI: *This is another must-have for Sherlockians.*

Part XXII: *Marcum's superlative 22ⁿᵈ Sherlock Holmes pastiche anthology features 21
short stories that successfully emulate the spirit of Conan Doyle's originals while
expanding on the canon's tantalizing references to mysteries Dr. Watson never got
around to chronicling.*

Part XXIII: *Marcum's well of talented authors able to mimic the
feel of The Canon seems bottomless.*

Part XXIV: *Marcum's expertise at selecting high-quality
pastiches remains impressive.*

Part XXV: *The variety of plots is matched by the contributors' skills.
Once again, those who relish traditional Holmes stories will be delighted.*

Edited by David Marcum
from MX Publishing
The MX Book of New Sherlock Holmes Stories
(MX Publishing, 2015-   )

Also by David Marcum
from Belanger Books

The Papers of Solar Pons

*"As a long-time admirer of the Praed Street sleuth,
I know no one better to chronicle his further exploits."*
– Roger Johnson, Editor, The Sherlock Holmes Journal (Summer 2018),
The Sherlock Holmes Society of London

Introduction: A Word from Dr. Lyndon Parker
The Adventure of the Doctor's Box
The Park Lane Solution
The Poe Problem
The Singular Affair of the Blue Girl
The Plight of the American Driver
The Adventure of the Blood Doctor
The Additional Heirs
The Horror of St. Anne's Row
The Adventure of the Failed Fellowship
The Adventure of the Obrisset Snuffbox
The Folio Matter
The Affair of the Distasteful Society
*And Forewords by August Derleth, Roger Johnson, Peter Blau,
Bob Byrne, Tracy Adam Heron, Derrick Belanger, and David Marcum*

Holmes Away From Home:
Adventures from The Great Hiatus
Volumes I and II

Sherlock Holmes:
Adventures Beyond the Canon
Volumes I, II, and III

Edited by David Marcum
from Belanger Books

Sherlock Holmes: Before Baker Street

Sherlock Holmes and Doctor Watson:
The Early Adventures
Volumes I, II, and III

Edited by David Marcum
from MX Publishing

Imagination Theatre's Sherlock Holmes

The Further Adventures of Sherlock Holmes:
The Complete Jim French Imagination Theatre Scripts

Edited by David Marcum
from MX Publishing

Sherlock Holmes in Montague Street
by Arthur Morrison
Sherlock Holmes's Early Investigations
Originally published as Martin Hewitt Adventures

Complete Hardcover Edition and Three-volume Paperback Edition

Edited by David Marcum
from MX Publishing

The Complete Dr. Thorndyke
by R. Austin Freeman
Volumes I-IX

Hardcover and Paperback

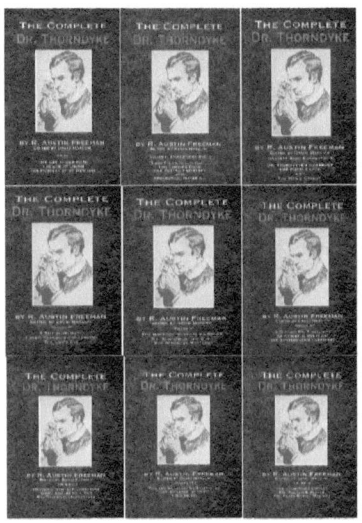

A Proof Reader's Adventures of Sherlock Holmes
by Nick Dunn-Meynell

Hardcover and Paperback

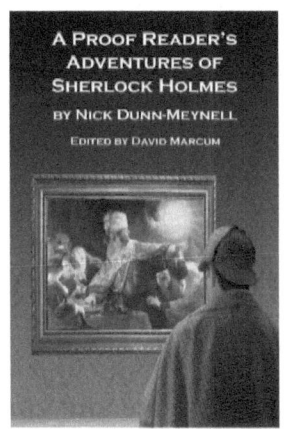

Edited by David Marcum
from Belanger Books

The Complete Solar Pons
by August Derleth

8-volume Paperback Edition

4-volume Hardcover Edition

Edited by David Marcum
from Belanger Books

The New Adventures of Solar Pons

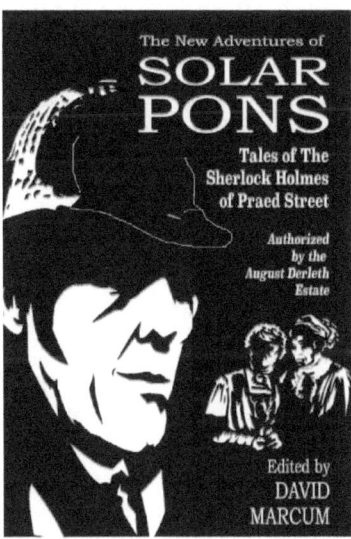

The Meeting of the Minds:
The Cases of Sherlock Holmes and Solar Pons

Edited by David Marcum,
Derrick Belanger, and Sonia Fetherston
from Belanger Books

Sherlock Holmes is Everywhere!

MX Publishing

MX Publishing is the world's largest specialist Sherlock Holmes publisher, with over five-hundred titles and over two-hundred authors creating the latest in Sherlock Holmes fiction and non-fiction

The catalogue includes several award winning books, and over two-hundred-and-fifty have been converted into audio.

MX Publishing also has one of the largest communities of Holmes fans on Facebook, with regular contributions from dozens of authors.

www.mxpublishing.com

@mxpublishing on Facebook, Twitter and Instagram

www.ingramcontent.com/pod-product-compliance
Lightning Source LLC
Chambersburg PA
CBHW020919020726
47495CB00002B/262